P9-DJU-418

AGE
OF
VICE

कलियुग

ALSO BY DEEPTI KAPOOR

A Bad Character

AGE

OF

VICE

कलियुग

DEEPTI KAPOOR

RIVERHEAD BOOKS · NEW YORK · 2023

RIVERHEAD BOOKS
An imprint of Penguin Random House LLC

Copyright © 2023 by Deepti Kapoor
Penguin Random House supports copyright. Copyright fuels creativity, encourages diverse voices,
promotes free speech, and creates a vibrant culture. Thank you for buying an authorized edition of
this book and for complying with copyright laws by not reproducing, scanning, or distributing any
part of it in any form without permission. You are supporting writers and allowing
Penguin Random House to continue to publish books for every reader.

Riverhead and the R colophon are registered trademarks of Penguin Random House LLC.

ISBN 9780593328798

Printed in the United States of America

Map by Malik Sajad

BOOK DESIGN BY LUCIA BERNARD

For *naga sadhus,* the *kumbha mela* disaster of 1954 was just another round of violence during an event predicated on violence among men whose profession was violence. If it was different, it was only because ordinary householders had gotten in the way.

—WILLIAM R. PINCH, *WARRIOR ASCETICS AND INDIAN EMPIRES*

And in consequence of the shortness of their lives they will not be able to acquire much knowledge. And in consequence of the littleness of their knowledge, they will have no wisdom. And for this, covetousness and avarice will overwhelm them all.

—THE *MAHABHARATA*

NEW DELHI, 2004

Five pavement-dwellers lie dead at the side of Delhi's Inner Ring Road.

It sounds like the start of a sick joke.

If it is, no one told them.

They die where they slept.

Almost.

Their bodies have been dragged ten meters by the speeding Mercedes that jumped the curb and cut them down.

It's February. Three a.m. Six degrees.

Fifteen million souls curl up in sleep.

A pale fog of sulfur lines the streets.

And one of the dead, Ragini, was eighteen years old. She was five months pregnant at the time. Her husband, Rajesh, twenty-three, was sleeping by her side. Both belly-up, tucked in with heavy shawls at the crown and feet, looking like corpses anyway save the telltale signs, the rucksack beneath the head, the sandals lined up neatly beside the arms.

A cruel twist of fate: this couple arrived in Delhi only yesterday. Taking refuge with Krishna, Iyaad, and Chotu, three migrant laborers from the same district in Uttar Pradesh. Each day these men woke before dawn to trek to the *labor mandi at Company Bagh, trying to grab whatever daily wage they could find—dhaba cook, wedding waiter, construction laborer—sending money back to their village, paying for a sister's shaadi, a brother's schooling, a father's nightly medicine. Living day to day, hour to hour, the working poor, struggling to survive. Returning to sleep in this barren spot after dark, beside the Ring Road, close to Nigambodh Ghat. Close to the demolished slums of the Yamuna Pushta that had been their home.*

But the newspapers don't dwell on these three men. Their names vanish at dawn with the stars.

A police van with four cops inside arrives at the crash site. They climb out and see the dead bodies, and the wailing, angry crowd that now surrounds the car. There's someone still inside! A young man, sitting bolt upright, arms braced at the wheel, eyes shut tightly. Is he dead? Did he die like that? The cops push the rabble aside and peer in. "Is he sleeping?" one cop says to his colleagues. These words cause the driver to turn his head and, like some monster, open his eyes. The cop looks back and almost jumps in fright. There's something grotesque about the driver's smooth, handsome face. His eyes are leering and wild, but other than that, there's not a hair out of place. The cops pull open the door, wave their lathis thunderously, order him out. There's an empty bottle of Black Label at his feet. He's a lean man, gym honed, wearing a gray gabardine safari suit, hair parted millimeter fine, impeccably oiled. Beneath the reek of whisky there's another scent: Davidoff Cool Water, not that these cops know.

What they know is this: he's not a rich man, not a rich man at all, rather a facsimile, a man dressed in the imitation of wealth: in its service. The clothes, the well-groomed features, the car, they cannot hide the essential poverty of his birth; its smell is stronger than any liquor or cologne.

Yes, he's a servant, a chauffeur, a driver, a "boy."

A well-fed and housebroken version of what lies dead on the road.

And this is not his Mercedes.

Which means he can be hurt.

———

He sobs in oblivion as the cops drag him out. Bent double, he vomits on his own loafers. One cop hits him with his lathi, hauls him up. Another searches his body, finds his wallet, finds an empty shoulder holster, finds a matchbook from a hotel called the Palace Grande, finds a money clip holding twenty thousand rupees.

Whose car is this?

Where did the money come from?

Who did you steal it from?

Thought you'd go for a joyride?

Whose liquor is it?

Chutiya, where's the gun?

Fucker, who do you work for?

In his wallet there's an election card, a driver's license, three hundred rupees. His cards say he is Ajay. His father's name is Hari. He was born January 1, 1982.

And the Mercedes? It is registered to one Gautam Rathore.

The cops confer: the name sounds familiar. And the address—Aurangzeb Road—speaks for itself. Only the rich and the powerful live there.

"Chutiya," an officer barks, holding up the car's papers. "Is this your boss?"

But this young man called Ajay is too drunk to speak.

"Asshole, did you take his car?"

One of the cops walks to the side and looks down at the dead. The girl's eyes are open, skin already blue in the cold. She is bleeding from the space between her legs, where life has been.

In the station Ajay is stripped and left naked in a cold and windowless room. He's so drunk he passes out. The constables return to throw icy water over him and he wakes with a scream. He is seated, and they press his shoulders against the wall, pull his legs apart. A female constable stands on his thighs until his circulation goes and he roars in pain and passes out once more.

———

By the next day the case has gained traction. The media is appalled. At first it's about the pregnant girl. News channels mourn her. But she was neither photogenic nor full of promise. So the focus shifts to the killer. A source confirms the car is a Mercedes registered to Gautam Rathore, and this is news—he's a fixture of the Delhi social scene, a polo player, a raconteur, and a prince, genuine royalty, the first and only son of a member of Parliament, Maharaja Prasad Singh Rathore. Was Gautam Rathore driving? That's the question on everyone's lips. But no, no, his alibi is watertight. He was holidaying away from Delhi last night. He was at a fort palace hotel near Jaipur. His current location is unknown. But he has released a statement expressing his horror, sending his condolences to the deceased and their kin. The driver, his statement reveals, only recently began working for him. He seems to have taken the Mercedes without Gautam's knowledge. Taken whisky and the Mercedes and gone for an illicit spin.

A statement from the police confirms as much: Ajay, employee of Gautam Rathore, stole a bottle of whisky from Rathore's home while his employer was away, took the Mercedes for a joyride, lost control.

This story becomes fact.

It settles in the papers.

And the FIR is registered.

Ajay, son of Hari, is booked under Section 304A of the Indian Penal Code. Death due to negligence. Maximum sentence: two years.

He is sent to the crowded courthouse and presented to the district magistrate, the magistrate takes two minutes to send him to judicial custody with no consideration of bail. He is driven with the other prisoners on a bus to Tihar Jail. They are lined up for processing; they sit in sullen rows on wooden benches in the reception hall, surrounded by placards with rules hammered into the damp, pockmarked plaster of the walls. When his turn arrives, he's taken into a cramped office where a clerk and a prison doctor with their typewriter and *stethoscope await. His possessions are laid out once more: wallet, money clip containing twenty thousand rupees, the book of matches bearing the name Palace Grande, the empty shoulder holster. The money is counted.*

The clerk takes his pencil and begins to fill out the form.

"Name?"

The prisoner stares at them.

"Name?"

"Ajay," he says, barely audible.

"Father's name?"

"Hari."

"Age?"

"Twenty-two."

"Occupation?"

"Driver."

"Speak up."

"Driver."

"Who is your employer?"

The clerk looks over his glasses.

"What is the name of your employer?"

"Gautam Rathore."

Ten thousand rupees are taken from his money, the rest is handed back to him.

"Put it in your sock," the clerk says.

He is processed and sent to Jail No. 1, led through the courtyard to the barracks, taken along the dank corridor to a wide cell where nine other inmates live crowded and packed. Clothes hang from the cell bars like in a market stall, and the floor inside is covered with tattered mattresses, blankets, buckets, bundles, sacks. A small squatting latrine in the corner. Though there's no room left, the warden orders a small space to be cleared out for him on the cold floor next to the latrine. But no mattress can be spared. Ajay lays the blanket he's been given on the stone floor. He sits with his back to the wall, staring vacantly ahead. A

*few of his cellmates come and tell him their names, but he says nothing, ac-
knowledges nothing. He curls into a ball and sleeps.*

*When he comes to, he sees a man standing over him. Old and missing teeth,
with frantic eyes. More than sixty years on earth, he is saying. More than sixty
years. He's an autorickshaw driver from Bihar, or at least he was on the outside. He's been here awaiting trial for six years. He's innocent. It's one of the
first things he says. "I'm innocent. I'm supposed to be a drug peddler. But I'm
innocent. I was caught in the wrong place. A peddler was in my rickshaw, but
he ran and the cops took me." He goes on to ask what Ajay is charged with, how
much money he has hidden away with him. Ajay ignores him, turns in the opposite direction. "Suit yourself," the old man cheerfully says, "but you should
know, I can get things done around here. For one hundred rupees I can get you
another blanket, for one hundred rupees I can get you a better meal." "Let him
be," hollers another cellmate, a plump, dark boy from Aligarh, who is picking
his teeth with a piece of neem. "Don't you know who he is, he's the Mercedes
Killer." The old man shuffles off. "I'm Arvind," the fat boy says. "They say I
killed my wife, but I'm innocent."*

*Out into the courtyard, break time. Hundreds of inmates piling out of their
cells to congregate. Men size him up. He's something of a celebrity. They've all
heard about the Mercedes Killer. They want a closer look, judge for themselves
his innocence or guilt, see how tough he is, how scared, decide where he could
belong. It only takes a minute to recognize he's one of the innocent, a scapegoat
for a wealthy boss. Men try to prize this truth from him. What was he promised to take the fall? Something sweet? Money, when he gets out? Or will his
sons and daughters be sent through school? Or did it come from the other side?
Was his family threatened? Was his life in danger? Or was he just loyal?*

*Representatives from the gangs that run the jail approach him in the yard,
in the dining hall, in the corridors, canvass his support, present their pitch. The
Chawanni gang, the Sissodia gang, the Beedi gang, the Haddi gang, the Atte
gang. The dreaded Bawania gang. The Acharya gang, the Guptas. As an in-*

*nocent man, as a man unaccustomed to the criminal life, he will need protec-
tion. He will soon become a target for extortion if he does not pick a gang;
without a gang's support, a man will rape him soon enough, a warden will
have him transferred to a cell, alone with another cellmate, he will be his sport,
no one will come when he screams. And they'll take whatever money he has.
They offer this as sage and neutral advice, as if they were not the threat. He is
pulled this way and that. What money do you have? Join our gang. Join our
gang and you'll have security. You'll have a mobile phone, pornography,
chicken. You'll be exempt from the "freshers party" coming your way. Join our
gang and you can fuck, you can rape. Our gang is the strongest. You should join
us before it's too late. He ignores each pitch. By the time he returns to his cell,
his blanket has been taken away.*

*He prefers to be alone and in pain anyway. The horror of the dead follows
him inside, he mourns them as he breathes. He refuses all the gangs, snubs the
emissaries and their overtures. So on the second day, outside the pharmacy,
alone, just after he's been called to visit the doctor, three men from another
cell converge on him. They stick out their tongues and remove the razor
blades they keep in their mouths; they set upon him, slashing at his face and
chest and the forearms he raises to protect himself. He takes the cuts in pen-
ance, making no expression of pain. Then his patience finally snaps, breaks
like a trapdoor. He shatters his first attacker's nose with the heel of his palm,
takes the second man's arm at the elbow and snaps it at the joint. The third
he sweeps down to the floor. He snatches one of their razors and takes it to this
man's tongue, slicing it down the middle, squeezing the squealing prisoner's
jaw open with his grip.*

*He's found standing over them, splattered in blood, the prisoners howling in
pain as he's locked in solitary in a daze. They beat him, tell him he'll be there
for a very long time. Once the door shuts, he goes wild, snarling and slapping
and kicking the walls. Screaming without language. Incomprehensible words.
He cannot control his world.*

———————

He imagines the end. Everything he is and all he's done. But no. The next morning, the door is opened, new guards enter. They tell him to come with them. He'll shower first. He's shivering naked and raw. When they approach, he curls his fists, back to the wall, to fight. They laugh and throw him fresh clothes.

He's taken to the warden's office. A pleasing spread: freshly cut fruit, paratha, lassi. A vision of paradise. The warden asks him to sit. "Have a cigarette. Help yourself. There's been a mistake. I wasn't told," he says. "If I'd been told, this would never have happened. Really, no one knew, not even your friends. But things will be different. You'll be taken to your friends here now. You'll be free, within reason. And this unfortunate business with those other men, this will be forgotten. They could be punished. Only, you punished them yourself, didn't you!? Quite a show. Oh, and this money, it's yours. You should have said something. You should have made it clear. You should have let us know. Why didn't you let us know?"

Ajay stares at the food, at the cigarette pack.

"Know what?"

The warden smiles.

"That you're a Wadia man."

MAHARAJGANJ, EASTERN UTTAR PRADESH, 1991

AJAY

(Thirteen Years Earlier)

1.

What you have to remember is that Ajay was just a boy. Eight years old and malnourished. Barely literate. Watchful inside the sockets of his eyes.

His family was poor. Wracked by poverty. Living hand to mouth in a hut patched with dried grass and plastic sheets on raised ground above the floodplain, by the ears of sarkanda beyond the shadow edge of the village. Father and mother manual scavengers both, scraping shit from the villagers' dry latrines with slate and hand, bearing wicker baskets on heads, to be dumped on farther ground. Pissing and shitting in the fields before dawn. Pissing after dark. Growing meager leafy vegetables in the filthy runoff. Drinking water from the brackish distant well so as not to pollute the common source. Knowing their limits. So as not to invite death upon themselves.

Ajay's mother, Rupa, is pregnant again.

His elder sister, Hema, tends to their goat.

This is Eastern Uttar Pradesh. Nineteen ninety-one.

The foothills of Nepal rise in the north.

The moon is visible long after dawn.

Before Ajay took a breath he was already mourned.

2.

It's nineteen ninety-one and the district is in dire need. The upper-caste landlords and their cronies thrive. The boy treks each day to the government school, an aging, unloved shell; a false hope of concrete without doors; wooden windows shuttered, splintered, and full of holes; rooms too small for the many children, snot nosed, hair combed, hair oiled, scrappy uniforms kept clean, fighting a threadbare tide. The teacher is missing, often drunk, often runaway, often collecting his government salary at home. Ajay is poor, less than poor, shunted to the back with the other Valmikis, with the Pasis and Koris, shunned, ignored. At lunch they are made to wait apart, on rocky ground, while the caste children sit cross-legged in rows on the smooth platform taking their meals on banana leaves. When their meals are over, it is the outcastes' turn, their portion meager, watered down. After lunch Ajay is put to work. He sweeps the floor, removes dried shit from the corners, sweeps lizard shit from the ledge. One day a dead dog lies beside the boundary wall, bloated and rotten and snakebit. He is made to tie string around its hind leg, drag it away.

In the afternoon heat he returns several kilometers home to help Hema with the goat. Past the Hanuman temple, past the boys playing cricket. He keeps a safe distance. Three years ago he made the error of picking up a stray ball, throwing it back with all his might. The ball was shunned like a leper, and Ajay was chased through the fields. He escaped across the sewage ditch. They told him: Touch the ball again, we'll hack off your arms and legs, set fire to them, throw you in the well.

It's nineteen ninety-one and his father has gotten into some kind of trouble. Their goat has broken free from its tether and entered a villager's field to eat the spinach there. Ajay and Hema retrieve it, but the owner of the field comes to know. He arrives late afternoon with the village headman, Kuldeep Singh. Kuldeep Singh brings with him a handful of eager goons. In their presence the landowner demands an explanation where none will suffice, while Ajay's father, all sinew and bone, begs forgiveness when none will come. It's the goat they deal with first. In clairvoyance, it spits and snorts and rears and brandishes its horns, so the goons shy away. It takes Kuldeep Singh to push them aside, to bring his brutish club down swiftly on its head. The skull cracks, the goat teeters on the void, legs folding—it looks, for a moment, like a newborn trying to walk. Kuldeep Singh places his knee on its head and slits its throat with his blade. Exalted by the hot blood, the goons move in on Ajay's father. They drag him to the ground, hold him down by his shoulders and knees, and take turns beating the soles of his feet with bamboo sticks, graduating in their zeal to his ankles, his shins, his knees, his groin. They deliver heavy blows to his groin, his chest, his arms. His wife and daughter cry out, wail, beg them to stop. Ajay turns to run, but he's held fast by Kuldeep Singh as he goes. Those heavy hands grip his shoulders. The breath of tobacco and liquor is a sour perfume for his nose. Ajay turns away, directs his eyes at the pinkish sky, but Kuldeep Singh twists his head so he must watch.

His father falls into a fever, bones purpling into dusk. In the morning, in despair, his mother turns to the local moneylender, Rajdeep Singh, begging enough to take her husband for treatment to the government hospital twenty kilometers away. Rajdeep Singh grants her two hundred rupees at 40 percent interest after a humiliating negotiation.

When Rupa reaches the hospital, the doctors refuse to admit her husband unless they are paid up front in full. They take 150 rupees, then leave him in a ward unattended. He slips from this world by midnight. She drags his body back herself, strapped to a wooden sled in the dark, reaching home after dawn. Denied access to the village's burning ground, they cremate him themselves with collected oil and cheap wood on a pyre near their home. There's not enough wood to finish the job. The stench is unbearable. They dig a shallow grave beside the woods and bury his charred remains there.

Next day, Rajdeep Singh's men come round to remind Ajay's mother what is owed. The goons surround Ajay's sister, pass lewd comments, suggest what she might do. Ajay watches hidden and mute among the stalks of the neighboring field. There's a cockroach in the cracked earth beneath his feet. He covers his ears to block the cries and stamps the cockroach into the dust. And then he runs. When he returns two hours later, his sister is sobbing in a corner of the hut and his mother is stoking the fire.

A few hours later, the thekedar—the local contractor—turns up. He offers his condolences and, knowing their parlous state, suggests he pay off their debt in full himself. They can pay him back in one simple, honorable way.

3.

Ajay doesn't get a say. The next morning before light, he is loaded into the back of a Tempo carrying eight boys he's never met. It's an old vehicle with a battered cabin and a greasy cage fitted behind that has a roof open to the stars so its human cargo can see but dare not risk escape. Ajay has nothing to show for himself save his old clothes and a soiled blanket. His mother and sister stand at a distance, then turn and walk away. The engine idles on the dirt track beside the gully. Then the contractor climbs in and the assistant climbs in and they drive from the crawling light along a potholed track toward a black horizon pierced by stars. Ajay sits catatonic among the sullen and shivering boys. A patchwork of blankets barely keeps them warm. They huddle together on the cab side of the cage, facing east, watching their homes recede, waiting for dawn.

They stop at a busy dhaba just before sunrise to piss. A mindless tube light gathers yearning moths. Steam escapes resting truckers' mouths. In minutes the sky has turned pale and the landscape grows distinct. Vehicles trundle down the highway. Wheat fields stretch in the mist on either side. The contractor's assistant, a wiry, dark, pockmarked man with a twisted mustache and a long face and narrow eyes, opens the back of the cage. He warns them not to run as he leads them to the trench to piss, and to make certain of this, he stands behind them toying with his knife. The fog sweeps in more heavily, the sun briefly appears as a pale silvery disk, then vanishes. Locked back inside the truck, the boys are given roti and chai as the thekedar and his assistant sit at one of the plastic tables in front and order aloo paratha.

This is the moment.

One of the caged boys, pigeon chested with curled hair, once passive, leaps up and scales the cage, throws himself down. He's running along the earth before anyone can react, down and running toward the backside of the dhaba, hands reaching out instinctively to grab him, but the boy slips through and leaps over piles of garbage, then over the stinking ditch into the shrouded field. The thekedar's assistant is quick on his feet, his plastic chair falling as he gives chase—running alongside the toilets, jumping over the ditch himself, pulling his knife. And then both boy and man are gone. The truckers, the dhaba workers, the boys, all watch expectantly in the direction of the escape, peering into the gray expanse, cocking their eyes to hear. Only the thekedar, a man of great experience, sits calmly sipping his chai.

Five minutes pass with no sign.

Normal life resumes.

Then there's a paralyzing scream, an outrageous howl somewhere in the fog. All the stray dogs begin to bark.

When the assistant comes back panting, alone, his white undershirt is flecked with blood. He spits on the ground and sits without a word.

No one dares meet his eye.

He finishes his chai, eats his paratha.

The moment is seared into Ajay's brain.

The mist in the fields rises and fades.

They drive all day and the sun grows sharp, burns captive the whole world through its towns with dusty junctions of trucks and vegetable stalls.

Some of the boys begin to stir as if waking from drugged sleep, whispering among themselves, trying to shield themselves from the glare of the sun and the dust and wind. Ajay squints and talks with no one; he tries to remember his father's face, his sister's face, his mother's face. He tries to remember the road home. In the afternoon he wakes without realizing he'd fallen asleep and sees a city with wide boulevards and grand buildings and gardens of bright blooming flowers, a world he thinks is a dream.

When he wakes once more, it's nearly sunset and they are on a narrow road rising into a mountain range, with a tumbling bank of scree at the right and rolling hills behind.

He looks at the eyes of the other boys and finally speaks.

"Where are we?" he says.

"Punjab."

"Where are we going?"

One nods above. "Up there."

"Why?"

The boy looks away.

"To work," another says.

They breach the mountains late that night, rising into the foothills, crawling the switchbacks there, the Tempo ascending no faster than a mule, its engine straining against the gorge torrent and the pitch dark. As they plateau, a humming sheet of river stalks their side. The moon shows again, waxing to full, the tall sky incandescent. But beneath the gliding fleet of cloud, there's blackness, grotesque shapes, dead drops, a world of shadow, the lull of the engine. The temperature drops and the boys draw close for warmth, rattling bones in cages, bracing themselves. Then the lava hours of nightmare begin, the ceaseless rise and rise, the sudden fall, hour upon hour wrapping around valleys and hairpins, with air so cold it scars, Ajay holding on for the next bend, for the plateau, for the sun to rise and spread itself on the unseen river, to be returned home, for his mother to wake him up from sleep, to drag dead dogs from school.

Then tendrils sprout and the night is done, the yolk of a sun cracks over the peaks and the blue death that filled the final hours is cast away. Pure light and the victory of dawn. Ajay examines the faces of the blinking boys, stirring dazed within their blankets. Faces older: fourteen or fifteen, a face that is younger, maybe seven. Checking to see if they have changed. They have not. But they have passed through a portal.

There's no hope of home now.

The truck stops for breakfast at a chai shop cut like a grotto into a sheer rock face high up on a mountain beside a shrine to the local deity, with barely enough room on the road for two vehicles to pass. Across the way, a soft river flows deep inside a gorge. The assistant leaps from the cab, stretches his arms in the air, lights a beedi, and wanders to the edge, where white-painted stones guard against the drop. He cleans his nails with his pocket-knife and spits into the void as grooming monkeys hiss their bare fangs and lope off to the next bend.

The boys still sit inside.

The dead engine is the loudest sound in the world.

The thekedar greets the chai wallah as he works the vat on a paraffin stove. The assistant returns from the edge to sit with him, flipping open the cage on the way. The three men gossip, catching up on the latest comings and goings on the road.

The assistant whistles at the boys. "Stretch your legs, go piss. You won't get another chance soon."

The men are relaxed, the incident at the dhaba the previous morning forgotten.

There's nowhere for the boys to run or escape to this time.

So they climb out and mill aimlessly, staring up at the corridor of lime-stone, taking in cool lungfuls of clean air. Ajay hears the river, out of sight, pouring from the top of the world.

One of the boys, the youngest maybe, the seven-year-old, walks over to the edge.

Ajay watches him stand there transfixed, balancing on the very edge, looking down.

Until the assistant grabs him by the arm and yanks him back.

And they're on the road again.

By ten the sun is harsh. Blankets worn loosely are turned into shade.

Flashing through the Himalayas.

Free of the night.

Ever more lost.

Now they sleep.

By midday the Tempo reaches a beat-up market town in a hot valley choked with grease and engines, a dumping ground inside the mountains, a bowl of filth. They cross a small rocky river snagged and dammed with garbage, the low metal bridge across woven with prayer flags. They join a new road out of town and follow the river upstream through the pines. Small grassy islands break the river's flow. North, through the breaks in the resin-scented trees, snowcapped mountains soar. A new colossal range, an impenetrable white wall. Ajay falls asleep again and dreams of his father carrying a basket on his head, his body below completely charred.

In the afternoon the truck approaches a large town wrapped in a forested hillside. It guards the mouth of a long steep valley slashing far ahead through the earth. Waterfalls hang above, splashing and easing through the rocks, joining the meandering river, turning it wild. Villagers wash their clothes a little downstream, whipping the fabric against the boulders. The truck turns a bend and the river is deadened by the heavy pine. They weave past neat wood-clad buildings, pulling into a parking space within the trees.

Just like that, the engine cuts, a new bereavement—the boys blink and stand unsteadily, like men coming ashore after months at sea.

A crowd is already waiting for them. The thekedar jumps out of the cab all businesslike, spits paan, and removes a small pocketbook. He wastes no time calling out names, while the assistant opens the back of the truck and hands the boys over, one after the other. Small disputes flare, money changes hands. Bonds that had barely formed are newly broken. A light rain starts to fall, and Ajay crouches in the cage, waiting. One by one, the boys are taken away. For the remaining three, an auction begins.

4.

Ajay is sold to a short, fat man with ruddy cheeks and fine clothes and a pompous air. "You can call me Daddy," the man says, taking Ajay by the hand, leading him to the nearby autorickshaw stand. "And your name is?"

But Ajay can't answer. He's too fixated on the shock of a big man holding his dirty little hand.

They ride up the east side of the valley in the back of an autorickshaw. The town folds away below in diminishing curves. Out the canvas flaps of the rickshaw, the higher ranges reveal themselves, glaciers like jewels, shining in the heavy rain that has started to fall. Ajay sits silently, pressed into the seat, shivering, while Daddy perches forward chatting with the driver. A few kilometers up, a smaller, more peaceful settlement emerges, a village dotted with dark houses in the old mountain style—thatched roofs, heavy stones, timber frames, ornately carved wooden balconies going to seed. They are threatened by new bullying homes of concrete, with piles of river sand under plastic sheeting next to piles of stone.

The rickshaw deposits them at what looks like a small cottage built on the hillside, but when they stand on the road, Ajay sees it stretches five stories down, as if leaking down the mountain in a landslide. They rush inside the top cottage along a short, bare passageway, emerging through a heavy wooden door into a place of light and warmth, a large, cluttered room with floor-to-ceiling windows on two sides that look out at the panoramic wonder of the valley. The room is full of sofas and woven carpets and ornaments and artifacts, the centerpiece a huge wood-burning stove waving tentacles of pipes vanishing into other rooms, while one belches smoke through a vent beside the window and into the sky. A huge vat of milk bubbles on top of the stove. The room is creamy with the smell.

A woman, plump and pink and fragrant, more glamorous than any Ajay has ever seen, stands up and smiles.

"This is Mummy," Daddy says, holding Ajay by the shoulders.

"Hello," Mummy says, extending her rosy hand. "What's your name?"

"Go on, take it," Daddy says.

But Ajay only stares.

"What's his name?" Mummy says, straining to hold her smile.

"Shake hands," Daddy says. "See." He takes Mummy's hand and shakes it. "Like that."

Ajay looks up at Daddy and grins stupidly.

"Have you eaten?" Mummy asks Ajay in a baby voice. "Will you have chai?"

Ajay only grins.

"He's shy," Mummy says, as if diagnosing a patient. She bends her knees and examines him a little closer. "Are you sure he can speak?"

"Of course he can speak," Daddy says.

But Ajay doesn't say a word.

"I doubt he can read or write," Daddy says. "But he can speak. Can't you?"

"Didn't you check?" Mummy says, mildly annoyed.

"He was the only one left," Daddy says.

"What's your name?" Mummy asks again, taking both his hands.

Ajay is mesmerized.

He whispers, so inaudibly he cannot be heard.

Ajay.

"Again?" she says, turning her ear to his face with a smile.

"Ajay," he says.

"Ajay!" she exclaims, victorious, pushing herself to her feet, repeating it as if it were the finest name in the world. "That's very sweet."

"I told you he could speak," Daddy says.

"Why don't you show him to his room?"

He leads Ajay back out; instead of joining the road, they turn round the side of the building, down a set of stone steps protected from the rain by the overhanging roof, past a series of small grassy terraces, all the way to the ground floor of the building, five stories down, and enter a room seething with damp, as if the rain-soaked earth threatened to spring through the bare concrete. It's a storeroom of junk and bags of cement with a grimy mattress and a few blankets.

"This is your room," Daddy says. "And here's the key." He hands Ajay the key. "Take care of it; if you lose it, you can't lock your door."

Ajay stares at the key in his hand.

"The bathroom is there," Daddy says, pointing to a door. "There's soap inside. Wash up and take rest. It's one now. I'll be back to get you at five, when you'll start work."

Ajay is staring at a shelf next to the mattress that holds some personal effects, two T-shirts, a school notebook, a deflated football, a wind-up duck on wheels, and a frosted mirror.

"You can take those," Daddy says, looking back in from outside as he closes the door. "They belonged to the last boy."

He falls asleep among the blankets, the motion of the Tempo still beating in his heart.

When he wakes, it's stopped raining, it's silent, and there's a weird glow throbbing in the dusty glass of the small window floating above the junk. He doesn't know where he is, then it slowly comes back to him, the journey receding like a dream, only the room solid, disconnected from everything else.

He lies motionless a long time in the blankets, his mind a bird sleeping above the ocean as it flies.

The sun is falling behind the mountains across the valley, the clouds have lifted to reveal a pure blue. The grasses of the terraces bristle with droplets. Loneliness throbs out of the building above. He climbs the steps to peer in, but the lights are off inside the main house. Now he doesn't know what to do. All the houses up and down the mountainside seem abandoned. So he returns to his room and covers his head with the blankets and waits.

"Have you washed your hands?" Daddy says.

Ajay lies and whispers yes.

"Wash them again."

It's the mantra of the house.

Wash your hands. Wash them again. Wash your feet, wash your clothes. Wash your snotty little nose.

Ajay is being fed. Daddy encourages him to eat. "For the work," he says, "you need to be strong. Eat rice with salt and ghee, drink milk, don't skimp on the good things, there's ghee and milk to spare."

Now he's being told about the work. He absorbs it all impassively.

Daddy has a small farm an hour's climb through the woodland in a high meadow. Ajay is replacing the last boy. His job is to tend to the milk, to make ghee, and to take care of the household chores, make breakfast, sweep and mop the floor, wash the clothes, tend to the fire, prepare lunch, and when lunch is finished, wash the dishes. He is given his own plate and cup and bowl and spoon.

"Do you know how to cook?" Daddy says.

Ajay shakes his head.

"Then you'll learn. Starting now. And tomorrow, after breakfast, we'll go to the farm."

Mummy shows him how she makes dinner that night, chicken curry, aloo gobi, palak paneer, rice. He gawps at the wealth of ingredients, the indulgent spicing, the spoonfuls of ghee. Mummy is a generous cook, a patient teacher. He is given drops of things to taste on the back of his hand, looking up as his tongue explodes each time with wide eyes of disbelief.

"Look at his smile," Mummy says. But Daddy is buried in the paper.

When it comes to the rotis, he is ordered to make them himself, and they are declared good, though he is too thrifty with the salt.

Now he is shown how to lay the table, how to arrange the serving spoons, the bowls, the plates, and when dinner's ready, he is asked to sit with them at the table.

He doesn't know how.

"Sit," Mummy says, pulling the next chair out. "Right here."

He climbs up the chair, gazing at her.

"Now, serve yourself," she says.

He looks at them both hesitantly.

"Go on."

He reaches for a serving spoon, clumsily bringing small portions to his plate, Daddy pretending not to watch as he spills food along the way.

When Ajay's plate is dotted with small mounds, Daddy finally succumbs to the urge to intervene. "You need more than that," he says, heaping large spoons of rice and dal on Ajay's plate and topping it all with spoonfuls of ghee.

"Isn't it the best ghee you ever tasted?" says Mummy.

"Yes," Ajay whispers.

He's never tasted ghee before.

"Your father died," Daddy says, as if his father had called on the phone to relay the news. "And your mother needed you to help her in the best way you can."

He is establishing a history.

"So you came here to work in order that everything at home would be OK."

Ajay just stares.

"Your mother doesn't have to take tension anymore. Your family is happy because you work."

Ajay pictures his mother's face, waiting in the dark as he's loaded into the Tempo. He pictures his father's smoldering corpse. He sees the wheat fields, he turns and runs away from his sister's screams. He crushes a cockroach with his bare feet, repeating in his head the names Kuldeep and Rajdeep Singh.

"I know you come from a place," Daddy says, "where they hold many backward customs and beliefs. Many rules and customs that are true to the reality of your world. But we're free of that here, and so you are free now. Do you understand?"

He looks from Daddy to Mummy, to the embers of the fire, to the chicken curry.

"In our household," Daddy says, "we have different rules. It doesn't matter where you come from. We're all human beings, and all humans are the same. Do you know what that means?"

Ajay says nothing.

"It means if anyone asks who you are and where you come from," Daddy goes on, "you tell them this: I come from a Kshatriya household."

Ajay lowers his eyes to the plate.

"Say it," Daddy says, elongating the words. "I come from a Kshatriya household."

Ajay looks to Mummy; she nods at him encouragingly.

"I live in a Kshatriya household," he whispers.

"No," Daddy says. "You come from one now, OK?"

Ajay nods. "I come from one."

"Very good," Daddy says, job done. "Now eat."

He tries.

He makes a ball of rice and dal. Stares at it.

But he cannot lift it to his mouth.

He seems paralyzed.

"What's wrong?" Daddy says, putting his spoon down pointedly.

"What's wrong, child?" Mummy leans toward him so he can whisper in her ear.

After he speaks, she looks at Daddy with troubled eyes.

"He wants to know," she says gently, "if he can eat down there"—she pauses and shifts her eyes—"on the floor."

Daddy takes a long deliberate breath that communicates his feelings better than any words.

"I told you," he says to Mummy.

"I know," she replies.

"Very well," he says to Ajay, switching back to Hindi. "Take one of the metal plates and go."

Ajay jumps down from the table and fetches one of the cheap metal trays. He transfers the contents of his china plate and loads up some more chicken and hurries to the corner of the kitchen, where he sits cross-legged, with his back turned, stuffing his face. It's more in one meal than he's eaten in a week—he feels that his stomach will burst.

After dinner, when Mummy and Daddy are resting, he is charged with doing the washing-up. When everything is clean, Mummy shows him how to make warm milk with turmeric.

"The day starts at five," Daddy says, as Ajay squats drinking his haldi doodh by the fire. The heat is hypnotic. He has the urge to lie down and sleep right there. But when it's done, he's given sandals and sent down the cold steps, shivering in the damp air, locking himself in the room, covering himself with as many blankets as he can find, lying in the grief-stricken dark, waiting for dawn.

5.

Winter is ending, spring is coming, the snow is clearing, and the cattle will be taken to graze again soon. At the farm he is shown the cows, taught how to give fodder to the animals and clean out their sheds, take them for milking, tie them up to graze. Every morning Ajay must run up and fetch two pitchers of milk for the house. The rest will be delivered by the farm workers for Ajay to process for ghee or bottle to be sold.

The work is hard and he's always tired, but he eats three meals a day and no one abuses him or threatens to kill him. It's a better life than any he's ever hoped for or known. Each morning he has his glass of fresh milk and several hot rotis doused in the finest ghee. The lunches and dinners he makes, using recipes passed on from Mummy, are full of fresh vegetables, and the rice never runs out.

In his free moments, when no one is looking, Ajay loves to roll around the stepped garden, muddying himself in the grass, jumping from each small terrace down to the next, descending just like the house toward the valley floor, toward the wide and powerful river. Over and over, every week a little more meat on his bones, a few more words in his mouth, a laugh, a smile. Then the guilt comes, and he comforts himself with the lie Daddy taught him. His family are living well now because of him. He builds a vision of their day. His sacrifice has paved the way for their prosperity. He tells himself this over and over until he can't remember the truth. He decides that he likes it here. He likes to run through the trees, to play with the farm dogs, to splash cold water on his face, to sit with Mummy beside the fire in the night. And he discovers something else: It gives him pleasure to please, it gives him pleasure to anticipate every possible need, not just Mummy's and Daddy's but everyone's, the farm workers', the animals', the shopkeepers' pleasure. Not just pleasure, not really, more like the stanching of a wound, more like the holding of a tide, a sacrifice, negating the trauma of his birth.

In the beginning of summer something unexpected happens; the foreigners come. They arrive in buses and on motorbikes, strange, wild, happy people with long hair who sit and smoke pipes like the sadhus and who make noise and play music and bring chaotic life to the mountainside, who appear to exist without structure or ritual or rule. When the first biker convoy arrives, it's the middle of the afternoon. Ajay darts from his room to find the source of the noise. He hears the rumbling far off, mistakes it for an avalanche or an earthquake, until he spies the bikes at the bottom of the valley sweeping up the river road and disappearing below the hump.

He waits, listening, not daring to run, not yet ready to be disappointed.

He spots them emerging half a kilometer away.

He leaps up the pathway two steps at a time, runs to the road as the first bikes roar through, jumping and whooping alongside them as fast as he can, cheering as they wave back, a blur of joy.

This summer is made of wonder. In the hours he is supposed to rest, he sneaks from his room and climbs into the village near the hot springs where the foreigners spend their days, gawping at these wonderful people who sit in cafés, smoking and talking and playing music, running away if they try to talk to him, in awe, wrestling with his shyness. They see him and wave and invite him to join them and every day his courage grows. When he gets the nerve to approach, they laugh and joke with him, they smile at him kindly. And when someone spills a drink, he runs to bring a napkin to them. When someone needs a light, he runs with the box of matches he keeps and strikes it and watches the laughter. He decides to carry a box of matches with him everywhere he goes. Lighting a chillum and a cigarette wherever he can. The Matchbox Kid. That's what they call him.

All summer long, the cafés and restaurants that were shuttered are now bright with music and light, with the smells of strange and exotic food, with men and women who wear flowers and bloom. Before the first month is out, he has learned a handful of English words. Please, thank you, yes and no. Sorry.

Daddy even opens up some of the rooms on the floors below, Ajay giving them a quick clean, and rents them for fifty rupees a night.

But when the long summer ends, the foreigners vanish as quickly as they came, a great exodus of bikes and buses to the south, down into India once again; and the autumn colors explode and the cold sets in, the earth turns hard and fades. The animals are brought down the mountain and kept in the winter sheds, and when the snow begins to fall, the household retreats to the central room with the fire burning day and night. Ajay sleeps through the winter in the main room next to the stove. He feels lonelier than ever here, and in the orange glow, with the snow falling thickly in the moonlight, he remembers his mother and sister as he dreams.

6.

Seven years pass in this place that never turns into home but is the only place he knows, to live, to breathe, to grow, tied to his body, the place he cannot leave. Ajay performing these chores, running after foreigners, learning Punjabi and Himachali alongside his Hindi, picking up a spattering of English, German, Hebrew, and Japanese, filling the hollow proofs of his existence, giving name to many things, Mummy kind to him—sometimes tearful or cruel—but she teaches him with great diligence to read and write, to write his name in English too.

And in the house and on the farm he becomes a strong and obedient teenager, muscled, lean; he learns to shoot, learns to hunt, helps birth the calves, keeps the dogs fed and trained, keeps a watch for leopards and bears, watchful as ever, always there, never quite there; the grains of life picked out and soaked, a functionary, loyal to Daddy, vital but so inconsequential in the scheme, exposed to the rhythms and terminal undercurrents of his domestic cove but somehow sheltered too; he eats, he drinks, drinks his milk, spurts in growth, grows an absurd little mustache, learns to shave—his work is relentless, how can he not become strong? His body inhabits adulthood though his mind is still somewhere behind, sometimes a child, always looking to be needed more than he really needs anyone. He sleeps alone every summer night in his room, listening to the parties in the apple orchards, every winter night upstairs, smothered by the hearth. Soon he's taller than Mummy, then Daddy, though they never see it like that. And in the village, every summer as the hippies come, clustered with them in the maze of cafés and guesthouses around the hot springs, he keeps learning his English, Ajay Matchbox, the Matchbox Kid, mute performer, silent clown, ever ready, learning to score charas for commission, roll joints for a rupee, pack chillum for five, keeping handy with the gauze; this boy who was once mocked by some strung-out German, some hardened Israeli, some Japanese acid freak, some hardscrabble Englishman, now strong and watchful and more beautiful than he ever had a right to be. But ready to serve above all else, delighting those who return each spring, saying, "Ajay, is it you? God, you've grown . . ." And those who ordered him so casually before become hesitant, and proprietorial too, seeking his good favor. And those who never laid eyes on him are eager to impress. Women joke about how handsome he is. "It's only a matter of time," one says, and they laugh at each other knowingly. Funny, the passage of time. Funny, this body. But Ajay isn't built that way. He has no guile and knows how precarious the body can be.

He learned the fates of those other boys by and by, the ones who traveled with him in his cage. One went missing in the woods and was found eaten by God knows what, one was drowned while swimming in the river in spate. Four ran away together after stealing from their employers, and of those four, two were convicted of dacoity and murder and two were known to have been shot before ever reaching jail.

"And why don't you run away?" Daddy asks each time a new report comes in.

"Because I'm not stupid," Ajay says.

"That's right," Daddy says. "Because you're not stupid, because you're a good boy too. Repeat after me," he says, switching to English. "There's no place like home."

Over the years Daddy expands that great, deep, empty home, renovating the shells of the lower rooms, making the place fit for guests, each floor painted and bright, bringing a summer profit. Another task: Ajay, now manager of the guesthouse alongside his farming chores, changing sheets, cleaning rooms, cooking food for the guests, running every errand that's required.

Sometimes the foreigners who stay here ask him questions: Where are you from? Where is your family? Do you go home? What's life like in the village you're from?

All of these he deflects with a shy smile.

"You go school?" the sun-leathered Italian asks when Ajay is fifteen.

Ajay shakes his head.

"What you do? To learn?"

"I work." He smiles.

"You go school before?"

"When I was little," he says, thinking out each word.

"When you leave?"

Silence. A shrug.

"When you come here?"

The Italian follows him with his eyes, persistent, trying to bore into his mind.

"You get the money, no?" The man makes the universal sign, rubbing his thumb and forefinger together, producing a ten-rupee note for good measure. "Money. Rupees."

Ajay pretends not to understand, continues making their lunch.

"Here, is for you, take it."

Ajay looks at the money and smiles and shakes his head.

"Go on, take it."

He takes the money and puts it in his pocket shyly.

The Italian leans back and watches him. "You don't get the money, no. Do you?"

It's true. Ajay has never been paid. Daddy has told him that his mother receives his salary every month. He has no reason to disbelieve, he takes it on faith.

But now he wants to know the details, like hearing the same fairy tale each night.

Picking his way through the forest from the farm one afternoon soon after, pausing every now and then so as not to leave Daddy behind, he asks offhandedly how it is that his wages reach his mother in his village.

Daddy remains silent awhile, as if he hadn't heard. Finally he says, "I put your wages in a bank account. And your mother takes the money out on her side."

"From a bank?"

"Yes."

"She has a bank?"

"Yes. The one in your village," Daddy says.

"I don't know it."

"There was no bank when you were there. It just opened."

"How did she get it before?"

"The man who brought you here paid her."

"How much money does she get?"

"Every month," Daddy replies, "she receives five hundred rupees."

Ajay spins the figure in his head, calculating all the things she could buy.

They walk on. In the sun the branches seem to catch fire. The sweet scent of resin fills the air.

"Can I see her?" Ajay asks.

"Of course," Daddy says, without missing a beat. "You can go anytime you want."

"I'd like to see her," Ajay replies.

"But if you go," Daddy continues, "I'll have to replace you and you won't be able to come back, you realize that?"

The thought of another boy arriving to take his place drives fear in his heart.

"I can't remember the way home," Ajay finally says.

Silence.

"But can I talk to her on the phone?"

"Perhaps," Daddy says, as if the thought had never occurred to him. "Does she have a phone?"

"I don't know," Ajay says.

"Even if she did, we don't know the number."

They dwell on this in mutual silence.

"What about the men who brought me here?" Ajay says. "Can we ask them?"

"They stopped coming years ago," Daddy replies. The trail widens, they pass an abandoned machine, the smell of rust and old oil hangs in the air. "Aren't you happy here?"

"I'm happy."

"You have everything you need. No hunger, no worry. You're surrounded by nature."

"I think about my mother sometimes."

Daddy sighs. "It's normal," he says.

"Sometimes I dream about her."

"Your mother wanted you to work."

"Sometimes I think of going back there after."

"After what?"

"After you're done with me. I want to go back there and be a big man."

"You do?"

"When I'm older."

"I feel bad that you want to leave."

"I won't leave," Ajay says.

They emerge from the woods and begin walking the short distance home along the road.

"Let's make a deal," Daddy says, his tone affectionate. "One day soon I'll tell you everything I know about your mother and your village. And then you can decide for yourself if you want to leave. OK?"

"OK."

"You understand no one is keeping you here against your will."

They walk on. The sky changes in the valley.

The glaciers toward Ladakh are melting.

"When will that be?" Ajay asks. "When will you tell me everything?"

Daddy frowns at the clouds.

"Let's say next year, when you turn sixteen."

Daddy dies a few months later, his Mahindra Armada colliding with a local bus late one night on a blind corner on the Bhuntar-Manikaran road. Twenty-six people perish. The driver was using an over-the-counter amphetamine; the conductor was the same age as Ajay.

Daddy's body is found the next day, sixty feet below the wreckage, cradled in the branches of a tree, soaked by rain, his bowels unspooled like a cassette tape in the gorge.

Ajay, all but forgotten in the outpouring of grief, takes refuge at the farm that day, tending to the animals, bringing down the milk, and slips down to his room at night only to sleep. The death, the cremation bring back frightening dreams. As soon as the final prayer ceremony takes place, four days after the crash, distraught Mummy is taken by her family back to her native place in another valley six hours away. Ajay watches as she's led to the car, driven away. He stands next to the window and reaches out to her, and she sees him but she doesn't speak or make a sign.

Then she's gone. The farm workers return to the farm and he's left alone in that house. He's been alone in the house many times before, but never like this, never without instructions, never without a horizon in sight. He builds a fire again, and when it's roaring, he begins to boil and skim milk. Then he cuts vegetables for a dinner that no one will eat. When all the dishes are done, sitting on the table with two place mats ready, he takes his metal tray and sits on the floor, eating his portion in silence. After dinner, after he's washed up, he takes a few tentative steps into the private section of the house, Mummy and Daddy's bedroom. He stands in the room, staring at the bed, the stuffed toys on Mummy's cabinet, the ticking clock on Daddy's desk. Finally he climbs on their bed, on Mummy's side, and curls up, smelling the pillow, hugging it, falling asleep. He wants to ask her so many things. He wants to ask about his mother's bank, the account number, where the branch can be found.

In the morning he wakes to find a man standing over him. He jumps in fright as he opens his eyes, scrambles to the corner of the room, head bowed.

"Dirty fellow," the man says. "Get out. Don't you have any shame?"

It's a relative of Daddy's come to take over the house and farm. He has brought his own boys.

Ajay is sent out into the main room. He stands dumbly between the kitchen and the stove, arms hanging limp. Things are already being shifted. The order he has helped to create, practiced and performed over the years, is being dismantled. The house already sounds wrong, it looks wrong, it's already no longer stable. He is told he has one hour to clear out.

"I can help," Ajay blurts out.

"I don't need help," the man replies.

"I'll work for free."

The man laughs bitterly. "You already do."

He's so desperate, he doesn't move. Hoping that might be an assent.

"What are you waiting for?" the man shouts, raising his hand in the air the way you wave off a stray dog.

"But where should I go?"

"What do I care? Go home."

It's April 1999. He has no papers, no identity card, no formal education, no wages, no security, only a few possessions: a wind-up duck, a collection of used matchboxes, his wits, his spattering of languages, his skill at serving a master. He climbs up to the farm and speaks words of good-bye to the cattle, allows their hot, soft tongues to wrap around his fingers, their nostrils and eyes flaring in pleasure and recognition. He has helped birth some of the cows. He has seen others die. When he comes down to the house, the furniture is already being rearranged; the rooms are being stripped of Mummy's things, which are to be sent away. There are other boys performing chores in ways he finds lacking. He waits for a quiet moment and takes his plate and his bowl from the kitchen and places them in a jute sack and steals his favorite kitchen knife, then runs down to his room and unlocks it and gathers the tips he has saved over the years, hidden deep in the clutter, in secret spaces, wrapped in several plastic bags against the damp. It's just under five thousand rupees, a fortune to be savored until this day, now a source of fear. When he leaves, carrying everything he owns in that one small sack, he locks the door behind him, then walks to the edge of the property. He stands on the lower wall, looking down over the valley and the river, down onto the field next door, takes his pants down and pisses toward the river, and when he's done, guessing he's being watched by the new residents of the house, he tosses his room key as hard as he can into the long, lush grass of the neighboring property.

He leaves that house, every inch of which he knows in his sleep, knowing he'll never see it again. Into the village he walks, through the inside paths, zigzagging on the steep slopes, cutting across the streams, through the orchards, around the backs of other houses, through yards of cats and dogs he knows. He climbs above the village, to the pine ridge, perches himself on a boulder.

What should he do? The world has opened up before him. He could travel to Delhi if he liked, and from Delhi he could fan out into UP. He could search out his mother and sister if he tried; if he really tried, he could still remember that land, how the foothills looked in the distance; given enough time, surely he would stumble upon it. He's strong now, he's smart. He can read and write, he can even speak some English. He could do it, it's not inconceivable. Only . . . every time his mind pursues that thought, it begins to shrink and crawl in fear. His mother's image withers, his sister's screams. Can he even remember what they look like now? He can still see them in his dreams, he sees their faces out of the corner of his eye, but when he tries to build their waking images, they crumble under the intensity of his grief. But surely, surely, they are rich now. They are happy because of him. That's why he worked so hard, that's why he sacrificed himself, that's why he was here so many years. Surely now they would be wealthy enough. If the money stopped appearing in her bank account, what would she think? That he was dead? Maybe. They would mourn him maybe. Maybe it was better to think of himself this way. He has paid his debt, now he is free.

He stands up with this sudden liberation and wanders down from the ridge, carrying his bag, into the village. It is possible now to see his freedom as an opportunity. He can live, if he wishes, as the foreigners do. Without ties, he can do anything. He can work in the city awhile, spend time in Delhi making money, discover the world and its wonders, go to far-off Bombay. He pictures it. He could work there awhile, get to know both places, find his mother and sister later on, at his own leisure, when he's a rich man. But then he wavers. He has no papers, after all. His identity is tied up in the farm, in Daddy, in this village. And what skills does he have for the city, a terrifying place?

He wanders into the village with these thoughts bubbling over one another and sits on the steps outside Purple Haze, one of the backpacker cafés in which he has spent so much time in his youth, tolerated then embraced the way stray dogs are embraced. The owner Surjeet has always been sympathetic to Ajay. He steps outside now to condole with Ajay on Daddy's death.

"Uh-ho, and what's this?" he asks, kicking Ajay's bag with his foot. "Going somewhere, are we? Do you have a holiday coming up or a pilgrimage?"

"No," Ajay shyly says.

"What then? Have you been thrown out?"

Ajay nods and smiles meekly.

Surjeet shakes his head. "I hear the new man is a thief. Where will you go?"

"Delhi."

"Hey! Don't go to Delhi," Surjeet says. "The city is a devil."

"I'll work there," Ajay says.

"More likely you'll be killed."

Ajay waits patiently, expecting more.

"Listen," Surjeet finally says. "My customers know you already. I know how hard you work. Why don't you just stay here and work for me? For money, like a real worker."

It's frightening how quickly Ajay agrees.

He slips into this life of service. He's paid two thousand rupees a month plus food and gets to sleep on a mattress on the café floor with the other boys at night, laid out when the tables and chairs have been packed away. Surjeet lives in a house in the village—he leaves around six p.m.; the café boys—all Nepalis who've been there years—stay up after the café is closed, cooking their own food, smoking cheap cigarettes, watching movies on laser discs, talking longingly about home, about what they'll do one day when they have enough money saved, the cafés they'll open, the farm machinery they'll buy. But not Ajay. He does his work, sweeps up, makes sure the café is in order, then he's the first to sleep, at ten on the dot, curled up at one side, oblivious to the noise, the laughter. It never occurs to him to be part of them, to ask to be part of them, and it never occurs to them to ask it of him—they accept him as he is, without malice or curiosity. He's the first to wake too, before dawn. He doesn't want to risk disrupting the fortune of finding this place, doesn't want to put his security at risk with irregular behavior. As soon as he wakes, after folding his bedding away, he climbs fifteen minutes through the forest, brushing his teeth with a twig as he walks, heading to a small waterfall he knows with a bar of soap in his hand. He strips and washes himself there naked in the freezing water, forgetting everything for a moment, then he returns to the café and takes the waste scraps from the previous day to feed to the cows and the chicken bones for the stray dogs in the square. When he returns to the café he quietly sweeps up the debris of the night as the boys still sleep, then as they wake, he begins to set out the tables and chairs. The Nepalis stretch, spit, brush their teeth, wrap themselves in shawls, look dumbly out at the mountains, light cigarettes, watch him pick up their slack, then they turn the burners on and make chai, cook breakfast, look on him in gentle puzzlement. Soon his hard work belongs to them, he is like a mascot. They let him be, indulge him, in a way. He works that first season in this manner, without flagging or wavering. He passes no judgment, makes no enemies, keeps his opinions to himself. Smiles and nods at every request. The boys take care of him. Cook extra food for him, which he eats gratefully. He inspires friendship and loyalty.

When the season comes to an end, he counts his money and collects his share of tips. He's made fourteen thousand rupees in all—he can't believe how easy it is. It's almost as if he'd been given money for doing nothing. It becomes magical, unreal. He likes the security it brings; he could go any-where now, live for a while, make his own choices. But that has its own peril—and now he has a decision to make. Winter is approaching, the cafés have shut down, the snow will come, the roads will be blocked off, the vil-lage will hibernate, as it has done every year, and he has nowhere to go. If he stays, he must find a house in which to work to live. He asks Surjeet if he can stay—Surjeet says he's going himself, to Chandigarh, his home here will be shut and locked. "I can take care of it," Ajay says.

"Alone? All winter?"

"Yes."

"No, why don't you go and find other work and come back in the spring?"

Surjeet and his Nepali boys confer; Ajay is invited to travel with them to Delhi and on to Goa to work. All but two of them are heading to a shack on the beach, a place they always go. They call the owner. When they finally get through, they ask. And, yes, Ajay is welcome to come and work as one of them. They leave for Delhi two days later.

On the way down, setting out long before dawn, sitting on the bus with his head pressed against the cold window, watching the blue mountains un-fold, following the lines of terrain he knows so well, Ajay has another plan. It entered his head overnight when he couldn't sleep, though he was too nervous then to give it words. But now it's there, confirmed in the glory of momentum. He will do it, he'll do what he was told, what he was too scared to do before: he will go home.

How could he not?

With the money in his pocket, he will go home.

He will make his way somehow. His money will be his guide and his protector.

He breathes deeply, says good-bye to the mountains; his heart flutters and his mind races at the immensity of what's ahead. And finally he falls asleep.

He wakes in traffic and heat, the sun beating down on the left side of the bus, blazing on his forehead against the glass. It must be only nine a.m., but it's already much hotter than it should be. He's dazed. "Are we in Delhi?" The boys laugh. They're still up in the mountains. "It's so hot," he says in wonder. "It's hotter down here," one of the boys replies.

They are in a jam in the center of a market town, several buses and trucks and Tempos trying to get through a bottleneck. It's true, the mountains are still around them—he can see their peaks—but they are different, the sky is different, the air is thick with the black smoke of engines. Anxiety engulfs him. The heat is sickening, the horns of the traffic assail his mind. The plan that seemed so certain and secure suddenly terrifies him, seems to slip from his grasp. How could he have thought such a thing?

The sensation builds and consolidates itself throughout the day. How is he supposed to survive this? To navigate this treacherous sea of bodies and objects? The money in his pocket seems barely adequate. The awful gnawing in his stomach won't go away. When they finally reach Delhi, he is in abject despair. The city overwhelms him; he's totally oppressed by the noise, the unrelenting concrete, the chaos of it. He can decipher no pattern at all. When they climb out of the bus, he sticks close to the Nepalis. They head off with purpose to the place they always stay—a rooftop adjacent to a hotel in Paharganj where other Nepalis work. Even as they keep telling him to stay close, he almost loses them several times, buffeted by the crowds, harassed by hisses and foul words. He keeps his bag at his front, his money close to him. He's relieved when they find their way to the hotel, wind through damp and stinking passageways, and emerge on the roof. It's placid up there, at least. The worst of the city is kept at bay. The boys warn him to keep his money and papers, anything of value, on his body all the time. Don't trust anyone here, don't wander off. They set up some mattresses on the roof, where they'll sleep huddled together under the stars. As the sun sets, the boys pitch some money together, the little they keep for their pleasure, which is not set aside for travel or sent back home, and go to the liquor store to buy a bottle of good whisky, their yearly indulgence. Then, with their friends from the hotel, they have a party on the roof, bring up a camping stove, make steamed chicken momos, pork sekuwa, tamatar jhol. They drink the whisky, finish the bottle between them, sing songs for hours. Ajay sits at the side, watching, always watching; he doesn't touch the liquor, barely touches the food. He asks why they don't stay and work in the city. The city is bad, they say, it's full of con men, criminals, it's ugly and dirty, it's no good, only rich people do well, everyone else suffers. They lay their mattresses out, lie down to sleep. It's September—the night has the slightest chill. It might rain, one of them says. He's heard it's raining in Goa, a late monsoon burst. Have you seen the ocean before? No, Ajay says. You'll love it, comes the reply. It's different down there, not hard like the mountains. In Goa life is good.

Throughout the night he feels the distant roar of traffic entering his soul, the great trucks and their horns, the plaintive bleating of exile. He follows their sounds and imagines this vast terrible land from which he was born. The idea to leave, to find home, seems pathetic to him. It is impossible. There is no home, he keeps having to remind himself, he has to let it go. He drifts to sleep with that idea in mind. And in the morning, as the temple bells sound and the bhajans begin their hypnotic rise and fall, Ajay stands ready to leave.

They arrive in Goa three days later and pitch up in a shack in Arambol called RoknRoll. It is here that Ajay sees the ocean, stands in front of it on the beach, lets the waves wrap around his ankles, suck on his bare feet. His days are full and empty at once, and work is the most pleasurable it's ever been. It's a good life, in Goa. They like him in the shack too, a hard worker who doesn't smoke or drink. A boy who can already speak basic English and Nepali. They like him because he knows how to behave, knows how not to look at the foreign women too long, not to ask too many questions. The foreigners like him too; he's diligent, he runs back to the kitchen with an order, hurries back with the food and a smile. The girls like him because he is shy and handsome and his teeth are perfectly white and his body holds no fat and he doesn't stare, doesn't try to charm them with cheap words and posturing. He is beloved. He only serves. Everything is forgotten. A season goes by like this. Mostly sun-blind. Sometimes reflected by violent shards. Keeping their toothbrushes together in the humid bathroom at the back. Sharing the leftover Axe deodorant, the leftover T-shirts and jeans. Ajay half adrift. Sunburnt and petrified. He learns to swim, first the doggy paddle, then as the season progresses, some foreigners show him the breaststroke and later on the front crawl. He learns to guide a motorboat too, goes crab fishing on the rocks at low tide in the moonlight and sleeps on the beach under the stars. He plays volleyball and cricket and football in the siesta of the afternoon, when business is at a lull. He eats fish and beef and chicken carbonara and french fries, mango, coconut water, pineapple; he becomes tanned all over.

He feels blessed, content. But he tells himself in the dark: *You know how precarious life can be.*

It's true.

Some of the Nepalis have been dealing their charas down here. They bring it from the mountains every season, one hundred tolas in total. Perfect mountain charas. Sticky and green, wrapped in cellophane. They sell it from the shack itself, take the order with the food order, it's the system: the customer orders the "special mountain sizzler," a dish not on the menu. They pay for it with their food bill, it's there on the receipt with the other dishes. The charas is passed to the customer in one of the little wooden receipt boxes along with their change. It's a good system. The landlord takes his cut, as do the police. But some of the boys are greedy, they deal on the beach alone too, without protection, and some deal in other bars and on the back roads at night. One day one of the boys is found dead in the jungle, tied to a tree, a rag in his mouth, his hands cut off.

He is cremated. It's forgotten.

It's never forgotten.

The boys, fraying at the edges, live quietly like there's no tomorrow. Some of them have foreign girlfriends, girls they meet in the café, get friendly with, give drugs to, take out to spots in the jungle or on motorbikes to waterfalls

far inland, show them hidden places, looking for that long-shot promise—
"I'll sponsor your visa, come live with me." The boys encourage Ajay to find
a girl. What is he waiting for? He has enough admirers. The girls often ask
about him. But he's too shy; he recoils. He cannot conceive of it, his own body
terrifies him, his own needs. He likes to set himself within limits; those limits keep him strong. He sleeps curled up on the beach, spooning the beach
dogs that are drawn to his gentleness and the scent of mutual need.

He builds a fantasy: He will return home to take his mother and sister
away. He'll arrive in a car of his own, a driver in front, he sitting behind, and
they'll all weep when he touches his mother's feet. And the whole village
will rejoice.

7.

It might have gone on like this forever, a life deferred, if it weren't for the
sudden appearance of Sunny Wadia. He arrives when Ajay has gone back to
the mountains, returned from Goa to Purple Haze for the summer season
of 2001.

Sunny is the leader of a small band of revelers, Indians who live like the
foreigners, still something of a rarity in those days. Who live like the foreigners but who are not like the foreigners at all, four men and one woman,
something dangerously new and bold; young, rich, and glamorous Indians,
not afraid to show it, not afraid to slum it, welcome everywhere, welcomed
by themselves. Travelers for whom authenticity is not a question, content to
sit in the cafés with the foreigners and smoke chillum and eat their backpacker food, who arrived in big, shiny cars without scratches instead of
buses and bikes and wore good clothing and stayed in the best new hotels in
the village, ones with bright pine balconies and expensive bars.

Ajay has never encountered Indians like this. In no time this small group
seems to take over the village. Shopkeepers are sending packages and par-

cels of goods to their hotel. Drivers are loitering, itching to serve, waiting to take them on tours, take them to parties so they don't have to drive themselves. And unlike the foreigners, who count every rupee, money is no object for this new group, money is nothing to be concerned with, there's no virtue in penny-pinching. They *spend*. They want their comforts; they make no romance out of misery. Word of their big spending and the high tips that go with it spreads. The economy of the village is redirected their way. All the workers want a piece of them, all the villagers want a piece of them. Everyone vies for their favor. But some of the foreigners begin to grumble. These Indians, some say, don't understand their own culture; they have been infected by the West. It's a sad sign, how they've lost their way.

But the boys in Purple Haze fall into animated discussion whenever they see them, analyzing this group's activities in great detail. Five of them! So glamorous. The men so handsome and rich. And one woman with the men! Who is she married to? Whose girlfriend is she? How is it possible? Where do you think they're from? Chandigarh, Delhi, Bombay? Someone decides the woman is a famous actress. Someone thinks there's a cricket player among them. These Indians sit in the cafés smoking charas every day, paying without hesitation for Malana Cream. They swallow up the places they go, they invade them, colonize them, move on. Money does that. They want the walnut cake here. They want the banana crepes there. They like this stroganoff. They order dishes from one café to be delivered while they sit in the next. They sit in Purple Haze and order dishes from MoonBeam.

"You have no respect," a voice says. It's a Spanish woman, rake thin and wrinkle tanned, in her forties, smoking a cigarette, sitting across the café, picking a fight with them. "You cannot just do like this," she goes on. She is waving her arms at them, worked up. "Doing like this is not right." She points to the owner. "He make his food." She points to her own dish. "And you bring in like that. You have no shame."

They watch, bemused, and begin to joke in Hindi. "Listen to this chutiya . . . Bitch is crazy."

"Don't you laugh at me," she yells. "Don't you talk about me."

"Ma'am," one of the group chimes in, speaking languid, London-tinged English. "With all due respect, if you learned the language of this country, you'd know we weren't talking about you."

"Don't give me your bullshit," she says, jabbing her cigarette his way. "I've seen you walking around here."

"Ma'am, there's no need for foul language," Sunny says with a faux earnest expression that makes his friends burst into giggles. In Hindi comes the muttered aside: "She's a psycho," and they laugh even more.

"Fuck you," she says. "You come here with your money and your big cars and think you can do anything you like, that you can order everyone around. You have your money, but you lost your culture."

The group explodes with laughter.

But the young man's mood darkens.

"Madam," he replies. "Don't tell us about our culture. We're not zoo animals for your pleasure, not the smiling native to accessorize your enlightenment. The simplicity and honesty you think you know is simply your eyes deceiving your brain. You see and hear nothing. And this guy," he says, pointing to the owner, "doesn't give a fuck if we bring food from outside. We paid him for that privilege. If you could speak our language, you'd know this. If you knew our culture, you'd know respect is one currency, but at the end of the day, money talks. Finally, understand this one thing. India is our country, not yours. You are guests here. We are great hosts, but don't disrespect us in our own home."

This young man is Sunny Wadia. Tall, imposing, charismatically handsome. Almond eyes, a pleasingly aquiline nose, a short beard of dense black. His hair is cropped, his chest is broad, his forearms strong. He wears a faded vintage T-shirt, aviator shades. He sits halfway between holy and profane.

After a few days, Sunny's group settles on Purple Haze. They like the feel, the service, the vibe. They charm the Nepalis; they are superior and fraternal at once, joking with the boys, asking favors, commandeering the sound system to play their music. Knowing the tips that come their way, the chefs have no problem making off-menu food.

Ajay, unsettled, full of nervous excitement, studies them intensely, fascinated by their behavior, by the wealth they bring, the ease with which they carry it. He watches all the time and tries not to stare. He watches Sunny closest of all, he's been watching him for days now. Sometimes Sunny laughs harder than anyone. Sometimes he cuts his friends down. But barring the one incident with the Spanish woman, he's courteous to a fault with strangers. He invites people to join them, he asks questions, he offers considered opinions. At every occasion, he is the one to pay.

Ajay takes it upon himself to make sure Sunny has everything he needs. If he sees a cigarette packet opening, he's there with a lighter. He's there with a napkin seconds after something spills. He brings Sunny's food first, clears his plates as soon as he's finished, makes sure the table is spotlessly clean. This isn't lost on the group. They're amused. "Look at him, he's your chela." To take advantage of his energy, they make him do other chores. Send him out to pick up groceries, pay him to get their clothes laundered, pay him to wash their cars. Use him to score their charas. When they realize that he excels at packing a chillum, he is employed in this manner. He's vigorous and meticulous when cleaning the pipe with gauze; he has the deft action of a shoeshine boy, the eye of a watchmaker; they laugh at him in admiration. Such attention to detail, such connoisseurship. Does he want to smoke up with them? He shakes his head with horror. No way. Good boy, they say. Soon he is going around to their rooms in the morning before he starts work and after, when he should be resting, fetching what they need. They find his eagerness extraordinary, sometimes endearing, sometimes a little pathetic. Someone comes up with a new name. Puppy. Puppy's here.

Sunny is interested in land. He's decided he wants to build around here. He wants his own villa or hotel, somewhere to escape to, to crash. Somehow word goes around. But land is hard to acquire up here. He needs a local partner, for a start. An outsider can't just buy land alone. Only, now that his hand has been shown, now that it is known he wants something concrete from this place, attitudes change: he has become an opportunity. Self-appointed property brokers loiter, villagers who "know a place" come to talk to him. He's offered inferior plots of land, and he knows how this works. They'll try to bleed him for everything he's worth. Sunny, circled by vultures, becomes annoyed by the stupidity of the world. He suspects some of his friends have talked about his interests. Ajay hears him chastise them one day as they sprawl on the cushions of the café, morning mist hanging on the mountains across the way, a little rain falling on the ancient cobbled alleyways. How else would word have gotten out? Sunny retreats moodily into himself. For several days he is sullen with everyone. He rarely leaves Purple Haze, smoking up all day, speaking to no one, plotting darkly. The fun stops when Sunny wills it. And Ajay stands and waits attentively by his side.

Then a few mornings into this grand sulk a new friend arrives to shift the mood. A tall, craggy Sikh wearing combat pants and a Superman T-shirt, a deep scar running down his forehead, splitting his nose. He comes in a souped-up Gypsy jeep, almost crashing into the café as he screeches to a halt, seventies' rock blaring from his outrageous speakers so loudly that a crowd forms from the shops and houses and cafés to watch him sweep in. Sunny runs to embrace him. Sunny's friends, who have been quiet, follow suit.

The man is called Jigs. "The Jig is up!" he cries.

He has come from the golf course in Chandigarh, he explains. He hit an albatross yesterday afternoon and was hoisted onto the shoulders of his brethren before they drank the clubhouse dry. At four in the morning, cruising the streets, he decided he would drive to the mountains to take the party up a notch. He'd heard Sunny was there. He went home and woke his wife, took a little speed and a little acid from his drawer, then set out from the city at five a.m., driving nonstop with a twelve-pack of beer and a pint of whisky to keep him company and a bunch of money to dish out to the cops.

He runs down to the Gypsy, strewn as it is with cans, and fetches from the glove compartment his hand-carved Italian chillum.

"Give it to him," Sunny says, pointing at Ajay. "He packs a killer pipe." He calls Ajay directly. "Hey," he says, snapping his fingers, "get the gauze."

Ajay's heart soars.

Sunny and Jigs party four days straight, trance music throbbing from Jigs's hotel room, the owner paid off handsomely. Ajay is charged with bringing beer to them, delivering charas and the occasional parcel of food. Sunny's other friends, the ones he came with, retreat to different hotels or drive home, fleeing down the mountain, unable to take the new pace. When Ajay makes his deliveries, entering the smoke-hazed room, with the UV lights Jigs has brought along in the car now glowing, with the curtains drawn, with the floor littered with pizza boxes and trays of food and overflowing ashtrays and used gauze, all semblance of propriety and sobriety gone, he shows no emotion at all, no judgment, no reaction. He only does as he's told.

On the fifth morning Sunny and Jigs disappear off in the Gypsy, bouncing down the road.

The village is suddenly silent. The whirlwind is over. Back in Purple Haze, back to his daily life, in the bad graces of the Nepali boys for shirking his duties there, Ajay is bereft.

But two days later Sunny returns, wandering into the village from the woods above, alone, barefoot, his clothes dirty and torn. He looks as if he had been to war, he seems not to recognize himself. He stutters here and there until Ajay catches sight of him and brings him into the café, guides him to a cushioned seat out of the way, and fetches a mug of green tea, rolls a joint for him. Sunny smokes the joint and sits like that for an hour, while Ajay serves other customers, then he calls him over and demands a beer, but before Ajay can hurry away to fetch it, Sunny says, "Ajay. Look at me."

Sunny's eyes are wide open, darker than usual. His breath is shallow. He is clinging to the edge of something no one else can see. It's the first time he's used Ajay's name.

"Where are you from?" Sunny says.

"From here."

"No," Sunny says in exasperation. "No." He taps his fist on the table. "No. You're not from here. You're not from here, you're not mountain blood." He peers into Ajay with his dark eyes. "So where are you from? Tell me."

"Uttar Pradesh," Ajay says in a whisper.

"Yes!" Sunny says. "Yes, you're from UP."

Sunny fills his chest with air and sits up.

"Where in UP?" Sunny says.

"I don't know," Ajay says.

Sunny stares hard into the boy. "It doesn't matter," he declares. "You and me, we're from the same soil. We're brothers." He closes his eyes and keeps them closed, sitting upright, forces a disarming smile. "Now go get my fucking beer."

"You take care of me," he says, when Ajay returns.

"Yes, sir."

"You don't want anything in return."

It is not framed as a question. Ajay doesn't know what to say.

"Where's your family?" Sunny goes on, trying to be more businesslike, taking hold of the beer.

"I don't know."

"Why don't you know?"

"My father died," Ajay says.

"And you ran away from home?"

Ajay shakes his head. "My mother sent me away."

"And?"

"I worked in a house here, but the man died."

Something about this image calms Sunny down. He leans back and closes his eyes for a moment, but then opens them as if the dark were too much for him.

"Do you like it here?" he asks. "Don't you want something more?"

"Something more," Ajay hears himself saying.

"How would you like to do something with your life? Something important?"

"Yes."

Sunny struggles with his wallet. He tries to look inside but has trouble focusing, so he hands it to Ajay instead.

"You've been good to me," he says. "You never tried to get anything from me."

Ajay holds the wallet, unsure what he's supposed to do. There's no money in there anyway.

"Take out," Sunny says, "one of the white cards."

Ajay fishes out a business card.

"Take it," Sunny says. "It's yours."

He hands back the wallet and examines the card. On the front, embossed in dark gray lettering, it says two words: SUNNY WADIA.

Ajay mouths the name.

"Give it here," Sunny says. "Go fetch me a pen."

Ajay hands it back and runs to fetch a pen.

"I'm leaving now," Sunny says when Ajay returns. "If you want to work"—he takes great effort scribbling something down on the back of the card—"come to Delhi to this address. Tell the guards you want to see Tinu. Hand them this card and say Sunny Wadia sent for you."

8.

Normal life resumes in Purple Haze, but for Ajay there's a big, Sunny Wadia–shaped hole in his heart. Everything that was once stable is subtly changed. He has not told anyone what Sunny offered. He only has the business card as proof. He keeps the card in his worn brown wallet, gifted to him by a German guest, folding too easily like old cardboard. He takes the card out often to turn in his fingers, to smell it sometimes, that faint smell of cologne, wealth, and happiness, always fading, the card beginning to fray if he touches it too long. He knows he should keep it put away, but he can't help looking, cherishing. It's the last thing he looks at before he falls asleep. But can he make this kind of leap? Six weeks pass, the mountain season draws to a close. Nothing changes, no one new comes to him, no new excitement pours into his life, everything is deaf and drained of color after Sunny Wadia. He begins to think about it seriously. He daydreams about what might happen if he turns up. Working in Delhi, working for Sunny Wadia. In a shop, maybe? Selling clothes? Or in an office somewhere? Wearing smart clothes himself, a shirt and tie, being modern like Sunny. But the dream gutters there. He can't imagine anything beyond it, how his life might really be. He puts the card back in the wallet and closes it away.

When the café closes, it's assumed that, as usual, he'll travel to Goa with the boys.

But the afternoon before the day they're due to leave, just after he receives his salary and tips, he packs his sports bag and walks away. Just packs his money and clothes and his few possessions and walks down the mountainside to where the bus waits. He catches the six p.m. bus to Delhi, sits staring out the window willing the engine to start.

He thinks he won't be able to sleep the whole way, but as soon as the bus starts moving, he's out like a light. It has a disorienting effect. He wakes in the dark hours later, hurtling down the many folds of mountain hundreds of kilometers to the plains. *I can come back*, he thinks. *I will just see what it's like*. But a part of him knows he'll never return. And there's something liberating about leaving, it's true, about throwing so many years over his shoulder and marching forward to a majestic life.

When he reaches the city, deposited at the Interstate Bus Terminal, he approaches a group of loitering men who are touting for business, trying to sell rooms, to ask if they can show him where he's going. He recites the address from memory, and they look at one another, one of them saying he's heading that way and can take him right there. Ajay climbs in an auto with him, and three others suddenly join. They take him a short distance, then stop in a quiet alley to beat him and rob him of all his things.

He roams the streets for the next few hours in a state of shock, bleeding from the nose and several cuts to his face, grieving the loss of everything he owns. Without the Nepali boys to guide him, everything is alien and threatening, everyone a potential assailant. He walks without a compass, hoping to stumble on an answer, but he cannot solve the puzzle of the city and is afraid to ask.

He wanders into a wealthier part of town, with wide boulevards and tree-shrouded bungalows guarded by cops. He passes a pair and they hustle him on as if he were a vagrant.

After an hour he takes the chance to sit outside a chai shop beside a busy junction. A perky auto driver takes an interest in him, asking him what happened to his face. When he summons up the courage to tell him about the theft, and why he's in the city in the first place, the driver buys him chai and bun-makhan and tells him he'll take him where he needs to go. In this moment of hope, Ajay remembers the card. He searches his shirt—yes, it's there! In his top pocket. He feels a burst of hope and pride and holds the card out, showing the address scrawled in slanting handwriting on the back. But the auto driver is only interested in the name on the front.

"You know who this is?" he says, whistling to himself.

"Yes," Ajay replies. "He's a good man."

"And you're gonna work there? Lucky kid. Who cares if anyone robbed you." He hands the card back. "Let's get going." He puts his arm round Ajay. "Just don't forget your friends."

It's turning to dusk when they pull into the narrow road full of shiny cars and piles of construction sand and blocks of inscrutable residential buildings hidden behind huge gates. Ajay is hungry and nervous, with bruises and cuts on his face, but his adrenaline soars when he sees these gates, the grandeur of the buildings they shield.

"This is it," the auto driver says, pointing toward the gate directly in front, where two armed guards stand outside. The building is a solid, dark, impregnable block, five floors high, its smooth, muscular walls obscured by creepers and vines and mirrored glass holding secrets inside.

As he climbs out, the men eye him distastefully, their hands tightening round their rifles.

"What do you want?" one says. "If you're begging food you can go to the temple."

"He's here for a job," the auto driver shouts. "Someone needs to pay me too."

"Get lost," one of the guards says to the auto driver.

"What do you want?" the other says to Ajay.

"I want to see . . ." Ajay's voice is so quiet they can barely hear.

"What? Speak up."

"I'm here to see Tinu," Ajay says in a clearer voice.

The guards laugh. "Tinu-ji? What do you want with Tinu? What does Tinu want with a dog like you?"

Ajay hesitates. Then he reaches into his top pocket. His fingers caress the card. He withdraws it and steps forward and holds it out nervously, as if it might disintegrate. "See," he says, praying it will work. "Sunny Wadia sent for me."

A phone call is made, the gates are opened, and he is led by a guard into a driveway packed with pristine cars, through a small side door into this monumental house. Along the brightly lit passage, like a cave, into another corridor and another, turning in a maze, waiting for a service elevator, going down a level, heading along another corridor. He passes dozens of people, kitchens and rooms with beds and offices, sees men and women in uniform.

He asks the guard, "Is this a hotel?" but the guard doesn't speak.

After several twisting minutes he is delivered to a small, stuffy room, like a cabin in a ship. A squat man of around fifty with a potbelly and a squashed face only a mother could love is reclining on a bed watching TV, wearing a white undershirt and dark pants. He stirs a little, belches inwardly, frowns as the guard salutes and leaves.

"So," he turns to look at Ajay, "what's this about?"

"Sir, are you Tinu-ji?"

The man puts on a shirt, combs his hair. He points to a strip of tablets. "Pass me those."

Ajay passes the tablets.

"Acidity," the man says, popping one in his mouth, then, "Yes. I'm Tinu."

Ajay holds out the card. "Sunny Sir sent for me."

Tinu reaches for a pair of glasses on his side table—with these perched on the end of his nose he looks like a small-town bureaucrat or a senior clerk, yesteryear's bruiser turned good. He looks between Ajay's face and the card. "What happened to you?"

"Sir, some men robbed me."

"You let them rob you. Never mind." He looks over the card, back and front, feels it between his fingers, and puts it down beside him. "Where did you get this?"

"Sunny Sir gave it."

"Yes," Tinu nods. "Where?"

"Manali. Six weeks before."

"Right," Tinu says, sounding unimpressed. "And he offered you a job?"

"Yes, sir."

"Why?"

Ajay is thrown by the question. He looks on helplessly. Tinu raises his eyebrows. "I asked a question."

"Sir, I helped him."

"You helped him?"

"Yes, sir."

"You're a shack boy?"

"Yes, sir."

"You helped buy him drugs . . ."

"No, sir."

"What did you help him with?"

"Errands, sir."

"Errands . . ." Tinu checks his watch. "It's late," he says. "We'd better put you in a room." He presses a buzzer and a boy not unlike Ajay arrives. "Give him a bed for the night, take him to the kitchen to eat." He looks at Ajay. "We'll deal with you in the morning. Go."

"Sir?" Ajay says, turning to leave.

"What is it now?"

"The card, sir."

Tinu rolls his eyes but hands it back and Ajay bows a little and is gone.

He is led along another set of corridors and another, down a flight of stairs to a cramped dorm room in the bowels of the building. He is led into one with four bunks, the bottom two already occupied.

"Take one," the servant says, pointing to the top. "The cupboard is for your things. Where are your things?"

"I don't have any."

"Go to the kitchen at the end," he points vaguely in the direction they've come from, "get some food. Then sleep."

It doesn't take him long to sleep. He's seen submarines in the movies. He imagines he's in one, that they're sailing under Delhi now. He listens to the clanking of pipes and the muffled noises of the kitchen down the end of the corridor. Some men come and go in the bunks, which have curtains to draw for privacy, like a sleeper bus.

In the morning the room is empty. He sits in the bed with the curtain drawn back, fully dressed, waiting. Another boy comes for him and takes him to the kitchen to eat breakfast, then takes him to a tailor's cabin in the basement, where he's fitted for a uniform, then given three white under-shirts, three powder-blue shirts, and two pairs of black trousers in his size, one belt and three pairs of socks and a pair of black shoes also in his size. At a small pharmacy window next to the tailor's he is given soap and shampoo and a toothbrush and some deodorant and nail clippers. He's told to shower using soap twice a day, to use deodorant, to wash his hands every few hours or after any activity where dirt might get on them, to always wash them before handling food and after he uses the bathroom, and to always keep his fingernails clipped and clean. He carries the clothes and supplies back to his dorm, showers and changes into the clothes, then he is brought up to the second floor in the building, seeing flashes of the outside world for the first time, to an office where one Mr. Dutta, graying and bookish with sprouting ear hair and a light mustache, sits behind a desk crammed with ledgers, smoking a cigarette.

"Who are you?"

"Ajay, sir."

Mr. Dutta pauses and inspects him closer, putting out his cigarette.

"You're the boy Sunny sent for?"

"Yes, sir."

"Lucky you," he says.

Then comes a long list of questions.

"Do you drink liquor?"

"No, sir."

"Smoke?"

"No."

"Take drugs?"

"No, sir."

"Sell drugs?"

"No."

"But you know what drugs are, don't you?"

"Yes, sir."

"Because you're a shack boy."

"I worked in a café, sir."

"Can you drive?"

"Yes."

"Two-wheeler, four-wheeler?"

"Everything, sir."

"Trucks and buses?"

"No, sir."

"So not everything."

"No, sir. I can drive a tractor, sir."

"You grew up in the mountains."

"Yes, sir."

"Doing what?"

"I worked on a farm. I made ghee."

"You made ghee? Very good."

"Then a café."

"You were in Goa also?"

"Yes, sir."

"And you didn't sell drugs?"

"No, sir."

"You must have seen all kinds of wrong things?"

"Yes, sir."

"Crazy people."

"Yes, sir."

"You know all the different things people do."

"Yes, sir."

"And you're discreet."

"Sir?"

"Careful. Quiet."

"Yes."

"You can keep secrets?"

"Yes."

"And you're loyal?"

"Yes."

"Do you know who Sunny Wadia is?"

"Sir, he's a big man."

"He's the son of a big man. Everything you see here is because of his father, Bunty Wadia. We all owe our happiness to him. He's a great man. You may answer to Sunny now, but we all answer to Bunty-ji. Bunty-ji is God. Remember that."

"Yes, sir."

"Have you been to school?"

"I left when I was eight."

"But you're smart?"

"I can read and write. I can understand English. Also some Hebrew, German, Japanese, sir."

"Married?"

"No, sir."

"No children?"

He shakes his head shyly.

"How old are you?"

"Sir, I don't know. Eighteen? Nineteen?"

"OK then, let's give you a birthday. Let's say . . . January first, 1982?"

"Sir, OK."

"You like girls?"

Ajay doesn't know what to say.

"One day soon you'll be working alongside girls. If you touch them, we won't spare you."

"Yes, sir."

"If you want girls, go to GB Road."

Ajay doesn't know where that is.

"If you fuck with the women here, we cut off your balls."

"Yes, sir."

"And if you're caught stealing, we cut off your hand."

"Yes, sir."

Mr. Dutta lights a cigarette.

"Good. Where's your native place?"

"UP."

"Your family is there?"

"I don't know."

"Why?"

"I left when I was small."

"You don't go back?"

"No. My father died."

"So no holidays for Diwali. You're not going to take three days' leave and come back three weeks later?"

"No, sir."

"Good. Do you have a PAN card? A bank account?"

"No, sir."

"Money?"

"Everything was stolen."

"What do you mean?"

"Yesterday, when I arrived in Delhi."

"That's what happened to your face?"

"Yes, sir."

"How much did you lose?"

Ajay lowers his head.

"Thirty-two thousand, sir."

Mr. Dutta whistles and shakes his head, makes a note, closes his book, and stares at the cover a moment. "Chalo. Go to Elite Saloon in the market for a haircut and shave. You won't have to pay. Then we'll have a doctor look at your face. We'll open a bank account and start you on five thousand a month. You'll get a phone. Keep it with you at all times, keep it charged. And here"—he opens a drawer and counts out five one-hundred rupee notes—"this is your advance."

"Thank you, sir."

"The rest is up to Sunny, you'll report to him. He's your boss now. Do what he says and you'll be fine."

"Yes, sir."

"And smile. You're a Wadia man now. No one will ever steal from you again."

He has a haircut and a shave in the market and when he returns a doctor tends to the cuts on his face, cleans his wounds, and hands him one pain-killer and one antibiotic. He is shown around the servants' areas below ground, shown where he is and isn't to go, then in the afternoon he is sent up to Sunny. He still cannot comprehend the dimensions of this house; this house is like nothing he's ever seen. A uniformed boy leads him back through corridors he thinks he knows, and when he reaches the ground floor through a small flight of stairs the surroundings abruptly change, the functional tiles and white lighting give way to rugs and ornate furniture, to paintings on the walls, to fantastic displays of wealth. They travel up a central flight of shallow marble stairs, with each floor leading off through several heavy wooden doors into different apartments, some he can see as servants pass in and out. On the third floor they turn into one of these doors and enter another maze of passageways, softly lit, decorated with stat-ues of gods and soothing sacred music, speckled white marble underfoot. At the end of one corridor there's an elevator. They enter, he and the silent, uniformed boy, and travel to the fifth floor. As soon as the elevator opens they are met by a red-leather-padded door and a stairway falling down to the right. The boy rings the bell on the door and a chubby young man with la-conic eyes opens up to let them in.

A burst of light and air. Sunny's apartment is the penthouse. Ajay enters a vast main room full of plush sofas and low tables full of hardback books, a raised level on the far-right side with more sofas and a giant TV; bright, gar-ish paintings on the wall; odd sculptures and lamps dotted around; trays of fresh fruit beautifully cut; and past the raised section a small, cramped-looking kitchen incongruous with the rest. On the left there's another sec-tion with a dining table and eight chairs, and beyond it a bank of glass doors leading to what looks like a pool, through which floods warm afternoon light. It seems to Ajay that this place exists in a universe of its own, detached from the working bowels of the vast mansion, the muted and austere opulence of the other upper floors. Yes, after the crushing authority of the building, after the windowless weight of his own dorm room, this apartment feels like paradise.

He stands dumbly, inhaling it all. Then he hears the voice he has yearned for for so long, coming from a door to the rear of the apartment.

"Arvind?" it shouts.

"Yes, sir?"

"Who's here?"

"Sir," the chubby servant replies, "the new boy is here."

"What new boy?"

"Sir, the one from the mountains."

There's a few seconds of silence.

"Send him in."

"Go," Arvind whispers.

Ajay heads toward Sunny's voice, pauses on the threshold.

"Get in here!"

When he enters, he's hit by the icy blast of the AC. The room is windowless, sparsely furnished. Marble floors, cream-painted walls, a large low bed in which Sunny sits topless, rolling a joint.

"Sir," Ajay says.

Sunny looks up and studies Ajay dispassionately. "What happened to your face?"

"Sir . . ." Ajay fumbles.

Just as he is about to regain his composure a door behind the bed opens, and the girl from the mountains, the "actress," walks out, dressed in short silk boxers and a man's shirt.

"It's Puppy!" she exclaims. "He's come. Oh, how sweet. But what did he do to his face?" She flops down on the bed and Ajay doesn't know where to put his eyes. "I want coffee," she says idly.

"Go make coffee," Sunny orders. "There are beans in the kitchen."

Ajay is frozen to the spot, overawed by it all.

"Chutiya," Sunny cries. "What are you waiting for?"

9.

His official workday begins at six a.m. He wakes each day at four, spends a good hour in the shared bathroom scrubbing himself, brushing his teeth, cleaning his nails, oiling and parting his hair, making sure his shoes are shined and his clothes are immaculately ironed and creased.

His job is to manage the mornings. When Sunny wakes, he does not want to see the debris of the previous night. Most nights Sunny has friends over until late. Sometimes when Ajay enters he feels he's missed them all by seconds. A cigarette still burning in an ashtray, a CD still playing low. He has his routine, collecting the empty bottles first, with great care so as not to make them clink. Then it's the empty glasses. Then the ashtrays. Then he begins to sweep. He checks empty cigarette packets for forgotten charas at the bottom, puts any he might find, or other drugs, in little baggies, away safely in a drawer. Then he checks the sofas for lost phones or money or credit cards, plumps the pillows, mops the floor.

He prefers it when he's alone. But two or three mornings a week he walks in to find Sunny with a handful of friends, shutters down, lights on low, a fug of smoke in the air, a movie on the TV, or else a group out by the pool, on the sunbeds listening to music. Then he has to take more care, be more discreet, balance cleaning with the mental hardship it might cause. He knows to listen to people's needs. He knows those who stay awake at this hour don't want harsh lights turned on, don't want to be asked frivolous questions, don't want to feel bad about themselves. He knows to make himself invisibly available here. Also, to bring out blankets and put them within arm's reach, to brew a pot of chamomile tea and leave it on the table, to massage Sunny's feet if need be.

Sunny, he learns, is meticulous about certain things. Hygiene, for example. Also, temperature. The air-conditioning must be running day and night at 17 degrees Celsius.

At seven thirty a.m., on a normal day at least, when the apartment is set to rights, he must deliver warm lemon water with grated turmeric root to Sunny's bedside and play the Gayatri Mantra at volume setting 14. This is followed twenty minutes later by a pot of filter coffee, a bowl of fruit, orange juice, and fresh croissants sent each morning from the bakery at the Oberoi. Next he draws Sunny a piping hot bath, filling the tub, tossing in scented oils or salts, scattering rose petals on the surface. At eight he fetches all the newspapers and the latest magazines. Around nine thirty, it's breakfast time. Sometimes toasted ham and cheese sandwiches, sometimes egg bhurji with white toast and ketchup, sometimes aloo parathas, sometimes nothing at all. After breakfast Ajay stands attentive while Sunny decides what he will wear that day, Ajay fetching the options from the walk-in closet, holding them up with accessories, listening to Sunny explain pairing and matching and the finer points of tailoring, which he says he learned about in Italy. Then, while Sunny dresses, Ajay prepares his briefcase for the day, packing his laptop and charger, his papers and documents, his cigarettes—Treasurer London—and his Zippo lighter. When Sunny leaves, Ajay takes inventory and restocks the fridge and the bar, which is depleted nightly. Beer, wine, and champagne are lined up in the vast fridge, vodka and gin enter the freezer, and the cupboards are refilled with whatever whisky, rum, and cognac have been consumed. The bottles are fetched from a giant storeroom in the basement, monitored by cameras and unlocked with a combination on the cage door. It has more varieties of alcohol than Ajay has ever seen, boxes and boxes and crates stacked high. Often Ajay spends time trying to memorize each brand, learning the colors of the bottles and their labels and their names by heart. If Sunny is home in the day, his lunch—dal, roti, chicken or mutton curry, sabzi—is served at one p.m.,

while Sunny catches up on emails or watches TV. He offers Sunny a cigarette once the meal is ended, lights it, and fetches coffee. Black, two sugars.

Ajay takes a break between two and three, during which he eats his own
lunch (leftovers from Sunny's menu). The afternoon and evening are unstruc-
tured. Sometimes he must clean the terrace pool, sometimes he is sent with a
driver on errands or else must deliver something to a hotel where Sunny might
be that afternoon. Sometimes he must do nothing but wait.

Six p.m.—his shift is ending. Now is the time for aperitivo, for saffron
almonds, oven-roasted olives, artichoke hearts, for Negroni Sbagliato (the
flavor of the month), the Campari, the Cocchi Storico Vermouth di Torino,
and the Bisol Cartizze Prosecco Valdobbiadenc laid out ready with the jig-
ger, the rocks glass, the ice bucket and tongs, the orange and lemon, the
paring knife, and the fresh cigarettes, unwrapped, packed down, opened,
the first two poking out, one slightly higher than the other.

Then he waits.

These are tense moments.

If Sunny's had a bad day, Ajay will know about it. He'll come in brood-
ing and sullen, pick fault at all he sees, sit and watch Ajay building the drink
and shake his head, make him throw it out and build it again. "You can't get
anything right, can you?" he'll say. But more often than not, Sunny will arrive satisfied with his life, will sit down and put his feet up and smile, will
lean forward and start to make the drink himself, will explain the mechan-
ics of it, give a little history, regale him with a Once upon a Time in Piazza
San Carlo, then encourage Ajay to make one himself (to throw away after
one sip, just to know the taste).

At six thirty, Arvind is supposed to take over, but he's often late. It frus-
trates Ajay, his colleague's sloppiness, but he's also grateful for a little more
time, to see Sunny's friends arrive, to see the nights he knows the embers of
take their first spark.

Relieved of duty, Ajay returns to his room, showers, changes, puts on
new clothes he has bought from the market—shirts and trousers he'd never
wear in the mountains. He takes his dinner at the small table at the back of

the central kitchen, eats slowly without conversation, going over the events of the day, then he's free to walk the streets. From seven thirty until ten most nights he memorizes the nearby roads, studies the shops, gets to know the neighborhood. He sits awhile at a chai shop or on a bench, watching people come and go, feeding stray dogs any kitchen scraps he could gather. He keeps moving, releasing the static energy of the day, fighting, in these hours, his loneliness, his longing for the mountains, for a path to climb, a forest to disappear inside. He walks as far as AIIMS, wanders the hospital grounds; something about the poor crowds desperate for some medicine, for news of a loved one's fate, makes him feel perversely safe. His face is bathed in the green neon of all the pharmacies lined up outside. He returns home. Yes, it's home now. He remembers the auto driver who helped him on his first day. He fantasizes about meeting him again, bumping into him in the street, showing the man his gratitude, buying him a meal, revealing how far he's come up in the world. Maybe the driver—what was his name?!—would invite him back home, he'd meet his family, be welcomed in by them, sit in the park with their son, maybe there would be a daughter, a niece. He tries to imagine something solid beyond that point, but he cannot remember the driver's face anymore, let alone his name.

Three months into Ajay's service, Mr. Dutta calls him to his office.

"You work evenings now too," he says. "In the evenings you serve Sunny when he entertains his guests. Can you do it? Day and night?"

"Yes, sir."

"You'll have some extra hours in the day to sleep. Remember, you see nothing."

"Yes, sir."

"Nothing leaves that apartment."

"Yes, sir."

"Your salary is now fifteen thousand a month."

"Thank you, sir."

"OK, go."

"Sir?"

"What is it?"

"What happened to Arvind?"

"That joker? I had to cut his balls off."

In these new and fantastic nights, Ajay witnesses the glory of what he's only seen echoes of before: the glamorous flames illuminating the apartment, igniting it with music and words and drunken howls, which seem to grow wilder and more extraordinary by the hour. In these flooded nights he sees the disintegration of some of the most beautiful people he has known, invisible as the crowds argue and laugh and debate and howl and kiss and fight and jump around. The men insult one another and tell stories. The women insult the men and tell jokes. People stop and peer over mirrors, fall into huddles of gossip and laughter, dive into the pool.

"Ajay." He has become a name. To be called and used. Turned on like a tap. Turned off again.

His name ringing out, hands raised, shaking empty glasses.

Ajay scurrying, refreshing their drinks, bringing fresh ice, cleaning the spills away.

He's a master of this. He discovers who is kind and who is cruel and makes a note to take care of cruelty first.

But Sunny.

Sunny is above them all.

Without Sunny, nothing exists. One invisible hand rests on his master's beating heart.

The gathering becomes riotous. Sunny tells the story of how Ajay came into being. "He was found in the mountains." To much laughter. "He's seen everything. *Everything*. Why do you think I got him here?"

In the middle of the evening, food is demanded. Ajay calls down to the kitchen. What can be made? Very serious now. Can we make it? Can it be done? Running down to the kitchen he's struck by how quiet it is, how the enormous building sleeps, how the staff sweep around in gilded silence, how desire spills like blood from Sunny's high life. Bring the food up, arrange it in the kitchen, serve it in bowls, arrange the plates, make sure everyone is served. Fresh roti with white butter. Chicken. Burgers and fries. Mutton biryani.

And sometimes he is sent out to pick up food from outside. He goes with one of the drivers in one of the many cars. Someone will say, "I want kebabs from Aap Ki Khatir," "Go to Karol Bagh for Chicken Changezi," and he'll ride in the steaming Delhi night with the driver and see the city from this place of power, gliding down the streets, listening to the driver hold forth on the universe, watching all the millions of faces like his, but without his fate or luck. And he strides into these places to collect the food, pays for it from the roll of notes that has been handed to him so carelessly. He learns to check whether the order is right, to make sure the food is fresh and hot, he waits on the moment he pulls out the notes, letting the restaurant know he serves a big man, and in the very best restaurants, where the bill is more than his monthly wage, he learns the power of a name, where a nobody like him is now treated with careful respect. He assumes the manner. He is becoming a Wadia man.

Often they'll vacate abruptly. Cut the music or the movie midway and pile out the door. He might be in the middle of serving food. He might be fixing someone's drink. But they go and Ajay is left alone, standing motionless in the silence, savoring the debris, savoring his life, before setting to work cleaning things so it will be spotless when Sunny returns. They could be back within the hour, or they won't be back at all. He'll go to bed with his phone and beeper next to his ear, waiting for Sunny to call. It's not always like this. There are low, slow days when Sunny doesn't get out of bed until the afternoon. Where it's just the two of them, Ajay serving tea and Sunny melancholy or rude. Days when Ajay knows to stay out of his way. There are days of women too. Ones he recognizes from the raucous nights. Turning up to see Sunny alone.

10.

A year passes in this rhythm, wanting for nothing, no time to think. He attends one of the gyms in the neighboring basti, a crumbling and swaggering box of testosterone and camaraderie, with a tin roof and old jury-rigged machines, a hub for migrant domestic servants and local braves. As a Wadia man, he's afforded extraordinary respect. No one forces him from the treadmill. No one teases his bench press and bar pull. No one asks questions. He takes his hour each day, building himself up with the weights. He goes running in the Deer Park in the morning, when he can, like the rich people do. In the mirror of the gym he repeats a name.

Ajay Wadia.

He is becoming aware of Sunny's fame. He knows his master is known in the city, it makes him proud. For the first time in his life he looks at himself as an object to be improved, he spends money on his grooming, gets a manicure once a month, a pedicure every other, takes a head massage from Dilip in Green Park. He shops. He consumes. He visits the new malls. He takes with him a handwritten list of the things he wants to buy. Searching out the alien words he has written down from Sunny's bathroom—Davidoff Cool Water, Proraso, Acqua di Parma, Santa Maria Novella, Botot, Marvis— sacred as an ancient text. He spends his free time and his salary in the malls working out the alternatives of these. Axe. Old Spice.

Those malls.

They're easier now.

But he remembers the first time he tried to enter one, on his first day off, his first month of service. There he is, waking before dawn. He can't sleep in. He has an idea to buy new clothes. But the bruises are still on his face; he looks like a nobody, worse than a nobody—in his old clothes from the mountains he looks like a poor migrant. Suddenly he is aware of his poverty. He turns up at the metal detector and he must reek of it, his poverty must betray him. The security guard, a man he now recognizes as someone who makes less money than he, bars his entry. It's humiliating, watching well-to-do families and smart young men in nice clothes walking past, watching young modern girls in skirts, linked arm in arm, eating ice cream, watching the occasional foreigner too, dirty and travel-stained and half naked, being given the royal treatment, saluted sometimes even, to their delight and amusement, while this gatekeeper pushes Ajay Wadia away. He takes half lessons from it. And he can only peer inside at the marble corridors, air-conditioned, with all the shops glowing, feeling slighted, ashamed like a beggar.

How am I supposed to buy nice clothes if I can't enter the place that sells them? The conundrum rattles around in his head. He devotes more attention to Sunny's wardrobe, learns the phrases, the terms—Rubinacci, con rollino, Cifonelli, pocket square, cap-toe Oxfords. He riffles through the magazines in the living room when he's alone, memorizes the fashions, the lines that differentiate weak from strong, he takes some pages he's torn out of the old ones to a tailor in the neighborhood and sits with him trying to explain what it is he wants to wear. Over some days they fix on an idea. The elegant blue suit that comes out of it, along with two shirts, a tie, and a pair of shoes, costs almost two months' wages, but it's worth it. When he tries this suit on, he is a man transformed, he's a someone in this city, someone beyond his job, beyond Sunny even, if he can dream of such a thing. He dresses up as this free man on his next day off and steps out, noting the whistles and murmurs of the guards, the giggles of the maids, then he hails an auto and goes to the mall.

And yes, he passes.

He passes for someone who has leisure time.

Despite his apprehensions, he's ignored by the guardians of the mall, not so much as glanced at as he sails through the arches of the metal detector and into the promised land.

Now he can do whatever he likes.

It's only when he walks around inside that his mood changes. With nothing left in his pocket, he feels an ominous burden, an oppressive sense of waste and fear. The landscape is of judgment; he begins to suspect everyone knows. He's a fraud. It's not only clothes, but bearing. He's never had this feeling before, never cared what anyone says of him. Now he clams up. He feels the shop assistants watching him, singling him out. They know he's merely trying to pass for the other side. So he doesn't dare go inside certain shops, even to browse. To open his mouth would be to give the game away. Finally he retreats to one of the bathrooms and sits sweating in one of the stalls. He looks down at his ridiculous clothes that feel so tight. What was he thinking? He looks like a clown. When he comes out of the stall he stares at his dumb clown's face in the mirror and wants to erase it. He resolves to flee as fast as he can. He breathes the air of the street, sucks in the fumes with gratitude, takes the bus back home, not wanting to waste money on an auto, not wanting to waste time on a walk. Once home he tears this suit off, showers, and puts his uniform back on, the blue shirt and worn-in black trousers, so comforting, so in tune with his soul, and locks that expensive suit away. He goes back to the mall several weeks later wearing his service clothes. He is taken for what he is, the servant of a rich man shopping for his master. If anyone asks, not that they will, he can say with confidence that he's on an errand for his boss, he can flash his money clip if need be. He can flash his shopping list. Davidoff Cool Water, Proraso, Acqua di Parma, Santa Maria Novella, Botot, Marvis. He can go through the shops slowly, pretending he's buying for his master as he gathers the replicas of Sunny's personal things.

One day, over a year in, when Sunny has gone away for three days, and Ajay has nothing much to do but wait around in his quarters and sweep the apartment occasionally and feed the carp or learn new recipes from the cookbooks on Sunny's shelf, he's called into Mr. Dutta's office and told he's been promoted to Sunny's personal valet; it's a role he all but inhabits anyway. Mr. Dutta tells him Sunny will one day soon be taking a great position within his father's empire, and as such he needs additional support. Alongside his existing responsibilities he will accompany Sunny whenever he attends the various family offices, he will carry his briefcase in the passenger seat beside the driver, he will run errands for him throughout the day when errands are required, carry his luggage when he travels, be his shield against the world, be at his beck and call around the clock, tie his shoelaces if he so needs; if he has to blow his nose, you will offer your handkerchief or your sleeve.

His salary is increased to twenty-five thousand a month and he is given his own room instead of a bed within a dorm. His measurements are taken again, and a week later he's given three new identical steel-gray gabardine safari suits with neat, minimal lines. "Mr. Sunny," the tailor beams, "designed them himself."

Security will be an issue. He is given training by the protection unit. He is taught by Eli, a young Israeli, ex-IDF officer. Eli comes from a family of Kerala Jews; he has golden skin and curly long hair, a tall rangy body. He went backpacking after his service, just like his fellow soldiers. He spent time in the Himalayas with his countrymen, getting stoned, riding Royal Enfields, until he found his way to Bombay. He tried his hand at modeling, but his temper was on a hair trigger, he was too volatile. He got into one too many fights, escaped arrest, made his way to Delhi. An old friend of his from Israel put him up, introduced him to Tinu. He was brought in for security, he rose up the ranks. Now he takes Ajay to the Wadia firing range out by the farmhouse in Mehrauli, in the plot of land with the woodland and orchards. He introduces Ajay to the one weapon he will keep by his side, the Glock 19. Over the next six weeks, in the spaces between his regular duties, Ajay becomes a master not only with the Glock but also with the Jericho 941 and the IWI Tavor TAR-21. He becomes acquainted with the AR-15, the AK-47, the Uzi, and the Heckler & Koch MP5. How to handle them, how to strip and clean and reassemble them, how to care for them, when to use them, when not to use them, how to make them part of his body. Ajay's marksmanship is exemplary. When the six weeks of firearms training is over he is given his license and presented with his own 9mm semiautomatic Glock 19, along with a shoulder holster and two boxes of ammunition, to be kept safe in the locker in his room, carried whenever he accompanies Sunny outside the family home.

Eli begins to train Ajay in Krav Maga.

Four days a week, for two hours at a time. But while Ajay trains diligently, following Eli's instructions to the letter, Eli is frustrated. Though Ajay can handle firearms, can make the metal objects sing, he lacks fluency with his own body. Though Ajay can follow each technique, can master the sequences and combinations, he lacks the spark.

"You too much hold back," Eli says in his broken English. "You have to go to the violent place. In here." And he slaps his heart. "Again."

Ajay drives Sunny around Delhi alone—his driver, his butler, his everything. He clocks up hours in the Audi, the Toyota Land Cruiser. He becomes familiar with their handling, their speed, they become extensions of his body, he takes pride in the way he can maneuver them through the city, he bullies other cars, feels extraordinary. Ajay is sent out on errands in the Land Cruiser. Mostly, he is sent to ferry other people, friends of Sunny's. Mostly these are girls, and mostly he recognizes them from Sunny's parties in his apartment. He's good at memorizing names, faces, favorite drinks, moods. He picks these girls up from wherever, a market, a restaurant, the entrance of a park, and delivers them, mostly, to the front entrances of five-star hotels, drops them off without a word. Picks them up several hours later unless Sunny tells him otherwise, takes them wherever they want to go. He speaks of this to no one. He hears other drivers gossiping about their masters and mistresses and what they're up to, but Ajay never says a word.

They travel out of Delhi more and more. Sometimes in a private jet. Ajay is the beating heart of Sunny's world. Wordless, faceless, content.

11.

After two years, a new girl enters the scene. She appears abruptly. Turns up one afternoon with Sunny at his apartment, and this is strange—he never brings girls back in the middle of the day. Masking his surprise, Ajay bobs his head and namastes, then slips away to the kitchen to fetch drinks.

The girl is different in many ways. She's unglamorous and not in Sunny's thrall. And what's more, she speaks to Ajay directly, looks in his eyes, asks questions. It unnerves him, to be made so apparent in the room. He makes drinks and snacks, then stands in the kitchen, at the edge of the door, eavesdropping as best he can, trying to figure out what's happening. She leaves after an hour. He learns her name, Neda. Neda Madam. Ajay escorts Neda Madam to her beat-up car. He sees the PRESS sticker on the back window and feels relief when she's gone.

He's waiting for Sunny outside the Park Hyatt several weeks later when he sees her again, exiting the hotel, distracted, waiting for the valet to fetch her car. She doesn't see him, she's preoccupied, pulling on a cigarette, talking on the phone. He recognizes a certain look on her face.

Soon after, she becomes a fixture in Ajay's life. She has succumbed to Sunny and he is the ferryman, from hotel room to home. From her place of work near Connaught Place to whichever five-star hotel Sunny is waiting in. She relies on Ajay. Conspires with him. Thank you, Ajay, stepping out of the rear door of the car at the end of the night.

About six weeks into this new phase, Sunny is watching TV at home. The news is on, there are disturbances in the city, some poor colony is being demolished. Sunny sits up and leans forward, stares at the screen with his hands clasped. He turns the TV off and just sits on the sofa in silence with a frown of puzzled concentration.

In the evening, Sunny goes out alone, but tells Ajay to head to the farmhouse on the edge of Delhi, the place where he learned to shoot, where a new mansion is quietly being constructed.

Sunny arrives with Neda several hours later, a somber mood between them. Ajay brings ice and vodka and is told to wait outside.

He feels it—something strange is happening here.

He paces the trees in the dark, holding his phone, watching the deserted construction site.

Shy of an hour, the headlights of three other cars approach from the end of the driveway.

They pull to a stop some distance from the villa.

He knows instinctively he must warn Sunny. He dashes in the dark; as he does so, many powerful lights turn on, illuminating the construction site outside. When he glances back, he sees Sunny's father emerging from one of the cars.

A race against time.

By the poolside.

"Sir, your father!"

Neda and Sunny are in the water.

No time to wait. Panic now.

Sunny orders Ajay to pull her out, to hide her. She's thrown inside the outdoor bathroom, just in time. Ajay retreats inside the villa and out a side door as Bunty Wadia and his unknown guests walk to the rear.

He doesn't know what's happening, but he knows Neda can't be here. So he does his duty.

When the coast is clear, when the men are inside talking, he smuggles her out and home.

After this night, Neda disappears from Sunny's life. And Sunny's life takes a drastic turn. In the coming days there's an awareness across the household that something terrible has happened, some dreadful confrontation has taken place between Sunny and his father—news spills out from his father's floor, it is heard by dozens of domestics and passed around in whispers. Tinu calls Ajay soon enough, orders him to his office. Once there he demands Ajay's SIM cards, his phones, his batteries, everything that Sunny has given him, he must hand them over. He is given a new phone, a new number. When he returns to the apartment Sunny is sitting in the living room in silence, staring at the wall, his back to the door, his fists clenched. As if he'd been waiting for some blow. There's a knock on the door. "Get it," he says.

Bunty Wadia enters the apartment, this sacred space, followed by seven men Ajay has never seen before, rough men stinking of tobacco and liquor, men from the street. They proceed to tear the apartment to pieces, smashing things with bats and rods, Sunny motionless while it happens, resigned, and Ajay paralyzed with shock. When the goons finish the job there's nothing left. Amid the rubble, the apartment is shockingly bare.

The next morning Sunny appears early, ashen, stern, dressed in a dark and somber suit. Ajay drives him out to one of the Wadia offices in Greater Noida—the headquarters of their real estate operation—and Sunny remains there all day. All day and every day thereafter.

The parties have ended. Neda has vanished. Sunny goes to the office every day and comes home in the evenings and glowers in his apartment alone. All of the dazzling, sparkling nightlife is gone. Sunny grows taciturn and secretive.

Weeks pass and this becomes the new routine. Sunny's mood cools and hardens. He shows no emotion, but he begins to entrust Ajay with new tasks, and Ajay must trust no one else. He must take the car out, make sure he's not being followed, then he must scope out various cheap, grubby, two-star hotels in the city, the names of which Ajay is given on sheets of paper. He must check their security, their privacy, their anonymity, and report back. Each hotel is given a code name, A, B, C, D, E, F. When they talk of them, they are not to use their real names.

Sunny begins to spend odd hours in these different cheap hotels, Ajay dropping him off, waiting several streets away in the car for the call to pick him up. At first he assumes Sunny must be meeting Neda, then he believes it's something else. There is talk among the staff of a crisis in the family, some kind of awful feud. Sunny has done something terrible. Some of the domestics in the house lean on Ajay for information about Sunny's activities. But Ajay plays dumb, says he knows nothing. Tinu calls him in when Sunny is busy and tells him to relay information about Sunny's state of mind, about what he's been doing, about the girl Sunny has been meeting. He reminds Ajay that Sunny is not his master. Bunty Wadia is the one he serves. Reluctantly, Ajay gives Neda's name. He tells them where she lives and where she works. But he does not say anything about the hotels Sunny has found.

Ajay feels like he's become trapped in a grotesque civil war, and somehow Neda is the cause. He imagines all kinds of vague and terrible things about her. That she has come expressly to ruin Sunny's life, to disrupt the gentle, luxurious harmony that had been put in place. Perhaps she was a spy all along.

Every day is loaded with a tension he can barely take, barely decipher. As if they were on a war footing. In private Sunny remains angry and withdrawn. In public, with his father, with Tinu, in the office, he maintains an aura of detached professionalism, robotic indifference.

One Sunday Sunny receives a phone call that causes him alarm. He pulls Ajay aside and tells him to drive out to the Greater Noida office immediately. Be discreet. Make it seem like you're going somewhere else. But go right now and keep watch on the office from the road. Watch out for Neda.

"Keep her safe," Sunny says. "I mean it. Keep her safe. Don't let anything happen to her."

Something does happen. He waits on the service road a short way from the office building. It's just off the main expressway, in a desolate part of the satellite city outside Delhi, all farmland and construction. He sits hours, watching for her, then he spots her car, driving back toward Delhi in the dark. He keeps his distance, driving at a steady pace a few hundred meters behind. Neda's car crosses into Delhi at the Kalindi Kunj Bridge, heading into Okhla.

The distance he has kept means he doesn't see the accident. He only sees the two cars smashed and at rest on different sides of a wide, deserted junction in an industrial area. He only sees two men surrounding Neda's car, banging on the bonnet and the windows, shouting inside, and another man pulling a cricket bat from the other car. He doesn't stop to think it through. He accelerates until he's almost on them, his headlights blinding the two men. Then he runs out and he attacks. Attacks with all the violence that's been coiled inside him. It's over in a few seconds. He doesn't even remember what he's done. He just knows there are men on the ground broken and bleeding and his gun is drawn and he's looking back into the car where Neda clutches the wheel, staring at him with her eyes wide.

Ajay calls Sunny and Sunny directs him to deliver Neda to Hotel D. She is angry, suffering from shock. When Sunny opens the door, she hits him. He drags her inside and sends Ajay away. She spends several hours in there, while Ajay returns to the crash site to take Neda's car for repairs. After he has dropped the car at a mechanic, he returns to Hotel D and waits. When he's finally called to take her back home, she is drunk and subdued and terribly sad, but her anger is gone. He keeps watching her in the rearview mirror.

After this incident, Ajay begins to have painful, unsettling dreams. Dreams of violence. Sometimes he dreams of broken limbs. Sometimes of burning bodies. Sometimes he dreams of Neda.

12.

Months go by without Neda. Sunny doesn't mention her name. Doesn't call her. Doesn't see other women. He begins spending time with a new friend, a man named Gautam Rathore, a cruel and frightening man who sneers at Ajay with a sick smile. Sunny is always dining with him, drinking with him. Sunny rarely sees anyone else. He's sinking into a morose state, a depression.

He asks Ajay, "What's the most important thing in life?"

"Work, sir," Ajay says, without looking up.

"Family," Sunny corrects him, without conviction.

Sunny is drinking more these days. Drinking alone.

Drinking with Gautam Rathore.

Doing coke with Gautam in the penthouse.

Ajay seeing nothing.

And soon Ajay is sent out to meet someone in a lay-by at night, to sit and wait an hour for this man. A young and friendly Nigerian man. He buys coke from him for Gautam Rathore. Sunny makes a point of this, makes sure Ajay knows it.

"It's not for me."

Without warning, in November, Ajay and Sunny fly out to Gorakhpur the next week. Sunny in first class, Ajay in economy. Ajay, who used to gaze at the sky in awe of planes, now sleeps before takeoff. When they land, the hostess touches him on the shoulder, he comes to with a frown, he can smell the tang of sweat in the stale air as the passengers stand up and grab their luggage while the plane taxis on the runway. The sky is dull and full of haze. Winter is sweeping down from the mountains to the north.

It is only now that Sunny tells Ajay they are here to meet his uncle, Vikram "Vicky" Wadia, a man about whom Ajay has heard a great deal, but only in whispers. "Vicky-ji is causing problems again." "Vicky-ji is handling things in UP." "Vicky-ji and Bunty-ji are having tension these days."

Ajay retrieves Sunny's bags from the carousel. They are greeted in the arrivals hall by a pack of goondas and an armed police escort. Ajay can see the apprehension in his master. He tries not to reflect it. He stands tall, drawing strength from his gun concealed in its holster. But Vicky's men are the real deal: rough-hewn, menacing, weighed down with gold. They smirk at Ajay, with his safari suit, his slick hair. They cut him off from Sunny, lead him to a separate car. *What would Eli say?* All his training leaves him. He mutely obeys.

They drive for three hours through this land of sugarcane and dusty, ramshackle towns, Ajay staring out the window with an unerring sense of déjà vu, a memory he cannot or dare not place.

Finally, in the middle of nowhere, they turn left off the road, through a set of iron gates below a crumbling concrete arch in the middle of precisely nowhere, drive along a wide track of dirt, past parked trucks and workers' tents, the sugarcane tall on either side, until they come upon a rusty, muscular island of industry, a sugar mill, in whose shadow they park.

The guards stream out of the cars, wordless, their weapons clicking and clanking. Throats are hawked, paan is spit red into the dirt where it thickens and dies. Ajay is held loosely by the bicep, as if he might bolt. He feels unnaturally oppressed, sickened. The sun dips behind the clouds, making a halo. One of Vicky's men casually urinates to the side.

He watches the lead car, waiting for Sunny to emerge. As the seconds tick by he steps toward it, but the hand grips him tight.

"Chutiya, don't move."

More men appear from the mill, all carrying AK-47s.

A sense of ceremony.

The roiling air before the storm.

Soon enough Vicky Wadia emerges. From where Ajay can't say. He seems to come midstride, fully formed, a giant of a man bathed in wilderness, wearing black kurta pajamas, his long black hair parted at the middle, tucked behind his ears, a red and yellow tilak slashing down his forehead, his flashing eyes lined with kohl, a thick, virile mustache bursting above his lip. He strides toward Sunny as if he'd been picking up speed his whole life. Ajay watches helpless, frozen. The sun comes out again and glints off the many golden rings on Vicky's fingers. They reach out, as if to grasp and smother and kill. But Vicky only embraces his nephew, pulls him close, cradles the back of his head as Sunny's arms hang limply by his side. Vicky steps back, examines him from this side, from that. Next, looks toward Ajay.

"The boy is yours?" The hand on the bicep is released, the goons clear a path. "A pretty doll," he says dismissively, "dressed up well." He beckons Ajay forward. He finds himself stepping into no-man's-land. He leers at Ajay. "Such an innocent face. Does he do what he's told?" Sunny doesn't speak. Then Ajay is forgotten. "Come, boy," Vicky says, clasping Sunny by the back of the neck, "tell me the news from home."

Vicky leads him toward a small bungalow beside the mill, and like that, they're gone.

Ajay stands alone below the fast-moving clouds with the men and their guns as they loiter in the dust. The line of tension between these men slackens as Vicky's presence recedes. Some shift and lean against their vehicles or move to sit in plastic chairs, others recline on rope beds under a canopy of tarp. Ajay feels naked, sick. Suddenly he has to get away. Feigning detachment, he turns and wanders away, heads down the long dirt drive. He waits for a voice telling him to stop, but nothing comes. So he walks, and with every step, a weight is lifted from his chest. He counts to one hundred before he turns to look back.

The men are smaller, not so threatening now. A small breeze kicks up. He unbuttons the top of his suit, rubs the grime from the back of his neck.

One hundred more paces.

The men receding into nothingness.

He takes time now to look, to smell.

To look at the sugarcane each side of the dirt drive, the birds flitting about in the sky. To smell the rich scent of earth.

He takes time to feel.

Something is stirring. The wind runs through the sugarcane. And it occurs to him, he knows this place. He knows it. He's been here before.

How? He searches his mind, finds deep black wells he cannot draw from, sees long, dark gullies he refuses to enter. He walks on a little more, goose bumps on his skin. Some wild impulse tells him to lean down and remove his shoes and socks.

He obeys. He obeys and his bare feet press into the earth. His feet have grown pale, soft. Was it so long ago he walked barefoot through the pine needles of the Himalayan forests, chary of leopards? And before that . . . before that . . . another kind of needle runs through his heart.

How far has he come?

He presses his toes deeper. He grinds them down, pushing dirt underneath the pedicured nails. A little way down the dirt track, the tents of the migrant workers stand humble, precarious. He is drawn toward their blue tarpaulin, forgetting his shoes and socks. Soon he's looking into this cluster of habitation, these jumbled, makeshift homes, observing the women scrubbing metal plates using sand and small stones, cooking a vat of rice over kindling fires. He sees the naked children with their malnourished bellies chasing chickens, chasing puppies, playing with tires and sticks. He's standing a few feet from the edge of this camp, staring at them as some look back. The eyes of the children, blank and expressionless, the eyes of the women, fearful. Suspicious, the eyes of the men. From the corner of his eye, he detects something below him: a large cockroach scurrying through the dirt. And with vicious intent, with such surprising violence in his heart, he stamps on it. He crushes it with the ball of his foot.

And in the instant of death, it all comes back to him.

His father's burning body.

His mother burying his charred corpse.

His sister surrounded by those men.

His cowardice in the face of Rajdeep and Kuldeep Singh.

Waiting for the last flight back to Delhi in the night, sitting in the miserable, shining departure lounge of the newly built airport, the flight delayed, both men silent and pensive, Sunny massaging his own neck, looking at messages on his phone, Sunny kicks Ajay in the leg.

"Chutiya," he says, "you abandoned me today."

Ajay says nothing.

"What's your fucking problem?"

"Nothing, sir."

"Bullshit. Do you know how you made me look?"

Ajay lowers his eyes.

"Sorry, sir."

"What did they say to you?"

"Sir?"

"What did they say?"

"Who?"

"Vicky's men. Who else, asshole? Did they talk about me?"

"Sir, no one talked."

Sunny narrows his eyes.

"So, what happened?"

"Nothing, sir."

"You made me look bad."

Ajay nods.

"You don't know what it's like. You don't know what it's like here. With my uncle. You have to toughen up out here. It's not like Delhi. Nothing is the same."

Nothing is the same. There's a ringing in his ears. He tries to let it go. But he can't clear the sound. He can't shake the image. The cockroach a messenger, a portal. And now a chord connects him to the child he once was. Time and space folded over, as if to erase the life in between.

13.

Since their trip, Sunny has grown more pensive. He drinks more into the night. He sends Ajay out to buy coke. Sometimes he sends Ajay away at night and when Ajay returns Sunny is still awake in the same place. Then Sunny sleeps until four and wakes up and drinks again before he goes out to see Gautam Rathore.

One foggy morning in January, Sunny wakes early and he wants to run. He's only had three hours' sleep, he's fizzing, restless, maybe still drunk. He looks like hell, but he tells Ajay to take him out to the city woodland of Sanjay Van. It's seven a.m. Sunny is awkward in track pants and running shirt. He knows it. Does he really want to do this?

"You're coming too," he tells Ajay.

Ajay removes his suit jacket, revealing his undershirt and the body beneath. Sunny's eyes pass over Ajay's lean muscles, his youth. Is that jealousy?

"Carry the gun," Sunny says.

It occurs to Ajay that Sunny is scared.

"You work out?" Sunny asks as he performs a few stretches.

Ajay nods.

"Do steroids?"

"No, sir."

Ajay removes his shoes and socks to run barefoot.

"Keep your shoes on. You'll cut yourself," Sunny says.

"Sir, I'm fine."

"No, you'll step on a needle. You'll get fucking AIDS. I don't want you bringing AIDS into my house. I'll put you down. Put your fucking shoes on."

They run for half an hour, Sunny pushing himself hard, punishing himself even, with Ajay at his heels barely breaking a sweat. But he's glad to be here with him, to share this moment. His brain has been on fire. He feels like this is the end of things. He feels they are both on the verge of collapse.

"Sir?"

"What is it?" Sunny pants.

They have returned to the car.

Ajay wants to speak, but he hesitates, so Sunny switches to English. "What? You're getting on my nerves."

"Sir, I want to ask . . ."

He can't . . .

"Just fucking say it!"

"Sir, what happened to your mother?"

The question stops Sunny dead. The impropriety of it. He's frozen.

He's never once spoken of his mother in front of Ajay, and Ajay has never asked such a personal question before, not about this thing or anything.

Stunned, he says, "Who told you about my mother?"

"Nobody," Ajay replies.

Sunny steps close to Ajay's face. "Fucker," he hisses. "Don't lie to me."

"It was no one, sir."

"It was Vicky, wasn't it?"

"No, sir."

"Don't lie to me."

"No one, sir," he says.

Sunny begins to shout. "Who the fuck told you about my mother? Who do you think you're talking to?" He removes Ajay's Glock from its holster. Points it clumsily in Ajay's face. "I should shoot you right now."

Ajay doesn't react, just stares into Sunny's eyes.

"Don't forget who you are," Sunny says.

"Who am I?" Ajay calmly replies.

The words unnerve Sunny more than anything his gun can do.

He lowers the gun, presses it back into Ajay's hands.

"Get in the car."

Sunny drives home himself, too fast, too reckless.

When they pull through the gates into the compound and park, Ajay can feel Sunny's heavy breath.

Still clutching the wheel, he turns to Ajay. "What the fuck is wrong with you?"

Sunny turns the engine off.

"Why did you ask about my mother?"

Ajay stares at the dashboard.

"No one ever asks about my mother," Sunny goes on.

He lights a cigarette.

"She's dead," he says, blowing on the cigarette.

"Do you think about her?" Ajay asks.

Sunny fights his instinct toward silence.

"I used to think about her a lot. Now I don't think about her at all."

"I stopped thinking about my mother too," Ajay says, "after I came to work for you." He thinks about it. "Maybe even from before. But she exists."

Both men are surprised to hear Ajay's voice so clearly.

"And I remember her now."

Sunny looks at Ajay as if he were a person for the first time.

"I didn't even know you had a mother."

"Everyone has a mother."

"I thought she was dead."

Emotion takes hold of him; it looks like he'll break down. "I've done a wrong thing," Ajay says.

"What thing?"

"When I was a boy," he speaks the words with great concentration, "my father was killed. To pay a debt I was passed to a thekedar and driven to the mountains and sold. I was supposed to help my mother live, I was supposed to send money home. The man I was sold to told me my wages would be sent to her. He said she would have money and live a good life because of me. But the money wasn't sent. I always knew it, but I pretended to believe. As I got older, I started to believe this lie. I decided my mother and my elder sister were fine. When I came here, when I started this job, I finally made money, I could do something to help them, but I abandoned them. I forgot." He gathers himself. "When we saw Vicky-ji, I remembered them. Now I need to find them again."

Sunny can't take any more of this.

He throws the door open, climbs out, and Ajay is left alone.

14.

Ajay circles Sunny for the next few days. Sunny closing himself off, Ajay performing his tasks with clipped professionalism. But he can barely look in the mirror anymore. He can't sleep at night for thinking of what he's done.

He returns to the edge of the field, running and hiding while his sister screams for him. He hears her now as she's taken away. He sees that cockroach in the earth. His cowardice defines him. The little runaway. He knows why his mother sent him away. His appearance begins to fray. Sunny watches him the whole time. Ajay fears he will be sent away. Cast out of the Wadia home.

"You really want to find her?" Sunny says out of the blue one morning, when Ajay carries the coffee into his room.

He doesn't hesitate to reply.

"I do."

"How?" Sunny asks. "How will you find her?"

"I don't know."

"Do you even know where you're from?"

"I think I grew up near that place we went."

"The sugar mill?"

"I recognized the land."

"That looks like a lot of places."

"But I felt it, sir."

Sunny weighs this up.

"I can't let you go," Sunny says. "I need you here. Things are going to happen soon."

Ajay nods once, turns to the door.

"Wait."

And Ajay does.

"Write everything you remember," Sunny says. "Names. Landmarks. Schools, temples. The names of people. Anyone."

"Yes, sir."

"I'll see what I can find."

"Thank you, sir."

"In the meantime, I need you by my side."

"Yes, sir."

"We're flying to Goa tomorrow."

That night Ajay sits up in bed and writes it all down. He writes everything he thinks he knows, the sight of the mountains from his hut, the shape of the fields, the school and the farmland and the temple, the long-forgotten names of places nearby, local names, the name of his schoolmaster, the name of his father and mother, and finally, finally, the names of the two big men, Rajdeep and Kuldeep Singh.

He hands the folded sheet to Sunny when they board the flight, as Ajay passes Sunny in first class to take his economy seat. Ajay can think of nothing on the way down but those two men, that place of his long-forgotten nightmares, all those things he spent his lifetime leaving behind.

They stay in a five-star resort hotel on the edge of the capital, Panaji, in one of the beachfront villas, with a servant's room. Wednesday and Thursday are spent at Sunny's side during different meetings in the city. In the evenings, after Sunny has attended the obligatory business dinners, he sits alone in the garden of the villa, staring out over the wall to the sea. He barely speaks, he doesn't eat or drink.

On Friday, Ajay is charged with renting a small car and a Royal Enfield motorcycle, to be paid for in cash. In the afternoon Sunny tells him to go and book a room in a cheap city hotel, the Windmill. Then he gives Ajay a flight number. "Go to the airport in the rental car," Sunny says. "Neda Madam's flight lands at eight p.m."

There is a great comfort in seeing Neda come out the arrivals door and fight her way through the taxi drivers. He's been waiting a little way off; he pushes through the scrum and takes her luggage, and she smiles at him shyly, with great familiarity. She places a hand on his shoulder as they walk to the small car, a Maruti with local plates, without a word.

He asks her to sit in front, so the police don't think that he's an illegal taxi driver.

It's strange, having her next to him.

For a moment he can take a flight of fancy—scandalous, unbearable to hold it for more than a second—that he is Sunny himself, that Neda is his, that he has a normal life, a life where he is in control.

With Neda back in Sunny's life he feels things might resolve themselves for the good.

"Is this your first time in Goa, Ajay?" she says.

It comes out of the blue.

He likes it when she uses his name.

"No, madam."

There is a safety in calling her madam.

They fall into silence again.

"Actually, madam," he says awhile later, surprised that he's talking un-prompted, "I worked here before."

"Really, you did?" she says, genuinely interested. "When?"

He feels shy. "Before."

She laughs quietly. "Where?"

"Arambol."

"Nice beach. In a shack?"

"Yes, madam."

"With friends?"

"Yes."

"Will you see them this time?"

"Madam," he says, "I'm here to work."

And they fall into silence again.

He delivers her to the hotel as planned and takes his leave. He goes back to Sunny's five-star, parking the local car in a residential street some distance away, alongside the Royal Enfield, and walking to the property, going through the metal detector, placing his gun in the tray, showing his license. He goes to the servant quarter in Sunny's villa and waits. Sits on the bed, bolt upright, hands on thighs, his eyes closed, as if he's meditating, thinking of Neda with him in the car, the warm wind blowing, no words. Then he's picturing her trapped while she's being attacked. Remembering the feeling of his fists pummeling her attackers. It's the first time he's really examined it. His teeth clench, his hands ball up into fists. He feels every blow, again and again, the commitment Eli talked about, the commitment to violence. What is it about her? His attachment. It is not desire. Is it mere protectiveness? Solidarity. Maybe. Or perhaps it is envy? He's envious of the closeness she shares with Sunny. A place he cannot reach. He opens his eyes before he gets too lost. Curls up on the bed. Tries to sleep. At midnight he gets a message from Sunny. Bring the Enfield to the hotel at five a.m.

It's a pleasure driving slowly through the dawn city on the Enfield, the warm air brushing over his face, the chop of the mighty engine reverberating through the empty streets bathed in the sulfur glow of streetlights. He waits outside the reception as the sky grows pale. Then they are here. He hands over the keys. The tank is full of petrol. Sunny's license is in the zipper pouch above the tank. Everything has been taken care of.

"Ajay," Neda says, "why don't you go see your friends?" She looks at Sunny. "Don't you think that will be all right?"

"Be back here tomorrow night," Sunny tells him. "Seven p.m."

Then they're gone.

He waits until they are out of sight, imagining himself a solid, stoic presence should they happen to look back, should they, for some reason, need to turn around and return to him. He waits a little longer, until the thundering engine is inaudible. At that moment he turns on his heel and goes inside to settle the bill and, when everything is settled, walks the five kilometers back to the five-star hotel.

He has thirty-six hours.

Thirty-six hours that are his own, that he must kill.

His mood clouds over.

What will he do, visit old friends?

He sits on the bed and waits. He thinks about locking up and leaving.

But are they even his friends?

He sits on the edge of the bed, eyes closed, back straight, palms on his thighs once again.

Thinking.

Picturing himself driving up.

He used to play it over, the scene. He could visualize it so well.

He'd turn up in a smart black SUV, in his uniform, but with the buttons open at the neck, to prove he was off duty. He'd have an easy manner about him, an enigmatic smile that would break into a laugh the second they recognized him. Someone would hug him and feel the bulge of his gun and they'd be in awe, they'd ask to see it. He'd take it out and remove the clip, check the chamber, pass it over. He'd laugh about the boy he used to be, reminisce about the old days, tell stories of Delhi, of how the big people live. He'd show that he was a man now, a man of the world. And they'd say: you made it, brother.

That's how he imagined it.

But what stories would he have to tell of himself?

What stories can he tell when he barely knows how to speak?

There. He sees it once again: the Tempo, the cage, his mother and sister watching as he's driven away. The other boys packed in with him in the night, his scared and frightened little self, receding from his wretched home, disappearing into the great blue mountains.

He sees it again: his father's half-burned corpse.

It's getting harder and harder to breathe.

At midday he removes his gun and holster and enters the villa proper and begins to tidy, making sure the kitchen is spotless and that Sunny's clothes are in order. He finds himself standing in the middle of the living room in dim light, thinking nothing with nowhere to go. He walks into the kitchen and opens the fridge, sees the beer and wine lined up in the door, the left-over food Sunny didn't touch. He closes it again. He's not even hungry. He doesn't drink. He has nothing to do.

But in the early evening as the sun is sinking into the ocean, he walks through the villa garden, out the white picket gate, down to the private beach. There are a few sun loungers with foreigners sipping drinks, a life-guard in a tower, two security guards patrolling the stretch, chasing off stray dogs or beach vendors, the white sand the preserve of the rich.

He is still wearing his uniform, sweating lightly into his undershirt be-neath. He unbuttons the top few buttons, rubs the damp skin around his neck, walks near the shoreline. He has the overwhelming urge to immerse himself. He takes off his shoes and socks, removes his suit jacket, and places it next to his neatly lined-up shoes. He walks toward the sea, his feet squeez-ing the moisture from the wet sand. At the first wave he closes his eyes and stops. Then starts to walk in.

He wades in slowly, with his eyes closed and a look of reverence on his face. All the way up to his waist.

Stands in the crashing waves, opens his eyes, and takes in the setting sun.

"Hey," a voice calls out. "Hey."

He looks round—the security guards are standing behind him on the shore.

"You're not allowed in there."

Ajay looks between them before returning his attention to the ocean.

"You're not allowed here. The beach is for guests only."

He holds out a few seconds more, but his rapture is already ended. He turns and wades back to the beach, passes between the two guards, picks up his jacket, his shoes and socks, and returns to the villa.

15.

He never sees Neda again in Goa. Sunny drops her off at the airport before he returns. Then the two men fly back to Delhi. Sunny seems calmer, re-solved. A few days later, he sits on the sofa with his laptop, looking through some architectural designs, when Ajay brings him coffee.

"Here."

Sunny removes a piece of notepaper from his notepad and holds it out.

"Sir?"

"This is the place your mother and sister live."

Ajay unfolds the paper and stares at it.

"You can thank my uncle," Sunny says. "Vicky found her."

He's speechless, lost for words.

"You have four days," Sunny says. "After that, I need you. After that, everything is going to change."

AJAY II

1.

Ajay travels from Delhi to Lucknow by train and from Lucknow he takes another train to Gorakhpur and from there he takes a local bus. It all comes back to him now. All that dust and all that smoke, the smell of burning plastic in all those towns, the buffalo herds and fields of mustard and corn and wheat and cane, all that engine oil dripping into the ground, mixed with the garbage and rotting vegetables. And the phantoms too. Arms cut off, throats slit, heads caved in. Corpses thrown into wells. The feces of men. Men on fire. But he has risen. Transcended. He sits by each passing mile a man remade, smuggling into his past, the past inside the present, with his safari suit and his handsome face, his lean body, his gun pressed against his ribs. And the money. Oh, the money. He is carrying three lakhs of rupees in the duffel bag at his feet, pristine, wrapped in brown paper, in turn wrapped in cloth. Three lakhs for his mother, all the wages in the world, next to a spare box of ammunition and a change of clothes and a toothbrush.

She will see him now, and all will be well. *They* will see him. His mother and his sister. And what else? His mother was pregnant as he left his old life, but he has lost this fact, just as he has lost the memory of pain. What will they say? In truth he has not considered what he will find when he finds home. He hasn't imagined anything save the broad lines—for himself he keeps it simple: they are alive, they exist. I exist. I am going home. I am returning just as I said I would, as was foretold. I am returning as a big man, a man of means, a success. Even as he imagines this homecoming, a dark part of him knows it is a lie.

The bus he is traveling in breaks down in the evening.

The passengers sit groaning in their sleep, wrapped in shawls, waiting for something to change. Nothing changes. Soon everyone is told to climb off. Most sit on the roadside, huddled against the creeping cold. Some who know the way begin to walk.

He climbs out with his bag and begins to walk too, hails a truck.

He sits in the cab beside the driver, careering into the night. They have been going an hour now, barely sharing ten words. He is studying the road ahead by the sweep of the lights. He begins, so he thinks, to recognize landmarks, monuments to the embedded memories of exodus.

The truck driver, a stout, bearded man in his fifties, chain-smoking beedis, studies the reverence in the boy's face.

"Where are you from?" he asks.

"Delhi," Ajay says.

Time passes.

"But you know these roads."

Ajay doesn't reply.

"What do you do?"

"Kaam." Work.

The trucker laughs. "We all work." He pauses. "What kind of work?"

Ajay unbuttons his suit, lets the chill draft of air from the night pour over his chest.

"Accha kaam." Good work.

They drive on with this phrase in the air, ambiguous and strange.

"There's been trouble this month," the trucker finally says. "Gangs fighting. Lots of hijackings. Maybe it's not safe."

Ajay turns toward him. "For me?"

Ajay's gun hangs in its holster inside his jacket.

The trucker averts his eyes.

For a moment Ajay has forgotten why he's there.

He leans back, closes his eyes, shivers, basks in his power.

"Who do you work for?" the driver asks.

His voice is flat, lacking pretense.

He wants to know.

"Vicky Wadia."

The driver's precipitous silence says it all.

They stop at a dhaba deep into the night. The glow of hypnotic striplights lashed to trees. Ajay sits alone at an outdoor table in the far corner, the legs of his plastic chair bowing under his weight. Steaming pots of food and drunken nocturnal voices reverberating with drunken desires.

He sees the truck driver watching from the other table, can guess the conversation with other drivers, with dhaba workers. Discussing him, pointing out the Wadia man, the one in the nice suit, carrying the pukka gun.

Debating his intentions.

He can't help but feel pride.

Feared, respected.

Unassailable.

He casts his eyes over the other men, truck drivers mostly. A handful of families, minding their own business. His gaze moves slowly through the dhaba. And then stops.

A dhaba boy, a worker. Big ears, a mop of black hair, painfully thin, twelve or thirteen years old. He's working the tandoor, sweat pooling on his forehead, a grimace on his face. Ajay scans his body, all the way to his feet. The chain. One bony ankle, shackled to the base of the oven. His eyes are glazed with the reflection of the flames flickering inside the pit.

Another memory resurrected. The dhaba, the fields behind it, lined with garbage. The concrete wall that hides the toilet ditch. How could he forget? The boy leaping from the cage that held them all, running from the Tempo into the misted fields, chased by the thekedar's assistant. The howl at the end of it. The bloodied knife. For a moment Ajay thinks he is there. That this, now, is then. The world unstable.

Is he? Is that the boy? Did they bring him back? Did he never get away?

He stands and walks slowly through the dhaba crowd, around the tables, all the way inside, knowing everyone is watching him. He passes the threshold of the kitchen, ignores the protests of the workers, and comes to a stop before the boy. The boy stops his work and looks at him, trembling like a whipped dog. A voice behind Ajay says, "Behenchod." He turns to find a potbellied cook with a cleaver in his hand. "What are you doing?" The cook raises the cleaver dramatically, but Ajay doesn't flinch, and another worker hurries to hiss something in his ear, pull him back. The cook lowers his cleaver and lowers his gaze and turns away, leaving Ajay alone.

The boy returns to the tandoor, and now Ajay sees he's a stranger. Just another boy who couldn't escape. What would be the use, he thinks, in freeing him. I have my own business to attend to.

He drifts back to his table with this thought in mind, and for the first time he thinks, I am me.

Chai is brought, along with a plate of rajma chawal slathered in desi ghee.

"From the boss," the waiter says, indicating a well-dressed man at ease at one of the tables near the cash till. "No charge."

The trucker waits patiently for Ajay to be done. When Ajay stands, he stands, and they are on their way. Before dawn the trucker says they're approaching town. "Pull over," Ajay says. "I'll walk the rest of the way."

He takes a moment to get his bearings as the truck pulls away, then he walks. He follows the sewage ditch into the slums, the unplanned colonies. He crosses a bridge made of metal sheeting to a scrappy cricket ground where goats graze. The day begins to show in the sky. He finds a group of men huddled beside a concrete building, warming themselves around a kindling fire. He shows them the sheet of paper he has. Asks where this colony can be found. They eye his clothes, his bag, his face, point out the way, but tell him, "You don't want to go there, those people are a waste."

He skirts the field where kids are playing cricket in the morning light. A shot goes for a four, rolls toward him, comes to a stop. The kids call out to him. They want him to throw it back to them. He finds he cannot.

2.

The colony is a wretched place. Rows of hovels of brick and wood, roofed with corrugated metal and tarp, built on dirt ground, surrounded by garbage dumps. Women cook on small fires outside their miserable homes. He stands among them, appalled. Appalled at himself for expecting anything more. But it will change now. It will all change. He walks down one of the rows, picking his way around the fires and the children and the dogs. Men and women look up at him with fear, contempt. They withdraw into themselves. He tries to smile. He tries to look out for her. It's supposed to be a surprise. It's not supposed to be like this.

A woman in an immaculate blue sari calls out. "What do you want?"

Ajay stops to look back at her.

He thinks about the words he's about to say.

Like trying to fling oneself off a cliff, the body won't obey the mind.

He must force himself.

"My mother." The words seem frail on his lips.

There's a hush, then muffled words, his words repeated, then a ripple of comprehension runs through the crowd.

Not entirely friendly. Not entirely welcome.

"So, you're the one," an old man lying on a charpoy says.

Another woman climbs to her feet, steps forward, examines him on all sides with contempt, derision. "They said you were looking for her."

"She's here?" is all he can manage to say.

"You have no shame."

He looks at her in bewilderment.

"Where is she?"

"You should have stayed away."

"Ma!" he shouts. He turns to the growing crowd. "Where is she?"

A gang of young men approach but keep their distance.

It's the old women who show their feelings.

With hostility, one woman points toward a small, low concrete hall at the end of their row, with a crowd spilling outside.

"She's there. But Mary doesn't want to see you."

"Mary? Who's Mary? My mother's name is Rupa," he says.

"Not anymore."

He stands on the threshold of the low hall. He has to stoop just to look in. Inside there are many chairs facing the front, where there is a platform with a lectern, behind which statues of Shiva and Krishna flank a large painting of Jesus Christ seated in the lotus position, his hands forming a mudra.

A church. It is a church.

He scans the crowd, his breath quickening, his heart throbbing in his temple. He cries out "Ma!" He cannot see her. But those inside turn, they gasp and whisper, a commotion builds. Almost every head now, watching him. Every head.

All but one.

He sees the back of it, the gray, thin hair, the bony shoulders, strong but shrunken.

And the young girl beside her, thirteen years old, locking eyes with him, pained. In her eyes he recognizes his own.

The sister he never saw, born after his flight.

"Ma," he calls out and begins to shove his way through the crowd.

The priest has not yet arrived. The service has not yet started.

Now he is the service.

Finally he reaches his mother, her face stern, jaw clenched, eyes not wavering from the portrait of Christ.

"Ma!"

The room is in uproar.

A voice cries, "Mary, see, he has returned!"

"Returned from the dead."

"Your son has returned!"

"It's a miracle, Mary."

Other voices. "He's an impostor."

"The Devil."

"Ma!" he says. "It's me. Ajay. Your son."

3.

She is before him, aged and withered, grief-hollowed, in a tattered lime sari, not the shining, terrible woman who visits in his sleep.

"Ma," he says.

The crowd has hushed.

"Ma," the sweet, frightened girl says, clinging to her arm.

His mother finally stands, turns, will not make eye contact. She crosses herself, says a silent prayer, and limps past him.

He cannot tolerate this. He grabs her by the arms.

And now she releases herself, her fury.

"Do not touch me!" she says. "I don't know you."

He has no words. His hand goes limp.

She hobbles through the crowd toward the exit. Doesn't look back at him.

Some in the crowd speak in his favor now, moved by the scene.

"Mary, it's your son."

"Forgive him."

She stops. Shakes her head.

"He's not my son."

His anger swells. He goes after her. "I'm here! I'm your son!"

She turns to him, her anger stiffened, tensed into stone. "You stand here, but you're not my son. My son is dead."

She makes her way for the exit, out into the hovel row.

"I'm not dead," he says.

As he tries to follow, a new disorder.

"Father, Father, Father," voices say. "Father Jacob . . ."

A man dressed in the robes of a priest enters, bald and chubby, with strong searching eyes. He stands in Ajay's path, holds out a peaceful palm.

"Father Jacob . . . Mary's son is here."

But Ajay just pushes outside past the father.

She is standing a short distance away, her back to him. Not moving.

"I came for you," he cries, a sense of rage and injustice filling his insides.

He understands as he says it just how hollow this sounds.

"I searched for you," he tries again. "I never forgot."

His head swims. He has money, good clothes, he has made it; against the odds, he is a big man. And he has returned. Dozens of colony dwellers have gathered, craning their necks, whispering, jostling to see this spectacle.

"Even though you sent me away," he says, "I returned. I know you had to do it. I know you needed to send me to work. I worked hard, Ma. I did it for you. They told me . . . they sent you money every month . . ."

She turns and limps toward him. "No one sent money," she says with scorn.

He lowers his eyes.

"No one would ever send money. I sold you," she says. "That was it. I sold you, but I would have given you away!"

Gasps from the crowd.

"Mary!"

"He's your *son*."

"He's not my son!" she roars. She turns on Ajay. "It would have been better if you died."

"Mary!"

"Ma..."

"It's because of you," she says. "All because of you."

"No, Ma... you sent me away. I did what you told."

"It was your fault."

"No, Ma..."

"You let the goat free! You let it roam into that field!"

"Ma..."

His mind reels. What is she saying to him? How can he...

"If it wasn't for you, they wouldn't have come!"

So many years of grief unraveling, charging her speech.

The sister Ajay never knew rushes to their mother's side, calms her, begs her to stop, but is thrown down.

"And then... when... after..." His mother's eyes well with tears.

And it hits.

Hema.

Where is Hema?

"You ran away!"

Where is his sister?

His mother goes on. "You ran when they came!"

"No!" he cries. "I fought them!"

"Fought them? You coward. You ran."

His young sister sobs on the ground.

"Where's Hema?" Ajay says in a low voice.

"And they came to buy you, and you were sold."

"Where's Hema?" he repeats again, searching his memory for her face.

"And now...," his mother rages, "now you come back. You dare to come back with no shame. A big man, with fine clothes. Working for the same demons who did this to us?!"

"What are you . . . ?"

"The Singh brothers! The ones who killed your father. The ones who ruined your sister. Their men came to tell me you were coming here. You work for them now." She launches herself at him, scratching, roaring. "How dare you show your face here!"

Men run to pull her away.

And Ajay?

He does nothing. He stands there.

Dumb.

He sits on the ground outside the church.

Disconsolate.

Catatonic.

His mother has been taken away.

The men still watch him, unsure what to do, unsure what he will do. They debate his case, but he doesn't hear.

Finally his young sister appears. She kneels by his side.

"She's in too much pain," the girl says.

It takes an age for the words to reach him. He turns his head to her.

"Who are you?"

"Sarah," she says.

His chest tight, his head dizzy. The churn of his mind makes it difficult to speak.

"Where is she? Where's my sister?"

"Gone."

"Gone where?"

"She left for Benares when I was seven."

"Why?"

"And she never returned."

"What happened?" he asks. "Why did she go?"

"You should leave now," Sarah says.

She gets up, but he holds her arm firm. She winces in pain. "What happened?"

"Please, it hurts."

The men and women around wait for what will happen next. "What happened after I was gone?"

"I don't know."

"What happened?!"

Another voice, his mother's, reaches him. "What happened?" it says.

She's standing nearby, watching.

"What happened to Hema?" he urges, letting Sarah go.

She runs to her mother.

"What happens to all girls," his mother replies, "when the men go away."

"I didn't do this," he says. "I came back for you."

"As one of them."

"I'm not one of them," he pleads. "I work for the Wadias. Not the Singh brothers."

His mother shakes her head, turns to walk away. "And who do you think they work for?"

He watches her go.

Watches Sarah go.

Nothing of his childhood left.

Everything shattered.

He turns to the crowd, still watching.

"Where are Rajdeep and Kuldeep Singh?"

"You should know."

"Ask your people."

"They rule our lives."

"They terrorize us."

He pulls the Glock from his bag. Considers it.

"Where are they?"

A young man his age steps forward. "There's a hotel in town," he says. "It's theirs. Palace Grande. You'll find them there."

4.

The Palace Grande is a four-story monstrosity beyond the noose of the traffic circle that marks the end of the road into town. All mirrored glass and cheap plastic panels, bad materials poorly fitted together with the illusion of glamour. An echoey lobby of marble, gaudy chandeliers, a sad palm tree growing inside. A corridor leads to a banquet hall, elevators up to the rooms. Men of dubious prosperity flashing their jewelry inside, on the sofas opposite reception, attached to their mobile phones.

And Ajay, entering through the revolving doors.

Eyes passing over him, considering him, factoring him into the equation.

He approaches reception, blinded by fury, by vengeance. And looks up.

On the wall beyond, a huge, gold-framed, soft-focus photograph with a saturated glow venerates two men in a street scene. A procession is taking place. The men are garlanded with flowers, jostled excitedly by an adoring crowd.

Rajdeep and Kuldeep Singh.

He's been smashed in the nose bridge.

White lights exploding in his brain.

The receptionist leers at him with an unctuous, weaselly grin.

"Impressive, aren't they?"

He has to control himself, guard his voice, keep his eyes from betraying his heart.

"I want a room," he says.

"How many nights?" the Weasel asks.

"One."

"ID."

Ajay hands over his driving license, the one Tinu has made for him.

"Just passing through?" The Weasel examines his card with great vigilance as he speaks, but Ajay doesn't hear, he's lost in the faces on the wall. "The honorable Singh brothers," the Weasel says, glancing up. "Rajdeep-ji owns this hotel. VVIP status. A very good man."

"And the other?" Ajay asks.

The Weasel turns to admire the two men. "Kuldeep-ji, he is our MLA. A hero in this town. He does great things. He has made us all prosper. Ask anyone."

Ask anyone.

The Weasel hands back his license. "You're coming from Delhi?"

"Yes."

"What line are you in?"

Revenge.

"Service."

"Service?"

"Yes. I want a room with a view of the road," he says.

Why? What do you think you're going to do?

"That will be difficult . . ."

Ajay draws his money clip, peels off several hundred-rupee notes, lays them down on the counter.

The receptionist smiles.

"But it can be arranged."

Room 302 smells of disinfectant and the ghosts of human desire. The AC rattles in fits. The windows are blacked out, the room is dark until the harsh fluorescent lights come on. Ajay locks the door and slides the chain and moves to the window, looks out at the traffic-snarled road leading to the horizon.

A wave of sorrow rises through his skin. Scars the tissue.

He sits on the edge of the bed.

Ajay Wadia.

Tetherer of Goats.

He puts his hand over his mouth in horror.

Did he cause all this? Is the whole world as he knows it his own doing?

He tries to think back, tries to see his childhood in his mind's eye, tries to remember, but his memory is only lined by absence. He has built his life around the story of exile. A convenient fiction that fueled him, gave him succor.

Now everything is a lie.

His life is a lie.

The pain of this is unbearable.

He can doubt her words, this woman who was once his mother, but he cannot doubt the reality in which he swims. He is despised. Reviled.

What can he do to fix this?

He begins to undress, removes his safari suit jacket and pants, lays them out on the bed. In his undershirt and briefs and socks and holstered gun, he turns off the light and approaches the window again, presses his hand against the glass, feeling the faint winter sun. On the main road, a legless beggar supports his torso with his hands. Three police Ambassador cars push their snouts through the traffic. Men sleep in the grass in the middle of the circle. Others play cards. A day like any other.

He turns his back to the window, removes his Glock, runs his fingers along the metal of the barrel, aims at the door. He catches himself in the mirror, the lean, muscled body of a man he never really knew.

His dream of unspeakable violence recedes as he wakes. He is lying on the bed, he has forgotten where he is. He thinks he's slept through the night and it's the bright morning in Delhi. Sunny must be waiting. He sits up. Then he sees the gun and remembers.

He is his own destroyer.

He has come to erase the wound.

Even now, he tries to imagine another way. He could call down to reception. Drink a cola, order dal fry. Go for an evening walk. Get drunk. Call for a girl to be sent to his room. In the morning, get the bus back to Delhi. Forget it all. Accept who he is.

But who is he? What use is a girl to him? With her, what would he do?

He is an island. Marooned.

No past, no future.

With the names of two men now carved in his heart.

Rajdeep and Kuldeep Singh.

5.

"Yes?" The Weasel looks up.

"Tell me one thing," Ajay says. "How can I meet with the Singh brothers?"

"It depends on what you want with them."

"I want to work for them."

"Many people do." The Weasel nods knowingly. "But you don't have to meet them for that."

"I want to pay tribute. I want to pay my respects."

"I see." He narrows his eyes, sizing Ajay up, trying to gauge from where the cash flows. "The brothers are usually here in town," he says. "We're often blessed with them right here in this very lobby. But"—he leans in—"right now things are very tense. There have been some complications. Between you and me, there is tension in the town. Enemies of the Singh brothers have been making certain moves. Now the brothers are with their men, discussing their reply."

"When will they return?"

"Impossible to say." A smile, outspread palms. "Like children, we are all waiting."

Ajay is standing outside the elevator, waiting to return to his room when a sly-faced young man in a brilliantly patterned shirt slips beside him. The doors open. They both walk in.

"You want to meet the Singh brothers?" this man says as soon as the doors close. "I heard you talking," he hurries on. "They all pretend it's impossible, but it can be arranged, just don't waste your time with that chutiya at the desk. He's full of big talk but he's small fry, he knows nothing."

"Who are you?"

"Vipin Tyagi," the man says, putting his hands together in namaste. "I fix things."

"I want to meet them," Ajay says.

"I understand."

"I want to see them face-to-face."

"Difficult. Not impossible."

The elevator opens at Ajay's floor.

"How much?" Ajay says.

Vipin uses his body to keep the door from closing. "Shhhh. This is not how good people talk. Why don't we meet tonight to discuss? Nine p.m.? Behind the Hanuman mandir. By the old cricket ground. Nice and quiet. Bring some goodwill with you and let's talk in the shadow of God."

6.

The town is stirring to dark. The thin light of day cracks and sinks into the frigid night. Vendors with steaming stalls sell aloo tikki, kachori, shakarkandi chaat, hot sweet tea. Plumes of smoke from wood fires rise against the dusk. Temple bells ring out. Ajay bathes with a bucket of cold water.

He knows there's a good chance he is walking into a trap.

But what else can he do?

At seven he dresses, checks the bulge of the gun under his suit, places the money in his bag. He eats an omelet at the cart opposite the hotel, kills time by wandering the lanes of the town, keeping to the shadows as much as he can. A febrile atmosphere. Groups of young toughs loiter. Cops man wary checkpoints. Whom they serve is unknown. He makes a distant pass of the

Hanuman mandir before returning to the market, watching from the shadows. By eight thirty, the streets are emptying out, the hotel lobby is deserted. He turns and makes his way through the backstreets.

He reaches the locked and desolate mandir a few minutes before nine. In the lane at the rear, he can sense someone within, watching him. He should turn around and leave. He should reach for his gun. He should . . .

"My friend, you came."

This is not a good place to meet.

Ajay begins to back away.

"Where are you going, my friend? Don't you want to meet Kuldeep Singh?"

"I made a mistake," Ajay says. His own voice startles him. Reedy, weak.

He turns to walk away, only to find a gun pointing in his face. A man he thinks he saw in the street? It's hard to focus on the face with this gun on him.

"You stick out here, brother," Vipin calls out affably. "Everyone sees you. You're already famous. Better step inside and talk."

The goon with the gun waves it toward Vipin Tyagi's voice, and Ajay steps inside.

"I hope you don't mind," Vipin says, flanked by another goon. "I brought my friends. After all, it would be foolish to meet a stranger alone in this town at night, don't you think?"

Ajay has no words. How foolish of him. How futile to believe he could alter the world.

Vipin steps forward. "It's better that you hand over that bag."

The goon beside Vipin draws a machete, while the gunman presses the muzzle into the back of Ajay's head.

"You don't know who I am," Ajay says.

Vipin Tyagi laughs and the goons' laughter follows. "Throw me the bag."

Ajay places the bag down at his own feet.

"I said throw me the bag, behenchod!"

"I work for Vicky Wadia," Ajay says.

Vipin pauses, narrows his eyes. Then the laughter rings out even more. "Is that right?! You work for Vicky-ji?" Vipin Tyagi wags his finger. "If you worked for a man like him, you wouldn't need to come to me." He nods to the gunman, impatient, bored. "Get the bag. Then kill him."

It all happens in a matter of seconds.

Of the three men, the gunman dies first. He's the one reaching for the bag, the one taking his eye off their prey. All Ajay needs is instinct, the split-second understanding that the gun is no longer in the back of his head but pointed at the sky. Ajay spins away. He doesn't think how he might die, how his brains may explode and splatter the earth. He spins and grabs the gunman's wrist and the gun goes off as they fall to the ground. He is the first to react. Thank Eli for that, all those hours of dry, mechanical training. But who to thank for the rage? Sunny? His mother? They fall and Ajay snaps the gunman's arm. The machete goon is already coming at him. But something about the sound of the arm bone cracking makes him come half-heartedly, and that's all Ajay needs to leap forward and take him down, pin the machete hand with his knee and smash the goon repeatedly in the face. Grab the goon's head in his hands and smash it against the dirt. Take the machete and slit his throat. Take the machete and hack at the head of the gunman with the shattered arm. When Ajay turns, panting, his eyes a film of blood, Vipin Tyagi is rooted to the spot, his own eyes wide, jaw agape. "I can take you to them, brother!" Vipin cries. But Ajay doesn't care anymore. The red mist has fallen. He strides toward Vipin, raises the blade, and brings it down into Vipin's face.

7.

It's two a.m. now, in the hotel room, sitting on the cold floor, his back up against the wall, gun pointing at the door. The town is ablaze with noise. Men chanting and roaring. Baying for blood.

Every cell of Ajay's body is on fire.

He is a killer. He has killed.

He'd staggered from the lane with his bag, machete still in hand, stumbled across the cricket ground, his face and suit jacket spattered with blood, his heart a jackhammer. Should he have fled right then? Straight to the edge of town? No, running was the worst thing to do. That would be his death sentence. Three corpses, and a stranger vanished from his hotel. A stranger who'd been asking about the Singh brothers. They'd have hunted him down. They'd have brought him back and finished him off. Tortured him. Tortured his mother and young sister. He would have failed in every way, and worse.

So he continued through the small streets in the dark until he came upon a hand pump, pumped the water and washed his hands and face, snatched a shawl from a line outside a house and wrapped it round himself, covering the blood. And he walked back into the shuttered town. Walked through the streets, quivering with adrenaline, trying not to be seen.

He had watched the hotel from across the road.

Waited twenty minutes until a large boisterous group emerged from the banquet hall.

Slipped in as they exited the lobby under the bright white lights.

The Weasel was not on duty.

He believed he had not been noticed.

In the room, he ripped off his bloody suit and stuffed it to the bottom of his bag. Then he scrubbed his skin clean under the shower, scrubbed his hair, until the water below him was clear. But every time he closed his eyes, he saw the machete strike, the body fall. Every time he closed his eyes, he saw Vipin Tyagi's face splitting open like a watermelon.

Now it's three a.m. and he is staring down the wreckage of his life.

Revenge. He can't even get that right.

He can hear the commotion in the streets.

Their bodies must have been found.

What is he good for?

He grips the gun.

Waits for them to come.

Should he shoot at them? Or shoot himself?

It's four a.m. and the horns and cries and engines have begun to fade. There is a lull outside, a pale light in the sky. Maybe at this point he can run? Check out of the hotel, be cool about it, and go. No. No. It would be suspicious. And run where? Back to Sunny? No, they'd find him eventually. And how can he work for this family anymore? Impossible. So, he'll disappear. Find refuge. In the mountains? In Goa? Or somewhere he's never been before. He can do it. Just run.

And then it comes to him.

Benares.

He will run to Benares.

He will search for his sister there.

The only thing he has left to hold on to.

He holds on to this thought.

He closes his eyes. The darkness swallows him.

He wakes and daylight is seeping through the glass.

He's still holding his gun, sitting against the wall.

What time is it?

He checks his watch.

Almost nine a.m.

His body is aching, but daylight brings fresh urgency. He combs his hair, shaves, tries to look like the bland, unobtrusive man of service he has become. There is a scratch on his cheek, a hollow look in his eye. Still, no time to think about that. He must go downstairs and pay. Hope against hope he's not challenged, questioned. Should he carry his gun? No. Wait until he's free to go. He removes the metal cover from the rattling AC and hides the gun in there.

———

When the elevator disgorges him into the lobby he's greeted by a sea of noise.

A TV is blaring. And the Weasel is there, waving at him with glee. "Full drama, my friend," he shouts, "high tension, come, see."

No indication of suspicion at all.

"I heard noises in the night," Ajay says, averting his eyes.

"How can you sleep at a time like this?" the Weasel cries, oblivious to Ajay's mood.

"I want to check out," Ajay says.

"How can you check out at a time like this!? Three of Kuldeep's workers have been killed, right outside the Hanuman mandir. Can you imagine? I'm sure it's the Qadari gang."

He points to the TV hanging in the corner wall. A crowd of men have gathered round. A reporter is standing at the crime scene in the daylight— the bodies of the men are covered with bloodstained sheets. The channel cuts to a group of around fifty men armed with swords, wearing saffron headbands, protesting loudly, marching through the town.

"God is angry," one of the men in the lobby declares.

Another says, "God only need worry about Kuldeep Singh."

"Nonsense. The Singh brothers are running scared. That's why they're hiding. They've been hiding for days . . ."

"Watch your mouth," the first man shouts, "or I'll shoot you right here."

Just as it seems a scuffle will break out, the news report cuts to Kuldeep Singh.

He is speaking outside his compound, in his white kurta and saffron scarf, his dark shades removed to reveal the rancor in his eyes, talking about this wave of violence that is staining the purity of their town, about the need for swift vengeance. He is addressing those who call him a coward. Yes, he has heard the lies. He will set the record straight.

"We will not back down," Kuldeep Singh exclaims. "We will show our

strength a million times. And if those people from a *certain community* oppose us, we will cut them down."

"Full drama," the Weasel says again, all but rubbing his hands together.
"The Singh brothers are taking out a march on town, this afternoon. And
guess what? It's true. The rally will end right here." He turns back to Ajay
with a searching smile. "But you, you want to check out I think, don't you?"

"No," Ajay says. "I'll stay."

8.

He hears the march long before he sees it. The revving of engines, the
screeching of horns, cars, and motorcycles, loudspeakers blaring slogans in
praise of God and Kuldeep Singh. He watches from his room as they emerge
on MG Road, several hundred men in saffron, wielding machetes and
swords and flags and banners, a few holding aloft old rifles or handguns,
and around them many hundreds more, gawping citizens, cheering onlook-
ers, an awesome sight, a vast human snake slithering toward him. As the
march draws close, he can make out the Singh brothers at its heart, riding
separate jeeps, Kuldeep standing with his arm raised, taking in the adulation of the crowd, Rajdeep waving a sword. Closer and closer to the hotel.
The noise deafening, voices chanting: *Jai Shri Ram. Jai Kuldeep Singh.*

He sees among the crowd many banners bearing the smiling, God-
fearing image of Vipin Tyagi, honorable citizen. The Singh brothers dis-
mount their jeeps. Grasping the outstretched hands of their followers.

There are five rows of plastic chairs facing the stage, a large, long sofa on
a raised platform behind them. Then a barrier of policemen, separating this
VIP area from the crowd. A worker is taking the stage, tapping the microphone, announcing the bravery and honesty of Kuldeep Singh.

Kuldeep Singh is ascending the stage.

Rajdeep Singh taking his seat on the VIP sofa, leonine.

Here they are, right in front of him.

And in their faces, he sees his father's face.

And all fantasies of flight go up in smoke.

He'll never have another chance like this. He knows what it means. He can finally find some purpose to his life.

He removes his Glock from inside the AC unit, tucks it into his waistband.

Wraps the stolen shawl around his chest.

Inside the shawl, one hand rests on the trigger.

He leaves the room, leaves his bag behind.

Walks down the corridor to the elevator.

Presses the button for the ground floor.

Emerging into the crowded lobby, he finds himself meditating on Kuldeep Singh, visualizing his death all the same. Once the pistol is out, he'll have, what? Two seconds to fire? Less? Will he run to him? Walk slowly? Say his name? Fire a shot into his head? His pulse races, his palms become clammy. Five seconds? Three seconds? It'll take a millisecond to explode. And then? Rajdeep Singh. There will be enough time for Rajdeep to watch his brother fall. And if he's calm, he can shoot Rajdeep from the stage. Unload the rest of the clip.

Or will he save one bullet for himself?

Will he even need it?

Surely their men will do the job themselves.

So, he's doing this.

This is his life.

He pushes his way through the crowded lobby to the front. A door at the side leads to a garden in which the stage has been erected. Workers mill around at the side.

Ajay spies the Weasel standing by the door.

He comes to stand at his side.

"Ah, you're here my friend!" the Weasel says.

"I was looking for you," Ajay replies.

"This is your lucky day!"

Does he know? Does he suspect?

"I want to get closer," Ajay goes on, slipping a wad of rupee notes into the Weasel's palm. "I want to see Kuldeep from the side of the stage."

"Come with me," the Weasel says.

From their position at the side of the stage they can see Kuldeep preparing to step forward, the thronelike sofa bearing Rajdeep Singh, and behind all that, the roiling crowd.

"So great, don't you think?" the Weasel yelps above the noise. "I told you, no man here is more powerful than . . ."

But as he says these words . . .

9.

Vicky Wadia arrives. The giant and terrible man. He wades through the masses of bodies, through the police barricade, up to the VIP sofa, dressed in his black kurta pajama, a shahtoosh shawl, the same long black hair, his body bullish and rangy at once, the rings glistening on his hands, and Rajdeep's smug face distorts in fear as Vicky stands over him, Rajdeep jumping to his feet, bowing his head, pressing his palms together and making room, relegating his body to the corner so Vicky can sit dead center, legs crossed, arms splayed along the back.

Now Kuldeep Singh comes to the front of the stage, to the microphone. He is talking up his power, his position, his defiance. "Our culture is under threat," Kuldeep says. "Our way of life. They want to kill us in the night. They want to make us live in fear. All the evils that plague us, the criminals who wish to prey on our good natures. Such things happening now. The smuggling, the trafficking of our children, the rape of our women, the murder of our brothers. They all come from a threat outside we know too well. We must resist it and keep our way of life. We must maintain order, through force if necessary. For too long we have been quiet. Now we must stand together, make noise against a common enemy."

Jai Shri Ram. Jai Kuldeep Singh.

This is his moment, he thinks.

Kuldeep Singh, hands aloft, milking the adulation and anger of the crowd.

This is the moment.

He reaches under the shawl for the gun in his waistband.

There's already one in the chamber.

He knows.

This is the moment.

He can jump onto the stage.

Get his shot off.

"Chutiya." A voice above him calmly speaks.

Laconic and baritone, laced with wicked humor.

Ajay looks up to see Vicky Wadia smiling down at him.

And the Weasel, averting his gaze, backing away in fear.

Vicky drapes his arm over Ajay's shoulder. "I heard you were in town." Lines up alongside him like an old friend, places a cigarette in his mouth, squeezes his rippling right arm tighter around Ajay's neck as he lights the tip. "I've had my eye on you."

And Ajay, frozen. *Wasn't he over there?* He looks toward the VIP area, expecting to see Vicky seated on the sofa throne. Expecting this to be an illusion. No.

No.

He's really here.

"You've been busy." Vicky purrs approvingly. "You've met your mother at long last. You've even had time to make new friends . . ." He leans so close to

Ajay's face that his mustache bristles against the soft skin. Vicky chuckles, blows smoke. "Then you've killed them."

Ajay instinctively tries to pull away, he tries to find a place of escape, but the enormous arm like a constrictor keeps him locked in place. His eyes dart about in alarm. He feels himself vanishing, vanishing, inside Vicky's enormous being. Only his hand, under the shawl, is free to grip the gun.

"Shhhh," Vicky soothes him. "Don't fear." He loosens his hold, slaps Ajay good-naturedly on the shoulder. "I'm good at keeping secrets." He drops his cigarette to the floor, crushes it underfoot.

Inhale. Breathe.

Ajay's hand inches the Glock slowly from his waistband. Slowly, slowly, finger trying not to quiver on the trigger.

"What exactly are you planning to do with that gun?" Vicky says. Ajay tries hard to swallow the lump in his throat, to keep himself together. "If you're not careful," Vicky goes on, "you'll blow your balls off." He smiles to himself. "Then I'll have some explaining to do."

Trapped.

You are trapped.

"Look at this," Vicky sighs, running his free hand across the horizon as if admiring a sunset, as the roiling crowd cheer Kuldeep Singh and bay, with weapons raised, for blood. "All these men. Ready to tear their enemies apart. Aren't they beautiful?" He inhales the air, the scent of anger and violence a fine perfume to him. "You should always have five hundred men on hand to tear a place apart. But more important are the ten thousand men behind them, cowards all." He laughs and holds Ajay's head. "You don't know what I'm talking about, do you, boy?" He begins to run his fingers through Ajay's hair. "But I'm proud of you. Killing three men is no small thing. I was twelve when I first looked into the eyes of a dying boy. I'll never forget the look on his face." He takes a moment to remember. "Surprise. He was surprised. And how did these men look? At the end of their lives. Were they surprised? Did they have time? No doubt they deserved it." He jerks Ajay's head back and forth on the pole of his neck as if he were a toy. "Don't worry, they won't be missed, despite what it looks like. This, this is all for show. In fact, you've done me a favor. This, all this chaos, it's good for business. But what were you even trying to do?" He motions toward Kuldeep Singh. "Get to this dog? This fucker? In order to kill him? Kill his brother? And then what? Were you just going to die?" He lets the question hang, and they watch the scene in dreadful silence as Ajay feels like his stomach is being ripped out of him, left on the floor. "I'll let you in on a little secret," Vicky says. "These men, these two men, Rajdeep and Kuldeep Singh, they mean *nothing*. They *are* nothing. Killing them right now would be a waste of your life. And besides, they're still useful to me. So I'll tell you what you'll do. You'll turn around, get your bags, and go back to Delhi. Go back to Sunny and forget all this, keep on playing nursemaid for a while."

Ajay's finger is shaking so hard on the trigger, tears are pooling in his eyes.

He feels like he's spinning, spinning.

Falling down a deep black well.

"And then, when the time is right, I'll give them to you. Rajdeep and Kuldeep Singh. You can kill them any way you like. You can pull their teeth from their jaws, cut their tongues from their heads, you can pluck their eyes out, you can rip their hearts from their chests. That's my promise to you. And when that's done, I'll give you something more. Your sister. Your mother may be lost to you, but you still have your sister. Yes, she's alive. In Benares. I've seen her myself. She thinks of you often. I'll take you to her. But only if you do what you're told."

10.

Ajay takes the overnight train and arrives in Delhi early next morning. He ignores the lighthearted joking of the guards, goes straight to his room, locks the door. He feels, even in the silence there, that he isn't safe, that

Vicky is watching him. Removing his gun from the bag, he remembers Vicky's parting words. "You are who you are, the past is gone. It's the present you must master now." He removes the money from his duffel, locks it away. He removes the crumpled, crusty, bloodstained suit from the bottom of his bag.

He had a chance, he thinks, in his life, to be a simple man. A good man. Now he's a Wadia man.

He reports to Sunny at noon.

"You're late," Sunny says, already nursing a whisky.

"Sorry, sir."

"I told you. I needed you."

"Yes, sir."

He starts to clear empty glasses, takes them toward the kitchen.

"Well?" Sunny says.

Ajay pauses.

"Sir?"

"Did you find your mother?"

He tries to sleep that afternoon, but he cannot. He goes to the local gym instead to lift weights. The strain, the extinction, that comes from the dead lift is a welcome for him. But when he drops the bar, when he can hold it no longer, a hand comes down on his shoulder, and he reacts violently, turns and grabs his attacker by the throat. It's only Pankaj, one of his gym friends. "Brother, it's me," Pankaj cries, stricken, then looks into Ajay's scratched face and is afraid.

"What happened to you?" Pankaj says.

He returns to duty at six p.m., makes Sunny an old-fashioned. Sunny retreats to his bedroom with the glass along with the bottle of whisky and slams the door. Gautam Rathore arrives at eight, breezing past Ajay, planting himself on the sofa, flicking through magazines, calling for a bottle of whisky himself.

He nods toward Sunny's bedroom.

"Does he have his bitch in there?"

Ajay brings Gautam his bottle along with ice and soda.

"He's alone."

"Well tell him to get out here! Chop-chop."

Ajay knocks once, discreetly, and waits. Nothing.

"What's he doing in there!?" Gautam drawls.

Still nothing.

"Sir," Ajay says, "Gautam is here."

Sunny emerges, sluggish with thought.

"Leave us alone awhile," he says. "I'll call when I need you."

Ajay returns to his room.

Two hours later Sunny calls. Ajay is to prepare a car. No drivers. Just him.

He gets up from his bed, dresses with his Glock under his jacket, and heads to the garage, where he takes the keys for the Toyota Highlander. He signs for it without a word, climbs inside, starts the engine. Then pulls it out beyond the gates and waits beside the Mercedes belonging to Gautam Rathore.

RAJASTHAN

THE DESPICABLE GAUTAM RATHORE

(Sixteen Hours Later)

1.

Gautam wakes.

With no idea where he is, no idea how he even got here.

Lying on his back, he stares vacantly at the dust motes floating in a sunbeam.

Like a lizard he blinks.

The film of consciousness breaks.

Then the pain begins.

The throbbing of his swollen brain within that proud regal skull.

These moments aren't uncommon.

If anything, he's made a sport of them.

But today something is different, there's something very wrong with this picture today.

He's the son of wealth.

But not like Sunny Wadia.

His wealth is ancient, storied.

Asset rich, cash poor.

Most wouldn't know it; appearances are deceptive, and he's a magician by blood, the firstborn son of the Rathores of Bastragarh, famed for their jewel-encrusted slippers and tiger hunts. Rulers, one way or another, of a vast swath of Madhya Pradesh.

But he is obliterating himself.

Turning himself inside out.

Turning himself away.

He despises Sunny Wadia.

But he was with him last night.

Wasn't he?

So what is he doing here?

He tries to see into the fog, the black hole of his mind's eye.

Deep inside there's nothing.

No, wait, a flash of white.

A face rising up.

Oh God, a girl dressed in rags.

Imploring.

Her eyes wide.

Widening.

Hand reaching out.

How vulgar, that can't be right.

He shudders, recoils.

She's engulfed in blinding light.

Silence in the room.

It's all so majestically serene.

The scent of luxury.

I'm OK.

I'm OK.

He was with Sunny last night.

Bleeding him dry, ho hum.

And then?

Think, brain.

It was more than that. Sunny had something grand to say.

He recalls arriving at the club.

Swaggering inside.

Behind the velvet curtain.

It was literally velvet. He entered the VIP room with his perpetual smirk on his face. And then?

Gautam's eyes fall on the naked laterite walls, the antique Rajasthani screen. The stillness in this place. It's so bright outside.

He loses his train of thought.

Where are you now, again?

Why are you here?

Do you know this room?

Men like him usually do.

He finds he does.

It's the Jasmine Villa of the Mahuagarh Fort Palace Hotel.

Yes, that's right.

Old Adiraj's place.

Two hundred kilometers from Delhi in the desert of Rajasthan.

What the hell are you doing here?

Technically, you're banned from the property. After that incident with the zip line and the Emirati's Pomeranian.

The room gives nothing away. Nothing says "blackout bender" like a room with no object out of place. No sign of another guest. No clothing strewn over the backs of chairs. No cigarette burns, no overflowing ash-trays, no broken glass, no empty bottles on the floor. No blood. It must all have happened somewhere else.

All he remembers is that he was with Sunny.

It must have been one hell of a night!

He checks to see if he's soiled himself; it's a coin toss on mornings like this.

But no! Clean as a pig's whistle.

God, and small mercies, eh.

Yet he *is* wearing someone else's pajamas: red pin-striped, a little too small.

And in the back of his throat, the leaky faucet of postcocaine drip.

But that's par for the course.

He scans the room for his wallet and keys.

For anything.

Nothing.

The plot thickens.

Ho hum.

He peels back the sheets, swings his legs to the terra-cotta floor.

God, the pain!

It's like he's fallen off, then been kicked by a horse.

He stumbles into the bathroom in a fit of coughs, doubles over, clears his throat, spits rust in the porcelain.

And rises to the mirror.

Dear God.

He daren't move.

A wild animal stares back at him.

A dictator, pulled from the rubble, ready for the gallows.

Two hideous black eyes, an equine nose fully taped.

He raises his hand to it.

Must have been one hell of a night.

"Wine," he croaks down the phone, cradles the receiver, straps the toweling robe across his chest, haughtily clears his throat.

"Yes, sir?"

"It's an emergency."

"Do you need a doctor?"

"No, I need wine."

"Wine, sir?"

"Do you wish me to repeat myself indefinitely?"

A pause.

"What kind of wine?"

"The kind that is wet."

A female voice, more polished, takes the phone.

"Sir, I'm afraid we cannot send alcohol to your room at this time."

Outrageous.

"Whyever not? I see no good reason."

"It's too early, sir."

"Nonsense. The sun is positively perpendicular. By any civilized metric it is reasonable to expect wine."

"Sir, I'm very sorry but it's . . ."

"What? A dry day? Gandhi-ji's hallowed birthday? Abstinence! What a way to celebrate! No doubt you've read what he did with his nieces. Are we all meant to suffer for that man's dreary austerities, for his dreadful lack of self-control!"

"Sir?"

"Send up a Bloody Mary then! An honest breakfast drink. Whisky in my porridge if need be."

"Sir, it's past noon."

"Are you saying if it were morning I would be indulged?"

"Sir . . ."

"Is Adiraj there?"

"Adiraj Sir?"

"Yes! Adiraj. The gentleman who pilots this static ship. Put him on the phone."

"Sir, Adiraj Sir is indisposed."

"Indisposed? *Dispose* of him then, put him on, or at the least have the decency to call him before I come down there myself! Let's get to the bottom of this!"

Does he really want that?

What will he find down there?

More dirt.

Always more.

He hangs up, shoves himself off the bed, hobbles to the front window, peers out the shutters with a paranoid eye.

"What the hell am I doing here? And what in God's name happened last night?"

He sees the terrace, empty.

Swings the door open, steps out.

It's well past noon. Two, maybe three p.m.

The desert dissolves into a wide blank horizon.

A few tentative steps.

Warm stone underfoot.

He shuffles to the edge, past his private pool, clambers onto the thick wall.

Hands on hips.

He's high on the far edge of the fort, looking down the sheer face of rock. The wind caressing his gown. Queasy.

His tour guide voice: *The Jasmine Villa is typically employed for the discretion of nobility. And the nobility of discretion.*

Looking back toward the main fort, so far away.

A deep sense of unease.

There's no one abroad. Not a soul in the mild winter light.

All gone out for an elephant ride, no doubt.

Bob and Peggy from Kansas City.

Getting the Full Indian.

What price a sniper rifle now!

He mimics the shot.

And there's that flash again.

Not a muzzle, a girl, and her eyes.

Her hand.

Her mouth.

Christ, I need a drink.

Something to steady the ship.

"I really must insist," he says into the phone.

"Sir?"

"On something to drink. And if nothing is forthcoming, I will come down there myself. I'm certain I *will* make a scene. Would you like that? I don't think you would. For a start, I'm wearing someone else's clothes."

"Sir, one second please . . ."

A glacial half minute.

"Hello! Gautam, dear."

A familiar voice.

"Adiraj!" Gautam winces. "I seem to have woken up in your hotel by mistake."

"Well now . . ."

"I know I'm technically barred, but really it's not my fault."

Adiraj says, "Speak no more."

Gautam cocks his head, narrows his eyes. "Hold my peace?"

"Yes, dear. Water under the bridge."

Something's not right.

Adiraj has never been so accommodating in his life.

"You wouldn't," Gautam ventures, "happen to know how I came to be . . . ummm . . . in your abode?"

"By taxi of course, last night, yes, late last night, around midnight in fact. Definitely midnight."

"Midnight?"

"Why, yes."

"In a taxi, you say?"

"Yes."

"Were you forewarned?"

"Well now. It was quite a surprise. Your spirits were high!"

"And you just . . . let me in?"

"Bygones, dear, bygones."

Gautam scrunches his eyes.

"Was I . . . alone?"

"Oh yes, very much so."

He's lying.

"You're saying I took a taxi from Delhi . . ."

"Quite alone."

". . . with the sole intention of coming to your hotel."

"Quite, quite alone."

"Alone."

He's lying.

"Absolutely."

"Well, why the hell would I do that?"

"It's not for me to say." A sudden flatline in his tone. "I cannot see inside your soul."

Gautam rubs his head, at a loss.

"I'm wearing someone else's clothes."

"Who am I to judge?"

"And my own clothes have been taken away. As has my wallet and my keys and I have no idea where I left my car. I have to say I find it all very strange and your answers are not apothecary at all!"

"Would you like a drink?"

"Yes, please."

An imperceptible sigh.

"I'll send something right away."

Dig deep, Gautam, dear boy, but beware!

Here be monsters.

What do you know?

Whaddayaknow?

You despise Sunny Wadia, but cling to him like a life raft.

Like a Saint Bernard, with his little barrel of brandy giving you succor in the snow.

Sunny, who turned up one afternoon at your apartment flaunting a bottle of rare Japanese hooch!

"Ah," you said, ever facetious, "you speak the lingo? Zenshin massāji wa ikagadesu ka? Waribiki shimasu!"

Sunny, pretending to look past all the mess, the carnage, the fall from grace, the lurid tales. Sunny, the latest Prince of Delhi, the young stud, the hot ticket in town, turning up with no warning, offering whisky to a man who just . . . didn't . . . give a damn.

What's your game?

Gautam took the whisky. Poured himself a glass and swallowed it down.

When was this? Seven or eight months ago? Eight whole months. August 2003 or so? God, your memory is shot to hell.

Has it been eight or seven months since Sunny nudged into your life? Offering cash, whisky, and what else? You know what.

In exchange for?

Advice? Friendship?

Consultancy fees.

"Consultancy fees?"

"Yes," Sunny said. He wanted to build hotels. This was his pitch. And Gautam had been in the hotel line, once upon a time, in that brief, bright window of his life when he had neither succumbed to his vices nor exhausted his father's credit line. Oh, those glory days. A thick head of hair, a virile pout, snipe-hunting calves, and polo thighs. A standard, upper-class addiction to booze. The keys to the kingdom! How had it gone so wrong?

Well, appetites, my darling.

He had a few.

When he was born, he sucked his wet nurses dry. He could never get his fill. Just as well his mother never spilled a drop. It would have been White

Russians all the way. And his father? Prasad Singh Rathore. A shrewd man, his only addiction a vice that cleans up its own trace.

Power.

He was the second generation of modern India, Gautam's father. In 1948, *his* father—Gautam's grandfather, the venerable Maharaja Sukhvir Singh Rathore (adored by the British, resolutely indifferent to the Independence cause)—saw his kingdom dissolved into the Republic, newly formed. How to compensate for this royal loss? Why, a "princely purse," a stipend designed for upkeep, which was used to barter feudal power and control.

It was good while it lasted. But then the '70s came along. Those Soviet times. The dictator Indira abolished that concession, and the Rathores were left with little more than a begging bowl and a handful of forts between which to string their washing lines.

Asset rich, cash poor.

It scarred them all.

Only Prasad, first son, Gautam's father, was wily enough to change.

Prasad Singh Rathore understood that politicians were the future kings. So he threw his hat into the ring, with noble disregard for his family's distaste of such grubby, earthen things, and was duly voted in as a hallowed MP. Soon after, he persuaded three of his cousins to stand for the legislative assembly. It wasn't long before Prasad's second cousin Sunil became chief minister of the state. Better the Devil, don't you know. And here they were, the family where they belonged. This was the world into which Gautam Rathore, Prasad's only son, was born.

2.

He reclines on his sun lounger under an umbrella on the terrace beside his private pool, impatiently awaiting his booze. Still trying to remember. He arrived here at midnight.

Really?

There's no way this timeline adds up.

He was with Sunny at midnight. This much he knows.

Why can't he remember why? Why, when he tries to dredge through the muck can he see nothing but some simpleton's face?

She reminds him of someone though.

He doesn't want to dwell on that.

He fixes on Sunny instead.

Their "whisky summit" wasn't the first time their paths had crossed, truth be told. They'd schooled together, very briefly. It was the early '90s. Gautam had been Sunny's senior by two years. He was cock of the walk, old money when old money talked, spiced with a dash of his father's political clout. And who had Sunny Wadia been? Just a nobody little gangster's son from UP, his English as coarse as his manners, someone to belittle, besmirch, an upstart who bought his way into school and snatched its good name like a common thief.

"You didn't last too long though, did you?" Gautam scoffed, Nikka in hand.

He was talking about Sunny's expulsion.

Sunny: a tight-lipped smile.

Gautam poured himself another glass. "But old Malhotra, he never saw it coming! He was never quite the same after you. He'd quiver anytime he so much as sniffed the crotch of a hockey player. It's a shame you didn't get to see the fruits of your labor, you would have enjoyed it, but I suppose one can't get away with such violence unpunished. What was it he did to you again?"

Sunny crossed his arms but said nothing.

Gautam could see he was pushing his buttons.

"Ah yes, I remember now . . ."

"I'm not interested in talking about the past," Sunny said. "I'm here about the future."

———

After school (Sunny vanished, forgotten) Gautam was sent off to Oxford (Brookes) to read finance. He had no interest in his books; by then he'd developed a rapacious appetite for sins of the flesh. In his teenage years he'd notched up several servant girls on the family grounds, local prostitutes outside the boarding school, and even one of his mother's friends with his louche cutting ways on the polo grounds. In England he bedded some minor royalty—the niece of an earl, the daughter of a baron, etc.—while developing a sideline in transactional sadomasochistic coke, using the "tart cards" in red phone boxes in town. He liked the schoolmistress. His weekend trips were pure bacchanalia. "Lashings of discipline," his favorite card. Alas, those salad days had a worm in their heart. His dismal 2:2 drew a recall to the family bosom, whereby he was lined up for marriage with the pliant daughter of a royal turned politician from Himachal. Desperate to escape the horrors of domestic life, he negotiated two years of grace, in which he would put himself to use transforming one of the family's dilapidated forts into a boutique hotel for the discerning elite of the world.

It was a triumph. At least at first.

He turned out to be a fine host. He organized press junkets, and during these, he plied the good men and women with precious vintages and exquisite meals, hosted elaborate dinner parties in Maharaja clothes. Gautam the raconteur, posing for photographers with his grandfather's big-game skulls, regaling journalists with tales from the Indiana Jones Playbook, massacres in courtyards, man-eaters, beautiful princesses in jewels tossing themselves into wells so as not to be defiled by rampaging hordes. It was a mishmash of true history from elsewhere and legends from his own mind. He followed it up with visits to the village to see the dancing girls, their gauzy pink veils, their shy smiles.

He enjoyed his success verily. Gained exposure in the right magazines.

He was Prince Gautam Good Times.

The Maharaja.

The Dynamic & Flamboyant Rathore.

The Remarkable Royal, Transforming Madhya Pradesh One Fort at a Time.

He partook in a glossy shoot for a fashion bible, posed by a renowned Armenian snapper before his deceased grandfather's portrait, wearing a turban to complement the Versace Cornici-print silk blazer he well adored, a tiger skin draped strategically around his loins.

The portrait was beamed around the world.

India was Shining.

But all the while, the stories began to swell, not only of the unspeakable amounts of coke he served along with the tawny port, or priceless vintage cars he wrecked on the potholed roads, or the antique gun he'd used to wing a journalist in a drunken duel, or the time he climbed on the table in the middle of a feast and relieved himself into the goat brain stew, but also of the staff—young girls who drew water from the nearby wells falling pregnant. One night one such girl threw herself off the fort wall.

She was three months' gone with child.

She left a note.

Word spread.

Mobs were formed. Vehicles were set ablaze.

The foreign guests were smuggled out in the night.

Some obscure local dispute took the blame.

Her family was paid off.

The police were employed to silence dissenters.

The media was sternly warned.

It all died down and went away.

But Gautam's father took decisive action.

He packed off his son to Delhi, to one of their apartments in a great building on Aurangzeb Road. He would cool his heels with a modest allowance—one lakh rupees a month—in quiet disgrace.

———

You would've thought he'd learned his lesson.

But no. Something took over him.

He'd always been stubborn, but in Delhi he doubled down. Tapped into some hitherto unknown crude despair.

It flowed.

He hit the city hard. Indulged in his vices unshepherded.

Went for the cheapest, dirtiest options and felt all the more gratified.

Whores from GB Road. Boys in Connaught Place. Inserted butt plugs into the rectums of school chums' wives. Imagine the club.

Young Royals Go Wild: The Musical.

Reveling in the reputation he gained.

The Grotesque Gautam Rathore.

Saving nothing for the return.

He would still drink with his old school friends, the polo crowd, and drink some more, peacocking. His tongue was loose. Insults, cutting remarks, let fly. Enemies would be made. Outrageous scenes would play out in the lobbies of hotels. Spill out into the roads. He'd lech and leer and grope and mock and snort and piss himself, until his erstwhile friends would avoid his calls. That suited him just fine.

Where were we, now?

His allowance was over by the middle of the month, and the rest would be served in desperate penury. His maids.

Unpaid.

Molested.

Fled.

Only his driver stayed.

He and Shivam sat and watched TV together.

Guffawed.

And late night he would go out to bring back more.

———

It was during these foul Delhi days that Sunny Wadia burst onto the scene. The upstart, transformed. In his tailored suits, his dewy skin, his parties, his vision. But what did Gautam care?

"I'll put you on a retainer," Sunny said. "Three lakh rupees a month."

"Make it five," Gautam countered.

"Five," Sunny said.

"Since that's settled," Gautam purred, "let's consummate."

He removed a baggie of shockingly white cocaine from his inner pocket. Tossed it onto the coffee table.

"It's of dubious origin. One part talc to one part aspirin to one part laxative to one part coke. And a part and a half of speed to spare. But boy, does it work."

Gautam ripped the head off the baggie with his teeth, swept away the debris from the glass tabletop, then dumped the entire gram down.

"Be my guest," he said.

"I'm fine," Sunny replied.

"Oh no, I'm afraid that's not the issue. You want my advice? On *hotels*? Then you have to mess yourself up with my bad coke."

He took a crisp note from his wallet and handed it to Sunny.

"You have experience?"

"Of course."

With a loose credit card, Gautam began to chop up four great ridged lines.

"Prove yourself to me."

Sunny ignored that but started to roll the note tight.

"You know," Gautam said, "I saw that advert of yours. Double-page spread. Very touching. All the best businessmen launder their reputations these days."

Sunny ignored him. "So, about the job," he said, "what do you say?"

Gautam stopped chopping, tossed the card onto the table, snatched the note.

"Job?" he replied, slightly wondrous, rolling the exotic term around his mouth. He leaned down and pulled one line, tilted his head, snorted hard again, blew his cheeks out, exposed his teeth, gripped the table, closed his eyes a long time, and just froze. Then he looked for a cigarette. "Almost too good to be true. But excuse me, I have to take a shit."

He held the note out to Sunny as he got up and walked away.

When he came back five minutes later Sunny hadn't touched a line.

"What?" Gautam mocked, cigarette hanging from his lip, debauched. "You already ate?"

"It's not that."

"What then?"

"It's yours."

"Oh, fuck off. Don't be a bore. This is the cost of business."

He detected the faintest whiff of regret as Sunny grasped the nettle, gripped the note, and bent down to snort the bad coke.

He could see Sunny didn't want to be there.

So what was his game?

3.

A man appears on the steps to the terrace, carrying a tray, a bottle of wine.

He's tall, dark, with long curly hair. From Kerala maybe.

Certainly not a Rajasthani boy. No gormless stare, no incipient mustache, just black wraparound shades, a crisp white shirt, dark pants.

An air of . . . security?

He stands above Gautam, staring down.

"And who might you be, young man?"

It's always good to assume indifferent command.

But the "young man" doesn't respond. He just puts the tray on the table and begins to open the wine.

"Are you new here?"

He can see the man's jaw clenching.

"You really are quite tense."

The wine pops open. The man places the bottle down and begins to remove the cork, and when he's done he places the cork next to the bottle and holds the corkscrew in his hand as if he just might use it as a gouging device.

"Go on then," Gautam says, "pour the damn thing."

The man places the corkscrew on the table, picks up the bottle and glass, and pours. Pours the wine slowly, slowly it fills, keeps filling to the brim.

"Steady on!"

It fills past, spills over, starts splashing onto the hot stone.

"What's wrong with you?!"

Gautam lurches up from the sun lounger, makes a lunge for the wine.

"For Christ's sake."

But the man just keeps pouring. Half the bottle is gone.

"Are you mad?"

"A little." He has a thick Israeli accent. He extends the glass to Gautam. Gautam reaches out to take it.

The next thing he knows he's coming up for air.

"What the hell!?" Gautam yelps. "You threw me into the pool!"

He splashes about, grips the side with his aching arms. The Israeli squats, balances his shades on the top of his head. His eyes are hazel, his expression hard. He nods toward a paper bundle wrapped in string.

"This is your clothes. We go inside and you put them on."

"Or what?"

The Israeli looks at the fort wall.

"We see if you can fly."

"You and I," Gautam says, "both know I can't fly."

4.

Half an hour later, the Israeli delivers dyspeptic Gautam through the fort grounds, along a path marked private that skirts the hillside, through a wooden gate, down a few steps onto a hidden terrace cantilevered over the plains.

Adiraj's terrace.

But Adiraj is not here.

It's an older man, spritely so, quite debonair, wearing an inconspicuously expensive cotton suit, his eyes protected by narrow shades. He sits at a wrought-iron table in the middle of the terrace, examining a sheet of paper. A decanter full of whisky, a water jug, and two tumblers sit in the middle, a manila envelope by his left hand.

Another chair is open, waiting at the side.

The Israeli stops at the bottom of the steps, holds his hand out, indicating Gautam should go on. "Keep walking, Johnnie."

Gautam, now dressed in his own salmon pink suit, says, "It's not really up to you, is it."

He has regained his bluster.

It's the clothes.

Also the understanding that this is a game.

The debonair man stands on cue, notes the time on his pocket watch, holds a hand to the waiting chair, calls out, "Please." To the Israeli he says, "Thank you, Eli, that will be all."

Gautam walks forward, running his hands over his jacket. "You picked one of my best."

"I assure you," the debonair man says, "I had nothing to do with that. But your driver was *very* helpful. He seems to know your taste." His accent is vaguely public school, clipped, impossible to place. "Please," he goes on, "have a seat. We've much to discuss and time *is* a factor in all this."

"How," Gautam replies, "did you get into my apartment?"

A pleasant smile. "Why, with your keys, Mr. Rathore."

"Ah, yes. I was wondering where they went. I'd very much like to have them back."

"All in good time."

Gautam considers the TB scars pitting the man's face.

"And you are, *exactly?*"

"My name is Chandra," the man says. "That's all you need to know."

Gautam splutters with forced jollity. "I need to know a hell of a lot more than that!"

Chandra smiles, takes his own seat. "Would you like some whisky, Mr. Rathore?"

"I would, as a matter of fact," Gautam says, his voice dripping with disdain. "I was on the verge of enjoying some mediocre wine earlier, but your Neanderthal in the bushes saw fit to throw me in the pool instead. You're lucky I'm suffering a particularly intense hangover or my ire would be worse."

Chandra takes the decanter and pours Gautam a large measure, adds the merest splash of water, slides it carefully across.

Gautam takes the glass, brings it to his nose.

A smile.

A frown.

"I know this."

"I'm sure you do. No doubt you're a connoisseur."

Gautam brings the glass to his lips, lets the whisky play on his tongue a moment before swallowing all of it down. "Yes. I'd recognize this anywhere. It's Japanese."

"Very good."

He drinks all the whisky in one go.

"More."

"Let's play a game. Whisky for answers. It has a wonderful dynamic."

Gautam taps his glass on the table. "Pour."

"You *are* keen."

"Pour."

Chandra does. A little less this time.

Gautam doesn't wait for the water. He swallows it impatiently.

"Not exactly playing your cards close to your chest, are you?" Chandra says.

"What does Sunny want?" Gautam snaps.

"I'll ask the questions, Mr. Rathore."

"He did send you though, didn't he? Or at least, you're here on his behalf."

He tries to pour another whisky himself, but Chandra pulls the decanter away.

"How would you characterize your relationship with Sunny Wadia?"

"Purely transactional," Gautam says.

"In what way?"

"I consult for him."

"On what?"

"This and that."

"Can you be more specific."

"Failure. I consult on failure. It's my specialty. I'm good at it. I notice he's good at it too."

Chandra sips his own drink.

"You consult for him on hotels."

"Yes. This is getting tiresome."

"Do you enjoy his company socially?"

"We're not fucking, if that's what you mean."

"The thought hadn't crossed my mind."

Gautam snorts. "I'm sure it has now."

Chandra, a wan smile. "Quite."

"For heaven's sake, man, give me a drink. A proper measure. Patiala at the least."

"How much cocaine have you been using in recent months, Mr. Rathore?"

"As much as Daddy will give me."

"Daddy?"

"The universal Daddy in the sky."

"Your relationship with your own father is . . ."

Gautam hoots, claps his hands together. "You're a psychologist!"

"Merely a lawyer."

"Do you think I got where I am today," Gautam says, "by being an idiot?"

"Your father has more or less disowned you, is that so?"

"I'd venture it's the other way round."

"And you're quite happy in your current situation?"

"Don't I *look* happy?" He taps his glass. "Drink."

"Tell me something about Sunny."

"He hates his father."

"Tell me something we don't already know."

Gautam hesitates. "He was planning to leave him. How's that for news?"

Chandra pours a drink.

"And you encouraged that?"

A bitter laugh. "I listened to his complaints, like a good and loyal friend."

"And the cocaine?"

"What about it?"

"Where did it come from?"

"A lady never tells."

"Was it his?"

"Pffft. Absolutely not. I have my people."

"But Sunny paid for it?"

"Naturally."

"And he took it too."

"Naturally. Now what's all this about?"

"Aren't you at all curious, Mr. Rathore, to know why you're here? To know why I'm here with you?"

A cloud passes over Gautam's face. A moment of seriousness. He swallows his whisky, pushes his glass forward. "More."

"What exactly do you remember about last night?"

"More."

"I need you relatively sober Gautam."

"It'll take a lot more than this to get me drunk."

Chandra pours him another small measure.

"And a cigarette."

Chandra offers him the pack. "Keep it."

"I *am* quite happy to talk," Gautam goes on, taking Chandra's gold lighter, lighting the cigarette, putting the lighter in his pocket. "As I said, I'm no fool."

"I'd like the lighter back."

Gautam looks perplexed, but removes it, slides it back.

"Are you in the habit of taking whatever you want?"

"Back to psychology now?"

"Do you see the world as essentially yours?"

"I'm quite happy to talk."

"Last night . . ."

"What has Sunny done?"

"Last night . . ."

Gautam suddenly sits up. "He's not dead, is he?" He frowns. "He didn't . . ."

"What?"

"What did he do?"

"What do you think he did?"

"I don't know."

"You were in the club together, do you remember that?"

There's that black hole again.

He shivers.

"Listen . . . Sunny turned up at my door one day. He didn't have to. He turned up and opened this bottle of whisky and asked me about hotels. Hotels? I'm not a fool. He didn't need to ask me about that. I know my reputation, I know exactly what people think of me. Frankly I don't care. Don't think I didn't ask why he was there."

"Why do you think he was there?"

"I don't know."

Gautam ashes his cigarette on the table.

"What do you think he wanted from you?"

"I don't know. But"—he lowers his voice conspiratorially—"he was weak. Lonely."

"You saw that?"

"I did."

"And then?"

"Nothing."

"You exploited him."

"We exploited one another. He needed a shoulder to cry on. Someone who understood his unique pain. And I needed someone to buy my coke for me. Everyone left satisfied."

"Sunny used the cocaine too?"

"Bien sûr! Naturellement."

"How much did he use?"

"Oh, he was a fiend."

"And what did the two of you talk about, broadly speaking?"

"What all boys talk about. How it would be better for us if our fathers were dead."

"Would that be better for you?"

"It wasn't really about me." He flicks his cigarette over the edge of the terrace. "Is he dead?"

"Your father?"

"Sunny."

"No."

"Oh."

"You sound disappointed."

"I suppose I am . . ."

"You don't have any loyalty."

"It would have been quite dramatic. Loyalty? To Sunny? No. I don't have loyalty to anyone." He swallows the whisky, then taps his glass. "Drink."

"No."

Gautam stares at the empty glass, the soft sun, the terrace, the desert beyond. "I'm tired."

"We're all tired."

"But no one is quite as tired as me."

"What do you know about Sunny's father?"

"Now *there's* a question."

The wind blows softly through Chandra's silken hair. He removes a mobile phone from his jacket pocket. He dials a number, puts the phone to his ear. Waits a moment. "Yes," he says, "he's here."

He places the phone on the table in front of them, puts it on speaker.

Gautam sits staring at it, waiting.

No voice comes.

Instead, Chandra takes hold of the manila envelope by his side, opens it, removes five large photographic prints from inside. Places them facedown on the table. Keeps his finger on them a moment. Then slides them across to Gautam.

"What is this?" Gautam glances uneasily at the phone, listening to the silence on the other end.

"See for yourself."

"No," he says childishly, "I don't want to."

No one speaks. No one moves.

Until a slow, narcotic voice emerges from the phone.

It says, "Turn them over."

Gautam's stomach drops.

"I don't want to." He runs both hands through his hair. "Give me a drink."

"Turn them over."

"It would really only take a second," Chandra says amiably, "for Eli to throw you over the edge. I believe he's already made the offer. And honestly, no one would think twice about your suicide now. Not with your blood alcohol levels the way they are. Not after the life you've led. Not after what you did last night."

"Give me a drink."

"And once it was done, everything would come out in the press."

Gautam is shivering. "I haven't done anything."

"Turn them over," the voice says. "And you'll have all the drink you want."

Gautam closes his eyes.

Places his hands on the paper.

Holds the edges.

Turns them round.

Bodies. Dead bodies. Dead bodies mangled and strewn over the road. Limbs broken and contorted, eyes wide open, lips curled in horrible smiles, teeth showing, eyeballs white, blood smears in flashbulbs. Police photos. Bodies on the sidewalk, bodies in rags, and a car, *his* car, his Mercedes, his license plate. Bodies. A teenage girl in rags, blood seeping from the void between her legs. Bodies. Now lined up in a hospital morgue. Five of them. Shattered and torn. Bodies. And finally, Chandra hands him a Polaroid. And there he is, Gautam Rathore, face crumpled up in an airbag at the wheel.

He turns them all back over, pushes them away so hard they scatter to the floor.

"This isn't real."

Chandra pours him that drink now.

Gautam takes it with shaking hands.

Then Chandra takes the phone, turns it off speaker, puts it to his ear, listens a moment, hangs up.

"It wasn't me," Gautam whispers. He drains the glass, takes out a cigarette, tries to get up, but he's dizzy. He sits down again, puts the cigarette in his lips. Chandra leans forward and lights it for him, retrieves the photos from the floor.

"Your car. Your fingerprints. Your face. Witnesses who place you at the scene."

"It wasn't me."

"Surely you must remember now."

That flash of light.

That servant girl reaching out.

Gautam's body sags.

Then his chest convulses, he retches.

Chandra stares at one of the photos a long while. Places it on the table. "The girl was pregnant," he says.

Gautam, empty.

"It wasn't me."

Chandra lights his own cigarette.

"It was. It was you. But . . . it doesn't have to be."

The words take a long time to become meaningful.

Gautam looks up.

"What?"

"Mr. Rathore. What if, by some miracle, it was not you."

He blinks stupidly. "What?"

"You'll be arrested soon enough. That is, if you don't jump. The police *will* take you in, I can assure you of that. You *will* go to jail. You can protest all you like, concoct strange stories, try to blame others, but that will only make things worse. Have you been to jail? I'm not sure you're suited. At least, not without money. Your family won't help you. Sunny's line of credit has expired. It's true you have your status, that will protect you to a point. But you also have enemies now. Would you like to be an enemy of my employer? Do you know what that means? We can make life quite miserable for you." He pauses. "But what if it weren't true? What if you could turn back the hands of time?" Chandra places the photos back into the manila envelope. "At present there is a young man in police custody, waiting to go to court. He has volunteered to take the blame, at great personal cost. He could just as easily change his statement, and this Polaroid of you could just as easily go to the press and the police."

Gautam closes his eyes.

"What do you want me to do?"

"That's the spirit."

"Just tell me."

"We want you . . . to get better."

Gautam looks up, screws his face.

"What?"

"There's a car waiting downstairs. Eli will show you to it. Inside there's a suitcase, your passport, other small effects, an amount of money to help you on your way, not that you'll need it, but it's psychological. You'll drive to Jaipur. From there you'll take a private jet to Bombay. From Bombay you'll fly to Geneva. Your visa is in order."

"It is?"

"Once there you will be escorted to a clinic. A lovely place in the mountains, conducive to recovery."

"Recovery?"

"From your vices, Mr. Rathore."

"You're sending me to rehab?"

"And you will stay there as long as it takes. You will work hard at your recovery, with the memory of this night and your liberty etched into your mind. And when you're fully recovered, be it three or six or eight months or two years if need be, you will return to your family home. You will marry. You will act with honor and propriety. You will take your rightful place as the heir."

"I don't understand."

"One day you'll be asked for a favor. It won't be anything onerous. In fact, in doing this favor, you will become powerful and also very rich. This wealth will snowball, as will the power. The only thing you must do is prove to your family that you are reformed. That you are worthy of your name."

Chandra stands up, buttons his suit, waves up to Eli to come join them.

"I don't understand."

"You don't need to understand, Mr. Rathore. You only need faith. Cheer up. You're with Bunty now."

AJAY III

Tihar Jail

1.

He is taken from the warden's office to a new cell in a different wing. He passes many crowded cells along the way, where prisoners whoop and cheer, snarl and spit, where some clutch the bars dead-eyed, some unblinking, some morose, others sleeping, cooking, sobbing in a corner. All the cells are overcrowded, twelve, fifteen men to a space, but the cell they stop outside holds just two. The scene within: sedate, bright, homely even. From a table against the wall, a TV plays a comedy show; another table, low and circular, holds a bottle of Black Label, two glasses, a pitcher of water, a sprawled deck of cards, a thick stack of rupee notes. Pictures of gauzy, hypercolored mountains and Bollywood actresses adorn the walls. There are two beds with thick mattresses, another mattress on the floor. The two men laze there, watching TV, eating from buckets of Chicken Changezi.

One is an ogre. Tall, powerful, grubby, in an undershirt too tight for his drum belly, wearing nothing else despite the cold. He has piggish eyes, a thick face on which the contours of his skull are weirdly displayed, an unruly head of wiry hair. The other is a small jackal of a man, sneering silently.

The guard slides open the unlocked door.

"What now?!" the Ogre roars.

"Your friend is here." The guard pushes Ajay in.

The Ogre pulls his head from the TV, looks Ajay up and down. "So you're the one," he belches, laughs. "You're prettier than I expected." He slaps the mattress, his eyes return to the screen. "Come on, sit, eat, don't worry, you're with friends." He nods to the jackal. "This chutiya's Bablu." He fetches a paper plate from the floor, loads it up with chicken and gravy and naan. "And I'm Sikandar the Great." He slaps the mattress again. "Whatever you did, you're a big man now. Time to rest. Time to enjoy."

Rest. Enjoy. Ajay's ears buzz with violence. His skin burns with razors and bruises and the cold.

"You sure taught those fuckers!" Sikandar says. "They were Guptas, you understand? They thought they were taking you for a fresher's party! Pretty boy like you. They thought you were fresh meat! They didn't know! But you showed them, didn't you? You almost killed one of them. You got them running scared. That's before they even knew who you were. Now everyone knows! Yes, my friend, the word is out! And now they're all scared. You showed them who's boss. But remember"—he wags his greasy finger—"there's only one boss here and that's me."

Sikandar is the jail boss of the Acharya gang. He represents Satya Acharya's interests inside. Acharya is from Lucknow; he started out in extortion, now he's cornered the Mandrax trade. His gang runs several labs on the streets, they make the tablets in the hundreds of thousands; their chemist, Subhash Bose, is a genius. His work has spread to South Africa, Kenya, Mozambique. They ship it out disguised as paracetamol. They ship it in here too, with the complicity of the doctors and the guards. Everyone wants a taste. You can pop the pill for an easy high. Even better, take a beer bottle, smash its body on the ground . . . instead of cutting someone's face, take the neck spout, fill its bowl with punctured cardboard, tobacco, and Idukki Gold, sprinkle in the crushed dust of the

Mandrax pill, light it all up, inhale through the neck, then prepare for euphoria and the inky blackness of the womb.

Sikandar was a coconut-wala outside. He ran a stall on the edge of Lucknow, a shed and a table and a white light, some goats tied up and some chickens running around. His uncle with a fruit stall next door. Sikandar told everyone he had a plantation in Karnataka, that he owned so much land you could walk across it for days, and everyone laughed, no one believed that. But he had the best coconuts, and often they were free. Someone would buy four and he'd throw in two more. "Baksheesh." He'd do it with everyone. You wanted one, he gave two. "Baksheesh." You wanted ten, he threw in fifteen. "Baksheesh." He'd toss a tender coconut in the air with his eyes closed, catch it in his left palm, chop the head at the moment of landing, toss in a straw. Chop, chop, chop. Laughing, wielding his machete. Joking with anyone who came. The cops came to be teased by him. The goons came to be teased by him. He knew everything that happened on the street. He was a butcher for Satya Acharya on the side. "A head is like a human coconut," he says. He's in a reflective mood. He swings his imaginary machete and sees the brain exposed as the body falls. He misses his favorite one. And his second wife. She died. We were here in Delhi, he tells Ajay. The city went to her head. She flirted with an ice-cream vendor; he saw it with his eyes. He couldn't accept that. He killed her in front of India Gate. All around him, the ice-cream-eating kids, couples lying on the grass, and there he was, beating her to death for the smile she gave. That's why he was in jail. But it's all right. He represents Satya Acharya from the cell. He has mobile phones, a TV, his heater, his AC, minions, he's doing just fine. He only misses his machete and his coconuts, and his second wife.

He is Satya Acharya's eyes and ears and teeth and fists and hammer and club and blade. He marshals troops with blood and sweat and fear. They have more than eighty men in here. They're at war with some, like the Gupta gang. They have uneasy alliances with others, like the Sissodias. When it's time to go out into the yard, they come together, the allied gangs, to trade information and goods. The Acharyas form a mass with Sikandar at the center, reclining on a cane seat, looking up at the winter sun with bliss in his heart.

"Is it true?" one of the men asks. "Is it true you work for him?"

The question is not for Sikandar. The "him" in question is not Acharya.

The huddle of men fall quiet and wait for Ajay to speak.

Ajay, a ghost in a safari suit.

"Shut up, fucker," Sikandar says. "Do you want me to break your skull?"

"How did you hurt those chutiyas so bad?" another asks. "Where did you learn to do that?"

"Shut up!" Sikandar yells. "Any fucker can do that. I'll break all your skulls right now."

"But look at him," one of the men cries, "he's half your size. He really taught those fuckers a lesson. Maybe he could even kill you!"

"No one kills me!" Sikandar says, rising from his cane throne, "except God himself."

"Gautam Rathore," Ajay says in a hollow voice. "I work for Gautam Rathore."

There's silence. Confused looks.

Sikandar laughs. "You hear that? He works for Gautam Rathore."

"Who's that?"

Sikandar lies back down. "Just some fucker out in the world."

Water becomes water, milk becomes milk. Everyone knows Ajay is Bunty Wadia's man. The prison telegraph is lightning fast. Ajay taught the Guptas a lesson, and he is Bunty Wadia's man. This is what they say. The name is whispered in the dark. He can hear you saying it. That's what people say. He sees it all. He hears everything. He rises above it all. Sikandar received word from Satya on his phone. Satya said, "We're getting a VIP. Take good care of him." "Who's this chutiya?" Sikandar replied. "One of Bunty Wadia's men."

———

He whistles through his teeth. One of Bunty Wadia's men. A child of God. But the child has been abandoned by God, by life, by fate. By the son most of all. Sunny's last words to him: "I'll take care of you." Before the gunmetal went into his face.

Now he is told to sit tight, don't take tension. You're exempt from chores. So sleep. Watch TV. Jerk off. Lift weights. Join the cricket team. Meditate. Smoke Mandrax if you like. Go fuck. That can be arranged. There's always fresh meat to go around. If one of the chikna boys takes your eye, go make yourself his friend. Enjoy yourself, you earned it. The only thing you can't do is leave.

Every day is submerged. He barely eats. Barely sleeps. Barely talks. Some say his mind is gone. They are afraid of him. They speculate on what he really did. He is a killer, they know that for sure. But there's madness there. No. The madness is an act. He's in here to kill again.

He doesn't hear it. Everything comes to him from far away. Words travel a great distance to reach him. A lifetime is returning through the moon and the mist. His childhood floods the landscape of his mind. Through the mist his childhood rises, through the mist his father burns, through his mind his sister cries, and through the night he goes away. The sun rises and burns. He wakes and doesn't remember who he is, why he's here. He wakes and he's in a Tempo and the mountains are above him. He wakes and the bodies are strewn across the road. He is waking to his pain, and he cannot hide. Old thoughts swoop like hungry demons. Dead men in alleyways. The crack of Vipin Tyagi's skull. Slick blood hair bunched in his hand, a crack of nasal bone, a squelch, slick hair with brain in hand. In his sleep he rolls the man over, wakes from the nightmare before he sees the face. In the darkness of the cell he sees Neda and Sunny, forever together in the back of a car. Time is elastic. His mother is gone. The woman, Mary, has taken her place. And his sister. Is she alive anymore? He's watching from the Tempo. Did he wave good-bye?

"What happened to her?"

"What happens to all girls when the men go away."

All those years in the mountains pretending everything would be OK. He lies on Mummy's bed and cries. He wakes to find himself punching the walls. Sikandar has to hold him down, hold him in a great stinking bear hug in his arms. Crazy fucker. Go outside. Run round the yard. Fight someone. See if anyone tries to kill you there. Kill them back. Go fuck someone. Get out of here.

Five hundred push-ups a day. Five hundred sit-ups. His watchful eyes. The husk of a body, meaning chipped away. To whom does he belong? Whom does he obey? What happened to the boy? What happens to all boys whose family goes away. At night, eyes open while Sikandar snores, he travels back in time.

He thinks of the Nepali boys.

Purple Haze.

The first time in his life he was free.

The first time he threw his freedom away.

Something is hardening. Hardening in him.

He buries all his past.

Buries his kindness.

Finds a new way to live each day.

2.

The air warms, the days begin to shimmer and bake. Some prisoners leave. New prisoners arrive. Fresh meat. They are sorted, graded, threatened, coerced. Those who are strong will pick a gang. Those who have money will buy their protection. Those with lots of money can buy anything. Those who have nothing are preyed upon. They can be servants, they can be slaves. Scrub the toilets, wash clothes. A nineteen-year-old boy comes in, skinny, milk skin, high cheekbones, *wide-set eyes, a pink bud of a mouth. Beautiful. Terrified. Jailed for stealing a mobile phone. Everyone takes notice. A flower, a prize. Sikandar licks his lips. He looks like a little calf, he says. Three Sissodia men surround the boy in the yard, make lewd comments, push him around. The kid withers as they caress him, grope him, whisper in his ear, take him by the wrist and pull away. At the last moment, Sikandar steps in. Shoves the Sissodia men aside, beats one of them to the ground, puts his arm around the kid, and leads him away.*

Tender Sikandar. He tells the boy not to cry, guides him back to their side. He has a friend now, he'll be taken care of. What's your name? Prem, the boy says. Prem. Sikandar toys with the name. He offers him a cigarette, some good food, some soap to wash, something to ease the pain. Arranges to have Prem transferred to their cell. Welcomes him with open arms. It's hard out there with no friends, no money, and so young. There are so many wolves out there, but not everyone is bad, not everyone is in it for themselves. You won't be preyed on now. I'm a big man here, you saw what I did. They're scared of me. Eat something. Take a blanket. Watch TV. Prem takes a seat on the mattress and hugs himself close. Have a peg of whisky. This is Bablu, he's your friend. This is Ajay. He's a killer, but don't worry about him. Just stay close to me.

Out in the yard, Sikandar keeps Prem by his side. There are jeers, cries of pleasure, taunting and mocking. Sikandar winks, grins, nods, plays the clown. To Prem he says, Don't listen to them. They're jealous. They want to take things from you. Prem is trying hard not to cry. What's wrong? Sikandar asks. Are you afraid? No, no. You don't have to be afraid. See across there, see the men who were going to hurt you? They're looking at us now. See them. They can't hurt you. They don't dare. See, I'll prove it. Go over there. Go stand right in front of them. Prem shakes his head. Come on, Sikandar says, and grabs Prem by the arm. Don't be scared. Let's go over now. We'll go together, you and I. He drags Prem across the yard. The Sissodia men stand unmoved as they get closer, Prem a child, Sikandar a harridan come to scold the neighborhood boys. Look at them, Sikandar giggles. Look at them, they're cowards. The men scowl and bristle at Sikandar's words. But they do nothing. Look at them. Sikandar grabs Prem's head and jerks up his neck. Look. A nasty edge to his voice. See. They won't do anything to you. He lets go and takes a step back. He grins and makes silent laughter at the crowd.

See. They're afraid. Stand there, look those fuckers in the eye.

Stay where you are. Stay where you are and look them in the eye.

Keep looking.

Sikandar steps back silently, across the yard.

Keep looking, don't turn around, look those fuckers in the eye. They're not going to hurt you. See.

Sikandar can barely contain his glee. He slaps his thighs and bites his fist.

See, he calls from the far side. There's nothing to fear.

Prem is left standing alone, face-to-face with the Sissodia men.

Now hit them! Sikandar cries. Hit them as hard as you can!

Prem is shaking.

ARGGHHH!

One of them makes a lunge at him.

Prem bolts as fast as he can across the yard, all the way back to Sikandar's side; Sikandar hooks him in his arm. And like that, it's known by all, he is Sikandar's boy.

Sikandar gets drunk and feeds Prem liquor too. Makes Prem sip liquor as he sobs, and as he sobs makes Prem massage his feet. Don't cry, Sikandar says. You're safe. No one is going to hurt you. You just have to realize one thing. Things work a certain way here. Everyone has their place. If you want to survive you have to know your place. Sikandar, ever more drunk, tells Prem the story of his second wife. How he loved her more than anything. But how she betrayed him. Her name was Khushboo, he says. When drunken Prem gets up to pee, Sikandar orders him to squat. "Do it like a girl," he says. And when he returns, Sikandar unbuttons the boy's shirt to display his smooth chest, ties the tails of the shirt together in a feminine way. "What's your name?" Sikandar asks. "Prem," he says, fighting tears. "No," he whispers, "that's not right." He pulls Prem down to his crotch, holds him by the shoulder with his dreadful grip. "Khushboo," he croons. "Khushboo is your name. Would you like to stay here, Khushboo? Or would you like me to throw you back out to the wolves?"

Prem turns his head to Ajay.

"Don't look at him!" Sikandar hisses. "What's your name?"

"Khushboo," Prem whispers.

The name from Prem's lips gives Sikandar goose bumps, ripples of pleasure.

"I'll make it easy for you, Khushboo, this life," Sikandar croons, stroking Prem's hair.

He pulls himself out of his sweat pants and forces Prem's mouth down.

When he's finished, he prepares a Mandrax pipe for the sobbing Prem. "Here, take your reward."

In the early hours there's no more noise. Prem lost in a Mandrax haze, Sikandar and Bablu snoring drunk. Only Ajay is awake, with death in his mind.

Now Sikandar has women's clothes brought. A blue-and-pink salwar kameez, chunni bangles, anklets. He presents them to Prem with great ceremony, tells him to put them on. Mute Prem offers no resistance. He does as he's told. Sikandar produces lipstick and kajal and applies them almost reverently to Prem's face, bewitched by the transformation. "Now, Khushboo," he says, "these are the rules." Prem is told he will perform the womanly duties of the cell: sweeping, washing, cooking, cleaning, and he will tend to Sikandar's needs. He will not speak unless spoken to, he will not pee unless he has Sikandar's say. He will talk like a girl. Walk like one. He will be Sikandar's wife in jail. If he does this right, if he repays Sikandar's love, he'll be a queen, lavished with beautiful things. If not, he'll be thrown to the wolves, or worse.

"Now tell me. What's your name?"

Prem stares at the cell floor. Holds back the tears. "Prem."

Enraged Sikandar grips him by the throat.

"Khushboo!" Prem cries.

Sikandar loosens his grip, smiles. "Again."

"Khushboo."

Sikandar inhales the fragrance of the name.

He holds Prem close, closes his eyes and strokes the fabric of the clothes, whispers, "Khushboo . . . Khushboo. Never lie to me again."

The heat creeps in, the burning sun of the day, the mosquitoes of the night. The stale sweat. Prem is Sikandar's prison wife, his slave, he works and serves and is raped. Day and night. Days and nights. Into May. Raped by Sikandar and then by Bablu too, by Sikandar's proud consent. "A good wife must do service for her husband's friends." Sikandar even tells Ajay to have a taste. But Ajay doesn't rise to the bait. "You'll change your mind!" Sikandar laughs, "soon enough, won't he, Khushboo!"

Prem, every day, in such spiritual and physical pain, every night, until the Mandrax dose. Mandrax, in such doses that the melancholic euphoria of the drug takes hold.

Into May. The heat unbearable. Sikandar suspects a member of their gang is passing secrets to the police and to other gangs—several of Satya's low-level men have been shot outside. Sikandar had Bablu investigate. He thinks they've got it all figured out. They decide to torture the suspect, Shakti Lal. Sikandar arranges for an ice block to be brought into their cell, a ridiculous slab, six feet long. It's dripping as soon as it arrives. He tells the gang there's going to be a party in his cell, they'll enjoy food and whisky and cold drinks and lots and lots of ice. There's cricket on TV turned up loud. Everyone marvels at the ice slab. Prem serves everyone's drinks. It's a raucous night. But at a prearranged signal, Sikandar and Bablu set on Shakti Lal, beat him as the others watch, stuff a rag into his mouth, gag him, strip him, place him on the ice slab, tie him down until his skin is burned with the cold. But he does not confess. So Sikandar has Bablu drag him to the shower room. He hangs him there, and the party goes on. They make their drinks with the ice they tortured him on, until it melts, soaks the mattresses, and they have a cool night's sleep.

———

Ajay dreams of a burning pyre, he dreams about his name. Sometimes in the night, he wakes with a start, from a cage, from a lonely room, from headlights on the road, and through the Mandrax haze, pressed against Sikandar's flesh, Prem looks at him and he looks at Prem and they watch each other, Prem's desperate, pleading, broken eyes, and Ajay's hard black pools of pain.

"Why don't you do it to me," Prem says, "like they do?"

Ajay watches snoring Sikandar for a sign of wakefulness, but he's dead drunk.

"I'm not like them."

"You have nightmares," Prem says. "I watch you crying in your dreams."

Ajay rolls on his back, looks away.

"You're a killer."

Nothing.

"Would you kill me?"

Nothing.

"If I asked you?"

"You should have fought the Sissodia men," Ajay finally says. "You should have fought them even if they beat you. You should have fought them with everything you had, instead of running away. Then you wouldn't be this way."

"I've always been this way."

It turns out Bablu was the snitch. Satya Acharya passes the word. Bablu's throat is cut in the corridor as they walk back from the yard. Sikandar does it himself.

Now he has a problem. Who will handle the Mandrax? That was Bablu's job. There's a meeting of the inner circle. Sikandar roars at them. He can't trust a single one. He can't trust them to do anything right. Maybe they knew about

Bablu all along. Maybe they're snitches too. He'll have to do it himself. Ajay speaks up from his spot against the wall. I'll do it.

Who is Sikandar to say no to a VIP? It's a simple enough job. He is to go to the prison doctor. The doctor prescribes certain legal pills, the warden signs off on the requisition form, Ajay collects the Mandrax in boxes from the pharmacy, carries them back to the cell, handing out Gandhis to the guards along the way. Then he does his rounds, deals the Mandrax out.

Ajay is happy here. Happily numb. Happy not to be preyed upon.
 He's a killer anyway. He has nothing to lose.
 Better to be like this than Prem.
 He looks on Prem with . . .
 Disgust.
 Or something else.
 Loathing, deflected from the self.

Sikandar sends Prem out on "errands" to his friends. He sends Prem out to whoever pays. A good wife does what her husband says. Members of their gang. Other gangs. Different Sissodia men. The three Sissodia boys from the yard, Pradeep, Ram Chandra, Prakash Singh, they pay a very good price, they pay extra to put cigarettes out on Khushboo's skin. Prem feels Prem is slipping away, vanishing between men, behind the Mandrax and the pain, behind the obedience and the fear and the psychological strain.

He smokes whatever he can get.
 He'll do anything for a lungful that will send shards of forgetting into his brain.
 Sometimes at the end of it, he can barely walk.
 Ajay discovers Prem collapsed in the hallway, laughing to himself.
 He stares down at him.
 Pity, horror.

Prem reaches out, grabs Ajay by the legs.

Ajay tries to pull away, but he can't bring himself to be so unkind.

He crouches down.

"Prem," he says.

Prem stares at Ajay with moist eyes.

"Prem is dead."

When Sikandar drinks, Khushboo drinks by his side. Black Label. Sikandar is onto the second bottle for the night.

> *Now chicken and roti.*
>
> *And fifteen men crowded into the cell, watching TV.*
>
> *The movie* Khalnayak *is on.*
>
> *Acharya members, some Sissodias too.*
>
> *They're watching so eagerly.*
>
> *Fifteen men, and Ajay, and Prem.*
>
> *Waiting for the song.*
>
> *The song comes on.*
>
> *"Choli Ke Peeche Kya Hai?"*
>
> *"Turn it up," Sikandar roars.*

It's miraculous, how Khushboo raises herself for the song. Like a marionette lifted from a drunken slump. Transfixed by the song. Eyes soaked with tears. Stands in front of the TV, takes on Madhuri's role. Smiles as if there's nothing in the world. Sikandar shouts at her, throws chicken bones. She's in such anguish. But she begins to dance. A soul transformed. The men delight, they begin to cheer. She moves around the cell with such grace. Dancing. Dancing away the pain. She dances up to Sikandar and she twirls and twirls.

> *The men cheer.*
>
> *Sikandar is enjoying his show.*
>
> *"See how my wife dances for me?!"*
>
> *"You should see how she dances for Karan!" one of the Sissodia men cries in reply.*

Sikandar's face changes in a heartbeat. He picks up an empty whisky bottle and hurls it at the TV. Knocks it over and cracks the screen.

"Karan?" he roars.

The song still plays, Khushboo still twirls and mimes, lost in a trance.

"You dance for Karan?"

Karan Mehta. A young man from a rich business family. An anomaly in this world. Handsome, soft-spoken. A downy beard, shoulder-length hair, soulful eyes.

He gave up his studies to join the Sissodias.

A sharpshooter.

He's killed eighteen, so they say.

Sikandar enters a jealous rage.

"Get out," he yells at them all. "Get out."

Khushboo is still twirling, laughing.

But when Sikandar starts the beating, it is Prem who screams. Prem, as the gang members flee, being punched in the stomach, kicked in the ribs. Prem grabs, pushes, begs for his life. Deranged Sikandar yells how she's always the same, she always cheats on him whatever he does. He starts to pummel Prem in the face. "I'll kill you," he says. The blood spurts from his broken nose. It's up to Ajay to intervene. He lifts a dumbbell from the floor and cracks it into the back of Sikandar's skull.

You've killed him.

There is silence, save the broken TV still blasting the music out. Sikandar sprawled above shards of glass. Ajay tosses the dumbbell to the floor.

You've killed him.

Bends down to look at him. No.

He's still alive.

He's breathing.

He'll wake in the morning with a sore head.

He fell when he was drunk.

That's all there is to say.

Ajay drags Sikandar to his mattress, rolls him onto it. Puts a blanket over him, places an empty bottle of whisky in his hand. Pauses a second. A guard passes by. Ajay looks up. "He broke the TV. He passed out drunk. He's sleeping it off."

The guard points to Prem, on the floor. "And this one?"

"I'll clean him up."

"Who are you?"

Prem is barely conscious. Ajay washes the blood from his face.

"Put your arms round me."

Ajay prepares the bottleneck.

Gives Prem a hit, though it stings his busted ribs to inhale.

"Hold me," Prem says.

Ajay puts him on the mattress.

Gives him another hit.

"Hold me," Prem says again.

He holds him for hours. And in the dark he speaks. "I'm from a village," Ajay says. "In Eastern UP. I am Dalit. My family were abused. My father was killed by a big man. I was taken to the mountains and sold. I worked on a farm. I was told to say I am Kshatriya."

He sees himself.

He's lying with his matchboxes and his wind-up duck toy.

Trying to remember his mother's face.

Daddy is upstairs, stoking the fire.

He has to make people happy to survive.

"I ran away when I was fourteen," Prem says as if in a dream. He picks out the words so slowly. "I grew up outside Kanpur. I had a sister and a mother, I loved my mother so much, but she died. My father married again. I cried all the time. His new wife hated me. She caught me sleeping with my mother's old clothes. I'd kept some hidden when that woman threw everything away. She beat me so hard. I ran to Delhi. I worked in a sweet shop. I made jalebi. I had

good hands. But the owner forced me to do things for him. He said if I refused he'd tell the police I was a thief and they'd lock me away. I ran away. I slept on the street, at the train station. I found other jobs. There was always somewhere to work. But there was always someone trying to take something from me."

"The day I came to Delhi," Ajay says, "I was beaten by a gang of men. They stole everything from me."

He falls silent.

"They didn't steal everything," Prem says.

Silence.

"I had one place to go. A place I'd been promised work."

"And?"

"I went."

"And then?"

"I served."

To obey. To serve. To be rewarded with protection, purpose, even love in the end. "I'll take care of you," Sunny said. It could have been so simple. There could have been a world in which these words rang true, provided succor, gave him sustenance, something to believe. A world where there was only duty, where he hadn't scratched that itch to find home. How simple it would have been. Loyalty, unquestioned. A desire to please. Sunny would have said, "You'll take the blame. I'll take care of you." And Ajay would have said, "yes, yes, yes."

But he had to scratch that itch that was always there. What had it been? Watching Neda and Sunny in love? He remembers wading alone into the ocean in Goa, before he was sent away. How many times had he been ready to break? How could he have gone on so long?

Who are you?

The words chase round his head.

Who are you?

Ajay Wadia. Sunny's boy.

Loyal.

Ready to serve.

In circles.

He'd rather not think about it at all.

He'd rather be here.

A killer VIP.

That thought surprises him.

Can it really be true?

Where did he leave himself behind?

Unraveling.

He keeps coming back to rooms. In the Palace Grande. Right after he'd killed Vipin Tyagi and his men. Waiting for the knock on his door. Waiting for the door to be broken down. Gun in hand. Waiting for death to come. And when it didn't, he went searching for it instead. Certain this was the end. He wanted to die. Yes. He's living in death.

He's still holding Prem long after Prem has fallen into a nullifying sleep.

Touching his delicate, broken face with his own once beautiful hands. The bloom of his split lip, his grotesquely swollen jaw. He runs his hands through the blood-dark hair, matted to the skull. He can't remember being so close to another human before, except when trying to kill or stop himself from being killed. His teeth begin to chatter. He doesn't want to let go.

He lets go of him.

Gets up and checks that Sikandar is still alive.

Then he begins to sweep.

He has cleaned the cell, placed the shattered TV neatly in the corner.

He is making chai, cooking roti on the gas burner.

Sikandar comes to with a jolt, the air caught in his throat, sitting up like a storybook monster and looking at the whisky in his hand.

He sees Prem, bruised and battered and shriveled in drugged sleep.

And Ajay at the stove.

Ajay glances at him, looks back to his work.

Waits.

Waits for it.

"What a night . . ." Sikandar moans.

He rubs the bump on his head.

Looks at the remnants of the TV.

Starts to remember things.

Stands over Prem.

Looks at Ajay.

"Women," he says sadly. "They're all the same."

Prem is sent to the infirmary.

Sikandar sits morose in the cell.

A new TV is brought. He watches it all day.

He can't remember all of it, but he remembers the name.

Prem is in the infirmary for a week.

Sikandar gets reports—Karan has been to visit him there.

Many times Karan has paid the guards.

Visiting Prem.

Holding his hand by the bedside.

Karan.

Sikandar knows he's been betrayed.

He wants to cut ties with the Sissodia gang.

But Satya says he can't.

Prem returns after the week.

Quietly to his mattress, with his broken nose, without makeup, wearing male clothes.

Sikandar ignores him, keeps watching TV.

Prem applies lipstick to his mouth, kajal to his eyes, crouches at Sikandar's feet.

Sikandar pushes him away. "No. You're not Khushboo," he says, as if he's only just learned the truth.

The next day he announces that he's divorced. He has no wife.

And Prem is for sale.

3.

An MLA from UP, Charanjit Kumar, comes visiting. He's conducting an inspection of the jail. Kumar is from Ram Singh's ruling party. Time to look busy. Ajay is assigned to an art class he's never attended, there to fill up the numbers, to look productive. The warden has told them: this is an art class, draw something nice, show it to our guest, everything will be well. The prisoners follow the teacher's instruction. They draw still-life pieces, flowers, plastic fruit. Then they draw from memory, as they are told, something that makes them happy. They make pictures of their mothers, brothers, families. Trees and fields and rivers. Ajay sits with his pad of paper and his pencil, his hand poised, and draws nothing.

4.

MLA Kumar is impressed. The prison is exemplary. Run to a standard even prisons in the West cannot reach. He's saying it for the cameras. He's brought a photographer with him, a journalist. At the end of the visit, the MLA asks to speak with some of the prisoners alone, to get their honest feedback. Prisoners are chosen at random. The interviews are held in one of the administration offices. Ajay is among the chosen. During Ajay's turn, Kumar asks him several banal questions, which Ajay answers monosyllabically. He dismisses Ajay and calls for the next prisoner. But on the way out he says, "Vicky sends his wishes."

5.

Ajay's legs almost go.

Outside the office, Kumar's aide takes Ajay aside. "Our mutual friend would like you to take care of something." He slips Ajay a scrap of paper. Tells him to read it.

It says: KARAN—SISSODIA.

The aide takes it back. "You know why you're here."

There is no stable ground.

He returns to his cell.

He thought he was safe.

He was never safe.

"Had fun?" Sikandar asks.

Is he in on it?

Is Prem?

Are they all?

Can it really be a coincidence? He gets the feeling things are being controlled, they can read his mind, they watch him all the time. That Vicky Wadia is playing some elaborate game.

Loyalty was not the reason he had agreed to go to jail. It was fear too. Fear of what Vicky might do. What he might make him do. Spy on Sunny . . . and what else? Harm his family. He thought in prison he would escape. How stupid could he have been?

Must he really do this?

It seems impossible.

Is there another way? If I could speak to someone, he thinks. Then he stops. Speak to whom? Speak to Sunny? And say what? Sunny is as remote as the sun, the moon. Sunny, whose life he once knew, is gone.

6.

Karan makes an offer for Prem. Twenty thousand rupees.

Tell him, Sikandar says to Ajay, that's not enough.

Go tell him. Go on your rounds, stop at his cell, and tell him.

It's the first time he's face-to-face with Karan. He has a calming presence, peace in his eyes, a gentle smile. He sends his cellmates away. He tells Ajay twenty thousand is a good price.

"The price is good for anyone else," Ajay says. "But not for you."

He has a razor in his pocket. He sees the blood pumping through Karan's neck. He looks him in the eyes.

He could do it right now, he could overpower him.

But then Ajay would have started a war.

Most likely, Ajay would be dead.

"Fifty thousand," Karan says. "That's more than fair, considering the damage that's been done."

Ajay nods. He'll take the message back.

He hesitates.

Wonders what makes Karan so calm.

Wonders what secrets he holds.

"What?" Karan says.

"Why," Ajay asks at the cell door, "do you want Prem so much?"

"Because I love him," Karan says.

———

He takes the offer back. Sikandar laughs. "Do you hear that, Prem? He loves you! He'll soon learn the truth."

Sikandar tells Ajay to make Karan sweat on it. Don't give him an answer yet.

No answer yet. Karan still lives. A letter arrives for Ajay. It's delivered directly to his cell. It doesn't even have a name on it, just a blank envelope. He's beckoned to the bars by a guard. There's no note. Only a photo inside. A woman in her midtwenties lying on a bed in a small cubicle of a room, neat and tidy despite the squalor, with a small shrine on a table next to the bed and a painting of a waterfall nailed to the wall. It's a brothel. The woman wears a floral sari, but her breasts are exposed. There is a man in the corner of the frame, at the foot of her small bed, drunkenly embracing her legs. Even through the years, Ajay recognizes the girl.

Hema.

"Arrey, chutiya, what's this?"

Hema, his sister.

Sikandar snatches the photo from him.

The sight of it is enough to get his mojo back. He whistles through his ugly teeth and laughs. "Look at this bitch. Is she waiting for you outside? So you're not a eunuch after all. But look, I don't think she's waiting for you anymore. She's got enough cock to pass the time!"

Ajay rushes to snatch it back, but Sikandar shoves him away. He laughs his ugly laugh. "Let me get a good look at her."

Sikandar turns the photo around. "And what's this?"

He reads out the words: "DO WHAT YOU'RE TOLD."

It's too much for Ajay to take. He launches himself at Sikandar, leaps up and grabs his arm, twists Sikandar's wrist, tries to prize the photo from his fingers. Fires his knee into Sikandar's chest. Sikandar is having none of it. With his free hand and his enormous strength, he grabs Ajay by the throat. Throws him through the air. He stands over him. Glowers. "You're protected, so I can't kill you. But no one touches me like that. And you still have to do what you're told."

TWO

LONDON, 2006

She'd always dreamed of living abroad.

She never wanted to do what she was told.

"Neda," her professor said.

She'd zoned out again.

"Are we boring you today?"

He's American, still young, likes to go for a drink with his students, likes to be their friend.

But Neda is a wall.

"No, sir."

It's the second term of her second year.

BA Social Anthropology at the LSE.

She's a straight-A student, mostly.

He plays to the room.

"So it's just me?"

A ripple of amusement, but from Neda, no.

He returns to the board.

"Maybe a full night's rest is in order? A little less partying with the boys?"

He reminds her of Dean.

"I don't party with boys."

Now the laughter is on her: of the students in her course, she's the least likely to party with anyone at all.

Yeah, she'd always dreamed of living abroad, of having an apartment of her own, a rich and stimulating inner life, tangled love affairs, true friends to whom she could confess. Something to write home about. A home to write home to in the end.

Not this.

She slips out of the hall, head down, hair over her face, books barricading her chest.

She doesn't even know why she's still there.

She imagines, when the time comes, she'll abandon it.

Just walk out the door the day before her exams and never return.

It's not like it matters.

It's not like the money matters.

Each day, at HSBC, she checks her account to see if it's still there.

It's always still there. One hundred thousand pounds.

Whatever she does: £99,878 becomes £100,000; £96,300 becomes £100,000.

Whatever she does, however much she spends, there it is, topped up with remorseless precision.

As if he were taunting her.

She taunted him back once by making a twenty-thousand-pound donation to a homeless charity.

Her balance returned to one hundred thousand pounds the next day.

Now she taunts him by barely spending at all.

She leaves the campus and walks up Southampton Row to the Polish vodka bar behind Holborn. It's slow at lunch; the suits like to come and get wasted in the evening after work. She takes her usual seat, back against the wall, watching the door. Orders śledź, a half pint of Żywiec, a shot of Chopin. Her one indulgence. The same thing every day. She eats in mechanical silence, sips her beer, saves the vodka for the end. She never orders more. To the outsider looking in, it's an eccentric's discipline.

Such is this habit, the owner has learned to bring her bill as she's nursing the vodka. He does it today, hands it over with his unobtrusive, sympathetic smile.

But today she does something unexpected.

Orders another Chopin.

His face betrays mild surprise.

"Celebrating?" he says.

"Yes," she replies. "It's an anniversary."

She arrived in London in April 2004, hurled from the wreckage of her Delhi life, parachuting into this gilded nothingness. The air smelled of nothingness. It would have been comical, if it wasn't built on death.

She arrived in April 2004, but today is February 24—two years to the day since her life irrevocably changed. In these two years, she has managed, more or less, to hold things together, to maintain the veneer of a respectable, steady life. She has done this through a form of self-abnegation—not merely financial, spiritual too. But today that goes out the window. Today, February 24, is the day for nasha, oblivion through intoxication.

He brings her shot. Without touching it, she looks up.

"I'd like two more."

The liquor is in her blood.

His hesitation, his curiosity, even his concern, are met by the cool desolation of her gaze.

And he nods. He understands something in this moment.

It is as clear as someone crying in church.

———

When the shots are brought, she slides them ceremoniously to the empty places at her table, to her left and to her right.

She lifts her glass and says a silent prayer.

Communing with her ghosts.

It's one thirty in the afternoon. A gloomy day, a day of umbrellas and head-lights. Clouds obscure the building tops. Rain swirls like a dancing kite. She leaves a fifty on the table, steps outside. At the ATM she withdraws four hundred more.

It's a short walk to the Princess Louise. She slips down the side, pulls up a stool in one of the ornate wooden cubicles facing the bar, orders a pint of Alpine, leans her shoulder against the stained glass. No one looks at her. No one talks to her. And if they did, if they asked her what she was reading, she would show them a printout of Dean's latest article, "Remembering the For-gotten: The Lonely Deaths of Five Pavement Dwellers and the Lives They Left Behind," and conversation would stop.

She doesn't even read it herself.

Instead she stares at Dean's byline, his name, below the masthead of the obscure magazine to which he's been reduced, though he'd never admit this finer point, never admit he threw away his glittering career for a principle, a scruple, a "boussole morale."

He'd say he was committed to the truth.

In the emails she never answers, he maintains she could commit to it too.

In the emails she never answers, he says, "It looks like you found your place."

But she's unfaithful. Unfaithful, also, to the idea of self; that which, after careful analysis, has been diagnosed as the cause of her ills. So she has found equilibrium in these two years by embracing nothingness, a radical emptiness. She works hard at maintaining this uncharismatic shell. She makes sure to stick to the facts and nothing more.

It's been a hard road. The first few months were the worst. Unmoored, adrift, in pain. Carrying a child. She drank herself almost to death. She doesn't like to think of those months now. She manages to block them out. But they come back when she drinks. And today, February 24, she drinks.

It's dark at four in the afternoon. She walks out of the Princess Louise four pints down, into the puddles and streetlamps, crosses the road and slips into the British Museum, past the busloads of tourists and the hot dogs and roasted chestnuts, through the throngs in the Great Court, through the back, down the stairs past the ancient Qur'an, and out to Senate House. A left toward Tottenham Court Road, doubling back and turning down the alleyway to Bradley's. She descends to the basement, to the smell of stale beer and urine, and listens to the jukebox, sinking into a pint of Spanish beer. She's crossing over the line. Inviting conversation. Fighting with herself. Why does she do it? As soon as she arrives, she wants to leave.

In these two years, walking has maintained her fragile stability. Walking with her Discman in her palm. Listening to the CDs she carried with her from home. Björk. Talvin Singh. Nusrat Fateh Ali Khan. Walking with nowhere to go, up to Hampstead Heath, Golders Green, out into the suburbs until she can't take it anymore. East to Old Street, Bethnal Green, Hackney, Clapton, Lee Valley, until she can't take it anymore. If she hasn't been studying, she's been walking. As long as she's walking, she's not drowning.

God, she misses Delhi. Misses roti and pickle and curd in the winter sun. Girls fussing over her in tiny, windowless salons. Golgappas in Khan Market. The crowds of Old Delhi. Sweet corn on the side of the road, dressed with chilli and chaat masala and lemon. Misses her dad so much just to think of him makes her cry. Misses her mum. But they barely speak. She doesn't answer their calls, refuses to have them visit her. To go there herself is out of the question. She has cut herself off. She has agreed to be exiled. "I don't understand what's happened to you," her mother writes. "I don't know what changed. Maybe you were always this way. You hurt your father so much. You broke his heart, my love."

Dean had been over to the house. He had written and told her so. "I'm not giving up on this," he wrote. What had he told them? What had he asked of them? Where had they surmised the money was from?

Maybe she'll just get up and vanish. Walk somewhere. Walk to Edinburgh, why not? Take her bank card, a backpack, a good pair of hiking boots, and walk. Walk from inn to inn, like in the olden days. Why not? Go up to the Highlands. Find a mountain hut. Live in a cabin by a loch. Speak to no one ever again. Why not?

She is swaying slightly with her eyes closed. A guy is shouting in her ear. Bradley's. The jukebox, the steam of winter bodies in the enclosed space. He asked her where she was from, and she made the mistake of telling him the truth. He'd thought as much. Either that or Israel. He showed her the sandalwood bracelet he bought in Dharamsala. He was there two years ago. And Goa. "Have you been? I read the Bhagavad Gita there!"

"Good for you."

"Once you've been to India," he shouts, "you're not the same. It gets under your skin."

No shit.

He nods. "And the philosophy! It's so much more profound. 'Consciousness knows itself,' didn't Krishnamurti say that?"

"You'd have to ask him."

"You're a funny one."

She puts a cigarette between her lips.

"Can I ask you something?" she says.

"Of course."

"What do you know about Maypole dancing?"

"Pardon me?"

"Maypole dancing."

He takes a moment, frowns, and shakes his head. "Nothing."

She lights the cigarette. "Then what the fuck do I know about Krish-namurti?"

For a brief moment, out in the street, exhaling smoke in the cold and the rain, she revels in her spite.

At least it is a feeling.

An old one. Like her old self.

She used to have a smart mouth.

She used to be, for want of a better word, "sassy."

It's dangerous, remembering that. That exuberance. Glib. She could be so glib. It would be easy enough to be glib again. What she fears most is joy.

She tries not to think about him and the time they had, and whether any of that ever qualified as joy.

She wants to say: I hope you die.

Die miserably of cancer. Catch Ebola and bleed out of your eyes. Get blown to pieces in a terrorist attack. Or just die alone.

She wrote him several emails she never sent.

She screamed and howled in those first four months.

She checked her email every day, waiting, dreading. She demanded something. A letter, a phone call. *Something*. She rehearsed what she'd say to him, she rehearsed the back-and-forth. But who was she to make demands, or expect them to be met? Who was she? He never wrote. He never called. There was only silence and that money in her bank account, the one his fa-ther's representative, the man who called himself Chandra, set up for her.

———

The bar at Dukes Hotel. The place Chandra took her the night they both landed from Delhi, when she was still numb and in shock and the pain hadn't set in, when she naively believed she could start again. Cheerful, avuncular Chandra. Hadn't she demanded this? Hadn't it been her idea? No, no, no!

She cries in the taxi. It's so foggy in her mind. She can't fix those days straight anymore, she had stopped trying, she'd buried them, and now when she digs, the carcass has been ransacked. "You all right there, love?" the cabbie asks. She nods, wipes the tears to the side. Puts on her dead face. Composes herself. They pull up outside Dukes Hotel. I'll be fine. She didn't wear any kohl yet today. She wore a nice shirt and black pants and black boots and a long black coat, because she knew she would be here tonight. She steps into reception and without emotion says she'd like a room, the best available, and a table for one, at the bar, in an hour's time. She slides over her Amex card.

Vomits in the room. Cries and screams on her knees, smacks her palm with a balled fist, curls up on the floor, then climbs into the shower and scours herself. Dresses again slowly. Takes the kohl from her bag and puts it on. Rings her eyes darkly. Then she takes the coke she's been saving for months, goes into the bedroom, and cuts herself a line. If they could see her now, her classmates. If they knew the half of it.

In the bar she takes her table, orders the Dukes Martini.
　　Lights a cigarette.
　　Looks at the two middle-aged businessmen looking at her.
　　The martini is poured ice cold.
　　It changes nothing.

She checks out at one a.m. She tells them she has changed her plans. Why do you do this? she asks herself on the cab ride home.

Her apartment is in Angel. A modern, luxury complex. Newly built. It wasn't her choice. She lives on the sixth floor. An open-plan one bedroom, all glass and metal and the smell of fresh upholstery. Surrounded by junior lawyers, investment bankers, anonymous young professionals. She meets them in the elevator sometimes. They smell of showers after the gym. When she gets inside, she throws her keys on the kitchen counter, takes a bottle of vodka from the freezer, cuts herself another line. The room glows blue and lonely in the night.

She hears a car door open on the street below. She can almost hear the light pouring out of it, smell the laughter. It's 2:20 a.m. Drizzling. Some birds are singing in streetlights. The pavement smells of rain. These voices cut through the dark, ricochet off buildings. She stands on the balcony looking down. The door slams and the car drives away; she's left with the click of heels and her own breath once again. She returns to the table in the living room. From the drawer she pulls out his Vietnam Zippo. Reads the engraving. "35 Kills. If You're Recovering My Body, Fuck You."

She lights her cigarette with it.

"Charming."

Sometimes she thinks they've hidden a camera in the apartment. She searched for it but found nothing. Now she treats it with the same shrugging formulation she once applied to gods and masturbation. Even if they can see it, what difference does it make?

But when it comes to her laptop, she keeps masking tape over her webcam. Always turns on the VPN. Stares at the screen. Lights another cigarette. Another careful line. Opens her Gmail, clicks COMPOSE.

Fine, Dean. You win.

Then she stops.

She can't help herself.

She opens a new browser tab.
Closes her eyes.
Takes a deep breath.
Opens them.
And Googles his name.

NEW DELHI, 2003

NEDA

1.

Sunny Wadia.

She'd been hearing the name for some time. Sunny this, Sunny that. Tall tales circulating through the veins and arteries of the city, until it felt like he was the city himself.

He was an art dealer, a party planner, a restaurateur, a provocateur. He was the son of a multimillionaire from the States. Or a dot-com millionaire himself. No one seemed to know for sure. But he was the vanguard, the architect, the patron saint, on the fringes of anything new or exciting or strange. And she was a junior reporter on the City Desk of the *Delhi Post*—even as she shirked her official duties, she took it upon herself to track him down.

But that wasn't why she was here, sitting in a circle with her old school friend Hari at a crumbling South-Extension rooftop terrace on a shimmering April night.

She'd called Hari up after a year of not speaking—a real "long-time-no-see" kind of deal. She'd seen a piece about him in another paper's culture magazine, hadn't even recognized him at first: in the badly printed photo in the top right there was this grinning facsimile of a guy she once knew by heart.

Only now he was wearing an acid-wash T-shirt, elbows askew, a set of Technics decks beneath his blurry hands. And a DJ name to hide behind.

WhoDini.

She peered a little closer into the ink. She was sitting in her old Maruti, pulling hard on a cigarette. "You're fucking kidding."

Shy, nerdish Hari was transformed the way everyone in the city seemed to be transforming these days. Everyone but her. She texted him on his old number thinking that would be gone too, but he replied right away, the same guy he ever was, excited and courteous, more than willing to meet, he'd even buy her dinner tonight (which was new), but only after they'd gone to pick up smoke. "It'll only take five minutes," he promised her as she climbed into the passenger seat of his Esteem outside her work. "This dude owes me big-time."

That was almost two hours ago.

Now here they were on the roof. She, Hari, a bunch of random stoner dudes.

As the bone-dry heat of the First Delhi Summer receded to a deep astral blue.

She was so blasted now, she closed her eyes and their voices all merged into one.

And there he was again.

Sunny.

The name.

"Yo, did you hear about Sunny's party? He flew in five thousand dollars' worth of caviar from Iran."

"No, man. It was Wagyu beef from Japan. On a private jet. Twenty thousand dollars' worth. It's insane."

"Were you there?"

"How much do you get for twenty thousand dollars? Is that one whole cow?"

"Were you there?"

"They airlifted a cow?"

"Ha-ha, shut up, man."

"Strapped beneath the jet, roasted on the way."

"Ha-ha-ha-ha."

"Picture it, a cow in a jetpack."

"Man, were you there?"

"Don't say that cow shit too loud, bro. Mr. Gupta will hear."

She contemplated their faces.

Who were these guys?

"I heard they flew up to Leh once on a private chopper, landed at a mon-astery, and put on a rave. The monks were still inside. They had all these oxygen masks and everything."

"Bullshit. You don't need oxygen masks."

"It was probably nitrous oxide!"

"You know he was brought up in Dubai."

"He was not."

"His mother's a famous actress."

"Ha-ha."

"Guess which one?"

"Your mom."

"No, shut up. Look at his eyes, you *know* her."

"I know your mom."

"Ooooh."

"He keeps a tiger in his bathroom."

"You don't even know what he looks like."

"Ha! That's too good. What are you smoking, man?"

"Same thing as you, asshole."

The chillum went round, staining the gauze, burning the night.

When it reached Neda, she sat up and said, "But who *is* he?"

"Dude," a voice said, "I thought she was a journo."

She took a Classic Mild from her bag, reached for the matches in the middle of the circle.

"She does real news," Hari said. "Crime and shit."

"Not fairy tales and myths." She placed the cigarette slowly in her mouth. Lit the match and watched it burn against the heat of the sky.

"I don't read the news," another sniffed. "The real news isn't there."

She laughed. "Amen to that." Then she lit the cigarette, leaned into the beanbag behind, flicked the match into the air, watching the glowing tip of the cigarette and the sky above, the kites circling on the thermals, the planes always landing in the distance, the rhythmic bells of a nearby temple, the many mosques' call to prayer strung across the coming night sky. She loved her city.

"It's not her fault," she could hear Hari saying. "Some chutiya's got her working every hour. I never see her anymore."

"What chutiya?"

"Some Dean."

"Who's Dean?"

"Her boss."

"He's not my boss," she heard herself say.

"Sorry," Hari said sarcastically, "her *mentor*."

"You mean she's fucking him?"

"Dude, she's not fucking him."

"How do you know?"

"I'm not fucking him," she said.

"Is he a gora?"

"Nah, he's from Bombay. A Bandra boy."

With her eyes closed tight she let it all wash over her.

"I'm not fucking him," she said. "I'm not fucking anyone." Then she added, "At least not today."

Why did she do that?

Because it sounded cool. She always liked men to think she was cool.

She *had* almost fucked him, hadn't she? At least thought about it. He was a catch, Dean R. Saldanha. That good, upright Bombay Catholic boy, Mount Mary born and bred: "You throw a stone from my childhood window, you'll hit a pig, a priest, or a Pereira." He'd been shipped off to New York at age thirteen to live with his aunt in Queens, to wind up at Columbia Journalism School, to cut a long story short, to return to Bombay as a hotshot young reporter, a little too eager. In his zeal he exposed a land corruption scandal in his old community, in the heart of the archdiocese. His father didn't take kindly to that. "Why don't you report on something real?" he'd said. That was when Dean knew it was time to leave.

He came to Delhi. The *Post* hired him in October 2001. He found himself vanishing inside the spaces of Delhi as the world reeled from 9/11, obsessed with land, what he referred to as "the dynamic instability of marginal urban life." He talked like this. He spoke of the tensions between the middle classes and the urban poor, of the evictions and demolitions of the slum settlements, which were happening all around them in plain sight. He spoke disparagingly of the neoliberal "discourse de jour," that of the "world-class city." He wanted to paint this shifting, unstable city in words, wanted to immortalize the daily struggles of its citizens. He had his own office, played classic rock on his earphones. A tobacco fug swamped the air. He dressed like a poet in the middle of a basketball game, tall and lanky with frizzy brown hair. In no time he got the names and numbers of all the right cops and goons and crooks. He ate and drank in the dives and the canteens. He developed contacts from the lowly beat constable all the way up the ranks to the mighty DGP. And he could write like a dream. He wasn't so old either, twenty-seven to her twenty-two. Of course they were going to fuck one day, right? Except it didn't take long for her to get bored.

"Don't listen to those assholes," Hari said.

They'd left the stoners behind. They were walking down the inner staircase of the building, past all the many doors decorated with gods, leading into God-fearing middle-class homes.

"I don't really know them," he said.

"It's all right."

"Besides," he went on, "they don't know what they're talking about."

They walked past an open door. Inside the room the ceiling fans were on so fast they sounded like they'd take the roof off. A soap opera was blaring on TV, crackling and distorted, turned up too high over the fans' noise. Somewhere, someone was frying onions.

"I'm pretty blazed," she said, "and hungry. What time is it?"

"Nine."

"Kebab?"

"Let's get some Coke first."

They cruised the wide boulevards of Lutyens' Delhi, smoking and sipping from their glass bottles of Coke, the ripe smell of flowering plants and wet grass coming from the traffic circles. Hari played new tracks on the stereo. The whomping bass squirmed below a tanpura drone. He said, "I'm glad you called."

"Yeah," she looked across at him and smiled.

"I was thinking about you the other day," he said.

"Oh yeah?"

She closed her eyes.

If he could just keep driving like this, everything would be all right.

"You dropped off the radar," he said. "At first I thought you might have finally done it, gone abroad."

She took a long pull on her cigarette and frowned to herself. "No, I've been here. Work is just . . . hectic these days."

"Yeah? You like it?"

"I didn't say that."

"I always keep a lookout for your name."

She smiled, "Of course you do. You're good like that."

Loyal, she meant. Like a puppy.

"It's always with his."

"My name? Who? You mean Dean?"

"Dean H. Saldanha. Additional reporting: Neda Kapur."

She shrugged. "He's got me doing his donkey work."

———

All of this was true. But it was an adventure too sometimes. Like the happy few months spent undercover researching corruption at a series of tourism ministry hotels, run as if they were private kingdoms, with lavish parties for senior bureaucrats, ministers' families taking up whole wings, hotel cars and furniture being smuggled away and sold off, all at the taxpayers' expense. She'd loved the gossip and intrigue of all that. And going undercover, pretending to be someone else.

"So you're not with him?"

"Hari," she sat up, gave him the eyebrows. "*Seriously?*"

"Yeah," he nodded. "Maybe he's not your type."

She relaxed. "Exactly not my type."

"I remember the guys you went for in school. Assholes with big cars."

"You know me, Hari. Mostly I just went along for the ride." She finished the Coke. "And now look, see, everyone's leaving me behind."

"Your old gang?"

She counted on her fingers. "London. New York. Boston. Manchester. Durham. Stanford. Geneva. One of them's even in Tokyo. I thought about going out there too to teach English. But . . . I'm stuck here."

"You're really not happy, are you?"

She tapped the ash. "I just can't deal sometimes."

"With?"

She shrugged, watched the roadside lights zip by.

"Your dad?" he asked. "I heard about his cancer."

"Yeah, it's no secret."

"So? Is it too much?"

"No. He's good now. And he's become so chill. It's almost scary how soft he is."

"So?"

"Mom pisses me off." She knew she was being unfair but couldn't help herself. "All the money ran out in the middle of Dad's chemo. I mean, it was almost gone before that, after the business went under, you know, but it was *really* gone. I told her to sell the house. Just sell it, but she said no, it's the house that keeps us together. If she'd sold the house, he could have had really good chemo *and* I could have gone abroad after. We all could have had our lives, but no, she's the one holding us all back."

"I'm sorry."

"Forget it." She sighed and mentally washed her hands, turned to him and beamed. "Anyway, look at you, all shiny and new with your clothes and your name. WhoDini. Hari fucking WhoDini. Did you come up with that yourself?"

"I had some help."

"You're an escape artist."

"I'm doing OK."

"Well, I want a copy of this CD, signed and everything."

"Sure thing."

"And a poster of you for my bedroom wall."

"Right next to Luke Perry."

"Ha!" She flicked her cigarette out the window, watched the end explode on the hot tarmac. "That came down years ago."

The night was heavy with the scent of jasmine.

"So are you seeing *anyone*?"

She shook her head.

"You?"

"On and off," he said. "Chicks from parties mostly."

"Oh-ho!" she laughed. "Listen to you. Chicks from parties!"

"But no one special."

"OK, lover boy, what does special look like?"

"I don't know." He became shy. "Someone to come home to. Eat Chinese with, in front of the TV."

"I can't tell if you're joking or not."

"No, I'm serious."

"Man, I wish I wanted what you wanted."

"What do you want?"

"I have *no* idea."

"You're always looking somewhere else, that's your problem."

"Maybe that's why I feel so old."

He laughed. "You're being such a drama queen. You're twenty-two years old. You know what you should do? Move out. Get an apartment, live on your own."

"Yeah, maybe. But then it's like I'm committing to Delhi."

"And? What's wrong with that? You really don't get it, do you? Big things are happening. Delhi's *the* place."

Hari began to describe this art project he'd been pulled into, some "happening" inside a warehouse on the edge of Delhi. It was meant to be this big, crazy, free party, like the stuff they were doing in New York. Not just music . . . "all kinds of crazy shit, everything free, food, drink, games, beds, food by real chefs, cocktail bars, hammocks, bunk beds, graffiti walls, laser tag, bumper cars, all really nuts shit, and secret. So this guy came to see me in my studio, shook my hand and started talking about this set I played last year, the one in this farmhouse near Jaipur. Then get this, he handed me a lakh of rupees in cash right there. Just handed it over. Something about good faith. He wanted me to play so bad."

"Sounds great."

He watched her closely. "Now guess the guy's name."

She thought about it a moment. "I have no idea."

"Think about it. It begins with an *S*."

"Ahhh," she said. "The mysterious Sunny Wadia?"

"The same."

"So you knew him all along?"

"I told you those guys don't know what they're talking about."

"Ha. How is he?"

"He's really cool."

"But what's his story? Does he come from the States?"

"Nope."

"He's not an internet millionaire?"

"Nah."

"Rich kid politician's son?"

"Uh-uh."

"So?"

"He's just . . . Sunny."

"But he's loaded, right?"

"His father's some businessman, yeah. But he's not a rich kid. He's, like, different."

"Where's he from?"

"Somewhere in UP. You'd never know it. He's so cool."

"So what does his father do?"

"I don't know, farming. Fertilizer and poultry and shit."

"That's a lot of shit." She lit another cigarette. "I was hoping for something more romantic."

"You're such a snob."

She shrugged.

"So what happened with this party?"

"The cops shut it down before it even began."

"After all that?"

"Yeah. They came and busted us on the first night. They wanted to arrest us."

"But?"

"Sunny made a call and it went away."

"Bribed them with fertilizer?"

"Man, I don't even know. They didn't search us or anything. He just made a call and we all walked free. Which is good because . . . we had a load of stuff on us. Anyway, we went to his place afterward—damn, his place is cool. So there were about ten of us, ten, twenty maybe, you know, the hard core, we'd been organizing it. We had this survivors' high, we partied for three days straight anyway. I played in his apartment. It was crazy. Full power. I lost track of the days. After something like that, you make a bond. He started a record label. He said he'd do it, like wasted talk, like people say. But a week later the label was up and running. He's going to put out my records."

"Are you gonna eat Chinese in front of the TV with him too?"

"Shut up. You're just jealous."

"So, when am I going to meet this man?"

"Where do you think we're heading now?"

"Seriously?" She began to check herself in the mirror. "I look like shit."

He said, "You know that's not true."

She grew up in her world of cultural elites, both parents from scholarly backgrounds, "impoverished," "proud." Highly educated families risen to subtle prominence in colonial days. Post-Independence, advantageously placed. Quote marks always needed to describe them. Words like "cash poor." Now they lived in a "modest" five-bedroom home in Malcha Marg, leafy and gated and close to Parliament, an address that reeked of proximity to power.

They made their money from handloom exports in the 1980s during the License Raj. Their success was a by-product of intellect, refinement, work ethic, and a wholesale bypass of the labyrinth of permits to gain tax-free contracts through their well-connected friends.

Still, they had been genuinely radical in their politics—marching, manning the barricades, organizing fundraisers. Justice was their concern. They viewed money—never wealth—as a mild shame they were eager to off-load.

True wealth was knowledge. When Neda had school friends over as a girl, the daughters and sons of new money, her mother made it a point to ask the question: "So, what are you reading?"

True wealth was the accretion of experience. As evidenced by the grace of their home, with the fig trees and the palms and the parakeets in the park, the faded Persian carpets lining the marble, the signed artworks that were gifts from friends who just happened to be famous now. Shelves of books lined almost every wall, their tattered innards releasing noble yellow perfumes. That home, a store of memory. A store of knowledge.

A cage to her.

"We want you to be the best you can be," her mother told her. "We want you to be happy." She should have been grateful for the qualifying clause— it was rare enough. But happiness had its interpretations. Her mother would have approved of her bringing a poor (secular) Muslim boy from JNU. But a guy like Sunny Wadia at her dining table? No way.

Hari pulled into the parking lot of a deserted shopping arcade.

"Where are we?"

"Moti Bagh."

She recognized it suddenly, she'd driven past a hundred times. One of those markets between colonies. In the daytime, shops selling plastic goods and household junk. In the night, everything shuttered and nothing stirred. Hari's stereo was replaced by a soundtrack of barking dogs, distant horns of trucks on the airport road, planes putting down their landing gear.

He led her over the gravel toward the arcade, a low, one-story brutalist concrete square of shops with an empty field of concrete in the middle. Weeds grew out of the cracks. A set of stairs led to the lower basement level, the underground run of shops. A solitary light bulb hung over the descent.

Hari lit a cigarette. Smoke puffed above the thick bush of his hair. She was still very stoned. His body loped ahead like a ranger in a forest. The comfort that had come from being inside his car leaked out into the sky. She was nervous. There were voices ahead. Hari skipped down the concrete stairs and turned a corner, disappeared from view. This was his world, and she was a stranger in it. She followed, saw desolate store after store, each with a number painted above its close-shuttered entrance, then Hari with his arms wide, crying out a greeting. One shop front was unshuttered and music and light were spilling out. As she drew near, she looked into the uncanny re-creation of a Soviet living room, like a bombed-out cross section of an apartment block. A long table with floral plastic cloth. Flowered wallpaper. East European TV playing high on the wall. The table was full of men and women engaged in the act of drinking. Many plastic trays, vodka bottles, and shot glasses. Great plates of stewed meat, potato salad, bowls of borscht. And there, standing at the head of the table, leaning forward, arms gripping the edge, his eyes blazing with all the possibilities of life, the mysterious, the immaculate Sunny Wadia.

"... and listen, listen ... I was there in England, I saw it, this 'Cool Britannia.' Oasis. Tony Blair. God Save the Bloody Queen. But you scratch the surface, it's crumbling, it's dying, there's no future on that miserable island. The same in America. You think India is poor? Go and travel around America. I couldn't believe it. Meanwhile some backpacker in Paharganj wanders around crying about our poverty, shaking his head, taking pity on us, taking photos for the people back home. Take a look at your own backyard. Study your history, man. You people looted us, took everything, stole our treasures. Now you look at us and say, 'You're so spiritual, you have so much wisdom, you're so wise, you're so ... simple.' Yeah, we're simple, fucker. We're simply going to destroy you. They don't want us to, they don't want us to be strong, to have heart, wit, resilience, ingenuity, wealth, power, but we are, but we do. We took their shit for so long, now the tables are turning. It's our time now!"

He raised his shot glass in the air. Everyone followed suit.

"What I'm saying to you is this ... We're going to transform this city, we're going to transform this country, we're going to change our lives, we're going to transform this world! This is India's century. Our century! No one's going to take it from us!"

"And bring back the Koh-i-noor," one drunken voice cried out.

"I'll bring back the Koh-i-noor!" he cried. "Right after I shove it up Prince Charles's ass!"

She watched this speech with an underwater detachment. He wore a casual dark brown linen summer suit, crisp white shirt, black tie. His rakish black hair fell about his face, his dark, almond eyes shone feverishly. His thick beard, neatly groomed, cut close to his skin, gave him a scholarly, revolutionary look. He kept running his hair back with his hand. He was tall, rangy, athletic. But she couldn't get a fix on him. While his accent seemed to belong to some international nowhere, there was a coarse rustic vigor to his speech that a few years of self-improvement couldn't hide. She liked it.

The tension of him.

She looked around the table and recognized some of the guests: a hotshot video artist, a model turned photographer, a Bengali director of short experimental films, a young fashion designer. She had interviewed a few of them for the paper. Here they all were at the altar of Sunny. She guessed he was bankrolling them too. She wondered if they would give him the time of day otherwise. But he was, and they were, and that's how the world worked. But beyond that, God, he was magnetic. Hari was now absorbed in the group. She knew she should introduce herself, but she became reluctant, shy. "Neda," Hari called out. She put on a faint smile, waved. A spare chair was found by Hari's side. Vodka was passed over. There were nods and looks of recognition among Neda and some of the people she'd interviewed. Recognition and what? Disapproval? She felt inferior to them all. Everyone was at ease, and she was out of place. Hari made up a plate of meats and salad and dumplings for her and she began to eat because she was so hungry and stoned, and she glanced at Sunny and looked away when he glanced back at her.

She did what she knew to do. A schoolgirl trick. She stood and stepped to the threshold of the restaurant and lit a cigarette, staring into the concrete of the deserted underground arcade, tapped her cigarette out a few times, waited, twisted the tip of her shoe into the small pieces of gravel.

Waited . . .

She felt someone behind her.

She could tell it wasn't Hari.

"I have a question," she said.

She was gambling . . . but yes. Sunny was holding a bottle of vodka and two shot glasses. He passed one glass and filled it.

"What's that?"

"Why would you want to shove a diamond up Prince Charles's ass?"

He laughed.

"Seems a bit excessive," she went on.

"It's a metaphor."

"Yeah, but *is* it?"

He gave a casual shrug. "I'm just playing to the crowd."

"I'll give you that." She glanced back at the room, caught Hari's eye a moment. "You have them eating out of your palm."

"And you?"

"I'm a cynic."

"So you weren't impressed?"

"I didn't say that. You certainly talk a good game."

"But you want to see if my money's where my mouth is?"

She offered her hand. "I'm Neda."

He offered the pinky of his shot-glass hand back at her. "Sunny."

She shook it with her thumb and forefinger. "Yeah, I know who you are."

"Neda?" he turned the name over.

"It's Persian."

"And you are . . . ?" he leaned back as if to reexamine her.

"Punjabi as they come."

"So let me guess." He furrowed his brow as if he were a vaudeville mind reader. "Your parents are leftist liberal intellectual types who don't believe in religion, caste, or class."

"Wow! You're good at this!"

"Actually, I interrogated Hari when he asked if he could bring a friend."

"Ah, so that's how he talks about my parents?"

"No, no. He said only nice things. He loves you, by the way. How come I never heard of you before?"

"He's been hiding me in his past life. The one that wasn't cool."

They both looked back at Hari. He was goofing around, telling a story to the gang.

"If he was friends with you he was always cool."

"Oh, smooth." She changed the subject. "Anyway, what's up with *your* name. Wadia. You're not Parsi, are you?"

"No."

"So?"

"There's a story to that. I'll tell you sometime."

"Tell me now."

"It's too intimate." He removed a pack of cigarettes from his jacket pocket—Treasurer London—and offered her one.

"This is an intimate setting." She took a cigarette. "Looks fancy." Crunched the one she was smoking underfoot. He lit the new one with his Zippo. She nodded to the lighter. "Can I see?"

It was silver, engraved. She read the writing on the front. "70–71."

"It's from Vietnam."

"Oh, no way! You fought in the war?"

She said it so earnestly, with such a straight face, he almost fell for it.

"Very funny."

She flipped it over, narrowed her eyes, read the other side. "35 Kills. If You're Recovering My Body, Fuck You." She handed it back. "Charming."

He opened it to show the inner chimney, diagonally cut away. "See this?"

"What am I looking at?"

"It was cut like that to light opium pipes."

"You're into opium?"

"No, no. I'm just a student of history."

"Ah, I see." She had to hide her amusement. His use of the term was quaint, gauche.

He picked up on it.

"So what are you doing standing out here?" he asked.

"Oh, I don't know. Separating myself from the herd."

"I get it. You're a loner, like me."

She laughed. "Yeah, just like you. You're the loneliest guy in the room."

"Where are you from?" he went on.

He had that look a guy gives, a look of pursuit.

"Right here. Delhi. I've lived here all my life. I'll probably die here too. What about you?"

"Me? I'm a citizen of the world."

"A student of history *and* a citizen of the world," she teased. "Next you'll be telling me you studied at the university of life."

She detected some kind of hurt in his eyes—she'd slighted him.

She knocked back the vodka to do something with herself.

He was still watching her intently.

She smiled as he refilled her glass.

"You look like you want to kill me."

He said nothing.

"I did enjoy your speech though," she went on. "I mean it. It was rousing. Even the cynic in me was roused."

"What do you do?" he said.

She decided to stop playing. She fixed him with a firm, cool look.

"I'm a journalist. I write for the *Post*."

He met her gaze. "I better watch what I say."

She was aware—intensely aware, intensely aware that the rest of the room was probably aware—that they were staring into each other's eyes.

"I'm off duty," she said.

"No one's ever off duty."

Before she could reply, one of the girls at the table cried out his name.

Neda nodded at the room. "They're missing their hero."

He broke eye contact, turned to go back in. "You can smoke in there too, you know."

"You go ahead," she said. "We wouldn't want to start a rumor."

More people arrived. A handsome minor film actor always in the gossip pages came with a TV star who played good girls in the soaps. It was a veritable who's who of bubblegum, not a camera in sight. All of them paying fealty to Sunny, who soaked up their attention and radiated it back out at them. More chairs were found. More vodka brought, some bottles of red wine were opened. More food. She felt she was backstage at a performance of Delhi, watching its players remove the paint, their masks. She was on the inside, the other side. The guy next to her said, "How do you know Sunny? He's the man of the hour." He extended his hand. "I'm Jagdish. Full of ideas." "You or him?" More voices were cutting in. "What this city needs." Neda smiled. They were all drunk. He curled his Dalí mustache. "A firm hand." "What?" "What do you do?" "I write." "I paint on walls." "What happened to your nose?" "I fell off a wall." Everything was spinning. Hari was smiling at her with fraternal pride. "Murals of a Future Delhi." "What?" "That's what I paint." "He has a grant from my foundation," Sunny shouted. He'd been listening in. "I got a grant from Sunny's foundation," Jagdish shouted. "Śūnyatā. Do you like the name?" Sunny said. "It means nothing. Literally 'Nothing.' Do you understand? Everything is connected." "That's what I tell myself," Jagdish said, "when I spend all his money." The room was red velvet and fairy lights of psychedelic wire. She watched the talk show on TV with great seriousness, men smoking cigarettes in armchairs, and below it all she saw Sunny raising a glass. "Neda here is going to write about me . . ." A bottle was knocked over. She grabbed another glass of vodka, and the room was falling out of orbit and she was spinning on her axis. She looked up and Sunny was looking at her . . . She saw the red lampshade sideways on the horizon . . .

She was in her own bed. There was birdsong and it was morning. Her leg was hanging out, touching the floor. She reached out and shut off the alarm, knocked it off the bedside table. Her clothes were strewn on the floor. Her mouth was an ash heap, her throat gravel, her stomach drying concrete . . . "Oh fuck." She couldn't remember how she got there. Or what she'd done. Then the restaurant came back to her. Standing on a table. She went to her bathroom and threw up.

———

"Cinderella," her father boomed. "Welcome back to the land of the living."

She dropped into one of the chairs at the dining table, picked up a piece of buttered toast, threw it down again.

"I think I made a fool of myself."

He watched her with patience and no small wonder. "Not for the first time, daughter of mine. I trust you had a good night?"

"How did I get here?"

"Home? Hari delivered you to the door. He was in good spirits. He's all grown up."

"Did we wake you up?"

He shook his head. "I was watching TV."

"What did Mom say?"

"Nothing. *She* was sleeping."

"That's good." She sighed. "I'm never drinking again."

"Here." He lifted his newspaper to reveal Sunny's pack of Treasurers and his Zippo. "I believe these are now yours."

"Oh shit, I think I stole them."

"Maybe from the one driving the fancy car."

"Which car?"

"Hari was not alone." He nodded wistfully at the cigarettes. "I can't say I wasn't tempted to have one."

"Dad?" she sat down.

"Yes?"

"Please stop talking."

He saluted her. "Message understood."

She took the lighter and cigarettes, looked at her phone. "I'm so late for work."

"Your powers of recovery are at their peak. Revel in them, child. Meanwhile, I already called you a taxi. Sardar-ji is waiting out front."

She kissed him on the forehead. "Thank you, Papa."

She felt anxious and skittish all morning at work, worrying about what she might have said and done, the regular hangover traumas, amplifying all those underlying fears. She was terrified of being irrelevant, of being found out, of being left behind. All those people there last night, they'd *seen* her. She'd thought she was being cool, but what if she'd been plain ridiculous? And now in the morning they were thinking how pathetic she was. And what if Sunny was laughing about her too, laughing with one of them right now? She reassured herself with the usual formulations: *Everyone was as drunk as you.* But they're not like you, she countered herself. They're rich or powerful or cool. What are you doing, Neda? She thought to text Hari, but she was too ashamed. But why? She'd done nothing wrong. She'd flirted with Sunny, but Sunny, he wasn't a big deal.

Was he?

She remembered his big words, his grand ideas, his promises and proclamations, which sounded so right at the table. But no, no, it was all hollow and dumb and he was just a guy. A guy like anyone else. Maybe he wasn't even real. Everything about the night was hazy, appearing to her memory as if in a funhouse mirror. She took out the lighter and examined it. It struck her as childish. What moron carried a lighter from a far-off, foreign, long-finished war? She put it away. She decided to just keep working. A weird night consigned to the dustbin of her life.

The hangover only got worse. Gone was the giddy stardust of waking. The sense of atoms twinkling. She was left with a viselike emptiness. A shrink-wrapped brain.

She went through the motions at work. It was only tolerable if she rolled downhill in neutral. She shifted a few sentences around a fraud story she'd been working on, filed it, made a round of phone calls of which she didn't hear a word, scanned the police bulletins, arranged an interview with the head of a trader's association for the afternoon.

At 3:38 p.m. her phone beeped.

A message from Hari.

Her stomach churned as she opened it. But it wasn't a horror at all.

—hey watt a nite!

    —:)

—just woke up. we kept going til 10

    —nice.

—u made an impression!!

As she was figuring out what to say, she looked up to see Dean standing over her. She put the phone facedown.

"Dean."

"Neda. You good?"

"Surviving."

"I wondered if you got a chance to go through the bulletins?"

"Yeah. Yeah, I did." She looked over her notes. "Kidnapping, kidnapping, kidnapping, spurious ghee, another kidnapping, an altercation at a paan shop, yet another kidnapping, some ransom demands but mostly they're missing with no trace." She flicked through her notes. "This one was interesting. An 'interstate car-stereo gang.' They were targeting Marutis, mostly. Remind me not to leave my stereo in my car."

"Don't leave your stereo in your car."

"Thanks."

"You want to get a smoke?"

"Sure."

Standing out in the corridor, she took a cigarette from Sunny's pack, lit it with his Zippo.

Dean motioned to the lighter. "May I?"

She handed it to him, he examined it all over, opened it, closed it, checked something on the base. He made a grunt of approval. "Seems legit."

"I wouldn't know."

He pointed to a detail. "There's a code right here."

"I really, really wouldn't know. I'm just holding it for a friend."

"Lucky friend. It's probably worth quite a bit."

"Maybe I should sell it?"

"In Manhattan, sure. Here it's just scrap metal. Anyway, the more you keep using it, the less it's worth. Tell your friend he should lock it away."

"You're assuming it's a he."

He gave her a look that said "Come on." "Anyway," he said. "What's new?"

"Nothing new. You?"

"I was at Nangla this morning," he said, frowning. "The high court put through another demolition order. It's just a matter of time before they execute it, rip it all down. They don't even name the settlement in the documentation. It's just called 'the obstruction.' The Obstruction. It's people's lives, their homes. Anyway, I might need you to transcribe some interviews later, if you're not too busy."

"Sure."

"Your Hindi is better than mine."

"Anyone's Hindi is better than yours."

"I'll leave them on your desk. I'm heading out to the Pushta now."

Yes, the Pushta. The Yamuna River and its banks and its "illegal" settlements, tens of thousands of households living on the edge of existence, tens of thousands of households already demolished, lives resettled, displaced. Dean was obsessed with it all. The slums, the demolitions. The courts were ordering demolitions all over the city, tearing down the poor, unplanned settlements that had grown up and become communities over decades, but the epicenter was the riverbanks, the Yamuna Pushta.

All Neda's life, this was a part of Delhi that she saw and didn't see. The slums had always been there; every time she crossed the river she looked down on the ramshackle city clinging to the banks. They were inevitable, they were ugly, they induced shame, guilt, in momentary flashes, but their people were submerged in her mind. If she thought about any of it at all, she thought it was Delhi, an eyesore, a sign of failure. But Dean saw the slums as people, and he saw their destruction as a tragedy.

She listened to him talk, indulged him, tried to learn from him, never spoke up herself. He said the Yamuna was seen as a "nonplace," a place without history or culture that flowed empty through the heart of commerce, that it was seen as a wasted space in the eyes of global capital, but the Yamuna and its banks were neither wasted nor dead nor empty, it was all alive. He'd been doing a series of reports from there, along the floodplains, among the fishermen and the subsistence farmers and the slum dwellers who made up the laboring classes, who made up the maids and servants and drivers of the city; he was tracking the government's eviction efforts, their plans of relocation. There were plans afoot for a World-Class Delhi, plans to turn Delhi into a "global city." The courts called it "the showpiece of the country." The riverfront should be a window to the world, a "public" space, a recreational and cultural landmark. There was a buzz of excitement about the future river. But all Dean saw was the damage done.

"So tell me," he said, walking back from the smoke. "How's the head? Because I know a hangover when I see one."

"It's that obvious?"

They entered the newsroom. "You know what, don't worry about the interviews. I'll get someone else to transcribe them."

"Actually," she said, as they reached her desk, "can I ask you something?"

"Shoot."

"There's this guy."

"Ah . . ."

"Not like that."

"Good, because I'm the last one to give relationship advice."

"I met him with my friend."

"Last night?"

"Right. I wanted to know his deal, professionally speaking. I wondered if you heard of him. If he was worth writing about. Maybe doing a profile."

"Name?"

"He's bankrolling a lot of art projects in the city. Sponsoring musicians, painters, designers. Putting on parties, this kind of thing. Something different. Something fun. I thought maybe I could do a profile on him."

"Neda, what's his name?"

She suddenly didn't want to say it.

"Sunny."

"Sunny . . . *what*?"

She braced herself a little. "Wadia."

"Sunny Wadia?" He shook his head. "That joker? Seriously, don't waste your time. He's just another rich kid in a sandpit. Empty calories. I don't mean to rain on your parade—I do actually—but he doesn't deserve your attention. He doesn't deserve anyone's."

"I don't know," she was flustered. "I'm just saying it's not all doom and gloom, it might be nice to cover some positive news once in a while."

"Do you know who his father is?"

"Some kind of farmer, I thought."

He clapped his hands together in glee. "Bunty Wadia, some kind of farmer? That's a hoot."

She hated him when he was like this.

He went on. "He's one of Ram Singh's mob."

"*The* Ram Singh?"

"Yes, chief minister of UP Ram Singh. None other. He's one of his cronies, and by all accounts he's a nasty piece of work."

She thought of Sunny, charming her in his suit, being a "citizen of the world."

"Still, you can't blame the sins of the father on the son."

"Listen, I know you think I'm old-fashioned. Or maybe just old. But these guys, with their dirty money, they get treated like gods now because money talks, but it stinks. They're gangsters, however you want to dress it up. And kids like Sunny, throwing their cash around, whatever they say, whatever they do, in the end it's always the same, they're always doing more harm than good."

She searched online for news articles on Bunty Wadia. There were surprisingly few, and none with photos. In the handful of pieces he was routinely described as "liquor baron Bunty Wadia." Or else the "controversial businessman" and once "the reclusive businessman." Another talked about his being the "chief beneficiary of the surprise election victory of Uttar Pradesh chief minister Ram Singh." According to reports, he bagged several lucrative contracts in the proceeding years, ranging from transport, sand mining, liquor, and construction, and had successfully completed the distress purchase of two apparently unprofitable state-owned sugar mills.

Another name kept popping up in her search. Vikram "Vicky" Wadia. He was a politician, an MLA out in Eastern UP, with a whole range of criminal charges against him: six of kidnapping for extortion, one of torture, four of rioting, three of attempt to murder. There were no convictions, only cases pending, stacking up, stacking up. No doubt about it, Vicky Wadia was a gangster, a dada, a rough-hewn country godfather. Several articles talked about the "Kushinagar incident," but none of them could tell her what it was. Eventually she found a grainy photo of him from a lurid piece on a Hindi news website, where he was referred to as "Himmatgiri," and my God if he didn't look like a more brutish version of Sunny.

She turned her attention to Sunny, but there was nothing there. He seemed perfectly anonymous—he didn't even appear in the photos of the society pages. And when she searched for the name of the foundation—the Śūnyatā Foundation, wasn't it?—she was disappointed by a simple page with no links and only a line of hackneyed, ungrammatical text espousing the transformative power of art in the urban landscape. Really? This was him? She examined the page more carefully for a sign, a hidden doorway, but it was bricked up and mute. She printed all the articles on Bunty and Vicky, put them in her drawer to read later, and returned to work.

That evening, sitting alone in her car outside Alkauser in Chanakyapuri with the window down, waiting for the boy to fetch her kakori in roomali, watching the charcoal grill glowing, the sparks leaping and blinking out of existence, she felt a vertiginous tenderness for the tangled complexities of her city. She took a photo of the kiosk with her Nokia and texted Hari.

—Guess where?

He replied almost immediately.

—home away from home:)

She waited a minute.

—Oh yeah I meant to ask. what did you mean when you said I made an impression?

Her kebab was delivered. She dipped the end into the chutney, garlanded it with onion, took a bite.

—u know wat I mean

Trust Hari to be difficult.

—I really don't know what you mean by impression. Did I embarrass myself?

She finished her meal.

Finally the phone beeped.

—FYI, he's seeing Kriti

Kriti was the TV actress from the other night.

—Yeah I knew that

She didn't. She thought the actress was with the film star.

—Ok gud

   —Anyway, he's not my type

—Yeah right

Sunny fit into the long line of boys she'd flirted with in school, slept with in college, all those boys she'd parked with on the ridge, whose daddies were wealthy businessmen, who represented the vulgar new India her mother railed against. He fit into that line, and he transcended it. While those boys had appealed by being so very different to her, they'd always disappointed in the end. They'd been conservative and dull at heart, or painfully dumb, or just plain boring. They had been her rebellion, but they themselves rebelled against precisely nothing, and that always ended dead. Sunny . . . he was something else. His family came from the soil. His family, his uncle at least, was dangerous. And what he represented himself was radical. Could he pull it off? Could she watch him try? Even to watch him fail would be a thrill. As the days passed by she smoked his cigarettes from her bedroom window and wondered what Sunny was doing, what adventures he must be having. Why wasn't he calling her? She felt like she'd had a glimpse through the clouds of a fantastic world below, only for the clouds to close again. She'd anticipated another party soon, one she'd be invited to, but no invite came. Hari didn't get in touch again. Every time her phone beeped or rang, she held her breath, but there was nothing. So, what should she do? Finally she texted Hari, asked if he wanted to meet for a smoke, but he was already up in the mountains, in Kasol, for the next three weeks. She stopped herself from asking if Sunny was there too. And then she got a grip on herself. Forget it. If he wants to get in touch, if he wanted his lighter back, he'll find a way. Assume whatever it might have been is over. After two weeks Sunny started to fade from the front of her mind. In the decadent night you might have heard his name, but in the harsh light of the city she inhabited, in the evictions and the police bulletins, in the spurious ghee and stereo gangs, he disappeared.

Then she bumped into him in Khan Market. She'd been sent there by her city editor to conduct a voxpop: "Will the new malls kill Delhi's traditional markets?" But she was mostly killing time, roaming the lanes, eating chaat, smoking cigarettes, chatting to the shopkeepers she had known since childhood. Occasionally she'd wave down shoppers: a couple of teenage girls, an upmarket housewife, a retired army man, the token white person. On one of her rounds, she glanced into the fancy electronics store that used to be a toy store when she was a kid. And there he was, in a straw cotton suit, the jacket slung over his shoulder, busy directing the various boys who were clambering up the shelves under his commanding gaze, hauling down bulky cardboard boxes containing all manner of gadgets and high-end equipment. She was still watching him when Mr. Kohli, the owner, waved at her from inside. "Neda, dear!"

Sunny glanced back and casually took her in. Had he already seen her? He seemed to betray no surprise.

Well, she could play that game too.

"Hello, Uncle," she said to Mr. Kohli. "How are you?"

"Very good, my dear, very good. And you? How's your mother?"

"Oh, she's very well." She stepped inside. "Having a good day of business, I see."

"Yes, Mr. Wadia here is one of my best customers."

"Really?" She drew level with Sunny. "Hello, Mr. Wadia here."

He glanced at her, nodded quite formally, but his eyes were smiling. "Ms. Kapur."

"I see," Mr. Kohli exclaimed, "you know each other."

"Ms. Kapur is a famous journalist," Sunny said.

"And Mr. Wadia is an outrageous"—he turned to face her—"flirt."

"I could think of some other words."

Mr. Kohli took his cue and buried himself in his books.

"You're looking well," he said.

She wasn't, unless he liked the tomboy office look, and who knows, maybe he did, so she ran with it.

"Thank you. You're dapper as ever. I never imagined seeing you in the day like this."

"I'm flattered you imagined me at all. I have to apologize," he said, quickly, "for not being in touch."

Her eyes roved over the boxes of toys and gadgets. "You've clearly been busy with very important stuff."

He laughed. "I like to get whatever's new, see what's out there. I usually give it away very soon."

"You go visit orphanages, do you?"

"Mostly I just let whoever comes to my apartment take things. I'm good like that. I don't get attached."

"I see. Remind me to visit your apartment."

"I look forward to it."

She laughed. "One day maybe."

"Why not now?"

"Because *I* am working. You know, that thing most of us have to do." She corrected herself. "Not that you don't work . . ." She was embarrassed, flustered. He was looking at her, watching her, intimidating her with his ease. "We're not all our own bosses. Some of us have people to answer to."

He just smiled.

Waited.

Smiled.

"What?!" she said.

"Nothing. You're cute, that's all."

"Oh, Jesus," she rolled her eyes. "That's the last thing I want to be."

"I'm serious though, why don't you come over? This is a serendipitous meeting. I have a free afternoon. We never really got to talk much the other night. It was mostly"—he reflected on the memory, and she braced herself—"shouting."

"*Shouting?*"

"Yeah, shouting. Lots and lots of shouting. Laughing too. Things getting knocked over." He scanned her blank face. "You don't remember anything, do you?"

She winced. "I remember the next morning."

Mr. Kohli had prepared the bill, he caught Sunny's attention, and Sunny took out an obscenely thick roll of cash and started counting it. "Excuse me," he said, "I'll just handle this."

"I'll wait outside."

Outside she weighed up the pros and cons of going back with him to his apartment. The only con was that she *was* supposed to be working. The pros were manifold. Mostly to satisfy her curiosity, to get a private audience with this mysterious young god of Delhi. She watched his back as he paid. So at ease, but so constructed too. But was she just projecting? Was she transposing the outlines of his father, his uncle, onto his body? Again the question entered her mind: Who is Sunny Wadia? She couldn't say. He stepped outside, followed by four boys, each carrying several boxes. Two TVs, several gaming consoles, a rice cooker, a fancy blender. He waved at her, pointed in the direction of the parking lot. "At least walk with me."

"Sure."

Immediately she became aware of eyes on them. Or rather, him. It wasn't as if everyone knew him, though some certainly recognized his face. It was more how he carried himself, a combination of stature and style, the way, she thought, movie stars carried themselves. Then there was the not insignificant train of boys carrying expensive objects behind, confirming his wealth. No one saw her, she was merely in his orbit; she felt, for a second, as if she were his secretary, his assistant. It wasn't an unpleasant feeling, but still, she felt she should assert herself somehow, get back to work at least . . .

"What are you thinking?"

She realized he'd been watching her.

"That I should get back to work."

"What are you working on?"

To say a voxpop seemed pretty lame.

"Well . . ." She cleared her throat. "I'm assessing the socioeconomic impact of the shifting commercial landscape through the oral testimony of consumers."

He made a show of concentration, mouthing the words back to himself.

"You mean you're conducting a voxpop?"

"Vox populi, to be precise."

He laughed.

"I'll give you some juicy quotes. We'll make some up together. Then you'll have no excuse not to come back with me."

They crossed from the shopping lanes into the parking lot.

She squinted at him in the sun. "Can I ask you a serious question?"

"Sure."

"Why are you so eager?"

He stopped, looked at her.

"Isn't it obvious?"

His smile said the rest.

Then she was saved. His driver saw them coming, came running, began to fret over the boxes, dashed back to the Land Cruiser, and popped the rear door. Sunny had clearly bought more than the driver or the SUV could handle.

"Besides," Sunny went on, "there's no room in my car. I need you to give me a lift."

It felt strange to have Sunny Wadia squashed in the passenger seat of her beat-up little red Maruti. His knees pressed against the plastic dash. Just ahead, his driver was guiding the box-cramped SUV through the streets.

"I like your car," he said.

She pressed a tender hand on the horn, gave it a little pip. "I know you're being sarcastic, but I love her. She's temperamental, she gets me from A to B, what more could you ask?"

"A bit more legroom," he smiled, trying to work the seat back.

"Oh yeah, that's broken."

He looked awkward and it amused her a little. This was her domain now.

"You like old things, don't you?"

"I like good things."

"That's more subjective."

"You don't think this car is good?"

"Let's put it this way, I couldn't pull it off. To do that, you have to be at the top of the food chain."

"So says the Crown Prince of Delhi."

"No, no. You're so far above me. I'm nowhere near your level."

"Rubbish."

"I mean it. You can get away with just about everything. I bet you insult cops when they pull you over, don't you?" Her silence told him he was right. "And you don't even need money. You have it rooted into you. Look at this shitty car."

"What about it?"

"I bet you can drive it right up to a five-star and jump out and swan inside and no one bats an eyelid."

"I never really thought about it."

"One look at you, in this shitty car, and everyone knows. You're right up there at the top. You don't know how lucky you are."

"I know I'm lucky," she said.

"Don't get me wrong," he went on, "I admire it. How easy it is for you. For me, no. I've had to construct myself. I'm reminded daily, in the mirror, I'm nothing without my suit, without my car, without my watch. Without these props, I barely exist."

"Speaking of props," she said, "do you have any more of those delightful cigarettes?"

"Sure."

"I finished all yours, by the way."

He took out his pack. Held one out for her. "You changed the subject."

She placed the cigarette in her mouth.

"I guess I was uncomfortable."

"You shouldn't be."

She gazed out at the road.

"It's hard for me to believe," she said, "that you're just a construct. I don't think of people that way."

"You don't have to."

"I feel like you're . . . like you're purposely devaluing yourself."

"No, I value myself."

"Like it's false humility."

"I never said I was humble."

She tried to follow the train of thought, to think of something witty to say. I mean, this *was* flirting, right?

"So how does it feel," she finally asked, "riding in this shitty car?"

"Honestly?" he grinned. "It makes me kind of nervous."

She laughed. "I can let you out *anytime* you want."

They fell silent.

Things had been reset.

She took a plastic lighter from the tray and lit her cigarette. "Oh, shit," she cried, slapping her head. "I needed to give your lighter back. It's in my drawer at work."

"It's OK," he replied smoothly. "I gave it to you as a gift."

She thought this over.

Took a short breath as if to speak, tilted her head, stopped herself.

But he caught it.

"What?"

"Just checking," she started. "But you're dating Kriti, right?"

He lit a cigarette for himself. "Where did you hear that?"

"I have my sources."

"Hari."

"Maybe."

Sunny smiled. "He's just jealous."

"Oh yeah?" she asked dumbly. "Is he into her?"

"Idiot. He's into you."

"Yeah, yeah . . . I don't buy it."

Ahead of them, Sunny's driver accelerated through an amber light. The light turned red, and Neda slowed to a stop while the Land Cruiser vanished into the traffic ahead.

"Asshole," Sunny muttered. "He should have waited."

He took his phone out.

"Chill," she reached over and pushed his phone back down. "You know the way home."

They were silent until the light turned green. The swarm of traffic and horns roared around them as her car groaned forward. But she was a master of the road, she cut in and out of spaces, all the while keeping the cigarette burning between her lips.

Its smoke was getting into her eyes.

"May I?" he reached out to take it from her mouth, ashed it out his window, stuck it carefully back in. "Take a right ahead," he said. "To Safdarjung Enclave."

She smiled but didn't say anything. This was a moment.

Fifteen minutes later, guiding her through the streets, he pointed to a huge gate guarding a monolithic block, five stories high.

She pulled the car to the gate. Two uniformed security men bearing automatic pistols approached, one with his palm raised for her to stop, peering inside suspiciously until they saw Sunny and snapped to attention. An order was barked, the gate was opened. On the other side, two more guards saluted as the car passed inside.

"What did you people do?" she said. "Rob a bank?"

The small driveway at the base of the building was packed with cars. Two servants hurried to open her doors.

"Leave it running," he said, "they'll park it."

He led her round the side of the imposing building through a small, nondescript door, down a corridor that felt like the staff area of a hotel. They emerged briefly into a brightly lit reception hall with marble floors, modern coffee tables and waiting sofas, freshly cut flowers, then away down another hallway toward an elevator. At all times he remained businesslike, as if he were escorting a guest to see "the manager." She made a mental note of this, along with the prevalence of security cameras lining the walls.

Inside the elevator, rising silently to the fifth floor, he was formal as ever. She could have laughed; instead, she waited emotionless, and when the doors opened she followed him along the windowless, red-carpeted corridor toward a single solid door that opened from the inside as they approached. Inside the bright room beyond, a uniformed servant greeted them both, bowing slightly, pressing his palms together in namaste.

After the strange, stifling ascent, the apartment felt like a sanctuary. The main room was bright, minimalist, its walls painted art gallery white, appropriately adorned with (he later told her) important works of constructivist and De Stijl art on one long side, and a vast piece of abstract expressionism on the end wall, where a TV might usually perch. A giant Bokhara rug held court in the center, upon which an antique Afghan wooden door, repurposed as a coffee table, sat squarely, surrounded by easy chairs, sofas.

To the left, blacked-out doors led to what she guessed was a roof terrace, while doorless arches hinted at more rooms beyond.

He spread his hands. "Well, what do you think?"

"This is . . . this is pretty special."

"I'm so glad you like it."

He directed her toward the sofa. "Please, sit," and he put his cigarettes on the table as he took his own place on a leather Falcon chair to her side.

As she balanced herself on the edge of the sofa, the servant who had opened the door, then quickly vanished into one of the arches, now returned with a tray containing glasses of water.

"Thank you, Ajay," Sunny said.

To Neda, he said, "Go on, taste it."

She studied the glass. "What is it?"

"Just taste it."

She did. It was pretty good.

"You never tasted water like that before, did you?"

She guessed she had to agree. "I don't think so."

"Guess where it's from?"

She smiled. "I don't know."

"Belgium."

"See, I'd never guess."

He sat forward. "It travels through prehistoric rock. It's purified by a thermal spring."

He was like a little boy, full of wonder, wanting to share his wisdom. She found it endearing.

"Will it cure me of my sins?"

"Take a seat," he said. "I'll be right back."

He vanished through an arch, and she was alone. She settled herself into the sofa, noticed how cool the air was, how the AC was hidden, as in a luxury hotel. Yes, that's what it felt like, a mishmash of gallery and hotel. She made an inventory of the magazines and books tastefully laid out on the coffee table: an array of Taschen's *Living In* series; back issues of *Architectural Digest, Robb Report, National Geographic*; *The Tale of Genji, Camera Lucida, The Art of War.*

She picked up a Taschen, *Living in Japan*, flicked through it idly.

"Madam?"

The servant, Ajay, stood before her, head bowed. "Drink, madam? Chai, coffee, juice, cold drink?"

Sunny approached. "Something stronger?" He'd changed, thrown on a fresh white shirt, wool pants. "What about a spritz? Ajay makes a great spritz."

"I . . . don't know what that is."

He placed himself back in the Falcon chair.

"Sprezzatura," he said grandly.

"Yeah, I don't know what that is either." She looked to Ajay. "I'll have a beer."

"Heineken, Asahi, Peroni . . ." He reeled off the names.

"No, no," Sunny waved his hand dismissively, "she'll try a Venetian spritz, with"—he cocked his head in delicate consideration—"Mauro Vergano Americano."

"Sir."

"I can't get drunk," she said.

"You won't." He looked to Ajay. "And I'll have an Asahi. Very cold."

She watched Ajay walk away. "He's a good one."

Before he could reply, the front door clicked open, and the driver who had been in the market passed through, followed by a procession of servants carrying the boxes from the store.

"And here come the toys."

Ajay emerged from the kitchen to direct proceedings, chastising the driver in a low, calm voice for some new offense he had committed, before returning to complete the drinks.

"Yeah," she said, "he's definitely a keeper."

"I rescued him," he said.

She looked puzzled. "From where?"

"The mountains."

"What, like, from an avalanche?"

"No," he laughed, "a backpacker café."

"Ah . . . so he rolls your joints for you?"

"Actually, it was the coffee that hooked me. He makes the most incredible coffee. In the macchinetta. He learned from some Italian guy."

"I didn't know coffee was so difficult."

"You should try it. He has a way, he has a, how do you say, international . . ." He clicked his fingers impatiently.

"Sensibility?"

"Exactly."

"And at the end of the day, he still rolls your joints for you, right?"

He smiled. "If he did, you wouldn't know about it."

"Discretion is very important in your line of work."

He nodded to himself, as if affirming a first principle. "It's important that I recruit my own people."

"I'd say it's essential." She thought: *Is he toying with me? Does he talk like this with everyone?*

"My father is . . . he has his ways."

"All fathers do," she replied, encouraging him to go on, but thinking of her own father and his ways or lack of, and how blessed she was.

"He brings people in from the villages," Sunny went on. "The workers. In from our"—he picked the next word carefully—"territories. They're very loyal, they have a network of loyalty, but"—he lit a cigarette, offered her one, which she took—"they're loyal to him, and I prefer—"

"Someone loyal to you."

"This is my sanctuary. I refuse to live a double life in here."

She nodded. "There's enough of a double life to live outside." She lived a double life all the time. Even in her own heart. Almost everyone did. It was just how things were. Someone was always watching, keeping a record of things to be used against you later. Who wouldn't want to be free in their own home? "India . . ." She sighed. "Land of traitors and double agents."

"Tell me something," he said, "be honest."

She finally lit the cigarette in her hand. "Maybe."

"Do you like your job?"

"What?"

"Your job. Do you like it?"

Her walls came up. "It's not my calling, if that's what you mean. But sure, it has its moments."

"What's your calling?"

"I don't have one."

"Everyone has one. I believe that."

"I don't. But I suppose that doesn't matter to you."

"You have a calling, I'm certain of it. We just have to find it."

"What's yours?" She wanted to talk about him.

He wagged his finger "All in good time, Ms. Kapur. I'm asking the questions."

"Bullshit. You can't do that. You claim everyone has—"

Ajay entered with drinks and some snacks. He laid a coaster, placed hers down, and announced: "Venetian spritz."

Neda examined Ajay with interest—he was powerfully built, but with a face of childlike openness. She smiled sweetly, pointed to one of the snacks. "And what's this?"

"Madam," he replied in English, in earnest, "this is fried, salted anchovy in zucchini blossom." He looked to Sunny for approval.

"Thank you, Ajay," Sunny said. "I'll call you."

"He adores you," she said as he slipped away. She held up her drink, examined the color. "And this is beautiful."

"Try it."

She took a sip. "Damn."

"Good."

"Bitter. But good."

"Your palate will adjust. And the snack?"

"You get off on this, don't you?"

"I enjoy giving people new experiences."

"You know," she said, examining the plate, "I actually never had anchovy before." She took a bite, chewed a moment, nodded affirmatively. "Yeah, that's amazing." She pointed at his plate. "What did you get?"

"Oh," he shrugged, "these are Japanese."

"Japan." She pointed at the Taschen book. "I'd love to go to Japan."

"It's insane."

"You've been? Course you've been. What's it like?"

"Insane. Impossible to describe. But you know," he motioned toward the drink in her hand, "I prefer Italy. The food, the culture, the passion, the style. I get all my suits made there. I have one tailor in Milan, another in Napoli. It's all . . . like I said . . ."

"Spritza-ma-somethin'?"

"Sprezzatura."

"That's the one."

"It means 'effortless cool.'"

"You could tell me it means 'asshole' and I wouldn't know the difference."

"But you'd believe me?"

"No," she shook her head.

He laughed. "You're funny."

"Am I?"

"And you talk back."

"Yeah, well . . ."

"No one talks back. Not anymore."

"No one?"

"Not to me."

"Not even your friends?"

"Not even my friends."

"Not even your bestest, bestest friends?"

He shook his head solemnly.

"Well, that's because they're scared of you," she laughed.

"They're scared of my money," he countered.

"No," she shot back. "I'm sure they love the money. What they're scared of is losing access. This is basic school shit. You're the cool new kid. You never watched *90210*? I mean, who wouldn't want to rest in the warm shadow of Sunny Wadia?"

He looked at the table momentarily. "I don't know." Then he looked up at her. "Me?"

She gave a mock cluck of sympathy. "Oh, is the poor rich kid sad?" She hadn't eaten since breakfast, and she could feel the alcohol working on her. It went like this sometimes, loosening her tongue so that she chose to prey on the traits she found intriguing when she was sober. Seeing his face, she tried to rein herself in, arranged her face accordingly. "But I remember now," she said. "We were talking in the restaurant that night. You said you were a loner. I didn't believe you. I thought you were being cute. But maybe it's true."

"You're perceptive," he said.

She batted it away. "I have two eyes and a brain."

"It's an attractive quality."

She knew he was playing a game with her, but still, she could feel herself blushing. "All right, enough of this," she said, placing the drink down and pushing it away. "I have a job to do, and you promised."

"Did I?"

"The voxpop."

"Right."

"Unless it was just a ploy to get me to your room."

He watched her with a sly smile on his lips.

"I need answers," she said. "You dragged me away from work, I have to file copy. So no excuses." She reached for her bag. "Oh, I'm going to record you."

She could see the hesitation in his eyes, but she fished out the Dictaphone anyway. "Don't worry," she said, "we'll change your name." She positioned the Dictaphone on the table. "OK?"

He assented, eyes calmly locked on her. "OK."

"First off, what's your name?"

He replied right away. "Vijay."

"Age?"

"Twenty-three."

"OK, let's go." She pressed RECORD, and the red light came on. "I'm here with Vijay, twenty-three, we're in Khan Market, and the question of the day is malls and markets. Vijay, please tell me what you do."

He took a long drag of his cigarette, frowned at the table a moment, placed the cigarette in the ashtray. When he looked up next, he'd not only switched personas but languages. "I work in a call center, madam," he replied, in strong, Western UP–accented Hindi.

It took her by surprise, the earnest, hopeful, confident voice. And it occurred to her: maybe this is his *real* voice, his *real* accent.

"OK, Vijay, twenty-three, call center worker," she replied, sticking to English, "here's the question: Are Delhi's new malls a death knell for the city's traditional markets?"

"Madam," he said, "the malls are very exciting for me."

"Why is that?"

"So much things, all under one roof, with the best brands. If you have no brand, madam, you have no style."

She had to stop herself from smiling. It teased her lips.

"Madam," Vijay cringed, "what is funny?"

"Kuch nahi," she said. "Nothing."

"Madam," he said, "you are making fun of me, but you don't understand what it is like, going here, going there, trying to find all the things a fellow needs in all the different markets. Also, mall has AC. Nice climate."

"OK, OK," she said, "so malls *will* destroy traditional markets? That's what you think?"

"No, madam," he smiled, "there will always be big men and women like you who like to use these markets, climbing out of your nice cars with your drivers."

"I don't have a driver!" she said.

He held up a hand for her to wait. "And there will always be the common man who cannot afford to go to the new mall, and they too will use the market. But in the middle, there is now a person like me." He switched to English and spoke one heavily accented word. "Aspirational."

He watched her in silence, perfectly straight faced, not breaking in the slightest.

"Oh, come on," she finally said, "this is just you giving your sales pitch."

"Madam," he said, almost cracking, "what are you saying?"

She threw up her hands, "Whatever!"

"Besides," he said, picking up the cigarette and returning to Sunny Wadia. "Do you even know how Khan Market started?"

She looked blank.

"Of course you don't," he went on. Now she listened for small tells in his honeyed, international voice, but it was flawlessly vague. "It started with Partition refugees. They came to Delhi and landed up in that colony with nothing. And they adapted because they had to. If they didn't adapt, they died. So more than anyone, they shouldn't be surprised when the city changes. And if they can't keep their customers happy, why should they stay in business? They have no God-given right."

"So the moral of the story," she said, "is adapt or die?"

He sat back in his chair. "Pretty much."

"Go on then," she said. "Say it."

"Adapt. Or die."

"Vijay, twenty-three, then . . ."

"Listen," he said, cutting her off, "seriously speaking, markets have their place. But there are thousands, millions, of young Indians who can't go to a place like Khan Market, who can't navigate Old Delhi all the time. Who don't want to, who don't have the time. Young people everywhere, from all backgrounds, are getting jobs, they're living alone or with friends, they have disposable income, and they want to get on with things. Our market research shows a high percentage of those entering the workforce want a more concentrated, immersive, convenient shopping experience *everywhere*, in B-towns, satellite cities, in places that people like you don't dream of going."

"*Your* market research?"

"Yes."

"You're building malls. Aren't you?"

"Of course," he said.

"You're twenty-three years old."

"Twenty-four."

"Wow." She glanced at the Dictaphone to see if it was still running. "And there I was thinking you were a patron of the arts."

"The two aren't mutually exclusive," he said.

"Well, no," she fumbled.

"Who do you think funded art, historically speaking? The Medicis were bankers."

"Yeah, I mean, of course."

"Besides, I have bigger plans than malls in mind. I want to turn Delhi into a truly global city."

"You?"

"Yes, me."

"Well, that's kind of insane."

"Are you happy living here?"

"Excuse me?"

"I hear you're not. I hear you want to leave."

She was taken aback. Hari must have told him.

"And I don't blame you," he went on. "Trust me, I didn't grow up with the West beamed into my living room like you, but I've traveled, I've seen how people live in other parts of the world, I've seen what's available, what's open, what's possible. We lag so far behind here. We have all the potential, the human capital, we just have to harness it."

Did he do this with everyone? Could he simply not help himself?

"Let me ask you something," he continued. "What do London, Paris, and Singapore have in common?"

"I don't know. Tell me."

"No, I'm asking you, what do they have in common?"

She shrugged. "Capital cities?"

"They have rivers."

"OK. And?"

"And what do we have here in Delhi?"

She was rapidly tiring of his rhetorical grandstanding.

"A river."

"Now listen," he said, launching into a monologue. "Throughout history, rivers and cities have been entwined. A river is a city's lifeline, its artery." And she knew as he spoke that he'd practiced this, that it was a speech he'd prepared. "At first trade, then industry, then leisure. And all the best cities in the world have something in common. They *face* their rivers. Their rivers become their centerpiece." Maybe it was even an essay he'd written once. "Now what do we do? Right here in Delhi? To the Yamuna?"

She shook her head, because she knew she was expected only to listen.

"We turn our back to it. Think about it," he said, slipping out of the prepared and into the evangelical. "Imagine the city from above, picture it, can you see it? Can you see the Yamuna running through? Now think about all the colonies, the things everyone does every day. Does anyone look at the river? Does anyone have anything to do with the river? No, we shun it, we ignore it. It should be *sacred*, but it becomes profane, fucked up with sewage, banked by slums. And we just accept this. Right?"

"Right."

"Now imagine the Yamuna sparkling clean. Imagine *swimming* in it. Imagine boating in it. Imagine marinas and promenades." He grew more animated as he spoke. "Imagine nature reserves, wetlands, opera houses! Imagine a business district, skyscrapers, trams, parks, coffee shops." He painted a vista with his hands. "Imagine finishing work and going down to the river for a cocktail, a Michelin Star meal, then the theater, then a stroll along its banks." She watched him, pleased with the vision he conjured in his mind's eye. "You can do it in London," he said. "Why not here?"

"I don't know."

"You can," he said. "Because I'm going to build it."

And with that, he was done.

"Well," she said, "that's . . ."

"Ambitious."

"That's one word. Another is crazy."

"You don't think I can do it."

"It's not that," she said, "it's just, you know, that's London, this is Delhi. I mean, how do you expect to . . . ?"

"That's for me to worry about."

Something about the way he spoke antagonized her.

She knew instinctively that he was wrong, that there was more to it than that, but she didn't have the ammunition to fight back his broad-stroked bravado. Still, he had started to irritate her. She thought, *What does he want from me?*

"What are you thinking?" he asked.

"Why?" she said.

"What do you mean 'why'?"

"It doesn't matter."

"You don't think I can do this?"

"No, it's just, what does it matter what I think?"

"Because I'm asking you."

"Then I think it's a nice idea."

"Which means bullshit."

"No," she replied, "it's a nice idea."

"But?"

"Nothing."

"Why don't you come work for me?"

She laughed out loud. "What?"

"You're clearly wasted in your job."

"Oh, I see."

"You could come on board, help with PR, media, whatever."

"Yeah, you can be my vocation," she said mockingly.

The venom did its thing. They lapsed into silence.

She couldn't get a grip on the situation, couldn't tell if he was serious, sincere, deluded, if he was toying with her, if this was just a circuitous routine to try to get her into bed (it was failing!), or whether he was just exercising his arrogance on her.

The silence went on, and he held all the cards.

So she thought: fuck it.

"You know," she said, "I was actually debating whether or not to do a profile on you. For my nonvocation. After I met you that night." Where was she going with this? "I was excited. It was going to be something frothy, fun, but with a serious undercurrent, for the culture pages, you know, about the parties, the restaurants. How the city was changing." She watched him listening to her.

"OK."

Was she really going to do this?

"And then I asked a colleague about you."

He placed his fingers together, touched the tips to his lips.

"OK."

"Do you know what he said to me?"

Why was she doing this?

He sat motionless, waiting.

"He said: 'Sunny Wadia? That joker?'"

She felt the rush of adrenaline up her spine, a scarcity of oxygen in her lungs.

He remained motionless.

"Right afterward he said, 'Do you know who his father is?'"

As soon as she said it, her stomach dropped. She felt sick. And she caught the red light of the Dictaphone in the corner of her eye. Surely he knew it was still running?

"Do you?" he asked, turning to look at her. They held one another's gaze. "Or did he tell you?"

"He told me something."

He inhaled long and slow. "You know, I've dealt with this all my life." He lit a fresh cigarette, drifted off into a private land of contemplation. "All my life."

She didn't dare move.

"So? What did he say?"

"My colleague?"

"Yes."

"He said he was a . . ." She couldn't finish.

"What?"

She resolved to be straight with him.

"He said your father was one of Ram Singh's cronies."

"Ram Singh . . ." He closed his eyes, smiled again, nodded to himself. Then he began to speak. "My father is a businessman, pure and simple. He wasn't born with money or connections; he had no friends in high places. His father before him was an alcoholic, a grain merchant. Papa left school and took over the business when he was fifteen. His father died soon after. He did what he had to do to survive. Out there in UP. Where no one helps you if you don't help yourself. Where the odds are stacked against you. He worked every hour God sent. He worked in his sleep. But he wasn't like other people. He had vision. He had a talent for making money. In every rupee note he could see three fifty-paisa coins. Is that a crime?"

"No," she said.

"The only thing he's guilty of is ambition. Of rising above his station. Did my father cut corners on the way? Yes. This is India. The game is rigged, the rules are stacked, you people make the rules in the first place. You already have everything, and you don't want to share. So sometimes things must be taken. But ultimately, he gives the people what they want. People like you, your colleague, they've always talked about him behind his back. I spent my school days listening to it. You know he sent me to a good school, he wanted to improve me, to mix with people like you. I was expelled. My classmates spoke just loud enough that I could hear. I could be reminded that we'd never be like them. Thing is, the world has changed. I don't hear them whispering anymore. Instead, they come asking for jobs. Instead, they come to the party. Of course, your colleague, he'll never change his opinion, I'm sure of it. He can afford not to. I bet he never really had to struggle, right?"

"I don't know. Everyone has their own struggle."

"But not like us." He put his cigarette out. "It's a struggle to get to the top. To get there you have to learn to be ruthless. But once you're there, then you can start to do good. My father is clean."

"And what about Vicky?"

There was a thrill in the dropping of the name.

His face was unreadable.

"I haven't seen him in years."

"He's part of your family," she said.

"But he has nothing to do with our future." He leaned forward and clicked the Dictaphone off. "We freed ourselves from him a long time ago."

"What do you want me to do with this?" she asked.

She waited for him to remove the tape, to put it in his pocket or set fire to it in the ashtray, but he just slid it over to her.

"That's up to you."

He stood from the chair, smoothed down his shirt and pants.

"If you'll excuse me, I'm late for a meeting. It was nice talking to you, Ms. Kapur. Ajay will see you out."

At home in her room, lying on the bed with her earphones on, she listened to the tape. She rewound it to Khan Market. First the voxpops, street noise in the background, then a click and the loud silence of his apartment. She closed her eyes and returned to the sofa, listened to Vijay, 23, Call Center Worker, listened to that voice and could not match it to the face, to the clothes, to the apartment. Then she mentally stripped him of the props, as it were, put him in cheap shirt and pants, placed him on the roadside, sitting on a motorcycle by a chai stall, and she was almost there, she could almost see him. But no, it fell away. Wasn't he faking it, after all? Wasn't his voice a caricature of all those men whose daily struggles he had as little insight into as she? He had merely been playing the role of one of his potential customers, putting words he wanted to hear into his doppelgänger's mouth. She paused the tape. She wondered how far he'd really come. And how fast. All that talk of Italy and Japan. How much was real? Stripped to essentials, relieved of his props, who was he?

She listened on as he talked about the river, opera houses and business districts and promenades. In the apartment all she'd heard was his pitch, but now she heard his hope, his enthusiasm, his energy. In hindsight, free of the temptation to intervene, to mock, to correct or challenge or adjust, free to listen and empathize, she found it all fascinating. He really believed it, she thought. This was the flip side of the misery, destruction, poverty, the world Dean waded through. And didn't she want Delhi to be like *this*? Wouldn't it be so much easier than the struggle? Dean's cold voice rose to meet her conscience. "Struggle?" it said. "You're not even in the struggle." She heard her own voice saying, "And then I asked a colleague about you." She winced. The words reached her ears. "Sunny Wadia? That joker?" She clicked off the tape a moment, braced herself, and pressed PLAY. "Do you know who his father is?"

She studied his responses, his speech about his father's struggles, and realized he'd deflected things, hadn't really answered anything. She'd let him, by being chicken. There'd been an opening for her, when he'd asked what Dean had said. "One of Ram Singh's cronies," came her voice. But if she'd been smart, she wouldn't have mentioned Ram Singh at all—the name was both too direct and too vague; instead she should have pushed him. A criminal. A gangster. Watched his response. She cursed herself for being too impulsive, not critical and objective enough. Still, she'd managed to get that question in about his uncle. She listened to herself.

"And what about Vicky?"

She'd said the name so casually, with such familiarity, as if they were talking about a family friend. It felt transgressive. She rewound the tape and listened to herself, tried to parse the second's silence after the question. But he'd given nothing away.

He had, however, thrown her out.

She tried to figure out what the hell had gone on in there. Flirting, definitely; they had chemistry. Had he bitten off more than he could chew? Despite his professing to liking her back talk. Certainly he couldn't have expected her to bring up his father, his uncle. Maybe he didn't think of himself as "known" in that way. Maybe he was too busy trying to be known himself, for his own deeds. So many questions. She was left with the image of an egoistic young man, swaddled in wealth and luxury, craving importance but cursed by a fatal insecurity. Just the kind of man she fell for.

She reached for her bedside drawer, pulled out his Zippo. Lit a cigarette.

She spent the rest of that evening writing up the real voxpop interviews she'd conducted and the fake ones she hadn't. Fake names, fake quotes.

She wrote up Sunny's last.

Vijay, 23. She added a later line, when Sunny spoke in his own voice.

"Adapt or die?" her editor called out from his desk the next day. "This fellow really said that?"

"He did," Neda replied.

"My God," he said. "This city gets harder by the day."

2.

She waited for some message from Sunny all week, some sign. She wondered if she should reach out herself, apologize. For what? Sorry I insulted your family. The more she thought about it, the more it seemed like a bad date. But still she was drawn to him. She thought about him all the time. On the other hand, she was always on the cusp of starting a dialogue with Dean. Saying: Listen, this thing happened, I think you should know. In her head she handed over the tape and he listened in his office, she sitting beside him, watching his face. Would he be proud of her?

"Good work," Dean said, in the bad version in her head. "Get close to him. Discover his plans."

In truth Dean might say, "That joker? Don't waste your time."

One day she asked Dean about the demolitions. (Another thing she'd been thinking of. Why hadn't she mentioned the demolitions to Sunny?

Why hadn't she articulated a vision of the city where land isn't just waiting to be commodified?)

"They're awful, I know."

"But?"

"Playing devil's advocate . . ."

"Go on."

"The Yamuna Pushta. Isn't that land better used for, I don't know, the city?"

"It is being used for the city. People are living there."

"But I mean, the city as a whole. Like London or Paris. Everyone's drawn to the rivers there. They're the heart of the city. Here we turn our backs to them."

She realized she was parroting Sunny's words.

He gave her a long, piteous look.

"India is not Europe," he said. "The Yamuna is not the Thames."

About two weeks had passed when her editor tapped her on the shoulder.

"Neda, what are your evening plans?"

"Nothing, sir."

"Here." He handed her a press release. "Sridhar can't make it. You go."

She looked at the sheet of glossy paper: "Dinesh Singh Kumar, President, RDP Youth Wing, invites you to attend the inauguration of the Uttar Pradesh Tourism Initiative: Toward the World Class."

"Toward the World Class," she repeated.

"The usual nonsense. So don't waste your time. In and out, write a few hundred words, file it, get your free drinks if you're lucky."

Dinesh Singh, son of Ram Singh. What were the chances of that? What were the chances Sunny would be there? Lurking in the background. If their fathers were in league, surely so were the sons, despite Sunny's protests.

She'd seen a lot of Dinesh in the papers recently, he was on a solid PR drive, trying to burnish the progressive credentials of his avowedly unprogressive father's government and not doing an entirely bad job of it. His image was a break from the usual entitled and frankly dumb politician's son. He'd studied history and politics in Canada, he'd imbibed the lessons of statesmanship, he was as urbane and chic (in a rural, son-of-the-soil, professorial, wire-rimmed sort of way) as his father was a hands-in-the-dirt political thug. He talked a good game, he wanted to build on his father's decisive victory and modernize the state. Naturally he had his eye on the chief ministership. But for now his mission was to promote tourism in UP. Tourism beyond the Taj Mahal. Tourism Toward the World Class.

Neda went to Dean before leaving. She showed him the press release.

"Toward the world class," he said distractedly. "That's cute."

"Do you have any questions? I'm taking requests."

He handed back the sheet. "Ask him how many hotels in the state are owned by politicians affiliated with his father, and of those hotels, how many are actively engaged in illegal activities such as prostitution and human trafficking."

"I get that on tape?"

"I'll buy you dinner."

The press conference was in one of the banquet halls of the Park Hyatt. They served drinks: there was a decent bar—four uniformed staff standing behind a long banquet table at one side of the room. It had been draped in a white linen tablecloth, there were prepoured glasses of red and white wine, along with orange juice and cola, then bottles of gin, whisky, and vodka under the watchful eye of the bartenders, along with ice buckets, bottles of mixers, the works.

"Quite a spread," one seasoned journalist crooned into Neda's ear. He smelled of talcum powder and Old Spice. Fifty or so chairs were arranged in eight rows, facing a raised platform with three chairs and a lectern to its side. A projector and screen had been set up, attached to a laptop. She took a glass of white wine and found a seat to the side in the second-to-last row. There was no sign of Sunny.

———

Dinesh Singh appeared on time and began with a presentation. He stood at the lectern, the image of a serious, engaged, civic-minded young man. He had a slightly brittle, insistent charm. He looked awkward on the stage, but not shy. He started well enough: he acknowledged UP had a long way to go, that there were all manner of problems in the state, issues that took precedence over tourism. Namely education, health care, security, jobs. But tourism was one industry that could be promoted alongside these, tied up with education, to stimulate progress and growth. Then he started to lose her. He began to drone on. Her heart sank. The room was hot despite the AC. The wine went to her head. She zoned out as he went through a slideshow of the various architectural wonders of the state. He shifted, after what seemed an age, to the ecological diversity. It was dark in the room. The bar had unexpectedly closed. She slumped in her seat and thought about texting Dean. She composed: "This is dumb." But just as she was about to press SEND, the lights went on. Polite coughs, the rustle of papers. The floor would be open to questions. She kept telling herself, leave after the next question, just get up and walk to the door and walk out. But she stayed. The questions asked seemed preapproved. What was the timeline for success? What was his favorite food? She was getting irritated. She put her hand up. He saw her and smiled and pointed. "Yes, the young lady right there." She took the mic from the assistant. "Neda Kapur, *Delhi Post.*"

"Please, go on."

"Before you invite the world to visit, will you be reviewing the number of hotels in the state involved in criminal activities such as prostitution and human trafficking?"

Dinesh didn't flinch or miss a beat.

"That's a very good question, and an important issue."

She felt a surge. "Especially since many of these are reportedly owned by associates of your father."

There was an audible intake of breath, voices chattering, but Dinesh kept his cool.

"There will be a comprehensive review of hotels, and those deemed worthy of international tourists will receive special certification. Thank you."

And he was done.

She watched him swamped by a group of lackeys, swept from the stage. Sunny was nowhere to be seen. She was buzzing with adrenaline. She felt the eyes of other journalists on her. She'd been too bold, reckless. Old Spice journalist leaned into her. "That was a sticky wicket!"

She gathered her things and hurried away. She felt sick suddenly. She was almost out of the hall when a voice called from behind.

"Ms. Kapur?"

She turned to see none other than Dinesh Singh.

"I'm running to another meeting, but I was wondering if we could talk?"

"Sure."

She found herself walking with him into the hotel lobby.

Expecting to be chastised, threatened even.

But no.

"I admire you," he said. "It takes nerve to ask a question like that. And you're right to ask it. Off the record, there's a lot we can do to clean up the state, and a lot of what's happening is happening on our watch. But you understand the nature of politics in UP. You can't win power without money and muscle, and that comes with compromises. You understand this is off the record?"

"Yes."

"The truth of the matter is, I want to clean all this up, but I can't do it alone. We need help, and you're exactly the kind of young person we're looking for." They entered the lobby. "Government should be transparent. It should be honest, vigilant, valiant."

His assistants and minders were herding them on.

He fished out his business card.

"I'd like to invite you to Lucknow as my guest. We're to have a youth summit soon. We need journalists to communicate our message."

"And if your message and practice don't match?"

"Judge me on my record." He wrote a phone number on the back of the card. "And get in touch anytime. This is my personal number."

She took the card. "What would your father say about this?"

"The defining question of my life . . ."

That's when she saw him.

Sunny.

Standing stiff in the lobby in a boxy navy suit and gray tie, his face fixed in pensive solemnity. He was playing with his BlackBerry. Her pulse quickened and her stomach dropped.

"Ah," Dinesh said, "my dining partner."

Sunny looked up with the same poker face from Khan Market, glanced at Dinesh, at her, back down at his phone.

She felt a wave of nausea. And anger.

"Neda Kapur," Dinesh Singh said, "this is Sunny Wadia."

Sunny didn't look up.

"Neda is a journalist," Dinesh said.

"Good for her," Sunny replied. "Shall we?"

Dinesh squeezed Sunny on the shoulder. "My friend here is shy."

"And shyness makes him rude, which is an unfortunate trait."

"Our table's waiting," Sunny said.

"He seems to have woken on the worst side of the bed. But please, do get in touch. Arrange that trip. And if you need anything, anything at all, just call me."

"Thank you."

"Now forgive me," Dinesh said, as Sunny turned away, "but I have to ask, what will you write?"

"Don't worry," she said, glancing at Sunny, "standard boilerplate." She looked back to Dinesh and smiled. "There's no reason to make an enemy of you. Yet."

He laughed. "I look forward to your call."

And he was gone, leading Sunny away. She watched them gliding toward the hotel's Japanese restaurant, waiting for either one of them to look back. Neither did.

What had she expected from Sunny? Civility at least? It felt cruel, the way he'd spoken. Though some part of her took heart from this—he cared enough. She walked outside the front doors, past the metal detectors, and lit a cigarette. She found her valet ticket, handed it over, and waited for her car. The cigarette was almost finished when her Maruti came creaking and chugging up the driveway and she thought of Sunny's words, how she can waltz in anywhere, but with the knowledge of that now pointed out to her, she became self-conscious, she felt ashamed.

Just as she was about to get into her car she heard a voice behind her.

"Ms. Kapur?"

"Yes?"

"My name is Amit." He issued an ingratiating smile. In his outstretched hand was a hotel key card wallet. "Mr. Wadia wishes to inform you he'll be late for your meeting."

"Our meeting?"

"In his suite."

She covered her surprise.

"How late?"

"No longer than an hour."

"An hour?"

She made a show of anger, but secretly she was thrilled. "That's difficult for me, Amit." She took the card. "But I'll manage. Which number?"

"Eight hundred."

Amit ordered the valet to return her car and swept her toward the lobby.

"I'll escort you inside." She was waved through the metal detectors. "Mr. Wadia told me to tell you to make yourself at home."

He led her across the lobby toward a waiting elevator.

She strained her neck to look inside the restaurant.

"If you'd like something else, I'm more than happy to help. This is my card, my personal number, call me anytime."

"Thank you, Amit," she said as she took his card and stepped into the elevator.

"Mr. Wadia's Business Suite," Amit said to the operator.

As they ascended, she was glad for the drabness of her work clothes, and the alibi they offered against the accusations in the operator's eyes.

The key card clicked open to suite 800, it was adorned with the usual luxurious anonymity, mosaic marble, a mahogany writing desk, a spacious living area, an office, a bedroom off to the side. There was none of the standard paraphernalia of hospitality though, no complimentary fruit basket, no wine bottle with a "personalized" note; the suite had been lived in, it was tense with Sunny's presence. Books, magazines. The writing desk in the corner spilling over with work, books on urban planning and history, architectural blueprints, logo designs. She leafed through the various sheets: the precise layout of a three-story mall, a pencil sketch of an elegant low-rise building sweeping across a hillside. Another showed a large, squat, modernist art gallery on a wide, reed-banked river, a sanitized, beautified version of the Yamuna. Below it, an architect's rendering of a riverbank full of smiling modern Indians, eating ice cream, holding hands, while corporate buildings and trams loomed in the background. There was an open notebook to the side, pencil set crosswise, but the handwriting, a mixture of Hindi and English, was utterly indecipherable.

In the recessed space below the TV there was a liquor collection. Black Label, Woodford Reserve, Wild Turkey, Patrón, Hendrick's. Inside the fridge there were a few bottles of Asahi, a few bottles of Schweppes Tonic Water, a few of soda, a few more of his precious Belgian mineral water, a bottle of Cocchi Americano, two bottles of Veuve Clicquot. She took a tumbler from the row of glasses and poured a large measure of the Woodford. Sniffed it as she carried it through to the bedroom. Just a quick look.

The bed was perfectly made, no sign of life, no sign of hurry. She opened the wardrobe. Eight white shirts, three blue, several others of various colors. Eight suit jackets, five pairs of trousers, several jeans. She ran her hand across the tailoring, the expensive material. She leaned in and inhaled his scent. She was strangely moved by their hanging helplessness, their passivity. The absence of his body in them. She shut the wardrobe door. Carried her whisky into the bathroom, examined his cologne: Davidoff Cool Water. She sprayed it on her wrist. Ah, yes, that was him.

Back outside in the main room, she waited. She found a pack of cigarettes in one of his drawers, lit one, dragged a chair across to the window, and pulled back the curtain. It was six thirty now. The traffic was crawling bumper to bumper, the headlights of cars on the roads in the distance twinkled at regular intervals. Delhi always looked its best from a distance. Never more beautiful than this, or from the air, flying in at night, tracing the concealed city of the ridge, the prehistoric backbone where no lights glowed, the regular streets of the Secretariat, the hive of South Delhi. From a distance, or very close up, standing at a chai stall surrounded by noise. No middle ground. What ground was this? She sipped her whisky and closed her eyes. What ground was this? His scent in the back of her throat. The AC hadn't come on, only a few sidelights were shining in the room. It was almost dark in there. She hadn't inserted the key card in its slot. She should get up and do that. But no, no. Better just to sit here in the dim light, waiting. The whisky slipped down. Why was she here? What did he expect of her?

She saw a shadow underneath the door and heard a key card sliding into the lock. The door opened, the key card was pushed into the holder inside, and all the lights turned on, the AC lurched into life, the twilight of the room was banished. Sunny stormed in and her reverie was broken, he was agitated, he glanced at her as if he were surprised, as if he'd forgotten she had been sent here. He said nothing, fixed himself a large Black Label, swallowed it in one mouthful, fixed another. A dark, tight energy radiated from him. She didn't move.

He took off his suit jacket and threw it on the floor, took his drink into the bedroom without a word.

She heard him sitting on the bed.

She counted to twenty.

Nothing.

She counted another ten, then walked toward the front door.

"Where are you going?" he said.

She froze.

"Home."

"Come here."

There was a cruelty in his voice.

"No."

She heard him sigh. "Please." And this time his words were drenched in loneliness.

She walked toward the bedroom door, stood on the threshold looking in.

He was sitting on the edge of the bed, crumpled, his clenched fists on his knees.

He was trying to control himself.

"What happened?" she said.

He seemed unable to speak.

"Sunny."

He looked up.

"What happened?"

"I can't stand him."

"Who? Dinesh?"

He loosened his tie, unbuttoned his shirt.

"He thinks he's the smartest person in the room."

"I got that impression," she said, leaning on the doorframe.

He rubbed his head with his hands. "Dumb fuck . . ."

"It's OK."

"No, it's not."

He reset himself, spoke softly, calmly. "What are you doing here?"

"You sent for me."

"No, I mean here with him."

"He held a press conference. It's my job."

His phone beeped. He checked it and put it down, got up and walked past her out into the main room. "I need a drink." She watched him at the cabinet. "You're not in a hurry, are you?"

"I have no pressing engagements, no."

He poured two large measures of Woodford. He walked toward her, passed one over. "I need to unwind."

She looked around. "I like your office. Your hideaway."

He sipped the whisky. "I have a few."

He took a seat at the desk, took the cigarettes from his desk drawer and lit one.

She drew closer, sat up on the edge of the desk.

She picked up one of the drawings, the pencil sketch of the house on the hillside. "What's this one?"

"A house in the Himalayas." Pride entered his voice. "I designed it myself. A retirement plan. A hotel maybe. I'm not sure yet." He took the drawing from her, laid it on the table, and fetched a pencil from the desk. He drew two parallel lines through the back of the structure, started them again at the front. "I wanted to build it on a stream, have hydro as well as solar power." In the background he drew mountaintops, making jagged snow lines near their peaks. "And I wanted it higher up. Somewhere near Rohtang. Or Auli maybe." She watched him working and was touched by the attention he gave to the work. He put the pencil down and slid the paper away. "But it's hard to build in Himachal. Permits, local objections. The local deities speak through local men and local men are hard to please."

"Can't your father help?"

He bristled at the question. "He's not God."

She studied his face.

"This Yamuna plan of yours. It's pretty godlike. I've been thinking of it."

"Yeah?"

"Thinking about it a lot. I work with someone who only sees the other side. The people being evicted."

"Is that the someone who called me a joker?"

"In this vision of yours," she went on, "where do those people go?"

"In my vision they've already gone."

"That's convenient."

"Because they're already getting resettled. You know that, right? They're getting fresh plots of land, pukka homes, electricity, running water, real toilets. They don't have to live in slums. They only lived there because the government didn't build enough housing, but that's been resolved."

She wanted to believe him.

He said, "Everyone can win here. We romanticize poverty too much. India doesn't need to be this way. We can raise everyone up."

She took a cigarette from his pack and lit it. Shook her head and sighed with wonder. "Sunny, Sunny, Sunny . . ."

He seemed surprised by her tone, the tender use of his name.

She slid off the desk and walked to the window. "We're *so* young." He watched her watching Delhi in the night. "And you make me feel like there's so much we can do."

He didn't speak, but she could feel his gaze enveloping her.

"You know," she went on, "I wasn't sure I'd see you again."

"I was waiting," he replied after a moment, "for some bullshit article to come out."

She glanced back at him. "I wouldn't do that to you. You should know that. I didn't play anyone that tape. I have it in my drawer at home."

"Yeah?"

"I listen to it. Listen to you speaking Hindi."

"That's not me."

"Listen to you talking about your father."

"You look good," he said.

"That's one way to change the subject."

"I want to fuck you."

She looked at him warily. "Is this how it starts?"

He stood, came up behind her slowly.

"If you want it to."

She could hear his breathing.

"And then?"

She felt his right hand on her waist.

His left.

His body pressed into hers.

His mouth on her neck through her hair.

"I like to get drunk," she said, staring out at the glowing city. "I like to see the city from far, far away. Is that so wrong?"

"No."

"I'm tired of being good."

She closed her eyes.

"Where are you going?"

She was sliding out of the bed.

"To wash out your cum."

He frowned and lit a cigarette. "Don't be so vulgar."

She laughed because he meant it.

She'd expected it. What she hadn't expected was the intensity. He'd barely pulled her into the bedroom, barely taken off her clothes, barely pulled her panties down before he'd climbed up behind her, held her wrists in his fists, braced her legs with his own. She was already wet, and he was hard as hell. He pushed himself inside and she'd collapsed to the duvet, buried her head in the pillow, let herself go. "I want you to tie me up. Blindfold me. Take all my senses away." She felt a flash of desire in him like white-hot metal in the sun.

———

"Why don't you come work for me?" he said.

She was in the bathroom trying to fix the kajal around her eyes.

"No. It's not a good idea."

She came back and lit a cigarette and lay on her belly with her legs in the air like she'd seen girls do in movies.

"Why not?"

"What would I do? Be your secretary?"

"Be anything you want."

"It's not a good idea."

"Why?" he ran his hand over her ass, slapped it lightly. "I already fucked you. It's not like you have to worry about that."

"Shut up." She rolled over onto her back. "And what about when you stop wanting to fuck me?"

He didn't have anything to say to that.

"Let's keep it simple," she said.

"You'll come around."

Her phone began ringing in her bag out in the living room.

She listened out, rolled her eyes. "Probably my mother."

It was probably Dean.

"Aren't you going to answer?"

"It can wait."

It stopped.

He closed his eyes and she ran her fingers through his pubic hair, cradled his soft dick. "Bigger than I'd hoped for," she smiled. He responded to her touch, or her words. "Ready to go again?"

"What happened earlier tonight?" she asked. They were drinking whisky. She was yawning. They had been napping.

"What do you mean?"

"Why were you so agitated?"

He opened his eyes and stared at the ceiling a long time.

Then suddenly he began to speak.

"One day when I was a little kid," he said, "my father took me to Lala Ka Bazar. This is back when we lived in Meerut. I remember being in a rickshaw with him, pressed up against his body, I'd never been so close to him. We climbed off and we walked through the alleyways. He'd never taken me out like this before. He'd never taken me anywhere. I was so excited. So happy because all my life I'd been ignored. We reached a toy store, and the other customers were asked to leave. There we were, he, I, the shop owner. I was told by my father to pick out any toy I liked, as many as I wanted. "Go," he said. So I did. I ran around. I spent a good long time searching and finally I settled on a few things—a red truck with flashing lights, a small, hard, yellow ball that bounced really well off the walls, and this toy gun that made different sounds when it fired. My father didn't say anything to me, but he had them set aside and then we left. I was confused, but I daren't ask why we hadn't taken them. I decided they were being sent home for me. I waited and I waited. Days. Weeks. But they never came. I never forgot. I never stopped waiting."

He paused, tangled up in his memories.

"Tonight," he went, his voice growing cold, "Dinesh said to me, 'Your father was like a father to me growing up. All the important moments in my life, he was there.' He meant it as a compliment. He thought he was flattering me. Then he described one certain birthday, the first time he met his Bunty Uncle. He said he'd never forget the gifts. A gun, a truck, a yellow bouncing ball."

"That's awful. Did you tell him your story?"

"Are you mad? Why would I humiliate myself like that?"

"I don't know."

They lay in silence for some time.

"What about your mother?"

He breathed slowly. "What about her?"

"Didn't she do something?"

He shook his head.

"She was dead by then."

"When did she die?"

"When I was five."

"I'm sorry."

He sat up, climbed out of bed. "Don't be. The bitch hung herself."

Her phone began to ring.

She ignored it.

"You should get that," he said.

"I don't want to. It's not important."

It rang off and went silent. Ten seconds later it started ringing again.

"Get it," he said, "or I throw it out the window."

It was Dean. She stood naked with the phone, looking at the twinkling sulfury lights of Delhi. He asked her where she was, said he wanted to meet her for dinner at 4S. He said, "How can you resist the lure of chilli chicken and cold beer?" She couldn't think of anything she wanted to do less right now. She calibrated her voice as if she were speaking to her mother. She told Dean she was having a drink with a friend, that she'd finish up and call back later. She was still reeling from Sunny's words. The practiced callousness that could not hide his pain. She wanted to know more.

But back in the bedroom Sunny was on his BlackBerry.

"I have someone coming over," he said. "So you should get dressed and go."

She was hurt.

"OK."

"It's work."

"I said OK."

They both began to get dressed in silence.

After he'd put his trousers on, he stopped to watch her.

"What?" she said.

"It's Dinesh. I was supposed to be with him all evening. I blew him off for a few hours to see you."

"Am I supposed to be grateful?"

"Don't get jealous."

"I'm not."

"I have a life."

"So do I."

"We're all good, then."

She finished dressing.

"Listen, about your mother," she said.

"I don't want to talk about it."

"Well," she continued, with a fake, breezy smile, "that was fun. I'll see you around."

She walked toward the front door, put the key card on the sideboard.

She was almost there when he reached her. Grabbed her and turned her around and pinned her against the wall.

"What?" she demanded. "What!? Get off, you're hurting me."

His eyes searched hers.

What did he want to say? Do?

Was he really hurting her?

She didn't know.

"You're not . . . ," he said, "like anyone else."

"Spare me."

"I mean it."

He tried to kiss her, and she turned her face away.

"I mean it," he said again.

Then he kissed her, and she didn't resist, and then he let her go.

She met the soft eyes of the elevator operator. Inhaled the nullifying scent of jasmine and lemongrass. The pain around her wrists. Too much whisky in her blood. Her head spun. She was grateful for the lobby. She was grateful for the hot summer air. She stood at the same spot, with the valet, waiting for her Maruti to chug its way up the driveway, but now everything had changed. She drove off and accelerated through the streets rashly until she got a grip on herself and pulled to the side of the road. Her hand was shaking. She lit a cigarette. The day had escalated from nothing, detonated. Laborers passed along the roadside in the dark, smoking beedis, glancing in without expression. She called Dean. "Hey. Yeah. I'm on my way. Yeah, I got out of it. I'll be there in twenty."

Dean was already sitting upstairs in 4S waiting for her. He'd taken one of the front two tables, where the light from the sign outside bounced and flashed through the plate-glass window and bathed his face in neon. The narrow space was packed, as usual, with students. Dark and a little grimy and so very comforting to her—the waiters knew her by sight, they greeted her as she came in and twisted up the steep stairs.

He saw her emerge at the top and he already had his hand in the air in greeting.

She smiled at the sight of him, a big kid among all the college kids, an amiable professor.

He'd already ordered two Old Monks and Coke and a plate of spring rolls. She picked up one of the spring rolls as she was sitting down and took a great bite. "God, I'm starving."

"So," he said, "how was boy wonder?"

She stuffed the spring roll in her mouth, spoke through the food.

Somehow it was easier to lie that way.

"Oh, you know, world-class this, world-class that, a lot of bullshit."

He shook his head. "If I hear that fucking word one more time I'm going to scream. I was at an RWA meeting in Sarojini Nagar, they kept saying it, they kept talking about the need to make Delhi world class. That fucking phrase. Global city, world class. The shop window of the world. Anyway, enough of that. I heard you actually asked the question."

"Yeah, it must have been the wine."

"I'm impressed. How did he take it?"

Her mind turned back to Sunny. She felt him inside her, smelled his cologne and his sweat on her skin, his tongue on her tongue. She could feel the weight of his arms like phantom limbs. She reminded herself to buy the Pill 72. Her mind fixated on him entering her, the intoxicating sensation of being filled and consumed.

"Hmmm?"

"How did Dinesh take it?"

"He offered to take me to Lucknow actually. He said I was the kind of fearless reporter the world needed, or some such rubbish. No way am I going. I don't fall for that kind of stuff." She waved for the waiter. "Shall we order?"

A couple of days later, in the morning, she got a message on her phone.

—9 pm Park Hyatt. Japanese. Dinner.

She finished work at seven thirty. She'd taken a change of clothes. A black dress. Thick kohl, but no lipstick. She became self-conscious when she entered. Felt awkward, visible. She spoke tentatively with the Japanese restaurant's maître d', said she was there to join Sunny Wadia's party. The maître d' became excessively deferential; he led her through a corridor inside the restaurant, down another private corridor into a passageway with several beautifully painted, lacquered sliding screens. He stopped at one and opened it. There was a long table with seating for twenty, but there was only Sunny inside.

The maître d' said, "Ma'am, enjoy."

She stepped in; he closed the screen door.

3.

So began a brief golden period. Two very different kinds of lives. By day the scorching, howling city, and Sunny Wadia by night. The cars would pick her up and transport her at speed through the sanctuaries of Delhi, beyond price or question or pain. She split herself in two. The monsoon hit at the start of

July. The evictions in the city continued apace. She was disconnected, she slid above. Dean was out interviewing, recording, collecting evidence, collecting testimony, fighting against the tide. The city was changing shape and character before their eyes, being hollowed out, gutted. Dean followed every demolition, followed the evictions, mapped out the routes from the scoured centers to the resettlement colonies. At work she transcribed the testimony he collected, interview after interview of citizens whose lives were being broken like quarry stones to be used elsewhere, building blocks for other, more profitable lives. At her desk, she swirled in the vortex of these words, she felt pity, sorrow, but when she was done, she packed up her things and drove out into the night to be with him. She knew it was wrong.

That first meal was perfection. Never again would she have that. Alone in that private banquet room, Kobe beef, a 1993 Romirasco Barolo, gourmet fries, his eyes taking pleasure in her every bite, every sip of wine, living his own pleasures through hers. They moved to a dazzling sake, drank in square wooden cups, followed it up with Cuban cigars, their feet up on the table, snifters of Venezuelan rum cupped in their palms, as Sunny regaled her with stories of his travels through Europe, his awakening to sex and drugs and the finer things of life. They retired through a private elevator to another one of his suites. Drunk, laughing, owning the world. In the room they fucked and barely spoke.

She was swallowed into his group. "Like Paris," someone said one night, "Sunny Wadia is a moveable feast." Their affair was kept in the gray though. She understood this. He had a persona, a court. She had no desire to become its queen. She was content to watch on the margins with a secret inside. She arrived at these grand meals, sometimes in small restaurants, sometimes in five-star banquet halls, always a little shy, a little reticent, always alone, always late. Hari returned to the city. He'd been in Bombay after Kasol. *He* noticed the change. They looked at one another across the table sometimes, across the penthouse when a party was full on and she knew he knew, and his face was sad, because he'd lost her again, but he was happy she was alive to the world. They didn't call one another, didn't speak anymore. She was someone else.

She came to understand going for a meal with Sunny was not about the food. It wasn't about the drink. It wasn't about the size of the bill at the end, which no one ever saw. It was the performance, it was waiting to see what would happen next in this city of theirs, in this world they had conjured. Sunny called them and they came, they ordered wildly and barely touched their plates, they drank and drank and laughed and screamed, howled and told stories and were scandalous and outraged, they made demands of the place, they threatened its foundations, then Sunny paid the bill of his indulged children and they left.

He was looking at her from his seat, drinking, laughing, watching, watching. Some of the men were debating property. Others were talking about the pranks they used to play in school. Food kept coming, dish after extravagant dish, waves of such fine food; it was relentless. At one a.m., the table a battlefield.

Sometimes she would turn up in an auto or a taxi. He would disappear after the meal, sometimes excuse himself, always discreetly pay, sometimes just disappear without a word and there would be a pall over the night with Sunny gone, newcomers nervous about its course. He had set them rolling. She would wait until an appropriate time and excuse herself for the night. Sometimes they would try to keep her, to take her to the next place. She begged tiredness or tomorrow's work. She knew when she left they were talking about her, especially since Kriti was no longer there. Maybe they would press Hari. *She's your friend, you brought her in. What's she doing with him?*

Sometimes she made a point to leave long before Sunny did. Sometimes Sunny spent time teasing her, insulting journalists in general. Accusing her of being a spy. Don't say anything in front of her! And she just smiled and made conversation with someone else. Then they were both gone.

Where do you think *they've* gone?

She didn't care.

Ajay would carry her. If Sunny had already left, Ajay would pick her up outside and deliver her to whichever hotel he was waiting in. If she left the party first, Ajay would deliver her to the hotel, she would be given the key card so she could wait. Silent, loyal Ajay, eyes lowered, never a word. They drove at speed through the night. Ajay never played music on the stereo, she noticed that. Sometimes she put her earphones in and pumped her music up so loud and stared out at the disconnected streets, the trash heaps smoldering by the roadside, the sleeping workers. The months of July and August, like this. Burning at both ends, never tired. Gilded hangovers. Iridescent with champagne.

She knew just how to take him in. She wanted all of him. To be full of him. There was no other way to say it. He talked about Italy in those moments after sex when they were lying on the bed smoking cigarettes. The atelier in which his suits were made, sun streaming through the Mediterranean air, dust motes in the skylight. The cafés he sat in during the day, the clink of spoon and coffee cup and saucer. He'd gone there when he was eighteen. He kept coming back to this memory. There was the toy shop in Meerut and there was Italy. There was an exhaustion in him sometimes, coming to meet her after she'd been waiting, sometimes an hour or two, drinking whisky and watching Star Movies with the AC on and the heat rolling in waves against the window from outside. He'd had no time to reset. And things were different then. She wanted to take care of him. People tire me, he said. They drain me. You're too generous, she said. She was lost in him and him alone. She wanted his scent. She wore his shirts in bed.

Money's a fucking curse, he said. It cuts out all the hard work. Before, you had to be kind or funny or fun. Interesting, intelligent. You had to take the time to know people. You had solidarity with them. Then you're rich. It annihilates everything. Everyone is nice to you. Everyone wants you there. You're the most popular person in the room. It's so easy to be charming when you're rich. Everyone laughs at your jokes, hangs on your word. You forget and think it's about you. Then sometimes you go somewhere and you don't spend, and it's so miserable, it's so horrible to go back to the drawing board, and you've forgotten how to earn someone's trust or love, and you know it's easier with a shortcut or two, so you bring out the cash in the end, the wad, the clip, the card, and the thrill of it is greater, because they didn't know, and now they do. You're rich. You're in charge. They love you. Money's a fucking curse.

"My grandfather," he said one night in bed, "was a Walia. That was his name. He changed it to Wadia after he met a Parsi trader who was doing very well. This was way back, just after Independence. He thought the change would bring him fortune. That's it. That's the story. It's not a story at all."

"Did it change his fortunes?"

"Two generations too late."

"Was he a religious man?"

"He died before I was born. I don't know anything except the story Tinu told."

"Tinu?"

"Tinu is Tinu. My father's right-hand man."

She paused. "What does your father believe in?"

"What?"

"What does he believe in?"

He thought it over.

"Why do you ask?"

"It's just a question."

"Money," he said.

"Lakshmi?"

"No. Just money."

"And to whom does he pray?"

He thought about it again.

"Himself."

"Do you love him?"

He thought about that even longer, and the silence was too long to bear.

"What about your uncle Vicky?" she asked.

He tensed up. She noticed him withdraw.

"We don't talk about him."

"Why don't you talk about him?"

He wouldn't say.

"What was the Kushinagar incident?"

"Where did you hear that?"

"It seems like it was a big deal."

He was quiet a long time, didn't move, didn't look at her.

"Just local politics. Things are different out there."

"I bet. They have another name for him, right? Like a mountain. What was it? Himmatgiri?"

He looked away.

"Don't ever use that name again."

This was only six weeks, but it felt like a life completely. From waking to sleeping, she was consumed by it. They met in hotel suites no more than twenty times. He brought her jewelry to wear. Clothes sometimes. She dressed slowly. Went out like that for the night, a different person. Vanished awhile. She became herself when she left him, when she went back to her world. But there was something she carried away.

Something eroding her.

Outside, the city was submerging, collapsing. The monsoon filled the drains and gutters. The roads spilled over with horns. They never talked about it. There were protests. Evictions. Demolitions. They never talked. She transcribed for Dean. They never talked. He talked at her from bed. From across the table. There was a necessity to this. Sunny cited the law. *Almitra H. Patel v. Union of India.* The court opined: Delhi should be the showpiece of the nation. Should one give a pickpocket a reward for stealing?

Her mother asked, "Are you seeing someone?"

"Yes," she said.

Sitting at the breakfast table.

"Hari?"

She laughed into her cereal. "God, no."

"What's wrong with Hari?"

"Nothing."

"Is it Dean?"

"It's not Dean."

"Will we meet him?"

"I doubt it."

"Are you taking precautions?"

"Of course."

4.

With all the precautions in the world, it was bound to change. This note could not sustain. The monsoon eased off. It was four a.m. on a Friday morning. They were lying in bed, half awake. He said he was leaving for Lucknow the day after, he'd be gone for work. Dinesh Singh, he said. When she was with him, she lost sense of the days. They fell asleep and when she woke it was 6:30 a.m. and he was already getting dressed.

"What happened?"

"Change of plan. These assholes are coming to Delhi tonight."

"Who?"

"Dinesh and his behenchod father. I have to prepare."

"How do you prepare?"

"Mostly by remembering not to talk."

"What do you do with them? You never say."

"It's my father's deal."

"And yours?"

"What do you mean?"

"What's going on with you, the river?"

"Don't ask."

"I just did."

"My father's looking into it."

He was about to leave.

She left the hotel that morning just after 7:30 a.m.

She was driving back home to change before work when Dean called. She didn't answer at first. She figured it could wait. But he called again seconds later, breathless. "Where are you?" Before she could answer, he said, "I need you to get down to Laxmi Camp right away."

"Now?"

"A demolition's happening this morning, the bulldozers are already there. The High Court sent a notice right now."

"OK."

"I need you to cover it. I can't get there, I'm in Meerut."

"Right now?"

"Yes! Right now!"

There had been protests over Laxmi Camp for months, court orders going back and forth, but now the bulldozers were moving in. It was true, a demolition crew had already arrived. The officer in charge announced work would start as soon as he'd finished his tea. A market had been designated on this land. Some residents on the site scrambled into action, tried to salvage their lives, dismantling their own makeshift houses piece by piece, others just made bags of belongings, leaving the structures to be destroyed. It had rained briefly overnight, but it was only hot and humid now. Many men had left for the labor mandi to find work, left their homes unguarded. They hadn't believed the threats, or they couldn't afford to take the time off work. She got there just as the officer was making his announcement. She was accosted by some residents of the nearby colony. One upright, white-collar gentleman with his fat Labrador wanted to go on the record. He was Ashok from the Residents Welfare Association. Age thirty-nine. Write it down. These people are a nuisance, a menace, they make the city filthy, they bring crime, they defecate in the gardens. Write it down. We built a wall, but they made a hole. They come through and use it as a path in the night. It's high time they were out. Why should they be rewarded for squatting on public land? The world is watching, he said. Write it down. He crowded her notebook as he watched her write it down. A plump, wearied woman from the jhuggi overheard what he was saying. I'm Rekha. Write that down! We helped build your homes! We cooked your food! We guarded your homes in the night! We chased away thieves when they came! And this is what you do! His dog started barking at her. Without warning the bulldozers fired up. People started to scream, back and forth. And this is what you do to us?! Where can we go?! Who'll work for you now?! The bulldozers drove their unerring path, crushing everything ahead. Homes of tarp and bamboo and metal sheeting and loose brick were crushed, entire livelihoods and lives summarily erased. Then a scream of a different kind ripped the air. It was so loud and sickening that everything stopped. The bulldozers cut their engines and ceased their march, police and citizens surged toward the source, the last, half-collapsed house. Ashok's dog continued to bark. A young woman in shredded rags was pulled away from the wreckage, howling and gibbering. Men dug up the rubble in a frenzy, but it was too late. The crushed bodies of two sibling infants were pulled out, held up in the air, whitened, covered in chalk and plaster, dead. She saw it with her eyes. She heard the people begin to wail, and saw boys pelt stones at the bulldozer.

She wrote a first-person account that afternoon—the chaos, the chain of events, the visceral shock. She had even managed to gather quotes. The demolition had been suspended, a protest broke out—it gathered strength, almost burst into a riot. But her copy for the newspaper was dry, functional, it communicated the bare bones of the situation and little more.

She realized she was on TV. The demolition had been filmed by a news crew. The moment of the kids' death was right there. She was gasping, crying.

Dean wanted to take her to dinner that night, but she declined. She said she wanted to be alone. He told her he would check in on her later.

The bereaved parents had been working on a construction site. They'd been assured the demolition would be delayed. They'd taken the risk, gone to work, left their kids at home. A neighbor was to watch over them, but the neighbor had been beaten by the police. In that moment they lost their children, their belongings, their life.

Neda's mother studied her with the minute care and attention she habitually employed against the world. Her gaze missed nothing. She was a hawk who never swooped, but Neda knew she was there.

"You're all we've got," her mother said, taking Neda's hand. "You know that, don't you?"

"I don't," Neda said, trying to pull her hand away.

Her mother wouldn't let it go. "And we're proud of you."

"You shouldn't be."

"What you're doing matters."

She blinked and the tears fell.

"Nothing matters."

Her head was fog.

"Shhhh."

"I can't take this," she said. She looked up to meet her mother's eyes and her voice changed to a plea. "Can I go now? I want to sleep."

Her mother nodded. "Shall I send up tea?"

"No."

"Whisky?"

"No."

"Will you share a cigarette with me before you go?"

She went upstairs and sat on the edge of her bed a moment, sick, immobile, then undressed and entered the shower and stood under the hot water, willing her mind to dislodge itself of the nightmare repetitions—the woman screaming, the tiny bodies, the frenzied barking of the dog, the guttural engine of the JCB, the glare of the TV cameras. She lived the moment again, seeing herself seeing the devastation, and her memory was grafted onto the TV cameras, making the event an out-of-body experience, detached from any discernible reality. The hot water ran out, the shower turned cold, but still she stood under it, letting the stream numb her body and so her mind. She lost sense of place and time; it might be a jungle, it might be the mountains, it was not Delhi.

She had no idea how to run from it. She heard the low hum of voices downstairs. Her mother speaking. A man's voice. It had to be Dean.

Yes, Dean was there.

She threw on a kaftan and crept down, hung at the curve of the marble stairs, peeking like a child.

It was not Dean.

It was Sunny, sitting with her mother at the round table in the heart of the home, dressed in his simple white shirt and chinos, sipping tea, looking tired, drained. He was listening to her mother speak, speaking in reply, her mother receptive, calm, nodding with him.

He must have heard or sensed or seen her from the corner of his eye. He looked up and made eye contact and she hugged the wall a little tighter. Then she took a few steps down, trying to be bold.

"What are you doing here?"

"I saw you on the news," he said.

It didn't seem real, Sunny sitting there, crossing this boundary, invading her life.

"I'm sorry," her mother said, "my daughter can be very rude."

"It's OK," Sunny replied. "She had a bad day."

Neda shook her head in disbelief. "A bad day?"

"I'm going to rest," her mother said. She turned to Sunny. "Take care of her."

Sunny stood, extended his hand. "It was lovely to meet you, Mrs. Kapur."

Her mother took it. "Ushi," she said. "My name is Ushi."

She glanced at Neda but said nothing and turned and retreated to her bedroom, and Neda watched her go without moving. She only came to sit at the table once she was gone. Only then did Sunny take his seat.

"She's like I imagined."

"Did she ask who you were?"

"I said I was a friend."

She spoke in a quiet voice. "You're not a friend." She closed her eyes. "What are you doing here? Aren't you supposed to be with Dinesh?"

"He can wait."

She shook her head. "I feel so stupid."

"Why?"

"I need a drink." She fetched a bottle of Teacher's and two brandy snifters from the sideboard. "What did you tell her?" She poured large measures into the glasses.

"Nothing."

She drank one of the glasses down. Looked at the other. Drank that too.

"What did she ask you?"

"Nothing."

She poured for herself again. "Slow down," he said.

"Don't lecture me."

"I'm not."

She poured him a glass too.

"It's not the good stuff, I know."

"Can I smoke?"

She waved her hand. "Sure."

He took out his cigarettes and lighter. Offered her one. "You grew up in this house?"

She took it, he lit it. "You know I did."

"You're lucky."

"So I'm told."

He spotted pencil markings on the white paint of one of the pillars. Lines with dates written next to them, marking growth. "Is that you?"

She nodded.

He stood and went over to examine them. The last one was marked 26.7.97. He ran his finger over it. "What happened after this?"

"I grew up."

He came back to the table.

"I don't want to fight with you."

She poured another whisky into her glass.

"It'll hit you."

"I'll hit you."

She drank the measure down.

"I feel like I've been sleepwalking," she said after a long silence. "And I've woken to another bad dream."

"What do you want to do?"

"I want to get out of here. Out of this city. Out of my life."

"So let's go."

"It's so easy for you, isn't it? There's nowhere to go."

"Let me take you somewhere."

"I don't want to go to a hotel room with you."

"I'm not talking about that."

"Not some private dining room, not some VIP fucking bar."

"No." He stood, walked to the door. "Where I'm taking you, you don't even have to change clothes. Are you coming?"

———

She lay across the back seat of his Audi as he sped her through the night, feet pressed against one of the doors. She wanted this cocoon. The AC was turned up very high, the upholstery fresh, the car an island. She felt the engine in her bones. Her teeth chattered with the cold and the adrenaline. He was on the phone, one hand on the wheel, speaking quietly. She watched the night city unspool like reams of ink ribbon while he managed the road. As they drove she felt she had been drugged. They were heading south toward the Qutb Minar. The car pulled along the straights at speed, the stretches between traffic lights devoured by the engine.

They traveled over the edges of South Delhi into Mehrauli. An inchoate world of farmland without farmers, their land hijacked and consumed by the secretive, the lucky, the adventurous, the strange, a labyrinth of dirt lanes and small holdings, shadowy, high-walled estates necklaced with barbed wired or crumbling villas grazed with goats. She'd been to a wedding reception here once, a school friend's elder sister. What surprised her was the space. Land. So much hidden land. Now it was being colonized by the wealthy, the super-rich. She should have guessed what was coming.

They came to a gleaming gate guarded by two old Rajasthanis with their mustaches and shotguns. They recognized the car, snapped to attention, ran to open the gate, and saluted as the car passed through. Beyond, the smooth dark tarmac of a private road. It was Delhi and it was not Delhi—lush verges, peacocks crying in the night, silent men tending to flower beds, no garbage, nothing broken. The engine hummed as the car moved at a stately pace, turning left and right as if on rails, as if this were a theme-park ride. The disorientation was intoxicating. She cracked open the window and even the air smelled different, moist and sweet, full of night-blooming jasmine. She watched the gates and high domes and gothic spires, guardhouses illuminated in white light, guards reading newspapers, listening to the radio, sipping chai, looking up to glance at the passing car. On the right there were no houses, no gates, nothing but a dark unbroken wall, almost as high as the trees that crowded the other side. They drove along this impregnable length until they reached a solid metal gate, built just wide enough for a car to pass, unremarkable after the other grand entrances. The car idled outside and a few seconds later a bolt was released from inside. The gate swung open inward. By the headlights she could make out woodland, a murky track that disappeared into a mass of trees. As the car drove in she saw Ajay holding the gate and they were swallowed inside.

They crept along the track inside the compound, through the woodland, Ajay trotting alongside. They traveled for a good few minutes this way. Then the track opened up, the trees vanished, and they emerged into a grassy clearing with another track leading out the opposite side. He stopped the car in the middle. Killed the engine and the lights. Climbed out and opened the rear door. She climbed out too, felt the grass underfoot, the soft purity of it. The moon came out and the clearing was illuminated. It was clean and empty. He took her by the hand.

"What is this place?"

"Wait," he said.

He led her through more woodland to a vast open space in which there stood a construction site of monolithic proportions. They were looking on the foundations of an extraordinary building, like an alien spaceship crash-landed. Around it were mountains of sand and gravel, piles of brick, and slabs of marble sheltered beneath tarp. There were several JCBs, a bulldozer, a huge cement truck, a dormant workers' camp of tents and firepits. But the site was empty.

He guided her with a flashlight across a manicured field, toward a squat building a hundred meters from the main site; when they got closer she could make out a single-story villa, sliding-glass doors, and horizontal slabs of rough-hewn stone, slightly run down, an older marker on the land.

"Ouch." She flinched and pulled her foot back.

She'd stepped on something sharp.

"What is it?"

He shone the torch down and saw that her foot was bleeding. She'd stepped on broken glass. A piece was still inside her skin.

He pulled it out. "Can you walk?"

She nodded.

They walked on to the villa, Sunny shining the torch on the ground, sweeping the path before her. He unlatched a gate at the side, led her down an alley to another. Outside that gate he opened a fuse box and snapped on several switches. Lights burst into life just out of view, and when they rounded the corner a swimming pool was glowing in the rear. By the poolside there was a bar, its many fridges jerked to life as Sunny flicked yet more switches. He led her to one of the deck chairs, sat her there with her leg up.

"I'll find something."

He got to work searching through some cupboards below the bar. She stared into the water of the pool. A few dead leaves floated in it.

He lifted his head from the cupboards.

"I don't bring anyone here," he said.

She turned back to the water. By the long edge of the pool toward the darkness, high, flowering bushes and palms peeked over the wall. An empty watchtower stood dormant in the night. Sunny straightened, placed a half bottle of whisky on the counter, and progressed to one of the deep freezers. "The assholes turned this off." He looked for a switch but couldn't find one. "Let me see inside."

He disappeared through an entrance hidden from view.

Some lights went on inside the villa.

She slid off the deck chair and hobbled to the pool. Her foot was bleeding quite badly. When she turned it toward her eyes, the cut throbbed, dripping onto the warm concrete. She hitched up her kaftan, slid her legs into the water, up to the knee. Bats flitted overhead. The faint roar of Delhi. She watched the blood leaking from her foot into the water.

"Madam," a new voice reached her ears. Ajay carried a large tray, its contents hidden beneath a white cloth. He looked at her with such an earnest expression.

"Sir is?"

She pointed inside the villa. He hurried in and emerged ten seconds later and hurried away again. Another minute passed before Sunny appeared carrying the same tray, now uncovered, revealing a bottle of vodka, an ice bucket, two rocks glasses, some lemon slices, a clean dish towel.

He set it down on the bar, carried the bottle over.

"You shouldn't put it in there. Show me."

She pulled her foot out. He took the clean towel to her skin, dabbed it dry around the cut.

"It's pretty deep."

She watched him closely.

"I don't feel it."

"You will in a second. Are you ready?" He tipped the bottle and poured vodka over her foot. "Stoli," he smiled. "Nothing but the best."

She laughed, then she started to cry.

"What's wrong with us!"

He tied the towel tight around her foot, placed it on his shoulder.

"You have to keep it elevated," he said.

But she was still sobbing.

"I'm *serious*. What the fuck is wrong with us?"

She pushed herself off him. Lay on the side of the pool staring into the trees. He walked back to the bar with the bottle, washed his hands in the sink, began to fix their drinks.

"Why are you doing this?" she said.

He squeezed the lemon, threw away the husks, added fresh slices, tossed in the ice, poured the vodka freely, carried the drinks over.

"What kind of host would I be if I let you bleed?"

He put the drinks down, removed his shoes and socks, rolled up his trouser legs, and sat next to her with both his feet in the pool.

"My blood's in there."

"I know."

She looked at the towel, red beginning to seep.

"It's still bleeding."

"I like what you're wearing," he said.

"Don't change the subject."

She considered the kaftan all the same.

"My mother got it from Jaipur," she said. "They used to export them." She pinched the material roughly between her left thumb and forefinger, let it fall. "This would sell for three hundred dollars in New York. So I'm told." She tilted her head toward the sky. "It might rain." The clouds had obscured the moon. "I hope it rains." She closed her eyes and felt wretched again. She drank her whole drink down. "I don't feel anything." She rolled the tumbler slowly toward the pool. It plopped in and sank.

He gave no reaction, just removed his cigarettes from his trousers and lit one.

"Is this what life's meant to be?" she said.

"You've had a rough day. You'll feel different tomorrow when you've slept."

"Why did you bring me here?"

"I'm trying to help," he said.

"We're fucking beyond help."

He reached for her hand, but she pulled it away.

She said, "Get me another drink."

As soon as he got up she untied her foot, tossed the towel to the side, lifted the kaftan over her head and slipped into the water naked. She disappeared underneath. The sounds of the world softened and distorted in the warmth of the monsoon night. She held her breath as long as she could.

By the bar, he stood and watched.

Eventually she let herself rise.

She made no sound as she breached the surface. Just floated, facedown, limbs spread, still holding her breath, letting out small bubbles. When she could hold it no longer, she rose and breathed deeply.

He was standing back at the side of the pool with her fresh drink.

She regained her breath. "I was imagining when I came up you wouldn't be here."

"You'd have trouble getting home."

"No, I'd be fine."

She began to swim lengths, front crawl.

"You're a good swimmer," he said.

"My dad taught me," she replied when she reached the end. Her hair fanned out around her shoulders. She swam into the middle of the pool and hung there, treading water. "I watched two children die today," she said. "Crushed to death in their miserable home. You could fit fifty of those huts into this pool, I swear. Their bodies were covered in this fine dust. There wasn't any blood. But they must have been broken up inside. I thought I was immune. I never heard anything like that woman's scream. I'd say it wasn't human, but that's not true. It was too human. I don't remember anything about myself at the time. But I saw myself crying on TV. I feel ashamed. I didn't deserve to cry. And after all that, I'm here with you like this. I have no courage, no heart."

"There's nothing you could have done."

"There's nothing I could have done! And it all just keeps happening." She let out a sob of frustration. Her blood was drifting around the pool. "What are we doing, Sunny? There's nothing we could have done, there's everything we could have done. We're all guilty. We're all the same. Even if you care, you can't get away. Especially if you care. How can you sleep at night? You have to be a saint. You have to wear a hair shirt and beat yourself with birch, give up all your belongings, go barefoot, sleep on the street, just to atone, and that won't be enough, it won't change anything. Or you just have to go on."

He peeled off his shirt and threw it down, removed his pants, walked around the pool to the deep end. He stood a moment as if still deciding, then dived in, pierced the water and swam underneath, all the way to the far end.

He came up gasping for air.

After a spell, he said, "It's better to have a plan."

"Oh," she laughed sarcastically, "a plan? You made your grand entrance to say *that*?!"

He swam toward her.

"We raise everyone up. So everyone can dream."

"God, spare me! This is ridiculous."

"You can't get lost in that world."

"Our dreams let people die." She turned away from him. "Tomorrow we move on."

At that moment a commotion rose outside, back toward the construction site. Powerful lights were turned on with an industrial clank, as if it were a movie set or a police raid. They heard the engines of cars, voices.

Neda turned to Sunny in alarm, but his face was more startled than hers.

"Fuck."

The side gate burst open.

Ajay, panicking, reported, "Your father's here!" then quickly disappeared again.

"Fuck," Sunny said. He was seized by fear, he looked to Neda. "You can't be here."

"Why?"

"Get out, now!"

His fear was contagious. "Where the fuck am I supposed to go? I'm naked."

She swam to the side.

"Sir," Ajay cried, returning. "They're coming here."

Sunny pointed to her kaftan. "Her clothes. Help her."

Ajay hurried to pick up her kaftan, ran back around with it, hauled her out of the water with his head turned the other way, and wrapped it round her body. Sunny pointed to a small changing room set back into the wall of the villa. "Go."

Ajay ran with her, dragged her past the bar to the changing room. She grabbed the bottle of vodka on the way. He pushed her inside.

The room had the ripe smell of disuse, the headiness of old chlorine and drains backed up with mulch. She caught her breath, unscrewed the vodka, and took a long drink. Then she began to shiver. There were small gaps in the walls where the wood had warped. She knelt down and peered through— there was room enough to see the rear of the villa, a part of the pool.

Sunny was dazed in the middle of the pool. Frozen.

What the fuck is happening?

Ajay emerged with a bucket of water, threw it over the stones leading to the changing room, to cover her bloody tracks.

This is crazy.

Then she heard voices.

Sunny heard them too, his body stiffened, a deer in the headlights. Ajay returned to the glass doors of the villa's rear and stood to attention. Footsteps. Many footsteps. Many voices. Across the pool, entering from that rear gate, she could make out three men. At the head, Bunty Wadia. She recognized him instantly though she'd never seen a clear photo in her life. At first glance he was benign, avuncular even, but he carried a cold authority that induced terror. There, alongside him, walked the famous figure of UP chief minister Ram Singh, and behind, patiently, deferentially, Dinesh.

Bunty and Ram were talking. Bunty glanced once at the pool and kept going, leading everyone inside past the upright Ajay as if Sunny weren't even there.

Sunny remained transfixed as the three men entered the villa.

Silence.

She wondered if she could make a run for it.

She couldn't take her eyes away.

In the empty space, Bunty reemerged.

Came to the edge of the pool and stared down.

She realized she was holding her breath.

All she could do was watch.

Bunty and Sunny below, facing off without words, without movement.

It was Sunny who made the first move.

He waded slowly through the water.

He came to the edge.

He said something Neda couldn't hear.

Sunny placed both hands on the side to haul himself out.

It all happened so fast.

As Sunny was halfway out, Bunty raised his foot. He met Sunny's chest with the sole of his black shoe. Pushed Sunny back into the pool.

Then he turned and he was gone.

She wanted to run to Sunny.

Instead she turned away into the blackness and drank from the vodka and closed her eyes.

How long had she been sitting there on the damp floor? Minutes or an hour? She was shivering, her teeth chattering, though the night was warm. However much vodka she drank, she couldn't get drunk. There was no sound from the pool. No sound from outside. When she allowed herself to check she saw nothing but the placid surface, the warm lights of the villa. Where had Sunny gone? Inside? Had he fled?

She was trapped in these thoughts when she heard a knock on the door.

"Madam," a voice whispered. It was Ajay.

She bit her lip and put her hand to the lock slowly.

"Madam, put your clothes on, please come."

She cracked the door open.

"Madam," he said, "You have to hurry."

She threw on the kaftan and slipped out still holding the vodka. He guided her silently around the back end of the pool, warning her to keep quiet. She could hear laughter and conversation inside the villa, saw the spilling light, and through a side window she caught a glimpse of Bunty and

Ram Singh. Then it was gone, and they were through the gate to the dim silence of the lawns. The uneven ground made her conscious of her foot. Ajay led her without a torch back through to the clearing in the woods where Sunny's car was still parked. The lights came on when she opened the door, they burned too brightly in the night. Ajay came round with a first-aid kit. With deference and care, he disinfected her wound, put a large plaster on, then a bandage. She watched him silently as he took care of her. Then she climbed in and slammed the door and pressed herself deep into the coldness of the leather seat and waited speechless and motionless as Ajay started the engine and the interior went dark.

They drove in silence to the rear gate.

Delhi returned.

Men on cycles, potholed roads, neon lights.

Noise.

They drove toward the Qutb, joined the main road, and slipped into the traffic. Just another car.

She sat so Ajay couldn't see her, slumped with her back against the door, her legs out across the seats.

"Ajay," she finally said, as the car waited at the red light of the IIT Flyover.

"Yes, madam."

"Is Sunny OK?"

He hesitated. Then said, "Everything is fine."

Silence hung until the light changed.

Fresh movement relieved them both.

Ajay turned the radio on low. The station was playing old film songs.

She asked him to turn it up loud.

The guards at her colony entrance opened the gate without question—they recognized the car, Ajay knew her house. He parked outside and waited for her to climb out. So this was how it ended.

Her hand opened the door.

"Ajay."

"Yes, madam."

"Thank you."

She climbed out with the vodka in her hand and closed the door and limped barefoot and bedraggled toward the safety of her home.

She entered using the key beneath the aloe plant, holding the bottle of vodka behind her back, listening to the Audi pull away. Her father was awake, sitting in lamplight in the living room in his favorite armchair, patched up many times over the years, watching a DVD. He looked over the top of his reading glasses. "Cinderella . . ."

He said nothing about her clothing, her bare feet.

"What are you watching, Papa?"

"*Apur Sansar.*"

She drew closer to him, kissed him on the forehead. His nose twitched.

"You smell like the Moscow Olympics." He reached behind her back, examined the vodka. "What's this? Gold medal?"

"The consolation prize."

"Well, let's be having some, daughter of mine. Just a small glass before we retire. We can have one of your mother's cigarettes too, and you can lie to me about your adventures in the night."

She fetched two glasses from the cabinet while he opened the bottle and sniffed. "Do you want ice?"

"No, no. You'll wake her. Just pour it neat."

She poured two stiff measures until the bottle was over, passed one to him, and fetched her mother's Classic Mild, then she pulled up a stool by his chair.

On-screen, a grieving Apu wandered the coalfields of central India, scattering his novel to the winds.

"So?" he said, enjoying the vodka sting on his lips.

"So . . . Did Mom tell you?"

She lit the cigarette.

"That a boy came to get you?"

"No, not that."

"Ah, yes, that other thing. She did, she did. I'm sorry, my child. I'm sorry you had to see that."

"If I could just disappear, I would."

He studied her. "Are you in trouble?"

She shook her head. "No." Then changed her mind. "Maybe."

She passed the cigarette to him. He inhaled once, very deeply, held the smoke in his lungs, tilted his head back, and, eyes closed, exhaled rings.

She laughed in childish pleasure. "You've still got it."

"I do."

"You used to do that for me all the time."

"It shut you up when you were crying." He ran his fingers through her hair. "I can't protect you anymore."

He knocked the rest of the vodka back.

There was nothing more to say.

He returned to the film, and she took the glasses to the kitchen, put out the cigarette, and slipped upstairs. She showered in very hot water. She was asleep the moment she crawled into bed.

She awoke from violent dreams with her head raging and went to the bathroom to be sick. It took awhile to remember what was real and where she was, and when she remembered she was more afraid than ever and there was no one she could talk to about what had happened last night. His father. God, his father. That foot in Sunny's chest, pushing him back into the water. Soon Dean was texting her, asking her when she'd be in the office. There was a lot of work to be done.

She and Dean went back out to the demolition site that next morning. It was chaotic, half demolished, full of government workers, NGO workers, journalists. Because of the deaths and the media outcry, the full demolition had been halted. But almost all the former residents were now gone. Some, eligible for relocation, had been bused out of the city, others had just drifted or run away. A few remained, picking through the rubble. She felt twice removed from herself. She kept forgetting things. Eventually Dean put her in an auto, sent her back to the office.

Dean wrote a piece about the demolitions, the children's deaths. "Tragedy and the Neoliberal Reimagining of Public Space." Late in the office that night, before heading home, she began looking through the first edition of the next day's paper. There, on page 8, only a few pages from Dean's piece, was a full-page, color advert:

The Wadia Charitable Foundation wishes to announce a 10 lakh rupee compensation (per child) to the parents of the children tragically killed in the Laxmi Camp eviction disturbance. We deeply regret their loss.

The intense, thoughtful face of Sunny looked out of the page. He was standing at the shoulder of his father, who was seated at a desk, pen in hand, looking up with a genial gaze as if caught unawares in the middle of signing a decree.

Dean slapped a copy of the same paper down on her desk.

"Can you believe this crap?"

She was paralyzed.

"It's in every damn paper," he went on. "The cost of the adverts combined is more than the compensation offered."

"It's a lot of money," she said.

"It's a lot of bullshit. Look at them," Dean said, opening his crumpled copy to the same page. He jabbed his finger into Bunty's face. "Who does this guy think he is?"

She thought: *It was Sunny. Sunny did this.*

"If they think they look good, they're wrong. It stinks. It stinks of a guilty conscience. You know what?" he snatched up the crumpled copy, leaving Neda's own looking up at them. "I'm going to find out what they're really about."

———

She texted Sunny from the bathroom.

—I saw the paper.

She stared at the phone a few minutes, waiting.

Nothing.

She wrote again.

—I know it was you.

She stared and stared at the phone. But there was nothing.

Nothing.

—I didn't ask you to.

Nothing.

—You still don't get it, do you?

Nothing came.

NEDA II

1.

Nothing came. Her phone remained quiet as a tomb. Days went by. She watched Dean's fury against the Wadias metastasize, and she carried her own confusion in her heart. She felt at any moment she would be caught. She worked on Dean's follow-up pieces, focusing on police indifference and judicial failures in light of the evictions. But Dean's was a lone voice at their paper. Op-eds appeared soon enough from interested parties, defending or excusing the demolitions. Dean charged her with tracking down the parents of the dead kids. All the while she waited for Sunny's call. She expected him the next day, the next, she expected to hear from him, for him to talk to her. But nothing came. She called him in the end, but his number didn't exist. She called Ajay and it was the same. She waited a week with no word or sign, and because there was no one she could confide in, it began to feel like all of it was a dream.

She replayed the night in the farmhouse, that terrible vision of his father looming poolside. His implacable foot into Sunny's chest, sending him under the water. The ride home with Ajay, fluid and inky, as if she were underwater herself.

———

She woke in the morning angry with herself. She missed him. In the glove compartment of her car, she kept a copy of the newspaper in which Sunny had placed his compensation advertisement. She folded back the page, sat with a cigarette at the side of the road, staring into his face. She tried to pull out clues. She was certain, absolutely certain, that Sunny had done this. He had put out the advert for her, as a message? As an apology? As a stupid thing done by a man in love? And then what? Regretted, repented, gone to ground? It was complicated by his father. The cruelty. The implacable foot. Had Sunny also put out that advert in rebellion? To stand up to his father? There were so many missing pieces, she was so in the dark. She examined their faces in the advert. His expression, his father's, the look in their eyes, the decor, the room. But there was nothing to learn. She didn't recognize the desk—didn't recognize the suit Sunny was wearing. "But I know you," she said to him. She turned to Bunty. How pleasant, how generous he looked. She inhaled on her cigarette until the tip was glowing bright, then pressed it into Bunty's face.

Three weeks passed. She slept, she woke, she worked in a haze of cigarette smoke. Dean was true to his word—he began looking more closely into Bunty Wadia and his business empire, his liquor, his mining, his construction, his timber out in UP, searching for a smoking gun, something to link them to what was happening in the city here and now. With Sunny she wavered between anger, fear, guilt, heartbreak. She missed him, she hated him. How hard was it to get in touch? How hard just to say he was OK? Or maybe he wasn't, maybe he was . . .

This would be the moment for her to confess. Go to Dean, tell him everything. *Dean, I've been stupid. I didn't mean it to happen . . .*

But what was she telling him? That she'd been having an affair with Sunny? Or that Sunny had plans for the city, this was the clue he might need. Could she tell him one without the other? *I discovered something... a friend came through for me...*

And then what? Sell Sunny out?

But why? Sunny had nothing to do with the demolitions, after all. His plans weren't for that colony. No, he was innocent!

She wavered back and forth.

What if she betrayed Sunny and he got in touch with her the very next day?

No.

She'd wait.

After all, *she'd* made Sunny put those adverts out.

She twinged his conscience.

She was the connection.

Finally, she drove to the Park Hyatt, stood inside the lobby, climbed into the elevator. She recognized the operator. As they were traveling to the eighth floor she said very casually, "Has Mr. Wadia been in today?" But he looked at her blankly and gave no reply.

She walked down the hushed corridor and stood outside suite 800. It was four in the afternoon. She put her ear to the door. Was there some noise inside? She thought she could hear the TV. What if she rang the bell, knocked on the door? Could she take it if Sunny answered? If some other woman answered? What would be the acceptable outcome? She prepared herself. She needed to know one way or another. She raised her fist, was about to rap on the wood, when she heard muffled voices and laughter approaching from the other side. She stepped back, ready to flee, when the door opened. A foreign couple looked out at her in surprise. American, she guessed. Heading out to see the Taj Mahal. Flustered, she turned and walked away. She took the stairs, stopped in the stairwell and caught her breath. When she was certain the couple had gone, she returned and took the elevator back to the lobby.

She spotted him outside.

"Amit," she said.

"Yes, madam," the pleasant voice replied.

"Amit, this is Mr. Wadia's friend. You helped arrange my interview with him a couple of months ago."

"I'm sorry, madam."

"In his suite. You sent me up. Gave me a key card."

"Madam, I'm very busy right now."

"Have you seen him?"

"Madam, if you please, I must go."

And he slipped behind the reception desk and away.

She went to the Japanese restaurant. She passed the maître d', ignored his polite attentions, followed the flow of the restaurant past the bar and waiters, past the main tables, into the private dining spaces. She began to pull back every screen and she knew it was a really crazy thing to do. She performed her search calmly enough, but the protestations of the restaurant staff, the manager, the maître d', the waiters grew more pronounced. Most of the rooms were empty. It was too early. Two were occupied with business meetings. She glanced in, shut the doors again, felt a fool at the end, and walked out without looking back. Despite the fact that she knew the staff, they looked at her blankly as if they'd never seen her before. She repeated her actions in other hotels. The other suites, the other restaurants. And the same thing every time. She turned up at the mystical Soviet restaurant where they'd first met, but it was blank and shuttered with the other shops.

She messaged Hari.

—Hey, what's up?

He didn't reply for a whole day.

—In Bombay. Kinda busy.

—When are you back? We should catch up.

He didn't reply.

How could a person just vanish like that? Very easily, when she had no foothold or claim to him. She'd always met him on his terms, in his spaces. She'd inhabited the bubbles he'd created within the city.

The evictions in the city kept up pace. The newspapers heralded the transformation of the urban space. The poor were no longer victims of an incompetent and corrupt state. They were encroachers and thieves. Their misery was not the misery of lives. As human beings they were being erased.

"Whatever happened to that boy?" her mother asked late one night. Neda was eating cold chicken at the dining table.

"What boy?"

"You know very well," her mother said. "The one who came over that night. The one you went out with, without your clothes."

"Without my clothes?"

"Yes, that boy."

"He's not a boy."

"Don't be smart."

"He's not around anymore."

"I didn't catch his name."

"It doesn't matter, he's gone."

"I see."

Neda just shrugged and kept eating.

"I thought he was charming," her mother said.

"Your radar is off."

Neda ate in silence awhile.

Her mother sat down opposite her.

"What's going on at work?"

"I'm not sure I want to keep working there. I want to study some more."

Her mother processed the words.

Neda said. "I'm tired of the job."

"Tired."

Neda fell silent.

Her father walked in.

"She wants to leave her job," her mother yelled.

"Love of my life," her father grumbled, "let me get both feet inside the house."

Neda got up from the table. "I didn't say that."

"Are you walking away?"

"Yes."

"She wants to quit."

She drove by Sunny's mansion that night. Turned and parked some distance down the road and watched the entrance. She'd done it before. She parked and sat with a cigarette, smoking, watching the comings and goings of servants, service providers, men and women, the comings and goings of blacked-out cars. She made a rule for herself. When three cigarettes had burned down, she would drive away.

She was sent out by Dean to visit the resettlement colonies, to get some quotes and a flavor of the scene and to try to find the parents of the dead kids. She drove at sunrise, fifty kilometers out, where Delhi became desolate, dusty, lined with derelict industrial complexes and dairies with emaciated cattle. A series of stinking canals bifurcated the land. On the patch of land that had been designated for the slum dwellers' resettlement, the recently evicted looked at one another in confusion. What were they supposed to do here? She began recording.

"They tell us this land will be worth something in fifteen years. That there will be everything we need. We had everything we needed there. We built it ourselves. Who can wait fifteen years?"

"What use is land if there's no work nearby?"

"It'll take four hours to commute to my job in the city. It used to take twenty minutes in all. How can we live like this?"

One of the men told her he was selling his deed to a property broker.

"We need money, we can't live here and starve, you can't eat a plot of land." Many others were doing the same. They told her several brokers were visiting the land daily, buying up their deeds for ready cash, enough money for them to start again somewhere else, or return to Delhi and take up in another slum. They pointed across the settlement plot a couple of hundred meters, where a broker stood with his men. She thanked them, walked over to this group. A fat, bald man in a white shirt and black pants stood in the middle of a group of toughs. She waved as she approached them. Could she ask them a few questions? The bald man turned away and began walking slowly. Not with fear but with contempt. She pursued him. She wanted to ask him some questions. Who did he work for? An arm stuck out to bar her from getting any closer. It belonged to a young man with a lazy eye. His face was froggish, fleshy, his hair thick with curls. He reminded her of a venereal boy in a Caravaggio painting. She recoiled.

"Don't touch me."

The broker was walking away, and the Caravaggio goon was facing her down.

She tried to step around him and he stepped with her.

Several poor men among the evicted came to her aid. They asked her to go back with them to her car. The goon's face was set in a snarl. She retreated. She asked her saviors about the parents of the children who had died. She needed to distract herself. Someone knew them. They were migrant laborers, they'd only been in the city three years. Did they come here? No, they weren't eligible for resettlement. What about the compensation money, the money announced in the paper? No, no one knew anything about that. She took some names anyway. She took the number of a man among them who had a mobile phone. She promised to return. "Why bother," the man said, "anyone with half a brain will be gone."

"Will you sell your plot to these brokers?"

"Of course."

"Do you have their names? Their cards? Anything?"

"No. They just turn up with cash and give us the money and take our deeds away."

She reported this news to Dean.

"Interesting," he said. "And what about the parents?"

"Nothing. They've gone."

"OK. I want you to do something for me," he said. "Get in touch with Sunny Wadia. You met him before. You must have a number. His official lines are shut, but let's try to see what he has to say."

"I never knew him like that."

"Get it from your friend."

She waited until the end of the day to come back to Dean.

"They say his number has changed."

After weeks had passed she tried Hari again.

She sent the text so breezily.

—Hey! Long time. Are you back? Do you want to catch up for that drink?

He replied an hour later.

—I'm here. Leaving tomorrow

—Oh wow. How come?

He didn't reply for another two hours, then he said:

—Meet at Market Cafe. Tonight. Six.

His tone was flat. There was none of his old warmth.

She met him on the small terrace at Market Café where everyone went to smoke pot. He was leaning over the railing, alone. He looked tired; he saw her and hesitated for a moment before giving her a hug. It had rained an hour earlier, the lingering tail of the monsoon. The cars in the outer parking lot shined.

They stood side by side, old friends who'd fast become strangers, with no word of the thing that had come between them.

"Did something happen?" she finally said.

"I'm just trying to figure out who my friends are."

"What's that supposed to mean?"

"Nothing."

"You're leaving tomorrow?"

"Yeah."

"You're in demand."

"I found an apartment."

"Where?"

"Bombay."

"But you love Delhi. You've been planning so many things."

"Plans change. You can fall out of love with a place."

She lit a cigarette. "Was it a girl?"

He glanced at her oddly. "No."

"What then?"

"People make promises they can't keep."

"It *definitely* sounds like a girl."

"Does it sound like you?"

There was spite in his voice.

"Have I done something to upset you?"

He closed his eyes and shook his head. "Why are you pretending you don't know?"

"Know what?" she replied in a quiet voice.

"Tell your boyfriend he's an asshole."

The shock made her laugh. "My what?"

"Your boyfriend."

"I don't have a boyfriend."

"Sunny."

"He's not my boyfriend."

"Right."

"I swear. I have nothing to do with him. Nothing."

"Sure."

"I haven't seen him for months."

"Come on, Neda, everyone knows you're fucking him."

"I fucked him once Hari, and it was a mistake. He's an asshole. I hate him."

"Really?"

"Listen, just tell me what happened."

It was another story of vanishing. Sunny had set up the record label he'd been talking about. He'd hired dozens of staff and they'd been spending wildly on it, having a good time. Hari was in charge; he was recruiting other DJs and artists. His future was set. Then one day Sunny just vanished. Stopped answering his phone, stopped replying to messages, stopped paying salaries and bills. His phone was disconnected, and the plug was pulled. The office was cleaned out by some goons, equipment and furniture taken away, the space sealed. Hari reached out to other friends in despair, thinking *he'd* done something wrong. But the story was the same. Sunny vanished from everything. And all the other projects he'd been funding, those restaurants and gallery spaces, all the money and support, it was cut overnight.

"He really fucked us all," Hari said.

"I didn't know," she replied.

"He's an asshole. He got bored of his toys."

"There has to be more to it than that. Has anyone seen him?"

"No one's seen him, no one's heard from him."

"Don't you think that's weird?"

"He'll be somewhere. Singapore. London. He was always shady. Should have known from the start he'd cut us loose."

"This is why you're going to Bombay?"

"Yeah. Fuck Delhi. It's too heavy these days."

Fuck Delhi. She drove back to his mansion that evening, parked her car a little way from the gates. Hesitated lighting the first cigarette. Wound the window down and killed the engine, put the seat back like a common driver waiting for a master and fixed her gaze on the comings and goings of the many dozens of staff, in and out. Where had Sunny gone?

Then he began to appear in public life again, but never in the flesh. He was an image, a projection. She saw his photos in the newspapers, his hair cut shorter, more precise, bringing out the sternness of his face, his high cheekbones and strong jaw. His eyes were blanks to her. She'd open the newspaper and there he was in the society pages, at some glitzy event, some grand wedding in Rajasthan, the opening of a new hotel, a Polo Club event, a charity gala, glad-handing everyone. A forced smile. Gone was the Neapolitan debonaire youth. He had been cinched and armored by Savile Row suits.

She was out again at night in her car, out in front of his mansion smoking. She was wearing down her third cigarette. What was she waiting for? He'd never step out. She'd only see cars. All their windows were blacked out. She could pick one, follow it, hope that it'd be him. It would give her something to do. One time she might get lucky. Then what?

She was angry with herself. But she couldn't let it go. Now that it was confirmed he was safe, she wanted to confront him for vanishing like that. For being a coward. At the same time, she couldn't forget that image—his father with his foot in his chest. What kind of father did that to his son?

She finished her fifth cigarette. She'd been there an hour. She'd broken her three-cigarette rule. It was stupid. She was wasting her time. She flicked it out the window. She almost hit a man passing by. He glared at her for a second before walking on. Her blood went cold. She recognized him instantly. It was the froggish goon from the resettlement colony, the Caravaggio boy. He was wearing tight jeans and a T-shirt. His boyish body seemed grotesquely muscled. He walked on ten or twelve paces, then stopped again, turned around slowly, and stood dead still, staring into the front windshield of her car. It was dark. He couldn't see inside. But he was just staring at her. What was he doing? Memorizing her plates? Trying to place *her*?

She dare not move. Dare not drive away. She moved her hand to the ignition just in case. She thought she could detect a smile on his face as he lit a cigarette and walked. All the way to the Wadia mansion. The guards opened the gate without question, and he stepped inside. She stared at the gate.

The fact of it sank in. She was still piecing together the connections—the goon, the resettlement plots, the Wadias—when Caravaggio emerged again, this time with three others. They walked straight toward her car. She panicked, turned the ignition on, and drove off fast, leaving them stranded in the road. She pulled a left and accelerated, turned left and right and left again through the colony maze, sped for several minutes before she pulled down a service lane. Even then she checked the mirror, kept the engine running. Her heart was pounding. She lit a cigarette. That was definitely him. This was proof. But proof of what?

2.

That Sunday she received a call on her mobile. A gentleman with a clipped, privately educated accent.

"Good afternoon," he said.

"Who is this?" she replied.

"Am I speaking to Ms. Neda Kapur?"

"Yes," she said. She sat on her bed, watching the street.

"Very good." His voice was delicate. "I'm calling on behalf of Mr. Wadia."

She half expected something like this, but still she was caught unawares.

"Mr. Wadia?"

"Sunny," the voice clarified. "He'd like to see you."

She checked the street doubly hard, answered cautiously, tried not to betray herself. "He wants to see me?"

"That's correct."

"Who are you?"

"An employee."

"Could I get your name?"

"Mr. Sengupta."

"OK, Mr. Sengupta, can you give me any idea of what he wants?"

"It's a private matter."

She hesitated. She should hang up now.

"And where does he want to meet?"

"He'd like to see you in his office."

"Which office?"

He gave the address of a place out of Delhi, across the Yamuna into Western UP, out on the Greater Noida Expressway. The desolate farmland regions being developed by Ram Singh.

"What office is this?" she asked.

"The headquarters of our property division."

"Your property division?"

"Indeed. Wadia InfraTech."

"And that's where he's working?"

"That's correct."

"Why can't he call me himself?"

"I make his appointments."

"And he wants to meet me when?"

"Today."

"It's Sunday."

"Indeed. It's his only free time."

"It's a little far out for me, this office."

"It's perfectly easy to find. There are signs along the way. Shall I confirm, let's say four p.m.?"

She checked the clock on the wall. It was 2:30. It would take an hour or more to drive out there with the bad roads. It was the kind of place she didn't want to be driving alone around after dark.

"I'd really like to hear from him myself."

She could hear the fear and sadness in her own voice, and it made her flinch.

"My dear," the man laughed, "he's a very busy man and he has only a small window. If you can't make it, I'll just cancel, and that will be the end of things."

"No," she replied. "I'm coming."

"Excellent. Give your name at reception when you arrive."

She hung up and cursed herself and then him.

She knew it was a bad idea. "This is a bad fucking idea," she told herself, crossing the Yamuna into East Delhi, lighting a cigarette. Over the river she turned south into Noida. The new city was still sprouting—there were tower blocks and apartment buildings interspersed with vacant plots of land and fields. By the time she got onto the highway it was already 3:15. Already the sun was beginning to dip in the sky. As she drove along the highway, the smooth construction of road began to fall away, and on either side the land turned into derelict waste, bulldozed mounds with diggers and workers, then there were long stretches of nothing, fields and farmers carrying loads on bullock carts. She'd been out here a few times, but not recently, and never on her own. As she continued south along the highway, she hit stretches where the tarmac was replaced with potholed sections through which she had to pick her way at a crawl. At some of these spots, men stood on the roadside or sat at stalls with umbrellas protecting them from the sun, holding out brochures for property developments. Their eyes fixed on her, alone in the car. What the hell was she doing here?

Finally, about thirty kilometers down, on the side of the expressway, a dreadful black cube looming in the middle of nothing, was the Wadia Infra-Tech HQ. She pulled inside the complex, past a guard who waved her into the parking lot. The difference from the outside was stark—the lot was perfectly paved in dark asphalt, with parking spaces demarcated by bright yellow lines. There were a handful of cars, mostly shiny SUVs. She locked hers and headed toward the main entrance. The building was imposing in an anonymous way. Aside from the glass doors of the main entrance, inside which she could see a lobby green with tropical plants, all the windows were tinted, impossible to see through.

The receptionist was a young man with baggy eyes, a high forehead, and gelled hair. He looked at her without smiling.

"I'm here to see Sunny Wadia," she said.

"Ma'am, do you have an appointment?"

"I'm expected," she said.

"You can't see him without an appointment."

"I have an appointment. I spoke with someone on the phone."

"Who did you speak to?"

"Mr. Sengupta. He told me Sunny wanted to see me today," she said, trying to sound authoritative.

"I don't know Mr. Sengupta."

Just then the reception phone began to ring. The man picked it up and listened. He looked her over. "Miss Kapur?"

"Yes."

He put the phone down and held out a hand. "Please, take a seat. Mr. Wadia will be with you when he's free."

She crossed the lobby to the waiting area. It was done up like the living room of a luxury apartment—she could detect Sunny's hand. There were cream leather easy chairs, a sofa, a low mahogany table covered with glass, full of magazines and brochures. Water ran through the whole lobby in small channels, trees and plants like a jungle. She took one of the easy chairs. A boy came out of nowhere carrying a tray with a single glass of water. He asked if she wanted tea or coffee. A snack? She took the water and nothing else and waited. There was a TV on the side wall. It switched on, as if by magic. She swung her chair to watch it. It played a promotional video—Sunny, wearing a power suit, addressing the camera. Behind him, superimposed images of luxury flats at regular intervals.

The video was twenty minutes long. She watched it twice, frowning at Sunny's banal appearance and unimaginative speech, before she approached the reception desk to ask how long she would have to wait. It was almost 5:30; she couldn't wait much longer. The man made a call.

"He's just coming," he said at the end of it. "Please, take a seat."

She returned to the easy chair.

Don't close your eyes, she told herself.

It's only for a minute, she said.

"Ma'am?"

The receptionist was standing over her. She opened her eyes, sat up in panic.

"I'm awake."

"Ma'am, I'm afraid we're closing the office, you'll have to leave."

"What time is it?" She looked around.

"Ma'am, you'll have to leave."

It was dark outside.

"What time is it?"

"Seven forty-five."

"You're kidding me."

"No, ma'am."

"Seriously? Where the hell is Sunny?"

She was getting agitated.

"I'm afraid Mr. Wadia had some business."

"No!"

She got up out of the seat, began to look around wildly.

She looked for the security cameras, spoke into them.

"This is bullshit!"

"Ma'am, please mind your language."

"Go fuck yourself!" She looked into the cameras. "Sunny! You fucking prick!"

"Ma'am, I'm afraid you'll have to leave."

He waved over two security guards.

She stood out in the parking lot beside her car. The guards were waiting for her to drive away. She looked up at the building, trying to see which lights were on. This was not a joke. She felt terrorized. She fished out her phone and dialed the number of the man who'd called her—the electronic voice told her the phone was turned off. She looked at the phone. "Asshole!" Then she got into her car and started the engine and sped away in anger, and suddenly she felt very alone.

She drove onto the highway—there was nothing there, the road was unlit and desolate at this hour, the men handing out brochures, selling dreams, had long since packed up and gone. She knew she shouldn't be out here. The roads weren't safe. There were carjackings all the time. She cursed herself for being so dumb. She drove along the highway toward Delhi, eyes open, adrenaline running. The absence of other cars unnerved her.

About fifteen kilometers along she realized there was a vehicle behind her at some distance. It had its full-beam headlights on. Maybe half a kilometer away. She kept a steady pace, continued to check the vehicle in the rearview mirror. It seemed to keep distance, whether she sped up or slowed down, too far to be anything other than a set of headlights, too close to be ignored. Five kilometers passed.

"Fuck you, Sunny."

She finally reached the stretch of highway close to Noida where the street-lights worked. She sped; several cars appeared around the service roads and joined the highway, there was normal life again. In the rearview mirror she saw many headlights and couldn't distinguish the ones she was sure had been following her. She felt idiotic. Sunny was an asshole, that was all. Right?

She decided to cross the Yamuna early at the Kalindi Kunj Bridge, and when she reached the other side of it and entered Delhi she felt an enormous weight lift. Her stomach unknotted, she was light and giddy. She started to laugh out of sheer nervousness. She decided she'd tell Dean everything, lay it all out from start to finish, explain how she'd drifted so far and vow to fix it. She entered the empty streets, the industrial units either side. She'd forget Sunny and all his games. She crossed a junction.

. . . the car was spinning wildly and her head was smashed against the frame of her door. She felt the g-force in her stomach. Everything in her ears was ringing. Then it came to a stop and there was silence. It was still. She tried the engine. She felt the warmth of blood on her head when she touched it with her hand. Where was she again? She tried the engine. It whined and clicked but wouldn't start. She looked up, around. Realized she'd been in an accident. She was vaguely aware of another car, maybe an Esteem, with its front smashed up, fifteen meters away. There was no one else around, an industrial district on a Sunday night. She should call someone. Her mother. As she was trying to remember how she'd gotten here, she heard a crunching of metal and voices raised and realized the doors of the other car were opening and the occupants were staggering out. Two young men from the front, a stout older man in the back. They stumbled, dazed, then turned to look toward her. They looked at each other.

They hit me, she told herself. They hit me.

The men started to walk across the junction toward her.

She realized one of them held a metal rod in his hand.

She tried to start her engine again, frantically turning the key, begging her little car to take her away, but the engine refused to start.

The men were getting closer, shielding their eyes from her headlights. She tried the engine over and over and the blood dripped down from her head. As the men drew up a few meters from the front of her car they seemed to hesitate. Maybe they couldn't see who was inside.

She held her hand down on the horn.

She locked all her doors.

But the men seemed to come to a decision.

They advanced on her.

They were closing in around the car, surrounding it, peering in.

"I'm sorry," she said.

The one with the rod stared at her.

"I'm sorry," she just kept saying. "I'm sorry."

The man with the rod smashed it on her bonnet.

"Do you see what you did!"

"I'm sorry," she said. And she tried the engine again.

This seemed to enrage them.

"Bitch! You think you can run!"

"Please. I'm sorry." She kept trying to start the engine. "I don't have any money!"

"Get out!"

"I'm a journalist!"

It was an absurd thing to say.

The one with the rod started laughing. The laughter spread among the men. One of them marched back toward their car.

"You hit us," the one with the rod said. "You need to pay."

"I'll send you money," she said. "Please, just let me go away."

"You need to pay," he repeated. He hit the frame of her door with the rod. The third man opened the rear of their car and came back out with a cricket bat. She kept slamming on the horn, helpless, terrified. The older man went round the other side. He was drunk or damaged from the crash. He rattled her door, leered at her. The young man with the rod was shouting at her and she was pleading with them to let her go. He was calling her a bitch, a whore. The one with the cricket bat was halfway to her car. She started to cry. The one with the rod was lifting the metal in his hand . . .

———

They were all taken by surprise. A new flood of light, a vehicle screeching from speed to a halt, a figure marching toward them. The one with the rod wasn't prepared, he underestimated the speed of this man bearing down on him. He spun and lifted the rod above his head, and the next thing Neda saw he was crumpled on the ground. The old man came round to the front of the car, fists raised, but it made no difference, the figure advanced on him, struck him with a flurry of punches and kicks, and he followed his friend into the concrete with a thud. Now she clearly saw her rescuer bathed in the headlights.

Ajay.

It was Ajay.

By now the man with the cricket bat was frozen.

Ajay pulled a pistol from inside his jacket and the one with the cricket bat turned and ran.

Ajay trained his gun on the one with the metal rod. He kicked the rod away, dragged the man into the headlights, examined him closely. She was half expecting to see the Caravaggio goon, but no, it was just a man. Any man on the street. Ajay smashed him in the head with the handle of his gun. He turned to the old man, looked down on him with coiled rage. She watched it all, trembling. The old man got to his feet, backed off. Ajay put the gun away.

"Madam," he said.

And he was back to sweet, loyal Ajay. "Open the door."

She did what he asked. She unlocked the door and opened it, and he took her by the arm and eased her out, and she leaned into him as he guided her to the SUV.

She sat shell-shocked in the passenger seat as he returned to her car and pushed it to the side of the road. Then he fetched her things, swept the seats, turned off the lights, locked it. He returned to the SUV, climbed in, and began to drive away. She just watched him. She couldn't find any words. He had hurt those men badly, but his face seemed perfectly composed.

"What just happened?"

He didn't reply.

"Ajay," she said.

His name on her lips seemed to startle him.

"What just happened?"

"I don't know," he said.

"They were going to hurt me."

"I wouldn't let them."

"I need my car," she said.

"Don't worry, madam," he replied.

He seemed to catch himself.

He dialed a number. Began to talk into the phone in a low voice.

"Is that Sunny?"

Ajay spoke in a quiet voice.

"Is that Sunny?" she cried. "Give me the phone."

She reached for it, but he hung up and clicked it off.

He drove her a short distance into Sarita Vihar. Eased the SUV into a narrow lane with shuttered travel agent offices and small warehouses. There was only one light glowing, inside a glass front with a faded painted sign: Hotel Ottoman. He stopped and climbed out, ran to the passenger side, guided her by the shoulder around the SUV and into the hotel. The bright white light was glaring and harsh. There was an elevator, and Ajay pressed the call button while the clerk at reception asked in an irritated voice what was going on. Ajay pulled out his money clip, peeled off a round of notes, and put them down, placating the clerk, saying something inaudible before returning.

As they rode up in the elevator, she braced herself.

"He's here?"

"Yes," he said.

She didn't know what else to say.

The elevator opened to a windowless corridor with wallpaper like green gemstones and a dirty marble floor. At the third room on the right, number 406, Ajay knocked three times, equally spaced, coded. She felt a surge of rage and began pounding on the door. Another door in the corridor jerked open and a paunchy man in undershirt and pants came out to scratch his ear and stare. A moment later the door to room 406 was thrown open, and there was Sunny, haunted and puffy and disheveled. He looked down the corridor at the man. Looked to Ajay. "Deal with him." Then he grabbed Neda by the wrist, pulled her inside, and slammed the door.

She almost fell onto the floor. "Hey! What the fuck?!"

The room was small, stuffy. Fluorescent lights gave it a sickly hue. There was a single bed with pillows in the shape of hearts, a synthetic bedspread with lace trills, a table at the side with a flask of water, a pack of cigarettes, a tumbler, and a plastic bottle of cheap liquor. A decrepit AC unit rattled in the wall. She got up ready to confront him, but then she saw his face. How ashen and pathetic, how diminished he looked. He grabbed her by the arms.

"What happened?"

A new kind of fear seeped into the anger and shock she already felt.

"They were trying to kill me." She stood rigid, her mind trapped in the memory of violence. "But Ajay . . ." She went on. "He hurt them. Oh God, he *really* hurt them." She frowned and looked up in a kind of concussed wonder. "But what was he doing there?"

"Are you fucking serious?" he replied.

His incredulous tone brought her back to the room. She pulled herself out of his grip, paced the floor. "Yes, I'm serious. What was he doing there, what are you doing *here*, where the fuck have you been!? What the FUCK is going on? I came to see you. You *called* me!" She froze, held her hands to her head. "You didn't call me. It wasn't you, was it? Oh God, I'm so stupid."

"Who called you?"

"But fuck you, Sunny. You vanished. You just vanished on me."

He approached, tried to corner her. "It's very important you answer me. Who called you?"

She was shivering. "I want to go home."

"And then?"

"And then nothing, forget I ever met you. Seriously!"

"You can't just go home."

"I can go where I want!"

"You have to tell me who called you."

"I DON'T KNOW! All right? I DON'T *KNOW*. I'm *so* fucking stupid. What's *wrong* with me?"

Tears started welling in her eyes. The adrenaline was wearing off, shock was fast approaching. She needed something from him, but there was nothing he could give, not like this.

"Don't touch me," she whispered, as she slipped past, sat on the side of the bed. She took one of his cigarettes from the bedside, lit it with shaking hands. The act of smoking soothed her. She examined the liquor bottle, held it up to the light. "You're really living it up."

He watched her motionless from the other side of the room.

"Someone called you out to the office," he said. "What did he say?"

She opened the bottle and took a swig and recoiled at the harshness, then she closed her eyes.

"He said you wanted to see me."

"Why?"

"How the *fuck* should I know. Because you *cared* about me?"

"No, why would he say this? Why would he call you out there?"

She gritted her teeth in frustration. "I *don't* know. You weren't there. It got late. I came back. Sunny, who were these guys out there who attacked me?"

"I don't know, they were just some guys."

"Are you serious? They were just some guys and Ajay just happened to be passing by and you just happened to be in this hotel. Yeah? I'm supposed to believe this? Fuck. They were going to *kill* me. Or worse."

"No one was going to kill you."

"Fuck you."

"Scare you, maybe."

"*Maybe?* Well guess what? I was scared." She took a deep breath. "God, Ajay was so . . ." She frowned. "If you didn't call me, why was he following me?"

"Because you were at the office! I have people there. They said you were at the office. I sent Ajay out to keep an eye on you."

"Fuck you, Sunny."

They talked at cross purposes awhile, over and over, each one giving the side of a story that made no sense, that went in circles. She was there because she'd been called. Ajay was following her because she was there. She wouldn't say that she'd been spying on the mansion, that she'd been seen by the same goon she'd encountered out in the resettlement plots. She refused to give this away. But slowly it made sense in her mind. They were screwing with her, sending her a warning, or maybe trying to get rid of her entirely. She thought about the goons surrounding her car, their bloodthirsty faces. Her mind went into terrible what-ifs, she saw herself being dragged out into the road, screaming, helpless, lost, and she knew she was going too far into something she hadn't bargained for. And Sunny, in this room, what the hell was that about? That was another story.

"Seriously, Sunny. Where the fuck have you been? The last thing I saw of you was your father kicking you into that pool. It was a nightmare. A nightmare. And you abandoned me."

He was sitting on the edge of the bed now. She could see him in profile.

"I had no choice."

"You could have made one call."

"You don't understand."

"I think I do. I understand them, I understand you."

"I didn't want to put you in danger."

She laughed bitterly.

"If I'm in danger it's because I came looking for you."

He turned to face her. "It's all gone to shit."

"Yeah? Whose fault is that?"

"It's mine," he said.

"My God, you're fucked up."

"Why? I should never have put that ad out. I was being weak."

"You were being human," she said. "But yeah, maybe you shouldn't have done it. Maybe we shouldn't have done a lot of things." She shook her head slowly. "It's such a mess. I don't want this violence. I don't want to be involved in this. I just want . . ."

"I miss you," he said.

"Oh, fuck off."

"I do."

He reached his hand out to her.

She held it.

"You really, really look like shit," she said. "What are you even doing here?"

"I don't know. Give me a drink."

She handed him the bottle, he took a swig, and she lay on the bed and he pulled himself up alongside her, and they were both on their backs looking at the ceiling.

"Sunny, what he did to you at the villa, in the pool . . . that's not normal. Fathers shouldn't do that to their sons."

"You live in a different world."

"Maybe. Maybe I don't anymore."

He smiled an empty, pitiful smile.

"The pool was just the start. After I put that ad out," he said, "he came

down on me so hard. He sent his men into my apartment, and they destroyed everything. They smashed it up, and he came in and stood there and
watched. He took my phones, my laptops. He shut my businesses down.
Took my cards away. Put me on a leash. He said, 'You never show our name
and our face like that again.'"

"Why do you think that is?"

He stayed silent for a long time without an answer.

She turned to face him.

"I saw something, Sunny. I found something out."

"What are you talking about?"

"These demolitions, these resettlements. Their homes are destroyed,
their land is taken away, they're sent off to the edges of Delhi, to waste
ground full of mosquitoes, next to garbage dumps, with nothing, no hope,
no future. But that's not all. There are people waiting there for them, goons,
terrifying people, pushing them into selling off this little bit of useless land
for a handful of rupees. The land that's being given after forced evictions is
being bought up by developers for nothing."

"So what?"

"I went there. I spoke with people on one of these sites. I was threatened
there by some goons. One guy I'll never forget. I call him Caravaggio. His
face is like a grotesque angel. I saw him there at the site and then I saw him
somewhere else. And he saw me."

"Where?"

"Where do you think?"

He didn't want to say.

"He was coming out of your mansion. He works for your family. And he
saw me, and then I got the call to come and meet you."

"No." He shook his head.

"What do you mean, no? Why is it so hard to believe? Your family is violence. Your life is violence. You're violent men."

"No."

She started to laugh it was all so absurd. "And now they're onto me.

They're onto me because they think I'm onto them. But all I did was stumble over it looking for you."

He had nothing to say. What was there to say anyway? It was the truth and they both knew it.

She closed her eyes and she was asleep before she even had time to see herself falling into the darkness.

She was awoken by three loud knocks on the door.

She guessed she'd only been down a minute.

She was about to speak when she saw Sunny holding his finger to his lips, a revolver in his hand.

She resisted the urge to scream as Sunny crept closer to the door.

"Sir." Ajay's voice came from the other side.

Relief spread through the room.

Sunny lowered the gun, opened the door a crack.

"Sir," Ajay said, "the car is taken care of."

"Good," Sunny replied. "Wait downstairs."

She came to understand as she gathered her things and Sunny watched her in silence that she'd been asleep almost three hours. When she was ready to leave, Sunny held her by the arm.

"What is it?"

"You can't talk about this to anyone."

She hesitated, thought it over.

"Who do I have to tell?"

"The guy you work with."

"You think I want him to know any of this? Where would I even start? But you should know, he's onto you anyway."

"There's nothing he can do."

"Yeah. You're probably right. But you could do something, you know that? You could just walk away."

"That's not realistic."

"Sunny, whatever dreams you might have, your father is going to destroy them, and he's going to destroy you. You want to transform Delhi, you want to make the city new, beautiful, you want to show it off to the world. But what does he want?"

He didn't answer.

"Sunny," she said, "he's a man, not a God. If you stay with him, I won't be there with you. All you have to do is walk away."

"I can't," he said. "That's suicide."

Ajay was waiting for her downstairs. He turned his head as soon as she stepped out of the elevator.

"Wait," he said. "I'll bring the car."

Ajay drove with great precision. She watched his hands on the wheel, his knuckles bloodied and swollen. She wondered what he thought. She began to get her story straight. Her car had broken down. She had taken a lift with friends. Her parents probably wouldn't even ask. They were like that. But as she neared home, she felt more scared.

"Ajay," she said.

"Yes, madam."

"Thank you."

"Madam," he said, "your car will be ready tomorrow."

Outside her house, Ajay turned to face her.

"Madam," he said, the engine ticking over.

"Yes?"

"He's a good man."

It broke her heart.

"So are you."

He averted his eyes.

Then she climbed out and closed the door and he watched her until she entered her house and then he drove away.

3.

Her car came back as promised the next day, a few hours after she'd taken Sardar-ji's taxi to work. All the denting and painting was done. Not a scratch on it. It was delivered by a rangy, cheery mechanic in blue overalls and a Brahmin's topknot; a boy following him on a scooter took him away again. As if nothing had happened.

She scoured the newspaper for any reports of an accident around Jamia or Shaheen Bagh or Kalindi Kunj. Nothing. No car crash. No injuries. No deaths. Everything erased. Everything smoothed over. As if nothing had ever happened.

She kept waiting for the terrible surprise. She didn't know what it would be. A visit from the cops. A visit from a goon. A phone call just like in the movies: I know what you did. I know what you did. Meet me here. Bring money there. Talk and you're dead. She kept waiting to hear from Sunny again. To see Ajay. But there was nothing. She avoided Dean that first day back in the office. Thankfully he was too busy to speak with her.

But she was going to tell him, wasn't she?

She just had to go to his office and knock on the door, step inside, close it behind her, sit down, and begin to explain.

That's what was going to happen, right?

But what would she say?

Was it an accident?

Had they been trying to scare her?

She still had no idea.

When she tried to sleep, she could only replay it all in her head. The phone call that drew her out. The nervy drive back into Delhi. The sudden smash of metal, the spinning confusion, the headlights on her face, the looming men. She kept making excuses to take taxis to work. Autos here and there in the city to do jobs. She left her car parked outside home, under the shade of the banyan in the park. She still shared nothing with Dean.

"By the way," Dean wrote in an email four days later. "This happy story might cheer your heart." His words were laced with irony. He sent her the link to a *Times* article. It was a color feature: "Picking Up the Pieces: A Family Makes Sense of Loss." The parents of the dead kids had been tracked to their native village, not far from Kanpur. There they were, Devi and Rajkumar, sad but hopeful, putting the past behind them. Devi was pregnant again. Rajkumar had used the Wadia Foundation compensation money to buy agricultural land. They had built a pukka house. Some good had emerged from the tragedy, the writer noted. Rajkumar hoped that one day his son would study in Delhi and speak English and live in a big man's house. He said Delhi was for modern people, progress was necessary, and God was looking over them now.

"Mystery solved," she replied.

Her regular beat continued. She was grateful for the uncomplicated monotony of these small stories. She avoided the southeast of the city if she could. She avoided late nights out driving alone. Even when she made peace with her car, driving home at night after dark made her nervous. She thought someone was following her. She began to imagine it was Ajay. He was following her everywhere. He would protect her. It made her feel better. The comfort never lasted. Her mind raced with the old questions.

In her dreams sometimes she saw the glare of headlights and felt Ajay's violence. She drummed up the courage to drive out one morning to the resettlement colony and found it was surrounded by a chain-link fence with warnings saying: PRIVATE PROPERTY.

Winter descended on Delhi. Woolens were removed from cupboards and steel trunks. Crisp, chill mornings of mist rose with the pale disk of sun, with boundless blue skies after. Lodhi Garden was full of walkers, vigorous, marching with purpose, while on the streets, the homeless lit fires in metal cans, squatting on the side of the road. There was a trip to Old Delhi for morning nihari. Diwali approached with its strings of golden light. Delhi burst into a frenzy of shopping and eating. Dean no longer confided in her. Sunny was not there. She spent it with her parents, lighting dias in the house, making a small puja, watching the kids in the park across the road with their sparklers, going up onto the roof terrace and viewing the fireworks over the city. The next morning a pall of smoke hung over the rooftops. The temperatures plummeted, the cold stole into the houses and squatted and refused to leave. She began to think about escape. Her heart was bereft and raging, a squall under the surface. She looked into taking the TEFL course at the British Council. Teach English in Japan. A friend had done it and never returned.

Christmas. Decorations with Santas in Connaught Place. Paeans to consumption. Paying lip service to religion. She went with her parents to St. James's Church for Midnight Mass. A secular family tradition—they went every year. The three of them in the pews, not quite understanding what was going on. She closed her eyes and said a prayer. She thought she saw Ajay in the congregation, sitting a little ahead, praying too. But when it came time for Communion, she saw it was just another man.

The desolation of January. The city choked by smog. The temperatures dipping toward zero some nights. Her first story of the new year: the lack of adequate shelter for the homeless, an organized blanket mafia. A mafia for everything. She took the TEFL course after work. She had given up on Sunny. And given up on herself. She knew it was too late. She wouldn't go to Dean. She could only plan to leave and never come back.

4.

On the morning of the last day of January 2004 she asked Dean to lunch at China Fare. She wanted to tell him her news: she was going to hand in her notice that afternoon. He agreed to see her, he might be a little late, he had a busy morning on the cards. She idled at her desk and saw his office locked. She went to Khan Market early and browsed the shops, everyone wrapped in sweaters and shawls. She wasn't sure if she was going to confess. She didn't know what she'd say until she was face-to-face, until he gave some clue from his end. All she knew was she was done. She took a table in China Fare at one and waited for him. Ate spring rolls and drank green tea.

When he came in she knew something was very wrong. He sat down at the table and held the edge with his fingers as if it were a cliff. He wouldn't even look up at her. He seemed only to care about breathing. He knows, she thought. But what? What does he know? It didn't matter. She was leaving. He lifted his hands from the table, rubbed his eyes under his wire-rimmed glasses, then removed the glasses entirely, placed them on the table, and covered his whole face with his hands. Finally he looked up and his eyes were shining and faraway.

"I just quit," he said.

Of all the things she'd expected him to say, this was not it.

"Seriously?"

"Or maybe I was fired." He frowned. "I don't know." He was talking to himself. "Maybe I jumped before I was pushed."

"Dean . . ."

He looked up. "Let's go get a beer."

They went to Chonas. He started to talk. "You know how I started investigating Bunty Wadia? I dug up so much dirt you wouldn't believe. I short-changed him when I called him one of Ram Singh's mob. Turns out the tail was wagging the dog. Ram Singh pretty much works for him."

His voice turned contemplative. "Seems like almost everyone works for him." She waited for him to go on. "I had a mentor," he eventually said. "An old editor at one of the papers here. I'm not going to say his name. Respected. A straight shooter. All the way down the line. I've only known him in person awhile, but I corresponded with him and read his byline when he was younger and he taught me how to be a journalist, a reporter, and it wouldn't be a stretch to say he taught me how to be a man. At least in my head. What's that saying? 'If you meet the Buddha on the road, kill him'?"

"Dean. You're rambling."

"I finished my exposé last week. It's huge. And it's completely fucking meaningless."

"Why?"

"The night I finished, this mentor of mine gave me a call. Ten p.m. He invited me to have breakfast with him the next morning at Yellow Brick Road. Nothing strange about that, right? Just a coincidence with the timing. I was buzzing with the story, the way you get when you've landed something big, something that'll make waves. So I was excited to meet him. But I didn't tell him anything about it on the phone."

"What was in the story?"

"Wait. This is the story. I turned up for breakfast. And there he was waiting, sipping orange juice, his coffee by his side, at one of the tables by the window, the one that looks out over the lawn and the driveway, it catches the sun. He was facing the room. I sat opposite him. He'd been ill last year but he was much better now. He looked tidy, tanned. That was unusual, to see him tanned. I asked if he'd been on holiday, but he said no, he'd been swimming a lot these days in an outdoor pool, he'd caught the sun that way and found it agreeable, though his wife nagged him relentlessly about it. All this pleasantry, small talk. 'So,' he said to me, 'what's going on with you?' And I told him I was about to send a story to my editor, a big one." Dean took a sip of beer, touched his hand to his forehead. "He nodded at me. 'Now,' he said, 'about that . . .'" And my stomach flipped.

"He knew about it."

"He knew the entire thing, paragraphs, sentences, the argument, the structure."

"How?"

"Because he'd already read it. I hadn't shown it to a single person, but he'd already read it."

"*How?*"

"They'd been on my computer." He threw his hands up. "He told me there was no profit in making this kind of trouble. No profit. I told him there was no profit in any of it. Profit isn't the point. Surely he remembered that. He said: 'It can be.' Profit *can be* the point. This guy, who was like a father to me, who I modeled myself on after a fashion, whose ethical standards inspired me, told me profit *could be* the point. I'd done great work, after all, and I should be rewarded for it. As such, the concerned party would be willing to buy my story back, because it was their story in the end and I'd just done the hard work of stringing it up. Yes, they'd buy it. He could see how disgusted I was. I thought I could see a moment of shame in his eyes, but all he told me was that the world had changed. Journalism was a business like everything else." Dean shook his head. "The distance between our thinking was not possible to bridge. The distance between the man who schooled me and the one sitting before me was unfathomable. But he was the same man. He had the same wife. The same dog he took for the same walks. The same routines, the same friends, the same restaurants he ate in. In fact, he'd always been this man. It was the world that had changed. But that's not me. I know who I am. 'What happened to you?' I said to him. He seemed to consider the question seriously, as if no one had asked it before, but he offered no answer. Instead, he wrote a sum on a napkin and slid it over and said this was his client's offer."

"How much?"

"I'm not going to dignify it by repeating it out loud. It was obscene. I tore it up. I left the pieces there on the table and I walked away. I took the story to Venkatesh that day. He read it. He thought it stood up. He passed it through legal. They were nervous. But they looked through my evidence and, yeah, it fucking stood up. V. said they'd run it. But he told me I should brace myself. And then . . ." He pointed his finger to the ceiling. "God. The man upstairs. The managing editor. The board. The owner. They stepped on it. They refused to publish. Twisted as it is, I'll give *him* credit, he came at me with the carrot first. Only later did he come with the stick. Well, I got stuck. The story got shut down this morning. I was put on paid leave. So I quit. Or I was fired. I don't fucking know. All I know is that I'm free."

She watched his face, trying to read his thoughts.

"What was in the story that was so bad?"

He gave a strange, polite smile, then reached into the satchel near his right leg and tossed a printout held together with a clip across the table.

"You tell me."

She started scanning the pages, counting them. She stopped at fifteen, flicked to the end, flicked back to the start.

She read out the title. "Hiding in Plain Sight?"

"Not very catchy, I know. It was a placeholder." He sank his beer. "V. was going to change it."

It must have been five thousand words or more. The narrative was clear: Bunty Wadia was the biggest player in the state of UP. He was the chief minister in all but name, and then some. His business interests spanned the state. He held a significant share of the state's wholesale and retail liquor business. For the sake of appearances, he ran the business through proxy members, who sometimes presented as rivals in public, but ultimately worked together and answered to him. They called themselves "the syndicate."

She read it out loud. "The syndicate?"

"I know," he said. "Straight out of a pulp novel. Though in fairness that's technically what it is."

She read on. It wasn't just wholesale and retail. It wasn't just vertical integration—sugarcane to sugar mill, distillery, distribution, wholesale, retail, the whole thing tied up, over the whole state, all the hundreds of millions of people, from nose to tail—it was monopoly. Sure, there were other players, other producers in the state, but since the Wadia Syndicate controlled the wholesale and retail licenses, they controlled who got to sell to the customer *at all*. Unless you paid handsomely, in cash, you were marginalized, made to disappear. At point of sale, Wadia's own brands, either the ones he made or the ones he imported, gained prominence. If you wanted a look in— and most ultimately did—you had to pay the price, in cash. So for every truck of liquor coming in, a suitcase of banknotes went to the Wadia/Singh coffers. Fifty-fifty. What was anyone going to do? Go to the cops? Go to the Excise Department? They were taking their cut too. The industry generated billions of dollars in white and billions in black, it kept everything in order and kept everyone paid.

And that was just the start of it.

The first two pages.

It went on and on.

Through sand mining, through transport, through toll booths and infrastructure. Through the control of the police and judiciary.

At every step, the Wadias and Singhs skimming off the top, the bottom, the middle.

The transport scam was fiendish in its simplicity. The state government systematically downgraded and shut down viable and profitable government bus routes only to grant licenses to private operators who ran those very same routes at considerably higher cost to the commuter. At first these private operators appeared to be competitors, but on inspection, eight out of ten were Wadia proxies, while the other two were run by extended family members of Ram Singh.

She skipped through, put it down. Picked it up again. Skipped through. There was a section of history, how Bunty Wadia had risen from a lowly grain merchant in Meerut. How he'd given Ram Singh his first boost in politics. How he'd shifted into daru production with the help of his elder brother,

Vikram. How Vikram "Vicky" Wadia had become an enforcer in Maharajganj, Eastern UP, then an MLA. Her eye caught something familiar.

"The Kushinagar incident?"

"Yeah," he laughed, "that one took a lot of figuring out. In the end I got it from the horse's mouth."

"The horse?"

"Vicky Wadia. He filled in a lot of the gaps."

"He spoke to you?"

"Where he comes from, this article is just good PR."

She read the paragraph slowly.

"Did he really do this?"

"I think so. The only ones who really know are the ones who were there. I asked the ex-DM of the district if it was true. I told him what Vicky told me. He said, 'If Vicky says it, then it's true.' In the end it doesn't matter if it's true or not, it's whether people believe it. And they believe it. They believe that he's a kind of God-man out there, that he does a powerful black magic."

"He burned someone alive in the vegetable market?"

A young man was caught stealing a housewife's gold chain, running through the market with it to escape. Vicky had been wandering through with his entourage. He saw the thief coming. Plucked him right into the air, so it was said. Flung him senseless to the ground. Took the gold chain back. Poured kerosene over him. Lit a match. The whole market watched it happen, the man screaming, running into the tomato stand.

"Go ahead, read his quote."

She read Vicky's words from the page. "'He was a thief, and thieves were plaguing the district at this time, and someone had to stand up for the people, someone had to make thieves understand there are consequences to their crime.' End quote. Jesus."

"He got voted into office later that year. They have another name for him, out there. Himmatgiri."

She threw it down, she wanted to change the subject. "I'm exhausted just reading it."

"Imagine how I feel."
Imagine how Sunny feels.

The weight of these men, the violence of their lives. It had been on top of her for days, weeks, months. For as long as she could remember, for what now seemed like years, years and years, hundreds of kilometers of black road. The money she had consumed, the wine, the whisky, the blacked-out cars, the black sole of Bunty Wadia's shoe, pushing Sunny deeper into the pool.

"These men," Dean was saying, "are heroes to the people from whom *they* steal, whose very lives *they* destroy."

She felt the foot.

She saw his face.

"Is there anything," she asked, "about Delhi?"

Dean laughed. His laugh was the laughter of the defeated, the man at the end of his rope, with nothing to lose, the man with whom the gods have done their business.

"Sure there is. Turn to the second-to-last page."

She watched him closely as she felt for the pages. Did he know?

She braced herself.

But there was nothing about demolitions and resettlement colonies or land grabs.

It was about Sunny.

"Read it out loud," he said.

She cleared her throat: "Bunty Wadia invests in none of the typical sig-nifiers of brand building. There are no sponsorship deals, no billboards, no interviews, no public events; no public profile at all. He is not so much building a brand as a silent, invisible web. Yet like so many so-called great men, his weakness appears to be his son. The yearning for dynasty blindsides such men to the clear and obvious flaws that come with nature's imperfect replication." She looked up at him. She carried on reading, but this time in her head. On he went, speechifying, writing on the neoliberal global order, the deafening clamor to transform Delhi. Then he came to the point. He had in his possession a copy of a proposal prepared by Sunny Wadia and an MIT graduate he had hired for the transformation of the Yamuna Riverfront from derelict, slum-ridden wasteland to "World-Class Business and Leisure Destination." It painted that same Utopian picture she had seen and of which she'd heard, of promenades, marinas, biodiversity parks, cultural centers, boating lakes, and boardwalks. It boasted computer-generated images of clean and happy families, their skin lightly toned, enjoying the blue skies and clean waters of a Yamuna "denuded of its very essence, it's very nature." Dean tore it apart. "The plans, according to those in the know, have been ridiculed. They are seen as both politically unfeasible and environmentally unsound. As one unnamed official commented, 'the Yamuna is an unchannelized Himalayan river, sitting on a floodplain, subject to monsoon pressures and at the mercy of nature's whims. To imagine otherwise is fantasy and folly of a gross nature.'"

Enough. She'd had enough. She flipped the stack of pages over, shook her head, gripped her beer.

"See," he said. "I told you Sunny Wadia was a joker."

5.

On Valentine's Day of all days, an unknown number called her phone.

She recognized Sunny's voice right away.

"Neda," he said.

It sounded so distant, so pained.

She waited for him to speak, but he only breathed heavily on the line. Not the heaviness of threat, but of oblivion, self-destruction. She was at home in the kitchen making chai. She took the call out in the front yard.

The parakeets were flitting, there was a chill in the air. It caught you hard if you stood in the shadows; she moved to the sun.

"What?"

"I need help."

She shook her head. Tears gathered in her eyes. "I can't help you."

"I can't do it anymore."

He sounded desperate.

"You can't do what?"

"You know what."

She blinked and the tears rolled down her cheeks.

"I thought you were going to fix this?"

"I can't."

Her shoulders slumped. "Where are you?"

"Goa."

"Why?"

"I can't do it anymore. I need help."

"OK. Calm down."

"Fly down."

"Sunny . . ."

"Fly down today. I need to see you. I need to speak to you. Face-to-face."

"Why?"

"I can't tell you on the phone. Just come. Just come and I swear I'll never ask you anything again."

"Sunny."

"What?"

"Honestly? This sounds like a trap."

"It's not."

"Are you fucking with me?"

"Book a ticket. Send the details to this phone. Ajay will meet you at the airport. Please, just come. Come now and I'll never bother you again."

———

She cursed herself. She waited an hour. Then she called her travel agent and had him book a ticket for the evening. She went to work but there was nothing pressing for her to do, her stories had been filed, and since she'd handed in her notice there were no new stories to pick up. The ticket was sent over to her office that afternoon. She messaged the details to the number from which Sunny had called. She didn't even go home to change or pack. She left her car parked at work and took a taxi to the airport. She called her house on the way; her mother answered.

"Hey, it's me. I'm in Bombay for a few days. There's a story I need to chase up. And I'm seeing Hari. I'll be home Sunday."

The flight down was only a quarter full. There were a dozen or so businessmen, a couple of travel-worn backpackers cheating on India by taking the plane. She curled up right away on three seats, put her winter coat over her, and tried to sleep. She didn't want to think. She had recently achieved some success by not thinking about anything at all. She was terrified of seeing him. As the plane began its descent she half hoped Ajay wouldn't be there. It was possible. There was a chance. And then? She'd take a taxi to Vagator, stay at Jackie's Day Night, eat crab curry at Starlight, go home. That would be the end of the line.

She arrived early in the night, the earth held the warmth of the day, tempered by the breeze that blew off the Arabian Sea. She peeled off her coat, hung it over one arm, left the tourists waiting by the luggage carousel, and stepped out to the arrivals strip with the hotel touts and the taxi drivers stirring to life. They advanced en masse at the sight of her, starting up their pitch. Taxi, madam. Hotel, madam. Come, madam, this way. She stood before them and opened her bag and took out her cigarette pack, removed a cigarette slowly, lit it and inhaled deeply, and blew smoke up into the night, where it danced with the moths and mosquitoes in the floodlights.

"Madam."

That familiar voice.

That face.

He led her away from the crowd to a parked car. A red Maruti like her own. Local plates. He said she should ride up front with him, so the police wouldn't think it was an illegal taxi. One had to follow the tricks here.

They drove beside a large river, past miles of palm trees and small white-washed chapels glowing with night-lights, past stray dogs barking in the headlights, turning to vanish in the groves. A few bars were open on the roadside, tiny concrete drinking dens with old wooden doors and weak bulbs inside. She wound the window down and let the sweet air fill her hair and her lungs. A sedative. They didn't speak. She watched his hands on the wheel, the knuckles that were scarred. After some time they joined a busy road, passed a police checkpoint. The traffic picked up and the way was dusty and potholed and slow. When they were stuck behind a truck, she felt compelled to talk.

"Ajay?"

"Yes, madam."

"Is everything OK?"

"Yes, madam."

"Is Sunny OK?"

"Yes," he said, but he didn't sound so certain.

She thought about pursuing that line, but decided against it, lapsed into silence again, but he overtook the truck soon after, and the act of accelera-tion on the narrow road roused her.

"You drive like you know the roads."

"Madam," he said, "I worked here."

"You did?"

"Yes."

"Where?"

"Arambol."

"You were a shack boy?"

"Yes."

"Before Sunny?"

"Before Sunny Sir."

She lit a new cigarette. "Have you been back there? To see your friends?"

He smiled shyly and shook his head. "Madam, I'm working."

They fell into silence again and crossed another bridge.

The image of that smile remained imprinted in her mind.

They entered the capital city, Panjim. Small, colonial. It made her think of a fairy tale. Ajay drove along the riverfront before turning inside, following narrow streets of yellow-painted colonial buildings with large-tiled roofs and narrow wooden balconies and screens made of oyster shell. Winding up a hill to a hotel called the Windmill, one of those once glamorous, now shabby, three-star joints. He found parking nearby and locked the car and asked her to follow him. Inside the small reception, a young man with frizzy hair and acne and a badly sprouting mustache greeted Ajay with warmth. He looked to Neda and addressed her in English. "You must be our guest. Your friend is waiting for you." He pointed to the elevator. "On the roof terrace."

"Madam," Ajay said, "I'll go."

Before she could reply he had slipped out the front door.

She rose in the cramped and clanking elevator. It opened to a dead roof. Chairs had been stacked, tables turned on top of others, lights switched off. But she saw a bartender standing in low light behind the bar, and when she moved ahead she could make out Sunny's figure seated, feet up on the concrete rim, staring out at the clouded, moonlit sky.

She approached silently. He was dressed in an old cotton T-shirt advertising a petroleum brand, the kind you get in backpacker towns in Thailand. She could see the bulge of his belly that had been hidden by his tailoring. His beard had grown unkempt. He wore a baseball cap.

An empty chair was waiting at his side.

She stood beside him, lit a cigarette but didn't sit.

She looked out onto the narrow, cobbled streets, the old stone churches, the palm-lined avenues. The air was fresh and smelled of brine. Beyond the city, trawlers bobbed in the wide, placid mouth of the river. On the far bank, a flamboyance of advertising hoardings, neon flamingos above a fishing village, irradiating the sky.

"Sit down," he said.

"Not yet. I've been sitting all day."

He offered her the drink that was in his hand.

She was cool with him.

"What's that?"

"Long Island Iced Tea."

"You're on vacation now?"

He shrugged.

She took it from him and took a sip.

"Shit, that's strong."

"Yeah."

"We used to get them in college, happy hour at TGIF, me and the girls, when I had my girls. Feels like another life."

"I never had one before," he said.

"Really?"

"I went straight from desi daru in the cane fields to martinis at Dukes."

"Why am I here?" she said.

"Because I'm a joker," he looked up at her. "Right?"

Dean's unpublished piece.

"You read it?" she said.

"Yeah."

"The whole thing?"

He nodded. "Maybe your guy was right."

She took a seat.

"I mean . . ." She was at a loss for words. "I don't think so."

He took the drink back from her, slurped it down.

He was on the way to being wasted.

She felt like getting to that place too.

"At least," she went on, "I now know what your uncle did in Kushinagar." She raised her eyebrows. "Local politics, right?"

"I used to love him so much. He always had good stories." He let out a long sigh, was about to speak but held back.

"What?"

"I don't know."

"No," she gently coaxed him, "what were you going to say?"

But he wouldn't go on down that path.

"The chutiya Dean should have taken the money," he said.

She shifted her lips into a joyless smile.

"He would never have taken it."

Sunny couldn't hide his irritation. "Ten crore rupees was more than enough."

Damn. Ten crore rupees. Enough to buy a whole new life.

"Your father ruined his career," she said. "Do you understand that?"

"It's all part of the game. He knew the risks."

"Do you even hear yourself? Do you know what kind of asshole you sound like? Seriously, Sunny. Why am I here? What did you bring me down for?"

"To tell you I'm done."

"Done what?"

"With all of it."

"Specific, Sunny. Be specific."

"You told me. I didn't have to take it. I could just walk away."

"Yeah . . ."

"I'm walking away."

"From?"

"Him, his money, his pressure on my head, his violence, his way of doing things. All my dreams are bullshit anyway. You saw what your journalist said about me. I'm tired. I'm stuck between the shit my father does and the things I can't do."

"What will you do?"

He closed his eyes.

"I'm tired," he said. "I'll tell you everything. Tomorrow. I have a room here for us for tonight. We have to leave early in the morning."

"Why?"

"We're going somewhere," he said. "A place I can talk. Where no one will find us. Then I'll tell you everything."

The room on the fourth floor was charming in a faded, musty way, jammed full of old-fashioned Portuguese furniture and fittings. She showered in the white light of the bathroom while she left him standing on the balcony smoking. She had questions. So many questions. She was desperate to hear him talk, but he was lying facedown on the bed when she came out, already sleeping, still wearing his shoes. She guessed he'd been saving all his energy for her arrival, for the news, and now he'd delivered it, he'd collapsed. She removed his shoes and socks, turned off the lights, threw down her towel, and lay next to him, pulling the blanket up tight. The city shimmered in the streetlights. It was near silent outside. The occasional bark of a dog, the buzz of a scooter on the road. He stirred. He mumbled without opening his eyes. "It's my birthday the day after, on the sixteenth."

Next thing she knew it was five thirty in the morning and he was up, boiling water in the small kettle in the faint light of the bedside lamp, pouring sachets of instant coffee into the chipped mugs on the dresser.

"What's going on?" At first she didn't remember where she was, what Sunny was doing in her room.

"We're leaving in half an hour."

"No." She pulled the covers up. "I want to sleep."

He poured the hot water, added a sachet of sugar, stirred it, and held one of the coffees under her nose. "Wake up."

He had a Polaroid camera on the table. He took a photo of her with the flash.

"It's cold," she said. "I want to sleep."

She watched him shaking the photo out. "I bet I look hideous."

He added a shot of Old Monk to his coffee.

"Hey! Pour me one too."

She could almost pretend it was normal. They were downstairs at ten past six. The morning was growing in the sky—strokes of amber among the lilac, the outlines of fast-moving clouds. Sunny handed the key to the receptionist, settled the bill.

Out in the street, Ajay was waiting, standing next to a Royal Enfield Bullet 500, holding her winter coat under his arm, along with a thick blue shawl and a helmet. She wore the coat, wrapped herself in the shawl. He passed the helmet to Sunny. The keys were in the ignition. Sunny climbed on, checked the amp meter, kick-started the bike.

"Get on."

She climbed on the back.

Sunny turned to Ajay and shouted over the engine. "Two days. We'll be back in two days. I'll call you. If anyone calls for me, you know what to say."

They cut through the narrow city streets in the dawn, past sleeping households and cats darting across empty roads. They were chased by a pack of barking dogs on the riverside, out of the city onto the highway south, toward the airport. She wrapped her hands around his waist, pressed her cheek to his shoulder as they picked up speed and the guttural chop of the engine turned into a high, smooth crescendo. He gunned the throttle harder, and she saw mist hanging over the paddy fields, and there was nothing so beautiful as the roar of the Enfield on that empty road. An hour passed. An hour of nothing. Palm groves, whitewashed chapels, ripe pools of mosquito swarms and resting buffalo, the first sun bursting over the horizon, dazzling her, spilling golden over everything. They roared over the airport plateau, descended toward the city of Margao. Life was beginning to stir, traffic trickling through the lanes, cafés opening for breakfast, seniors exercising in the parks. They crossed over the train tracks, pulled out of the city and onto the highway again. A short while later he broke away, turned toward the coast, down small roads of dusty churches and football fields, weaving through villages where schoolgirls in pigtails walked arm in arm and hungry cats and housewives waited for the fishmonger's horn. Sunny removed his helmet, handed it back to her as they entered a hamlet crowded with palms and crows, and suddenly there was a beach, visible only for a second, glorious, before they veered toward the jungle and began to rise. For the next half hour they climbed inside the hills of the Canacona coast, straining around corners, up and down. She removed the shawl, the coat, held them over her lap with the helmet, soaking in the hot wind, closing her eyes and giving herself over to the sweep of the road. She was happy in being lost. They crested a hill. Suddenly he cut the engine and there was silence. The bike slowed, then picked up speed again. She opened her eyes. The jungle spread for many miles around, and ahead the sea, shimmering in the distance, with a handful of rocky islands around the headland, waves crashing into their many coves, spray refracted by the sun. Gravity carried the bike downhill, runaway, the squeak of the suspension felt precarious without the torque of the engine, and she understood in that moment how the sources of strength are illusory.

They stopped in a small market town, ordered poori bhaji and chai at the Udipi, ate and smoked cigarettes after, barely exchanging a word. He paid the bill, left a twenty for the waiter, a fifty for the beggar woman standing patiently by the bike. To a bunch of kids, he gave nothing. And they were off again.

It took another half hour to reach their destination, cruising with full bellies through the one-track hamlets with their sloped-roof houses and roaming chickens and their tulsi shrines. They crossed a palm-fringed river on a narrow iron bridge and the water was a turquoise she'd never seen.

And then the beach, the ocean, the bite of salt air. Kilometers of untouched sand, with only a few fishing boats and simple huts signaling life. He eased the bike down a sandy track toward a cluster of palm-roofed huts.

"We're here," he said.

"Santosh!" Sunny walked between the huts, calling out the name. A boy playing football with a deflated ball saw him and went hollering and jumping through the air. A moment later a cheerful young man stooped out of the darkness of one of the huts. Compact and muscled, with soft, pleasant skin, he wore nothing but Bermuda shorts and a silver Om pendant that dangled from his neck.

"Sunny, my friend!"

He wrapped his arms around his shoulder.

"Santosh," Sunny smiled. "How are you?"

"Very good, now you are here. I was waiting too long."

She saw how shy Sunny was, how happy.

"You've grown up. Santosh, this is Neda."

"Most welcome," Santosh said, holding his hand out very formally for Neda to shake.

He led them away from the huts, up toward a dune and a bank of pine trees.

She could hear the sea behind.

"Where are your things?"

"This is it."

"This is it? Just this. OK, very well. This is all you need. How long you stay? A week, a month, a year?"

"Just one night."

He clucked his tongue. "No good. How long has it been? Three years since you come? Look at you." He stopped and stood back and examined Sunny and laughed cheerily. "Now you look prosperous," he said, patting Sunny's stomach. Santosh turned to Neda. "Before he was never eating. He was too weak."

The hut was separated from the beach by a strip of wind-blasted pines, trunks tilted like calligraphy strokes. To the south, the pines ended at a tidal lagoon that connected the mangrove swamp to the sea. Beneath the trees sat a red plastic table, two chairs, two hammocks. The beach sand was soft and golden and piled up in powdery drifts. The high tide lapped the shore.

"Come. Sit," Santosh said. The boy who was playing with the football now waddled up carrying a huge metal bucket of beer and ice. He placed it in the shade next to one of the trees.

"See," Santosh declared as the kid ran off again, "I am prepared."

Sunny touched Santosh's arm with great affection. "Thank you."

"Anything for you, my friend."

Sunny kicked off his shoes and socks and collapsed into one of the chairs.

He lit a cigarette.

"Always working too hard, this one." He gripped Sunny's shoulders in his strong hands. "Now you relax."

Neda threw her coat and shawl and bag onto one of the chairs, walked up a little, and scanned the beach.

"What time is it?" Sunny said.

"Nine maybe," Santosh replied.

A handful of empty fishing boats bobbed in the surf.

Neda stretched. "Santosh, this place is incredible."

"I was born here," he said. He fished out two ice-cold Kings from the bucket, opened them on a row of nails hammered into one of the trees. He handed one to Sunny, then Neda. "Are you hungry? Let me go see. Maybe food is ready."

Santosh strolled back toward the huts.

"We just ate," Neda said.

"It's OK," Sunny replied, "even if it's ready Sushma will take another hour."

"Sushma?"

"His mother. She works on Goa time."

She sat, placed her beer on the table, removed her boots and socks. She buried her toes in the cool sand and lit a cigarette. A scruffy beach dog wandered up and curled itself under her chair.

"How do you know this place?"

"I spent a few months here a couple of years ago. Santosh was just a kid then. He flagged my bike down when he was walking home from school and demanded a ride. I ended up living with his family awhile."

"Good days," she said.

He nodded.

She said, "You'll have them again."

They spent the morning in a suspension of light and heat. Sunny retreated to the other hammock, drank more beer. Neda drifted in and out of sleep while Santosh made the occasional round, opening a fresh beer for Sunny, indulging him. Soon Sunny was sleeping too. When she woke next, Santosh was smiling as he stared out to sea.

"What are you thinking?"

"Fishing," he said. "Later we go fishing."

She stretched. "Do you swim?"

He giggled. "No."

"Is it safe to go swimming?"

"Not if you can't swim."

She laughed. "I can swim. But I don't have anything to wear."

"It's OK," he said. "You go how you like here; no one cares."

Around noon he arrived with plates of rava-fried prawns, shark curry, rice, papad, mussels with fresh pao. They devoured it with lemons and raw green chilli and drank more beer. When they began to eat, she recognized how hungry she was. As they were eating, Santosh told them he was heading out, he'd be back in several hours. Sunny opened his wallet and counted a thousand rupees for Santosh to take.

———

She waited for Sunny to continue their conversation from last night. It was the *only* thing she wanted to talk about, but she couldn't bring herself to start. She couldn't understand if it was the sun and sea air making her lethargic, or her reluctance to pick at the wounds, to ruin this idyll he had conjured around them, which felt like the end of something. She could feel Sunny's tension. The ride down had done the opposite of its stated intent. He seemed more tightly wound than ever. Every time he finished a beer, he opened a new one.

"You might want to pace yourself?" she said.

But he ignored her.

She climbed into the hammock and slept.

When she woke, Sunny was still sitting at the table with his shades on. The tide was receding, revealing a deep shelf of sand that caused the waves to roll and crush wildly. She climbed out of the hammock. "I'm going in the water," she said. "Are you coming?"

He shook his head minutely, his aura oppressive. She turned and undressed without a word, stripped to her underwear. She checked the beach—it was still deserted. She ran down through the sand. It burned the skin of her feet. She charged through the waves, broke free of the undertow, dived under the swell, and emerged beyond the breakers, where it was smooth and calm. She swam front crawl straight out to the horizon until her arms began to ache. She floated in the sea and looked back at the land; it looked so different from out here, the beach vast yet insignificant against the jungles and the Western Ghats that rose in green undulating waves, higher and higher to the mountains inland. She could make out Sunny at his table, his shirt open, smoking, sitting in his shades, surrounded by dead beer. Trails of dark smoke rose from hidden homes along the beach. She let herself float and drift, and the only thing she could hear was the gentle slap of water against her skin. Every time her brain tried to ask necessary questions, the ocean intervened. She felt as if her memory were being wiped clean. She closed her eyes and tried to rise from her body, look down on herself, see herself as nothing but a speck, an insignificance, nothing at all. From the heaven of her mind she looked down on the coastline. Bombay to the north, Sri Lanka off the southern tip, higher, higher, rising into space, the Arabian Peninsula, the East African coast, Europe, the Americas, the curve of the planet, the deep, impenetrable void.

She came out refreshed. "You should go in." She sat next to him, dripping wet, pooling water in the sand around the plastic chair. She couldn't see his eyes behind his shades.

"I will."

"It clears your head."

He said nothing, didn't move. He was like a stone. She ran her fingers through her hair, started squeezing the ocean out. "It'll help."

"I said I will."

"At some point we have to talk."

"Don't . . . ," he said.

"Don't what?"

"Ruin this."

They fell into silence, then he stood and walked wordless through the trees, down toward the beach, crossed the sand toward the waves, tottered up to his ankles and peed into the surf. He stripped off his T-shirt when he was finished and immersed himself. His body had become soft in the last six months. She felt such sadness seeing him, bloated and broken, floating just beyond the breakers.

The day drifted away from them. She wore the spare dress she'd brought, and Sunny sat on the beach with his T-shirt and pants back on his damp body, staring at the ocean. She sat at the table reading an old copy of *The Rough Guide to Goa*. Pages had been torn out. People sometimes used them for toilet paper. It was almost five. The sun was sinking toward the ocean, turning amber.

Santosh walked up from the huts. "Where's Sunny?"

She pointed to the sand.

"What happened?"

She didn't reply.

Santosh placed his hands on his hips. "He has too much thinking." He waited for her to respond. When she didn't, he asked her if she wanted a beer.

"Just water."

"Sunny wants beer?"

"Wait until sunset." She offered him a weak smile. "Please. It's not good for his head."

She walked up the beach with the setting sun, accompanied by the scruffy dog, who refused to leave her side, and when she returned she walked to Sunny, carrying two burning cigarettes, squatted beside him in the sand.

"The day just went by," he said.

She handed him one of the cigarettes. "You spent it avoiding me."

"I don't know what I was hoping for."

"Why don't you just talk to me?"

"I don't know. I don't know anything."

She brushed the hair out of his face. "No one knows anything."

"My father knows." He spoke with such certainty. "He knows the when, the what, the why, the where, the how."

"You forgot the who."

"He knows that too."

"Does he know we're here now?"

"Probably."

She thought on that.

"What does he even want from you?"

"Control." He held a handful of sand. "The perfect son, the one that thinks like him, acts like him. But I don't know who that is. I don't know how to be that person. The one he wants."

"You shouldn't have to be that person at all."

"I wanted to please him. I wanted to make him proud. If I could just unlock the code, everything would follow. But I can't unlock the code."

"So you have to leave."

He nodded slowly. "Yeah."

"Will he let you go?"

He tossed the sand back down. "I don't know."

She watched him closely. "Have you stood up to him before?"

"I put those ads out."

"Sunny . . . That wasn't you standing up to him. That was spiting him."

"I told you what happened after that, didn't I? He sent his men into my apartment, they smashed everything, right in front of me. Furniture, paintings, sculptures." She watched him reliving it in his head. "Things I'd bought, collected, things that meant something to me, things that had beauty. Only the things that had beauty. Priceless things. Not priceless in money, priceless to me. He stood and watched as his men destroyed them all. He didn't say a word while it happened, but he was telling me something, sending me a message, I could hear it in my head, like telepathy. There was no room for beauty, no room for mistakes. He was saying I'd forgotten who I was. I'd forgotten that he was the person who made me."

"But he *didn't* make you."

"He *did*, Neda. He did. He and Vicky. They made me. How do I escape it?"

"You walk away."

"I feel like I'm trying to swim to shore all the time, but I'm being pulled farther and farther out by the tide. I'm exhausted."

"I know that."

He turned to look at her. "You know you're the first person to ask me about Vicky. No one ever asked me."

"People don't know he exists."

"They do. They're just afraid of him."

"And you?"

He smiled awkwardly. "I used to see him a lot when I was a boy. I remember him, before my mother . . . before my mother, now and then . . . He was . . . exciting and he was kind and he was brave. I think . . . And after she . . ." He couldn't bring himself to say it. "I saw him less. Once a year. Then after I went to boarding school, I didn't see him at all."

He drew shapes in the sand. "He became this legend in my mind. A hero . . . So different from my father. When I left school, I knew my father was a big man. We had this gated, white-walled villa in Meerut, security, important people visiting day and night, coming to him. Ram Singh, coming to him. And I had all the toys I wanted. But he wasn't a hero to me at all. Maybe he knew that. I don't know. But he sent me out into the fields, out into Eastern UP, where Vicky lived. To learn to be a man."

He stopped talking a second and thought about those words. When he started again his voice became quiet, she had to strain to catch the words. "I lived beside a sugar mill we owned. I stayed in a cottage on the grounds. Cooked for myself, washed my own clothes, grew this shitty little beard. I went running every morning. Every morning. I became lean and strong and fast. I led this . . . pure life. I went running through the fields every morning, past the workers, I could smell their food on the wood fires, I could see their girls. Watching me. Handsome. I had this desire . . . I hadn't been with anyone before."

He smiled. "I did all this. It went on and on. For months I was there, living with the mill workers like I was one of them, happy, humble. I wrote all this in my journal. My hopes and dreams, my desires. All that time I was waiting for Vicky, but he never came. He never came. No one even spoke his name. Then, one night, he came. He arrived with this entourage. Their jeeps came down the long road, pulled up outside the mill."

He flicked his cigarette into the sand. "He stepped out. He was huge. All the workers were terrified. He rounded them up, intimidated them. I just stood at the back of the group, waiting. Waiting for him to look at me. He didn't even acknowledge me. He went off with his men to inspect the workers' camp, and I went back into my cottage. I still waited. It got late. It must have been eleven when he walked in. He was a mountain. His men were there too. They were . . . *wild*. They filled my room. He scared me. He took my seat. Handed me a bottle and told me to drink. He told his men stories about my childhood. My mother. Then he started reading my journal, started reading passages out, private things, things that hurt me. But there was nothing I could do. There was"—the memory was becoming very painful—"a knock at the door. Several of his men entered with three girls. They were young, fifteen maybe, I don't know, but I recognized them from the laborers' camp. They were as scared as I was. Well, two of them were. The third was . . . defiant. She looked defiant . . . she looked us all in the eye in turn. She looked at Vicky. He stood and walked toward her. He turned to me. He said I could stay if I wanted to or . . ."

"Sunny . . ." She put her hand on his arm.

"I ran." He pushed his hand through his hair. "I just ran. I ran to the fields and I hid in them for hours. I didn't recognize this man. I watched their jeeps leaving in the early hours and crept back. The cottage was a wreck, empty. It smelled of liquor and sweat and worse. I made a space on the floor, curled up, and went to sleep. When I woke up it was chaos outside. The workers were screaming, shouting, they wanted to tear the place apart."

"Jesus."

"The police were there. They took me to safety . . . They sent me back to my father."

He fell silent, stared at the ocean.

"What happened?"

"Two of the girls were found hanging from a tree. The third was never found."

She felt herself shivering, speechless.

"I was sent to London after that. My father said I'd 'earned it.' I was given a first-class ticket. Credit cards. I was sent to a man who gave me cash. I was told to do whatever I wanted. No one spoke about what happened. So

I tried to forget it. I tried to change myself there. I partied. A lot. Did a lot
of drugs. Acid. MDMA. I went to galleries, museums. I tried to construct a
new self. The one with the sculptures and the paintings. The one with the
big ideas. And I was good at it. I carried him back to Delhi with me and I
pulled the trick off for a while. I thought I could be that man forever. But
look at me. I can't be that man. I can't keep it up. I can't do it anymore. I
can't. It was all a lie . . . I love beauty. I want to create beautiful things. But
that's the last thing they understand. They want me to have a beautiful surface and be rotten to the core, like they are."

The crows flew round the pines, the wind whipped along the tide, the sun
dipped into the Arabian Sea. After a long silence he described the biolumi-
nescence of the ocean, as if nothing else had been said. It was growing cold.
Her skin was stippled with goose bumps. He remained in the sand with his
arms wrapped around his knees as the sky grew dimmer by the second. She
stood and slouched to the water and the water was warmer than the air. She
waded in and soon enough she let the tide push and pull her body. When
she climbed out again, he was still there, like a petrified nobleman in the
ashes of a volcano. She pulled him by the hand and said, "Let's build a fire."

Santosh dug the pit. A basket of firewood was brought from the huts. The
beach dog came and watched. It didn't take long for the whole thing to wheeze
and crackle and pop, roaring magnificently, sparks spewing and blinking out
in the night. When it calmed, more logs were loaded on top and the three of
them stood, admiring the work that pitched the rest of the beach into dark.

Santosh was the first to pull away, returning to the huts. Neda climbed
into one of the hammocks and felt the heat spread over one side of her body
as the other received the cool air. When she closed her eyes she saw the imprint of flame. Santosh returned shortly with three other men, from where
he brought them she didn't know. They were dragging cushions and mattresses. They spread them around the fire.

"My mother brings food in one hour."

Another man brought blankets.

"Don't you need them?" she protested.

"We don't sleep," he said.

"What do you do?"

He pointed to the sea. "We fish tonight."

The fire became something solid, permanent. They lay cozy in their hammocks while Santosh and the men hauled their boats out into the waves. It couldn't have been more than eight. When night fell, it fell.

By an unspoken agreement they descended from the hammocks and arranged themselves low down on the mattresses near the now hot sand, the blankets loosely draped around their bodies. Neda's feet toyed with the cold sand away from the fire until the sand became too cool, then she moved her feet near to the flame. The beach dog crept closer on the other side and curled up to sleep. Santosh had left them a bottle of water and a bottle of Old Monk. Sunny poured large measures of rum into two chipped glasses, squeezed a little nimbu with the seeds falling in, threw in the husks, passed one glass to her, wedged the bottle in the sand. "I have some grass," he said. "We can smoke."

In her mind she stood and stretched and looked out to sea, though she lay still. "They're out there now. In the dark. I've always been afraid of the sea. Not the surface, but what's underneath."

He passed her the joint.

She propped herself up on her elbow to smoke.

"I bought those boats," he said.

"What?"

"The boats they're in. I bought them."

"You own them?"

"No. I gifted them. So they could make money. They sell the fish in the market in Karwar, him and his brothers."

"Real brothers?"

He laughed gently. "I don't know."

She passed the joint and pulled the blanket round her shoulders and held her hands out to the fire.

"Damn, it gets cold."

"Did you ever think about something like this?" he said.

"Like what?"

"Buying a plot of land, having a kid, building a house, learning to fish."

"Selling it in Karwar?"

"I'm serious."

"Because I'm warning you, I already know how to fish."

"I'm serious. Do you think about it?"

"No."

He paused. "It's not a bad life."

"It's a fantasy."

"Yeah. I'd probably drink myself to death."

She waited awhile, then went to pee in the surf. For some minutes she was lost in the blackness of the water. When she came back to him she pulled her dress off and hung it over the edge of the hammock and stood glowing naked in front of him. He was smoking a new joint, smiling up at her, absorbing her body in the firelight.

"I haven't seen that in a while," he said.

He held out the joint and she took it. She was swaying above him. She fell down and wrapped the blanket around herself.

"I turned my phone off on the way here. God knows what will happen when I turn it back on." She shivered. "But fuck it." She mimed the banishment of thoughts from her head.

"I liked your mom," he said.

The words took a long time to reach her.

She turned to him and said, "Who they are, they're not you. They're not you. You're here with me now and you're real."

He looked at her but didn't speak. He didn't speak again for what felt like an hour. She put on her dress.

"Have you heard of this guy called Gautam Rathore?" he finally said.

"Yeah, everyone has. He's a cokehead degenerate. I've seen you with him in the paper."

"You know he's from this royal family in Madhya Pradesh. They have a lot of land. Like, half the state. There's talk of iron ore deposits in some of their land near the Chhattisgarh border. My father wants a piece of it. Gautam's the heir. The only son. My father thought I could influence him. Bring him in line with our way of thinking. That was my punishment. My test. Gautam had checked out completely from that life. He was never going back home. I was supposed to get him on the side. Get him to clean up. I was supposed to lure him with . . . I don't know, power? So he could go back into his family as a proxy for my father. He wants a piece of that mining. He wants to expand out of UP, but Gautam doesn't want to go home. He doesn't want to do any of this. So we've been talking."

"You and Gautam?"

"Yeah. We've been saying 'fuck you' to our fathers."

She felt nauseated.

"So?"

"We'll leave together. We'll go into business together."

"With what?"

"Our brains. Our savings. Our contacts."

"And?"

"He used to run a hotel. We'll build a new one, up in the mountains. Something special. Remember the sketch I showed you once, my retirement plan? Cantilevered off the hillside, a stream running through the heart of it, through a courtyard, great bukharis heating every room in the winter, a grand view of the Himalayas, a solarium on an upper deck with a pool, heated by solar panels, tunnels through the mountainside connecting underground saunas and steam rooms, trees growing up inside the structure itself."

She could feel him waiting for her to say something.

"That sounds like a dream."

"It's going to come true. And we'll be free."

There was a long silence before he spoke again.

"I took this girl once," he said, "you know her, Kriti."

Neda smiled gently. "She's a type."

"I took her with me up to Himachal once, on a road trip. It was a disaster. She was too precious."

"She thought she had to behave that way."

"She could see she was pissing me off."

"She was trying to please you."

He shrugged. "We drove up past Shimla, there was this village I wanted to get to. Sarahan. Not the big Sarahan, this other one, small, high up, hard to get to. There's a waterfall and an old wooden temple. We were driving there in the afternoon, there was a herd of goats on the road below Hatu Peak. I called out to the shepherd to buy a goat, take it up to the village and offer it for a feast. It was the right thing to do."

"Was it?"

"Sure. You know what happens when you turn up with nothing?"

"What?"

"Nothing."

She laughed. "But when you turn up with a goat, everything changes?"

"Exactly."

"So, what happened?"

"I bought one. Threw it in the back seat. It shit everywhere and she bitched about it nonstop, then she gave me the silent treatment. I almost stopped and threw it off the side of the mountain just to make a point. We reached the village miserable. I stayed in a shed attached to one of the houses, slept on straw, drank whisky, gave the goat to slaughter." He laughed to himself. "I told everyone it was called Kriti. Kriti ended up sleeping in the car. She got a ride down to Kullu the next morning. Didn't call for two months."

"Is there a point," she said, bemused, "to this story?"

"The point is, I wish you'd been there."

She smiled and nodded to herself. "I would have loved it."

"I know." Then he said, "Come live with me. Don't go abroad."

Sushma brought food by lamplight. She was a wisp of a woman in a purple sari, strong and weathered from a life of work. She placed the tray on the table a little way off from the fire, retreated and returned with a metal bucket under her arm, which she placed in the sand. Neda was stoned and motionless and she was thinking about a life in the mountains, a life both like and unlike hers. It was always intruded on by Gautam Rathore. By the foot in Sunny's chest. By the rubble of slums and empires. By her own heart. The flames of the fire were low. Sushma slipped away without a word. When Neda got up to bring the food she saw there was a bottle of champagne in the bucket, packed in ice. Sunny sat up and placed another log on the fire. "What's this?" she said, carrying the bottle. He smiled. "I had Santosh pick it up from the Marriott down the road."

They drank the champagne solemnly in cracked china cups, along with plates of grilled mackerel and mounds of red rice. There was more: rava-fried prawns, a huge spicy bowl of crab curry, the pieces of crab taken up in their hands, broken open, the meat sucked out noisily. She threw the fish heads to the dog, who ate them out of the sand. They drank more champagne, rinsed their hands with water and settled by the fire.

When she woke the fire was low and Sunny sat staring into the flames. She feared the night was already dissolving, the world no longer at bay. She pulled her blanket tighter.

"What time is it?"

"Past three."

"I passed out."

"It's OK."

"It's cold."

"There's more wood to burn." He reached out and built up the fire, then shifted back and lay down. "Come here."

She crawled in the space between his body and the flames. He wrapped his arms around her, and she shivered and pressed herself into him. He slid his warm fingers under the blanket, under her clothes, rested their tips around her belly button, toyed with the cold flesh. She closed her eyes again and her breathing shallowed, and he slipped his hand inside her.

"It can't stay like this," she said.

"No," he replied. "It can get better."

She turned to him. "You promise?"

He lifted his fingers and touched them to his tongue.

"You taste like the sea."

"An oyster," she said.

He settled his hand on her hip.

He couldn't promise her anything.

But she could feel his hardness.

"I love," he said, "that you never asked if I loved you."

"I love," she replied, "that you never needed me to say it."

It was five a.m. He'd come inside her, and holding her, he'd fallen asleep. Now the crows were calling from the pines.

"They're coming back in."

Sunny opened his eyes.

Santosh and his brothers were hauling their boats up the beach.

He still had her in his arms.

She rolled free and turned to him.

"The chains of existence," she said, "have to be weak enough to break." She kissed him. "But strong enough to carry you through in the first place." She turned to face the stars. "By the way . . . Happy birthday."

LONDON, 2006

FROM: NEDA.KAPUR@XXXXXX.COM

TO: DEAN.H.SALDANHA@XXXXXX.COM

DATE: 2/25/2006

SUBJECT:

Dean,

Do you know how many times I've composed this mail? This fucking mail
to you a thousand times, in my head, in so many ways, when I'm walking,
walking is the only time my thoughts flow, so long as I'm walking I can
justify it all, but to compose I have to stop, and the page robs me. It's even
worse when I begin to write. Every pretty phrase that rolled off my tongue
becomes a trap. I can't tell the truth. I don't know how to anymore. I used
to be so good at telling the truth. I was so good at telling the truth that I
discovered it was easy to tell a lie. Do you understand me? I told enough
lies to you. I couldn't tell one from the other in the end.

What I'm trying now is to tell you about Sunny Wadia.

I hate the name. I avoid it if I can. Those syllables. But I can't avoid them
today. Right now, the early morning of the 25th. Two years since that night

where everything was destroyed. The ghosts come out tonight. I'm drinking vodka. Remembering. When I remember I'm a mess. But forgetting is even worse, forgetting is memory's lining. I thought I could escape, I've been rubbing pages out, but it doesn't work.

What I'm trying to tell you . . . I'm trying to tell you what you already know. India is so far away. So far away but I'm there every day.

You wanted to know what happened to me, you wanted to know why I disappeared, where I was. You've already guessed. What I'm trying to tell you, I was there, there at the end, in the crash. I was there on the road. I was there with Sunny. Gautam. Ajay. I was there with the girl. I held her when she died. I didn't know her name. I read her name later in the news. One of your pieces, one of someone else's I don't know. You were always there to record the names, weren't you. All their names. I saw the broken bodies. Dean, I don't remember everything . . . I'm back in Delhi suddenly, a teenage girl in my room. The monkeys have come down from the ridge and they're jumping in the trees in the park. My father used to carry a stick every morning on his walks. I want to go back there. Go back there more than anything, that time, that Delhi, and take another path. But I can't. It's impossible. To dream it is intolerable. I can't bear it anymore. I know I don't deserve your sympathy. I imagine your stoneface . . . Dean, let's set this straight . . . you want to understand. First it was Sunny, Bunty, the Wadias, what you learned, what they did to you, and I was there on the side, then it was something new. You want to know everything, you want to know how I was involved. It still confuses you. You still can't find a thing. Here it is now. The first thing I can give you: I shouldn't have been in that job. You know my mother flexed her muscles and found that position for me. Good, old-fashioned nepotism. Or something about idle hands. My father had been sick so I couldn't go abroad. You've heard this story before. And on paper at least I was some kind of match. I studied the liberal arts. My English was beyond reproach.

I'm upper caste and fair. What's not to love? So I started work and of course I didn't have any ethics. I didn't even know there was such a thing as ethics in journalism. I knew injustice when I saw it, in a novel, on the news, but I never understood the process of its creation. I never considered complicity, or the obligation to guard against it in yourself. I was interested in a good story above all else. And yet you pursued me. Or you let me pursue you. I often think you missed your calling. You should have been working with the lepers in East Delhi, you should have been giving sermons at Tis Hazari Church. Did you see something in me worth saving? I don't know how you lasted so long. See, your problem was decency and mine was being afflicted by the toxic compound of curiosity and passivity. Passivity is normal—most people suffer from it. They watch the woman being beaten in the street. They watch the accident from the car window. They're frozen, expecting someone else to intervene. I'm the same. Only I'll go and stand right next to the beating and take notes. Remember this. Remember this. Write it down. Remember the light. Yeah, I just want to see where the story goes, it's my privilege to observe the futility of life. But life isn't futile if you live it right. I want to live it right, I want to but I can't! Let me just confess something else: I was interested in Sunny from the start. He was the smoke that told me there was fire. I was bored of Delhi, of the job. Of you. I was restless. I wanted more. I was twenty-one and he was promising to make Delhi the center of the world and I believed him. Why not? I remember you called him a joker that first time, you dismissed him as another rich kid, and that stung, it stung like you'd insulted *me*. You were coming from the States. You hadn't lived through the nineties in Delhi. You hadn't seen how dusty and dull and sleepy it was. You couldn't understand how someone like Sunny made me feel. I was coming out of the years of dealing with my father's cancer too, of the disappointment of not being able to escape, when everyone around me had left and gone. Then he came along with his ideas, his words, his wealth and glamour, and it just seemed like the most incredible trick in the world. Do you think any of us asked where his wealth came from? Seriously? We grew up watching *Beverly Hills 90210*. We treated our servants with kindness, but they were still our servants. That was the way it was. We wanted above all else to live like the West. We never thought about the consequences of that, the misery our desires were built on in the Indian context. What did you expect me to do? Put on a hair shirt? Renounce it all and go live in a slum? No. He looks at you and says, "let's go." What would you do? So I started with him. And I saw no conflict of interest. I had nothing to declare. Even when you mocked him, wondered about his background. I just thought, there goes Dean again, American Dean. Like when foreigners came and discovered poverty and wept, started giving out money in the street, gave away their shoes. They could afford it. But I'm Indian. I could live with our work by day and be in Sunny's world by night and it was fine, it was fine until it wasn't fine. I have had so many lives, and I've lived them all apart from the other, it's what you do, a woman, a woman in Delhi of means. It was fine until it wasn't. So yeah, I started seeing Sunny, and there was this small window of joy. Do you know what it feels like to have power? Real power. To sit all of a sudden inside the wheels of power and speed through the city with your eyes wide, watching everything, making eye contact with everything—it was intoxicating. To roar through the city at speed and have no fear, and to see, to be able to see, the way a man sees, to stare, be able to do it without blinking, my God. I don't know, maybe as a man it's something you can't understand. Your fear arises from the things you do, not the things that are denied to you. But Sunny gave the city to me. And here's the thing you didn't understand about him, here it is. He wasn't his father. Sunny wanted to leave his father behind. He hated his father. He wanted out. He wanted to go his own way. I wanted to help him. Why would I have come to you with any of this? Why would I have abandoned him? I wasn't living like a journalist. I was living like someone in love.

Where did it go wrong? Was it the deaths at the demolition site? The adverts he put out as a consequence? It locked us all in a death spiral. You were offended by what you thought was hypocrisy. You thought it was his father, but you weren't looking at it right. It was all Sunny. He was trying to placate me. Trying to impress me, to spite his father. I was distraught, as you saw. I had some rage by then, a little of you had already seeped into me. I repeated your lines. But I used them quite cynically, to wound him. I started to question his world without really believing in the question. Just to taunt him. Only my grief was real. I'd been immune for so long to the city and suddenly there I was, confronted by it in the shape of dead children. Not on TV, in front of my eyes. Their ashen bodies. I was a mess, and he wanted to protect me. In his wisdom he took me away, smuggled me to his farmhouse, where I could escape the city, inoculate and isolate myself for a while, recline in luxury. It didn't work. It only upset me more. I should have walked away, I should have come to you. I might have, if something hadn't happened that night, if I hadn't seen his father and understood so much . . .

. . . I won't go into that night. You can't have it . . .

But I barely saw him again after. I saw him on three occasions in seven or eight months after that night, and after the last night, never again, though he has haunted me all this time . . .

What am I supposed to apologize to you about? What is mine to confess? I've made excuses for myself, I've tried to make you understand why I was with him, why I didn't betray him, how I got to that point. But all you want to know from me is what really happened that night.

Tomorrow I might tell this story differently. I'll have changed again. Only the words will remain, and what truth they hold I can't tell. I can't remember. I don't know what else to say. So let me tell you.

Sunny had made a decision in the weeks before—he was finally going to leave his father. He was going his own way. Taking what he could and making a fresh start. He had convinced me that Gautam was his friend. Oh, it's so ridiculous . . . but this is what I understand: his father, punishing him, controlling every aspect of his life, charged him with taming Gautam, making him loyal to them for some future use, something about their land back in Madhya Pradesh. It was one of a thousand schemes his father had, he just happened to use his son for this one. But Gautam only dragged Sunny down. It's clear to me now he'd got him hooked on the blow. Oh, these men, these fucking men . . . two heirs who hated their fathers, using the other for escape. The way Sunny painted it, they would survive. He called me that night. He called me and Gautam to the club and he was giddy. I went there with some kind of hope, but as soon as I walked inside, I knew all the things Sunny had been trying to convince me about Gautam were wrong. I could read it in his eyes. I looked at Sunny, he seemed so pathetic. I could see what was coming, it was so plain and clear. Sunny called for another bottle of champagne. When it arrived, he put one arm around Gautam's shoulders, another around mine, pulled us close together and said . . . "Well, it's time . . ."

"Well, it's time," he says.

"Sunny . . ."

"We're getting out."

"Sunny . . ."

She tries to stop him, but stopping him is as good as killing him right now.

Still, she tries.

"Sunny, don't."

Bloated, exhausted. On edge.

"You don't know what's on my mind. But we've talked it to death. Tomorrow morning, I'm doing it. I'm telling him I'm leaving him behind. I've tried to prove myself, I've tried to do what's asked of me, and nothing works, nothing makes him happy. There's nothing left for me. I don't have to live like this."

He's staring at the bottle in his hand; the bottle in his hand is shaking.

"We can start from scratch," he says. "We can build our own world."

He's never looked so naked and scared, never looked so vulnerable, and she's never loved him so much as she does right now.

He pops the cork and charges her glass, Gautam's glass, his.

She looks to Gautam.

Gautam looks to her.

And she knows.

Just knows.

Sunny sees the nausea in her face.

"What's wrong?"

She keeps her gaze on Gautam.

Gautam on her.

"Go on, tell him," she says.

Sunny frowns. "What?"

She's not even sure.

But Gautam takes the bait.

"Here's to Neda." He makes a toast, swallows his champagne, and refills his own glass. "The smartest bitch in the room."

The look of confusion on Sunny's face breaks her heart.

"Tell me what?"

Gautam begins to laugh.

"That you're a fool."

Sunny laughs too. For a second, it's a joke. Then he has the sensation of being exposed.

"Why," he asks, "am I a fool?"

Gautam tells him. "It's as plain as your nose. You actually think I want to go off and make a hotel with you? A hotel?! Pull myself up by my bootstraps?

With you?! Sunny, my boy, you're nothing on your own. You think you could survive a minute in this world without your father? You would be a losing proposition. You're too gullible. You lack what's called a cutting edge. The only reason I'm sitting with you right now is because of Daddy Dear. Take away Daddy, and you're just a . . ."

"But we . . ."

"But we," Gautam cuts back. "But, but, but . . ." He stands. "But you said you were my friend." He raises his glass, saunters across the room, turns at the door. "It was good while it lasted, Sunny boy, you got me on my feet, that's true enough, but it's time for the next adventure."

He might have left it at that. But he goes on.

"You know what? Maybe I'll go *right* now and wake Daddy Dearest. Tell him what a fool his son has been. Do you think he'll adopt me? Do you think he'll greet me with open arms?"

Sunny has been sitting dumbstruck listening to him speak. Now it's dawning on him: it's over. All avenues are shut. A new thought: maybe he will. Maybe he'll greet you with open arms. She says his name. She reaches for his hand, but he pulls it away. "What did you do?" He might be talking to himself. He reaches for the bottle, grips its neck.

She's shouting his name. He pushes past her. Shouting his name over and over as he holds the bottle like a club and pushes past the curtain and enters the main room. She thinks: He's going to kill him. Or get himself killed. She puts her head in her hands. Then she hears the screams. Not one, but many. The sound of broken glass. Of a brawl. A man falls through the curtain into the VIP room, his face streaming blood. She runs.

She enters into chaos. Twenty, thirty sweaty and drunken men punching and kicking one another, falling over one another, shirts being torn. A dozen women too, in tight dresses, kicking, pulling, scratching. Blood on the floor. How did it happen so fast? She gets knocked to the ground.

Through the melee of legs she sees Gautam running down the stairs to the street. Sunny is not far behind.

By the time she's on the street, men are assaulting him. He manages to punch one cold, but the others take him down. More fights are breaking out. More screaming. Men and women are running. Men and women are climbing into their cars. A gunshot rings out. Clear in the night. Everyone freezes. Everyone scatters, Ajay is pointing his Glock at the crowd of men. He bears down on them, pistol-whips the first. The rest flee. Ajay pulls Sunny to his feet. Drags him away toward his SUV.

Gautam is climbing into his Mercedes, shoving his own driver out into the road. "Stop him," Sunny says, even as he bleeds. He's pointing Gautam's way. Ajay sees. She could have left him right then. She could have run to her own car. She runs to Sunny's SUV. Climbs in the back with Sunny as Ajay takes the driver's seat.

Gautam is headlong through the streets, searching for the colony exit, racing around the corners for the open gate. She is in the back, pleading with Sunny to stop. Just stop. Just give it up. Think it over. He pushes her off. Scrambles from the back into the front seat. She tries it with Ajay instead, puts her hand on him, pulls at his shoulder as he drives, says his name, tells him to stop, but he turns to look at her with such bloodlust that she's afraid.

Then they're out of the colony, then they are out on the ring road. She expects the police will come. There will be a roadblock. She expects this madness to end, for sense to prevail. But no. Gautam is speeding ahead and there's no one on the road, no one in the night, nothing but the roar of their engines, Sunny's empty vengeful face, Ajay's vengeful empty face, they look like twins of pain. For a moment time slows, speed and distance have no meaning, like those dreams or nightmares where you're just falling, falling into infinity. And then it happens. A stray dog runs across the road.

———

She remembers her father. She was seven years old, it was her first time out in their new car, an Ambassador. Her father let her ride in front. She'd never sat up front with him before. They went on a tour of Lutyens' Delhi. On the way he said something she's never forgotten: Whatever you do, whatever happens, however much you love dogs, however much you care, never stop or swerve for a stray dog on the road, just drive on through it, there are too many of them, and it's just not worth the pain. Even if it breaks your heart.

There's a streak of burned rubber on the road. The tracer red of a brake light. The Mercedes swerves, veers toward the curb, pops up in the night air. The men and women are sleeping just ahead. That image is fixed. Then it lands.

If only Gautam had as much compassion for Sunny as he did for a stray dog. My memory is dark after that. It comes in pieces. I'm outside on the road on my hands and knees screaming into the pavement. I'm covered in someone else's blood. I'm cradling the girl who is dying. I can see that she is pregnant. I can feel her hand pressed in mine. I still feel it. Sometimes I wake up and think I'm holding it. I wake up sometimes and I think she's standing by my bed looking down at me, but that's only my conscience. On the road, I look down and she has died. The baby could still be saved. Sunny is behind me, and he's looking down on us all. I stand. I stagger away from him. I see Gautam unconscious in his Mercedes. I think he's dead too. I can keep telling you what I see and feel, but what difference does it make now? And I don't even feel it myself. It isn't happening to me, it's happening to someone else. I tell Sunny to call an ambulance. I try to pull his phone from his pocket. Mine is still in my bag in the car, I must have left it there. He pushes me away. I cry at him. What the fuck are you doing? Call an ambulance. Call an ambulance. Call somebody. Do something. I'm back where I've been before. He turns to Ajay instead and orders him to take something from the car, it's a Polaroid camera, the one

I saw in Goa. He takes a photo of Gautam in the car, then he orders Ajay to pull Gautam out. I think they are going to put him on the roadside. But they take him out and carry him between them and place him into the back of the SUV and I think is this really happening, is this how it happens? I get up and stumble after them. Ajay and Sunny face one another in the road. Sunny has taken a bottle of whisky from the back of the SUV. He keeps a bottle there. He guides Ajay over to the Mercedes. They speak. Ajay hands over his gun and takes the whisky in its place. Then he climbs into the Mercedes and starts to drink, he drinks the bottle until it's done. And when he's done, Sunny takes the butt of the gun and smashes it into Ajay's face. When I cry, Ajay and Sunny both look at me. Then Sunny steps toward me. Nothing in his eyes. I am afraid of him. He closes his fist. He raises his hand.

The next thing I knew, I was in a room. A white little room, clean, bright, with a garden outside and little birds singing. It was midmorning and I was in bed, looking at a man who was a stranger but who I know now as Chandra. There was a small TV mounted on the wall, an electric kettle, a bedside table with a phone. A government guesthouse. That's how it felt. He's sitting in an armchair. I think we've been talking but I don't know what about, it occurs to me I don't know where I am, I can't remember how I got there. I'm wearing pajamas and my face is sore and bruised but otherwise I'm clean. This is what I remember. He had exceptional manners. He was soothing. He was laying it out for me. He was saying: there's nothing you could have done, and there's no profit from dwelling on it. It's done, my dear. Decisions were made in the heat of the moment and none of them were yours and for that you can be grateful. And rest assured, the decisions that were made were in the interests of everyone. I stared at him blank-eyed. I didn't have a thought in my head. Then I remembered. He must have noticed. He said: it was a bad night for everyone. I must have expressed a desire to go home because he told me I couldn't go home just yet. Why not? He told me I was in Amritsar. He said I had driven to Amritsar with friends on a whim in the night. We had wanted to see the border at dawn and eat chole kulcha for breakfast. Such is the life of a carefree young Indian. He handed me the phone and warned me not to complicate my parents' lives, knowing how sick my father had been. I found it surprisingly easy to lie when my mother came on the phone. I didn't betray a shred of fear or grief. Just the exhaustion of a young girl who drives to Amritsar on a whim. After the call to my parents, he told me to call in sick at work, to keep it brief. I did as I was told. Then he gave me a glass of nimbu pani. I drank it all and it must have been laced with sedatives.

When I woke it was evening. The sun was setting, the birds outside were in full song. I was groggy. A sweet lady was bringing me a bowl of khichdi. I asked the woman where I was, but she didn't say. When she left, I heard her lock the door from outside. So I was a prisoner. I didn't try to escape. Chandra came back just before dark. It took him a moment to get into character. He must have caught that look in my eyes. He crossed his legs and smoothed his thighs with his palms. He said: You want to confess, I know. You want to go to the police and tell them everything. I didn't agree or disagree. But what will you tell them? What will you actually say? And who will believe you? It had already come down to a question of belief. I asked where Sunny was. "Sunny? He's on a business trip in Singapore. He has been for the last three days." I saw where this was going. Gautam? "Mr. Rathore," he replied, "is far away." Ajay? He just smiled and shook his head. "Mr. Rathore's driver is in jail."

The light outside was almost gone, someone was turning lamps on around the garden, lighting dhoop. "And you're driving back from Amritsar. You'll be home soon." He half stood and turned on the bedside lamp. It cast a deep shadow on his face. I asked him what's going to happen to me? He said, what do you want to happen? I didn't know what to say. I really didn't know. So he told me. It's time for you to leave, Neda. That's what you always wanted. You wanted to go and study and live abroad. I said yes, I'm going to Japan. He said why? You can go anywhere now. He told me I'd been dragged into a situation not of my making, which I didn't fully understand, and it could easily destroy me and my family. Or I could go anywhere. Anywhere at all. I would be given money, an apartment, my tuition would be paid for, the visas would be arranged. I could have a new life now. A happy life. How does that sound? Does that sound reasonable? I was so very tired. Does that sound like something you'd want to do? He handed me a handkerchief from his pocket for my tears. Does it? Neda, dear, does it sound reasonable? He was all kindness. He said all I had to do was forget this night, forget Sunny, forget the last year of my life, never speak about that night, never contact Sunny again. Wipe my slate clean. I was tired. I said yes . . .

I said London, that's where I want to be. I still don't know why. I don't know anything anymore. I never did, but at least I could lie to myself, say something good was coming. Now. No. I'm hurt. The hurt won't go. But what's my hurt to those lives? Dean, what's my hurt to the truth? What did Sunny do and why? That's the question I've gone over a thousand times. Every night before I sleep and I don't sleep until dawn. Why did he save Gautam? He made a decision on the road to save Gautam's life, to sacrifice Ajay and me and himself in order to keep Gautam safe. Why? If he'd left Gautam to his fate, if he'd called the police, the ambulance, if he'd just driven off, he would have been free. He would have had his solution. Whatever Gautam claimed would be void. He'd have solved the unsolvable problem of his life. He could have left his father, he could have been with me, he could have not been with me. It was his father all along. I didn't understand it before, even when he spoke about it, even when his father pushed him down into the darkness. It was his father from the start. He was the only thing he cared about. The clues were there. He said it to Gautam in front of me: I can't prove myself to him. He couldn't find the code, the combination, to unlock his father's heart. And finally, by chance, by brute luck, there it was before him in the road. Gautam's prone body. Sunny could display the ruthlessness he had lacked, which he found inexpressible through design. He could throw away all those things he loved in order to save the life of someone who meant nothing but a measure of profit to his father, and in doing so he could secure what had eluded him for so long. I wouldn't ever call it love. I don't know what it is. I didn't think about this at the time. I can't remember what I thought. I wanted to get away from the pain. I wanted to take the chance to escape.

It went so quickly after that. I had agreed, and everything was arranged, and I barely remember any of it. I was awarded a fake scholarship. I had the letter sent to me. Who knows, maybe the scholarship was even real. I opened the letter and I cried. My parents thought it was joy. They were overjoyed, they comforted me, and I fled to my room. I packed my bags and very soon after I left. Somewhere along the way they knew everything was wrong. I don't remember half of it. What I know is this: a month later, I discovered I was pregnant with Sunny's child. You must feel such revulsion. I was in London then. Chandra met me every few days, took me out to an expensive restaurant. He called me his niece to waiters, it was his joke. It was the seventh or eighth meeting. I started to cry, I'd just taken the test that morning. Taken it three times to be sure. It was only Sunny's, no one else's. Chandra tried to coax words from me. I confessed; though I wanted to keep it from him, how could I, they knew everything in the end. He wasn't laughing. He was very serious. Tell Sunny, I said. Tell him. At least tell him, tell me what he says. I wanted to keep it if he did. I was still . . . He came back to me the next day. He was very sympathetic. He said, Sunny says it's not his. He doesn't want anything to do with it. And if you keep it, he'll take all of this away . . .

He made the arrangements for me. He took care of it for me. I didn't argue. I was broken. I was drinking so much, I was in such grief. My heart hardened because it had to, Dean, but it never hardened enough. I'm consumed by such remorse and horror at the direction my life has gone, how I let it go there. You can only be judged by your actions. But my God! There's so much more to it than that, isn't there? I don't know what's left for me now. I don't know where I'm supposed to go, what I'm supposed to do. When I arrived here I was bereft. I had no shortcuts to help me process life. I had no comfort to help me manage. I watched all my life torn away. I watched the life I could have had evaporate. Why did I do that? And yet I'm no victim. Everyone thinks of themselves as a victim, Dean, not a willing accomplice. But there I was. I have no right to anything anymore. I have to suffer . . .

You know I see Sunny everywhere. I see him in so many faces on the street. Punjabi men with their baseball caps and beards, in their jeans and tight T-shirts over their rice bellies. He could have just been a man. I read about him in the papers. I don't know this man. He's thriving, it seems, though I know him enough to know he's damned himself. But Gautam, I doubt Gautam has one sleepless night. He was born to rule, and to escape punishment is his God-given right.

I'm going to stop writing now, I'm done. I'm left alone in this lonely gray city in the dark, far from home. Can you do anything with this? Is it any good to you? Or will it just cause more pain? You can use it if you like. I allow it. I don't know if I'll be around to face it. I've already decided to leave. If you use any of this, just remember, nothing will change, this is Kali Yuga, the losing age, the age of vice. The people on the road will remain dead. The baby will still be unborn. The Gautams of this world will thrive. The Ajays of this world will always take the fall. And Sunny? I don't know. I don't know anything anymore. The wheel will keep turning toward the dissolution that will swallow us all.

Her finger lingers on the trackpad, moves the cursor over SEND. But she lacks the courage again. She discards the draft. She still won't take a stand.

THREE

MEHRAULI, 2004

SUNNY

1.

He woke the afternoon after the crash in the villa at the farmhouse estate.

In the bedroom with the plate-glass windows looking out at the pool, and the skylights above like the eyes of a corpse staring up at the sun.

The sun was strong. Hot glass on sun. Cold, empty air. Tangled in the white duvet. The creamy sheets soaked with sweat. A perfect late winter's day.

Remember it. Turn your head to look outside. Bare trees. Leaves falling into the pool. Remember it. Clouds pass quickly through the blue and cover the sun. Brightness muted, heat scattered, hiding. The damp sheets remember it. His perception not connected to his senses. Still a ringing in his ears. The sun returning.

He rolled over. If he stared hard enough at the pool it began to tremble.

He could see the wind through the trees.

But couldn't hear it. He thought about the ocean, far away. "Ajay . . ."

He called out the name, impatient, forgetting Ajay was just a name now and nothing more. He was waking from a drugged nothingness. Valium, 30 milligrams. Xanax, 5 milligrams.

The bliss of a void. He shifted his body from the damp sheets, but the bed was cold there too. Sat up and reached for the cigarettes. The lighter. Artifacts of the night.

He still had Gautam's coke in his trouser pocket.

His suit jacket had fallen from the back of the chair.

He wandered around the villa in his boxers with a thick blue blanket around his shoulders, one hand drawing it across his belly, listening to the cigarette burn.

Suppose it was a nightmare?

His nose was crusted with coke and blood.

He turned on the kitchen tap, spat dry, sticky blood into the sink.

Blew each nostril.

From the freezer, a bottle of Grey Goose.

He poured the viscous spirit down his throat.

A coughing fit. Doubled over. Retching.

Swallowed more vodka, waited until the sharp edges of his soul began to swoon and fray. He had to do something.

He kept seeing it.

The turn.

The river.

The cards in his hand.

The hand of his life.

2.

And driving through the Delhi night in the SUV with the two unconscious bodies in the back, with Gautam and Neda in the back, leaving the dead behind. Ajay, and the dead. Not too fast, not too slow.

Waiting for the sirens.

For the checkpoint.

But no one is coming. No one is flagging him down.

His car is not damaged.

He did not crash it; he did not kill anyone.

He has done nothing wrong.

His car is pristine.

No different from the truck that had passed.

The auto that had passed.

Not guilty.

He passes through the city.

Nothing has changed.

We're all still dying stars.

He drives through a checkpoint.

The cops glance sleepily at his car.

Another rich man's car.

He almost gives them a salute.

Now slow along the quieter streets, into an oak-shrouded service lane, bringing the vehicle to a stop, turning the lights off, gripping the wheel.

Now what?

He fumbles with the door. Climbs out, bends double and vomits. A few rickshaw pullers are sleeping. Some dogs are barking. Nothing more.

He finds water in the door pocket, rinses, spits, climbs back in.

Looks at both of them, Neda and Gautam.

Gautam closest to him, smashed in the face, bleeding from his nose, his contemptuous face serene in spite of it all.

Neda, makeup smeared, head tilted back, almost snoring, ugly looking, mouth open to bare her teeth. They could be two kids, exhausted from a big day out.

He can hear sirens. But the city carries on.

And what has he done?

He glances at the passenger seat and sees Ajay's gun.

What has he done?

He reaches in and takes it, feels its weight in his hand, opens the rear door on Gautam's side, gently presses it to the flesh of Gautam's cheek. It would be so easy to pull the trigger.

No.

His hand is beginning to shake. He is fearful of the weight, he suddenly can't remember if there's a bullet in the chamber. His brain is fogging, shutting down. With great force of concentration he removes the clip, places it in his pocket, pulls back the slide, and ejects the bullet from the chamber. It falls into the road, rolls in the dark.

Fuck.

Should he get on his hands and knees?

No.

It's not about time. It's about dignity.

He searches Gautam's pockets and pulls out two baggies.

He climbs back into the driver's seat, puts the unloaded gun and clip in the glove box. And in the sulfur glow of the streetlight he uses his car key to scoop out a large bump of coke.

Sunny dials the number.

And Tinu wakes. Groans.

"What is it?"

He's trembling. "There was an accident."

Tinu takes a pause, turns on his bedside lamp. "Tell me."

"Some people are dead."

Lights a cigarette. "Who's dead?"

"People. On the road."

"Did you kill them?"

"No. It wasn't me. It was Gautam. He hit them with his car."

"Are you with the police?"

"No."

"Where are you?"

"On the road, somewhere else."

"Far away?"

"Far away. I'm safe."

"Are you sure?"

"I'm sure."

"How many dead?"

"I don't know."

"Are you sure they're dead?"

"Yes."

"Where's Gautam?"

"With me."

"In your car? Or his?"

"In mine."

"Where's his?"

"Back on the road. It's a wreck."

Tinu puts out the cigarette. "OK, is this right? He crashed his car, you pulled him out, you left with him in yours. Is this how it is?"

"Yes."

"And no one else saw you? No crowd, no scene?"

"Nothing."

"Where did it happen? Where *exactly*?"

"On the Inner Ring Road, by Nigambodh Ghat."

"Which car of his?"

"His Mercedes."

"And you're in?"

"The Toyota. The Highlander."

"Who else is there with you?"

"Gautam, me, this girl."

"Neda?"

The pause of fear. "Yes."

"And where's Ajay?"

Sunny braces himself.

"In the car."

"In the car with you? Let me speak to him."

Silence.

"Put him on the phone . . ."

"I can't."

"Sunny . . ."

"He's in the car on the road."

It sinks in.

"You left him there?"

Eyes closed. "I had to."

"Is he alive?"

"I made him drink whisky . . ."

"Sunny, is he alive?"

"Yes!"

Tinu collects himself. "OK. There may be time. Listen carefully."

Sunny begins to sob. "I did it for him, Tinu!"

"Don't fall apart."

"Tell Papa. I did it for him."

"Listen carefully."

It happened like it was happening to someone else. Tinu gave an address on Amrita Shergill Marg. "A man called Chandra will meet you there. Do everything he says."

The man called Chandra was waiting on the lawn of the high-walled compound with the three-story bungalow looming behind, sitting on a deck chair in the moonlight, smoking a cigarette. He wore a camel-hair overcoat over a pair of powder-blue pajamas. His rubbery face under the floppy fringe had an aspect of weary bemusement. Seven or eight men in black Pathani suits and surgical gloves were waiting on the driveway ahead. When the

SUV came to a stop and the gates were closed, they opened its doors and got to work.

Neda and Gautam were removed from the rear seat first, their phones and wallets and other personal effects stripped from them, placed on the low wooden table at Chandra's side. Gautam was carried across the lawn to a second driveway. There were two cars: a white, government Ambassador at the front, a BMW behind. Gautam was placed inside the rear of the Ambassador. A police driver and a Black Cat Commando sat inside. A uniformed cop climbed into the back alongside Gautam, propped him up, pulled the rear net curtains shut as the driver put it into gear. Then the gates were opened, the Ambassador pulled away, and Gautam was gone.

As this was happening, two men carried the still unconscious Neda round the side of the main building.

Sunny gripped the wheel of the SUV and watched her go.

Chandra rose from the deck chair, buttoned his coat, came to stand beside the front window. Tapped on it.

"My dear, it would be wise if you stepped out now."

Sunny did as he was told. "I didn't hurt her," he said.

Chandra nodded absently. "That's not for me to say."

"What will happen?"

"She'll be afforded every courtesy."

"What happens to me?"

"Are you in possession of a firearm?"

"In the dash."

"Drugs?"

He fingered the bags of coke in his pocket.

"I threw them out."

"Where?"

"On the road."

"Where on the road?"

"Nowhere. In some bushes."

Chandra examined Sunny coolly.

He pointed toward the BMW.

"Get in the car and go."

The BMW slipped through the streets with funereal calm. The city reeled through the black glass, signs of morning emerged in the sky.

He began to search the back.

The driver glanced in the rearview mirror.

"Looking for something?"

It was Eli, the Israeli, the Cochin Jew. A member of his father's security detail. The one who'd trained Ajay.

"I need a drink."

Eli raised an eyebrow. "You and me both, buddy."

"Do you have one?"

"This is more than my job's worth."

But a minute later he produced a hip flask from his pocket and passed it back. "Don't finish, OK?"

Sunny unscrewed it, sniffed, recoiled.

"What is this?"

"Israel arak, my friend."

Sunny took a hit and winced.

"No good?"

"Tastes like shit."

"So give back."

Eli held his hand out.

But Sunny drained the flask all the same.

They entered the farmhouse estate by the service gate that passed through the woodland. It was nearly five a.m., and the BMW went slowly along the shadowed track, the lights picking out the moths and potholes, the dark blue sky elusive in the trees. The arak burned. But it was an abstraction. Eli's phone rang. He picked up and listened and held it back toward Sunny.

"It's for you."

It was Tinu.

"You were at the farmhouse all night, in the villa. Put that in your mind. There's Valium by your bedside, the correct dose. Go to bed, take the pills, close your eyes."

"Did you tell Papa?"

"Yes."

"Did you tell him I did it for him?"

"Just go to bed."

"What did he say?"

"Give the phone back to Eli."

"What did he say?"

"He'll come to you soon."

3.

Sleep.

Noon sun drifting to set.

The rays still soaking the bed.

The damp sheets drying out.

In the kitchen the ice-cold vodka down his throat until he can't take it anymore.

He opens the sliding door and walks barefoot to the pool, tastes the sun through his skin, and thinks things like: a new dawn. Drinks from the bottle and walks around the pool slowly three times. Walks back inside into the bedroom, takes the coke and his wallet into the bathroom. Locks the door and removes the huge mirror from the wall, lays it down on the floor, wipes the mirror clean with damp toilet paper, dries it assiduously with more, pours out half the gram. Crouched in his boxers, straddling the mirror, reeking of vodka, cutting lines, staring into himself, muttering, puffing. On his knees. A long line. A long slug of vodka. A long line. A slug of vodka. A line. And the shock of the pool. The thumping of his heartbeat. What was he searching for? The cold water, the bright sun, his burning mind, his body out of time, the vodka numbing his pain, the coke making him brave. He remained underwater as long as he could, his heart hammering, looking up at the sun . . .

. . . looking down at the wreck of Gautam's Mercedes, Gautam unconscious inside, Neda crying over the dead bodies, urging him to do something. What could he do? What was he supposed to do? What more? What could anyone expect of him? Take charge, call an ambulance, call the police, try to help the dead and dying while he waits for the authorities to arrive?

Really?

Laughable.

Absurd.

Maybe in Sweden.

But this is India.

If he'd stayed, a mob would have had them.

This is India.

Yeh India hain.

Here's another version: they watch the crash and just . . . drive on.

Drive on as if nothing ever happened. No contact. No engagement.

Gautam left to his fate.

That would have been something.

To keep driving through the night. Drive on to Chandigarh. Then what? To the mountains, stop for breakfast at Giani Da Dhaba, go on, all the way to Jalori, to Baga Sarahan. They slaughter a goat. Stay for a week, a month.

And then what?

Stay up there forever? Run farther? He and Neda. Start a new life, free of everything? Another country, another city, a humble life.

A regular job.

Imagine it.

Neda comes home to find he's quit, he's been drinking all day. She's had enough. She screams at him. He slaps her. She spits at him, throws a plate. He grabs her raised hand with his left fist, punches her in the ribs.

See how that worked out.

No, there is no way out of this.

There is no way.

He bursts from inside the pool. And his father is standing there, right above, at the villa end, the sun in his face, a navy suit, black shades, a solid, stark figure in the winter haze. He's been watching him. How long? How much does he know?

Now neither of them moves, nor do they speak.

Until Bunty raises his hand, motions ever so slightly for Sunny to approach.

That's all it takes.

Sunny slides toward him.

Everything is keenly felt.

The cold water, the weak sun on his back, the light shimmering on the surface, bouncing off the villa windows. And his father, the bright, dark center of everything.

He reaches the edge, looks up.

"Papa . . ."

Then it happens.

Bunty holds out his hand.

Holds it there, palm open, waiting.

For Sunny to take it.

To be pulled into a new life.

He feels a cold, hard certainty blooming inside him, which he hopes will never leave. His father's hand on the scruff of his neck, guiding him inside.

DEEPTI KAPOOR

In the bathroom he looks down at the mirror on the floor, the remnants of lines, the baggie still half full.

"That poison," his father says. "You don't need that poison anymore."

Sunny doesn't say anything in reply, he just watches the coke.

"Flush it," comes the command.

Even now, he's thinking about saving something somehow.

One last line.

"Put the mirror back on the wall."

He does.

He won't look at himself until he does.

When he does, he sees.

There's nothing there.

He showers with scorching water once his father is gone.

Combs his hair.

Dresses in a crisp white shirt and wool pants.

When he comes into the living room his father is sitting in one of the armchairs smoking a cigarette, his great hulking mass so at ease with itself, one leg over the other, head tilted to the ceiling in an aspect of poised contemplation.

"Sit."

Sunny sits on the footstool, far too small, diminishing himself.

"Papa, I . . ."

Bunty holds up his hand. "Don't speak. There's nothing to say."

Silence. In the warm shadow.

He goes on.

"You cannot undo what's done."

Sunny feels his throat narrowing, clogging, burning.

"I did it for you," he says.

He just might break down. He wants these words to be believed over everything.

"It was smart thinking with the Polaroid." Bunty taps out his cigarette ash. "Did you sleep?"

Sunny composes himself, nods meekly.

Bunty nods along too. "It was a bad night. But it could have been far worse. And now I know something very important."

Sunny's eyes dart around the floor as he waits. Bunty, in no rush, only stares into his son's anguished face.

"What, Papa?" Sunny whispers.

Bunty leans forward. "That you know what it means to be ruthless."

Sunny wells up, all but cries.

Satisfied, Bunty leans back in his chair. "Why don't you make yourself a drink?"

But Sunny shakes his head. "I'm fine."

His father studies his broken expression, his downturned eyes.

The coke is losing its power.

The yawning emptiness is swallowing him.

"Where is he?" Sunny asks.

"Who?"

"Gautam?"

"He's far away now."

"What will happen to him?"

"He'll become useful."

He daren't ask.

But he has to.

"What did he say?"

Bunty feigns ignorance. "About what?"

About what? About what a fool I've been. Exposing myself to him, being played for fun.

"About last night."

Bunty smiles. "Does it matter? Do you think I don't know everything anyway? Your plans with him. Your plans with the girl. Do you think I didn't know?" So there it is. His father knew it all. He watched quietly, waiting for Sunny to ruin himself. Waiting, waiting, until . . . "But you've wiped the slate clean." Bunty stands. Shifts his body close to Sunny and Sunny looks up as Bunty speaks. "I always worried for you. Worried that you didn't have it in you to be my son. But you destroyed everything you held close in a heartbeat." He reaches for Sunny's face, holds his cheek in his great hand. "You did good, son." Tears well and fall. Then just as suddenly Bunty is gone, walking across the villa floor. "You didn't ask about the girl," he calls back brightly. "She didn't ask about you either." He pauses at the sliding doors. "You'll stay here in the farmhouse for four nights. As far as the world is concerned, you're in Singapore."

"Yes, Papa."

"Eli will keep an eye on you here."

"Yes, Papa."

"When you return home we'll get to work."

4.

He returned to the city mansion on the fifth day, Eli driving him home. To his penthouse, still almost empty since it had been torn apart. He walked into it, and he was glad all the memories were gone. He was with his father now. He ate with his father, he sat with his father, he listened to his father's calls in the evening in his father's great mahogany-paneled dining room, the two of them alone.

He told himself a story. He had been playing different roles all his life, testing personas, like all young people test themselves. Seeing who it was possible to be. Seeing which one fit. For a while he had enjoyed building a scene, projecting himself in a certain way, as an avant-garde philanthropist, a patron of the arts, as a good man with a moral code. There had been that flourishing cult of personality around him, and this he had greatly enjoyed. He had enjoyed the attention, the importance he was afforded by a small band, which he craved as a proxy for what he really needed. He had lavished them with generosity.

And the more he exercised his incredible generosity, the more he felt the desire to corrupt grow in him. He had seen it again and again inside himself. He lavished his friends with wine, whisky, champagne, five-star meals. He let them know everything was free, everything was on him, they needn't worry about this ridiculous little thing called money because it would keep pouring from his body, his wallet, his card, his father. He watched their pleasure, especially those who were not conditioned to wealth, who otherwise had to count their rupees. He forced luxury and pleasure upon them so readily. It was only inevitable their tolerance, their threshold would increase. That they would slowly stop expressing delight and guilt and joy at what came from him. That they would slowly come to expect everything. And then he would pull the plug on them.

Now when these old friends came back to him, in the weeks and months that followed, as Gautam got clean in the Alps, as Neda vanished into London, as Ajay was just a name gathering dust, as the crash was forgotten, never spoken of, never raised, never even known, as all the tension of the last year washed away, he watched with numb pleasure as these parasites devoured everything around them without a second thought, and those he'd rejected so cruelly and arbitrarily turned up once more as if it had never happened, and partied without question, consumed without question, took everything from him. But now he succumbed to that desire within him to see them suffer, to see them fall prey to their vices. He surveyed them, his false friends, and despised them all, and was secretly glad in his heart because he was corrupting them. He was giving and giving and giving in the knowledge that when they needed him most he could take it all away.

In a globalized world given over to solitary consumption, his desires found expression in the anonymity of expressways and the suites of luxury hotels, pleasure in their streamlined ease, liberation in their frictionless navigation. He only need withdraw his card, only need direct his driver, sit back and close his eyes, let the blue glow of the future wash over him. The car would do the rest, the card would do the rest, the driver would do the rest. He despised public contact, dust, noise, failure, sorrow. He'd dream of waking in a city of the future, depopulated, full of elevated walkways, paths to nowhere on which no one walked.

When he was called in to his father, he was told he would get his reward. Now he would build. But not in Delhi. Delhi was dead to him. He would build across the border in UP. There was land, land given to them, land that Ram Singh had acquired, which Dinesh Singh would oversee, as was the deal. It was a blank canvas of nothingness upon which he could finally construct his dreams.

AJAY IV

Tihar Jail

1.

It was a lesson to him, the photo of his sister. You're never comfortable. You're never happy. Thinking you have power, you're in control, this is a mistake. Never make that mistake again. He keeps hold of the photo in the brothel, it's in his hand all day, in his hand at night, a double-edged sword, a double-sided coin that's the price of life. Obedience and slavery. He can't bring himself to look at her face. He can't stomach the words on the back of it. But he holds it. All day long he torments himself. He just holds it, keeps his eyes averted. An act of torture, an austerity. His sister. He wants to see her again. He wouldn't judge her. He would save her. At night before he sleeps he allows his eyes to fall on her.

Is it possible to withdraw? Disappear? Be erased? Can one do it by doing nothing? Or must one make the choice? Must one take the drastic step? There it is, the thought that's been dogging him, at his heel his whole life. He, Ajay, can die. He can just die. It would be quick. It would only take a moment and all the pain would end.

The idea, coaxed into the light, becomes his friend. He tends to it kindly. Where? When? A bottle shard in his wrists. A sheet round his neck in the shower. Or a

· 379 ·

Mandrax overdose. But he must get it right. He mustn't slip up, lose his nerve, be found out and saved. If it was done, it should be total. Death would be a relief to him. Justice, perhaps, for everything he's done. For the men he killed, and for the ones he saw dead in the road, who, though he didn't kill, he betrayed. Strange though . . . now these thoughts run freely in his mind, others run too. Options he never thought he had. Saying no to Sunny—this is the first thought he enter-tains. Sunny tells him to get in the car, to drink the whisky. And he, Ajay, says no. The very thought of it is thrilling. He says no. He says: no. It's like the dreams of a blind person who has sight. It's a deaf person dreaming they can hear. A mute dreaming they can speak. Everything is turned up loud, in color. No.

 Why don't you get in the car?

He plays his life in reverse.
 Each time saying no.
 No, he won't chase Gautam.
 No, he won't fire the gun into the air.
 No, he won't decide to kill the Singh brothers.
 No, he won't try to find home.
 No, he won't go to Delhi to work for Sunny Wadia.
 No, he won't get in that Tempo.
 No, he won't let the goat free from its rope.

He's back there, eight years old, back with Hema. He's supposed to be tying up the goat. He's supposed to be tying the rope. He doesn't tie the rope. The goat goes free. He watches it go. This is what he realizes. He watches it go, and it eats the spinach in the neighbor's field. Hema, where is she? She sees and comes running. She doesn't chide him. She runs straight for the goat. Pulls it away, though it won't come. He watches. He tries to see her in his mind's eye. But now all he sees is the woman in the photo.

And he's back here, yes, with the same intractable problem. How long can he wait? How long before the next photo comes? His sister lying in that same brothel bed, eyes forever open, blood pooling the sheets from her fatal wounds. It all comes back to this. His sister must live. She is the last part of him that is real, the last part that is true. Everything else has been taken from him. His father dead, his mother someone else, his little sister someone he never knew. But Hema, she's part of him. She cannot die. He cannot die. He must kill Karan and save her.

2.

It seems to be his inevitable fate.

The price for Prem has been fixed.

Karan will pay fifty thousand rupees.

The handover is due to take place the next day.

This is his chance.

Only, Sikandar wants to do it himself.

Ajay approaches Sikandar, asks to speak to him.

Prem watches carefully.

Sikandar says "Speak."

Ajay whispers something in his ear.

Long. Serious.

He talks for a while.

Then Sikandar bursts out laughing.

Slaps Ajay on the back.

"He's taking you!" Sikandar says.

That night, when Sikandar snores, Prem is awake.

"What did you say to him?"

"Nothing."

"Why are you taking me?"

"I'm trying to protect you," Ajay says.

"I don't need you. Karan will take care of me."

The fans whir.

"He loves me."

Time passes, heavy with unsaid words.

Prem's voice, a tiny vessel of sorrow on a vast ocean of pain.

"Who is she? The girl."

Ajay feels his heartbeat in his throat.

"The girl in the photo."

"My sister," Ajay says.

"Your sister?" Prem replies, surprised. "I thought . . ." Then he trails off.

There is nothing left to say.

The morning comes. There are no more words to say.

Sikandar waits by the cell door.

He nods at Prem, offers his hand.

As if they met once or twice and conducted some business together.

"Be good," he says. Then slaps Ajay on the shoulder, laughs as he pushes him out the door. "Make sure you get the money first!"

Down the corridor they walk.

Ajay with a razor beneath his tongue.

And Prem, looking like hope, like love.

"Thank you," Prem says.

The handover is taking place in one of the bathroom blocks, out of sight.

Karan has a man with him.

Ajay shakes his head.

"Just us."

The goon checks Ajay for weapons.

Nothing.

So Prem and Ajay and Karan go inside one of the shower rooms.

The money is in a jute bag.

Ajay counts it first.

Pushes Prem toward Karan when it's done.

He doesn't look at him.

Watches Karan's face as Karan takes him by the hand.

Puts his arms around his waist.

"Now leave us alone," Karan says.

What's that Ajay feels?

Jealousy.

A loneliness of his own.

A failure of nerve.

He should make his move.

In that moment he can't.

Outside, Ajay and Karan's man eyeball each other, nod. It's done. But as soon as Ajay walks past him, he drops the jute bag, lunges back, wraps his arm round the man's neck in a sleeper hold. He brings him down to the ground as he struggles, drags him into a bathroom stall. Puts him to sleep.

Ajay strips quickly to his underwear.

Takes his sandals off.

Creeps back into the shower room.

Karan has his back to the door, naked from the waist down. Prem is up on the counter, facing him, legs open, legs hooked round his waist. Karan is inside him. Ajay holds the razor in his hand.

Approaching barefoot, trying to calm his heart.

Prem has his eyes closed in joy, taking Karan inside.

Prem opens his eyes.

Sees Ajay.

Razor in hand.

Ajay puts his finger to his lips.

In what world would he think Prem would respond in anything but a scream.

Karan's body locks up.

Then he understands the look in Prem's eyes.

Before he can react, Ajay lunges forward.

Grabs Karan's hair and pulls it back, cuts wildly with the razor. Blood begins to spray from his throat, but the arteries are too deep. Karan is fighting back, trying to protect himself while Prem struggles and screams and cries beneath. Ajay holds Karan's head in the crook of his arm, squeezing it as he digs deeper and deeper with the blade, blood spilling and splashing now and Karan, gurgling, falls down and Ajay falls with him.

"What did you do?" Prem is screaming and Karan is twitching below Ajay, the life draining out of him, the razor lodged in his throat.

"What did you do to me?" Prem collapses to the floor, holds Karan, kisses his face, tries to block the bleeding with his palms.

But Karan is gone.

"Why?"

Ajay doesn't say anything anymore.

Prem is shivering, his face contorted.

Ajay opens his mouth to speak.

But Prem doesn't give him a chance.

He does the only thing he can think to do.

The only thing he has left.

He pulls the razor from Karan's throat and digs it into his left wrist. Gouges it open. Does the same to the right.

Lies down next to Karan.

Looks Ajay in the eyes.

Ajay looks down, turns his back.

Walks away.

FOUR

LUCKNOW, 2006

DINESH AND SUNNY

"So?" he says.

"So what?" Sunny replies.

"So you got what you wanted . . ."

They sit in the private room of the five-star hotel restaurant, Sunny and Dinesh Singh, hushed in the AC, looking out through one-way glass at the elite of Lucknow living their best lives.

". . . but are you happy?"

Sunny winces like he swallowed something bad.

"What?"

"It's a simple enough question," Dinesh says. "Are you happy?"

"Right now?" Sunny puts his lips to his whisky. "The conversation is a little lacking."

Dinesh smiles. "You know what I mean."

"What are you?" Sunny says after a long pause. "My shrink?"

"Do you have one?" Dinesh replies. "Do you *want* one?"

"Jesus."

"Either way, the question stands."

Sunny stares straight ahead, crunches the ice, signals to the attendant for one more.

Dinesh echoes the wave as Sunny lights a cigarette.

Endorsing Sunny's order.

Being a good host.

This is Lucknow after all. His turf.

Also, there have been problems. Sunny, intoxicated in the past, has caused a scene, sometimes merrily, sometimes angrily, before blacking out.

At some point Dinesh may have to make a call: no more drinks for Sunny Wadia.

But he'll cross that bridge when he gets to it.

As for the question: Is Sunny Wadia happy?

File that away under Who the Fuck Knows?

If Sunny's not on the way up, he's coming down. Lurching from one position to the next, avoiding the horror of an equilibrium that can only reveal his face in the mirror.

In his midtwenties, already starting to look old. Fat and old. Held together by shoestrings of misery, dark energy, expensive suits. It's incredible, the extent to which he's letting himself go.

Sunny turns his head.

He can still arrange his face just so.

Do I really have to sit through this? Listen to this from you?

And Dinesh's face is saying:

Yeah, you do.

They have a little bit of telepathy by now.

Sunny gets up, and Dinesh gently pushes him back down.

"Chill," he says. "I'm just fucking with you."

Sunny had come to Lucknow to finalize the land acquisition. Today the deal was done. The land in Greater Noida was going to be all theirs. The farmers were to be bought off. This so-called Megacity would take root.

The details had already been thrashed out by their fathers. All Sunny had to do today was dot the i's and cross the t's. Dinesh had to be there to facilitate. Dinesh had nothing exceptional to do.

But Dinesh also has plans of his own. In the past couple of years he has grown in myriad ways. Developed into a striking young man. An ambitious, effective leader in waiting.

Before, he was simply playing the part.

He was, in many ways, aping Sunny Wadia. The truth is, Dinesh used to be a little gauche. A little bit "village." Sunny had always been the more stylish, the more worldly. But then Sunny stood still, and Dinesh worked on himself. He traveled extensively. To seminars and museums, galleries, auctions, fashion shows, opera houses. He befriended writers and thinkers and grilled them extensively about matters unknown to him. His English became nuanced. He learned to express himself colloquially, modulating his delivery to include a sense of play, irony, delight. People once laughed behind his back, thought he was a striver. They don't laugh anymore. To reflect all this, he has developed his style as well. He still wears kurtas, but he accentuates them with elegant scarves, jeweled brooches, with pocket pins and pocket squares. He wears designer spectacles modeled, it has been noted, to both approbation and approval, on Dr. Ambedkar.

Yes, he is well groomed.

He is well put together.

It shows.

Next to Sunny now, it definitely shows.

"I'm not going to let it go," Dinesh says. "I want to know what's going on in that head of yours."

It's the next morning.

Monsoon clouds fill the air.

They're in Dinesh's Pajero 4×4.

Sunny is smoking a cigarette, staring forward at the road, clammy in his fine white shirt, knees up, feet on the dash, one hand across his gut. In intense negotiations with his own hangover.

Last night, he sat obstinate in the booth. Dinesh's entourage joined, talked rumor, policy, social justice, election tactics, hip-hop, eventually "the bitches," and he was a coiled serpent of misery. The hotel bar became increasingly busy beyond the isolation of their room, and Sunny became increasingly withdrawn.

Out in the main section, another drunk man began playing the piano badly, bashing at the keys in what could only be called an act of provocation. Free jazz, Dinesh joked.

But when a tipsy young woman objected in her own brash manner, the man pulled a revolver on her, waved it around the crowd. Then Dinesh was up and out before you knew it, defusing the situation.

Dinesh the Peacemaker.

He disarmed the rowdy in full view of the room, put an arm round his shoulder and led him to the exit, listening to his woes, handing the gun to security, all witnessed by the pack of city journalists, formerly huddled in one corner, drinking hard.

Sunny made the revolver incident his excuse to escape. He slunk upstairs to his suite without a good-bye, opened the bottle of whisky he'd had Eli buy. Drank a good two thirds of it before he passed out cold.

He'd woken to his own screaming at four thirty a.m.

A nightmare. Someone had been pulling him somewhere he didn't want to go.

Turned out he'd been clasping his own hands, holding them tight above his head, lying on his belly, trying to prize them apart in his sleep. He sat at the side of the bed trying to remember himself, shaking off his fear. He poured a large glass of whisky, slung it back, lit a cigarette, smoked half of it, poured more whisky, knocked that back too, went back to bed and focused on the humming of the AC.

"Nothing's going on with me," he says. "Nothing."

The morning becomes bright with the sun between the clouds scorching the earth, making Sunny's skin itch, turning the puddles in the road into obnoxious mirrors.

Dinesh looks him up and down dubiously.

"Yeah, right. I mean, you look like shit."

"That's because you dragged me out of bed."

They're an hour out of Lucknow.

Out in the countryside. The green fields, the bicycles, the buffalo. The life-giving monsoon air streaming through the windows like a fresh current in the ocean over this lush and bountiful land.

Dinesh is dressed casually, in navy APC chinos and a red Loro Piana wool polo shirt with Loro Piana suede moccasins.

He's saying something.

"What?"

Dinesh shakes his head. "Do you even know who you are?"

They'd called Sunny's room at seven a.m.

Ringing on and on until he was roused from his sleep.

Reception on the line. Then the phone passed to Dinesh.

He'd been smart enough not to call Sunny on his mobile.

"Hey, listen, bro. I need you to get down here. I want to show you something."

"How long is this going to take?"

Sunny did not expect to be driving into the countryside. Driving out alone, without guards, without security, without a driver? In UP?

His father would not approve.

There is, as has been impressed upon him, a real and ongoing kidnap threat.

Sunny tosses his cigarette. Lights another cigarette almost immediately.

"Oh why?" Dinesh says. "Is there somewhere you need to be?"

Sunny slips farther down in his seat, closes his eyes entirely, and concentrates on the cigarette between his fingers and on his lips. The very real tangible cigarette and the smoke that goes in and out of his lungs. Is he asleep?

"I like to slip out," Dinesh says. "Go into the villages and towns. Take the pulse of the common man. You should try it sometime. You might learn something."

The engine has stopped. The air is moody, pregnant with the monsoon.

They're in a lane in a scrappy little market town. An oppression of horns, bodies streaming past. The stench of everything. How did they . . . ?

"You were out cold," Dinesh says. "But you looked so angelic. I thought: just let him sleep."

Sunny sits up. Still vulnerable. Senile, momentarily.

"What happened to my . . . ?" He looks at his fingers.

"I took it right out of your hand, bro. You were ready to burn yourself. Come on."

Dinesh climbs out, breezy, ready for the world.

They take a table at a simple dhaba overlooking the main road, quietly bustling, red plastic chairs, stained tablecloth, surly no-nonsense waiters. One arrives and Dinesh orders a plate of parathas, two nimbu panis.

They look like a couple of big city folk on the way to somewhere else.

"It's funny, I'm out of uniform, so no one recognizes me. I realized, they all know me by my kurta. If I turned up wearing a beautiful white kurta, maybe they'd recognize me. If I turned up next to my father, well! Then they'd know who I was. Everybody knows what my father looks like. My father, and his famous mustache. The second most famous man in this state. You could draw that mustache on a cartoon face without eyes, ears, nose, and I swear, voters would know who it was. I used to say, you should put that mustache in the ballot box. You know, I saw him once, when I was a child, without his mustache. I don't remember why. He turned up at home one day with it shaved off. I cried and cried like crazy. I didn't recognize him at all!"

Sunny says nothing.

"But you know what really interests me?"

Still nothing.

Dinesh taps the table. "The most famous man."

Sunny lowers his shades, looks at him warily.

"I bet my shirt," Dinesh says, "no one here has the slightest clue what he looks like. And yet"—he presses the tip of his finger down until it turns white—"and yet if I stood up and shouted his name, what do you think would happen? Shall I try? Do you want to see what happens when I call out your father's name?"

Sunny stares at him with a face like murder.

The waiter arrives with the parathas and drinks.

"The sooner you tell me what you want . . . ," Sunny says.

Dinesh comes back in, leans both elbows on the table. Gently, he tears a small triangle of paratha apart, places it in his mouth. He eats with tiny, controlled gestures.

"What I really, *really* want," he says, "is to know what the fuck is going on with you."

Sunny rubs his face, growing in agitation.

"And I keep telling you."

"So tell me again."

"There's *nothing*. Nothing is going on." A long pause. A small concession. "What do you think is going on?"

Dinesh nods once, firmly. "I think you're depressed, man. Frankly speaking."

"Fuck off."

"And, you know," Dinesh goes on, "that shit really affects me. Not just in our business relationship. I mean it affects me here"—he slaps his hand to his heart—"right here, it hurts to see you like this." He cracks his knuckles gently. "You may not know it, but I used to look up to you. I used to hang on your every word, brother. You *knew* shit. I'm talking about those good old Delhi days. I was stuck here, dreaming, learning my trade, and you were in Delhi like a . . . like, like a fireball, blazing through the sky."

"Spare me."

"No. To talk to you was to travel the globe. Look at you now. You're . . . you're like . . . frankly, I don't know what you're like. *But look at you.* You look like shit, Sunny. Yes, it's true, don't look at me like that, look at that belly instead. Do something about it. Because, bro, you look like shit. And some people, they just get fat because they love life. You know. They eat, drink, and be merry. But you? No." He wags his finger, crosses his legs. "You're not loving anything anymore. You're miserable. That's what it is. You're *depressed*. And it can't go on like this. Look," he says, lowering his voice to a whisper against the morning thrum, holding what he knows is Sunny's eye through the black glass of his shades. "Look, I *know* what it is. I know what happened. That night, that business with Rathore. It's no great secret."

He watches Sunny clench his jaw.

"These things eat at you."

Sunny shakes his head, stares into the middle distance across the road.

"You don't know shit."

But Dinesh has the scent.

"It's the girl, isn't it?"

"What girl?"

"What girl!" Dinesh laughs in mock surprise, claps his hands together. "You were in love with her, no?"

Sunny snorts a laugh. "You're fucking retarded."

"What was her name?"

Nothing from Sunny.

"Neda," Dinesh says. "That was her name."

He watches Sunny for a reaction.

"Oh, yeah, that bitch," Sunny says, as if recalling a long-forgotten acquaintance. "She was a bad fuck. Nothing more. I threw her out."

"Right." Dinesh brushes crumbs onto the floor. Pinches off another piece of paratha. "I'm glad you cleared that up. That makes a *lot* more sense than the story I heard."

Dinesh is waiting for him to take the bait.

It takes awhile to come.

But it comes.

"What did you hear?"

"Oh no, forget it, it's nothing."

"Fuck off, what did you hear?"

"You really want to know?"

"Fucking tell me or shut up."

"Your father sent her away. That's what I heard. With, pardon the expression, an offer she couldn't refuse. A very generous one, monetarily speaking."

Sunny is a picture of nothingness.

Dinesh pushes the plate his way.

"Why don't you have some paratha?"

"Why don't you shove your paratha up your ass."

It makes Dinesh laugh.

"You really think you're something, don't you?" Sunny says.

Dinesh ignores him, picks up the nimbu pani. "When I taught myself about art," he says, "I did it because I thought it was something modern people do, people like you. I taught myself about art like I was ticking off a shopping list. But I found it fascinating. And I discovered," he frowns in thought, "in the Old Masters, in hushed galleries, and then later, in certain photographers, I discovered something in them that I later discovered was in me. Empathy. It was empathy. I was scared of it at first. I reserved it for the frame. But then I sometimes walked from my hotel and wandered. I did this in Paris, around the Gare du Nord, saw the bums and the down-and-outs. I looked at them like I was looking at a painting, then I took that painting into the world. I told myself, these men and women, they have autonomy, they are fully formed, I can look at them, I understand their pain."

"What the fuck are you on about?"

"Empathy, Sunny. When I returned from that trip, I started to think. About the things we said in the past, and what we really meant, and about what was possible with the power we have. Would you like to hear my conclusion?"

"Do I have a choice?"

"I choose morality over aesthetics. I choose empathy. That's my conclusion. In the current moment, morality should be above everything."

"What's the 'current moment'?"

"The moment of our fathers."

Dinesh sits back, lapses into silence.

Sunny's head is foggy.

"I might look her up," Dinesh says. "When I go to London next. I always liked her. I hear she's doing well. With the apartment she was given, and the money . . . it must have been hard for her to go through what she did all alone."

"Fuck off."

"The real fool," Dinesh says, "such as the gods mock or mar, is he who does not know himself."

"Oh great. Quoting Shakespeare at me now."

"It's not Shakespeare."

"And we're not having this conversation."

"OK," Dinesh says brightly. "Let's talk about something else. Tell me what you're into these days. Talk to me about architecture, cocktails, watches. Sunny, talk to me about the big fucking cities you're going to build on the land my father has given to yours."

"Fuck you."

"But this is our time, Sunny!"

Sunny just stares out.

Across the road, a liquor vend is opening.

Men line up before the metal grilles waving their rupee notes into the darkness within, until they are snatched away and replaced with little plastic bottles and clear plastic bags of hooch.

Dinesh's voice becomes hard, flat. "You aren't enjoying any of this, are you? Tell me. When was the last time you enjoyed anything?"

"Fuck off."

"Tell me, the guy I once knew, who wanted to change the world, did he even exist?"

"He grew up."

"Who wanted to make things better."

"I never wanted to make things better."

"Because it's something we can actually do, you know that, right?" Dinesh becomes animated, passionate. "You do understand, it's in *our* hands to do something good, not to make their mistakes. To do the right thing. Listen to me. Look at me. Take the shades off. Look at me."

Sunny slowly lowers his shades.

His eyes are bloodshot.

"You'll never be your father."

The words strike Sunny terribly. Split his brain in two.

"You'll never be your father, and that's a good thing. It's a *good* thing. I'll never be mine, you'll never be yours. But we can be more than both."

"What do you want?"

"Do you know," Dinesh says, "how many people there are in this state? Two hundred million, give or take. If we were a country, we'd have the fifth-largest population on earth. And it's ours. *All* ours, you and I, we're supposed to inherit it all. But look at it! Look. The people are miserable. This state is almost as miserable as you are!" He pauses meaningfully. "What's the common denominator? Our fathers." Dinesh lowers his voice. "We both know the pact our fathers made: yours bankrolls mine into power, then mine makes them both richer than anyone can imagine. That was the deal. That was the dream, right?"

"If you say so."

"But it's turned into a nightmare. Why?"

"Because your father got greedy."

"No! Because your father is relentless."

"You're blaming my father for making too much money now?"

"I'm blaming him for trying to control the world. He wants it all, all the power. He's a vampire. A locust. He consumes it all. Health care, education, infrastructure, mining, even the media. He has his hand in everything. But he takes from the people."

"He takes from no one."

"Don't be so naive. The hospitals have no medicine. Why? It gets stolen, sold on the black market. To whom? Private hospitals? Who steals it? Who sells it? Who owns the private hospitals? You know who. There's a pattern emerging. Everything public ends up stripped down, sold, taken away. But what is there in abundance? Liquor. Your father's liquor, from the sugarcane he grows, through the distilleries he owns, the distribution he controls, to the shops he sells out of. Like the one right across the street. Look at it. It shouldn't even be open this early in the morning, but there it is. Just so you can forget the misery of your life. It goes round and round. The poor get screwed, and I can see it on your face that you act like you don't care. And I guess you don't. So let me put it another way. The poor get screwed, but the poor also vote. They fucking vote, Sunny. It's the one thing we can't yet take away from them. We can try to buy them off. More liquor, meat, money. But sooner or later they'll kick us out."

Sunny gives a strange, self-satisfied smirk.

"I advised against this land deal of yours," Dinesh goes on, "this deal to give you your fantasy city. You should know that. I advised against it *completely*. It's political suicide. It's self-immolation. It's going to be the death of us. The farmers won't forgive us. They'll tip things over. Come election time, we'll be done."

"Correction. *You'll* be done. They'll vote *you* out. But the next guy who comes along will smell the money, he'll smell it and run to my father and fall in line."

"You believe that, don't you?" Dinesh replies. "But sooner or later the people will vote in someone who can't be bought."

Sunny gets up from the table.

Lights a cigarette.

"Everyone can be bought."

Reaches into his pocket and tosses several hundred rupee notes down.

Dinesh shakes his head. "You don't know the monsters you're letting in the door."

But Sunny is already walking to the street.

Across to the liquor vend.

He turns, shrugs, give a bitter smile that says: *I. Just. Don't. Fucking. Care.*

2007

DEVELOPMENT BEAT

Tales of Precious Dirt

DEAN H. SALDANHA | WEDNESDAY, FEBRUARY 7, 2007

*Forced Acquisition serves private investors under the guise of
"public interest." But farmers in Greater Noida are banding
together across caste lines to fight back.*

IT's a kidney-rattling ride to Maycha village in Western Uttar Pradesh's Gautam Buddh Nagar. The potholed stretch of dirt betrays the dire state of development in this fertile agricultural zone, yet neither road nor settlement will witness the improvements they deserve: both sit within the catchment zone of the UP government's proposed eight-lane Delhi-Agra Expressway. When completed, this "modern marvel" will reduce travel time between the national capital and the Taj Mahal to little over two hours. Meanwhile, Maycha village will be destroyed.

By and large, villagers had made peace with this fact. When the Ram Singh government acquired Maycha and thousands of other farming villages late last year, under the controversial "Urgency Clause" of the Land Acquisition Act, 1894, the affected farmers were offered "market value" compensation, ranging anywhere between 250 and 400 rupees per square meter, turning many landowners into dollar millionaires overnight. While gossip in New Delhi spoke of the uncomfortably close connections between the Ram Singh government and Wadia InfraTech Ltd—the private company behind the expressway contract—opposition on the ground was mostly muted, limited to niggles over pricing calculations. If anything, farmers grudgingly accepted that such a modern and prestigious project served the greater Indian good.

But that situation exploded during a subsequent round of acquisitions a mere three months later. A further 400 villages were notified, in some cases as far as five kilometers from the proposed expressway. Here, it was announced, a company by the name of Shunya Futures would begin construction of the state's first "Tech City," a vast development "modeled on Singapore," replete with "elite" residential colonies, commercial and industrial units, schools, hospitals, nature reserves, and even a waterpark. Further investigations revealed the Shunya Futures CEO to be none other than Sunny Wadia, dilettante son of shadowy Wadia InfraTech boss Bunty Wadia.

Anger and agitation swiftly followed, with farmers balking at the relatively meager compensation provided when measured against Shunya Futures' projected revenues. Some even suggested the expressway itself was a smokescreen to benefit Ram Singh's cronies.

On the back foot—with strikers blockading roads—the state sought to nip the protests in the bud. But the cat was out of the bag; in response to draconian tactics, in an unprecedented show of solidarity, farmers began to organize across caste lines, with Jat and Thakur landowners joining forces with cattle-rearing Gujars and the poor, uncompensated Jatav and Dalit workers who farm their lands.

According to Manveer Singh, one of the agitation's leaders, "Farmers are not against acquisition blindly. In the past, many good things have come. But this project does not serve the common man. We have worked the land for generations, now we have been cheated of our birthright. But we will not give up our land without a fight."

It should be noted this is not the first time the Wadia family has displayed such insensitive ambitions. Several years ago, Sunny Wadia's proposed vision for Delhi's "Yamuna Redevelopment Project" was roundly condemned before being unceremoniously shelved. Whether the Wadia scion's much vaunted "techno-utopian" dreams can be realized in the more amenable Singh-Wadia Oligarchy of Uttar Pradesh, only time will tell.

DEVELOPMENT BEAT

A Tale of Two Singhs

DEAN H. SALDANHA | FRIDAY, JUNE 8, 2007

The proposed Shunya Futures Megacity project at the Yamuna Expressway has been the subject of fierce opposition in recent months. The deadlock seemed intractable, but intervention arrived from an unlikely source.

THE ongoing mass protest against the controversial Shunya Futures Megacity project has taken a surprising turn. As the violent demonstrations showed no sign of abating, the UP chief minister's son, Deputy Leader Dinesh Singh, stepped into the fray.

In a dramatic twist, Singh arrived in Chanyakpur village yesterday morning, with an entourage of party youth workers and sympathetic members of the media in tow. Word had been passed to the protesters in advance regarding his arrival, while notorious local criminal Shiny Batia guaranteed his safe passage. Once inside, with TV cameras rolling, Singh gave his explosive speech.

"We who are in power can no longer treat our citizens with contempt. We can no longer fool ourselves by thinking you cannot see our ill intentions. You deserve more. I have no quarrel with development, I champion it. But this? This is not development. This is looting. If land is to be acquired, it must be done fairly. The people must be compensated, not only monetarily, but with jobs, with dignity, with a future. Not a Shunya future, a real future, a people's future. Do you know what Shunya means? Nothing. It means emptiness. The poisonous and empty dreams of Bunty Wadia. They cannot go on. I stand here in solidarity with the men who toil this land and who are being cast aside. I send a clear message to my party, and to my father. Do not forget where you came from. Do not forget the people you serve, who gave you power. They can also take it away."

GREATER NOIDA

ELI

Friday, June 8, 2007, 3:18 p.m.

"That motherfucker."

Eli looks at Sunny's juddering face in the rear mirror, grapples with the wide wheel of the Bolero, driving his master through the wasteland of fallow fields and derelict machinery that is now his kingdom.

Weeds sprouting.

Untended shrines.

Mangy dogs loitering beneath trees.

The black-shaded expression on his face.

His complexion like a coffin opened.

"He went over the line. He went over the fucking line. Who the fuck does he think he is?"

And Eli says, "Boss. Boss! Notice anything different about me?"

Sunny lights a cigarette.

His hands are trembling.

He takes a hip flask from his trouser pocket, fixes himself with a slug of vodka. "You shaved your pubic hair."

"No. Very funny. This I do last week."

Sunny almost laughs, takes another hit of vodka, looks out over the land. Calms a little. "What is it?" he says. "What's different about you?"

"I give you small clue. You see *Terminator 2*?"

"What?"

"*T2: Judgment Day*. Have you seen?"

"Am I Osama bin Laden? Living in a fucking cave? Of course I've seen it."

"So then?" Eli grins and touches his hand to his shades. "Look! See! I got this morning. Persol Ratti 58230. Count them, five-eight-two-three-zero. Very rare. Hard to find. Exactly same as in movie."

Silence. Then . . .

"What movie?"

Eli is about to erupt in exasperation.

But he catches himself.

"Ahhh, very funny boss. What movie?"

"So," Sunny says, "how much did you pay for them?"

"Ahhh," Eli shakes his head. "I buy in auction. Cannot find in shop."

"Yeah, but how much?"

Eli sighs. "Even you cannot afford."

That makes Sunny laugh for real.

Before the silence swallows him again.

They drive on.

More scrub.

"You think you're the Terminator?" Sunny says.

Eli shrugs. "I'm pretty tough."

"If you're the Terminator, what does that make me?"

"Easy! You the kid."

"The kid," Sunny says, "who tells you what to do."

"Yes! I know this actually. This my job. Do what you say. Make you happy. You ask me stand on one leg. I do. Shoot that asshole. Sure, why not? Drive you into enemy territory. Oh look, this is what we do right now. You want me to wipe your ass? You want maybe I give hand job?"

"Fuck you."

"No! Thank you! This I draw the line."

Miles of dust and nothing.

Eli shakes his head.

Sucks his teeth.

"Boss, where we going? Because all this," he pats the gun in his waistband, "with only Eli and Mr. Jericho for company, is really bad fucking idea. You don't see what I see."

"What do you see?"

"Trap."

They pass through a small settlement of half-finished plots.

Migrant laborers have set up fires; washing lines are strung between poles.

"I need to know what this motherfucker's doing."

"So pick up the phone, dial number. Seriously!"

Sunny shakes his head, opens the window, and flicks the cigarette out.

"The phone isn't safe."

"*This* is not safe, driving alone in this pile of shit." Eli begins adjusting the stereo. "Doesn't even have Bluetooth!"

"It's your car, fuckface."

"This I know," Eli nods. "This I use for driving to shops, buying milk." He gives up on the stereo. "Not for bringing knife to gunfight. Should have brought Porsche Cayenne. Porsche Cayenne has Bluetooth. Porsche Cayenne is bulletproof."

"Porsche Cayenne is conspicuous. You know what that means?"

"Yes, I know what means."

"How you say in Hebrew?"

"Is bolet."

"Bullet?"

"No, asshole. Not bullet. Is bolet."

Ahead, on a lonely crossroad, a small, canopied kiosk. A man stands outside.

He sees the car coming, holds out a hopeful armful of brochures.

Brochures for property developments.

"One of yours?"

"No," Sunny watches with disgust.

"You want maybe I run him down?"

"Maybe on the way back."

"Ha! But I scare him, no?"

Eli accelerates the Bolero into the crossroads, the boxy metal shell bouncing around the road, swerving toward the man before pulling back at the last.

Sunny watches with relish as the poor soul dives out of the way.

And when the dust settles . . .

"Seriously, boss. I should've called Papa. Uncle Tinu. Tell them, Sunny is crazy."

A motorbike rises from behind a mound of earth on a parallel dirt road thirty feet away.

Two men riding, their heads wrapped in white cloth.

Both turn to watch the car.

"Don't look," Eli says, his hand creeping toward the gun.

But the bike peels away on another track and heads west.

And they are alone again.

Nothing for miles.

Twenty minutes later, and they are there. Dinesh's hideout, a villa on the edge of a farming village, fortified, guarded by his loyal men.

Ahead, the road is blocked by tractors and men with rifles.

Eli slows. "Yes, this is bad fucking idea."

Sunny pulls out a cheap Nokia phone, dials a number. "Motherfucker," he says, "I'm here. Yeah, a Bolero. Let us through." He hangs up.

Eli brings the Bolero to a crawl, the roadblock is a hundred meters away, the men and their guns are taking form. Then movement, the tractors begin to reverse, opening a path forward.

"Here we go," Sunny says.

Eli drives through, along the rubble road to the villa, a raised track packed with fresh, soft dirt. And either side, vegetables.

"Thinks he's a real fucking farmer."

When they arrive at the metal gate it opens to show eight men with assault rifles inside.

"This is bad," Eli says. "This very bad."

"Keep your mouth shut."

And there's Dinesh, emerging from the villa in his white kurta and round glasses, hands clasped behind his back, a grave expression on his face.

Eli eases the Bolero to a halt.

And Sunny opens the door. "Stay here," he says, then pauses uncertainly. "This motherfucker better have something good to say."

Two Hours Pass

Eli sits alone on a charpoy under a canopy of white cloth, smoking his Marlboro Reds, his long hair unbound, his legs rakishly crossed, his wrist hanging dandyishly limp as his cigarette burns between his fingers. But the eyes behind the Persol Ratti 58230s are sharks watching the guards patrolling the forecourt. They wear white open-neck shirts and black suits, dark wraparound shades, gold jewelry; they are dressed to appear like government security, but they're not. They carry Type 56 assault rifles. Fully enclosed front sights. No side mount plates. Probably Vietnam War stock, or sourced from the Nepalese PLA.

Whatever, they don't know how to use them, he can tell. If it comes to it, he can kill four with his Jericho before they get off a single shot. He plays it through in his head, two would be dead before they even knew what was happening, the other two would be lucky enough to see him fire. Then? Then it would be down to luck, skill, and fate. He allows himself a wan little smile. But how many more are there inside? And what to do about Sunny?

Beyond the bounds of professional objectivity, Eli wavers between pity and contempt when he thinks of his boss. Even with eighteen hundred daily dollar reasons to stay—wired to an account in Zurich—he's begun to reconsider his position. There's something soul destroying about being Sunny Wadia's shadow. His Rottweiler. His court jester. His nursemaid. Eli's almost nostalgic for the good old days of his youth, when all he had to do was shoot and stay alive. He's seen a lot of shit these last few Wadia years. More than he bargained for when he signed up.

It started so well.

"Securing venues and working out schedules for a wealthy New Delhi family" was how it was sold in the brochure. A well-paid monotony with all the perks. On his days off, Eli wandered the shopping malls dressed in his favored big-collared floral shirts, his curls splayed on his shoulders, his panther limbs ranging, grinning at the girls.

Then he got selected—for his skin tone, he wagered—to teach a few choice servants how to shoot, how to fight, how to think on their feet in a tactical situation. He kept his mouth shut (his Hindi almost nonexistent anyway) and got on with it. There was a certain pride in guaranteeing these kids wouldn't blow their faces off loading their own guns.

Then came Ajay.

Dutiful, diligent, burning with hidden fire.

He trained Ajay to be Sunny's bodyguard, to fight in Krav Maga, Brazilian jiujitsu, or at least know the fundamentals. Gave him dedicated firearms training too. Grew close to him, was proud to watch him bloom. Sunny was just the asshole upstairs. He remembered this one time Sunny decided to learn Krav Maga too, crashed a couple of Ajay's classes with some ditzy model on his arm, used Ajay as a human punching bag, Ajay never fighting back, never laying a finger on Sunny, just crouching like a dog with his tail between his legs, taking his licks. Eli willed Ajay to give it back just once, to wipe the sanctimonious smile off Sunny's face. He wanted to see Sunny hurt.

Then he wanted to see him dead. It was the morning after the night he was called to the lawyer's place, no idea what was going on, even when he was ferrying Sunny to the farmhouse.

It was only when he turned on the TV in the villa as Sunny slept that he got to know. Seeing Ajay's face projected on-screen, seeing his cuffed hands as he was led out by the cops. He understood enough to know that Ajay had been offered up as a sacrifice. Full of rage, he turned off the TV and crept into Sunny's room while Sunny slept his sedative sleep. He could have done anything in that brief moment. Put a pillow over his face and pressed down. But no, no. He was a professional. He valued his own life. He went back outside and played cards and waited for orders. By eleven a.m., a new directive—go with the lawyer to Rajasthan. In the SUV he was told: you can take your anger out on Gautam Rathore.

Amazing how these fuckers read your mind.

His career followed the trajectory usually reserved for a laser-guided bomb. He was assigned to guard Sunny full time. Guard, babysit, protect, spy on, whatever. It was surely going to blow up in his face. At least he didn't have to wear a bow tie and make drinks. And why him? He didn't know for sure. He guessed it was due to his being alone with Sunny on the dark, downward slope of that fateful night. He'd seen the worst of it already (or so he thought), and they had sealed a bond in arak and blood. At the start of this tour of duty, Eli was granted his one and only personal audience with God himself.

Bunty Wadia, wandering through his hothouse in that roundabout, mellifluous way of his, said: all Sunny needs is saving from himself.

"That all?" Eli deadpanned.

"And if he ever speaks about the Neda girl . . ."

Eli finished the sentence in his mind.

It was understood.

And of course he was still angry with Sunny deep down, but the wanting-to-kill part of it quickly waned. I mean, he was *so* miserable, so pathetic, so lost. So adaptable Eli still carried a flame for the fallen Ajay, but switched allegiances in his mind and bore his mission with the same droll sense of humor he was famous for among his friends back home. Risus sardonicus, you could call it. Sardonicism under fire.

It sat well with Sunny, truth be told, the backchat, the fuck-you cynical asides. Maybe that's what he'd been missing most of his life. Maybe he needed a punching bag that fought back. No, no. He needed much more than that. But it was a start. In their grimly invigorating dialogues—no sub-ject taboo (save father, Neda, Ajay, crash), no joke too far (save see above)—their twisted, inexplicable companionship grew. Truly, Eli was the only real person left in Sunny Wadia's life, present for every minute of the masquer-ade, biting his tongue, averting his eyes, shit-talking when shit-talking needed to be done, watching Sunny eat, drink, drug, and fuck his way to the hills and back again. He'd never known anyone show so little pleasure, so little joy in the business of living. He told him so, when they were alone, and was invariably told to fuck off in return.

Then there were the times they weren't alone, and Eli had to fall silent and position himself behind the line. This was genuinely exhausting work. Yeah, there was something corrosive about Sunny Wadia. Something corro-sive about standing guard as Sunny taunted so-called friends, used them, mocked them. Tempted and humiliated them. There were the sudden out-bursts of manic violence to take into account too. How many times had he dragged Sunny away from a trashed hotel room, a punch-up in a nightclub. Smoothed things out after the fact with a wad of cash, a splash of humor, the knife-edge of his right hand in the bridge of a nose. One time, to Sun-ny's grotesque amusement, all of the above (in that order). Then there were the sojourns to Dubai. In Dubai, all Sunny wanted to do was go over the edge. That one time with the Siberian escort . . . my God, some things you couldn't unsee. If you're going to pay a beautiful woman that much money, the least you could do is have sex with her.

Eli shakes his head, spits on the ground with such venom all the guards look. He waves a dismissive, clownish hand.

Fucking Sunny Wadia! Crazy guy!

Dinesh, on the other hand—he knew the time of day. This shit with the farmers, Eli was sure it was a smart play, a masterstroke. Who wanted to build these shitty apartment buildings anyway? Not Sunny, not really. In his heart Sunny seemed to hate the whole thing. In his heart Sunny seemed to hate . . . well . . . no . . . Eli wasn't about to manifest that thought.

After all, they could read minds.

Truth be told, if he could, he'd work for Dinesh Singh in a heartbeat. Calm, resolute Dinesh, the man with the plan. But he also knew, if he *was* to go to the other side, he'd just as likely find a bullet in his . . .

Friday, June 8, 2007, 5:28 p.m.

"We're leaving!"

Eli is smoking his seventh cigarette when Sunny staggers out the front door.

Staggers like he's been knifed between the shoulder blades, eyes wild, face drained of color. Eli springs to his feet and Dinesh's guards come forward too, and Dinesh, he's right there behind Sunny, pulling him by the shoulder, calmly whispering something in his ear, pressing an A3 manila envelope into his hands. Sunny regards the envelope with dismay, then reels toward the Bolero as Eli lopes over, climbs in, starts the engine, spins the Bolero round. One of the guards walks over to the gate, a little too casually.

"Motherfucker," Sunny cries, clambering into the passenger seat, slamming his hand on the horn.

"Boss . . ."

Sunny tries to light a cigarette.

The guard pulls open the gate and smirks.

Eli is scanning the horizon for threats. The sky burns an intense blue. And Sunny is still trying to light the cigarette, becoming more agitated, to the point where he opens the window and tosses the lighter out into the dust. So Eli has to light it for him, his eyes darting between the cigarette and the road and Sunny's sweating, clammy brow. Sunny sucks it down to a stub in record time. All in silence. And when it's done he turns his attention to the envelope on his lap.

"Boss. What happened?"

"He's fucking crazy," Sunny mumbles.

"Who? Dinesh? Yeah, sure, he crazy. This we know."

"He's lost it."

"Yes, he lost it. But what's in envelope, boss?"

Sunny runs his hand over it and winces. "I don't . . ."

"You don't?"

Sunny reaches for his hip flask, unscrews it.

"I don't want . . ."

"Don't want what?"

He swallows all the vodka that's left, holds his tongue out for the last drop, screws the cap back on, collapses back in his seat, and closes his eyes.

"Don't want to know."

It's forty minutes since Sunny spoke. They're three kilometers from the expressway, almost back in civilization. The words *don't want to know* rattled hollow in their respective brains.

The vodka has stunned Sunny, for now. He's sluggish, glassy-eyed.

"Eli?"

"Yes, my friend?"

"How many people you kill?"

Eli sucks the air between his teeth, takes some time to organize his thoughts. "With respect," he replies, "you do not ask."

"I'm asking you," Sunny slurs.

"And I tell you," Eli replies, "you do not ask."

"More than ten?"

Eli glances at Sunny, slumped, leg up on the dash, leg slipping now and then.

"How many people you fuck?" he counters.

"Twenty?" Sunny goes on, ignoring the question.

"How many people you fuck?"

The words reach Sunny late. "What?"

"You tell me," Eli states firmly, "how many people you fuck, and I tell you how many I kill."

"Literally?" Sunny asks, seeming surprised. "Or metaphorically?"

Eli shakes his head. "You're a mess. Why we play this game?"

"Because I want to know."

They're approaching the expressway.

"But what good does it do?"

They can see it in the distance.

Trucks and cars and bikes.

"I said you tell me!"

Eli sighs. "Who you want me to kill?"

There's a brief moment when it looks like Sunny has blacked out. But then he sits up straight and sucks in a lungful of air and opens his eyes and he's animated, manic even. "Fuck it." He rips open the manila envelope.

Pulls out what's inside.

A single, dark plastic sheet.

Like an X-ray.

Stares at it.

And behind the sheet, several photographs, some from a CCTV camera, some taken with a telephoto lens.

Eli cranes his neck but can't quite make out what it is.

Either way, there's no mistaking Sunny's reaction.

Shock.

Nausea.

He starts to tremble.

"Boss?"

Sunny quickly stuffs the sheet back inside. Sober, instantly. "I want you to take this," he says.

"What is it?"

"Put it somewhere safe. No one ever sees it. Ever."

"OK, boss."

"If anyone tries to see it, shoot them."

"What if I try to see it?"

"You shoot yourself."

"What if you try to see it?"

"Eli. I'm not fucking around."

"OK, OK." Eli's spooked. "But what if your father tries to see it?"

"Then I shoot you."

"OK, boss."

The Bolero creeps into the narrow underpass.

Eli turns the headlights on.

Pitch darkness and deep holes where the concrete has worn away.

Sunny begins to speak in the dark.

"Dinesh Singh wants to bring his father down. And if my father goes down with him . . ."

When they emerge into the light, rising onto freshly paved tarmac, Sunny is staring at Eli with plagued eyes.

Eli is staring back at him.

It's 5:49 p.m.

Friday, June 8.

Eli doesn't see the masked man stepping out from behind the parked truck, wielding an antique shotgun.

Sunny does.

But by the time he cries out, it's too late.

THE GODOWN

There's this dream he keeps having.
    Culled from life.
    Back home in Meerut, aged five,
    sleeping next to his mother,
    the whir of the ceiling fan,
    the cotton of her nightdress bunched in his fist.
    It's the dream he keeps having.
    Only it's real.

He's five and awake, and his mother is no longer there.
    Empty hand clenches empty fist.
    The sheet still carrying her outline and her scent.
    He calls out to her, but his voice is swallowed by the ceiling blades.
    He must jump to reach the floor.

Tinu is sleeping in the kitchen.
    In the study, a light is on. His father's frame in the frosted glass.
    He moves away, calls through rooms.

In the violence of the blades, his voice goes unheard.
But when he enters the sitting room,
the fan does not spin in there.

She hangs from it by her own dupatta,
    tongue out,
    eyes bulging,
    void.

He comes up like he's coming up for air.
From the turbulence of the ocean floor.
Rag-dolled.
Rasping.
Howling.
And the dream he was having is receding,
sucking up boulders, hurling them toward the shore.
Leaving only enough oxygen
for the scream.

"Namaste ji," the Incubus says.
"You pissed yourself."

And Sunny thrashes like a caged animal in this dank and humid room, with the monstrous presence in front of him and the ropes that bind him to the chair.

The Incubus watches his rage.

An ink blot in black jeans and blue-checked shirt.

"For a while I thought you were dead," it says. "Then you started to scream. And you pissed yourself."

Gnashing, gasping. The whites of his eyes. Teeth bared.

Sunny comes out of this twilight.

Breathing, panting, spent.

The Incubus holds his head and pours water over his cracked lips.

He chokes, then begins to groan.

Sunset leaking through the walls.

The stench of manure, buffalo, blood.

The pain across his nerves, inside his bones.

Taking him outside himself.

"I asked," the Incubus says, "what's he dreaming of that could make him so scared? I've had dreams like that myself."

Sunny tries to gather the fractured parts.

"Where am I?"

His body won't respond.

"You're here."

"Where's here?"

"You don't know?"

He doesn't know.

"What's happening?"

"You're lucky to be alive," the Incubus says. "You weren't supposed to be in the front."

Front of what? He doesn't remember. He tries to stand.

"If you died, Sunny Wadia, so would I."

Sunny's eyes flicker at his name. "I don't know you," he says.

"But I know you," the Incubus replies. He places a hand on Sunny's cheeks. "I know this face."

He takes a pill from his pocket and slips it into Sunny's mouth.

"Take your medicine."

He pours more water in, covers Sunny's mouth, and pinches his nose with his spidery hand.

"Papa's going to kill you," Sunny says.

The Incubus runs his hand through Sunny's hair. Drenched in sweat and blood. Presses his thumb down on the deep gash at his hairline.

"He can try."

He's in a hotel suite.

No place or time.

It could be Europe.

Milan.

Zurich.

It could be Paris.

He's in the marble bathroom, under the shower.

Long, hot shower.

The beep and thrum of traffic outside.

Night, opera. Night, restaurant.

Vicky says, "You were born on the day of the solar eclipse."

Vicky holds his face.

His mother has been cremated.

He climbs out, stands dripping on the marble floor, the white towel wrapped halfway up his chest.

He looks at the mirror. The mirror steamed.

There could be someone in the room, in the bed.

There could be a woman.

But in the bathroom he's alone.

He locks the door.

Gold taps. Marble.

Turns off all the lights but one, small and recessed, so the room is womblike with the heat and dark corners and the extractor fan rattling in the wall.

It's the noise of the fan that's important here.

He takes another towel and places it over his head.

Eases himself to his knees and crawls like a penitent into the corner.

Here he admits the smallest sliver of light.

Considers nothing but this light, which grows to the size of the universe.

He can hold himself here.

Here he's safe,

beneath the table below the mirror,

as his mother combs her hair and sings to him.

He wishes he could stay here.

But he's waking.

Waking.

What's changed?

The pain has made a bed for itself.

And he's back in the world.

A godown of sorts.

Farm machinery, bags of fertilizer, animal feed.

The floor of compacted dirt, the walls of brick.

A weak light bulb hangs from a cord.

What day is this?

He tries to lift his head. He's on a filthy mattress.

Mosquito and flea bitten, staring up at a corrugated metal roof.

His wrists bound together with rope. The stench of soiled bodies, his pants and shirt soaked with dried blood.

His ribs broken, certainly.

His nose too. Maybe his jaw.

He's been kidnapped, this has become clear.

He can't remember how or when or where.

There's a great black hole where his memory has been.

He twists his neck.

An oaf of a man is sitting against the wall, his limbs like spades, his face all nose and ears. He wears a faded blue tracksuit, the cheap knockoff kind.

There's an old shotgun by his side.

An Oaf, he thinks.

An Oaf who's sleeping.

So Sunny tries to stand.

But his legs are weak and numb, and what's more, his left ankle is clapped in rusty metal, chained to an old machine.

Now the Oaf is pulling the white rag that hangs around his neck up over his mouth.

Reaching for the shotgun.

He disappears out the door.

A flash of evening sky, a golden field, hot wind.

An old man, body bent like a question mark, leading a herd of buffalo.

Think. Think.

It's hard to think beyond the immediacy of the pain, but he tries to string his mind together, to make a thread of things.

Where was he?

Where has he been?

What day is it? What month?

He latches on to Dinesh Singh.

Dinesh Singh and the farmers and his Megacity. All this bullshit, these Shunya things. Dinesh making his stand while he was in his office, watching it unfold on the TV.

Drinking vodka from the bottle in his bottom drawer, blinds drawn, a cliché.

From there he reaches across the chasm.

Eli.

He was driving with Eli in his beat-up old SUV.

Heading to meet with Dinesh Singh.

That motherfucker better have something good to say.

———

Minutes pass. Or has it been hours? The godown door opens. In comes the Oaf again. There's another man behind him. He recognizes him as if from a dream. Yes, it's the Incubus, swaggering, fishing out a Nokia phone.

"About time, Sunny Wadia," the Incubus says. "No time to waste. Give us the number."

"What number?"

"The one that will make this all go away."

Two rings, three rings.

A click on the other end.

The Incubus speaks.

"Good evening, sir. I have someone for you."

He thrusts the phone to Sunny's ear.

"Papa . . . I . . . ," Sunny fumbles the words.

The Incubus snatches the phone from him.

"Hear that?" he says. "Your boy is alive. But for how long, that depends on you. I'll call again in one hour with our demands."

He hangs up, removes the battery and the SIM, looks to the Oaf.

"I'll be gone for a while. Keep an eye on him. Give him food."

With that, the Incubus stalks away.

He's left alone with the Oaf.

But he isn't really there.

He's slipping down the cliff face of consciousness once more, toward the roiling sea.

Vicky was the one to tell him about the date of his birth.

The auspicious date. February 16, 1980.

The day of a great solar eclipse.

He was there. He saw it with his own eyes.

Vicky was the one who told him of the demon women who rode naked from the sky, fangs bared, when the blood sacrifice was made, who conferred power on those who had conjured them, or else tore them limb from limb. The boy sat on the hard mountain of his thigh, lost in his words while the long black strands of hair spilled over like night water falling.

"One day," Vicky whispered in his ear, "you'll be stronger than them all."

But he is shriveled.

Shriveled.

Everything is dry and tight and hard.

A barren rock face where water once flowed.

There's a gap he cannot bridge.

    A distance he has crossed and cannot return.

    He has sacrificed everything.

    Love, adoration, respect, loyalty, companionship.

    He has nothing left save his ruthlessness.

    A fleeting ruthlessness he cannot own.

He's back there on that road. That forever road.

Ajay is helping him, carrying the limp body of Gautam Rathore.

Ajay has not yet handed over his gun.

Sunny has not yet punched Neda in the face. The forever face.

Why was she there?

Why do anything?

Time goes both ways.

He's there on the road.

She's crying in the road.

He's angry with her.

He thinks she's performing grief.

He'll never leave.

The Oaf returns sometime later carrying a metal tray. A jug of lassi, a clay cup, three parathas.

The Oaf pours the lassi into the clay cup. "Drink." His voice is grudging, halting, maybe even scared.

"What happened to the guy I was with?" Sunny says.

No response.

"Who are you?" he tries again.

No response. Just those sad, lonely, pinprick eyes.

"You're not a monster," Sunny says.

A flash in those eyes. "Shut up."

"You don't have to do this," Sunny goes on, for want of anything real to say.

"Shut up!"

"You've proved you're a big man. Now we can talk. We can use a man like you. A man like you can get rich."

The Oaf lumbers to his feet, scrambles to the door.

"Hey!" Sunny calls.

The Oaf halts, freezes, half turns.

"Where's your boss?"

The Oaf bristles. "He's not my boss."

"He'll get you killed."

"He's not my boss."

"Who is he?"

"Stop talking."

"Do you really think you'll get away? You know he'll take the money and run. Even if he doesn't, how long do you think you'll last? You'll be dead soon enough. Worse than dead. Or you could live and get rich. You could help me. You could help set me free."

The Oaf puts his hands over his ears.

"Shut up!!" he cries.

And with that he's gone.

The hours tick by.

Night falls, and the Oaf returns.

He sits on the floor near Sunny, sullenly stares.

He seems calmer now.

He and Sunny both.

"Why are you doing this?" Sunny says.

The Oaf finally looks Sunny square in the eye. His voice is flat.

"Because you ruined my life."

"I ruined your life?"

"You ruined my life," the Oaf repeats himself.

"How?" Sunny says.

"You took our land away."

"You're a farmer."

"You ruined my life."

"You got paid."

"Money didn't help anything!" the Oaf snaps. "Anyway," he says after some time, "the money is all gone."

"The money is gone," Sunny repeats, testing the words.

"It's gone."

"How much did you get?"

"Eight crore."

Sunny whistles long and slow. "Eight crore rupees. It should have changed your life."

"It did. It made it worse."

"Where did it all go?"

The Oaf closes his eyes as he speaks.

"We married off our sisters in big weddings. We bought cars, TVs, washing machines. We built big mansions like you people. The whole village became crowded with mansions. But all our fields were gone. After all the celebration, what then? Everyone was lying around all day with money and nothing to do. No fields to work in, nothing to work together for. People turned to drink. Drugs. All I knew was to work together. Now everyone was just in their own worlds. Buying more cars. You couldn't move for all the new cars. The lanes were blocked for hours sometimes, and people would fight and shoot at each other. Everyone was sick. My brother bought a fancy car from Delhi."

"What car?"

"A fast car."

"What brand?"

"Lam . . . Lamb . . ."

"Lamborghini," Sunny smiles. "He bought a Lamborghini."

"Yes."

"That must have cost, what? Two and a half?"

"Two point eight crore."

Sunny nods to himself. "It was the Gallardo."

"I don't know."

"What did your brother do with it?"

"The same day he bought it, it got stuck in an alley between two new mansions. The more he tried to get it out the more it got stuck. The noise of the engine was so loud everyone came to see and watch and give advice. But my brother was drunk and angry and he kept pushing the engine. It was so hot the engine caught fire."

"And?"

The Oaf's eyes give the hint of a smile.

"The whole car burned."

"So what did your brother do?"

"He went to the showroom. He said the car was faulty. The dealer told him it wasn't. The fault was with him. My brother got angry with that. He pulled out a gun. Demanded his money back. But they wouldn't give it."

"So?"

"My brother shot him in the head."

Sunny lets it sink in.

"Your brother's a hothead." Sunny stops a moment, thinks. "What can I call you? What's your name?"

"I'm not telling you my name."

"Make one up. I have to call you something."

The Oaf hesitates, his eyes search the room. "Manoj," he finally says.

"What happened next, Manoj?"

"My brother went to jail. I had to go every week to give money to the cops. Four lakh a month to keep him well. Good food and blankets. I had to keep going to Lucknow to bribe people to get his bail. Soon the money was gone. We were left with nothing and he was still in jail."

"That's too bad."

"I went so many times. He was so angry. Then one day his mood had changed. He was smiling. He said he'd met a friend who had suffered too, and this friend knew how to win our money back. He told me to trust this man, pay his bail. He'll take care of you."

Sunny smiles and nods. "This man you're with now?"

"Yes."

"And this was his plan?"

Manoj looks down. "Yes."

"He's running away with the money, Manoj. He's long gone, he's running with the money or he's already dead. And soon enough my father will be here. And then you'll be dead too. Nothing I say will stop it. But you could just let me go, Manoj. Let me go and I'll make you rich."

"I don't want to be rich."

"Then why did you kidnap me? What do you want?"

"I want my life back."

"No one gets their life back."

No one ever gets it back. Life just runs away from you. It never comes back, however hard you try, however much you want it to. This is the lesson you should know. You have to adapt or die.

"I've made up my mind," Dinesh Singh said.

Sunny had driven to the villa that morning.

Called Eli from his office and told him to get the Bolero ready.

The Bolero, not the Porsche.

It's coming back to him.

Eli pulled the Bolero into the compound.

It's coming back to him.

Dinesh came out to meet them.

"This motherfucker better have something good to say."

It's coming back to him.

Something Dinesh said to him.

"I've made up my mind."

"Yeah. You've decided to fuck yourself. And you're fucking me too."

"I'm trying to save you."

Sunny swallowed his whisky. "Fuck you."

"I warned you about this," Dinesh said. "It shouldn't be a surprise."

"You're destroying yourself."

"No, I'm making my move."

It's coming back to him, through the fog, it's coming back to him.

Something Dinesh knew.

"By siding with some fucking farmers?"

"Yes. And you're going to side with them too."

"You're insane."

"After we get rid of them both, we're going to change this world."

"Get rid of them both?"

"My father. Yours."

"Fuck you. Why would I do that? I'm not betraying my father for you."

"Then do it for yourself." Dinesh walked to his desk, picked up a manila envelope. "He never stood by you."

"He always stood by me."

"He never did. And I have the proof."

He held the envelope out to Sunny.

"What's this?"

"I know you don't care about the world, and the suffering taking place in our names. But maybe you'll care about this. Your father lied to you. Controlled you. Took the only thing you've truly created away."

In an almighty flood it returns to him.

The envelope held in his lap as he and Eli drove away.

The envelope opened, the documents spilled from inside.

Patient's name: Neda Kapur.

And the sonogram.

The image of his unborn child.

Alongside the photos of Neda and Chandra at the clinic in London where his child returned to atoms and stars.

He sits stunned in the dark.

When dawn finally comes a figure sits before him on a stool, swigging from a plastic bottle of country liquor.

"Manoj?" Sunny groans, through the pain and the sorrow.

"Oh no," comes the reply. "Manoj is gone."

It's the Incubus. His rasping voice unmistakable.

"Gone?"

Sunny feels the floodwaters of panic rise in his chest.

"Gone where?"

"To get the first payment, of course." The Incubus laughs. "Your people have come through for you."

Sunny squeezes his eyelids shut. "They're going to kill him," he says.

"No, no, no," the Incubus replies. "You're the heir to the kingdom. You're much too precious for them to risk that." He gets off the stool, tosses the liquor bottle to the floor, slowly circles around behind Sunny. "Besides," he goes on, "you're the one who's going to kill him."

"I don't understand."

The Incubus pulls a long, greasy rag from his pocket as he edges out of Sunny's vision, like a bad magician performing a bad trick.

"Just not yet."

"What are you doing?"

Unable to see.

Unable to turn or break free.

Writhing in his ropes.

Until the Incubus looms above him, a nightmare in flesh.

"What are you doing?!"

Brings the rag down over Sunny's gaping mouth.

Ties it tight.

"Telling you my story."

ALL GLORY MUST GO TO GODS

1.

It's the story of my life, Sunny Wadia. Here I am, Sunil Rastogi, crippled and scarred. But not so long ago I was a young man of nineteen on the back of my brother's brand-new Pulsar, and my brother, twenty-five years on earth, riding up front. On that day it was just before dark, when the birds are loudest above the fields and the sun is a ball of fire in the sky. We were riding slow. The road had been paved only three months before, but it was crumbling already. Such is life. Sunny Wadia, listen. A man flagged us down at the Bulandshahr junction, stepped out and waved us down in a panic, and we saw another man lying motionless in the road beside him. "Don't stop," I said, "it's a trick," but before my brother could react the first man pulled a gun and the second leaped to his feet. My brother stopped the bike in a calm manner, and as we climbed off, he said, "Do what they say," then he whispered to me, "We can always kill them later." Some gust of wind must have carried his voice to them like a stray spark igniting my life, for the one with the gun laughed a moment later and said, "Oh really?" then he shot my brother in the chest. "Behenchod!" I cried as they jumped on our bike and escaped toward the sunset, while my brother collapsed into the dirt.

Some other men on bikes passed by as I held my hand to the wound, tried to stop the blood that was pumping out of him. One of these men turned and hurried off to fetch a police Gypsy they'd seen parked just down the road. As we waited, my brother slipped out of consciousness. "Why did you do that?" he said. "Do what?!" I replied, but I would never find out, for those were his last words.

The cops in their jeep arrived soon enough. They looked down on us as if we were dogs. I shouted at them to take us to hospital. "Take him yourself," one of them said. The other said, "Do you think we're charity?" "But, sirs," I cried, "you have your Gypsy right here. He's dying." They looked on. "Please, sirs," I cried, "it's nothing to you, but it's my brother's life." "Oh, it's *nothing*?" the first cop sneered. And with that he turned and the other followed. I ran after them, Sunny Wadia. I fell on my knees. "Please, sirs, just take him, please, why won't you take him?" The first one looked at me and said, "We don't want his blood on our seats." I said, "Sir, if that's the case, I'll clean the blood. I'll scrub it off with my own hands, you won't see a single stain when I'm done." Do you know what he said to that? "But where do you expect us to sit while we wait?"

2.

Such is life, Sunny Wadia. My brother died there in the road. My mother blamed me for his death, then collapsed and died herself from shock during his cremation. My father had already died from alcohol poisoning when I was small, so now I was left alone with my brother's widow and their little son. My uncle lived in the next house with his fat wife and their own stupid sons, and on the pretext of helping they came and took hold of our animals and land and my brother's widow as well. She wailed and wailed in my uncle's house, and I lay listening to her in the night. I knew soon enough one of my uncle's sons would take her as his own.

Oh, Sunny Wadia, I was full of rage, staring at the ceiling. Do you know how much it burned? I wanted to kill them all, smash their heads with rocks, slit all their throats, kill all the cops in the world. But who was I in this world? Without money, without power, without even a bike or a gun or an iron rod to my name. I said to myself, You must find a way out of this place or you'll be ruined. So do you know what I did? I applied to join the police force.

You look surprised, Sunny Wadia, but understand, I knew what it was like out there. I didn't want to be next in line. I wanted to be sitting in a Gypsy instead, handing out tickets for life and death. But in the meantime, I started roaming the area, snatching gold chains. It was so easy! The cops didn't care about this kind of thing, they were too busy protecting men like you, making money for themselves. I loitered in the markets, and one day a man left his scooter running while he went to buy medicine. I stole that and rode off and sold it, then I used the money to buy an old Pulsar like my brother's. Then with the money from the chains, I bought a country pistol of my own. Now I was riding along on my bike with a gun stuffed down my pants. It was so easy. Yes, I thought, *this* is the life! Only at home, I was still under a cloud and in such a rage, watching those fellows looking down at me. So I went out and stayed out. I was free when I was on my bike, robbing chains.

Only, I couldn't get my brother's widow from my head. I had always caught her eye looking at me. And now I was thinking she should be mine. I found myself daydreaming of this, killing everyone else and taking her back, making inside her a son of my own. As I was riding one evening on the road, I saw a girl walking just ahead of me. A maid from one of the new apartment blocks, fifteen or sixteen years old. She was Bihari, not from here. I saw her and thought it was too late for her to be walking alone, that's no good, and as I got closer to her I watched the way she walked, I saw her long braids and . . . Oh, don't look at me like that, Sunny Wadia, with your eyes full of contempt, you know those desires. I'd been so lonely for so long, it was only natural I should fulfill my needs.

I brought the bike to a crawl beside her, smiling, until she turned and looked at me. I was wearing my good shirt, my hair was oiled. I asked if she was tired of walking by herself. She kept her head down and looked away. Did she want a ride? No, she said, but then she turned again to look, and I saw that she wanted it, so I pulled up ahead of her, blocked the path. "Sister," I said, "it's dangerous out here, there are many criminals and thieves, I can take you where you need to go very quickly, don't be afraid." I asked her name. It was Asha. "I'll take you wherever you want, Asha didi. Your brothers don't need to know." She blushed at that. How charming I'd been. I imagined she'd never been on a bike before. She tried to walk past me but this time it was a game. I held out my hand to stop her and she froze, and I showed her my gun and told her to get up on the bike, sit in front of me. She did as she was told.

As we rode off like that, I became aroused and angry all at once. I could smell her sweat and washed clothes and skin, could feel her hair in my face. I'd never been so close to a woman before. I felt like retching. I kept thinking, why hadn't she run? If she had any honor at all, she would have resisted me until her dying breath. And I thought of my brother's widow now, and realized what was in her heart, how she was happy now with my uncle and his sons. A whore! I pictured her sleeping with all of them. Oh, it drove me into such a rage. I became disgusted, betrayed, humiliated. So I went faster on the bike. I accelerated the bike as fast as I could on the road. For the next minutes there was nothing but speed, nothing but her hair in my face and her whimpering and crying in her body and the engine between my legs as I roared this way and that on the potholed roads so at any moment both of us could have flown and smashed our brains out on a rock. The madness passed. I brought the bike to a halt beside a field. Then I told her to get off before it was too late.

3.

Oh, Sunny Wadia, I felt like the most impotent man. At home I cowered in the dark and I dreamed of the girl on the bike, felt her hair, the stink of her sweat, the sourness of her breath on mine. I could clamp my teeth down and feel them tearing into her skin, could see in my mind's eye her dupatta stuffed inside her mouth as I dragged her into the field and sprayed my seed. Why had I let her go, why hadn't I taken what was mine? I was such a weakling, a coward, even though I had it all, a gun, a bike. No, no. I was in such turmoil, Sunny Wadia. I kept going out again and again, roaming the land, looking for something. Then I made a mistake. I was riding around on my bike when I spotted another girl. She was already running, dressed strangely in revealing clothing. She had no shame. I didn't realize it at first, but she was one of those rich girls you see in the movies and in Delhi. Running for fun, like rich people do. It was stupid of her, running on the streets so far from home. Maybe she thought being rich would make her safe.

Well, I followed her. I kept a distance and followed her a long time, until she went through an isolated spot, and when she did I accelerated and pulled the bike up ahead of her, and then I smiled and said, "Hello, sister." Something in that smile must have scared her, because she slapped me hard in the face and started running away through waste ground where my bike wouldn't go. I jumped off and chased her on foot, to teach her a lesson for striking me, but she was too fast, she escaped to a busy road. And from there I could do nothing. She must have had a good memory, because the cops came to pick me up soon enough. They took me to the station house and beat me very badly. But when the girl and her father came to the station, they must have felt bad for me, seeing all the bruises and cuts on my face, because she came to my defense. She told them I had simply smiled at her, and she had hit me herself. The case against me fell apart and I was released.

But when I returned home later that day, I found more cops waiting for me. My uncle was smirking as they took me. I said nothing, only glared back. I went with them quietly, did as I was told. I climbed in the back of their Gypsy, remarked to them how fine and stain-free the upholstery was, though they didn't get the joke. As we drove, the cops either side took hold of my hands and shoulders and the one in front placed a jute sack over my head. Everything went dark, and we drove around for a long time, here and there. I expected I would be taken out and beaten or shot; I thought this would be the end for me. Finally we arrived in a compound and I was led out and taken inside a room. Only there was the sack removed.

Rather than being tortured, I found myself sitting alone in some police camp office, a fine wooden desk before me. Staring at me from high on the wall ahead was the painted portrait of a lady officer in uniform. The portrait was crude, but even so, I could see she was very upright and moral and very beautiful. I knew from the insignia she was an SP, and on her desk I saw the name: Superintendent of Police Sukanya Sarkar. I'd never seen a lady SP before, much less sat before the portrait of one. After a long wait the door beside the desk opened and out walked the living version. Oh, Sunny Wadia, the blood flowed through me. She looked so powerful in her uniform, so stern and unforgiving, so unlike all those other girls. I can tell you the feeling in my heart. Violent and strong. I watched her closely as she sat down at her desk, her womanly nature encased in khaki. For a long time she didn't look at me, she acted as if I were not there, and I waited, happy to play my part in this game. Then she picked up what I realized was my wallet and looked through my identity cards. She said, "You're a bad man, Sunil Rastogi." It pleased me to hear my name on her lips. I said, "Yes, sir, I am." "Madam," she corrected me, with a withering eye. "Yes, madam-sir," I replied. She asked if I knew why I was there and not in the lockup, where a chain snatcher belongs. I shook my head. She said, "Because you work for me now." "Yes, madam-sir, yes!" Such music to my ears!

4.

She said a vile gang was roaming the land, robbing, raping, murdering. Twenty-two rapes and sixteen murders in eight months; hijacking cars at night, pulling passengers out, raping the women, slitting the throats of the men, taking all their jewelry and cash. At first the news had been kept quiet, but with each new case the details were spreading, and now the rich people like you, who lived in their fancy villas, were getting nervous, so the cops were desperate to crack the case. What made it more terrifying was the gang's appearance. They traveled in bands, barefoot, naked except for undershirt and underpants, their skin smeared in engine grease, these vile, stinking men, blackened, slippery as fish, their eye whites glowing in the dark. The newspapers called them the Chaddi Baniyan gang. Ah, yes, I can see you've heard of them. They were much feared. Some said they were a legendary criminal tribe, in their hundreds or thousands, living among us by day, striking at night. Others said they were supernatural beings, demons out to cause chaos. "Find a way to infiltrate this gang," SP Sarkar said. "And once you're in, feed me their information so I can bring them to justice fast." I was taken aback. "But madam-sir," I asked, "how will I join this gang?" She gave me a cool gaze and said, "A man like you will find a way." I was confused, Sunny Wadia. A man like me? What did she know? Had she picked up the wrong person by mistake? I wanted to protest. I was certain I could not find a way, but then I didn't want to displease her, I didn't want her to discard me in the street, so I summoned all my strength and nodded and said yes, I would find a way. "Good," she smiled, "I knew you would." And I felt powerful again, I felt the blood surge through me as she looked on me with that disdain and contempt. She said they would pay me a stipend once a month to aid my work. Then she nodded to her ASP, stood up, and left the room. Her ASP hooded me again, took me into the vehicle, and threw me out in the middle of nowhere with a wad of cash and a phone number to call when I had something to report. How giddy did I feel? I walked back to the farm and sneered at my uncle and laughed and got my things, and without a backward glance to any of them I rode off to Kasna, where I took a cheap room and fell in with the card players and the drinkers and the thieves.

5.

So there I was Sunny Wadia, mixing with those nefarious criminal types in the service of Madam-Sir, seeing what information on this gang I could find. The only problem was, no one spoke of the gang, not a word, no one cared one bit, and when I brought them up, everyone just laughed and shrugged and said it was old news, this gang, if it even existed, was far away, in Haryana or Rajasthan by now, and wouldn't return for a year or more. A year? Yes, a year. They roamed with the seasons, like herders, like the cattle themselves, grazing on the land. For me this was a blessing and a curse. On the one hand, so long as there were no more attacks, Madam-Sir could not accuse me of failing in my job, but on the other, I could not please her, I had nothing to say. Six weeks went by like this, drinking and gambling, indulging in petty crime. I grew disheartened. My lust and ardor fell, I slipped into a dark place. It all felt pointless. I could not rouse myself to do anything. Dreams of murder and escape began to gather around my head like dark clouds. I despised all those I consorted with. I was ashamed to call Madam-Sir, but on the other hand, I yearned to see her strict face, to hear her berate me, to order me to do more or face the consequences. So I called the number. It was the ASP who answered the phone. I told him I had nothing to report. "Madam-Sir is very disappointed in you," he replied. "If you cannot be of use to us, we'll send you straight to jail." I tried to protest, I demanded to see Madam-Sir myself. He was offended by that. "Have more respect, Sunil Rastogi. If you're not careful, we'll pin the whole gang on you instead." He said this as a terrible threat, but it was a moment of great excitement for me, because in that instant, I had solved the case.

6.

From that point on, during every drunken night with my new friends, I began to push the idea: one fine moonless night, wouldn't it be smart to imitate those devils ourselves, strike the unsuspecting public as the Chaddi Baniyan gang? They roared with laughter. "Sunil Rastogi, you're a crazy sort!" But I kept sowing the seeds in their liquor-addled brains, explaining over and over how we could use the fear and terror of this notorious gang for our own purposes. Since this gang was long gone, we, the petty criminals, thieves, gamblers, addicts, sometime rapists, occasional murderers, could take ownership of this gang. Sunny Wadia, it was a masterstroke! Don't you think so? A perfect way to get out of this hole. I worked on them and worked on them, I wouldn't let the idea rest. I told them how the rich people in their cars driving late at night would be so scared at the sight of this gang they would give everything up without a squeak. We didn't even need to hurt anyone. I continued to work on these men. When they were at their most drunken I would fill their heads with lust and greed and wounded pride. All those rich people, laughing at us, having what we cannot have. What harm would it be to teach them a lesson? Slowly, slowly, the idea took root, until one fine day they were talking about it as if it had been their idea from the start.

On a moonless night a few days later, with many bottles of daru inside them, with charas in their blood, I laid out the plan I had already made, the stretch of road, the precise method. I would play lookout; when the right vehicle was coming along I would signal and they would throw a piece of metal into the road, beneath the wheels, forcing the car to stop. Then we would hold them up, take all their things, and vanish into the night. They cried, "Let's do it! Let's do it!" Someone went to fetch some engine grease, then we raced away on our bikes to the country road, hid the bikes in the fields a little away, stripped ourselves down to baniyan and chaddi, and covered our bodies in that grease. I collected their wallets and identity cards and kept them in a sack for safekeeping, and when the transformation was complete, I plied them with even more liquor and charas, and they howled and cried and danced around in the road, taking on the manner of demons. I positioned myself a little farther along the road, sober, my wits sharp, marveling at the weakness of men. Several cars went by until I finally saw the right one, packed full of plump women and weak-looking men. I flashed a light three times at my partners and the metal was thrown into the road under the coming car. As it screeched to a halt, my men pounced. They surrounded the car as the occupants screamed. Metal rods and bats smashed at the car and its windows, clawing hands ripped out the men and women jammed inside. The fear they showed intoxicated my men further. One of the gang picked up a heavy rock and smashed it into a woman's skull. When one of the men cried out and tried to save her, another of my men began to beat this fellow to a pulp, and incited by the violence and screaming, the rest followed suit. Sunny Wadia, they wouldn't stop. It was a frenzy of metal and eyes and teeth. They slit the throats of the men, stabbed them in the eyes and the stomach, ripped off their clothes. The women they dragged into the fields and raped before strangling them and crushing their heads. When it was done, there was no one left alive. And now all my men looked at one another in a daze. They stumbled around in silence awhile, wiping at the grease and the blood, looting the bodies and the car, before retrieving their bikes and riding away.

7.

The frenzy didn't take me by surprise. I knew what rested in the hearts of all men. So in the morning I woke and stepped outside and took in the cool spring sun, went to eat an omelet at the nearby cart, watched the local boys throwing firecrackers at stray dogs. Then I called the ASP. But before I could give him the good news, Madam-Sir snatched the phone from him and began abusing me in the harshest words. It was already all over the news. She went on and on. I had failed, the gang had been more brutal than ever, they had killed everyone, left no survivors, you did not do your job. But, madam-sir, I said. I was there. She was silent awhile. "You were there?" she said. "I was lookout, madam-sir." "Then this is your fault, Sunil Rastogi. Why didn't you call me?" I told her I only got to know in the last moment and I had to give my phone away. "This is bad," she said, "this is very bad. Now let me think. Call me back in one hour." She hung up and I waited, and I did as she asked. Now she wanted me to tell her everything, who they were, how I managed to infiltrate them. I had anticipated the questions. I hewed close to the truth. I told her it was a gang of criminals, gamblers, and drug addicts who passed themselves off as a secret tribe to strike fear into the souls of men. She listened silently while I talked; she seemed skeptical. She said, "They have become more brutal. The next time the gang decides to strike, call me, however you can, and we will ambush them." She gave me her private number. "What about me?" I asked. "Don't worry," she said, "I will keep you safe." I wanted to believe her. I wanted to be her loyal dog, I daydreamed scenes of her taking vengeance against this vile gang, gun in hand, and setting me free.

8.

But I knew I wasn't safe. And now I was in a quandary. If my gang committed a crime again, and I didn't give them over to her, she would come after me. And if I gave them up, I would be implicated too. What if I was to do nothing? What if they never struck again, and I simply ran away? This was the sensible thing, Sunny Wadia. But what then for Madam-Sir? She would not solve the case. I only wanted her to be happy. So I made my choice. I went to meet my gang that day. I discovered them overwhelmed by what they had done. The news kept pouring in. The Hindi channels showed gruesome cartoon reenactments on TV. My men had taken to drinking hard to live with their memories. I sat with them at a back table of a gambling den, our secret between us, and I watched them drink more and more. Slowly through the drink they began to speak, slur, curse, recount their excitement, the feelings of power they had had. The police, the TV said, had no leads, none at all, and I smiled at that, because it meant Madam-Sir was looking out for me, and my men smiled at that, because it meant they were free. They all agreed, in whispered words, to lie low for some time, a week or so . . .

9.

. . . and then do it again. The hungry demons that they were, they were itching to go again. Be careful what you wish for, Sunny Wadia. When the night was upon us, I gathered them, plied them with drink and drugs, and arranged to meet at a certain godown, this very one we're sitting in now. Then I called the SP, victorious. I said, "Madam-sir, I have done it. They're going to strike again." I told her where the gang would be lying in wait. She was excited. "Sunil Rastogi, you have done good for once in your life." Of course she had already come up with a plan. She had been waiting for this. She told me she and her fellow officers would be traveling in a white Esteem, dressed as jewelry-laden wedding guests. They would be a target impossible to refuse. So it was, I would give the signal to the gang, and the gang would strike. And then? Well, the counterambush would begin. "Will you shoot at sight?" I asked. "No, Sunil Rastogi, I respect the law. I will arrest them." Then she faltered and said, "Unless they shoot at me first."

10.

I had counted on that. All I needed now was a trigger; a trigger I had already seen on the street. You see, I had to eliminate my gang, Sunny Wadia, for her, and for me. When I went to meet my men later I found that they were not wild with lust and rage, they were nervous and scared, timid human creatures, and that wouldn't do. I gave them liquor, I gave a rallying speech, I spoke of the whores and chutiyas who were laughing at them, who lived a high life while they suffered. I made them drink more and more, I managed to get the wind in their sails. I led them on, collected their identity cards, promised them pleasures and riches and blood, then took them out in the night to the fields, to the hiding places. Made them undress and cover themselves in that grease, which they did with anxious ceremony. And I snuck off to my spot, where I waited as lookout, waited and waited and waited as several cars passed in the dark, praying the men wouldn't jump the gun. All was quiet and still, then I saw the car in the fog, its lights on inside, saw Madam-Sir sitting in the back, dressed as a wedding guest, in a bright red sari, as pure as any goddess. I wanted to run away with her. I flashed my torch to the gang as the car passed. Three flashes. I swear I saw Madam-Sir turn her head and look at me. For good measure I cried out, "This one!" Then I darted through the field toward my men. They threw the piece of metal into the road as was planned, and the car came skidding to a halt before their spot. It all happened so slowly and so quickly then, Sunny Wadia. The fake wedding guests, guns at the ready, spilled out of the doors, while my men stepped out with their rods and knives, pathetic in the headlights in their grease and their undershirts and their underwear. They dropped their weapons. Put up their hands. Then I did it. I hatched my plan. Firecrackers, like the boys tormented the dogs with in the streets. I lit and tossed a strip through the air, exploding with a flash at the foot of my men. This caused panic. The whole night turned into flame. Not only from the cops in the fake wedding car, who let rip with their guns, but also from the other side of the road, dozens of small bursts of muzzle fire. A batch of sharp-shooting cops had been hiding there all along. Now they were slaughtering my men, cutting them down without mercy. I turned and ran through the fields into the night with my heart beating hard.

11.

I ambushed a man on a motorbike around dawn, bashed in his head, took his clothes and money, and rode several hours, then dumped that bike and hitched a ride on a truck, reaching Benares by dark. I made my way to the Holy Ganga, bathed myself, threw my gang's identity cards into the river with the other relics of life gone, and said a prayer. By this time, the encounter with the cops was all over the news. I saw it on TV channels everywhere. The dreaded Chaddi Baniyan gang had been slain. Slaughtered in a gun-fight as they attempted to commit another heinous crime. In every report, on every TV, there she was, the young SP, Sukanya Sarkar, Madam-Sir, tough in her wedding sari, slinging her pistol, the hero of the hour. Later, she was back in uniform, cleaned up and stern-faced, and I liked her best like this, standing over the corpses that were lined up on the roadside cov-ered in white sheets. I could recognize each one of my gang by his toes. I spent days in the brothels then, exhausting all my money, but soon I got bored. Sunny Wadia, I decided to give the SP a call. I went to a booth and dialed the number she had given me. As soon as I heard her say "Speak," I said, "Congratulations, madam-sir, you cracked the case." She was silent. She seemed afraid. Then she said, "Sunil Rastogi, is that you?" "Yes, madam-sir, the one and only." "Where are you?" she asked. I said, "Madam-sir, it would be foolish of me to tell you." "Why would it?" she asked. "Because you will come to kill me." I should have left it at that and hung up the phone. But I wanted to keep hearing her voice, I felt it important that she knew how much I had sacrificed for her. So I confessed it all. I said, "Madam-sir, please listen to me one time, I have something important to say," and I told her everything, I said the whole gang was a lie, I created it myself from my friends. "Why?" she said, in little more than a whisper. "I was scared," I said, "the pressure was too great, and besides all that, I wanted to please you. I wanted to make you happy. I wanted you to crack the case." She went silent at the end of that. Silent for a long time. "Madam-sir?" I said. Then she said, in a very thin and lonely voice, "Are you telling me the truth, Sunil Rastogi?" I said, "I'm telling you the truth, I swear, I will do anything for you." She was silent, then she uttered one word down the phone. "Behenchod," she said. "Madam-sir," I replied with a joyful heart. Then she said, "Never call this number, and never speak of this to anyone ever again."

12.

I began to roam now. South, into Bundelkhand, then east, toward Bihar, wandering from town to town, stealing when I had to, committing small and petty crimes. I ended up in Ballia, on the Bihar border, a perfect place for a man like me. I started working for one of the local MLAs. His name was Ajit Singh. Nothing moved in the town without his say-so, this was what I heard, so I turned up at his party office one morning and said I was a man who liked hard work. A senior worker there directed me to speak to a man in another office a few streets away. He asked me what I wanted, and I said I'd do anything for a little money and some liquor, though I wasn't a drunk. He quizzed me a little, asked what my experience was. I told him I'd worked for my local party back west. Teaching our enemies a lesson. It was all he needed to hear. "What's your name?" Chotu Raj, I said and that was it, I was in. I learned a great deal about politics then. See, Ajit Singh was the biggest goon in town. He had many interests. Dredging the riverbeds for construction sand, cutting down trees for timber on Forestry Department land, mining quarries for stones, stealing medicines from the government hospitals. So long as we did his work, whatever else we did, short of killing cops, we had protection. I had a great education there, I understood the turning of the wheel, how the cops and the politicians and the bureaucrats were all working together to keep this wheel in motion, how every spoke of the wheel was important, how the wheel was the system itself. How men like you are the shit that sticks to the wheel. How a wheel crushes everything in its path. And oh, what crushing it was. We indulged in extortion, collecting protection money from businesses or else burning them down, we'd commit many kidnappings for ransom. We'd kill our opponents, stage riots, manage protests. If the minority community became upstarts, we'd burn their neighborhoods down. If some misguided citizen tried to complain about us, go to the media, or the new district magistrate, we'd break their legs, or else we'd kill the journalists themselves. We had to make sure the message was clear: so long as you know your place and don't interfere, the wheel turns very well, but if you wish to be a hero, good-bye! And yet for all that, I was dissatisfied. It was monotonous work, lacking any creative spark. I had no real chance to distinguish myself. That changed when one of Ajit's upstart rivals, a man by the name of Govind Chaudhary, a gangster who'd started in scrap metal, began to step up, planning to contest the next election and win. Any man who stands for election in our part of town is a threat. He has his own money and muscle behind him. So Ajit Singh wanted to send a message his way. There was a meeting, it was debated: what kind of message would be sent? Now, Govind Chaudhary had a right-hand man, Shiv Kumar. Shiv Kumar was an old associate of Ajit's, who had gone to the other side. It was understood that without him, Chaudhary would be lost. So it was decided that Shiv Kumar would be killed, in front of the court-house, no less, in three days' time, the day an extortion case was to be settled in his favor. It would be a powerful message indeed. The only thing to decide now was who would do the killing and how. Oh, my God, Sunny Wadia, in Ajit's headquarters the debate was going back and forth, back and forth, everyone talking for the sake of it, loving the sound of their own voice. I'm not much of a talker, so I was listening silent in the back. When I grew bored of the false bravado, I stood and called that I would do it. Then I walked out. But I would not wait three days, nor would I restrict myself to Shiv Kumar.

13.

I went back to my room and spent the rest of the day with several bottles of daru and some charas, preparing myself. Some of Ajit's men came to find me to tell me they had their own men, that I was not part of the plan; I laughed and waved them away. Please yourself, I said. I finished the last bottle and waited for night to fall, and when my blood was in nasha, went out into town, giddy into the dark, avoiding the police posts, avoiding everyone, and when I was close to Shiv Kumar's house in one of the fancy colonies, I went into one of the dark alleys and hid among some trees until late in the night. Then I stripped down to my chaddi and baniyan, stashed my clothes away, rubbed grease that I'd carried with me over my limbs, wiped my hands clean and wrapped them in clean rags so I could climb. The street around his house was guarded by cops and his house itself had two armed guards. So I climbed onto the roof of a house some distance away, stalked over the tops of others until I reached his place. I leaped across to their balcony and landed without sound. It was a fine house, the kind all big men keep these days. But it made no difference to me. I unseated the balcony door from its slider and went inside, across the cool marble floors of the hall until I found the bedroom, and inside the bedroom I looked down on the bodies of Shiv and his wife. It was so easy, Sunny Wadia. Shiv Kumar was just a man. Just a man. I wasted no time. I slit the man's throat in his sleep. The blood drained out everywhere as he gurgled his last. Then his wife awoke with a start and I pressed my hand across her mouth. Her eyes widened in terror and she bit my hand like a rabid dog. I was so incensed, I had to fight my urge to carve her up, but it was necessary to my plan that she stay alive. I fought her. She was stronger than most men in her desperation to survive. She bit my hand so hard it drew blood, but as soon as she pulled away I was able to twist myself and beat her with my fists. I beat her until she was unconscious, then tied her up and searched the rest of the house. The sound of the ceiling fans had muffled the noise of our scuffle, so the others inside hadn't heard a peep. There were two servants sleeping downstairs, two guards posted out in front, and two children. Shiv Kumar had been blessed with two boys. I slit the throats of the servants first. Then I crept into the kids' room and looked down. Should I kill them or let them sleep? I had too much time to think and this was my mistake. See, Shiv Kumar's wife had woken, and as I stood in front of the children, she began to cry. The boys woke and looked up at me standing over them in chaddi and baniyan, covered in grease and blood. Their screaming was immense. By now the guards outside were forcing their way in, so I took flight. I sailed out the window, scrambled over the roofs and into the nearby trees just in time to avoid the rifle shots. I grabbed my clothes from the bushes and managed to escape through the town, hiding in the forest all night.

14.

By the next morning, word was out. The dreaded Chaddi Baniyan gang had surfaced once again, killing the notorious Shiv Kumar. The guards, wife, and children confirmed one another's account. There had been five at least, they said. Horrors in dark grease, their eyes glowing in the night. It was all anyone talked about. The fear in the town was extraordinary. The whole place buzzed with demonic energy. The killers were described in extreme terms. They were not human. Their eyes glowed red and their fingers were claws. Word then leaked out that Kumar's wife had bitten one of the monsters. Everyone said she would become infected by his blood, that she would turn into one of them now. I had to laugh at their stupidity.

I returned to Ajit Singh's headquarters after dark. I slunk in, in the shadows, to hear the fear and terror in the gang members. "Did you hear? Did you hear?" they cried. "The Chaddi Baniyan gang is here! They got to Shiv Kumar first! But who knows who they'll target next?!"

As I slipped farther inside, I heard Ajit Singh's unhappy voice, raging against the fool who had done this thing! Shiv Kumar was supposed to die in public, his death a political message, a statement of Ajit Singh's power and intent, not a ghost story to frighten the common man.

"What if," I said, stepping into the light, "the common man thinks the dreaded Chaddi Baniyan gang works for you?" At that I held up my hand and unwound the bandage to show the deep bite marks. "She put up more of a fight than the men." I laughed.

"Who are you?" Ajit Singh finally said, his voice much altered by fear.

"My true name is Sunil Rastogi," I replied. "My gang lurks in the shadows and lives for death." As soon as I said this, the room fell silent, these hardened expressions changed, they backed away from me. It felt good, Sunny Wadia, to be given the respect I deserved.

Barely saving face in front of his own men, Ajit Singh thanked me profusely for what I had done. Nonetheless, he urged me to leave; the cops would be coming down hard on everyone. He said activities would cease for a while, I would have to lie low, there would be nothing to entertain a man like me. "I make my own entertainment," I replied, reveling in his groveling plea. Then one of his aides whispered something in his ear. They conferred for some time, casting sharp glances my way. When they were done, Ajit Singh said he had a new proposal that he would reveal alone, in one hour. "Reveal it now," I replied. He said he must speak with someone more important than he, and I would have to wait. I was careful not to overplay my hand, so I agreed. I passed that next hour smoking blissfully as I waited, while the eyes of Ajit Singh's men fell on me from afar, like the delicate rays of sun on a winter's afternoon.

When the hour had passed, I was taken to Ajit Singh's private room, and he told me this: in the north of the state, within the Terai forests that border

Nepal, there was the shadowy dera of a great and powerful man who had heard my story, and who now wished to meet me.

"Who is he?" I asked.

"His name," Ajit Singh replied, his voice falling to a whisper, even though there was no one else in the room, "is Himmatgiri. He is a warlord, and his knowledge of the dark arts, kala jadoo, is stronger than any man alive."

Kala jadoo? Black magic? I had to stifle a laugh at this. There was no black magic in the world, only the actions of men. So here was a trickster hiding in the woods, preying on the idiocy of stupid men. To be clear, I was laughing at the foolishness of men like Ajit Singh. But this Himmatgiri I liked the sound of very much. To Ajit Singh's relief, I said I would be glad to journey to this man and take the measure of him. By midnight, I was gone.

15.

So there I was, Sunny Wadia, at the pinnacle of my career, passed from gang to gang like an idol, fed and venerated and feared. My reputation always preceding me. Often no one would talk, only stare from afar, or sneak little glances, as if they couldn't quite believe who I was and what I'd done. And who was I anyway? A killer? A demon? At heart I was a young man, wronged many times, who had merely survived. I thought of my past deeds, my many scrapes, and of Madam-Sir on this journey of mine. I wondered what had become of her. But as I got closer to my destination, all such thoughts began to fade. I began to wonder about this Himmatgiri fellow instead. Who was he, exactly? What had he done? My transporters gave conflicting reports, were often vague. Sometimes they cringed at the name, turned to look here and there as if there were ears in the room. Others murmured that he was a great rishi, a sage, or the reincarnation of past warrior saints. Only once or twice did a goon, surly, cynical, or brave, laugh and declare this Himmatgiri was a fraud, or that he didn't even exist at all, and this kind of talk triggered intense debate. How do you know? Isn't it obvious? How can you say such a thing? Be careful when you go to sleep at night. Himmatgiri will come for you. I asked the question: "What does he look like?" "He's a giant," they said. With dark hair falling in strings from his high forehead, animal eyes, and rings glistening from his fingers. He carries an ax the size of a man. No, he carries a sword. No, he carries nothing, for no mortal weapon can touch him. I laughed myself at that one! They fell silent around me. It was in this climate of uncertainty that I entered the Terai forests north of Maharajganj, and this is where my story gets strange.

16.

The gang I joined was part of the timber mafia. The timber mafia was very powerful up there. They were involved in the cutting and smuggling of khair wood. Maybe you have some in your home? All the big people do. Or maybe in those grand apartments you've been constructing all over the land. Anyway, I was attached to this certain logging crew. Tough guys, with experience. They were supposed to escort me to a place in the forest where my journey would be complete, where I would be passed over to Himmatgiri. In exchange I would act as security on the way, as they carried out their logging missions in the night. "Where would this place be," I asked, "where we would meet the mysterious Himmatgiri?" They said this would only become clear over time. I found this all quite hard to understand, but I did not raise my voice in questioning, because I knew silence was my friend. But after some time trekking through the forest in the evening light, I decided to provoke them. I laughed. "You know, some people don't even think this Himmatgiri is real." I felt a collective shudder run through the ranks. One old logger said, "I will say a prayer for you tonight." No more was said on Himmatgiri. I traveled silently, a rifle in my arms.

And so the work began. It was very scientific work. We only worked at night. We had these cycles on which the timber was transported through the forest trails onto the roads, and on the roads the timber was loaded up onto trucks and mixed in with legal wood bought at auction at the Government Depot. We sent these trucks through selected checkpoints, where those officers stationed at certain times had been paid to turn a blind eye. If that sounds dull, it gives no indication of the land we were in.

I've never been religious, Sunny Wadia. My brother was, my mother too. But not I. I bathed and performed puja like everyone else, but I never felt God in my heart. Not until I stood in that place. Have you ever seen the Terai forest in the night? I'm sure you've seen many things, but there are places men like you don't go. Places and ways of being. If you went, you'd go with your big cars and your suit and your men. You wouldn't trek alone into the depths in the night. There are all kinds of spirits and gods in there. Leopards and elephants and tigers. And then there was Himmatgiri. The farther we went into the forest, his unspoken name seemed to hang over all. No matter we had the firepower—Chinese AKs, Sten guns, grenades, shotguns, pistols, machetes—it felt like we could be doomed anytime. The superstitious men kept charms, said prayers, offered sacrifices in our camp. They slaughtered goats and chickens to the local deities and prayed before they went out to cut the first trees of the night.

How had I come to be there? Where was I going? I couldn't seem to remember clearly anymore. There was a blank behind me, and only the endless trees in the night. I had vague snatches of the journey I had taken, the killings I had done, but even these now felt unreal, as if I had dreamed them all up, as if they had happened in another life. I felt removed from the self I had held so tight. When I talked to the logging crew, it was as if they were talking to someone else, someone who had been with them in the forest for a long time, who had lived with them for years. Sometimes I even forgot my name. Sunil Rastogi. I had to repeat it to myself when we returned to our camp in the safety of the morning light. Sunil Rastogi. Sunil Rastogi. But even this name lost its meaning, detached from its object, like any word said over and over in time.

It was on the fifth night, or maybe the five hundredth, that it happened. We were out there cutting in the dead of night, three a.m. There was a chill in the air. We were just over on the Nepal side. We'd been cutting for two hours by then. I was patrolling the edges of our zone, a cigarette in my mouth, watching the jungle, watching out for rangers, for leopards. Break time came and the cutting stopped. The saws and axes fell silent. As soon as they did, I noticed the fog creeping in, arriving on all sides, so suddenly I couldn't see. An uneasy feeling stole over me, something very bad was close at hand. I listened without moving, without speaking, straining my eyes into the forest, until I imagined many things. Things moving in the dark. I grew panicked, crashed through the fog calling out to my men, but no, there was nothing. I stumbled farther and farther, until the fog dissolved and I found myself lost and alone. Then I heard a voice in the wind. Sunil Rastogi, it said.

I did not want to be there anymore. I did not want to meet this man. I wanted to go home. I wanted to run. I turned to find a path. I turned to run. I gripped the gun in my hand. And that's when I saw her. A sight one could not imagine in a thousand years. There was a girl. A naked girl, with long black hair, running through the trees. Running, not more than ten meters from me, ghostly pale in the bare moonlight, running across from me. She seemed beautiful, but there was something dreadful hanging over her. When I caught a glimpse of her face I understood what it was: though no sound came out, her face was contorted into the rigor of a scream. I stood there paralyzed as she crossed my path, and when I turned to see her running away from me, I saw a great square pink bubbling patch on her back where the skin had been peeled away. I watched in awe as she disappeared into the fog, and when she was gone all sound returned to the world, and I was crying out in terror and firing my AK up into the night.

With the gunfire the men in my logging crew dropped their tools and ran toward me. Yes! They had been there all along. "What is it?" they cried.

"An elephant? A leopard." I looked at them in disbelief. Hadn't they seen it? The fog? The girl? They looked among one another. "Where did you go?" I shouted. "Where have you been?" They grew reticent. Their expressions were knowing and wary. "We're here," one said. "Where?" I replied. "We go no farther" came the answer. One of the other guards spoke up. "Let me see your gun," he said. "It looks like it jammed." With that the gun was snatched from my hands, and not a moment later I was being grabbed from all sides, pulled toward a tree, and lashed to its trunk by heavy rope. A gag was tied around my mouth. Another round my eyes. I couldn't move, see, or scream. I could only hear the men marching away until the silence of the forest returned. I'm being sacrificed, I said in my mind. And then footsteps. Footsteps approached through the forest floor. Coming closer. Until they stopped before me and I heard steady breathing and hot breath, and I shivered as I heard my name emitted from the depths of a stranger's chest.

"Sunil Rastogi," it said. "So you're the man who will not die."

And his hands peeled back the rag that covered my eyes.

17.

That was the last thing I remembered. I woke up four days later, lying beside a canal among the beggars in a market town I didn't know, dressed in tattered clothing, covered in my own filth, an empty liquor bottle in my hand. My feet were raw, my body bruised. It was the middle of the day, the sun beat down. The market was lively and I was ignored, taken for a drunk, a madman. A crone without legs howled at me. I staggered up and on in agony. As I hobbled, trying to remember what had brought me to this place, I stopped to examine my face in the mirror of a bike. I almost jumped out of my skin. My cheeks had been clawed, my lips had burned and blistered. I had aged, it seemed, many years. What I saw was the man you see now. I knew in that instant; something had been taken away from me. Something here, in my head. Here, in my heart. Even down here, in my balls. I tried so hard to recall how I ended up this way. All I could remember was my name. Sunil Rastogi. But I was not myself. I was not the man I used to be. I was penniless and haunted. Without luck. I tried to beg, and I was spat on. I tried so hard to beg, and I was beaten by the cops. Left to bleed. I crawled through ditches. I was bitten by stray dogs. Me! Me? No . . . there was no me. I had been hollowed out. I escaped at night and walked through fields. I slept in temples and old buildings. But I couldn't bear to be around men. I took to sleeping in the wild. I hated sleeping at all. Sleep was full of monsters. Even when I was awake, I felt something watching me behind the lids of my eyes. But when I tried to understand what had happened, my brain fell into darkness. I could only see life out of the corner of my eye. I knew I had to flee.

18.

But flee where? The only place I could think was west, all the way back home, back where everything started. You have to understand, Sunny Wadia, I was desperate in that moment, desperate and afraid. The amnesia that haunted me was the worst of all. But what's that you're thinking? Wasn't home just as unsafe? Weren't they waiting to arrest me there? It was possible. But at the same time, I doubted it. The only one who knew me as a criminal was Madam-Sir. But to protect herself, she would never have uttered my name. Besides, it seemed to me that years had passed, that old sins had been forgotten. No, I would go back home, show humility, take my family land. Live a life of solitude and simple work. This thought sustained me as I begged and stole my way west. Several weeks later I arrived. Imagine my surprise, Sunny Wadia, when I reached Greater Noida and came to find all the farmland gone, whole villages erased, huge apartment complexes rising, and mansions for former farmers springing up from the soil. With some difficulty I located the place where I had been born, found the village house had been replaced by a compound with tall metal gates and video cameras on top. I called my uncle's name; there was no reply. I pressed the buzzer on the gatepost and a voice buzzed back. Who was I? What did I want? If I didn't leave they'd come out with the dogs. Even though I was no longer wearing rags, I looked a sorry state in that grand light. One part of me wanted to turn and leave. Another said no, this is your land. In my inde-cision, a door within the gate burst open, and one of my young cousins stepped out, dressed in a shiny suit, sunglasses, big watch, wielding a huge American gun. Ah, I said, so it runs in the family! What are you talking about, crazy man? I asked him if he didn't recognize me. Especially since he was standing on the place of my birth. He told me to get lost or he'd shoot me. I managed to smile at that. I am your cousin, I said. "Sunil?" I heard a woman's voice behind him. It was my brother's widow. Plump and covered in jewelry and dressed in jeans! She had a queenlike manner, she was in charge of the home now . . . my loins burned on seeing her, my heart raged . . .

19.

She told my cousins to let me in. Within the compound walls, next to brand-new marble palaces, our old brick houses remained. Buffalo still snoozed alongside the SUVs. And in the courtyard, our old toothless dadi slept on a charpoy. My uncle emerged at the commotion. He'd grown so fat and grand. He wore so much gold I don't know how he didn't fall down. All my cousins lined up, they glared at me, they were spoiling for a fight. "Sunil," my uncle said, "you worthless fellow, you chor of a man. What is it you want?" I told him I didn't want trouble, I had traveled very far, and now at the end of my wanderings, I wanted to return home. He replied, "There's nothing here for a thief!" I became hot in the head, I forgot myself. I said, "It is you who is the thief, uncle, because this land is mine and mine alone, you have taken it from me." He laughed and dismissed me. "No land is owed to a beast like you." I stood there humiliated, seeing they wouldn't budge. I realized how much things had changed, how weak and worthless and unlucky I had become. They all began to laugh at me. They could see it dawning on my face, how my future lay out there on the road, a vagabond. What could I do? I lowered my head, stepped toward the door out to the road. But before I crossed the threshold, I heard my brother's widow call my name. I turned yet again, and there she was, removing her heavy gold chain. "Take this," she said, "for the things you have done in the past." I took it humbly. She remembered the person I had been. When she was in my brother's bed, I had barely been able to look her in the eye from shame. Even now, it was hard to look her in the face. But with that gold chain in my hand I would begin a new life. My reverie was short-lived. Ten minutes later, as I trod the dirt road, a police Gypsy arrived to cut off my path. A man matching my description had snatched a woman's chain.

20.

Yes, my uncle had my brother's widow do his dirty work. The police took me away, registered a case, beat me in the cell, transferred me to Dasna Jail. After so many years, after all I'd done, it was a fitting fate. To be caught right back at the start. And what did I feel now? Nothing more or less than relief. A weight had been lifted from me. I was a chain snatcher, after all. I decided to give in to this. To let go of life, to let prison take hold. Inside, I lost all desire, I wanted for nothing anymore. I was left alone. My face, my scars, my air of decay, meant no one challenged me. I was neither hunted nor hunter. I lived like an ascetic. I was ignored by those men who look for fresh meat. If I was to catch my reflection, I knew there would be no trace of the "Chaddi Baniyan" Rastogi there. I did not catch my reflection at all. I assumed an air of disinterest; I was someone who could smile down on the follies of youth. That's how I met Sonu, Manoj's brother. He was a hothead, as I had been at his age. He was always eager to find someone who would hear his story. I listened to him. He said he had killed a man in a dispute. He had entered a showroom in Delhi and fought with a salesman over a car; this fight ended in the salesman's death. Yes, Sonu shot him in the head. Now he had no hope of being released unless a vast sum of money could be found. Enough money to bribe everyone to secure bail. How will you find that money? I asked him. There's only one way, he said, his eyes fixed in a violent glare. I'll have my useless brother kidnap and ransom the behenchod responsible for all our misery. This fucker by the name of Sunny Wadia.

21.

Maybe things are becoming clear now? You think my rambling story is merely leading to this. Think again! We're entwined more than you know. When Sonu told me this plan of his, I barely gave it any thought. It sounded like something I would have done in the old days, but those days were over. I didn't think of that stuff anymore. I didn't care for his dreams of revenge and escape, despite his goings-on. But everything changed, Sunny Wadia, when I saw your face. Up there, on the TV screen on the cell wall of one of the dadas inside. "There he is! That's him!" Sonu screamed. "There's the fucker who stole my life. I'll take my revenge!" And everyone began to laugh at him. "How will you take revenge? Don't you know who he is?" "He's the fucker who ruined my life," Sonu shouted. "Taking our land with his money, spoiling us all." "No, no, no," came the reply. "That's not who he is." "Who is he then?!" "He's Bunty Wadia's son!"

I said nothing while this debate was taking place. But back in the cells, I was a man possessed. I pulled Sonu aside, looked him in the eye, and said,

"Get me bail." He shoved me away. "Get you bail?! Why?" he said. "Get me bail," I repeated. "What's come over you!?" he cried. "Nothing," I said. "I'm myself again." "You're talking nonsense," he went on. "No, I'm talking sense. Now use whatever money you have to get me bail. Then I'll kidnap Sunny Wadia for you."

22.

Even a man as stupid as Sonu wished to know why. I had to come up with something. So I regaled him with the story of my life. Told him I was a dreaded criminal lying low, whose deeds had not yet been found out. But now I was getting nervous. I had been here too long. So for a small percentage of the ransom fee, I would commit the perfect kidnapping, leave the money with his brother, and hit the road. After hours of coaxing, he was convinced. From that point on I had to keep him close. Tell him nightly stories of my deeds as he arranged with his brother to pay my bail, until finally it was done.

That was three weeks ago. And now here we are, Sunny Wadia, face-to-face. And now the question you must be asking. What happened in that jail? When you appeared on TV, what happened to me? What is the real reason for my being here? Would you believe me if I told you that it was your face? Something in your face spoke to me. Something in your face left me transfixed. From that very moment, I was compelled, beyond my own reason, to escape and meet you in the flesh. You, Sunny Wadia, you were all I thought about. I had to get to you, and I had no understanding why. Even as I spent these weeks stalking you, working out a plan, waiting for the right time, the deeper reasons evaded me. I didn't even know what I would do when I had you. Then the chance came. You and your friend, alone in that Bolero, in the middle of nowhere. We took it. We shot your friend. Crashed your car. Put you here. I pulled the blindfold off and looked into your eyes. I understood why I was here. I remembered those four lost days.

23.

How could I have let them go, those days that were stolen from me, those days that stole my life, where before I was beholden to no man and after I was a shell. How could I have not inquired? Why did I run like a beaten dog back home? I tell you, Sunny Wadia, it's because those days were black holes. But now, here they are, there they were, the fog blown away, days resting before me plain. I felt the hand in the forest pull the rag from my eyes. I felt my body released from the rope and tree. I saw men around me, all wearing black, each carrying swords, carrying guns, armed, as they say, to the teeth, each with dark-ringed eyes and long black hair bundled high on heads, secured with sharp chakrams, with many more chakrams around their forearms and necks, like acolytes, like monks. Something was blown into my face, and within seconds I couldn't move or speak. Somehow I had no desire to scream. Now I found myself carried through the air by many hands, carried through the forest, and I lost sense of time. I lost sense of space. It felt like hours or minutes had passed. It felt like I had been carried one hundred miles or remained in one place. We reached a camp, a series of barrack-like buildings with watchtowers and barbed fences inside the forest, in the cleft of a ravine. I was carried through the gates and placed in a small room with a mattress and a blanket and left there at dawn. The sun rose and I watched its shadows on the ceiling, then I watched it fall again. A whole day had passed. At no point in time could I speak or move. Sunny Wadia, I was scared. I had never been so afraid. Not to be able to scream, not to move, this is unbearable. A nightmare. But even worse, not to know what was in store for me. To my relief, my limbs began to regain their motion at dark. First my fingers, then my toes. I wiggled them back and forth, delighted in their motion. But joy was short-lived, replaced by a new fear. I recalled the ghostly girl running through the woods with her skin cut out, running without noise. I still could not speak. Would that be my fate? I tried to calm myself. You're Sunil Rastogi. The luckiest man alive. With this lodged in my head, I stilled my wilder thoughts and comforted myself with one more simple truth: I was a man and not a girl. This eased my soul. Now I listened for some clues as to where I was. Funny, the day before, during my paralysis, I hadn't heard a thing. Only birdsong and animal call. I had wondered if this camp was deserted, if I'd imagined everything I saw. Now I heard human voices, the bustle of enterprise. Slowly I got to my feet. Unsteadily I crept to the metal bars that gave me a dim view of the world. I saw those black-clad men all around in lantern light, wielding their weapons, and beyond the fence a procession of female bodies, being taken from one of the barracks and loaded onto a truck. Not dead, you understand, but enslaved. The handle of my door turned. I was caught in that pose, peering out.

"So you're the one," the voice said.

That's when I saw him. This giant of a man.

"The one who will not die."

What was I supposed to say in reply? I froze. I felt like I was caught. He stepped in, wearing a long black kurta, his hair streaming onto his shoulders, his eyes like coals ringed with kohl, tilak of red and yellow slashed down his forehead, I had to look up to see him, crane my neck. I was captive to him and the glistening of rings on his hands. Himmatgiri. He was flanked by two of his men. One carried a wooden stool, the other a lantern. He gave a signal and they turned away, left the stool and the lantern and us alone, closed the door. I noticed as he stalked the room that he had a gentle manner, a feline grace. I felt like he knew me. He came close. I was dumb, still holding the metal bars. I could smell a strange metallic sourness on his breath. "How is it," he said, placing his hand on my head, "that you will not die?"

24.

He interrogated me all night, perched on his stool. What could I say? I was lucky. That was my only word. I was a lucky man. He wanted to know more. He said a man like me should have died many times. He had been following my progress since Ballia, since the killing of Shiv Kumar. How had I done it? I didn't know. What knowledge did I have of the Chaddi Baniyan gang? I didn't, I said. It was all concocted. That gang, he said, knew certain things. They practiced certain austerities, sacrifices. I am not them, I said. But Sunil Rastogi, he smiled, you're a killer of men. He made me go back. He made me tell the story of my life. From birth to there. This is why I tell my story to you so well, Sunny Wadia. It has already been rehearsed. Yes, he would not let me rest. All night the interrogation went on, the night rolled and spun. I recall nothing but his voice. As day rose I was brought a special drink, thick and pungent in a clay cup. He drank it with me too. He went back over certain points. What had I thought at the moment of crisis? How had I made a decision? I didn't know. I didn't know. He seemed to be searching for a key. When the daylight filled my cell, he left. I lay awake, frozen in the light, with visions of my life. I did not see him until the next night, when he returned with lanterns and food. He sat on the same stool. "I have decided," he said, "that you tell the truth. You are a vessel."

25.

His phone is ringing. One moment, Rastogi says.

He steps away from the stool, answers the phone.

"Hello?"

He smiles.

"Yes."

He looks back to Sunny.

Manoj will be here soon, this will all be over for you. Let me finish my story.

26.

Where was I? Ah, yes, Himmatgiri. He sat before me and smiled. "I've decided," he said, "that you tell the truth. You do not know from where this magic comes. You do not know why you cannot die. But you have come to me for a reason, Sunil Rastogi." He left his stool and came close to me, crouched down and retrieved a chain that hung inside his clothing. On the end of that chain was a golden ring and inlaid in that ring was a stone of such bright green it was all I could see. He said, "You've traveled all your life to be here, and now you are a servant to me." I found myself trembling. I could not disagree. "But soon," he said, "you will leave." "Where will I go?" I replied, blinking back tears, for I was moved by his faith in me. "West," he said, "to the place you were born. You will follow fate, fate has carried you everywhere." "Yes," I whispered. "And once there," he went on, "you will forget everything until you see a face; that face will guide your hand. You will seek out that face and deliver a message." I asked him, "What message will I give?"

27.

In the godown, with those words, Rastogi gets up from his stool, pulls from his pocket an ivory handle, and with deft fingers reveals the killing blade within.

"He said first you will deliver the message of pain."

Sunny begins to squirm and cry out.

"Then you will deliver the story of your life."

Sunny fights against his ropes, strains every muscle to find one bit of freedom.

Tries to stand with the chair attached to him, tries to bring it down again to break its legs.

Something.

Anything.

But he's in agony and weak and nothing works.

"Your life is also pain. The pain that is native to our land."

Rastogi crouches so close and searches Sunny's eyes.

"And then? I asked him. Do I kill him then? Oh no, he replied. You let him live. And I asked him, Why?"

Rastogi reaches out and cups Sunny's cheek in his palm.

All Sunny hears is the hammering of his heart.

Not the sound of the motorbike in the distance.

"Do you hear?" Rastogi says, suddenly standing up. "Yes. Manoj is here."

He steps back from Sunny toward the door.

Backing away.

Backing away.

The sound becomes solid, a bike racing at speed.

Rastogi presses his back flat against the wall beside the door. "As Himmatgiri lifted me to my feet and held me in his arms I asked him that question. *Why?* Why all this to let him live?"

The bike is almost on them.

Sunny can see the jagged sweep of the headlight under the door.

"Do you know what he said, Sunny Wadia?"

The bike's engine cuts off.

The sound of feet across the dusty ground. "Sunil bhaiya, Sunil bhaiya!" Manoj rushes in full of joy, cradling a duffel bag in his arms, bursting past the concealed Rastogi. "Sunil bhaiya, I have it!"

He skids to a halt, sees Sunny bound and screaming with the rag in his mouth.

Before Manoj can think, Rastogi steps forward and grabs him by the hair, yanks his head back, and gouges the flesh of his throat. Digs deep and vicious until the opened artery sprays.

Manoj drops the bag, raises his hands to his neck, tries to say something, but he's drowning in himself.

Rastogi holds his head back, pulls Manoj's arms away.

Sunny watches the life vanish from Manoj, his eyes wide in sorrow.

His legs buckling.

He's gurgling.

Trying in vain to reach the gun in his waistband.

But he's already leaving this world.

Rastogi eases him to the floor.

He lets the limp Manoj go, takes the gun, picks up the duffel bag of cash, walks to the door. Turns one last time.

"'Because the face you will see,' Himmatgiri said to me, 'is the face of my son.'"

NEW DELHI, JANUARY 2008

THE KING WAS EXTREMELY ALTERED

MORNING

1.

Sunny wakes naked beside the girls from last night. Maria and ? He doesn't even remember the other's name. He plied them with so much vodka and LSD even they hadn't remembered by the messy end. He'd coaxed them into fucking each other while he watched, made them do it like that scene from *Requiem for a Dream*. It got him going, knowing they'd have to face each other in the morning.

He's a dog digging a phantom hole. A needle gouging the skin to find a vein.

Now the light hurts, the day hurts, everything fucking hurts. He strains up from the bed, stumbles across the marble floor to the bathroom that's bigger than Maria's apartment in South Ex. He climbs inside one of the floor-to-ceiling shower cubicles designed to look like teleporting pods, but which today resemble the psychic cages in which Bacon condemned his Popes. He pisses long and hard, a malevolent stream of raw malice, pushing each palm to the glass, head raised in a silent scream, watching his life go down the drain.

He climbs out and wraps himself in one of the Langham bathrobes hanging from a portable rack in the middle of the floor.

When he reenters the bedroom, the girls don't stir. He looks at Maria, facedown. Feels nothing. Bored even of his own emptiness, he pops out three two-milligram bars of Xanax from the stash in his bedside table, swallows them with the dregs of a beer, picks up a pack of Dunhills, pads through the bedroom door, a nine-foot high, silent, swinging beast, out into the cool corridors of his mansion wing, a maze that resembles a museum, little sealed glass boxes containing artworks: gruesome figurines in the Mojave desert, a piece of the Berlin Wall, a female mannequin in a silk kimono and fencing mask, suspended in the air by kinbaku ropes in the style of Araki.

He opens a door into a vast and gaudy ballroom, fifty meters long, the ceiling adorned by small lamps mapping the constellations of the night sky. An archipelago of velvet sofas, big as beds, dot the room below, with sleeping bodies strewn like the victims of a poisoning cult. Chill-out music plays low from the stereo system installed in the walls, the bass vibrates from the panels beneath the floor. He picks his way through the mess, runs his hand along the sweeping curve of the bar, the Platonic form of all the nightclubs he has known. Rounding the business end, there's Fabian, the wealth manager from Paris, the one Ashwin brought. He's slumped against the wall with a thousand-yard stare, a loaded crossbow in his arms. Sunny steps over him, plucks a bottle of tequila from the shelf.

He approaches one of the giant bay windows that look out over the mansion grounds. Like an imprisoned Emperor he surveys the manicured lawns, the amphitheater beyond, the sanctuary of woodland on the horizon, the hundreds of workers in the crisp sunlight of the February morning pegging tents, setting tables, constructing the stage upon which the artists will perform, building and stocking the bars, assembling the mini Ferris wheel, the fairground attractions: the hall of mirrors, the ghost train, the shooting range.

He unscrews the bottle and pours tequila down his throat. Takes a breath.

"Fuck."

He pours again, first down his throat, then over his head, drenching his hair, streaming tequila into his eyes, into his beard, inside his robe. He drops the bottle to the floor, then fishes the pack of Dunhills from his pocket, inserts a cigarette in his mouth, considers the consequence of tequila and fire . . .

Thwack!

A crossbow bolt embeds itself in the ceiling.

He lights the cigarette anyway.

Today is Sunny's wedding day.

In the prison cell Ajay looks down on the brand-new safari suit laid upon his mattress. The skin of another life. He is told to dress in it. An escort will be here in half an hour. They will drive him to the Wadia mansion, then bring him back to jail before the night is out.

A compassionate day release.

He has no say in the matter.

His presence has been requested.

He does not know why.

What he'll do when he's there, he doesn't know either.

Will he be made to serve drinks?

Stand by Sunny's side?

Or just linger in the back, head down, out of sight?

The absurd reward for four silent loyal years as an undertrial.

"Have fun!" Sikandar roars.

He'd just as happily kill them all.

In the brothel photo of his sister, the man who once shared the frame is torn from view. Now the words on the back only say . . . WHAT YOU'RE

TOLD. He places her image in his inside pocket. He picks up the bottle-neck with the fresh foil, pierces holes with a toothpick, spreads out the to-bacco, sprinkles the crushed Mandrax, lights it, inhales.

Sunny comes back into the bedroom and the girls are still there. He can't bear the sight of them. He looks at the clock on his wall. Eight fifty-two a.m. The wedding ceremony is scheduled for the Gurdwara at noon. And here he is, soaked in tequila, smoking a cigarette, watching Maria with her back to him.

The other one is lying on the far edge, curled up alone, hugging herself.

"I know you're awake," he says.

He gets up and retrieves the ornamental Kashmiri box he keeps on his bookshelf, brings it to the bed, removes a small mirror from his bedside drawer, an old Amex card, a crisp yen note. Only when he opens the box does he discover his emergency coke is already gone.

It's 3:22 a.m. in London and Neda is sitting at the long wooden table in the living area of the Old Street loft conversion that's now called home.

Saturday night, Sunday morning.

Waiting. Not waiting.

She couldn't sleep. University students were chanting and drinking and knocking over rubbish bins outside. She put the radio on low, smoked a cigarette, grated ginger and haldi into a pan, boiled the water, let it steep.

Now she sits at the table with the mug between her hands, looking at the exposed brick walls, the faded Persian rugs on the wooden floor, the elegant lighting, the tropical plants, figuring out just how she got here.

Her partner, Alex, is design director at the small Soho ad agency where she now works as a copywriter. He's thirty-five years old. Scottish. A tidy but playful mind. Likes the outdoors. Likes to snowboard. He noticed her from Day One. He was kind to her, covered her mistakes, looked at her like he was trying to see her. It just happened. She let it. She doesn't love him. Or maybe she does. It doesn't matter.

She works hard. Keeps her thoughts to herself. Watches words like a hawk. Tries to be tidy too.

He says, "Sometimes I think you're asleep at the wheel."

"Very poetic."

"Drifting into the headlights of a car."

"Are you the car?" she asks, stroking his hair.

"I think I'm more likely the car behind."

"Then that makes you a voyeur."

She has not touched the Wadia money in a long time. She cut up their credit cards, their debit cards. She stopped meeting Chandra and Chandra stopped calling. She even stopped Googling Sunny's name. She waited for the hammer to fall. But they just stopped pursuing her. They let her be. It was as if her life before had never existed.

Then she heard the news. Sunny was getting married. Fucking Facebook. All those old Delhi people who'd added her in the last years, this had been her weakness, the link she maintained. Now she saw the photos posted. The mehndi, the sangeet. The farmhouse villa and its pool. It triggered everything. And now she's awake. Waiting for the day itself. Waiting for something. Living on India time again.

She hears the key in the front door.

Alex coming home after a poker night with the boys.

"Christ," he says upon seeing her. "Second night in a row."

He's pleasantly drunk. Smells of cologne and whisky and cigar smoke.

She turns gently. "I wasn't waiting up, if that's what you're worried about."

He comes to greet her, gathers her hair up in his hands, kisses the back of her neck. "Still can't sleep?"

She shrugs, ignores the question. "What's the gossip your end?"

"The gossip my end is I'm getting broke and old."

"How much did you lose?" she asks.

"Enough," he says, then corrects himself. "No, seriously speaking, it's all right."

"You at least smell like you had a good night."

He heads toward the bar. "You want a nightcap?"

She shakes her head. "No."

"Can I ask you something," he says, his drunkenness loosening his tongue. "Were you an alcoholic?"

She gives a calm, placid smile. "Where did that come from?"

"It's a reasonable question."

"If I were, I'd still be one."

"Drug addict?"

"Nope."

"What then?" He pours a snifter of Cognac, inhales it, walks to the bedroom.

"A recovering coward," she says.

Maria wakes to see Sunny reclined in a vintage leather armchair, robe open, smoking, staring into space.

"Teresa," she says, and rolls over to shake Teresa awake.

Maria's from Mexico City, she's been running a restaurant in Delhi for a year now. Teresa's from Madrid, she's been backpacking in the south for three months. When she flew into Delhi three nights ago, she got fleeced by the taxi, dropped off in a desolate spot, then creepy guys followed her to her Paharganj hotel. People had warned her about the city, how hard it was. She went to a travel agent the next morning and booked a bus to Jaipur. Then she went to an internet café and looked for anything that looked like home. A Mexican restaurant in South Ex was good enough. She spent the day at Lodhi Gardens, Khan Market, and Humayun's Tomb, then went out for dinner at seven. When she walked in, Teresa was surprised to see the modern design and the young Mexican woman running the place. This wasn't the Delhi she expected at all. Since it was early, and the place was still empty, Maria made a beeline for her. Maria's authority and the relief of the shared language made Teresa's exhaustion and loneliness melt away. Maria made sure Teresa got the best of everything, gorditas, mutton cabeza tacos, tamales oaxaqueñōs. Whenever there was a lull in service, she sat at Teresa's table, drinking a beer. They got talking about India; already jaded by Delhi, Maria was glad to hear Teresa's complaints, and knowing she couldn't be understood by the rich English-speaking Indian clientele, unloaded her grievances as well. Purged, they moved on to what they loved about the land. They were still talking when the other customers faded away. Maria brought out a bottle of mezcal. "I have to go to Jaipur tomorrow!" Teresa exclaimed. Maria declared it impossible. "You're staying with me," she said, "at least for tonight." Teresa just smiled and said OK.

In the car back to Maria's place, Teresa thought she was picking up a vibe.

"I have someone," she said, feeling foolish as soon as the words came out of her mouth.

Maria looked at her quizzically. "Someone?"

"At home."

"Boy or girl?"

"A boy."

Maria nodded and smiled but said nothing more.

Teresa passed out on the couch.

In the morning Maria brought her coffee, said she'd send Teresa with one of her drivers to the hotel, pick up her things. "Crash with me a few nights," she said, "no strings. Only one thing: I have to go to my financer's wedding. I'll need a friend."

"An Indian wedding!" Teresa cried. "I went to one in Kottayam!"

Maria blinks through her comedown haze and shakes Teresa awake.

—Oye.

Teresa opens her eyes. Looks at Maria with unvarnished disgust.

She gets out of bed, starts to dress.

—Ya me voy.

—¿A donde?

—A la recamara.

—Yo también.

Teresa doesn't look at her.

—Quiero estar sola.

Sunny stares at Maria as Teresa slips away.

"What did she say?"

Maria climbs off the bed, covering her breasts, gathering her own clothes.

"She wants to be alone."

"Why?"

"So do I."

"Why?"

"Why did you do this?"

"You did it yourself."

She turns on him.

"It's your wedding day!"

"So what?"

"I didn't want this."

"Didn't look like it from where I was standing."

"You're sick."

He just stares and smiles.

"There's something wrong in your head," she goes on. "What I have to do, that's business. But why do it to her?"

"I didn't know you were such a dyke," he says.

"You don't know me at all. You know she's never going to speak to me again."

"What do I care?"

"No mames, güey." She pulls her dress on, gathers her panties and bra in her hand, heads to the door. "I've never met someone as sick as you."

"Fucking rug muncher," he says.

"Chinga tu madre! Suck my dick!"

"Suck mine," he replies.

She throws open the door.

"No, really," he says, in a cold distant voice. "Suck my dick or I shut your restaurant down, then I throw you out of that apartment and get your visa revoked."

She freezes at the door. "You can't do that."

"You know I can."

She turns to face him. "Why would you?"

"My cock's not good enough, is that it?"

"Why are you doing this?" she whispers.

"Because you're a whore."

"You can't do this to people." She shakes her head. Then walks out the door.

Eli is perched on the metal counter in the staff kitchen sipping a Nescafé when he sees Teresa fleeing on the CCTV screen that hangs in the corner. He rotates his aching pellet-ridden shoulder, where the brunt of the shotgun blast was felt, and mutters to himself. "Fucking Sunny Wadia." He turns to the chefs. "You see nothing, OK!"

Sunny's bedroom door has been a source of great entertainment for the chefs in recent months. Eli has observed how they glance toward the monitor reflexively while they work. Another screen, in the other corner, is trained on the entrance to the ballroom, but that doesn't distract them at all. Sunny's bedroom is where the magic happens.

Now this morning they're rewarded by the sight of a half-naked foreign girl running away.

They grin at one another in reflected glory.

"Savages," Eli says.

He jumps down from the counter, winces at the remnants of pain. The broken collarbone, the collapsed lung.

"You're lucky to be alive," the doctor had said.

He hadn't felt lucky, waking in that hospital, not knowing if Sunny was dead, having to explain himself to the family, feigning amnesia for a while.

He hadn't considered himself lucky until he heard Sunny was recovered alive. Until he managed to retrieve the file from the hidden compartment in his car.

Still, he'd been in the doghouse for a while. He'd expected to be fired. He'd thought about quitting too. But he discovered he couldn't leave Sunny behind. He needed to see this thing through.

Oh shit.

On the screen: Maria marching away.

It takes forty-two seconds to reach Sunny's room. Sixty measured steps. Eli counts each one, hands clasped behind his back. He passes the girl on the twenty-seventh, nods to her respectfully as she wipes her eyes, and when he reaches the door he draws a breath, covers his own eyes, peeks through the fingers. "Knock, knock," he calls, "safe to come in?"

He waits to be screamed at.

When no sound materializes, he pushes the door open a little. Tries to make light of it all. "Sunny Wadia, last night of freedom, feeling like lion? Yes?"

But inside he sees Sunny on the edge of the bed, a rolled-up note shoved into his nose and a line of blue powder resting on a small mirror below.

"Oh no, my friend!" Eli rushes forward. "This is not normal."

By the time he reaches Sunny, the blue line has been vacuumed.

"What is this? You snort Xanax now? You are crazy." Eli snatches the mirror as Sunny slumps back and closes his eyes. "How much you take?"

Eli searches Sunny's robe pockets for the pack. "You're sweating tequila, baba! Why like this? Do I need get flumazenil?"

"Flumazenil," Sunny slurs.

"You go to temple in three hours."

"Gurdwara . . ."

"Temple, Gurdwara. Whatever. God is looking at you. Papa looking at me."

"Leave me. . . ."

"Come. We take cold shower."

He hauls Sunny's mass toward the bathroom.

Heaves him into the shower cubicle.

Turns the jets on cold.

Eli doesn't flinch at Sunny's drug-fueled nakedness, his rolls of fat, his fresh scars. He removes his own wallet and phone, gets into the shower fully dressed after him. Grabs the soap and begins to scrub.

What he flinches at is Sunny's yearning to annihilate himself.

Still, he tries to keep it light.

"I was beyond enemy line in Lebanon one time," he shouts over the rush of water. "Only me. Not official. I get sent because I look Arab. You know that? In truth I had no choice. This between you and me. I do something very wrong. Now they say, go to jail or go to Lebanon. You decide. I choose Lebanon. I almost die. Twice!" He slaps Sunny round the face. "But you know what? Even Lebanon better than scrubbing Sunny Wadia's asshole."

Nothing. Sunny doesn't stir.

Eli turns off the jets, looks down on this ungodly form.

"Sleeping like baby. Is flumazenil time."

Flumazenil has become an essential component of life since Sunny's kidnapping.

Flumazenil: a competitive benzodiazepine receptor antagonist inhibiting activity at the benzodiazepine receptor site on the GABA/benzodiazepine receptor complex.

AKA: righting Sunny's Xanax OD.

Onset of action 1–2 minutes; 80 percent response within 3.

Eli pulls Sunny out onto the bathroom floor, fetches a vial and syringe and rubber tourniquet from the medication fridge.

How many times has he done this in the seven or so months since Sunny's release?

Five? Eight? He's lost count.

He preps the syringe, binds the tourniquet to find the vein.

Sticks it in.

The bedroom phone begins to ring.

Eli releases the solution into Sunny's bloodstream. Immediately unties the tourniquet.

The bathroom extension starts to ring too.

"I think it's for you," Eli says.

And Sunny begins to growl like a dog.

"OK. I answer. I say you're taking big shit, yes?" He draws himself up tall, lifts the receiver with a great false smile. "Hello," he booms. "Eli speaking." He listens awhile. "Yes, sir. Yes, sir."

Sunny opens his eyes. Takes a great breath. Sits his naked body up.

Rubs his face.

"I want a Diet Coke," he says.

"Yes, sir, one second, he just walked in now." He covers the receiver and hisses. "Is Papa. He wants to speak to you."

Sunny sighs, hangs his head, takes the phone.

"Yes. I'll be right down."

2.

Sunny stands before Bunty Wadia, more or less alert.

With the eyes and face and hangover expected of a wedding day.

There are masseuses and beauticians to fix such cosmetic things.

But what can be done about his soul?

Since Sunny's rescue, he and Bunty have barely talked.

Bunty has taken a lenient, compassionate line.

Has given Sunny space and time.

Has vowed to hunt Rastogi down.

He sat in on Sunny's debriefing, his treatment for dehydration, bruised ribs, a broken wrist, infected wounds.

A tracking device had been placed in the bag of notes.

It had been found, minus the money, next to Manoj's bike.

They had an artist come in and sketch the face Sunny saw.

But what about the faces he sees when he closes his eyes?

Manoj, bleeding out.

Lost words gurgling pink blood bubbles in his mouth.

And the other face.

The one whose name he does not speak out loud.

Sunny told Bunty, the cops, everyone who'd listen, that it was all about the land.

The story checked out.

Manoj's brother Sonu was inside.

Rastogi's uncle was found.

Sukanya Sarkar, too, with her awful secret, was quickly tracked down.

But despite all this, despite the cops, the informants, the insiders, the undercovers, the snitches, Rastogi disappeared. Just a few sightings, a few traces.

Why?

How could he so easily evade?

Maybe one vital part of the story was left out.

The bit that starts with Ajit Singh and ends with . . .

"I know," Bunty says, "it's been hard for you, since the incident with this . . ."

Sunny shudders at the absence of the name.

"But we'll find him," Bunty continues, "we'll bring him in."

"I want him dead," Sunny says.

Bunty holds Sunny's gaze.

"That's a matter of time."

I want him dead.

It's an earworm, an unending refrain.

It spreads through his brain in the darkness, and there are so many more things that go unsaid.

"But that's not what I want to talk about," Bunty says. "I want to talk about the future. You've long been a man, but today with this union, you'll become my heir."

Of course, Sunny suspects. He suspects Bunty knows more than he lets on.

And though Bunty has become kinder to him, he looks at Bunty with a righteous contempt.

It overwhelms him.

You killed my child. You are not my father.

Or maybe you didn't. And you are.

He doesn't know, which is worse.

There's only so much of it he can take.

Hence the Xanax, the flumazenil.

Hence the spreading of pain.

"And I wanted to tell you," Bunty says, "that you were right. You were right about our future. You were right about leaving UP behind. This is partly what this union's about. With this marriage, we align with Punjab. And what you've done for me with Gautam Rathore, Madhya Pradesh can be ours. What you choose to do yourself . . . you take your time. You're not only marrying into a family today, you're marrying a woman. I expect she'll take care of you. I expect she'll give you a son. But what you do next, that's your choice. We can leave UP behind. Ram Singh is yesterday's news."

"And what about . . ." Sunny balls his fists . . .

"Vicky?"

"Today will be the last time you'll ever have to see him."

"Why?"

"I'm selling off the sugar mills."

"Why?"

"It's something I should have done a long time ago."

Sunny clasps his arms behind his back. Takes a deep long breath.

"I should go."

He takes a half-turn.

"I should have protected you."

Bunty speaks these words with more emotion than Sunny has ever felt.

"I should have protected you," Bunty says again.

"When?" Sunny replies.

"When I sent you off to the mill. When Vicky . . ."

Sunny closes his eyes tight a moment.

"I knew what he was doing," Bunty says. "I shouldn't have sent you."

"But you did."

"Everything since then was to protect you."

Sunny nods dispassionately. "I should go."

"I may seem harsh in your eyes."

Sunny can't take much more of it.

"I'll be late."

He turns and heads toward the door.

"But I'm your father and you're my son."

Back in his room, Sunny finds his phone. He calls Eli.

"Bring me whisky. Bring me coke."

He rocks back and forward while he waits.

3.

For the past few hours Neda has been reading the gossip online. The snippets in the Delhi tabloids. The Punjab papers. Now she knows all about the Enfield-riding, golf-playing bride. Farah Dhillon, rebel Queen of the Chandigarh social scene, with her heart-shaped face and crooked smile.

She's upset with herself for even feeling this pain.

She conjures Delhi in the late winter. Crisp air, thin blue skies, a lazy mist bathing the lawns under the pale morning sun. Her father smoking a cigarette somewhere. Sunny somewhere. She opens her laptop again, checks Facebook once more, scrolls through the pictures of the party in Sunny's farmhouse that have been posted in the night. She recognizes almost nothing, but there's that pool again. Some of the old gang are there, bottles in hand. More foreigners than there used to be. No pictures of Sunny at all.

She thinks of that pool. Thinks of Ajay. Considers him her own.

It's four thirty in the morning.

She lights a cigarette, walks to the bedroom door, listens for Alex lightly snoring. Walks back out and stands by the window. Watching the sheets of rain. Waiting for the day to come. Waiting for the day to end.

Then what?

Get on with it, she supposes.

She studies the bar trolley, selects the bottle of Absolut, places it in the freezer, lights another cigarette.

Eli pushes the door open five minutes later, dressed in new clothes. A big-collared Hawaiian shirt, black skinny jeans. He carries a tray with a bottle of Yamazaki 50-year-old, an ice bucket, a rocks glass, two cans of Coke. Places them on the coffee table.

"As requested."

"Where's the coke?"

He points to the cans. "Right here, motherfucker."

"Asshole," Sunny says, putting ice into his glass, breaking open the whisky. "I want *cocaine*."

"What am I? Drug dealer? I don't have."

"So get some."

"From?"

"One of those pricks in the ballroom. It's all mine anyway."

————————

While Eli hunts the coke, Sunny drinks down a large glass of whisky. He intends to get to the very knife-edge of oblivion, then bring himself back with a massive line.

The force of the coke will be like coming up through waves.

By the time Eli returns, he's on his third glass.

"You killing yourself," Eli says, sitting beside him.

Sunny stares at the floor, glassy-eyed. "I don't care." He looks up. "Where's the coke?"

Eli fishes a baggie out of his top pocket, places it on the table.

"Do you know what I had to do for this? Some guy tried to shoot me with a crossbow."

Sunny holds the bag up to the light.

Nearly a full gram in there.

"Assholes." His movements are sluggish. He slurs his words. "Get me a mirror and a card."

"Please . . ."

"Fuck you."

"How about thank you?"

"Fuck you."

"You know something," Eli says, fetching what Sunny needs, "you cannot talk to people this way and expect to survive." He points to his chest. "I take shotgun for you. I lie in hospital. I lie to your father. I hide your secret. I do everything you ask. Not once you say thank you."

He wipes the mirror down with a Kleenex, tips out the coke, cuts three huge lines, rolls a note.

"Fuck you," Sunny slurs.

"Why you do this?" Eli says, handing him the note. "You know when someone talks like this to me, I cut their tongue out."

Sunny smirks. Bends down to take the first line with one eye closed. Misses it.

"You think I'm fucking joking," Eli says. "But no, I serious. I do it. Cut out their tongue, stick it back down throat. Watch them choke on it. No problem. Sleep just fine. Dream of kittens."

Sunny sets himself up just right this time. Pulls the whole line.

"But you," Eli goes on. "With you I don't do nothing. You know why?"

Sunny looks up at him with the false clarity of a brain exploding with coke. "Why?"

"Because you already fuck yourself."

Sunny sits back, closes his eyes.

Eli says, "I know suffering when I see it, my friend."

"You can go now."

Eli walks toward the door. "You know something, I think you used to be good guy."

Sunny shakes his head. "You don't know who I am."

Now, in his hand, he holds the sonogram of his unborn child.

He holds the report.

Patient name: Neda Kapur.

One last thing, one piece of doubt.

He has to know.

He takes out his phone, dials the mobile number listed on the report.

She has her phone on the table in front of her.

The cigarette burning down in her hand.

When it rings—unknown number—she answers right away.

Clairvoyance.

Despair.

Puts it to her ear.

Hears the silence of a sealed room, a sealed mind. And all these fucking years.

What if he'd called once? Just once?

She hears him breathing.

Heavy but regular. So brutal.

The ocean, the sand, the fire.

"Sunny," she says.

The last thing she wants to do is cry.

She forces a false smile. "I hear congratulations are in order."

Nothing.

She waits.

Waits.

He keeps breathing.

Is he going to stay silent after all these years?

Then he speaks.

"I need you to tell me something."

His voice so measured, so clinical.

She feels like she's going under again.

The anesthetist's needle in her vein.

Her insides pulled out.

She puts her cigarette out, gets up and walks to the freezer, places the phone between her shoulder and ear.

She retrieves the ice-cold vodka. Brings it to the table with a shot glass.

So unexpected, how life goes.

She swirls the bottle, releases the vodka into the glass. Drinks it down.

"What do you want to know?"

Pours another shot.

"Did you kill my son?"

The abruptness, the impropriety of it.

It makes her laugh.

"You think it's funny?" he says.

"No," she cuts him. "It was never funny. None of it." She walks to the window, looking out on the wet street, the orange lights. The N55 bus passes, early workers sit gloomy below, a few ravers up top. She knocks back the shot once more. "Is this really why you called? On your wedding day?"

"Did you kill him?"

Silence. She gathers herself.

She feels the vodka burn, her belly slowly becoming warm.

"You should have told me."

Incredulous.

"Fuck you," she says. "I should have told you? *I* should have told *you*? Fuck you. You *abandoned* me. After everything we did and said and went through. You abandoned me. I thought you loved me. I really thought it. I thought you didn't need to say it because it was true. And what did you do? You left me there."

A pause.

And then a flat, callous voice.

"I didn't know."

"Listen to yourself." She returns to the kitchen, finds a rocks glass, sits at the table, and pours the vodka. "I'm tired, Sunny."

And his voice reveals the smallest crack.

"I didn't know."

She closes her eyes.

So it's true.

The shock in this moment is profound.

But it passes.

"It doesn't matter now," she says. "But when did you find out?"

The rain trickles down the window.

He doesn't answer.

She lights another cigarette.

"She's pretty, your wife."

"Tell me one more thing," he says calmly. "Did he make you do it?"

She's been through this a million times.

"Did he force you?"

"You want to put this on someone," she says, "I understand."

"Did he make you? Was it him? Or was it you?"

She can hear him pulling a line.

"What does it matter?"

"My son is dead."

"My son is dead too. We all have to pay somehow."

"Was it him?" he says. "Did he make you do it?"

"Let's play a game, Sunny. An answer for an answer. I'll tell you what you want to know. All you have to do is tell me one thing too: was it worth it? Everything you've done, the life you have, all the people who loved you who you threw away, lurching from one thing to the next, always finding someone to blame. Showing your broken heart, showing what was done to you, then doing it back to them. In the balance of things, was it worth it?"

"Him or you?"

"You seem to think it hinges on this. Who made the choice, him or me? Him or me? Which one of us killed our son. Are you sad, Sunny? Are you lost? Will knowing close the wound? Well, here's my answer, Sunny. Here's the truth." She looks up to see Alex watching her from the doorway, but it's too late to stop. "Your father didn't kill our son. I didn't kill him either. You did, Sunny. It was you."

In the emptiness of his room, Sunny stares into his phone.

Takes a moment. Composes himself.

Calls Dinesh Singh.

"Bro!" Dinesh answers cheerily. "Why you calling? It's your wedding day!"

"Is it on?" Sunny says.

"Your wedding? You tell me, man."

"Is it on?"

"Shut the fuck up," Dinesh says.

"Is. It. On?"

"Get the fuck off the phone."

"The phone is safe."

"No phone is safe, you fucking idiot."

"Just do it," Sunny says. "Just do it. I want him gone."

"Bro," Dinesh says. "Pray no one's listening. Because it's already done."

AFTERNOON

1.

They are married.

Sunny and Farah Wadia.

They sit beside one another in the Gurdwara congregation hall, Farah resplendent in crimson lehenga, dripping with exquisite jewels, smiling demurely, her chin poised for the occasion, bow lips parted to reveal that perfectly imperfect smile and the single crooked tooth in that heart-shaped face. And Sunny, in his turban and sherwani, stone-faced behind Ray-Ban shades, looking like a Bollywood badass, or its waxwork at Madame Tussauds.

Back at the farmhouse estate, Tinu is perched on the edge of his daybed, smoking, waiting. Three phones laid out on the table ahead. Three phones, for three specific reasons.

One begins to ring.

He takes another drag of his cigarette and gets up.

The police van drives through South Delhi with Ajay in the back, dressed in that new safari suit, as if nothing had ever gone wrong. His eyes stare forward in a Mandrax haze, his wrist cuffed to his guard's wrist.

The van pulls up at the Mehrauli Police Outpost, half a kilometer from the estate. Extra security has been posted in the neighborhood. The colony gates that lead to the farmhouse boast half a dozen private guards waiting to check IDs, open trunks, use telescopic inspection mirrors to examine the underbellies of the cars.

Sniffer dogs roam the lanes.

Soon there'll be a torrent of luxury cars. Now there's only the black Land Rover going the other way.

The guards salute as it approaches, run to open the gate.

Tinu speeds through and turns south toward the Police Outpost. When he nears, he slows, beeps once, turns into one of the back lanes.

The van with Ajay follows.

They both park. The engines ticking and cooling. And Ajay is led out, uncuffed.

He watches Tinu climb out of his Land Rover, walk around to the passenger side door, open it, and beckon him in.

"Go on. Enjoy yourself," his guard says.

"Have you eaten?" Tinu asks. Ajay sits beside him in the Land Rover as Tinu examines the man, notes his empty eyes, the hardened flesh. He's a soldier now. Or a shell.

"Why am I here?" Ajay asks.

"What I want you to do," Tinu replies, "is take rest." The Land Rover is ushered inside the mansion gate. "Enjoy the day. Feel at home. You're our honored guest."

They sweep up the drive to a vista of lawns and statues and fountains and flower beds. At the very end, the mansion itself, seventy rooms, three stories high.

They pull up at the gravel entrance. Tinu cuts the engine and climbs out.

Ajay climbs out too, doesn't wait to be told.

A staff driver runs to take the Land Rover away.

"What can I get you?" Tinu asks, when the car is gone. "Chai? Pani? Cold drink?"

"A cigarette," Ajay says.

Tinu considers this response with a faint smile, offers him a Classic Mild. He takes one, pulls the filter off, stares out evenly over the lawn to the side, the tables of food and drinks, the stages, the fairground rides. As Tinu lights it for him, Tinu's phone rings. An important call. "Why don't you wait over there," he says, pointing toward the first set of tables. "Eat something, have chai. I'll be back soon. Don't go far." Tinu hurries toward the mansion, hand cupped around the mouthpiece of his phone.

Is this a test? Ajay walks across the gravel to the lawn and looks down. Green, green grass. He removes his loafers, his socks. Takes a long, long drag of the cigarette, smoking it through his balled fist, prison style.

What am I doing here?

They're watching him, he knows.

He wanders onward, stands among a bunch of workers, fancy people, even some foreigners. Stuffing themselves with samosas, pakoras, sandwiches, pizza slices. Drinking from cans of cola, bottles of mineral water. Pouring cups from giant thermoses of coffee and chai. There are three ice buckets full of Heineken. A foreign guy smiles at him expectantly.

"Could I have one of those?"

But he's soon unnerved by Ajay's motionless stare.

And the realization, upon closer inspection, that this young man isn't as servile as he thought.

Still, Ajay grabs a bottle. Opens it with his teeth, passes it to him.

Walks off with a bottle of his own. Looks out at the woods in the distance, the old villa with the pool. Stops and opens the beer and pours it down his throat, eyes closed.

Curls his toes into the grass.

Feels the gentle breeze, the winter sun on his face.

Soft, perfect, alien.

Numb.

His reverie is disrupted by a tide of applause: the wedding convoy has arrived.

Ten black Audis snake up, four come to a halt outside the mansion, six peel off along a lane cut through the lawn, cruise toward the guesthouses a quarter kilometer away near the modest zoo. Ajay keeps his eyes fixed on those four that sit outside the Wadia home. From the first two, bodyguards in black suits and shades emerge and disperse, their job done. From the third comes Bunty, alone, in his Armani and shades. He stops to light a cigarette, which is dwarfed by his huge hands, his bearded face. He looks around at his world with all the time it affords, then heads up the mansion steps. From the fourth car, the happy couple emerge. First Farah, still laughing, still joyous, waving at the gathering staff and workers, rushing up the steps to catch her father-in-law. She whispers something in his ear and Bunty laughs too. She lays a hand on his lapel, for all to see. Her claim staked, she turns and skips down the steps with catlike grace, dances across the lawns, drawing delighted gasps as she goes. Bunty watches her go, then turns and disappears inside the mansion.

And that black car is left on the gravel alone.

Ajay watches it, with what in his heart?

And finally, *he* steps out.

Sunny Wadia.

Impenetrable behind his shades.

He stands a lonely figure.

He lights a cigarette for himself.

Doesn't look.

Heads inside.

2.

Farah's relatives are lodging in both guesthouses, two fourteen-bedroom delights, linked by gym, sauna, cinema hall, industrial kitchens, spa, heated Olympic swimming pool.

The servants housed in a humble building behind.

Children run, screaming, jumping into the pool. Her paternal grandfather breaks the whisky out. Most of Farah's close relatives—mother, father, father's parents, two aunts on her mother's side, aunt and three uncles on her father's, their children, her cousin brothers and sisters, her own brother and two sisters and their spouses and children—will reside here for the next two days.

Only Farah's maternal grandfather is missing. He is already flying back to Amritsar on one of Bunty's private planes. It does not matter. His work here is done. It was he who officiated the wedding, reading from the Guru Granth Sahib.

He is Giani Zarowar Singh, a religious leader of authority second to none, one of the most respected men in the community, one of the most revered. He remains the moral and spiritual adviser to the chief minister of Punjab, who is himself a not-too-distant blood relative of the bride on her father's side.

It was Giani Zarowar Singh whom Bunty was really marrying.

Farah was simply the way in.

Her family had run to ruin. Her father was a generous, hopeful, sloppy man, a cheerful and hungry man, a gambler, an alcoholic taken up by impossible schemes.

Get rich!

He dared to dream at the roulette wheel of life and lost his shirt every time.

Among his follies, an ill-conceived medical supplies company, making parts for MRI scanners. Badly managed, profligate, it cost a great deal to set up and bled money from the start. Instead of listening to Lovely, his wife, he tried to compensate with farmland in Sierra Leone (failed, fifteen crore rupees down the drain), gas stations in New Jersey (watered-down gas, fell foul of the authorities, fined to the tune of eight crore rupees), and a diamond mine in Ghana. This was the worst of them all. He sent his eldest son to set that one up. The son came back after six months, five crore rupees down, with the Ghanaian management team all hooked on cocaine.

Farah saw all this play out as she grew into a woman all men adored. She was sent to a boarding school in the Himalayan foothills at the age of three. When she was seven, the European ski holidays dried up. The first-class air travel stopped at eight. The apartment in Mayfair was sold when she was ten. The house in Zurich when she was thirteen. In her teens, she and her siblings were reduced to holidaying in Shimla, playing Monopoly, placing plastic houses on the same streets on which real apartments had been owned.

They did what they could to keep up appearances. Every Sunday they dined out at the Taj hotel. And still they had their bungalow, with its luscious lawn and servants who stayed because this was also their land and they had nowhere else to go. They all lived together in asymmetric poverty, her mother and aunts, sitting out on the lawn sipping gin under the parasol, conducting affairs with strapping young army men, while the men of the home were out squandering the last things they owned.

Farah learned to fend for herself, harnessing rugged boyfriends, paragliding, hunting, riding motorbikes, playing and cheating at cards. Back in society, her charm, her intelligence, her ruthlessness worked its magic kindly on authoritative men. Her gymnastics tutor waived his usual fee. Her tennis coach was always free. Then there was her venerable grandfather. She was the apple of his eye. Because of their bond, no one could afford to get on her bad side.

By the time Bunty was readying his approach, she was a perfectly put together young woman of twenty-four. Bunty had met her once, a year before, at a VIP wedding in Chandigarh. He'd clocked the family first, then made a mental note of her: she had brains, fire, poise, she drank and smoked, but not excessively so, and not to make a point. She was *ambitious*. She was *in control*. The more he inquired, the more she suited Bunty to a tee.

While Sunny was recovering in hospital, he flew out to Bhutan, where Farah was holidaying in the Aman hotel with a wealthy and anonymous male friend. He sent a message: Would she come to meet him in the pine-shrouded Paro Lodge? He had a business proposition to make. Sitting on the deck, sipping a Château de Montifaud X.O., looking out over the misty valley and the monastery-clad mountains, she smiled and said, "This is irregular."

And Bunty said, "I know."

3.

Back out on the lawn, Ajay flicks the cigarette away, considers the green bottleneck of the beer, places the empty bottle down. He crosses the grass, the gravel, barefoot, to the mansion steps.

Follows Sunny inside.

No one there, no guards to stop him.

Inside. Silent and cool. Two sets of marble stairs curving either side of the enormous hall, in which an exquisite thirty-meter Persian rug stretched toward an ornamental pool. On the wall, a portrait of Bunty fifteen feet tall. In the distance, a few servants walking back and forth.

Ajay follows his instincts. Half-remembered memories of blueprints, plans. Heads up the right-hand staircase to a mezzanine floor, turns right again and pushes open a leather-paneled door.

Before him, a maze of corridors. All empty, cool, echoing, hung with artworks. He walks slowly, silently pressing the marble with his feet, expecting to be stopped anytime, not caring either way. He passes door after closed door, hears the displaced sound of laughter. He walks past a snooker room. Another full of arcade games and pinball machines. Empty, unused. But the laughter grows.

He finds its source.

An industrial kitchen with three chefs inside. One of them is miming a story. Someone running away. They keep laughing and look up at a video screen in the corner of the room. Then they see Ajay and stop. He stands in the door, but he doesn't see them. He's staring at a jar of fig jam, a hunk of Parma ham, a slab of cheddar cheese.

He remembers that combination.

One of Sunny's favorite sandwiches.

Only, the ham is cut too thin, they should be using Gruyère for cheese.

He steps in and they look at him, startled. This strange, almost familiar uniform, this drawn and weathered face. "Who are you? What do you want?"

A mild alarm.

He doesn't answer.

He only walks to the sink, pulls back his sleeves, washes his hands.

Says, "You're making it wrong."

Refreshed from a nap, a joint, and a dab of speed, Eli dresses in a fresh floral-print shirt. He's looking forward to the reception tonight; he's decided something important, something liberating. In the morning he'll resign. This shit has gone on too long. His babysitting days are done.

Time to go to the kitchen and grab a beer.

The first thing he sees are the chefs.

Standing horrified, agape.

Then the man at the counter destroying the slices of bread.

Swiping them back and forth with the butter knife until they fall apart.

Then the ham cut roughly.

Slapped onto the bread with furious hands.

Hands that smother the bread.

Hands that pause, clench into fists, raise the plate in the air and bring it down.

Shattered plate on the countertop.

Silence.

"Go wait outside," Eli says to the chefs. "Now."

"Ajay?"

Eli holds his hand out slow, as if Ajay were a lost animal returned from the wild.

"Remember me? It's Eli. Your friend."

He watches Ajay take a long deep breath.

"You shouldn't be here," Eli says. "This isn't the place for you. But I understand. I get it. They did you wrong. Why don't you and me we take a walk. Go outside. Sit on the roof maybe. So long as you don't push me off. Are you listening to me?"

"Where is he?" Ajay says.

Eli wags his finger. "That's not your problem anymore."

"Where?"

"Ajay, do I need worry about you?"

Ajay turns to look at him, and in turning his eye passes up to the TV screen.

And there he is: Sunny Wadia. Walking down the corridor, gliding into his bedroom. Without warning, Ajay is off, toward the kitchen door, and Eli is surprised to find himself backing away, letting Ajay pass. The chefs outside grow in alarm. "Find Tinu," Eli says. "Now."

"You have to tell me," Eli says, overtaking him, walking backward while Ajay searches single-mindedly for Sunny's room, "are you doing something crazy? If you do something crazy . . ." He doesn't finish his words.

Ajay keeps marching.

"Maybe you want to kill him. Really I don't blame you. I want to kill him myself sometimes."

Looking left and right.

Turning into the corridor.

Seeing the door.

Eli puts his hand out. "I know what they do to you," he says. "I know what they do. And is not right."

Ajay comes to a halt.

Eli stands between him and the door.

He drops the smile from his face.

Adopts a fighting stance.

"Let him in," Sunny says from the door.

4.

In the guesthouse, Farah wastes no time getting her people settled in.

Strides around barking orders at servants and family alike, commandeering the Wadia staff with such natural authority they fall not only in line but in love.

What this household has missed is a firm female hand.

When she's satisfied with the order of things, dressed in the Benares silk sari Bunty gifted her, she tosses her empty beer to the maid and sweeps out of the building back to the mansion she as good as owns.

But as she's about to enter, she's intercepted by one of Bunty's bodyguards.

Bunty is waiting for her in his glasshouse. A golf buggy will take her there.

Twisting and turning through the wooded path.

Two more guards stand across the entrance.

Farah strides toward them, head raised.

"Papa!" she says when she sees him inside.

She gives him a great, lingering hug, presses her cheek to his chest, inhales his cologne. When they part he says, "Let's take a walk."

They stroll in silence.

"What are you thinking?" Bunty asks.

"How happy I am today." She glances at him. "Here with you."

"You don't need to flatter me." He smiles. "I know you're asking: What does this old man want with me?"

She pulls a horrified face. "Papa, you're not old."

He frowns slightly. "I feel it today, after all these years."

"It's natural on a day like this."

He nods. "It marks a change."

They walk on. There's a cloud over him, she sees.

"What are you thinking, Papa?"

"All this will be his one day."

"And you worry."

"About many things."

"That's normal."

"I told you," he says, "about his incident last year."

"You did."

"It left him changed. He's angry. Never satisfied."

"What man is?" she says.

He touches her arm. "The man who's married to you."

"Don't tease, Papa."

"He's too emotional." He pauses. "He goes on his mother that way."

She nods sympathetically. "Fortunately that's not me. I can't work miracles, but I promise," she stands to attention and gives a chirpy salute, "I'll whip him into shape."

He laughs. "I'm sure you will."

"I've managed men like Sunny all my life," she says. "It's child's play. I'm good with children. When I'm in charge, they never misbehave."

"He's lucky to have you."

They walk on.

"What I'm more concerned about," she says, "is learning from you. Do you remember what you said to me in Bhutan?"

"I said many things."

"You said, 'I don't expect you to marry the man, or even the family, I expect you to marry the business.' You were honest from the start and I liked that. I saw it as an opportunity." She points to a plant. "What's this?"

"Solandra maxima. The Golden Cup Vine."

"And that one?"

"Fire lily. Gloriosa."

"It's lovely."

"And poisonous."

"This is my favorite," he says, leading her on a spell. "The Shenzhen Nongke orchid."

"It's quite plain."

He smiles. "It's not in bloom. But it is very expensive. Do you know why?"

"Because it's rare?"

"Because it's man-made."

He slips his hand into his pocket and pulls out a jewelry box.

"What's that, Papa?"

"I have something for you."

Inside: a huge diamond ring.

"Papa!"

"A gift for a girl without sentiment."

"It's beautiful."

"I took care to pick it out. It's from Sierra Leone."

She looks at him with a mischievous smile. "Where my family's dreams went to die."

"Consider them reborn." He lifts it from its nest and places it on her index finger. "A perfect fit."

"Now," she says, taking out a pack of cigarettes from her purse. "Let's talk business."

He opens his hands wide. "Proceed."

"I'm not that pretty," she says, "and any fool can give birth to a son. You want to expand territory. Am I right?"

He smiles. "You are."

"This being the case," she goes on, "a decision has to be made."

"A decision?" Bunty replies, amused.

"Do you only want to capture the Punjab liquor trade? Or do you want it all?"

5.

They sit facing one another.

Ajay and Sunny Wadia.

On the red plastic chairs at the coffee table.

Sunny in his Ray-Bans. Ajay making no attempt to lower his gaze.

"Drink?" Sunny says. He doesn't wait for a reply. He pours two tumblers of whisky, large. "For old times' sake." Drops ice cubes in each. Slides one across the table, Ajay reaching for his, his jacket sleeve riding up to reveal the base of a tattoo. "What's that?" Sunny asks.

Ajay pauses, pulls the sleeve higher.

A crude dagger, coiled by a crude snake.

"You did it yourself?" Sunny asks.

Ajay lowers his sleeve without a word, brings the tumbler to his lips, takes a tentative sip, then a deeper one. Puts the glass down. "Give me a cigarette," he says.

Sunny holds out his open pack, looks into Ajay's bloodshot eyes, sees the slightly trembling hand. "We've both changed."

Ajay takes the cigarette.

Sunny leans across with a flame. "What were you going to say?" He lights his own, and they sit there smoking in silence for a while. "Do you even know?"

Ajay only stares.

"Were you going to hurt me?"

Was he?

"I heard you killed some men inside."

Ajay looks around the room. "One or two."

Sunny removes his shades. "I know," he says, "you don't work for me anymore. But soon everything is going to change."

"That's what you said last time."

"And I could use a man like you."

Tinu bursts through the door into this scene, looks between the two men drinking whisky with incredulous eyes. "You," he barks, "I told you to wait outside." Then he sighs, shakes his head. "Now come with me. Bunty wants to talk."

Sunny begins to stand.

"Not you," Tinu says. He points to Ajay. "Him."

6.

Ajay stands in front of Bunty's desk, Tinu on guard just behind him. In a fug of cigarette smoke, Bunty says, "This is the first chance we've had to talk."

Ajay watches Bunty, glances at Tinu, resigned. "There's nothing to say," he replies.

"You're not in trouble," Bunty smiles, then nods to Tinu. "You can leave us now."

On the wide verandah of the mansion, Sunny smokes another cigarette. He scans the horizon. Checks the discreet watchtowers with their hidden gunmen on the perimeter fence. Thinks to himself: Dinesh better get this right.

He tries to get it all lined up in his head. The who, the what, the when, and the where. The only thing he doesn't try to know is the why.

He hears a door opening inside, sees Tinu stepping out.

Sees Tinu answering his phone.

Bunty stands and comes round the front of his desk. Inches away from Ajay's face. Looks him up and down.

"I have a question for you. I'll be happy for you to tell the truth. Before this unfortunate business with my son, you returned to your home. What happened when you were there?"

Ajay looks him square in the eye. "I killed three men."

"Why?"

"They tried to steal from me."

"What did they try and steal?"

"Money."

"And you didn't get caught?"

"I came back here."

"I see. And in jail?"

"I killed again."

"For whom?"

Ajay wavers. "For myself."

Bunty thinks this over.

"What my son did to you was wrong," he finally says. "I won't deny it. But it was part of a bigger plan. And whatever has happened in jail, I know you are still loyal to me." He lays a hand on Ajay's shoulder. "The reasons for your imprisonment are difficult, but they'll soon come to an end. Soon a deal will be put in place that will guarantee your freedom. My question is, what would a man like you do next?"

Ajay thinks of his sister. Remembers Vicky's words.

DO WHAT YOU'RE TOLD.

But now's a chance to confess.

He's about to talk.

But . . . too late . . .

———

Sunny is lost in his turbulent thoughts when Tinu calls out to him urgently from the office door. "Sunny, get in here, now!" Tinu disappears inside.

By the time Sunny follows, Tinu is whispering into Bunty's ear.

Do they know?

"We have news," Bunty says. "Something we can't ignore."

Tinu turns to Sunny. "We found him."

He feels his stomach drop. "Found who?"

Sunil Rastogi. He has been spotted in the alleys of Old Delhi. It was a rumor at first, from an informant, now Tinu's men have it confirmed. He's been sighted in Darya Ganj. He's been followed to an old Christian community, a colony bungalow forgotten in time, hidden behind rose gardens and hedges in Civil Lines.

"He's going by an alias. Peter Mathews," Tinu says.

The sweat creeps on Sunny's brow.

"We have people watching the perimeter, we have eyes on the escape routes. We have eyes on the wider roads. We have to be careful not to spook him or he'll escape again. Like he did in Saharanpur."

"In Saharanpur," Bunty adds, "he didn't get away on his own."

From the front gate, six black Subaru SUVs cruise toward the mansion. Sleek, muscular, covered in dust.

"Kill him," Sunny says.

Bunty looks to Tinu. "We could fly in Shiva or Dadapir from Bombay."

Tinu holds up a cautious hand. "But we should watch him first."

"There's nothing to watch," Sunny says. "I want him dead."

Tinu looks at his phone, offers another way. "We can bring some UP contacts in tonight. I can make some calls."

From the corner of his eye, Ajay sees the video screens hanging on the wall.

Black SUVs arriving at the front of the mansion.

From the frontmost, Vicky steps out, dressed in his long black Pathani suit, his forehead daubed with red and orange tilak, his eyes covered by wrap-around shades, his fingers glistening with his rings.

Bunty looks from Ajay to the screen.

Back at Ajay.

Notices his eyes are wide, his hands are trembling.

"He'll do it," Bunty says.

It takes a moment for Ajay to realize everyone's looking his way.

"He can't," Tinu protests. "He's only here for the wedding. He's still in jail."

"He'll do it," Bunty persists. "He'll kill this Rastogi for me." Bunty looks to Sunny. "For you."

But Sunny's eyes have already traveled to the wall.

The distraction outside.

The many goons pouring out of the other cars.

Vicky at the heart of it all.

"I'll do it," Ajay says. "But, sir, do one thing for me."

He reaches into his inner pocket, pulls out the torn, worn photograph.

His sister.

Naked.

Alone.

Holds it out.

Bunty examines it, the woman on the bed, doesn't flinch. Turns it over, reads the cut-off words: . . . WHAT YOU'RE TOLD.

"What's this?"

"She's my sister."

"What do you want from me?"

"She's in Benares. Make her safe."

Voices outside. A rabble.

Bunty looks into Ajay's eyes. Hands the photo back to him. "Bring this to me once the job is done. Then we'll find her. You have my word."

With that said, Vicky Wadia swaggers in.

"Looks like the party started without me," Vicky purrs, "but where's the whisky, brother?"

Sunny looks to be in pain.

He puts his shades on. "I have to go."

He turns to march past Vicky, but Vicky grabs him by the arm. "Congratulations, son."

But Sunny pulls his arm away.

"I didn't think you'd come," Bunty calls out in a measured tone.

Vicky approaches his desk. "You thought wrong."

He stops beside Ajay. "How's your mother?" he says in a mocking tone. "And your sisters? Are they all well?"

"Let's go." Tinu gives Vicky a foul look, leads Ajay off by the arm.

"We'll catch up later!" Vicky calls.

7.

In the corporate competence of Bunty's office Vicky's eyes probe with pointed interest the photographs on the walls: Bunty outside a sugar mill, Bunty on a construction site, Bunty and Ram Singh. He pauses at a yellowed photo of two teenage boys, posing outside the cabin of a truck, one shielding the sun from his eyes, the other with a pistol in his hand.

"Ah, there we are." Vicky smiles. "I thought I'd been erased completely."

Bunty sits on the edge of his table. "You were never fond of photos."

"Look at us," Vicky says, almost wistful.

"We were just boys."

Offhand, with a gleam in his eyes, Vicky turns. "And what did you want with this other boy?"

"Ajay."

"Is that his name?"

"You know it is." Bunty takes a seat behind his desk, lights a cigarette. "I wanted to thank him, that's all. He's been a loyal servant."

"And a good soldier."

A pointed glance. "To you maybe."

Vicky wags his finger. "Nothing gets past you."

Bunty regards Vicky with an unhurried eye. "Now tell me, brother, what else have you done?"

"Done?"

"Behind my back."

"Impossible, brother. You see all."

"Not out in the darkness where you choose to live."

"Choose?" Vicky turns from the photo. "If I recall, I was exiled."

Bunty's voice is flat. "You exiled yourself. You were in no fit state."

"And you were always the one to decide." Vicky checks himself, grins, opens his arms. "But look at me now!"

Bunty takes a deep breath, pulls his chair close to the desk, examines the papers lying there, like a father who's had enough of an impertinent child.

"Some of the things you're doing," Bunty goes on, "they have to stop."

"Like what?"

"You think I don't know," Bunty says, "about the trafficking. About those girls?"

"I assumed you turned a blind eye."

"How much do you even make from them?"

"Nothing in your league." Vicky stands in the middle of the floor, pulls himself up tall, clasps his hands together at his front. As if from nowhere, the giant emerges. "But then, money isn't everything."

Bunty shakes his head. "The world has changed. We're not goondas anymore."

"I was never a goonda," Vicky says.

"I forget." Bunny smiles. "You were a God-man."

"God is everywhere."

Bunty opens his drawer, takes something metal in his hand, flicks it through the air.

"God is a paisa coin."

Vicky catches the money and with sleight of hand makes it disappear.

Their argument is as old as the trick that always calms it.

Bunty softens, eases back into his chair. "You were always a hothead."

Vicky approaches him. "And you were always the rational one. But still," he leans forward across the desk, "it was your violence that started it all."

Bunty looks at him impassively.

"You know what I want," Vicky says. "Show me."

Bunty shakes his head dismissively. "This again?"

"For the sake of the past," Vicky persists. "Show me. Show me your hands."

Bunty hesitates, holds Vicky's eye.

Then he stubs out his cigarette.

Holds out his hands.

Turns them slowly, like secret cards.

Reveals two great scars.

Canyons slashed diagonal across his palms.

"I remember that day," Vicky says, his eyes bright. He reaches out and takes Bunty's hands in his own, runs his thumbs reverently along the gouged lines. "It gave me power. But it gave you so much more."

Bunty says nothing, but his eyes don't disagree.

"Do you still have it?" Vicky asks.

"The kite?" Bunty nods. "Of course."

Vicky closes his eyes. "Remember how it would fly?"

In his mind's eye, he sees the kite of their childhood, flying in a blue, cloudless sky.

The kite and its long string, laced with powdered glass.

Dancing, jerking, fighting other kites on rooftops in the sky.

Slicing through them, cutting them down.

In that mind's eye of his, he sees a face.

The grotesque face of a boy.

"Who's still alive, from that day?"

"Tinu. Me. You," Bunty replies.

A boy, covered in blood.

"We were wild," Vicky laughs, opening his eyes, letting go of the hands.

"We did what we had to do," Bunty replies. "And we moved on."

"Yes," Vicky says, waving his hand around the room, "and now you live in this airless hole, hiding from the world." He pulls the paisa coin from behind his ear, flicks it back across the room. "Power for power's sake." The coin bounces on Bunty's desk. "That's what you crave. For me, power was always something else. Pleasure. Pain."

Bunty lights a fresh cigarette. "That's why you didn't grow."

"Oh, I grew, brother. I grew away. That's the tragedy." Vicky draws a long deep breath, making a show of peering into the past. "I often think about those old days. Memory's a funny thing, don't you think? Who's to say what really happened. Not the history books. Not the mouths of the dead. Of course, there must be records *somewhere*. Of the things we did."

These words cause Bunty to withdraw. "Enough of the games," he says. "I have work to do. Go enjoy the evening."

Vicky heads to the door. "It's an auspicious day. The heavenly bodies are aligned."

"Just try not to cause any trouble."

Vicky grins and shrugs. "I have nothing planned."

At the quiet side of the mansion, away from the lights and workers and buzzing stalls, a Bolero sits parked. Ajay and Tinu appear from a side door. Ajay has been given new clothes. Black jeans, a plain black T-shirt. He's been given a mobile phone. A hand-drawn map with a sketch of the target on the back. A small wad of rupee notes.

"I don't like this," Tinu says. "I don't know why he sent you. But it's done." He looks into Ajay's bloodshot eyes. "How do you feel?"

"I'm fine."

"You have everything you need." He opens the rear door. "Take the first shot you get. The driver has your gun."

Ajay climbs in.

"He'll take you to Kashmiri Gate, then you'll go on foot."

He shuts the door on Ajay.

He turns away.

"The world's gone mad."

NIGHT

1.

Darkness falls like a curtain, guests spill in, spread like ice floes through the grounds, escorted by Siberian hostesses, tall, blond, sympathetic, displaying just enough skin. Powerful men form confidential rings. Drinks and canapés are passed around. The road outside is crammed with gleaming metal, an impatience of horns. Inside, everything strewn with flowers, light. The reception is a festival, a mela.

In Sunny's realm: men and women; drunk, hungover, high, drunk again. His friends, those men he has tempted and courted and ruined, those who are yet to be ruined but waiting, who are curious and foolhardy, the ones who have demeaned themselves long enough to be barnacles on a hull, those insignificant enough to be more or less ignored, or those who have just enough power not to care. They have colonized the distant villa and pool. Their comedowns have been massaged all day. They have begun to ride intoxication's next wave.

They march out from the mansion, skirting the large bright lawn in the dark, heading for the woodland behind, where, in a hidden hollow, the parallel party is due to begin. DJs from Tokyo and Berlin play psytrance and deep tech and tech house. Bartenders from the speakeasy Death&Taxis

craft bespoke cocktails of exotic ingredients. Farah's cousin Randy has managed the drugs. One hundred grams of cocaine, fifty grams of MDMA. Cream has been carried down from Malana. Grass up from Kerala. Eye drops of white fluff LSD have been shipped from Amsterdam. Some of the drugs have been stashed inside ornamental wooden eggs, waiting to be found. Others are handed out in goody bags, along with watches, perfume, and in one lucky bag, the key to a Maserati Quattroporte.

The main lawn is a more sedate affair. Sixty tables, each seating twelve. Each table with four bottles of Johnnie Walker, six bottles of Pol Roger on ice, boxes of Montecristo No. 4, all to be replenished at the blink of an eye.

There are thirteen separate stalls, with street foods of the world.

And a long, long bar with almost every drink under the sun.

There are ice sculptures, five thousand paper lanterns arranged in the trees, strung across invisible wires. Beyond the sea of tables and lights, two stages dominate the lawns. A company from Tel Aviv is in charge of lighting, sound, and set design. One stage for the classical musicians, the other for Bollywood stars. Right now, the old musicians play a gentle evening raag.

The guest list is a who's who of modern India. There are senior bureaucrats, police chiefs, ministers from across the political board, aviation ministry, environment, health, transport, mining, to name a few; there are God-men, retired bureaucrats, four media barons, editors and columnists of all stripes, a fierce and muckraking journalist known to hunt down the corrupt; there are film producers, directors, actors and actresses, legends and starlets and upcoming heroes; there are representatives from multinationals and major NGOs; there are captains of industry, mining barons, steel billionaires, property developers and shipping tycoons, three different jailed ministers, ostensibly on medical leave. There are royals, of course. There are poultry kings and Formula 1 drivers. There are cricketers and hockey stars, wrestlers and shooters, there are the TV anchors, noted surgeons, and cardiac specialists enjoying their fat cigars.

Everyone knows this is a rare sight; they may never see this again. Bunty Wadia and anyone who ever leaned on him, or has been leaned upon, all in one place. For this moment in time, they can try to guess how far his web has been spun.

2.

Ajay holds on to his precious minutes in the back of the car, knowing how soon they'll end. He has freed himself of all masters in his heart. And yet here he is once more, picked, chosen, delivered toward death. Why is he doing this? Ah yes. He looks at the photo of his sister again. The only thing in the world tying him to control. But even when he's rescued her, will he be rid of them? Cut adrift? No, they'll always have something over him. They can take her away any time they want. His mother and younger sister too. He can only pretend he doesn't care so much. The city swims in his head, the sulfury light. He hasn't seen the city at night since the night it all changed. He sees it now through the Mandrax, the whisky, through murderous eyes. He watches the world pass by, counts the money Tinu gave.

Two thousand rupees.

Would that be enough to . . . ?

He looks to the driver. "Show me the gun."

The driver looks back in the rear mirror. "When we arrive."

Sunny and Farah Wadia sit upon the throne, upon the dais, on the main lawn, side by side, receiving the blessings of guests. Their gifts are placed by several bearers on tables to the side, which groan under the weight. "You could at least smile," Farah grins through her teeth. "Why can't you be happy? You've got everything you could ever want or need."

Sunny says nothing in response, mutely accepts each guest's blessing and gift, presses his palms together in thanks each time.

"You're the most miserable sonofabitch in the world."

He's scanning the crowd behind his shades.

Looking for Dinesh.

Looking for Eli.

Trying to stave off a panic attack.

It's happening now. There's no turning back.

Gautam Rathore gets up from his table to join the queue. A passing waiter offers him a glass of champagne, which he politely declines. He's four years sober; bright-eyed and bushy-tailed. He has assumed gray hairs and a certain gravitas, ever since his father died in that helicopter crash. He's a property magnate now: his political contacts buy up and flip agricultural land, the kind of land where cities love to spread. Very soon he'll have the wealth and connections to become a major power broker in his state. When the proper kinds of leaders come in, who knows where the mining rights could land?

He stands before Sunny, hands over a simple envelope, lingers just a moment, perhaps hoping to hear a word. But no, Sunny only nods, presses his hands together in thanks. Looking at him for the first time in years, Gautam has a sudden Pavlovian urge to say something cutting and unkind.

Then he remembers his Twelve Steps.

Steps One through Twelve: Bunty Wadia.

He compliments Farah with sincerity and is gone.

"I need a bump," Farah says, when there's a lull. "I'd seriously consider one too." He doesn't move. "Trust me," she slaps his thigh, "I have everything you need." With that she gets up, waves at everyone, gives him one last look. She says, "I'll be by the lake, between here and the woods," and is gone too.

Alone.

Now Sunny is left alone.

On that throne, looking out at the guests, he has never felt so alone.

And it hits him, the panic attack he has been fighting all day, all week, all month. The panic of years. The loneliness of a lifetime. The rage. The knowledge that tonight, it is happening. It is most definitely happening. And he doesn't even know what *it* is. He's left all of *it* in Dinesh Singh's hands. All he knows is that their fathers will soon be pushed aside, embroiled in some business that will wear them down, allow Sunny and Dinesh to take the crown.

The crown.

Oh God!

The throne and the crown.

He can't even sit on *this* throne let alone that.

He looks out and comprehends the vastness of his father's world.

The intricacy of the ledger Bunty keeps in his head.

And he . . .

He can't even think two moves ahead in chess.

Why is he doing this?

Why?

Dinesh, he knows why. For power. And maybe even for the good of the state. For a belief in democracy, the rule of law, whatever that means. But he, Sunny Wadia, why? For revenge. For hatred. For a broken heart? For no reason at all. For a wish to erode everything associated with everything he's done wrong. Yes, once again he's detonating his life. Setting fire to the oceans, the atmosphere, turning his world into a dying star.

And what will be left when he's done?

Will they even pull it off?

No, he's so unfit for this.

He looks at Bunty at his table, cigar in mouth, as well-wishers clap him on his back, whisper in his ear.

He can't do this.

He can't even breathe.

Sweat is dripping down his forehead. Oh God.

It's one thing to privately nurture grudges, another to throw them out at the world.

Can he reach for his phone, call it off?

No. No.

Bro, it's done.

And what if Farah's right?

You've got everything you could ever want or need.

Why can't you be happy?

Why?

Then he remembers.

The sonogram.

The floating image of his floating child, lost forever in space and time.

He's submerged in an instant into the cold black ocean of his mind.

To the sand, the sea, the fire. The moment he believes his child was conceived.

Can't he stay here?

No.

He's taken to the night of the crash.

Blood. Whisky. Coke. Rage.

The smell of metal and petrol.

Ajay's bloodied face.

Neda's broken face.

And his father's words that have followed him all his life.

Ruthless.

You *have* to be ruthless.

Well, father, here I am.

Oh God.

Father.

Yes, he's drowning.

Drowning.

All I ever wanted was that life.

He clenches his fists.

Tells himself to stay calm.

That's when he sees Ram and Dinesh Singh arrive.

Fuck this.

He turns and flees toward the woods.

Farah is gazing into the water of the lake, the moon reflected above.

She doesn't look up.

"I wasn't sure you'd come."

"I need something," he says, stumbling forward, pulling off his shades to reveal his frightened eyes.

"Something is always better than nothing." She smiles.

Her voice soft, reassuring.

She takes him by his clammy hand and pulls him into the trees.

Back toward the mansion, the party is glowing. And from the hidden hollow, the thudding bass of psytrance drifts on the wind.

But here, it's just the two of them.

He shivers. "I need something."

"Shhh." She strokes his cheek, takes a baggie of coke from between her breasts. He considers it, shakes his head. "I need something more. I need . . ."

"Tell me what you need."

"I need . . ."

"Tell me."

His voice starts to break. "To be happy."

"Honey," she whispers, putting the coke back and bringing one hand down toward his cock. "I can make you happy."

He closes his eyes.

Holds back the panic.

With practiced fingers she finds her way in, runs her thumb gently up and down his lifeless shaft.

"With me," she says, "happiness is guaranteed."

"Not that," he says. "I need something more."

"I've got what you need."

With her free hand she unclasps her purse, reaches in for a pill box.

"Open it," she says. She feels his cock going soft as his attention goes to the box, so she gives it a little squeeze. "Ah, ah, ah, you only get the good stuff if you're good to me. *Concentrate*."

But it's no use.

"What is it?" he asks.

Six big bombs of MDMA.

"The happiness," she replies, "that you seek."

3.

Ajay stands on the edge of Kashmiri Gate, the bus terminal lit bright behind him, with its many families wrapped in shawls, sleeping among their bags, waiting for their departure in the cooling night as other buses pull away. This is the place he arrived full of hope, with the card of Sunny Wadia in his hand. Now he holds Tinu's map of the grounds he must infiltrate, the gun he must use, and the sketch of the man he must kill. One way or another, he's come a long way.

He looks out over the road toward Nicholson Cemetery, the flyover under which the junkies live off to the right. He dashes out, dodging the traffic, leaps over the divider, clears it to the other side. He buys a pack of cigarettes and a box of matches and enters the colony of Civil Lines.

At the reception, Ram and Dinesh Singh take their tables with their entourage.

All talk of a rift between father and son has been put to bed. Dinesh brokered a deal with the farmers that left everyone satisfied. Their dynasty is heading into the next election weakened but still strong. Ram Singh makes a beeline for Bunty while Dinesh sips a soda and does the rounds.

In the darkness of an unlit pavement beneath a neem tree, Ajay smokes a cigarette and takes a closer look at his gun. An 8-round Luger with the serial number shaved off. The driver told him: it's tough, it'll do the job. He checks the safety by the grip, slips it into the front of his jeans. He opens the map again, gets his bearings, heads into the alleyway ahead of him. Halfway down the alley, on the left, a change in the brickwork marks the place where one property turns into the next. This is the point to climb in. Once over, he leaps into bushes and crouches, listening for dogs.

Feels his heart and his head throb.

With great care, he looks out onto a pristine lawn and the squat colonial bungalow beyond. The place seems quite deserted, only some lights on at the front.

He crouches, silent.

Waits awhile.

Waits.

Feels the reassuring weight of the gun.

Sunny sits alone on the crest of the mound that shields his wilder party from prying eyes, peering down into the strobe-lit hollow with its sweaty, dancing bodies, its laughing, screaming faces, its bar, its tent, its fires. He can't touch a thing of it. But he's waiting with a stomach full of butterflies for the fruits of the MDMA to arrive.

The MDMA.

Yes.

He's taken a heroic dose.

He can feel it in his nausea, in his glitchy eyes, in the ebbing molecules of life.

He's waiting for it to tell him everything will be all right.

He feels him before he sees him.

"You're looking the wrong way," Vicky says. He eases himself to the grass with a surprisingly vulnerable groan. "I'm getting old," he says, and looks at Sunny tenderly.

Sunny shudders at his immediacy.

"What do you want from me?"

Ajay makes his way around the perimeter to the front of the bungalow. The front door is open, and there are lights on inside.

How long should he wait here?

Should he climb onto the roof?

Should he peer into every window? Or should he just walk in?

He tries to get his story straight, but he doesn't have one. Only withdrawal from Mandrax and a gun. He takes a step into the driveway, and a fat black dog trots out from behind the door. Waddles toward him, leg wagging.

"I see you've made a friend!"

From the garden to the right, a young, stocky, bearded man appears, wrapped in a heavy shawl. He shows no surprise, no fear. He doesn't seem to think Ajay is out of place.

Ajay doesn't know what to say.

"Don't worry, she won't bite. She only farts! But that's a small price to pay for keeping me warm at night." He puts his palms together. "I'm Brother Sanjay, by the way. Are you lost?"

"Yes," Ajay hears himself say.

"Can you speak?"

"Yes."

"Perhaps you need to rest?"

"I'd like some water."

"Of course, of course! A fundamental right to all!" He guides Ajay inside by the arm. "And where are you coming from, my friend?"

"Nowhere," he says.

"Oh dear," Brother Sanjay replies. "A bad place to be! Though they say 'ignorance is bliss,' don't they? But I prefer knowledge, isn't it? Well, you're clearly in need of a wash and meal. Believe me, you're not the first!"

Beyond the reception room, an ancient book-lined study with a fireplace.

Warm light.

Peace of mind.

"What do I want from you?" Vicky acts surprised. "Nothing! Nothing at all!"

"Then leave me alone!" he cries, and he's sickened by the way he sounds like a petulant child.

Vicky lays a hand on his shoulder. "It just hurts my heart, that's all, to see what you've become."

What is he supposed to say to that?

"Yes, it hurts my heart," Vicky reaffirms.

"What have I become?"

"You're falling apart."

Sunny shakes his head.

"But it's OK," Vicky goes on. "I've studied your charts. I saw it all from the start. Everything you've done, the depths to which you've sunk, the misery you've endured, it's leading you to this. Today's the day you'll become a man."

"Who's there? Who's there?"

Brother Sanjay leads Ajay deeper into the bungalow.

"We have a guest!" Brother Sanjay shouts.

They pass through an inner arch into a dining room, where a solid hardwood table, space enough for twenty, runs lengthways down the middle of the room. But there's only one man, an elderly white priest, hairless, almost deaf and almost blind, sitting at the head, eating sausage and mash.

"What's this!?" he shouts.

"A weary traveler!" Brother Sanjay replies.

"No, I don't want to buy a radio!"

"Ignore him, he gets like this." Brother Sanjay pats Ajay with a reassuring hand.

With that said, the old priest retreats into his own world.

"Here," Brother Sanjay says, "sit, I'll bring you food."

Ajay looks around him, shaken and confused.

Moved by the spontaneous kindness.

Mindful of the gun.

The mission at hand.

Sanjay returns with two plates of rice and dal, sabzi on the side. He looks at the clock on the wall and makes a tutting noise. "He's always late."

"Who?!" the old priest shouts.

"Peter Mathews," Brother Sanjay replies.

"Leave my sausages alone!" the old priest shouts.

A gruff, bearded cook appears. "Father! Everything OK?"

"He wants my sausages!"

The cook winks at Ajay. To the priest he shouts, "I'll keep him away."

As the cook disappears, another figure enters the hall. Silently, meditative, head down, his hair cut into an unfashionable bowl.

He bows to the old priest first, takes a seat opposite Ajay, next to Sanjay.

"Good evening." He places his hand on his heart. "I'm Peter Mathews."

"Why are you doing this to me?" Sunny holds his head in his hands.

"I remember the day you were born," Vicky replies. "It was an eclipse. A beautiful day. I wished I could have been by your mother's side."

"Please. Stop torturing me!"

He can feel the MDMA rising, unmooring him from reality, loosening the mortar of his rage.

"I regret all these years," Vicky says.

Sunny turns to look at him and he clearly sees his own face.

"What are you doing to me?" he says again.

Vicky gives him a distorted smile.

"Nothing you haven't already done to yourself." From his pinky finger he slides off a gold and emerald ring. "She wanted me to give you this."

Sunny stares into the emerald pulsing green.

"I told her I would wait."

"I've been through my life convinced more and more," Peter Mathews says, "that I'm dying all the time. I can't help this feeling. Every time I cross the road, I believe I've been hit by a car. One version of me keeps walking, but the other has died. These are terrible thoughts to have, I know, but it's something I can't shake. Have you heard of the multiverse, Brother Sanjay?"

"I can't say I have."

"There are infinite worlds where every possible world plays out. In this one, I could stab myself right now," Peter Mathews says, "or you, Brother Sanjay, or our new friend here, who has just arrived."

"Oh dear."

"Here we'd all be dead, but in the other worlds we'd still be alive."

"It doesn't bear thinking about," Brother Sanjay says, before perking up. "Still, it's no excuse to be unkind."

Ajay keeps staring at Peter Mathews.

Does he know?

Does he suspect?

Should he pull his gun out and shoot him dead?

Peter Mathews looks back at Ajay and smiles.

"Where have you come from?" he asks.

"He's from nowhere," Brother Sanjay jokingly replies.

Mathews pours himself a glass of water. "No, he's come from somewhere else tonight."

"I came from jail," Ajay says.

"Yes," Mathews nods, "I could guess from your tattoo. I work with prisoners all the time. And what did you do?"

"Killed people."

"Oh dear," Brother Sanjay laughs, "maybe *you'll* be the one to kill us to-night."

Sunny holds the ring in his hand, shimmering, pulsating.

He starts to grin.

He says the word.

"Rastogi."

Vicky nods sympathetically and smiles.

"Rastogi," Sunny says again and climbs to his feet.

Starts to laugh.

Uncontrollably.

"Yes," Vicky nods, "yes, Rastogi!"

"No," Sunny shakes his head. "No. You don't understand!"

His laughter fills the air.

"I'm free of both of you!" he cries.

He tosses the ring toward Vicky.

"Where do you think Ajay went?!"

Vicky's smile vanishes.

Sunny staggers backward laughing.

"Sunil Rastogi's going to die!"

He doesn't know whether he's tripped or he's pushed.

But Sunny comes tumbling down.

A monster from the hills.

He lands with a bump on the ground.

In time with the thumping bass.

A dreadlocked hippie is juggling fire to his left.

The fire elongates in Sunny's mind.

Says good things about the world.

Tells him it's going to be all right.

He jumps to his feet, starts to dance, throws his arms in the air.

They're all watching him.

Calling out his name.

Sunny Wadia is returned!

SUN-NY!

SUN-NY!

And above them, unseen by all, Vicky Wadia takes out his mobile phone.

"One second, please," Peter Mathews says, removing his battered Nokia, holding a finger in the air. "Yes?" he answers pleasantly. "I see. I see," he sighs. "I can't promise anything. But I'll try."

He hangs up the phone, slips it back into his pocket again.

And Ajay's finger flicks off the safety around the Luger's wooden grip.

"Is everything all right?" Brother Sanjay inquires.

Peter Mathews says, "Ev . . ."

But before he finishes speaking, he's on his feet, wrapping his arm round Sanjay's neck, pulling him to his feet, grabbing the old priest's sausage knife from the table as he goes, dragging Sanjay at knifepoint toward the rear pantry behind.

It happens so quick, and Ajay is slow.

By the time his gun is out, Mathews and Sanjay are gone.

The old priest shouts, "What the hell is going on!?"

In the pantry, Mathews drags the protesting Sanjay toward the outer door. As Ajay turns the corner in pursuit, Mathews smashes Brother Sanjay's head against the wall, shoves him forward through the air so that Ajay can't take a shot. And when Ajay stumbles over him, Peter Mathews is gone.

A three-story guesthouse rises behind.

Ajay hears footsteps up the stairwell.

Hears the cries of the cook.

Looks up to see Mathews turning the corner of the stairs on the first floor.

———

He's in pursuit, racing up the stairs, as the cook dashes out with a cleaver in hand.

On the first floor, all the doors are closed on either side.

And he hears footsteps going higher.

He runs after them, stumbles in his haste.

When he scrambles up to the second floor, he sees an open room.

Without thinking he lurches in.

Runs across the threshold gun drawn, ready to fire.

But there's no one there.

By the time he hears the footsteps again, it's almost too late.

He turns to see a metal pipe crashing down toward his face.

He raises his left hand.

The crack of bone.

And now Mathews is on top of him.

They tangle, grapple, Ajay holding the gun for all he's worth while Mathews tries to prize it from his right hand.

"You're ruining everything," Mathews yells.

Ajay's left hand is in agony now.

So he kicks up with his legs instead, tries to throw Mathews off, but Mathews is disturbingly strong. With no choice left, Ajay steels himself. With all his strength, he jabs his throbbing left hand into Mathews's throat.

The terrible pain shoots straight up Ajay's arm.

But the deed is done.

Mathews falls back, choking.

Gasping for air.

And now Ajay has the freedom to put this monster in the sights of his gun.

All he has to do is pull the trigger.

But he can't.

"Wait, wait!" Mathews cries, tears in his eyes.

And Ajay waits.

That's all it takes. Mathews's lips start to curl into an eerie smile.

And Ajay says: "You're Sunil Rastogi."

Mathews nods.

"I am."

Ajay watches as Rastogi comes to the fore. The remnants of meek Mathews evaporate.

Now Rastogi glances toward the door, at the growing commotion downstairs. "They'll come for you," he says, "you know this, yes? You better shoot me now, or you better run."

"I have to shoot you," Ajay replies.

"Then do it."

Ajay's hand trembles.

"I can't," he says.

"Why?"

"I don't know."

"I think I know why." Rastogi smiles.

Ajay's voice is a whisper. "Tell me."

"You don't want to be a slave anymore."

"But I have to kill you," Ajay says. "I have no choice."

"You're in pain." Rastogi smiles. "I can see it in your eyes. I've been there too, we're like brothers, you and I."

"I have to shoot," Ajay says.

"Remember downstairs," Rastogi says, "what I talked about. Imagine a universe where you didn't need to kill. Where would you be?"

He can see Ajay's hand losing focus, shaking.

"Home," Ajay says.

"Home?"

Ajay closes his eyes. "In the mountains."

"So go back there."

"I can't!" Ajay cries.

With great distress and searing pain, Ajay slides his fingers into his jeans pocket and pulls the photo he's been carrying for so long.

He holds the photo pinched in his swelling hand.

Rastogi takes it from him, brings it to his eyes. He devours the image, the girl in the bed, in the brothel, so fierce, so afraid. Rastogi looks from the photo to the man before him.

"Who's this?" Rastogi says, his voice softening, conciliatory.

"My sister!" Ajay sobs. "My sister! I have to kill you to save her."

"Brother." Rastogi begins to laugh. "That's not your sister."

"What do you mean?"

"I mean they lied to you."

"What do you mean?!"

"I mean to say, that's not your sister."

"How?!"

"Because I know this girl. I know her only too well. She hails from Bihar, my friend. Her name is Neha. This is a brothel in Benares. I know because I used to work there."

"No. That's not true! She's my sister."

"Maybe she is and I'm wrong,"

"She is!"

"Or maybe they lied to you, brother. Listen, I *know* this girl. Look at her! She doesn't even look like you."

Rastogi holds the photo to Ajay's face.

Ajay looks at the girl as if for the first time.

And his whole world falls away.

Maybe it's true. Maybe this is not her.

And what if that's so?

"Yes, they lied to you," Rastogi says. "Like they lie to everyone. They promised to save her, didn't they?"

Ajay looks up. "Yes."

"But really they sent you here to die."

Ajay's head throbs and pounds, the mandrax comedown, the shock, the agony of confusion, the agony of his swollen hand.

From downstairs, the sounds of a mob.

Rastogi points to the open window behind.

"You can wait here for them to catch you. Kill you. Turn you in. Or you can run. You can run and be free."

Up the stairs, the cook leads the way, followed by several neighborhood boys wielding cricket bats, hockey sticks, kitchen knives. They huddle together, move forward fearfully, shouting among themselves. There! They yell at the door, stumble in.

Peter Mathews lies sobbing on the ground.

"He tried to kill me!" he cries. He points at the window. "He ran."

The cook darts to the window, slashing his cleaver at the night.

"Go after him," Peter Mathews cries.

The mob complies, running out the door, down the stairs, spreading out, yelling for the property to be searched.

Sunil Rastogi picks himself up off the ground, retrieves the photograph that Ajay, in his desolation, left behind.

He smiles to himself.

Considers her body, her face.

He's never seen this woman before in his life.

Now on the approach road to the Wadia mansion, a new convoy arrives.

A fleet of vehicles from the Special Task Force and the CBI.

Rastogi strolls through the heart of the bungalow while the search for the intruder intensifies. Across his back, a long green zip-up duffel bag is strapped.

He walks straight out the front door, grabbing a bike helmet as he goes.

As he passes out the front gate, he takes out his phone.

He dials a number. "The problem's solved."

In the lane, he climbs on a Yamaha sports bike for which he has the key, starts the engine, revs it hard, and rides out toward the bus terminal.

At the reception, the Bollywood stars are dancing onstage.

Bunty is smoking his cigar, content with the world.

Dinesh Singh looks at Vicky.

Vicky smiles at his phone.

And in the hollow, Sunny's mind explodes.

Pleasure. Pain.

He has no masters.

He forgives the world.

Everything is going to be OK.

The convoy is now at the Wadia gates.

Security comes to greet them. What do they want?

Don't they know who lives here?

Don't they know there's a wedding on?

They do.

They don't care.

They have a warrant to search the property.

And to arrest Ram Singh and Bunty Wadia.

A signature is required.

Vicky looks across to Bunty as Bunty answers his ringing phone.

Puts his feet up as he watches the disquiet among the staff.

Watches several VIP guests answering their phones.

Watches the head of security rushing to Tinu.

Tinu's face turning gray.

In the distance, the many police vehicles glide up the driveway.

All the while, Bunty remains seated, wearing a dignified smile.

But several government officials, bureaucrats, ministers, are rising from their seats. Phones are lighting up. Calls are made.

What's happening now?

Does anyone know?

To arrest a sitting chief minister and the father of the groom on a wedding night. And Bunty Wadia no less. In front of guests.

It's unheard of.

Someone will pay.

The warrant is shown.

Chaos reigns.

Ram Singh begins to rage.

Documents have come to light—photos, letters, tapes, videos, sound recordings. A series of murders, ransoms, corrupt undertakings, committed from the 1990s until the present day. Raids are being conducted right now across UP. Everything comes back to Bunty Wadia and Ram Singh.

Ram Singh loses his head.

Insults the officers, shoves them away.

The fact that this has been done to him. It's a sin.

That someone could fear him so little.

What's more, he knows that it's his son.

Although Bunty maintains his calm, the reception is teetering on the brink.

The many flashing lights.

The men in uniform.

Ram Singh making a scene.

A scuffle. A small riot.

Ram's men attack.

Weapons are drawn.

And now the crowd is in complete disarray.

Some VVIPs are already fleeing, heading for their drivers and cars.

Others are wading over to speak with the police.

And Bunty is smiling genially.

This is what Sunny sees, pulled by Eli from the paradise of his oblivion.

In the swarming driveway of the mansion Tinu pulls Sunny aside.

Drags him toward one of their SUVs.

"They're taking him in and we're following."

He shovels the sweating, wild-eyed Sunny into the back seat.

Eli jumps in beside him, stowing his Jericho.

The police are taking Ram and Bunty in separate SUVs.

Streaming down the driveway toward the gate.

Tinu on the phone, shouting.

And Sunny lost in all the lights.

"It's beautiful," he cries. He puts his hand on Eli's shoulder. "Is it real?"

"Yes, you fucking moron," Eli says. "Is fucking real."

The convoy emerges from the colony road and speeds away.

Tinu, Sunny, and Eli three cars behind the one in which Bunty is held.

"Who is doing this?" Tinu shouts. "Find out!" He hangs up. "Whoever has done this is worse than dead." He turns to Sunny. "He'll be out in an hour. They have nothing on him. This is a disgrace."

Sunny nods emphatically.

"Everything's going to be OK."

Ahead, in Bunty's SUV, studied quiet.

The officers are deferential, respectful.

Bunty sits bolt upright, betraying no anger or fear.

The convoy reaches Mehrauli.

A Tempo has broken down ahead. A bottleneck.

The police at the head of the convoy climb out.
Begin to direct cars, get others to push the Tempo out of the way.
Sunny winds down the window and puts his head out.
Tries to climb up to see.

The whine of the high-pitched engine is what they hear before they see.
The high-pitched whine of a Yamaha sports bike shifting down the gears.
On the other side of the central divider, against traffic.
Speeding from behind.
Sunny watches it glide past.
Coasting.
Slowing.
Stopping.
Level with Bunty's Task Force SUV.

The helmeted rider plants his left leg into the ground.
Removes the object from his duffel bag.
Locks it in his arms.
Metal.
Dark.
Long.

Bunty glances to his right.
In that split second he sees.
He pulls the cop across him as a human shield.

The muzzle flash.
The ear-splitting chunk.
Of the fully auto AR-15 with the hundred-round drum.
Decimating the police SUV.

Slicing through metal and flesh.
Before the bike kicks into gear again.
Spins east at the junction toward Sainik Farms.

Eli is on the far side.
By the time he's out firing shots it's in vain.
The cops are next, with their Glock 17s.
But the bike is gone away.

Sunny staggers onto the road.
Stares at what's left.
Of the shredded, slaughtered meat inside.
It was once his father.

Past one a.m., somewhere in Punjab, the HRTC bus to Manali pulls over at the dhaba on the side of the road. The passengers file out sleepily, Ajay among them in his black T-shirt, his black pants. His Luger has already been thrown. In this world all that belongs to him is a few thousand rupees, and his grief, and his freedom. He'll vanish into the mountains of his youth. He takes his seat, orders chai and dal fry. Then he looks up at the newsflash on the TV.

CONCORD REBEL

Other Books by AUGUST DERLETH

Walden West
Village Year
Village Daybook
The Wisconsin: River of a Thousand Isles
Still Small Voice: The Biography of Zona Gale
H. P. L.: A Memoir
The Milwaukee Road: Its First 100 Years

Wisconsin in Their Bones
Country Growth
Sac Prairie People
Place of Hawks

Bright Journey
The House on the Mound
The Hills Stand Watch
Wind Over Wisconsin
Restless Is the River
Shadow of Night
Still Is the Summer Night
Evening in Spring
The Shield of the Valiant

Hawk on the Wind
And You, Thoreau!
Rendezvous in a Landscape
Selected Poems
Country Poems
West of Morning

And, for Younger Readers

The Moon Tenders
The Mill Creek Irregulars
The Pinkertons Ride Again
A Boy's Way
The Ghost of Black Hawk Island
Sweet Land of Michigan
The Country of the Hawk
The Captive Island
It's a Boy's World
Land of Gray Gold
Land of Sky-Blue Waters
Fr. Marquette and the Great Rivers
St. Ignatius and the Company of Jesus
Columbus and the New World
Oliver, the Wayward Owl
Wilbur, the Trusting Whippoorwill

CONCORD REBEL

A LIFE OF
HENRY DAVID THOREAU

By AUGUST DERLETH

CHILTON BOOK COMPANY

PHILADELPHIA   NEW YORK   LONDON

PS
3053
.D4

For

WALTER HARDING

*who has earned the gratitude of Thoreauvians
throughout the world . . .*

Foreword

The single business of Henry Thoreau, during forty-odd years of eager activity, was to discover an economy calculated to provide a satisfying life.

VERNON L. PARRINGTON
Main Currents in American Thought

IT is seldom in the history of mankind that a writer, generally ignored in his lifetime—one whose work has been dismissed by critics and largely gone unread by the public in his own time—should achieve many years after his death an eminent place among the leading writers of his country and among the most influential writers in the world.

Henry David Thoreau was such a writer.

Yet Thoreau was a rebel against the commonly held social credos of his time, a profoundly religious man who had "signed off," as he put it, from his church, a rigid disciplinarian and believer in order who had denied the authority of the state, a poet whose preferred medium of expression was prose, an exponent of freedom of thought in a society which followed the contemporary patterns in popular thought—and valued what Thoreau scorned—material success.

His work is the testament of his rebellion, from *Walden*, which has become the companion of thousands, to *Civil Disobedience*, which was the inspiration of Mahatma Gandhi and other liberal leaders throughout the world.

ix

His life was not one of physical action, but of adventure in the domain of his mind. He found his "occasions" in himself, as he said, and in so doing he achieved the distinction of being "the only man of leisure" in Concord, Massachusetts, because the work he did was less visible to his fellow-citizens than the labor of a ditch-digger. Writing was his "business," he said, and he walked abroad in the environs of his native place "to see what I have caught in my traps, which I set for facts."

Thoreau's vision is one which ought to make an irresistible appeal to the young. No mentally alive young man or woman can read *Walden* and come away from it willing to accept readily the common conventions of the world or the shabby goals set for the mass of men by their materialistic society. "The cost of a thing is the amount of what I call life which is required to be exchanged for it," he wrote, and he went his way through life determined to exact the most from every moment at the least cost in living, and this, despite his limitations—for he was a bachelor, and he made his sacrifices only for himself, which is considerably easier than making sacrifices which might involve dependents in deprivations—he did.

G RATEFUL acknowledgment is made to Houghton Mifflin Company, as the authorized publishers of the works of Henry D. Thoreau, for permission to quote at will from *The Writings of Henry D. Thoreau;* and to the New York University Press, for permission to do likewise from *The Correspondence of Henry D. Thoreau,* edited by Walter Harding and Carl Bode, as well as to the owners of previously unpublished letters appearing for the first time in that book.

Contents

CONCORD REBEL

CHAPTER 1

"If I Knew How It Began . . ."

I came into this world, not chiefly to make this a good place to live in, but to live in it, be it good or bad. —WALDEN

THERE was little in Henry David Thoreau's background and youth to foretell his course in life. He was born July 12, 1817, at his Grandmother Minott's farm on the old Virginia road not far outside Concord, of French-Huguenot and Scottish-Quaker ancestry. When he was baptized three months later by Dr. Ezra Ripley, the leading divine of Concord, he was named David Henry Thoreau, and so he was called until he chose to reverse his given names when he was twenty, at about the time he was graduated from Harvard.

His father was John Thoreau, born in 1787 in Boston. His mother was Cynthia Dunbar, born in the same year in Keene, New Hampshire, the daughter of the Reverend Asa Dunbar. Henry had an older sister, Helen, an older brother, John, and was yet to have a younger sister, Sophia. His father, following the family tradition, had learned storekeeping in Salem and Concord before going into business on borrowed money. He had failed in business, and at the time of Henry's birth the family was quite poor even by the standards of 1817.

Thoreau's earliest years were unsettled because of his father's attempts to establish himself. His father tried his hand at various enterprises. For a while he farmed for

1

his mother-in-law, but he was ill-suited to farming. He next tried keeping a store at Chelmsford, but he failed at this, too, and he turned to keeping a school in Boston, but he had little talent for teaching. He then tried to become a salesman, directing his attention to the Indians who were still to be found in various places throughout New England. This proved so unrewarding that finally, in 1823, when Henry was six, he moved back to Concord and set himself up as a pencil-maker, at which he presently made a modest success.

The Thoreaus were a closely-knit family of lifelong duration. John was a relatively grave man who said very little. He stood somewhat shorter than his wife, and had a tendency toward deafness. He was not prepossessing, but likable, and was far more studious than his wife. Mrs. Thoreau was lively and bustling, with an inclination toward gayety. She was a kindly, shrewd woman, who could sometimes make sharp observations about her fellow-citizens, though she was not in any sense mean and she was very much liked. She loved to talk, and soon had the reputation of being the biggest talker in all Concord. She was also a great reader, much given to sentiment and emotion, and capable of very strong opinions, particularly on such subjects as slavery, to which she was strongly opposed.

Concord was at this time—and remained for most of Thoreau's life—a village of something less than two thousand inhabitants, though the country men who lived in the surrounding township of Concord brought the total population to a little over that figure. It was a typical New England village, one of tree-naved streets lined with white painted houses—as well as some which were not painted at all. There was a village square just past rows of shops put up on a one-time mill dam along a brook. It was a village weighted with ministers at the one end of the social scale, and tavern-keepers at the other. Its most substantial citizens during most of Thoreau's life were Samuel Hoar, the lawyer who owned the most imposing house in the village, and the Reverend Ezra Ripley, pastor of Concord's First Parish, Congregational.

It was a village open to the country on all sides, and the country, so easy of access, was singularly beautiful, not any longer as wild as it had been in the years of Concord's founding over a century and a half before, but still offering the walker in its precincts sight and sound of many a wild creature, furred and feathered. It was a country of little rivers—the Musketaquid or Grassgrown River—the meadow stream, the Sudbury, flowing into the Assabet—which, together, made up the Concord River on its way through marshes and meadows toward the Merrimack. The rivers were bounded by low, glaciated hills, among which were lakes and swamps—one of them, on the way to Cambridge, a pleasant, tree-girt lake named Walden, which charmed Thoreau even as a child. It was a country of pine and hardwood trees, of maple and spruce swamps, of huckleberry and cranberry stands, of knolls like Fair Haven, from which the eye fell upon Wachusett, a small mountain standing solitary in the landscape, and Monadnock.

Except for isolated journeys and his Harvard years, Thoreau's life was bounded by Concord village and town, by Walden and Fair Haven and the rivers. In this setting he spent a boyhood like most boyhoods in New England villages. He drove the cow to pasture, ran barefooted, went fishing—sometimes of nights beside a blazing bonfire to attract the bullheads in Walden Pond—hunted a little, though he abandoned this relatively early in life, and flourished in the aura of his affectionate family. He

3

could hardly help, as a boy, being somewhat dominated by women, for not only was his mother clearly the dominant force in the Thoreau household, but the regular boarders which the Thoreaus took in were all women, not the least among them being Aunt Louisa Dunbar, who joined the household when Grandmother Minott died.

Despite a good sense of humor and easy gregariousness, Thoreau was a grave boy. His gravity earned him the nickname of "Judge," bestowed upon him by no less a local eminence than Samuel Hoar. He soon grew interested in books and learning. He began to go to school in Boston, but he subsequently attended Concord grammar school. He wrote his first essay, *The Seasons,* at the age of ten; it offered no startling clue to what he was to do later in life and demonstrated only that he had a well organized mind, a love of nature, and an ability to write, none of which was unusual among alert children. He had already developed a boy's affection for the countryside and an inclination toward solitude though this was not an indication of the pursuits of his maturity, however much it may seem to have presaged his later life. In his mature years, he referred to his early years in glowing terms, writing in his *Journal,* "My life was ecstasy."

Following grammar school, Thoreau prepared for Harvard at the Concord Academy, which offered courses in Latin, Greek, and French, and where he could learn music and dancing as well. Either here—or from his lively Uncle Charles Dunbar, who led a roving, carefree existence, and of whom Thoreau was very fond—he first learned to play the flute, which was ever afterward to remain part of his life. Certainly here he learned to dance, which was hardly necessary for entry to Harvard.

4

He was ready for Harvard at sixteen. There was scarcely enough money at home to send Thoreau there, though his father could help pay his expenses. By this time Thoreau's sister Helen had begun to teach, and offered to help; so did his aunts. With this support, and sharing the beneficiary funds offered by Harvard to worthy and needy students, Thoreau went to Cambridge in August, 1833, and was entered at Harvard on September 1.

He roomed at Hollis Hall throughout his Harvard years, sometimes alone, sometimes with a roommate. His meals at commons cost him $1.35 a week. Having not yet "signed off" from his church, he attended chapel; he did not wear the required black, but went in a green homespun coat because he did not own and could not afford a black one.

He studied the classics under Professor Felton and Jones Very, a poet who also tutored him. He took rhetoric under Professor Edward Tyrrell Channing, from whose exacting requirements it took Thoreau some time to escape. He was primarily interested in the classics, mastering Greek and Latin early, though he also studied mathematics and, by means of books from the Harvard library, science. Since he knew French, he may also have studied this language at Harvard, and he took an informal course in German at which Henry Wadsworth Longfellow talked about German literature with an informality which, combined with Longfellow's wine-colored waistcoats, very probably left Thoreau cold.

He stood close to the top of his class, but he went his own way too much to reach the top. He made few friends, though there were brief friendships—A. G. Peabody, Henry Vose, Charles Wyatt Rice—evidence of which exists in letters, but none of these was a lasting friendship. One of his classmates, John Weiss, remembered Thoreau at Harvard in a reminiscence-review published in *The Christian Examiner,* July, 1865.

"He would smile to overhear that word (career) applied to the reserve and unaptness of his college life. He was not signalized by a plentiful distribution of the parts and honors which fall to the successful student. . . . We could sympathize with his tranquil indifference to college honors, but we did not suspect the fine genius that was developing under that impassive demeanor. Of his private tastes there is little of consequence to recall, excepting that he was devoted to the old English literature, and had a good many volumes of the poetry from Gower and Chaucer down through the era of Elizabeth. . . .

"But he passed for nothing, it is suspected, with most of us; for he was cold and unimpressible. The touch of his hand was moist and indifferent, as if he had taken up something when he saw your hand coming, and caught your grasp upon it. How the prominent, gray-blue eyes seemed to rove down the path, just in advance of his feet, as his grave Indian stride carried him down to University Hall! This down-looking habit was Chaucer's also, who walked as if a great deal of surmising went on between the earth and him . . .

"He did not care for people; his classmates seemed very remote. This reverie hung always about him, and not so loosely as the odd garments which the pious household care furnished. Thought had not yet awakened his countenance; it was serene, but rather dull, rather plodding. The lips were not yet firm; there was almost a look of smug satisfaction lurking round their corners. . . . The nose was prominent, but its curve fell forward without firmness over the upper lip . . . Yet his eyes were sometimes searching, as if he had dropped, or ex-

6

pected to find, something. It was the look of Nature's own child learning to detect her wayside secrets. . . .

"Thoreau was always indisposed to call at the ordinary places for his spiritual refreshment; and he went farther than most persons when apparently he did not go so far . . .

"But he had no animal spirits for our sport or mischief."

Thoreau was not at home at Harvard as he was in Concord, nor did he make much effort to be. He had come to study. He showed no interest in any of the literary groups or social sets which then flourished at Harvard. He did not contribute to the *Harvardiana*. He appeared to prefer—if not outright solitude—at least obscurity, though he happily accepted the friendship of Charles Stearns Wheeler, one of the promising scholars at Harvard, and went camping with him. Yet he was not lonely, however much alone he was.

He was happy with the library. He read Virgil, Cicero, *The Greek Reader, Adam's Latin Grammar,* Horace, Demosthenes, *Roman Antiquities, Greek Exercises,* Seneca, Euripides, Homer—he read, in fact, all the classics he could get his hands on. To some extent, that reading— and the rhetoric he was taught—was reflected in the themes he wrote for his Harvard classes. Of more than fifty, he saved thirty essays; they were on such topics as *Punishment, The Morality of Lying, The Simple Style, The Superior and the Common Man,* and, curiously, *Shall We Keep Journals?* Yet in his last year at Harvard, he indicated the direction of his thoughts when he wrote in *Conformity in Things Unessential* that duty consisted "in conformity to the dictates of an inward arbiter. . . . Mere conformity to another's habits or customs is never, properly speaking, a duty. . . . The fear of displeasing the world ought not in the least to influence my actions."

Thoreau was not in unbroken attendance during his four years at Harvard. It was the custom of Harvard to allow needy students one leave of absence to earn money. In December, 1835, Thoreau took his leave. He was then 18, and he planned to earn money by teaching. He taught in Canton, Massachusetts, for a period of six weeks, and at Canton stayed with the Reverend Orestes A. Brownson. Brownson was not quite twice Thoreau's age. His own children were in the Canton school, and it was Brownson who examined Thoreau for the position and who recommended him to the board of education.

Brownson was an extraordinarily vital man, hardly the ideal model of a country minister. His mind was ever searching; he was seldom contented with any situation, and he was turning more and more toward the socialist ideal, with a kind of infectious enthusiasm. He was hungry for any new idea and had an idealistic notion of helping labor in his support of the Workingmen's Party. He had only recently gone into the ministry in the Unitarian church, then a great force for intellectual growth within a socio-moral frame. It was perhaps inevitable that something of his enthusiasm would rub off on to Thoreau.

At the time of their introduction to each other, Brownson was studying German. Thoreau joined him in this—perhaps not alone because Brownson was doing it, but because Carlyle, in whose writings Thoreau had developed a strong interest, had done so. In the course of this study Thoreau listened to a flow of ideas the like of which he had not encountered at Harvard. Brownson was Thoreau's first stimulating encounter outside Harvard, and though Thoreau was actually a teacher in the

8

Canton school but a month and a half, yet he was to write to Brownson almost two years later,

"I have never ceased to look back with interest, not to say satisfaction, upon the short six weeks which I passed with you. They were an era in my life—the morning of a new *Lebenstag*. They are to me as a dream that is dreamt, but which returns from time to time in all its original freshness. Such a one as I would dream a second and a third time, and then tell before breakfast."

In the spring of 1836, Thoreau was at home. He may have been ill. He was not teaching. And he was not ill enough to be prevented from accompanying his father to New York to peddle pencils. Tuberculosis was the family illness—as it was that of many families—and Thoreau may have been afflicted with it early in life. Thoreau's absences from Harvard probably did not trouble him overmuch; he was scarcely at ease there as he was in Concord, and his ability to keep up his grades was not in doubt.

Harvard may have made Thoreau scholarly—the point is moot, but his years at Harvard certainly opened to him a world of books to which he had no access in Concord. Other than the Greek and Latin classics, he had read Thomas Carlyle, particularly *Sartor Resartus,* and Carlyle had impressed his youthful mind. He was to write of him later that in his work Carlyle made "the world seem richer for us, the age more respectable, and life better worth the living . . ."

Perhaps more than any other contemporary work, Ralph Waldo Emerson's *Nature* influenced Thoreau. *Nature* was published in 1836; two years earlier Emerson and his family had taken up residence in Concord, and was thereafter to draw to that village many intellectuals. *Nature* was a relatively brief book, but its impact on young readers in the 1830's was tremendous. Thoreau was ready for it. The very first lines of *Nature* must have appealed to him instantly. "To go into solitude, a man needs to retire as much from his chamber as from society. I am not solitary whilst I read and write, though nobody is with me. But if a man would be alone, let him look at the stars." And, a few paragraphs further along, "The lover of nature is he whose inward and outward senses are still truly adjusted to each other." And, still farther along, "We are taught by great actions that the universe is the property of every individual in it."

The man who could write ten years after his graduation from Harvard, in response to an inquiry for a class record, "Though bodily I have been a member of Harvard University, heart and soul I have been far away among the scenes of my boyhood. Those hours that should have been devoted to study, have been spent in scouring the woods and exploring the lakes and streams of my native village."—the pursuits of that boyhood—was clearly ready for Emerson's philosophy.

There is a time in every man's life that is the right time for enlightenment, for exposure to the life of the mind. For Thoreau that time coincided with his reading of *Nature,* though perhaps he was not yet sufficiently impressed by Emerson's, "Each particle is a microcosm, and faithfully renders the likeness of the world," to implement it by deciding then and there to return to Concord and remain there. This came later, though by only two or three years.

But it is not too much to suppose that his quest for truth and his drive toward simplicity began with *Nature.* "A man's power to connect his thought with its proper symbol, and so to utter it, depends on the simplicity of his character, that is, upon his love of truth and his desire to communicate it without loss. . . . All the uses of nature admit of being summed in one, which yields the activity of man an infinite scope. . . . The best read naturalist who lends an entire and devout attention to truth, will see that there remains much to learn of his relation to the world, and that it is not to be learned by any addition or subtraction or other comparison of known quantities, but is arrived at by untaught sallies of the spirit, by a continual self-recovery, and by entire humility." The entire course of Thoreau's life thereafter is evidence that these words of Emerson either profoundly impressed him with a new direction in life, or, what is far more likely, reinforced a bent already firmly rooted.

Life for Thoreau meant living in the environment of his boyhood. He left letters to attest to his friendship with a few classmates—he wrote to Henry Vose in the summer of 1836 urging him to arrange to secure a room for Thoreau ("Your humble servant will endeavor to enter the Senior Class of Harvard University next term, and if you intend taking a room in College, and it should be consistent with your pleasure, will joyfully sign himself your lawful and proper 'Chum.' ")—he wrote to Charles Wyatt Rice urging him to visit ("It would afford me much pleasure if you would visit our good old town this vacation; *in other words, myself.*")—but there is no record to show that Thoreau ever mingled with the students en masse. He never attended his classmates' "evening entertainments" and he ignored his professors' receptions.

Thoreau was ill again for a while during the summer of 1836, for he wrote to Rice that the doctor had forbidden him to indulge in his favorite pastime—which was

11

hunting for Indian remains, in which the Concord area abounded, since Concord had been Indian country before the coming of the white men, and it was possible to find arrowheads and other artifacts anywhere in the vicinity. But "digging and chopping" had been forbidden Thoreau that summer, and perhaps for longer, for Thoreau wrote of his pastime, "the season is past with me."

He was back in college at the end of that summer, and he resumed his more or less restricted way of life—haunting the library, studying, and being relatively reclusive. The tenor of the essays improved; what he had to say in them was more sound and indicated a personal philosophy taking shape, one which owed some debt to Emerson. His essays in this final year of college were more individual and somewhat set apart in content from the typical student's essays he had written earlier.

He was graduated on August 16, 1837. His Commencement address was on *The Commercial Spirit,* in the course of which he said, "This curious world which we inhabit is more wonderful than it is convenient; more beautiful than it is useful; it is more to be admired and enjoyed than used. The order of things should be somewhat reversed; the seventh should be man's day of toil, wherein to earn his living by the sweat of his brow; and the other six his Sabbath of the affections and the soul,— in which to range this widespread garden, and drink in the soft influences and sublime revelations of Nature." —sentiments which come through Thoreau from Emerson's *Nature,* but with Thoreau's own views coloring them.

So he left college. He was not an outstanding student, and he went through his college years leaving not a hint anywhere of what he might become. That his work was satisfactory was attested to some months later when, in response to a request for a recommendation, President Josiah Quincy of Harvard wrote, "I certify that Henry D. Thoreau, of Concord, in this State of Massachusetts, graduated at this seminary in August, 1837; that his rank was high as a scholar in all the branches, and his morals and general conduct unexceptionable and exemplary. He is recommended as well qualified as an instructor, for employment in any public or private school or private family."

CHAPTER 2

First Love

If a man does not keep pace with his companions, perhaps it is because he hears a different drummer. Let him step to the music which he hears, however measured or far away. It is not important that he should mature as soon as an apple or an oak. Shall he turn his spring into summer? If the condition of things which we were made for is not yet, what were any reality which we can substitute? We will not be shipwrecked on a vain reality. Shall we with pains erect a heaven of blue glass over ourselves, though when it is done we shall be sure to gaze still at the true ethereal heaven far above, as if the former were not? —WALDEN

THOREAU returned to Concord. Though he was happy to be back home, he was not yet committed to living in Concord for the rest of his life. He had some thought of teaching. He had been prepared for it, and it seemed to him then the most likely way to make a living. His family found him not quite the same Henry he had been when he left for Harvard in 1833; he was less content to accept opinions as facts, more argumentative, and entirely apt to shock his aunts with his own independent and unconventional opinions.

Secretly, Thoreau wanted to be a poet, but there was no very great drive in him toward that goal. He had no illusions about the economic position of the poet, though a proportionately respectable number of people read poetry in his time. What he wanted most of all was to live as he wished, with freedom to think and act as he pleased; what he had not yet discovered was some kind of economy which would permit this way of life. This was to be his primary concern for the rest of his life.

The only immediate source of income which seemed open to him was teaching. He applied for the public elementary school in Concord and was accepted. In September, scarcely a month after his graduation, he began to teach. He had some vague ideas about education which, by the standards of his day, were decidedly progressive. He let it be known that he would abandon flogging as a punishment, and deliver moral lectures instead. This course hardly impressed the school committee, who were of the opinion that moral lectures did little to enforce discipline.

For two weeks, the committee—and, no doubt, Concord—waited and watched. At the end of that time, one of the committee members visited school and instructed Thoreau to resume the use of the flog and ferule, or the school was likely to suffer in discipline. Thoreau had no intention of being told how to teach. Moreover, he firmly believed that physical punishment should have no part in education. With a fine contempt, he lined up six pupils after school that day, flogged them, and handed in his resignation.

More than all his independent talk, this deed set Thoreau apart. From that moment forward, he was looked upon as queer—which is to say, unconventional to the point of having the wrong values—as people customarily react to everyone whose values differ from their own. He was, in short, a rebel, who showed by his actions that he intended to remain one.

Thoreau went back to pencil-making with his father,

though he had not yet given up the idea of teaching, and made at least one application to a school in Maine. Nothing came of this. Still he cast about; he looked to Virginia, he spoke of going west for a school either alone or with his beloved older brother, John.

Yet the business of making pencils was not onerous. It had grown into a respectable business by this time— though not yet such a business as to place the Thoreau family in the first rank of Concord businessmen. Moreover, it was a happy occupation for a man of Thoreau's temperament; it did not keep him tied down; he kept no regular hours. It was just the sort of occupation which would allow him to do what he liked best—it gave him time for reading, study, and walking about Concord looking for the facts he expected to catch in his "traps."

Thoreau walked the environs of Concord day after day. His favorite walk was to the southwest, which took him through deep woods from Concord toward Sudbury, along the Sudbury River—and south to Fair Haven Hill, Fair Haven Pond, and Walden Pond. It took him past the Hosmer farm, where he liked to stop, for he was already beginning to enjoy the company of people who lived close to the earth over that of the presumably "best" people of Concord. Northeast of Concord lay the Great Meadows and Ball's Hill, along the Concord River, and directly north rose Ponkawtasset. Thoreau had known them all from his earlier years, and he set about now to improve his acquaintance with them.

Late in October of that year, he began his *Journal*. Journals were commonly kept by men and women in that day, and diaries were even more common. Under date of October 22, 1837, Thoreau recorded that someone had asked him, "What are you doing now? Do you keep a journal?"—and added, "So I make my first entry."

16

It was to be a life's work, though at first it may not have seemed so to Thoreau.

A little later, under the same date, he wrote, "I seek a garret." He preferred living in a garret, and that preference remained with him. The Thoreau family were then living in the Parkman house, and Thoreau lived "upstairs"—in the garret, if there were one to be had. "The spiders must not be disturbed, nor the floor swept, nor the lumber arranged."

On his walks Thoreau carried with him a notebook and pencil, so that he might jot down such thoughts as occurred to him, or those incidents of the life of woods and marshes and rivers that might catch his eye, to be expanded later in the solitude of his garret. He frequently also carried a spy-glass with which to watch birds and animals going about their affairs, and also a *Primo Flauto*—his father's old music book—in which to press plants he gathered as specimens.

He used his journal also very largely to copy lines and paragraphs from the books he was then reading. These were chiefly classical—Ossian, Homer, Donne, Chaucer, Anacreon, Pliny, Aristotle, Virgil, Tasso, Goethe. Generous quotations from these sources vied for place with accounts of his walks—like the story of a walk taken with John in the course of which, by coincidence, after a conversation about Indians and Henry's declaration that "There is Tahatawan's arrowhead," they found an arrowhead on that fanciful spot—and the direction of his thoughts—"My desire is to know *what* I have lived, that I may know *how* to live henceforth." He also set down in his journal the gist of essays he hoped to write later, and, perhaps, publish in the magazines of the day, as well as later, in a book.

Thoreau's journal was no private affair. It was read

by the members of his family, especially his sister Helen, and it was drawn to the attention of one of the ladies who had boarded at the Thoreaus earlier in 1837, Mrs. Lucy Jackson Brown. Mrs. Brown was visiting one autumn afternoon and the two ladies were discussing a recent lecture of Ralph Waldo Emerson's, when Helen said that Henry wrote similarly in his journal. At Mrs. Brown's request, the journal was produced—far be it from Thoreau to keep it under lock and key—and Mrs. Brown read in it. Not surprisingly, some of the notes Thoreau had set down paralleled things Emerson had said or written.

Mrs. Brown happened to be an older sister of Emerson's second wife, Lidian. It was only natural that she should bring to Emerson information that there was in the immediate vicinity a young man whose thoughts echoed Emerson's. Emerson, who was always interested in the young—though he was only fourteen years older than Thoreau—asked that he be brought to the house. Emerson may not have known who Thoreau was at that time, but certainly Thoreau knew all about Emerson, for, as a younger schoolmate of Thoreau's, George Hoar, chronicled in his own autobiography many years later, Thoreau had walked eighteen miles from Concord to Boston—and back by night—solely to hear Emerson lecture.

Emerson was in these years an inspiration to the young. He encouraged them to revolt against outmoded beliefs, to challenge conventions, particularly in thought, to strive toward knowledge of themselves and to express themselves. It was typical of Thoreau that he had made no effort tc call upon Emerson previously; it was like him to pursue his own solitary way without regard for the opinions of the famous, the godly, the wealthy, or the learned neighbors of Concord; but an invitation to visit he did not turn down.

Thoreau left no record of his first meeting with Emerson, the beginning of an important, if not always easy, friendship. Very probably Emerson saw Thoreau, then in his twenty-first year, as a disciple. By early February of 1838—not long after their first meeting—Emerson was writing of Thoreau in his own journal, "I delight much in my young friend, who seems to have as free and erect a mind as any I have ever met."—and, a week later, "My good Henry Thoreau made this else solitary afternoon sunny with his simplicity and clear perception. . . . Everything that boy says makes merry with society, though nothing can be graver than his meaning." It was not improbable that Emerson saw in Thoreau a reflection of himself, ground which had proved fertile for Emerson's ideas.

On another score there was sufficient evidence to persuade Emerson in his lighter moments to fancy that he had invented—or at least prophesied—Thoreau. Three years before, while Thoreau was still a sophomore at Harvard, unknown to Emerson save as a lad from the village, Emerson had written in his journal, "If life were long enough, among my thousand and one works should be a book of nature whereof Howitt's *Seasons* should be not so much the model as the parody. It should contain the natural history of the woods around my shifting camp for every month of the year. It should tie their astronomy, botany, physiology, meteorology, picturesque, and poetry together. No bird, no bug, no bud, should be forgotten on his day and hour." By 1838 Emerson had put aside this dream, but here was young Henry Thoreau traveling widely in Concord and setting down just such a record in his journal.

From that initial visit onward, Thoreau was welcome at the Emerson house, and particularly at those evenings of stimulating conversation so much a part of Emerson's life. These evenings could hardly have been described as ordinary. He might meet there Edmund Hosmer, his farmer friend, but he might also meet the versatile and colorful Margaret Fuller or Jones Very, the poet. He saw citizens of Concord next to people like Elizabeth Peabody, a distinguished educator, or Sarah Bradford, a renowned Greek scholar, or Bronson Alcott, the idealistic pioneer in education, who was himself to take up residence in Concord in 1840. Thoreau took part in the stimulating gatherings, but he was not essentially a part of the group which came together at Emerson's. He took what he liked of the ideas which were scattered there like chaff, and rejected the rest, quite as at a table he was wont only to partake of those viands which suited his palate.

The visitors at Emerson's were interested in anything new, particularly new avenues of thought. Freedom of thought was their ideal—it was Thoreau's, too. Many of them called themselves Transcendentalists after a pattern of thinking which took its ideas from life's laws and looked for truth, however idealistically, in consciousness and awareness itself, rather than in sense. Constantly in search of the ideal, always embattled against materialism, the Transcendentalists appealed to Emerson, but the movement—such as it was—never completely involved him, much though he enjoyed listening to the ideas of his guests. He might lend them his prestige now and then, or offer them a protecting wing, but never his mind's independence. Nor did it involve Thoreau. If now and then he called himself a Transcendentalist, he forgot it in a few days. From the ideas of the Transcendentalists he took, too, what suited his nature, and ignored the rest; he took only what seemed to him of help in his struggle to come to terms with life in Concord.

Undeniably, these evenings stimulated him. He was a member of the Concord Lyceum, where audiences listened to lectures by local luminaries as well as by hired speakers. On April 11, 1838, Thoreau delivered his first lecture on *Society*. It was not such a lecture as to set minds afire, but rather more rhetoric and pedanticism, but now and then there were glimpses of the later Thoreau. He said, for example, that some of his fellow citizens were "newly shingled and clapboarded," but a knock brought no answer for there was no one at home. *Society* was only the first of a series of lectures, though Thoreau performed other services for the Lyceum, not the least of which was the programming in one season, when he retained twenty-five speakers at a total cost of a hundred dollars.

In May of that year he set out by boat from Boston for two weeks in Maine. From Portland he went to Bath and Brunswick. "Each one's world is but a clearing in the forest, so much open and inclosed ground," he wrote in his journal. He went to Augusta by way of Gardiner and Hallowell, and then on to Bangor and to Oldtown, where he encountered an Indian. He was much interested in Indians and hoped some day to write a book about them. "I had much conversation with an old Indian at the latter place (Oldtown), who sat dreaming upon a scow at the waterside and striking his deer-skin moccasins against the planks, while his arms hung listlessly by his side. He was the most communicative man I had met."

By May 17 he was back in Boston and once more on

his rounds. He had put in an apprenticeship in poetry, and his journal contains many of the poems he wrote celebrating a variety of things—*May Morning, Cliffs,* truth, goodness, beauty, *My Boots, Friendship, The Blue-birds, Walden*—

> . . . Only the practiced ear can catch the surging words
> That break and die upon thy pebbled lips.
> Thy flow of thought is noiseless as the lapse
>   of thy own waters . . .

and *Fair Haven*—

> When winter fringes every bough
> With his fantastic wreath,
> And puts the seal of silence now
> Upon the leaves beneath;
>
> When every stream in its penthouse
> Goes gurgling on its way,
> And in his gallery the mouse
> Nibbleth the meadow hay;
>
> Methinks the summer still is nigh,
> And lurketh there below,
> As that same meadow mouse doth lie
> Snug underneath the snow. . . .

Meanwhile, there was still the problem of making a living other than in manufacturing and selling pencils. Teaching continued to seem to Thoreau the only course open to his limited talents. In June, 1838, he established himself as master of a private school held in the Parkman house. His reputation as an eccentric had not injured his standing as a teacher, for he had enough pupils to keep him occupied. Presumably the school made progress, for in three months both he and his brother John were teaching in the newly reopened Concord Academy.

The Academy soon had a waiting list. There was a widespread distrust of public schools among the leading citizens of the region. Boys came not only from Concord but from beyond. Some of the boys boarded with the Thoreau family, so that Henry and John saw them not only in school but out. John was in nominal charge of the school, and was especially popular with small children. Henry taught mathematics and the classical courses, and either he or his brother opened each day with a little talk to preface the lessons of the day.

The Thoreau brothers offered a curriculum that satisfied the educational standards of the day, and more. They took the students out for hikes through the countryside, trips on the river, in search of arrowheads, birding, on flower hunts, in the course of which Henry or John shared their knowledge with the students in their charge. It was a happy school for the children. Small wonder that discipline was no problem; there was no flogging and there were no moral lectures, for lack of need.

Yet the school seems not to have fulfilled Thoreau's expectations financially for, in early October of that year, he wrote to Taunton, Massachusetts, seeking a position in a school there because his "present school . . . is not sufficiently lucrative." Nothing came of this, and the Academy continued with John and Henry Thoreau to serve its students.

Dissatisfied Thoreau might have been, but he could hardly have been unhappy. He fed his soul on his long walks into the country around Concord, and his mind basked in the reflected brilliance of the gatherings at Emerson's or in its own white light. To Emerson, Thoreau was already *"the* man of Concord," which was a salute to the quality of Thoreau's thinking, rather than to his written work, which was to Emerson no more than

23

"good poetry and better prose." He walked frequently with Emerson, discoursing on philosophical matters and on life. Their relationship was that of master and pupil—Thoreau absorbing Emerson's ideas, Emerson delighted to see his ideas fall upon such fertile soil.

The year turned.

In that year of 1839 there were, among the Thoreau boarders, the Wards. Miss Prudence Ward taught drawing and gave some lessons in botany. She wrote at great length about the Thoreau boys to her sister, who was the wife of the Reverend Edmund Sewall in Scituate, and they exchanged frequent visits. In June, young Edmund Sewall came along to visit, and Thoreau found himself so much attracted to this eleven-year-old boy that he wrote a poem, *Sympathy,* to celebrate the boy's "pure, uncompromising spirit," as Thoreau put it in his journal under date of June 22. "Some persons carry about them the air and conviction of virtue . . . when they are near it is like an invisible presence which attends you."

The following month Edmund's sister Ellen came to Concord. She was a beautiful, gay, affectionate girl, and she arrived in midsummer, the time of vacation at the Academy. The Thoreau boys showed her about Concord. Henry squired her up and down the Assabet. Aunt Prudence chaperoned. She was in Concord for three weeks, and both the Thoreau boys fell in love with her, apparently without mutual knowledge.

On the day of her arrival, July 20, Thoreau put into his journal a poem titled *The Breeze's Invitation* which contained such lines as "I the king and you the queen . . . To our music Time will linger . . ." and clearly celebrated her arrival. Five days later he wrote a single, poignant line, "There is no remedy for love but to love more." Thereafter there is no entry in the journal until

24

late August. Undoubtedly Thoreau's thoughts were taken up by Ellen Sewall, and his feelings for her must have given him many troubled hours.

On that last day of August, Ellen Sewall had returned to Scituate, and the Thoreau brothers were embarking on a holiday together, one much to their liking. They were going by boat down the Concord River, and meant to take the Middlesex Canal into the Merrimack River to follow that stream as far as the vicinity of Hooksett, New Hampshire, from which they intended to walk deeper into New Hampshire before returning to Concord.

The trip was an idyll which Thoreau never forgot. Out of it was to come his first book. Undoubtedly he kept copious notes, but what remains in his journal gives little clue to the material which ultimately appeared in that first book. His initial entry sets forth what he saw, the things that his senses apprehended. On that first day the brothers "Made seven miles, and moored our boat on the west side of a little rising ground which in the spring forms an island in the river, the sun going down on one hand, and our eminence contributing its shadow to the night on the other."

Thoreau continues: "In the twilight so elastic is the air that the sky seems to tinkle over farmhouse and wood. Scrambling up the bank of our *terra incognita* we fall on huckleberries, which have slowly ripened here, husbanding the juices which the months have distilled, for our peculiar use this night. If they had been rank poison, the entire simplicity and confidence with which we plucked them would have insured their wholesomeness. The devout attitude of the hour asked a blessing on that repast. It was fit for the setting sun to rest on. . . .

"From our tent here on the hillside, through that isosceles door, I see our lonely mast on the shore, it may be as an eternity fixture, to be seen in landscapes henceforth, or as the most temporary standstill of time, the boat just come to anchor, and the mast still rocking to find its balance. . . .

"The musquash by the boat is taking toll of potatoes and melons. Is not this the age of a community of goods? His presumption kindles in me a brotherly feeling. Nevertheless, I get up to reconnoitre, and tread stealthily along the shore to make acquaintance with him. But on the riverside I can see only the stars reflected in the water, and now, by some ripple ruffling the disk of a star, I discover him."

By the second night, they had reached Tyngsborough on the Merrimack where they "camped under some oaks . . . on the east bank . . . just below the ferry." By Wednesday they had reached Hooksett, and on the following day, September 5, they "Walked to Concord (New Hampshire), 10 miles." Thereafter for a week they walked—to Franconia Notch "and saw the Old Man of the Mountain," and to other places in that state before riding back to Hooksett and rowing to Bedford "near the ferry, by a large island, near which we camped." After that they rowed and sailed back to their home village.

Each must have been secretly engrossed with thoughts of lovely Ellen Sewall, for they were no sooner back in Concord than John went to visit in Scituate and walked out with Ellen. And in December both the Thoreau boys visited the Sewalls, taking Miss Prudence Ward along with them. Returning, John sent Ellen opals for her collection, and Henry sent her some of the poems he had written.

The winter put an end to visiting, if not to correspondence. By this time Thoreau's interest was being enlisted in the Transcendentalists' newest venture—a magazine. In common with literary groups since the dawn of time, the Transcendentalists were planning to publish a magazine so that they might have a rostrum from which to announce their beliefs, vague as they were, to the world. It was to be called *The Dial,* and Margaret Fuller was to be its editor. Perhaps Thoreau could contribute?

He sent her *Sir Walter Raleigh,* which she rejected. Then he sent her *Aulus Persius Flaccus,* a study of the Latin poet, which she accepted for the first number, which was to be dated July, 1840. Thoreau now intended to try his hand at writing, but he could hardly have had any conviction that a creative career was the answer to his economic problems.

Teaching still remained to him the only answer, and even this was not entirely satisfactory. It may have begun to pall. In spite of it, Thoreau had ample leisure in which "to improve his soul's estate." On March 21, 1840, he recognized his position in the world when he wrote in his journal: "I am freer than any planet; no complaint reaches round the world. I can move away from public opinion, from government, from religion, from education, from society. Shall I be reckoned a ratable poll in the county of Middlesex, or be rated at one spear under the palm trees of Guinea? Shall I raise corn and potatoes in Massachusetts, or figs and olives in Asia Minor? sit out the day in my office in State Street, or ride it out on the steppes of Tartary? For my Brobdingnag I may sail to Patagonia; for my Lilliput, to Lapland. In Arabia and Persia, my day's adventures may surpass the Arabian Nights' Entertainments. I may be a logger on the head waters of the Penobscot, to be recorded in fable hereafter as an amphibious river-god, by as sounding a name as Triton or Proteus; carry furs from Nootka to China, and so be more renowned than Jason and his golden fleece; or go on a South Sea exploring expedition, to be hereafter recounted along with the periplus of Hanno. I may repeat the adventures of Marco Polo or Mandeville.

"These are but few of my chances, and how many more things may I do with which there are none to be compared!" But Thoreau did none of them; he was actively about the exploration of Concord and its environs, and he recognized that "Our limbs, indeed, have room enough, but it is our souls that rust in a corner," knowing that it was not important who one might be or where he might go, but *what* he was that mattered.

His love for Ellen Sewall continued unabated. One might guess that he walked all that winter and spring on lighter feet, waiting upon renewed sight of the visitor from Scituate.

In June she came. No doubt the Thoreau brothers vied for her attention. Henry took her rowing one day, and on June 19 wrote in his journal, "The other day I rowed in my boat a free, even lovely young lady, and, as I plied the oars, she sat in the stern, and there was nothing but she between me and the sky. So might all our lives be picturesque if they were free enough, but mean relations and prejudices intervene to shut out the sky, and we never see a man as simple and distinct as the man-weathercock on a steeple."

Perhaps he was already aware that the elder Sewalls, while accepting the Thoreau boys as acquaintances or friends, had some reservations about their becoming relatives. The Sewalls were conservative Unitarians, and the Thoreaus, by their standards, were radical. Late in July Ellen returned to Scituate, with her Aunt Prudence, her Grandmother Ward, and John Thoreau. While he was there, Ellen later related, John proposed. She accepted his proposal, but the engagement did not last long—less than a month. It was broken amicably, for John and Ellen continued to correspond.

Henry's turn came next. At the end of October he wrote his proposal to Ellen, but he had no great confidence that it would be accepted, and his journal entries for early November offer evidence that he anticipated her rejection.

It came with almost crushing finality. Her father directed her to write to Henry as coldly and briefly as possible in rejection. Though she wrote her Aunt Prudence that she "never felt so badly" at having to do so, she was herself of essentially the same mind. She enjoyed the company of the Thoreau brothers, but she never had any real intention of marrying either one of them.

It is doubtful that Henry had any real longing for the married state, either.

Though he never lost the memory of Ellen Sewall, Thoreau was speedily resigned to her passing out of his life. He dreamed of her, he made references to her in what he wrote, however disguised, and in January he wrote in his journal, "To sigh under the cold, cold moon for a love unrequited is but a slight on nature; the natural remedy would be to fall in love with the moon and the night and find our love requited."

He could now give all his attention to devising some means of making his living by writing.

CHAPTER 3

"A Singular Character"

> *Time is but the stream I go a-fishing in. I drink at it; but while I drink I see the sandy bottom and detect how shallow it is. Its thin current slides away, but eternity remains. I would drink deeper; fish in the sky, whose bottom is pebbly with stars. I cannot count one. I know not the first letter of the alphabet. I have always been regretting that I was not as wise as the day I was born. The intellect is a cleaver; it discerns and rifts its way into the secret of things. I do not wish to be any more busy with my hands than is necessary. My head is hands and feet. I feel all my best faculties concentrated in it. My instinct tells me that my head is an organ for burrowing, as some creatures use their snout and fore paws, and with it I would mine and burrow my way through these hills. I think that the richest vein is somewhere hereabouts; so by the divining-rod and thin vapors I judge; and here I will begin to mine.*
>
> —WALDEN

MORE than ever, Thoreau sought the solitary instruction of the woods and fields, the rivers and hills of the town. He still taught with his brother, but he had not given himself to teaching. Little of those hours in the classroom made its way into the pages of his journal, and increasingly more of the countryside and Thoreau's experience—both physical and mental—was set down.

30

On the 30th of January, 1841, Thoreau walked to Fair Haven Pond, marking the trails of foxes, and then suddenly saw a fox down river—sixty rods away, heading for the woods. Five inches of snow covered the ground, and the fox, he saw, was experiencing some difficulty. Thoreau decided to chase him and took off with "head aloft . . . snuffing the air like a fox-hound, and spurning the world and the Humane Society at each bound. It seemed the woods rang with the hunter's horn, and Diana and all the satyrs joined in the chase and cheered me on. Olympian and Elean youths were waving palms on the hills."

The fox, however, was Nature's own child, and Thoreau not alone Nature's. The fox doubled and "I wheeled and cut him off, bounding with fresh vigor, Antaeuslike, recovering my strength each time I touched the snow. Having got near enough for a fair view, just as he was slipping into the wood, I gracefully yielded him the palm."

This was Thoreau in his element.

The journal for that year was filled with observations of nature, with aphorisms, and thoughtful passages testifying to Thoreau's growth. "There is always a single ear in the audience, to which we address ourselves," he wrote—and if that ear were his own. "We are constantly invited to be what we are; as to something worthy and noble. I never waited but for myself to come round; none ever detained me, but I lagged or tagged after myself." And, "My life must seem as if it were passing at a higher level than that which I occupy. It must possess a dignity which will not allow me to be familiar." And, "Brave speaking is the most entire and richest sacrifice to the gods,"—like that, perhaps, which made him seem argumentative at some of those gatherings at Emerson's.

He was happy to be a part of Nature. "I feel slightly

complimented when Nature condescends to make use of me without my knowledge, as when I help scatter her seeds in my walk, or carry burs and cockles on my clothes from field to field." Many passages in the journal testify to his delight on his hikes into the country. "My life at this moment is like a summer morning when birds are singing. Yet that is false, for nature's is an idle pleasure in comparison: my hour has a more solid serenity. I have been breaking silence these twenty-three years and have hardly made a rent in it."

He kept his journal with more than one purpose. He was setting down in it notes he hoped to use in work he could publish later in his life. He was improving his prose style, slowly escaping from Professor Channing's rhetoric. He was keeping a literary—rather than a sci-entific—record of Nature in the environs of Concord. In its fourth year, he saw his journal as "that of me which would else spill over and run to waste, gleanings from the field which in action I reap. I must not live for it, but in it for the gods. They are my correspondent, to whom daily I send off this sheet postpaid. I am clerk in their counting-room, and at evening transfer the account from day-book to ledger. . . . It is always a chance scrawl, and commemorates some accident,—as great as earth-quake or eclipse."

Another objective beyond mere hiking and observation was gradually taking shape in Thoreau's mind. He wanted a place of his own—some country retreat not too far from Concord, so that he might still make his regular way along the Mill Dam and take part in the current of village gossip, as always, and be in attendance at Emerson's gatherings, and drop in on his mother and sisters from time to time. He wanted such a place as

32

might still permit him to teach and make pencils, thus doing the things he must do to earn some income while he perfected his writing to a point where it might either supplement his small income or replace it, which he would much have preferred.

He thought about buying the orchard side of Fair Haven Hill, the Baker Farm, the Cliff Hill, and Weird Dell, but he finally fixed upon Hollowell Farm, which served all his requirements. He set down its attractions—"its complete retirement, being at least two miles from the village, half a mile from any neighbor, and separated from the highway by a broad field; its bounding on the river; the pleasing ruin of the house and barn; the hollow and lichen-covered apple trees gnawed by rabbits; above all the recollection I had of it from my earliest voyages up the river, when the house was concealed behind a dense grove of red maples, which then stood between it and the river, through which I once heard the house-dog bark; and in general the slight improvements that swayed, though I did not mention them to the proprietor. To enjoy these things I was ready to carry it on and do all those things which I now see had no other motive or excuse but that I might pay for it and be unmolested in my possession of it; though I knew all the while that it would yield the most abundant crop of the kind I wanted if I could only afford to let it alone. Though it afforded no western prospect, the dilapidated fences were picturesque. I was in some haste to buy, before the proprietor finished getting out some rocks, cutting down some hollow apple trees, and grubbing up some young birches which had sprung up in the pasture, all which in my eyes very much enhanced its value."

He was aware that ownership of such a property entailed certain responsibilities, even though those responsibilities might earn him an income. "I must not lose any of my freedom by being a farmer and landholder," he wrote in his journal. "Most who enter on any profession are doomed men. The world might as well sing a dirge over them forthwith. The farmer's muscles are rigid. He can do one thing long, not many well. . . . I can leave this arable and grass ground, without making a will or settling my estate. . . . I would buy a farm as freely as a silken streamer. . . . My life must undulate still."

He was not called upon to make any difficult choice. He had no money with which to buy the Hollowell Farm or any other. He wanted to buy the farm on credit, and, while the owner was willing, his wife was not. This ended his hope of owning the Hollowell Farm, but did not put an end to his aspirations. "I only ask a clean seat," he wrote in his journal on April 5. "I will build my lodge on the southern slope of some hill, and take there the life the gods send me. Will it not be employment enough to accept gratefully all that is yielded me between sun and sun?"

His economic circumstances were not to improve. Indeed, they weakened. Early in 1841 his brother John took sick, very probably with an attack of tuberculosis, the family ailment. He struggled along with the school for a while, but not for long. On April first, the school was closed, and another source of his income was at an end. He very likely saw the end of teaching without regret, for he certainly found it onerous and an interference with his inspection of the countryside around Concord. Nothing of the school's closing appears in the journal, unless a curious poem, *On the Sun Coming Out in the Afternoon—*

34

> Methinks all things have travelled since you shined,
> But only Time, and clouds, Time's team, have moved;
> Again foul weather shall not change my mind,
> But in the shade I will believe what in the sun I loved.

may be considered an indirect reference to it.

Thoreau may have wondered what he might do to earn money while he improved his writing, still hoping to make a living by writing, which was scarcely a rational hope in his time, but he made no effort to do anything but the most casual kind of occasional labor. However, his friend Emerson was not unaware of his situation, and was convinced that one so full "of buds of promise" ought to be given a helping hand.

Emerson asked Thoreau whether he would not like to come and take the place of the chore boy he had had. Emerson was frequently away from home, lecturing—sometimes for months—and he wanted someone who might serve as a handyman at the house. He had grown weary, too, of caring for the property. All this Thoreau could do, and none of it would tax him very much. It was the kind of position which fitted Thoreau in that it would still permit him to take his jaunts along the river and into the woods.

Less than four weeks after the school closed, Thoreau moved into an upstairs room at Emerson's. What Thoreau's intimate thoughts about this shift in his fortunes were is not recorded. His journal for the day—April 26, 1841—is laconic in its entry. "Monday. At R. W. E.'s." There follows a paragraph about the charm of the Indian—a lifelong interest of Thoreau's—and one pungent line—"It is a great art to saunter."

He discharged those duties which he had accepted and still had ample time to pursue his favorite occupation. A month later, at May's end, he was at Walden Pond. "I sit in my boat on Walden, playing the flute this evening, and see the perch, which I seem to have charmed, hovering around me, and the moon travelling over the bottom, which is strewn with the wrecks of the forest, and feel that nothing but the wildest imagination can conceive of the manner of life we are living. Nature is a wizard. The Concord nights are stranger than the Arabian nights." His life was perhaps more idyllic than he knew, even though it was understood that, apart from his board and room, there was to be no payment for Thoreau's services.

Emerson meant Thoreau to have the leisure to develop. He wrote to his brother William that if Thoreau could only fall in love, it might "sweeten him and straighten him."

His sojourn at Emerson's enlarged Thoreau's horizons and in a sense also his family. Not only did he have his own closely-knit family to visit, but he had recourse to the pensive Lidian Emerson, Emerson's second wife, and the Emerson children. He was also in more intimate touch with the Transcendentalists and others who regularly called at the Emerson house, but he continued to hold himself a little aloof from them. He took part in their discussions, but a prickly sort of part, on his own terms, unwilling to accept without challenge what the Transcendentalists held to be gospel.

For Mrs. Emerson—and her sister, Mrs. Lucy Jackson Brown, with whom he corresponded—Thoreau had an affection not unlike that he had for his mother and sisters, but an affection uncomplicated by family obligations. He felt that he could open himself to these sisters as to few other women. He could write to Mrs. Brown, "We always seem to be living just on the brink of a pure

36

and lofty intercourse which would make the ills and trivialness of life ridiculous." But at this brink Thoreau was happy to remain. "I am very happy in my present environment," he wrote.

He was more likely to write of himself—"I grow savager and savager every day, as if fed on raw meat"— and indeed, he had begun to eat woodchuck, as indulgence in a new experience, one of which he soon had enough—"and my tameness is only the repose of untamableness. I dream of looking abroad summer and winter, with free gaze, from some mountain-side, while my eyes revolve in an Egyptian slime of health,—I to be nature looking into nature with such easy sympathy as the blue-eyed grass in the meadow looks in the face of the sky. From some such recess I would put forth sublime thoughts daily, as the plant puts forth leaves. Now-a-nights I go on to the hill to see the sun set, as one would go home at evening; the bustle of the village has run on all day, and left me quite in the rear; but I see the sunset, and find that it can wait for my slow virtue."

Living at the Emerson house had one more important advantage—it gave Thoreau access to Emerson's library. There he made the acquaintance of Hindu philosophy in *The Laws of Menu* and, later, in the *Bhagavad-Gita*, which had as profound an influence on him as anything he ever read. He had not been in residence five weeks before he was reading these books. He mentioned *The Laws of Menu* in his journal as early as May 31; by June 7 he wrote, "I know of no book which comes to us with grander pretensions . . . What wonder if the times were not ripe for it?" Thereafter he recorded his enthusiasm frequently—

August 6th, for instance—"I cannot read a sentence in the book of the Hindoos without being elevated as upon the table-land of the Ghauts. It has such a rhythm as the winds of the desert, such a tide as the Ganges, and seems as superior to criticism as the Himmaleh Mounts. Even at this late hour, unworn by time, with a native and inherent dignity it wears the English dress as indifferently as the Sanscrit. The great tone of the book is of such fibre and such severe tension that no time nor accident can relax it."

And the next day, "The impression which those sublime sentences made on me last night has awakened me before any cockcrowing. Their influence lingers around me like a fragrance, or as the fog hangs over the earth late into the day." And later—"Any book of great authority and genius seems to our imagination to permeate and pervade all space. Its spirit, like a more subtle ether, sweeps along with the prevailing winds of the country. Its influence conveys a new gloss to the meadows and the depths of the wood . . . All things confirm it." And later still—"In the Hindoo scripture the idea of man is quite illimitable and sublime. There is nowhere a loftier conception of his destiny. . . . There is no grander conception of creation anywhere. It is peaceful as a dream, and so is the annihilation of the world."

He did not abandon the Greeks for the Hindus, however. He read voraciously, but there is less of the Greeks in his journals for the years he spent at Emerson's house. And nothing he read shook his foundations, but only reinforced them. He continued to write, and some of his verses appeared in 1841 in *The Dial*, which offered an outlet for so many of Emerson's young friends when other markets, more staid, were closed to them.

And he held to the ideal of a place of his own. On Christmas Eve that year he wrote in his journal, "I want to go soon and live away by the pond, where I shall hear

38

only the wind whispering among the reeds. It will be success if I shall have left myself behind. But my friends ask what I will do when I get there. Will it not be employment enough to watch the progress of the seasons?"

Thoreau's idyllic life was, however, to sustain a new and profoundly shaking experience, which was to bring home to him the aloof impartiality of Nature as perhaps nothing else had done to this time. Early in January, 1842, his brother John, while shaving one day, cut himself. The wound healed, but tetanus set in, and on the 12th John died in agony. Thoreau, ever close to his older brother, was deeply affected; he was unable to set down a note in his journal, and his grief was compounded when Emerson's son, Waldo, died of scarlet fever only a fortnight later.

It was five weeks before he made another entry in the journal. "I feel as if years had been crowded into the last month, and yet the regularity of what we call time has been . . . preserved . . ." he wrote on February 21. Three weeks later he wrote to Emerson, "How plain that death is only the phenomenon of the individual or class. Nature does not recognize it, she finds her own again under new forms without loss. Yet death is beautiful when seen to be a law, and not an accident—It is as common as life. Men die in Tartary, in Ethiopia—in England—in Wisconsin. And after all what portion of this so serene and living nature can be said to be alive? Do this year's grasses and foliage outnumber all the past?

"Every blade in the field—every leaf in the forest— lays down its life in its season as beautifully as it was taken up. It is the pastime of a full quarter of the year. Dead trees—sere leaves—dried grass and herbs—are not these a good part of our life? And what is that pride of our autumnal scenery but the hectic flush—the sallow and cadaverous countenance of vegetation—its painted throes—with the November air for canvas—

"When we look over the fields are we not saddened because the particular flowers or grasses will wither—for the law of their death is the law of new life. Will not the land be in good heart *because* the crops die down from year to year? The herbage cheerfully consents to bloom, and wither, and give place to a new.

"So it is with the human plant. We are partial and selfish when we lament the death of the individual, unless our plaint be a paean to the departed soul, and a sigh as the wind sighs over the fields, which no shrub interprets into its private grief."

And under that same date—March 11, 1842—Thoreau cried out in his journal: "My life, my life! why will you linger? Are the years short and the months of no account? How often has long delay quenched my aspirations! Can God afford that I should forget him? . . . Why, God, did you include me in your great scheme? Will you not make me a partner at last?"

With John's death, Thoreau came to not only the fullest realization of the meaning of death, but also presently to acceptance of it—an experience which every young person must know at least once in his life, and one that comes usually with the death of someone dearly loved, as Thoreau loved his brother. The experience tempered him, but only confirmed him in his directions.

Meanwhile, the intellectuals were moving into Concord to add lustre to that village's fame. Bronson Alcott, with his wife, Abigail May, and their children, had come to live there in 1840. William Ellery Channing, nephew of Thoreau's professor of rhetoric, himself a poet, came with his bride, a sister of Margaret Fuller, to spend some time in the Emerson cottage in 1841. Since the cottage was on the grounds, it was inevitable that Thoreau should see something of him, though at this time Channing had come principally to see Emerson. It was only later that he became Thoreau's best friend, though in many ways Thoreau's opposite.

In September, 1841, Dr. Ezra Ripley died; he had been vaguely troubled by the Transcendental thinkers; he thought them "speculators" and not very firmly grounded. In the following July, Nathaniel Hawthorne and his wife, Sophia Peabody, came to live in the Old Manse. Emerson sent Thoreau to help put the garden in order. So the two men met, and, since both of them felt more kinship for the common man than the Transcendentalists, they became friends.

Hawthorne left in his notebook a description of Thoreau in 1842. He called him "a singular character; a young man with much of wild, original Nature still remaining in him; and so far as he is sophisticated, it is in a way and method of his own." He thought Thoreau ill-favored in looks—"long-nosed, queer-mouthed, and with uncouth and somewhat rustic manners. . . . But his ugliness is of an honest and agreeable fashion, and becomes him much better than beauty. . . . he has repudiated all regular means of getting a living, and seems inclined to lead a sort of Indian life. . . .

"He is a keen and delicate observer of Nature . . . a *genuine* observer, which I suspect is almost as rare a character as even an original poet. And Nature, in return for his love, seems to adopt him as her especial child; and shows him secrets which few others are allowed to witness. He is familiar with beast, fish, fowl and reptile, and has strange stories to tell of adventure and friendly passages with these lower brethren of mortality. Herb and flower, likewise, wherever they grow,

41

whether in garden or wildwood, are his familiar friends. He is on intimate terms with the clouds also, and can tell the portents of storms. He has a great regard for the memory of the Indian tribes, whose wild life would have suited him so well; and, strange to say, he seldom walks over a plowed field without picking up an arrow-point, spearhead, or other relic of the red man. With all this he has more than a tincture of literature; a deep and true taste for poetry, especially for the elder poets; and he is a good writer. At least he has written a good article,—a rambling disquisition on Natural History, in the last *Dial,* which, he says, was chiefly made up from journals of his own observations. . . ."

Hawthorne's reference was to *The Natural History of Massachusetts,* which had just appeared in *The Dial,* in which in 1842 many of Thoreau's poems also appeared in print—*To the Maiden in the East, The Moon, The Summer Rain, To a Stray Fowl,* and others. As Hawthorne revealed, Thoreau was beginning now to draw upon his extensive journal for "pieces"—hardly essays—for the magazines which would publish them. There were not many such.

In mid-July of 1842 Thoreau took a long walk to Wachusett with Richard Fuller, Margaret Fuller's brother. This walk was later to become the subject of an article, and Thoreau kept an account of the journey. The two young men took their time, now and then resting on the rails of a fence, learning "that man's life is rounded with the same few facts, the same simple relations everywhere, and it is vain to travel to find it new." They stopped to bathe their feet in every brook, dawdled on every knoll, and spent their first night out at an inn four miles from the base of Wachusett.

Next morning before dawn, they began the climb of

42

Wachusett, following the Stillwater River to the mountain, gathering raspberries for breakfast. In this leisurely manner they reached the summit, which consisted "of a few acres, destitute of trees, covered with bare rocks, interspersed with blueberry bushes, raspberries, gooseberries, strawberries, moss, and a fine wiry grass. . . . This clear space, which is gently rounded, is bounded a few feet lower by a thick shrubbery of oaks, with maples, aspens, beeches, cherries, and occasionally a mountain-ash intermingled, among which we found the bright blue berries of the Solomon's seal, and the fruit of the pyrola."

They pitched their tent here, after which they had blueberries and milk for supper. "Before sunset, we rambled along the ridge to the north, while a hawk soared still above us. It was a place where gods might wander, so solemn and solitary, and removed from all contagion with the plain." By night, under the almost full moon, they strolled the summit and fed their spirits on the view. "There was, by chance, a fire blazing on Monadnock that night, which lighted up the whole western horizon, and, by making us aware of a community of mountains, made our position seem less solitary. . . . It was thrilling to hear the wind roar over the rocks . . . The night was, in its elements, simple even to majesty in that bleak place,— a bright moonlight and a piercing wind. It was at no time darker than twilight . . . and . . . there was the moon still above us, with Jupiter and Saturn on either hand, looking down on Wachusett, and it was a satisfaction to know that they were our fellow-travelers still, as high and out of our reach as our own destiny."

With moonset came the dawn. They were up before the sun, watching upon its rising, and taking in the splendid view. "We could see how ample and roomy is nature. . . . On every side, the eye ranged over suc-

43

cessive circles of towns, rising one above another, like the terraces of a vineyard, till they were lost in the horizon. Wachusett is, in fact, the observatory of the State. There lay Massachusetts, spread out before us in its length and breadth, like a map. There was the level horizon, which told of the sea on the east and south, the well-known hills of New Hampshire on the north, and the misty summits of the Hoosac and Green Mountains, first made visible to us the evening before, blue and unsubstantial, like some bank of clouds which the morning wind would dissipate, on the northwest and west."

At noon they went back down the mountain, and, traveling with more dispatch, they reached Concord early the following morning. With scarcely any transition, Thoreau slipped back into his pattern—making pencils, continuing his sojourn at Emerson's, resuming his exploration of Concord town. From time to time he shared his company with Hawthorne and Emerson, as on the winter occasion when they went skating together and were later remembered by Rose Hawthorne Lathrop, Hawthorne's daughter, as a remarkable trio skating down the Concord River—Thoreau "an experienced skater—figuring dithyrambic dances and Bacchic leaps on the ice," Hawthorne "who, wrapped in his cloak, moved like a self-impelled Greek statue, stately and grave," and Emerson "too weary to hold himself erect, pitching headforemost, half lying on the air."

His journal grew in the sense that it was less derivative; he drew less upon other writers he read—save for the Hindus—and more upon himself, reflecting his attitudes. "I have been making pencils all day, and then at evening walked to see an old schoolmate who is going to help make the Welland Canal navigable for ships round

Niagara. He cannot see any such motives and modes of living as I; professes not to look beyond the securing of certain 'creature comforts.' And so we go silently different ways, with all serenity, I in the still moonlight through the village this fair evening to write these thoughts in my journal, and he, forsooth, to mature his schemes to ends as good, maybe, but different. So are we two made, while the same stars shine quietly over us. . . . So does the Welland Canal get built, and other conveniences, while I live. Well and good, I must confess. Fast sailing ships are hence not detained."

He linked his fate "in some sense" with the stars, "and if they are to persevere to a great end, shall I die who could conjecture it?" His association with the villagers opened to him many profound truths—"Man's moral nature is a riddle which only eternity can solve."—and, apart from expressing his dislikes and enthusiasms, he did not set himself in judgment upon his fellow citizens.

He had, too, already discerned an important fact about writing. "Those authors are successful who do not *write down* to others, but make their own taste and judgment their audience. By some strange infatuation we forget that we do not approve what yet we recommend to others. It is enough if I please myself with writing; I am then sure of an audience." And he had learned, too, that "Poetry cannot breathe in the scholar's atmosphere," and that "One does not soon learn the trade of life."

Despite the greater number of his contributions to *The Dial,* now that Emerson had assumed the editorship of that magazine, despite the security of his position, despite his freedom of movement, Thoreau was uncomfortable in his place in the Emerson household, and he evidently made Emerson, too, somewhat uncomfortable. Early in 1843 Hawthorne set down in his journal that

"Mr. Emerson seems to have suffered some inconvenience from his experience of Mr. Thoreau as an inmate. It may well be that such a sturdy, uncompromising person is fitter to meet occasionally in the open air than as a permanent guest at table and fireside." Thoreau, in short, was not a sycophant; he was not at Emerson's simply to agree with Emerson's propositions in an intellectual discussion; indeed, he was inclined rather to disagree. Emerson was frequently contradicted by Thoreau, and he found this somewhat wearing.

Well aware of Thoreau's desire to write and publish, Emerson enlisted his aid in the editing of *The Dial,* which he had taken over from Margaret Fuller early in 1842. The experience was salutary. With Emerson frequently away, Thoreau did more editing than he had contemplated—the entire April 1843 issue was edited by Thoreau, at about the same time—in February—that he wrote to Emerson that he was pondering "some other method of paying debts than by lectures and writing," and asking Emerson to look about in New York for something "of that 'other' sort" and "to remember it for me?"

Not long after, Emerson found some "other" occupation for Thoreau. It was as tutor to his brother William's son, Haven, on Staten Island. It was the kind of position which would put Thoreau next to the center of American publishing in New York. It would give him opportunity to meet editors and fellow writers other than those who belonged to the Concord group, though Thoreau had already met John O'Sullivan, one such editor—of *The Democratic Review*—at the Old Manse at Hawthorne's invitation earlier that year. Thoreau was promised board and room, as well as $100 a year—which was $100 more than he received at his present post.

On May 6, 1843, Thoreau left for Staten Island, by

boat. In a matter of days he was writing to "Dear Mother and Friends at Home," "I am seven and a half miles from New York, and, as it would take half a day at least, have not been there yet. I have already run over no small part of the island, to the highest hill, and some way along the shore. From the hill directly behind the house I can see New York, Brooklyn, Long Island, the Narrows, through which vessels bound to and from all parts of the world chiefly pass,—Sandy Hook and the Highlands of Neversink (part of the coast of New Jersey)—and, by going still farther up the hill, the Kill van Kull, and Newark Bay. From the pinnacle of one Madame Grimes' house the other night at sunset, I could see almost round the island. Far in the horizon there was a fleet of sloops bound up the Hudson, which seemed to be going over the edge of the earth, and in view of these trading ships, commerce seems quite imposing."

And he added, "But it is rather derogatory that your dwelling-place should be only a neighborhood to a great city,—to live on an inclined plane. I do not like their cities and forts, with their morning and evening guns, and sails flapping in one's eye. I want a whole continent to breathe in, and a good deal of solitude and silence, such as all Wall Street cannot buy,—nor Broadway with its wooden pavement. I must live along the beach, on the southern shore, which looks directly out to sea,—and see what that great parade of water means, that dashes and roars, and has not yet wet me, as long as I have lived. . . .

"I must not know anything about my condition and relations here till what is not permanent is worn off. I have not yet subsided. Give me time enough, and I may like it. . . . it will be long before I can make nature look as innocently grand and inspiring as in Concord."

Though he was by no means sure that Thoreau would ever find time enough to like any place but Concord, Emerson did everything he could to introduce Thoreau to the literary life of New York. On the day of his departure, he wrote a letter to the senior Henry James introducing Thoreau, and James immediately wrote to Thoreau at Staten Island inviting him to call at his convenience. After he had gone to New York—but not to see James—Thoreau wrote to Emerson, "You must not count much upon what I can do or learn in New York. I feel a good way off here . . . Everything there disappoints me but the crowd—rather I was disappointed with the rest before I came."

He was homesick for Concord and resumed the writing of poems, which he had abandoned for most of the time since John Thoreau's death. He did resolutely try, however, to meet people who might be of use to him. O'Sullivan, whom he had met at Hawthorne's Old Manse, bought *The Landlord* from him, and ordered a book review. He visited James early in June and liked him "very much. . . . I never was more kindly and faithfully catechised. It made me respect myself more to be thought worthy of such wise questions. He is a man, and takes his own way, or stands still in his own place." But on the whole, as he wrote to Emerson in the same letter in which he reported on James, "I always see those of whom I have heard well with a slight disappointment. They are so much better than the great herd, and yet the heavens are not shivered into diamonds over their heads." And, at the same time, he admitted, "I don't like the city better, the more I see it, but worse."

Of the people he thought genuine, and with whom he felt kinship—and there were not many in the setting where he found himself in 1843—there were two above all others—Henry James and Horace Greeley, who was to remain his friend for life, and who was to do all in his power to find an audience for him. Of the others, Thoreau thought but fleetingly. He tried every way he knew in which to increase his income—to make a living—even to selling subscriptions to *The Agriculturalist*, but he failed in all of them. As for his own writing, he wrote Emerson, "Literature comes to a poor market here, and even the little that I write is more than will sell."

He wrote many letters home—nostalgic letters. He wrote to his parents, to his sisters, to the Emersons, and their replies linked him to Concord. He came to Concord for Thanksgiving, returned briefly to Staten Island, and then finally, Concord being more vital to him than any other place, he returned to his home place early in December. There he meant to stay.

CHAPTER 4

A Place of His Own

I went to the woods because I wished to live de-
liberately, to front only the essential facts of life,
and see if I could not learn what it had to teach,
and not, when I came to die, discover that I had
not lived. I did not wish to live what was not life,
living is so dear; nor did I wish to practise resigna-
tion, unless it was quite necessary. I wanted to live
deep and suck out all the marrow of life, to live so
sturdily and Spartan-like as to put to rout all that
was not life, to cut a broad swath and shave close,
to drive life into a corner, and reduce it to its lowest
terms, and, if it proved to be mean, why then to get
the whole and genuine meanness of it, and publish
its meanness to the world; or if it were sublime, to
know it by experience, and be able to give a true
account of it in my next excursion. —WALDEN

HE settled back into life in Concord as easily as if he had never left it, as if he had
gone to Staten Island with no intention of remaining away
from the place he liked best of all those he had known, and
wished to know no other. He had told George Ward in
New York that, having studied books, he now meant to
study nature and his fellowmen, and he set about it. He
was back at making pencils once more, and he was occupied in helping his father to build a house across the new
railroad tracks which had been put in from Boston through
to Fitchburg. This house was called the "Texas house,"

either because it was so far from the Mill Dam or because of the current agitation of the Texas question. The Thoreaus had been building it, off and on, for three years.

He resumed his exploratory acquaintance with the woods, the rivers, the fields and ponds, very often alone, but sometimes with William Ellery Channing, who had come to live in Concord, or with Emerson, and perhaps on occasion with his idealistic friend, Isaac Hecker, who was studying Latin and Greek under the schoolmaster, George Bradford, in Concord, and rooming at the Thoreau house. Channing was a lively companion, in many ways the opposite of Thoreau. He was gay, witty, much given to flowery speech and not above telling a risque story once in a while, perhaps as much to annoy Thoreau as to entertain himself, for Thoreau frowned on levity in dealing with matters of sex.

On Town Meeting day that April of 1844, Edward Hoar, home from studying at Harvard, went along with Thoreau on a trip up the Sudbury River, and, having caught some fish, the two stopped along shore to fry them. They took the usual precautions, but the day was a windy one, and the grass along the edge of the woods caught fire. They had intended to camp out, but the fire drove all else from their minds. They tried to stamp it out, then got a board from the boat and tried to beat out the flames, to no avail. The wind spread the flames along the hillside away from Fair Haven Pond.

While the flames would be halted on one side by the Well Meadow Brook, there was a distinct possibility that they might get to Concord on the other. Edward Hoar took the boat down river, and Thoreau ran through the woods to arouse the town. On the way, he met the owner of the woods, and told him what had happened; the two ran all the way back to the scene, meeting a carpenter

51

who had been driven from the woods by the approaching flames. He went on to give the alarm, together with the owner; Thoreau, tired from running, stayed behind. "What could I do alone against a front of flame half a mile wide?" he asked when at last he recorded the incident in his journal six years later.

He climbed to the highest rock on Fair Haven Cliff and sat down to watch the flames move toward him. They had by this time traveled a mile. The alarm bell rang, and Thoreau knew that help was on the way. "Hitherto I had felt like a guilty person," he wrote in his journal, "—nothing but shame and regret. But now I settled the matter with myself shortly. I said to myself: 'Who are these men who are said to be the owners of these woods, and how am I related to them? I have set fire to the forest, but I have done no wrong therein, and now it is as if the lightning had done it. These flames are but consuming their natural food.' (It has never troubled me from that day to this more than if the lightning had done it. The trivial fishing was all that disturbed me and disturbs me still.)"

Pressed by the approach of the fire at last, Thoreau went down to join the fire-fighters reaching the scene from Concord. For several hours they fought the flames with hoes, shovels, and back fires. Before they had contained it, the fire had burned over a hundred acres of woodland.

The experience was instructive for Thoreau. "When I returned home late in the day, with others of my townsmen, I could not help noticing that the crowd who were so ready to condemn the individual who had kindled the fire did not sympathize with the owners of the wood, but were in fact highly elate and as it were thankful for the opportunity which had afforded them so much sport; and it was only half a dozen owners, so called, though not all of them, who looked sour or grieved, and I felt that I had a deeper interest in the woods, knew them better and should feel their loss more, than any or all of them." At least one of his townsmen called Thoreau a "damned rascal."

That night Thoreau returned to the woods to wander through them, among the burning stumps, and "far in the night I threaded my way to the spot where the fire had taken, and discovered the now broiled fish . . . scattered over the burnt grass." What his inmost thoughts were as he walked through the blackened waste is not recorded. One can imagine them. He who had loved the woods had, even if by accident, destroyed them.

More important, the incident showed him the Thoreau his townsmen saw. He regarded himself as an individual, a nonconformist in thought. At this point he must have learned that his fellow townsmen looked upon him as an eccentric, more or less a loafer, and, to cap this low opinion, as an irresponsible rascal. This is the kind of discovery almost every creative solitary sooner or later makes when some such incident brings him face to face with what has been smoldering in the thoughts of his fellowmen for a long time.

In subsequent days, as he walked the familiar Concord streets and lanes, he learned to grow accustomed to anonymous jeers and shouts sent toward his retreating back. "Burnt woods!" some of his fellow townsmen called after him. It must have hardened a resolve which had long been growing in him—to put a little distance between his townsmen and himself. This had been a goal ever since he had failed to acquire the Hollowell Farm, and as the year wore on, he came closer and closer to it.

Isaac Hecker left Concord and made his way into the Catholic religion, asking Thoreau to go on a hiking tour of the Continent with him. Thoreau declined. But that summer he went on a walking tour of the Berkshires and the Catskills with Channing. When his friend Emerson announced an address—*On the Anniversary of the Emancipation of the Negroes in the British West Indies*—and the Concord churches, with that timidity which always afflicts settled social units at any criticism of the status quo, refused the use of their buildings for this purpose, Thoreau managed to persuade the authorities to permit Emerson use of the Concord courthouse. Thoreau himself rang the bell to announce to Concord the hour of the address, delivered on August 1, 1844.

Thoreau's disaffection with his fellow townsmen—or, more importantly, their attitude toward him—was aggravated by the end of *The Dial* and the consequent closing of an outlet for Thoreau's writing. The last volume had contained his essay, *A Winter Walk*. There was no other magazine of the day which was inclined to look favorably upon Thoreau's work. It was time for Thoreau to take stock of himself, to find opportunity to prepare a book which had been in his thoughts ever since his brother's death.

The opportunity lay before him. In October of that year Emerson bought eleven acres of land along the shores of Walden Pond. He wrote his brother William that "As . . . for years I had a sort of daily occupancy in it, I bid on it and bought it, eleven acres, for $8.10 per acre." Shortly after, he bought a few more acres of adjoining woodland from Heartwell Bigelow—a woodlot of scrub pine, white pines, briars, blackberries. Channing had once called the place "Briars" and Emerson also referred to its thorny nature. But Channing thought it might be ideal for Thoreau to occupy. "I see nothing for you in this earth but that field which I once christened 'Briars'; go out upon that, build yourself a hut, and there begin the grand process of devouring yourself alive," he wrote to Thoreau early in March, 1845. A little farther along in this letter he refers satirically to Thoreau in the third person as "too dry, too confused, too chalky, too concrete."

The idea of a retreat at Walden Pond fitted in with Thoreau's scheme of things. This was only another version of the "garret" he constantly sought; it was, in effect, an attic room in an ideal setting. Emerson was delighted with the idea of having Thoreau once more as a tenant, albeit two miles off where his social truculence would hardly be apparent to the talkers who gathered at Emerson's Concord house. Before the end of that month, Thoreau began to clear the briars from the field above Walden. In his own way, he was already paying rent on the land he hoped to occupy.

"It was a pleasant hillside where I worked, covered with pine woods, through which I looked out on the pond, and a small open field in the woods where pines and hickories were springing up. The ice in the pond was not yet dissolved, though there were some open spaces, and it was all dark-colored and saturated with water." He walked to and from Concord on the Fitchburg railroad, which ran along the west end of the pond, though his site was closer to the road that ran along the east end toward Cambridge.

"So I went on for some days cutting and hewing timber, and also studs and rafters, all with my narrow axe, not having many communicable or scholar-like thoughts, singing to myself,—

Men say they know many things;
But lo! they have taken wings,—
The arts and sciences,
And a thousand appliances:
The wind that blows
Is all that anybody knows.

I hewed the main timbers six inches square, most of the studs on two sides only, and the rafters and floor timbers on one side, leaving the rest of the bark on, so that they were just as straight and much stronger than sawed ones. Each stick was carefully mortised or tenoned by its stump, for I had borrowed other tools by this time. My days in the woods were not very long ones; yet I usually carried my dinner of bread and butter, and read the newspaper in which it was wrapped, at noon, sitting amid the green pine boughs which I had cut off, and to my bread was imparted some of their fragrance, for my hands were covered with a thick coat of pitch. . . . Sometimes a rambler in the wood was attracted by the sound of my axe, and we chatted pleasantly over the chips which I had made.

"By the middle of April, for I made no haste in my work, but rather made the most of it, my house was framed and ready for the raising. I had already bought the shanty of James Collins, an Irishman who worked on the Fitchburg Railroad, for boards. James Collins' shanty was considered an uncommonly fine one. . . . I took down this dwelling . . . drawing the nails, and removed it to the pond-side by small cartloads, spreading the boards on the grass there to bleach and warp back again in the sun. . . .

"I dug my cellar in the side of a hill sloping to the south, where a woodchuck had formerly dug his burrow, down through sumach and blackberry roots, and the lowest stain of vegetation, six feet square by seven deep, to a fine sand where potatoes would not freeze in any winter. The sides were left shelving, and not stoned; but the sun having never shone on them, the sand still keeps its place. It was but two hours' work. I took particular pleasure in this breaking of ground, for in almost all latitudes men dig into the earth for an equable temperature. . . .

"At length, in the beginning of May, with the help of some of my acquaintances . . . I set up the frame of my house. No man was ever more honored in the character of his raisers than I." The men who helped him in this were his friend Channing, George William Curtis, who was then living with Edmund Hosmer, Bronson Alcott, and Hosmer himself. The cabin cost Thoreau $28.12½, by his own careful reckoning.

Channing wrote of it, "As for its being in the ordinary meaning a house, it was so superior to the common domestic contrivances that I do not associate it with them. By standing on a chair you could reach into the garret, and a corn broom fathomed the depth of the cellar. It had no lock to the door, no curtain to the window, and belonged to nature nearly as much as to man. . . . It was just large enough for one, like the plate of boiled apple pudding he used to order of the restauranteur. . . . It was . . . a sentry box in the shore, in the wood of Walden, ready to walk into in rain or snow or cold. . . ."

Into this cabin Thoreau moved a bed, a desk, a table, a few utensils, three chairs, and a tiny looking-glass but three inches in diameter. One of the chairs Thoreau used for the purpose of announcing that he was open to visitors by dint of setting the chair outside his door. On the fourth of July, 1845, Thoreau moved into the cabin on the shore of the cove on the north side of Walden Pond. Two days later he wrote in his journal:

"I wish to meet the facts of life—the vital facts, which are the phenomena of actuality the gods meant to show us—face to face, and so I came down here. Life! who knows what it is, what it does? If I am not quite right here, I am less wrong than before; and now let us see what they will have."

He set about his business at Walden Pond without delay. He had his previous journals with him—and the material he wished to draw upon to write *A Week on the Concord and Merrimack Rivers*—the two weeks he had spent on this excursion with his brother he saw best as a week for the purposes of his account, which was to be much more than a simple record of the journey. At the same time he was putting down his notes for *Walden,* however unconsciously.

He reveled in his freedom, in his solitude—which was not quite the solitude of a recluse, for the retreat at Walden Pond was not a hermitage. He was visited by Hosmer, Alex Therien, a garrulous wood-chopper, Channing, members of his family, and others; he walked into Concord whenever the mood was upon him—for conversation, or to find some food not of his own baking—for he baked bread for himself at his own hearth—or to see people or to attend a lecture at the Lyceum. He did not pretend to be a hermit. He had but established a listening post in a familiar wilderness with one foot, as it were, on the threshold of the village, so that he could withdraw in either direction, as his inclination dictated.

He accepted his animal neighbors and they accepted him. A mouse nested under his house "and came when I took my luncheon to pick the crumbs at my feet. It had never seen the race of man before, and so the sooner became familiar. It ran over my shoes and up my pantaloons inside, clinging to my flesh with its sharp claws. It would run up the side of the room by short impulses like a squirrel. . . . At length, as I leaned my elbow on the bench, it ran over my arm and round the paper which contained my dinner. And when I held it a piece of cheese, it came and nibbled between my fingers, and then cleaned its face and paws like a fly."

He sat outside of evenings and played his flute and heard the echo from a nearby wood—"a stolen pleasure, occasionally not rightfully heard, much more for other ears than ours," and pondered his position: "A man must find his own occasion in himself. The natural day is very calm, and will hardly reprove our indolence. If there is no elevation in our spirits, the pond will not seem elevated like a mountain tarn, but a low pool, a silent muddy water, a place for fishermen.

"I sit here at my window like a priest of Isis, and observe the phenomena of three thousand years ago, yet unimpaired. The tantivy of wild pigeons, an ancient race of birds, gives a voice to the air, flying by twos and threes athwart my view or perching restless on the white pine boughs occasionally; a fish hawk dimples the glassy surface of the pond and brings up a fish; and for the last half-hour I have heard the rattle of railroad cars conveying travellers from Boston to the country."

He spent a little while from time to time tending his "garden." Even before he had finished his house, "wishing to earn ten or twelve dollars by some honest and agreeable method, in order to meet my unusual expenses," he had planted over two acres in beans, with a small part reserved for potatoes, corn, peas, and turnips. He did not "quite hoe it all once. I got out several cords of stumps in plowing, which supplied me with fuel for a long time, and left small circles of virgin mold, easily distinguishable through the summer by the greater luxuriance of the beans there. . . . I was obliged to hire a team and a man for the plowing, though I held the plow myself. My farm outgoes for the first season were, for implements, seed, work, etc., $14.72½. The seed corn was given me. This never costs anything to speak of, unless you plant more than enough. I got twelve bushels of beans, and eighteen bushels of potatoes, beside some peas and sweet corn. The yellow corn and turnips were too late to come to anything."

His net income from the venture at farming was $8.71½ "beside produce consumed and on hand at the time this estimate was made of the value of $4.50,—the amount on hand more than balancing a little grass which I did not raise. All things considered, that is, considering the importance of a man's soul and of to-day, notwithstanding the short time occupied by my experiment, nay, partly even because of its transient character, I believe that that was doing better than any farmer in Concord did that year."

Whatever his townsmen thought of his venture—and among them, Channing had spent some months in a hut on the Illinois prairies—he himself did not think that he had gone into any wilderness to live in isolation. "It is in vain to dream of a wildness distant from ourselves. . . . I shall never find in the wilds of Labrador any greater wildness than in some recess in Concord, i.e., than I import into it." The townsmen—save for Alcott, Emerson and Channing—saw no evidence that Thoreau at Walden Pond was other than a farmer, in a small way; the creative life seldom leaves evidence of work immediately apparent, as, for instance, the mound of earth left by a ditch-digger.

His chief concern at Walden was not, after all, raising beans. It was in a sense an attempt to justify his way of life—the rightness of doing what he wanted. In the course of it he intensified his study of nature and of man—just as he had said he would do—not so much the men of Concord village, whom he had known before, as the men who were his fellows in the wilder areas of the town— Alex Therien ("a Canadian now, a woodchopper, a post-maker . . . and who made his last supper on a woodchuck which his dog caught")—to whom Thoreau occasionally read—the Irish laborers settled in the vicinity after building the railroad, among them John Field, and Hugh Quoil ("He was a man of manners and gentlemanlike, as one who had seen the world, and was capable of more civil speech than you could well attend to.").

In the course of his enquiry he also worked on his first book.

He had begun the writing of *A Week on the Concord and Merrimack Rivers* even before moving to Walden. As early as March, 1845, he had delivered before the Concord Lyceum as a lecture the opening chapter of that book, *Concord River,* and he now set himself to raiding his earlier journal for the material to round out the book so begun. He intended it to be a compendium of verse, quotations, essays all hung loosely within the frame of a seven-day excursion on the Musketaquid or Grassgrown River now called the Concord.

Since the early journal was filled with quotations, there was no dearth of them. He began by quoting Ovid and ended with Virgil; between them he used Donne, Pindar, Spenser, Emerson, Chaucer, Channing, Quarles, Bishop Percy, Anacreon, Tennyson, George Herbert, and others. Within the frame of the excursion he had taken with his brother, he set down whatever seized his fancy, taking off from paragraphs in the early journals. He included no less than half a hundred of his own poems or fragments of poems. He put in essays on prose, on Christianity, friendship, history, satire. Yet, while the title he chose for his book invited prospective readers to join him and his brother on a leisurely trip on the rivers, it was his primary purpose to offer his essays in some acceptable frame. These little essays, so carefully wrought, were for Thoreau the heart and substance of this first book he put together.

The book occupied him, but not exclusively. He found time to tend his beans—but less in the spring of 1846, when the book was nearing completion, and when he recorded that he planted fewer beans and more "sincerity, truth, simplicity, faith, innocence," which may have been a reference to the work in progress. He found time to prepare material for his most unified and best work, yet to come, and to write *Thomas Carlyle and His Works* ("It is not in man to determine what his style shall be. He might as well determine what his thoughts shall be. . . . No, his thoughts were ever irregular and impetuous. . . . Who cares what a man's style is, so it is intelligible,—as intelligible as his thought. Literally and really, the style is no more than the *stylus,* the pen he writes with; and it is not worth scraping and polishing, and gilding, unless it will write his thoughts the better for it. It is something for use, and not to look at. . . . Translate a book a dozen times from one language to another, and what becomes of its style? . . . We believe that Carlyle has, after all, more readers, and is better known to-day for this very originality of style, and that posterity will have reason to thank him for emancipating the language, in some measure, from the fetters which a merely conservative, aimless, and pedantic literary class had imposed upon it, and setting an example of greater freedom and naturalness.")

Like most authors, he tried out selected portions of his book on his visitors. Bronson Alcott was especially impressed by what he heard in the course of his various visits to the cabin at Walden. In his own journal, Alcott wrote, "The book is purely American, fragrant with the lives of New England woods and streams, and could have been written nowhere else. . . . There is a toughness too, and a sinewy vigor, as of roots and the strength that comes of feeding on wild meats, and the moist lustres of the fishes in the bed below. It has the merit, moreover, that somehow, despite all presumptions to the contrary, the sod and sap and fibre and flavor of New England have found at last a clear relation to the literature of other and classic lands."

He read part of the book to Emerson, "under an oak on the river bank the other afternoon," as Emerson wrote. "In a short time, if Wiley and Putnam smile, you shall have Henry Thoreau's *Excursion on the Concord and Merrimack Rivers,* a seven days' voyage in as many chapters, pastoral as Isaak Walton, spicy as flagroot, broad and deep as Menu. He read me some of it . . . and invigorated me." Emerson's reference was to a firm of New York publishers with which he was acquainted. At the time of this letter—July, 1846—the book was ready for publication, though it was yet to undergo further revision.

Thoreau had high hopes for it. What budding author does not have such hopes for his first book?—unaware of the often painful realities of publishing, which are so different from what the author conceives them to be. Very probably Emerson himself sent it off to Wiley and Putnam. Thoreau had some reason to be hopeful, for, through the good offices of Horace Greeley, he soon learned that he had been accepted elsewhere.

Greeley, impressed by his essay on Carlyle, had undertaken to send it around, and presently wrote to say that Rufus Griswold, editor of *Graham's Magazine,* had accepted it for his magazine "to be paid for at the usual rate." Thoreau began to feel that a way to maintain himself in his modest way was being opened for him by his pen, and he entertained visions of a large edition of his first book at a popular price, so that it might have a wide circulation. He waited for Wiley and Putnam to smile upon his fledgeling.

He waited in vain.

CHAPTER 5

Journey to Maine

The authority of government, even such as I am willing to submit to—for I will cheerfully obey those who know and can do better than I, and in many things even those who neither know nor can do so well—is still an impure one: to be strictly just, it must have the sanction and consent of the governed. It can have no pure right over my person and property but what I concede to it. The progress from an absolute to a limited monarchy, from a limited monarchy to a democracy, is a progress toward a true respect for the individual. Even the Chinese philosopher was wise enough to regard the individual as the basis of the empire. Is a democracy, such as we know it, the last improvement possible in government? Is it not possible to take a step further towards recognizing and organizing the rights of man? There will never be a really free and enlightened State until the State comes to recognize the individual as a higher and independent power, from which all its own power and authority are derived, and treats him accordingly. I please myself with imagining a State at least which can afford to be just to all men, and to treat the individual with respect as a neighbor; which even would not think it inconsistent with its own repose if a few were to live aloof from it, not meddling with it, nor embraced by it, who fulfilled all the duties of neighbors and fellow-men. A State which bore this kind of fruit, and suffered it to drop off as fast as it ripened, would prepare the way for a still more perfect and glorious State, which also I have imagined, but not yet anywhere seen. —CIVIL DISOBEDIENCE

ONE July evening in 1846, planning to go berrying next day, Thoreau walked into Concord from Walden to get a shoe he had left at the cobbler's for mending. He was accosted by Sam Staples, the Concord jailer, and charged with not having paid his poll tax. Thoreau had not paid poll tax since 1843— when Bronson Alcott had spent a night in jail for refusing to pay his. Why should he? He had never voted, and such a purely political tax as a poll tax was allied to such political acts as the Mexican War, which had begun that May, and the maintenance of slavery.

Without more ado, Thoreau was clapped into jail, "mad as the devil," as Staples recalled it later. His anger cooled. He heard Staples lock up, take off his boots, and close the jail for the night. Here Thoreau was, and here he had to stay. He grew philosophical.

"As I stood considering the walls of solid stone, two or three feet thick, the door of wood and iron, a foot thick, and the iron grating which strained the light, I could not help being struck with the foolishness of that institution which treated me as if I were mere flesh and blood and bones, to be locked up. I wondered that it should have concluded at length that this was the best use it could put me to, and had never thought to avail itself of my services in some way. I saw that, if there was a wall of stone between me and my townsmen, there was a still more difficult one to climb or break through before they could get to be as free as I was. I did not for a moment feel confined, and the walls seemed a great waste of stone and mortar. I felt as if I alone of all my towns-

66

men had paid my tax. . . . I could not but smile to see how industriously they locked the door on my meditations, which followed them out again without let or hindrance, and *they* were really all that was dangerous. . . .

"It was like travelling into a far country, such as I had never expected to behold, to lie there for one night. It seemed to me that I never had heard the town clock strike before, nor the evening sounds of the village; for we slept with the windows open, which were inside the grating. It was to see my native village in the light of the Middle Ages, and our Concord was turned into a Rhine stream, and visions of knights and castles passed before me. They were the voices of old burghers that I heard in the streets. I was an involuntary spectator and auditor of whatever was done and said in the kitchen of the adjacent village inn—a wholly new and rare experience to me. It was a closer view of my native town. I was fairly inside of it. I never had seen its institutions before. This is one of its peculiar institutions; for it is a shire town. I began to comprehend what its inhabitants were about.

"In the morning, our breakfasts were put through the hole in the door, in small oblong-square tin pans, made to fit, and holding a pint of chocolate, with brown bread, and an iron spoon. When they called for the vessels again, I was green enough to return what bread I had left; but my comrade seized it, and said that I should lay that up for lunch or dinner. . . .

"I saw yet more distinctly the State in which I lived. I saw to what extent the people among whom I lived could be trusted as good neighbors and friends; that their friendship was for summer weather only . . ."

Some years previous to Thoreau's imprisonment, he had "signed off" from his church affiliation. "The State met me in behalf of the Church, and commanded me to

67

pay a certain sum toward the support of a clergyman whose preaching my father attended, but never I myself. . . . I declined to pay. . . . However, at the request of the selectmen, I condescended to make some such statement as this in writing:—'Know all men by these presents, that I, Henry Thoreau, do not wish to be regarded as a member of any incorporated society which I have not joined.' This I gave to the town clerk; and he has it. The State, having thus learned that I did not wish to be regarded as a member of that church, has never made a like demand on me since. . . ."

In prison, Thoreau made friends with his cell-mate; Staples told Thoreau that he was "a first-rate fellow and a clever man." He had been put into prison accused of arson, but Thoreau was of the opinion that "he had probably gone to bed in a barn when drunk, and smoked his pipe there; and so a barn was burnt." He pumped his fellow-prisoner "as dry as I could," but eventually they turned in.

In the morning Thoreau was released because someone—probably his Aunt Maria Thoreau—had paid his tax. He was even angrier at this. His fellow townsmen "first looked at me, and then at one another, as if I had returned from a long journey." Undoubtedly they were not as surprised as Thoreau thought they might be, for patently a fellow who did nothing much but walk around and make notes in his journal, with enough time to set the woods on fire, instead of being engaged in some socially approved venture which would make him money, could be expected to land in jail sooner or later.

Once released, Thoreau went on about his business. He had been on his way for a mended shoe; so he got it. He had intended to lead a berrying party into the hills and in half an hour he was "on one of our highest hills, two miles off, and then the State was nowhere to be seen."

Out of this experience grew his first statement of his individual philosophy, originally titled *Resistance to Civil Government,* and written two years after, at almost the same time that Karl Marx was setting down *The Communist Manifesto.* But Thoreau's concern was with principles, not the reform of society, and he celebrated the individuality of man and the problems which do not yield to solution by any political structure or philosophy.

The imprisonment left an indelible impression on Thoreau. He could be amused by it later, but he thought about the principles involved a long time, for it was almost two years before he wrote about it in the essay which was eventually to be titled *Civil Disobedience.* It was not such a paper as would inflame to mass rebellion, but only an account of the individual of integrity, who has no recourse but to oppose the oppression of the State by means of passive resistance.

"Action from principle . . . changes things and relations; it is essentially revolutionary," he wrote when in retrospect he considered his arrest and the reasons for it. "If the injustice is part of the necessary friction of the machine of government, let it go, let it go: perchance it will wear smooth. . . . But if it is of such a nature that it requires you to be the agent of injustice to another, then, I say, break the law. . . . I was not born to be forced. I will breathe after my own fashion. . . . If a plant cannot live according to its nature, it dies; and so a man. . . . I am as desirous of being a good neighbor as I am of being a bad subject."

For the nonce, however, he was berry-picking, heading a party in the hills, and presently, finishing with this, he walked back to Walden and resumed where he had left off—the affairs which had brought him to this place, which now included the beginnings of his second book, *Walden*. This did not occupy him so exclusively that he found it impossible to leave the area; on the last day of August, 1846, he set out for a trip through Maine.

"I left Concord . . . for Bangor and the backwoods of Maine, by way of the railroad and steamboat, intending to accompany a relative of mine . . . as far as a dam on the west branch of the Penobscot. . . . From this place, which is about one hundred miles by the river above Bangor, I proposed to make excursions to Mount Ktaadn, the second highest mountain in New England, . . . and to some of the lakes of the Penobscot, either alone or with such company as I might pick up there."

In Maine, as was the case wherever he went, Thoreau set down voluminous notes. Everything was grist for him. He went, as always, in wonder, clear-eyed, anxious to miss no detail which might enlarge his horizons or add to his knowledge of nature and his fellowmen, and enable him to draw sound conclusions about man and his place in the universe. Whatever he saw might be turned into lectures, articles for the magazines, or perhaps even a book.

He was prepared to learn more about the Indians and how they lived, for the Penobscots roamed the Maine wilderness. He hoped to study them at first hand, but the Indian guides who had been arranged for, did not show up, and George McCauslin was persuaded to take the party instead. "McCauslin was a Kennebec man, of Scotch descent, who had been a waterman twenty-two years, and had driven on the lakes and headwaters of the Penobscot five or six springs in succession, but was now settled here to raise supplies for the lumberers and for himself. . . . A man of dry wit and shrewdness, and a general intelligence which I had not looked for in the backwoods. In fact, the deeper you penetrate into the woods, the more intelligent, and, in one sense, less countrified do you find the inhabitants; for always the pioneer has been a traveler, and, to some extent, a man of the world; and, as the distances with which he is familiar are greater, so is his information more general and far reaching than the villagers'. If I were to look for a narrow, uninformed, and countrified mind, as opposed to the intelligence and refinement which are thought to emanate from cities, it would be among the rusty inhabitants of an old-settled country, on farms all run out and gone to seed with life-everlasting, in the towns about Boston, even on the high-road in Concord, and not in the backwoods of Maine."

They went into country of bear and moose and added to their supplies by fishing. "Seizing the birch poles which some party of Indians, or white hunters, had left on the shore, and baiting our hooks with pork, and with trout, as soon as they were caught, we cast our lines into the mouth of the Aboljacknagesic, a clear, swift, shallow stream, which came in from Ktaadn. Instantly a shoal of white chivlin (*Leucisci pulchelli*), silvery roaches, cousin-trout, or what not, large and small, prowling thereabouts, fell upon our bait, and one after another were landed amidst the bushes. Anon their cousins, the true trout, took their turn, and alternately the speckled trout, and the silvery roaches, swallowed the bait as fast as we could throw in; and the finest specimens of both that I have ever seen, the largest one weighing three pounds, were heaved upon the shore . . . While yet alive, before their tints had faded, they glistened like the fairest flowers, the product of primitive rivers; and (the angler) could hardly trust his senses, as he stood

71

over them, that these jewels should have swam away in that Aboljacknagesic water for so long, so many dark ages;—these bright fluviatile flowers, seen of Indians only, made beautiful, the Lord only knows why, to swim there! I could understand better for this, the truth of mythology, the fables of Proteus, and all those beautiful sea-monsters,—how all history, indeed, put to a terrestrial use, is mere history; but put to a celestial, is mythology always."

The party traveled until they broke a pike-pole and ran short of provisions, then turned back. Thoreau was so favorably impressed with the Maine woods that he resolved to return, if opportunity came. "What is most striking in the Maine wilderness is the continuousness of the forest, with fewer open intervals or glades than you had imagined. Except the few burnt lands, the narrow intervals on the rivers, the bare tops of the high mountains, and the lakes and streams, the forest is uninterrupted. It is even more grim and wild than you had anticipated, a damp and intricate wilderness, in the spring everywhere wet and miry. The aspect of the country, indeed, is universally stern and savage, excepting the distant views of the forest from hills, and the lake prospects, which are mild and civilizing in a degree. . . . The aborigines have never been dispossessed, nor nature disforested. . . .

"What a place to live, what a place to die and be buried in! There certainly men would live forever, and laugh at death and the grave. . . .

"I am reminded by my journey how exceedingly new this country still is. You have only to travel for a few days into the interior and back parts even of many of the old States, to come to that very America which the Northmen, and Cabot, and Gosnold, and Smith, and Raleigh visited. If Columbus was the first to discover the islands,

Americus Vespucius and Cabot, and the Puritans, and we their descendants, have discovered only the shores of America."

Back in Concord, he took up where he had left off— at Walden. No matter how much he might move out from the cabin along the shore of the pond, this was his retreat where he might come face to face with himself. He continued to write, perhaps with a certain desperation. He was now in his thirtieth year, he had yet to have a book published, and his magazine appearances, apart from *The Dial*, were few and far between. He worked at *Walden*, and from his journal drew material for lectures to be given at the Concord Lyceum, and, hopefully, elsewhere at a fee.

In February, 1847, he lectured twice at the Lyceum— once *The History of Myself*, the second time on *Walden*, and his life there; these were the first public revelation of any part of that second book. But his primary concern was still publication, and he must have been understandably nettled at the lack of it—his first book had yet to find a publisher, and *Graham's Magazine* had not yet printed his *Thomas Carlyle and His Works*.

He wrote to Wiley & Putnam asking that his book manuscript be sent back so that he could revise it yet again, and he wrote to Horace Greeley to suggest withdrawal of his article from *Graham's*. Greeley replied in haste to say that the article was in type and destined for the leading place in the March issue of the magazine, and to beg Thoreau not to be "unreasonably sensitive at the delay." He was somewhat troubled by Thoreau's suggestion that the article be withdrawn and pointed out to him the advantages of appearing in a magazine with so much prestige as *Graham's*. At the same time, he suggested to Thoreau that he might soon have material

73

enough for a volume worth publishing, and promised to "see what can be done" about publishing it. He also offered to publish any article Thoreau might care to write about Emerson or Hawthorne, and pay him well for it; but Thoreau was deaf to this offer because he would not take advantage of friendship for money.

He had, this year, at least one different commission. When Horatio B. Storer, a young naturalist studying at Harvard, asked him whether he collected specimens of birds' eggs, Thoreau confessed "to a little squeamishness on the score of robbing their nests, though I could easily go to the length of abstracting an egg or two gently, now and then, and if the advancement of science obviously demanded it might be carried even to the extreme of deliberate murder." But he was less loath to collect live specimens for Louis Agassiz, who had come to Harvard from Switzerland to lecture, beginning in October, 1846. By way of his friend, James Cabot, Thoreau sent to Agassiz a collection of fish, turtles, a black snake, and a mouse he had put together at Walden.

Cabot reported that Agassiz was delighted with the specimens and would like to see more. Some money was paid to Thoreau for them, but it was very probably paid to cover expenses incurred in obtaining them. That spring of 1847 Thoreau gathered many fish and reptiles and sent them to Agassiz through Cabot. He suggested that Agassiz himself might like to come to Walden for "a spearing excursion," but his lectures so occupied Agassiz that he could not accept Thoreau's invitation to join him.

In May Thoreau sent Cabot a long letter listing the fish commonly found in the Concord waters—pickerel ("Those caught in Walden, hard by my house, are easily distinguished from those caught in the river, being much heavier in proportion to their size, stouter, firmer fleshed, and lighter colored. The little pickerel which I sent last, jumped into the boat in its fright."), pouts, breams ("Some more green, others more brown."), suckers, perch ("I have counted ten transverse bands on some of the smaller."), lampreys ("Very scarce since the dams at Lowell and Billerica were built."), shiners, roach or chiverin, trout, eels, and red-finned minnows ("I have never recognized them in any books. Have they any scientific name?"), and asked, "What of the above does M. Agassiz particularly wish to see?" Agassiz particularly wished to see "the pickerel with the long snout, which he suspects may be the *Esox estor*, or Maskalongé."

On June 1, Thoreau sent in "15 pouts, 17 perch, 13 shiners, 1 larger land tortoise, and 5 muddy tortoises . . . 7 perch, 5 shiners, 8 breams, 4 dace? 2 muddy tortoises, 5 painted do., and 3 land do." variously from Walden Pond and the river. He sent also "one black snake, alive, and one dormouse? caught last night in my cellar," and promised to send "the pickerel with the longer snout" when he met with it. He was anxious to have for himself any scientific information about the specimens which he himself did not yet have, and was as delighted as Agassiz to learn that he had probably turned up one or two new species.

Meanwhile, Thoreau's first book was going the rounds of the publishers in vain. By late August Thoreau was inquiring of James Munroe & Company how much it would cost to publish the book at his own expense. And on September 6 of that year he left the Walden cabin as abruptly as he had come to it. "There was a little stagnation, it may be. About 2 o'clock in the afternoon the world's axle creaked as if it needed greasing. . . . I left the woods for as good a reason as I went there. Perhaps it seemed to me that I had several more lives to live, and could not spare any more time for that one. It is remarkable how easily and insensibly we fall into a particular route, and make a beaten track for ourselves. I had not lived there a week before my feet wore a path from my door to the pond-side . . . I did not wish to take a cabin passage, but rather to go before the mast and on the deck of the world, for there I could best see the moonlight amid the mountains. I do not wish to go below now."

Within a month, Thoreau was once more at the room at the head of the stairs in Emerson's house—invited to stay there by Lidian Emerson with Emerson's approval while Emerson himself went on a lecture tour of England. And that autumn, too, he cut the tie to Walden Pond and his haven there even more definitely by selling the cabin at Walden to Hugh Whelan, Emerson's gardener. That autumn, also, he took a little stock of himself when he finally answered an inquiry from the secretary of his Harvard Class of 1837—

"I don't know whether mine is a profession, or a trade, or what not. It is not yet learned, and in every instance has been practised before being studied. The mercantile part of it was begun *here* by myself alone.

"—It is not one but legion. I will give you some of the monster's heads. I am a Schoolmaster—a Private Tutor, a Surveyor—a Gardener, a Farmer—a Painter, I mean a House Painter, a Carpenter, a Mason, a Day-Laborer, a Pencil-Maker, a Glass-paper Maker, a Writer, and sometimes a Poetaster. If you will act the part of Iolas, and apply a hot iron to any of these heads, I shall be greatly obliged to you.

"My present employment is to answer such orders as may be expected from so general an advertisement as the above—that is, if I see fit, which is not always the case, for I have found out a way to live without what is commonly called employment or industry attractive or otherwise. Indeed my steadiest employment, if such it can be called, is to keep myself at the top of my condition, and ready for whatever may turn up in heaven or on earth. For the last two or three years I have lived in Concord woods alone, something more than a mile from any neighbor, in a house built entirely by myself."

He might have added that he had lived at Walden Pond for two years and two months at an average cost of twenty-seven cents a day. He did add in a postscript that if any members of the Class of 1837 "are in want of pecuniary assistance, and will make known their case to me, I will engage to give them some advice of more worth than money."

The resumption of his life at the Emerson house meant a renewal of his entertainment of the Emerson children and their guests, of the trivial cares of housekeeping and caring for the grounds. Though his journal contained little of his daily chores, the letters he wrote to Emerson in England did. "I have banked up the young trees against the winter and the mice, and I will look out, in my careless way, to see when a pale is loose or a nail drops out of its place. The broad gaps, at least, I will occupy. . . . The world is a cow that is hard to milk,—life does not come so easy,—and oh, how thinly it is watered ere we get it! . . .

"Lidian and I make very good housekeepers. She is a very dear sister to me. Ellen and Edith and Eddy and Aunty Brown keep up the tragedy and comedy and tragic-comedy of life as usual. . . . Eddy . . . occasionally surveys mankind from my shoulders as wisely as ever Johnson did. I respect him not a little, though it is I that lift him up so unceremoniously. . . . He very seriously asked me, the other day, 'Mr. Thoreau, will you be my father?' I am occasionally Mr. Rough-and-tumble with him that I may not miss *him*, and lest he should miss *you* too much. So you must come back soon, or you will be superseded."

He wrote Emerson of the little affairs of Concord. "Mr. Hosmer has been working at a tannery in Stow for a fortnight, though he has just now come home sick. . . . Mrs. Hosmer remains here, and John looks stout enough to fill his own shoes and his father's too. . . . Mr. Blood and his company have at length seen the stars through the great telescope, and he told me he thought it was worth the while. . . ." And the affairs of Cambridge—"Cambridge college is really beginning to wake up and redeem its character and overtake the age. I see by the catalogue that they are about establishing a scientific school in connection with the university . . . Agassiz will erelong commence his lectures in the zoological department. A chemistry class has already been formed under the direction of Professor Horsford."

He informed Emerson, too, that he had had "a tragic correspondence, for the most part all on one side" with Miss Sophia Foord, who had not long since lived under the same roof, where she had tutored the young Emersons, though she had been gone over half a year when she had written to Thoreau, proposing that they be married. "She did really wish to—I hesitate to write—marry me. That is the way they spell it. Of course I did not write a deliberate answer. How could I deliberate upon it? I sent back as distinct a *no* as I have learned to pronounce after considerable practice, and I trust that this *no* has succeeded. Indeed, I wished that it might burst, like hollow shot, after it had struck and buried itself and made itself felt there. *There was no other way. I really had anticipated no such foe as this in my career."*

He wrote little of himself. "I do not know what to say of myself. I sit before my green desk, in the chamber at the head of the stairs, and attend to my thinking, sometimes more, sometimes less distinctly. I am not unwilling to think great thoughts if there are any in the wind, but what they are I am not sure. They suffice to keep me awake while the day lasts, at any rate. Perhaps they will redeem some portion of the night erelong."

He had "nothing worth writing" about his book. "Wiley & Putnam, Munroe, the Harpers, and Crosby & Nichols have all declined printing it with the least risk to themselves; but Wiley & Putnam will print it in their series, and any of them, anywhere, at *my* risk." Nevertheless, he was concerned about his book, though he wrote to Emerson that he was "indifferent." He was in the process of settling in his mind whether he should continue to hope for a publisher who might take on his book, or whether he should frankly arrange for its publication himself; it was a problem that touched less upon his vanity—that did not concern him at all—than it did upon the simple finances involved, since the sum required would not be one that could be worked up at twenty-seven cents a day.

He bent himself to do more lecturing. Late in January he delivered *The Rights and Duties of the Individual in Relation to Government*—the first public version of *Civil Disobedience*—to the Concord Lyceum. Requests to lecture outside Concord, however, were not easily come by, though before 1848 was done, he had such invitations, principally because Nathaniel Hawthorne persuaded the managers of the Salem Lyceum to ask Thoreau to lecture, which he did, on the economy of student life in New England, in some part a portion of *Walden*.

In 1848, too, Horace Greeley managed to sell *Ktaadn and the Maine Woods*—for which he had paid Thoreau $25 himself—to the *Union Magazine* at three times that fee, part of which he sent Thoreau. Greeley had faithfully represented Thoreau, who was not a prolific writer and who was, from the point-of-view of an editor, not easy to deal with in his impatience and his desire to make constant changes in his manuscript and his objection to any editing.

Perhaps the most important event of 1848 for Thoreau was the opening of a correspondence of ideas with Harrison G. O. Blake, of Worcester, Massachusetts, a Harvard graduate, once a Unitarian minister, who had reread Thoreau's article on Aulus Persius Flaccus in *The Dial*, and had seen new depth and meaning in it. He wrote with the enthusiasm of a sycophant asking about the "significance" of Thoreau's life on the threshold of Thoreau's fourth decade. Late in March, 1848, Thoreau answered him.

"I do believe that the outward and the inward life correspond; that if any should succeed to live a higher life, others would not know of it; that difference and distance are one. To set about living a true life is to go a journey to a distant country, gradually to find ourselves surrounded by new scenes and men; and as long as the old are around me, I know that I am not in any true sense living a new or a better life. The outward is only the outside of that which is within. Men are not concealed under habits, but are revealed by them; they are their true clothes. . . .

"I do believe in simplicity. It is astonishing as well as sad, how many trivial affairs even the wisest man thinks he must attend to in a day; how singular an affair he thinks he must omit. When the mathematician would solve a difficult problem, he first frees the equation of all incumbrances, and reduces it to its simplest terms. So simplify the problem of life, distinguish the necessary and the real. Probe the earth to see where your main roots run. I would stand upon facts. . . .

"My actual life is a fact in view of which I have no occasion to congratulate myself, but for my faith and aspiration I have respect. It is from these that I speak. Every man's position is in fact too simple to be described. I have sworn no oath. I have no designs on society—or nature—or God. I am simply what I am, or I begin to be that. I *live* in the *present*. I only remember the past—and anticipate the future. I love to live, I love reform better than its modes. . . .

"If you would convince a man that he does wrong, do right. But do not care to convince him.—Men will believe what they see. Let them see.

"Pursue, keep up with, circle round and round your life as a dog does his master's chaise. Do what you love. Know your own bone; gnaw at it, bury it, unearth it, and gnaw it still. Do not be too moral. You may cheat yourself out of much life so. Aim above morality. Be not *simply* good—be good for something.—All fables indeed have their morals, but the innocent enjoy the story.

"Let nothing come between you and the light. Respect men as brothers only. When you travel to the celestial city, carry no letter of introduction. When you knock ask to see God—none of the servants. In what concerns you much do not think that you have companions—know that you are alone in the world."

Thus opened a correspondence which was to continue for the rest of Thoreau's life. For some time, while Blake probed Thoreau, the tenor of their correspondence continued on this level of ideas; Blake manifestly wanted to know all he could about Thoreau. "If one hesitates in his path, let him not proceed," wrote Thoreau in his second letter to Blake, less than six weeks later. "Let him respect his doubts, for doubts, too, may have some divinity in them. That we have but little faith is not sad, but that we have but little faithfulness. By faithfulness faith is earned. When, in the progress of a life, a man swerves, though only by an angle infinitely small, from his proper and allotted path . . . then the drama of his life turns to tragedy, and makes haste to its fifth act. . . .

"I am of kin to the sod, and partake largely of its dull patience,—in winter expecting the sun of spring. In my cheapest moments I am apt to think that it is not my business to be 'seeking the spirit,' but as much its business to be seeking me. I know very well what Goethe meant when he said that he never had a chagrin but he made a poem out of it. I have altogether too much patience of this kind. I am too easily contented with a slight and almost animal happiness. My happiness is a good deal like that of the woodchucks.

"Methinks I am never quite committed, never wholly the creature of my moods, being always to some extent their critic. My only integral experience is in my vision. I see, perchance, with more integrity than I feel."

In July of 1848, Emerson returned from England, and Thoreau left the Emerson house to live once again with his family, resuming his endless walking and writing, and once more making pencils and surveying when called upon to do so, biding his time until the dream of book publication became the reality.

CHAPTER 6

Cape Cod and Concord

There is a sort of homely truth and naturalness in some books which is very rare to find, and yet looks cheap enough. There may be nothing lofty in the sentiment, or fine in the expression, but it is careless country talk. Homeliness is almost as great a merit in a book as in a house, if the reader would abide there. It is next to beauty, and a very high art. Some have this merit only. The scholar is not apt to make this most familiar experience come gracefully to the aid of his expression. Very few men can speak of Nature, for instance, with any truth. They overstep her modesty, somehow or other, and confer no favor. They do not speak a good word for her. Most cry better than they speak, and you get more nature out of them by pinching them than by addressing them. The surliness with which the woodchopper speaks of his woods, handling them as indifferently as his axe, is better than the mealymouthed enthusiasm of the lover of Nature. Better that the primrose by the river's brim be a yellow primrose, and nothing more, than that it be something less. . . . But a good book will never have been forestalled, but the topic itself will in one sense be new, and its author, by consulting with Nature, will consult not only with those who have gone before, but with those who may come after. There is always room and occasion enough for a true book on any subject; as there is room for more light the brightest day and more rays will not interfere with the first.

—A WEEK ON THE CONCORD AND MERRIMACK RIVERS

By 1849, Thoreau was committed to the publication of *A Week on the Concord and Merrimack Rivers* at his own expense. He had had estimates from W. D. Ticknor & Company ("Say—1000 Cops. 448 pages like Emerson's Essays 1st series printed on good paper @ . . . $501.24") and from Munroe, also of Boston. It was to Munroe that the manuscript finally went early that year. Thoreau had committed himself to a financial obligation greater than any he had heretofore assumed.

His income to defray the costs he had agreed to pay for his new book did not materially increase. He lectured for a second time on his Walden experience in Salem in mid-February. A month later he lectured in Portland, Maine, on the same subject. His cousin, George Thatcher, asked him to address the Bangor Lyceum, since he was already in Maine and thus not far away; he quoted a fee of twenty-five dollars. Thoreau, however, was busy with the proofs of his book and did not want to go to Bangor for but one lecture, writing, "unless I should hear that they want *two* lectures to be read in *one* week or nearer together, I shall have to decline coming, this time." Thatcher was not able to arrange for two lectures and wrote Thoreau to this effect; his letter was waiting for Thoreau at Portland. Thoreau was not displeased; he had not wanted to go, having grown somewhat disenchanted with lecturing at relatively limited remuneration. "I am just in the midst of printing my book, which is likely to turn out much larger than I expected. I shall advertise another, 'Walden, or Life in the Woods,' in the first . . ." Presumably his second book was ready in manuscript by this time, though it was certainly not yet in its final form.

In April, Elizabeth Peabody asked him to retouch *Resistance to Civil Government* for use in a periodical she intended to publish occasionally. "I have so much writing to do at present," he wrote her, "with the printers in the rear of me, that I have almost no time left, but for bodily exercise; however, I will send you the article in question before the end of next week. If this will not be soon enough, will you please inform me by the next mail?" He added a postscript: "I offer the paper to your *first volume* only." *Resistance to Civil Government* appeared in the May issue of *Aesthetic Papers*—Miss Peabody's first, and, since public reception was disappointing, her only issue. Busy as he was, Thoreau went in mid-April to lecture at Worcester, the first of a series of lectures Harrison Blake obtained for him there; this lecture was followed by a second only a week later.

Late in May, James Munroe brought out *A Week on the Concord and Merrimack Rivers*. At the time of its publication, however, Thoreau was caught up in the slow dying of his older sister Helen. Her death occurred on the fourteenth of June. She had been declining in health through the winter and spring, and was the second of that congenial family circle to die. She was but 37, three years short of normal life expectancy for women in Massachusetts at that time. Though Thoreau's new book was in hand, she had very probably read the work in manuscript or had had it read to her by Thoreau himself. Thoreau's concern for her took precedence over the publication of his first book. He had written his cousin George Thatcher in February—taking the occasion of the Portland lecture to inquire about "statistics of a winter excursion to Chesuncook" in Maine—that he did not "wish to foresee what change may take place in her condition or in my own" in reference to Helen's "gradually failing" health.

After her death, he looked to his first book. Like every author, Thoreau was buoyed aloft by his hopes. Like every author, he expected to be acclaimed by reviewers and accepted by enough of the reading public to make a little money, not only through sales of the book, but through the increased demand for his lectures brought about by his mounting prestige as an author. Perhaps only the author who has passed through the fire of experience can look upon publication of a book with more tempered judgment. Only that author who has already had his hopes dashed has learned not to raise his hopes too high.

Copies of the book were sent to selected readers and critics in England, particularly to those who might be thought sympathetic. Copies for review went to the leading newspapers and magazines of the day, and, of course, to Thoreau's friends. Like all other authors, Thoreau could not believe that his friends, out of various motives, were apt to be his least reliable critics. Alcott's enthusiasm may have been balm to Thoreau. Alcott thought that the book would be "a popular book with our people here." Emerson thought it "fresh as the wild flag," and a beautiful book in the poetry of its descriptive passages.

Alcott's judgment, however sound in regard to the book's literary value, was wide of the mark insofar as public reception was concerned. In New York, Horace Greeley, anxious to do everything he could for Thoreau's book, assigned it for a feature review to George Ripley. The *New York Tribune* had a wide influence and Greeley hoped to carry word of Thoreau's abilities throughout its range. Unhappily, his choice of reviewer was not a good one for that purpose. Though Ripley thought *A Week on the Concord and Merrimack Rivers* "very near a fresh, original, thoughtful work," in which the "observations of Nature are as genial as Nature itself, and the tones" of Thoreau's "harp have an Aeolian sweetness," and while Thoreau's "reflections are always striking, often profoundly truthful, and his scholastic treasures, though a little too ostentatiously displayed, are such as the best instructed reader will enjoy and thank him for," he was repelled by Thoreau's philosophy, "which is the Pantheistic egotism vaguely characterized as Transcendental." He said, "It seems second-hand, imitative, often exaggerated—a bad specimen of a dubious and dangerous school."

All this was set forth in the very first paragraph of the review. Many a reader of book reviews goes no farther than the first paragraph if he finds in it such disapproval that strikes a note of harmony in him. No matter what Ripley might write farther along in his review, he had done the book irreparable harm in his opening paragraph. He went on to quote liberally from the book after setting forth that Thoreau was "a scholar, a laborer, and in some sort a hermit" whose main purpose in life seemed to be "to demonstrate how slender an impediment is poverty to a man who pampers no superfluous wants, and how truly independent and self-sufficing is he who is in no manner the slave of his own appetites." But he inevitably returned to the attack on Thoreau's philosophy and charged him with an attack on the Bible. "Can that which Milton and Newton so profoundly reverenced . . . be wisely turned off by a youth . . . ? Mr. Thoreau's treatment of this subject seems revolting alike to good sense and good taste." Ripley concluded his review by inviting Thoreau to answer in his defense through the columns of the *Tribune*, but Thoreau had no taste for theologic controversy and made no reply to the review.

Ripley's review appeared within a month of publication—on June 13, 1849—and it unquestionably had an adverse effect on sales. But it did not alone slow sales of Thoreau's book. The fact remained that Thoreau's was as yet a new by-line on a book; at the same time it was true that his book was launched into a reading world which still held that practically all the worthwhile books written in English were written by British authors; and it could not be denied that the average reader who approached the book, invited by its title to a leisurely and pastoral journey along American waterways, was not prepared for Thoreau's philosophical digressions—the jewel-like essays which Thoreau had mined from his journal.

By the time James Russell Lowell's more favorable review appeared in *The Massachusetts Quarterly Review* for December, 1849, it was too late to do Thoreau's first venture between hardbound covers much good. Though not without criticism of the book, Lowell's review was on the whole a gratifying one. "It is like a book dug up, that has no date to assign it a special contemporaneousness, and no name of author. It has been written with no uncomfortable sense of a public looking over the shoulder. And the author is the least ingredient in it, too." If, in Lowell's opinion, Thoreau, "like most solitary men, exaggerates the importance of his own thoughts," it was also true for him that Thoreau's style was "compact and the language has an antique purity like wine grown colorless with age," and that the book "abounds in fine thoughts, and there is many a critical *obiter dictum* which is good law . . ."

By the time that Lowell's review appeared, it must have been brought home to Thoreau that his first book was a failure insofar as public acceptance and sales were concerned. It was comforting to be told by the English historian, J. A. Froude, in a letter from England, "In your book . . . I see hope for the coming world. . . . I wish to shake hands with you, and look a brave honest man in the face. In the mean time I will but congratulate you on the age in which your work is cast, the world has never seen one more pregnant."—but this praise from Britain was offset by condescending notices in British periodicals.

Thoreau spent no time mourning its failure. He went about his business in Concord, as always. He frequented the woods and the river, and from time to time went to Emerson's, not so much for intellectual stimulation as simply to befriend the children, as on one summer day when Ellen, now ten, was visiting her cousins at Staten Island, and Thoreau wrote her engagingly about his own visit at her home—"Eddy has got him a fish-pole and line with a pin-hook at the end, which he flourishes over the dry ground and the carpet at the risk of tearing out our eyes; but when I told him that he must have a cork and a sinker, his mother took off the pin and tied on a cork instead; but he doubts whether that will catch fish as well. He tells me that he is five years old. Indeed I was present at the celebration of his birthday lately, and supplied the company with onion and squash pipes, and rhubarb whistles, which is the most I can do on such occasions. Little Sammy Hoar blowed them most successfully, and made the loudest noise, though it almost strained his eyes out to do it. Edith is full of spirits. When she comes home from school, she goes hop skip and jump down into the field to pick berries, currants, gooseberries, raspberries, and thimbleberries; if there is one of these that has thoughts of changing its hue by to-morrow morning, I guess that Edith knows something about it and will consign it to her basket for Grandmamma."

That summer, too, Harrison Blake began to visit Thoreau—sometimes alone, sometimes with Theophilus Brown, a Worcester tailor, and they accompanied Thoreau on his excursions into the woods. On at least one occasion they discussed Thoreau's book, which Blake

89

liked, and later Thoreau wrote him, "I thank you for your hearty appreciation of my book. I am glad to have had such a long talk with you, and that you had patience to listen to me to the end. I think that I have the advantage of you, for I chose my own mood, and in one sense your mood too, that is a quiet and attentive reading mood."

In October, 1849, Thoreau set out on a trip to Cape Cod with Ellery Channing. They went by way of Cohasset, where a hundred forty-five lives had been lost, impelled by curiosity. The lost lives were principally Irish immigrants. "We found many Irish in the cars, going to identify bodies and to sympathize with the survivors and also to attend the funeral which was to take place in the afternoon . . ." His first sight of the coast was at the scene of the tragedy—"said to be the rockiest shore in Massachusetts,—from Nantasket to Scituate,— hard sienitic rocks, which the waves have laid bare, but have not been able to crumble.

"The brig St. John, from Galway, Ireland, laden with emigrants, was wrecked on Sunday morning; it was now Tuesday morning, and the sea was still breaking violently on the rocks. There were eighteen or twenty . . . large boxes . . . lying on a green hillside, a few rods from the water, and surrounded by a crowd. The bodies which had been recovered, twenty-seven or eight in all, had been collected there." The scene did not make the impression on Thoreau he had thought it would. "If I had found one body cast upon the beach in some lonely place, it would have affected me more. . . . If the last day were come, we should not think so much about the separation of friends or the blighted prospects of individuals."

Thoreau carried with him the eighth volume of the

Collections of the Massachusetts Historical Society, containing information about the Cape towns, and used it for reference. Undoubtedly he intended to use his excursion in his lectures; the journey to Maine had earned him some money in subsequent lectures; there was reason to suppose that Cape Cod would make as interesting a subject. His account, however, was more that of the traveler than of the naturalist, but very often there was a pleasant combination of the views.

"The windmills on the hills,—large weather-stained octagonal structures,—and the salt-works scattered all along the shore, with their long rows of vats resting on piles driven into the marsh, their low, turtle-like roofs, and their slighter windmills, were novel and interesting objects to an inlander. The sand by the roadside was partially covered with bunches of a moss-like plant, *Hudsonia tomentosa,* which a woman in the stage told us was called 'poverty-grass,' because it grew where nothing else would."

Among the common people of the Cape Thoreau was thoroughly at home, as he was with Therien, the woodchopper, and Hugh Quoil the Irishman, and the Hosmers and others of his townsmen who lived close to the land and pretended to no eminence of mind or material possessions. "I was struck by the pleasant equality which reigned among the stage company, and their broad and invulnerable good humor. They were what is called free and easy, and met one another to advantage, as men who had, at length, learned how to live. They appeared to know each other when they were strangers, they were so simple and downright. They were well met, in an unusual sense, that is, they met as well as they could meet, and did not seem to be troubled with any impediment. . . . It was evident that the same foolish respect was not

91

here claimed for mere wealth and station that is in many parts of New England; yet some of them were the 'first people,' as they were called, of the various towns through which we passed. Retired sea-captains, in easy circumstances, who talked of farming as sea-captains are wont; an erect, respectable, and trustworthy-looking man, in his wrapper, some of the salt of the earth, who had formerly been the salt of the sea; or a more courtly gentleman, who, perchance, had been a representative to the General Court in his day; or a broad, red-faced Cape Cod man, who had seen too many storms to be easily irritated; or a fisherman's wife, who had been waiting a week for the coaster to leave Boston, and had at length come by the cars.

"A strict regard for truth obliges us to say, that the few women whom we saw that day looked exceedingly pinched up. They had prominent chins and noses, having lost all their teeth, and a sharp W would represent their profile. They were not so well preserved as their husbands; or perchance they were well preserved as dried specimens. (Their husbands, however, were pickled.) . . ." He added to this note a whimsical aside about his "own dental system" being "far from perfect,"—and two years later had false teeth.

Thoreau noted the dwarfed apple trees ("One, which had been set ten years, was on an average eighteen inches high, and spread nine feet, with a flat top. It had borne one bushel of apples two years before."), the strangeness of the Cape landscape ("to an inlander . . . a constant mirage"), the prevailing "crops" ("The shores are more fertile than the dry land. The inhabitants measure their crops, not only by bushels of corn, but by barrels of clams. A thousand barrels of clam-bait are counted as equal in value to six or eight thousand bushels of Indian

92

corn . . ."), the emetic quality of clams ("In the course of the evening I began to feel the potency of the clam which I had eaten, and I was obliged to confess to our host that I was no tougher than the cat he told me of . . . and I was made quite sick by it for a short time, while he laughed at my expense.").

On the third day of their excursion, they came to the beach beyond the Nauset Lights on the way to Provincetown; it brought out again the poet in Thoreau. "The white breakers were rushing to the shore; the foam ran up the sand, and then ran back, as far as we could see (and we imagined how much farther along the Atlantic coast, before and behind us), as regularly, to compare great things with small, as the master of a choir beats time with his white wand; and ever and anon a higher wave caused us hastily to deviate from our path, and we looked back on our tracks filled with water and foam. The breakers looked like droves of a thousand wild horses of Neptune, rushing to the shore, with their white manes streaming far behind; and when, at length, the sun shone for a moment, their manes were rainbow-tinted. Also, the long kelp-weed was tossed up from time to time, like the tails of sea-cows sporting in the brine.

"There was not a sail in sight . . . and the only human beings whom we saw on the beach for several days were one or two wreckers looking for driftwood . . . We soon met one of these wreckers,—a regular Cape Cod man, with whom we parleyed, with a bleached and weather-beaten face, within whose wrinkles I distinguished no particular feature. It was like an old sail endowed with life,—a hanging-cliff of weather-beaten flesh,—like one of the clay boulders which occurred in that sand-bank. . . . He looked as if he sometimes saw a doughnut, but never descended to comfort; too grave

93

to laugh, too tough to cry; as indifferent as a clam,—like a sea-clam with hat on and legs, that was out walking the strand. He may have been one of the Pilgrims,— Peregrine White, at least,—who has kept on the back side of the Cape, and let the centuries go by."

They roamed the Cape for a week and then turned back to Concord. "When we reached Boston . . . , I had a gill of Provincetown sand in my shoes, and at Concord there was still enough left to sand my pages for many a day . . ."—and enough material for a lecture or two.

By 1850, Thoreau had resigned himself to the failure of *A Week on the Concord and Merrimack Rivers*. Nothing of the book appeared in his letters or the entries in his journal. He wrote long letters to Harrison Blake, still absorbed in philosophical matters, sometimes with theological references—("Let God alone if need be. Methinks, if I loved him more, I should keep him,—I should keep myself rather,—at a more respectful distance. It is not when I am going to meet him, but when I am just turning away and leaving him alone, that I discover that God is.")—and he wrote a pungent note of advice about conforming—("As for conforming outwardly, and living your own life inwardly, I do not think much of that.")— as well as some preaching ("Drink deep or taste not of the Pierian spring. Be not deterred by melancholy on the path which leads to immortal health & joy. When they tasted of the water of the river which they were to go, they thought that tasted a little bitterish to the palate, but it proved sweeter when it was down.").

That year the Thoreau family left the Texas house and moved into the Yellow House on the Main Street of Concord, Thoreau's final home. For a brief time that May Thoreau had a surveying job in Haverhill, found for him by his cousin Charles Dunbar, but he was back

94

in Concord by the end of May. And in July Emerson called upon him to discharge a melancholy commission; Emerson had learned that their mutual friend Margaret Fuller—now Margaret Ossoli, she having married in Italy —had drowned at Fire Island in the wrecking of the ship bearing the Ossoli family home; he asked Thoreau to go at once to Fire Island and salvage any of her property that could be found. Thoreau went, but reached the scene five days after the accident, and found little to recover. He did not linger at the scene any longer than he needed to—five days—returning home virtually empty-handed. Scarcely a fortnight later he wrote of the event to Blake—

"I find that actual events, notwithstanding the singular prominence which we all allow them, are far less real than the creations of my imagination. They are truly visionary and insignificant,—all that we commonly call life and death,—and affect me less than my dreams. This petty stream which from time to time swells and carries away the mills and bridges of our habitual life, and that mightier stream or ocean on which we securely float,—what makes the difference between them? I have in my pocket a button which I ripped off the coat of the Marquis of Ossoli, on the seashore, the other day. Held up, it intercepts the light,—an actual button,—and yet all the life it is connected with is less substantial to me, and interests me less, than my faintest dream. Our thoughts are the epochs in our lives: all else is but as a journal of the winds that blew while we were here."

He developed this theme at greater length in his journal. He was once again making many entries in his journal, including paragraphs which he added to the manuscript of *Walden,* that second book he still dreamed of seeing in print, and which he revised from time to

95

time. Between periods of employment as a surveyor—employment which he performed with highly satisfactory precision—he continued his solitary walks, striving, as always, to avoid people who might take his precious time with small talk he did not want to hear.

Concord by this time had learned to accept him for what he was. There might still be those who scorned him as a loafer, but, after all, he did help make pencils, he was the local surveyor, and he went about lecturing—for money. Undoubtedly his walks and his attitudes made him a local "character," which he was already on the way to becoming when, some years before, Dr. Ripley had dubbed Thoreau and his walking companions the third church in Concord—the Walden Pond Association.

Gone from the journal now and thereafter were the multiple quotations from what Thoreau read—and he did still read, having only late in 1849 persuaded President Jared Sparks of Harvard to permit him to take books from the Harvard Library ("I ask only that the University may help to finish the education, whose foundations she has helped to lay. I was not then ripe for her higher courses, and now that I am riper I trust that I am not too far away to be instructed by her."). His observation now was sharper, and his appreciation of his native countryside went deeper.

"In all my rambles I have seen no landscape which can make me forget Fair Haven. I still sit on its Cliff in a new spring day, and look over the awakening woods and the river, and hear the new birds sing, with the same delight as ever. It is as sweet a mystery to me as ever, what this world is. Fair Haven Lake in the south, with its pine-covered island and its meadows, the hickories putting out fresh young yellowish leaves, and the oaks light-grayish ones, while the oven-bird thrums his sawyer-like strain, and the chewink rustles through the dry leaves or repeats his jingle on a tree-top, and the wood thrush, the genius of the wood, whistles for the first time his clear and thrilling strain,—it sounds as it did the first time I heard it. The sight of these budding woods intoxicates me . . .

"The life in us is like the water in the river; it may rise this year higher than ever it was known to before and flood the uplands—even this may be the eventful year—and drown out all our muskrats.

"There are as many strata at different levels of life as there are leaves in a book. Most men probably have lived in two or three. When on the higher levels we can remember the lower levels, but when on the lower we cannot remember the higher.

"My imagination, my love and reverence and admiration, my sense of the miraculous, is not so excited by any event as by the remembrance of my youth. Men talk about Bible miracles because there is no miracle in their lives. Cease to gnaw that crust. There is ripe fruit over your head. . . .

"My friends wonder that I love to walk alone in solitary fields and woods by night. Sometimes in my loneliest and wildest midnight walk I hear the sound of the whistle and the rattle of the cars, where perchance some of those very friends are being whirled by night over, as they think, a well-known, safe, and public road. I see that men do not make or choose their own paths whether they are railroads or trackless through the wilds, but what the powers permit each one enjoys. My solitary course has the same sanction that the Fitchburg Railroad has. If they have a charter from Massachusetts and—what is of much more importance—from Heaven, to travel the course and in the fashion they do, I have a charter, though it be from

Heaven alone, to travel the course I do,—to take the necessary lands and pay the damages. It is by the grace of God in both cases. . . ."

He was traveling ever more widely in Concord, expanding his range in his own corner of the earth.

CHAPTER 7

Action from Principle

*However mean your life is, meet it and live; do
not shun it and call it hard names. It is not so bad
as you are. It looks poorest when you are richest.
The fault-finder will find faults even in paradise.
Love your life, poor as it is. You may perchance
have some pleasant, thrilling, glorious hours, even
in a poorhouse. The setting sun is reflected from the
windows of the almshouse as brightly as from the
rich man's house. The snow melts before its door as
early in the spring. I do not see but a quiet mind
may live as contentedly there, and have as cheering
thoughts as anywhere, and, indeed, the town's poor
seem to live the most independent lives of any.
They are simply great enough to receive without
misgiving. Cultivate poverty like sage, like a garden
herb. Do not trouble yourself to get new things,
whether clothes or friends. That is dissipation.
Turn the old; return to them. Things do not
change; we change. If I were confined to a corner
in a garret all my days, like a spider, the world
would be just as large to me while I had my
thoughts.* —JOURNAL, 1850

IN September, 1850, wanting "one honest
walk" in Canada, Thoreau set out with Ellery
Channing on an inexpensive journey to Montreal and
Quebec. He carried the baggage he took wrapped in paper, and meant to rough it. They went by train.

Thoreau had not traveled far in Quebec before he was aware of the inadequacy of his clothing. "It already looked and felt a good deal colder than it had in New England, and we might have expected it would. I realized fully that I was four degrees nearer the pole, and shuddered at the thought . . . It was an atmosphere that made me think of the fur-trade, which is so interesting a department in Canada, for I had for all head-covering a thin palm-leaf hat without lining, that cost twenty-five cents, and over my coat one of those unspeakably cheap, as well as thin, brown linen sacks of the Oak Hall pattern, which every summer appear all over New England, thick as the leaves upon the trees. It was a thoroughly Yankee costume, which some of my fellow-travelers wore in the cars to save their coats a dusting. . . . I never wear my best coat on a journey, though perchance I could show a certificate to prove that I have a more costly one, at least, at home, if that were all that a gentleman required. . . . Honest traveling is about as dirty work as you can do, and a man needs a pair of over-alls for it. As for blacking my shoes in such a case, I should as soon think of blacking my face. I carry a piece of tallow to preserve the leather and keep out the water; that's all; and many an officious shoe-black, who carried off my shoes when I was slumbering, mistaking me for a gentleman, has had occasion to repent it before he produced a gloss on them."

Along the heights at Quebec he and Channing walked, plucking flowers. "There was an abundance of succory still in blossom, broad-leaved goldenrod, buttercups, thorn bushes, Canada thistles, and ivy, on the very summit of Cape Diamond. I also found the bladder campion . . ." They walked to the Falls of St. Anne, thirty miles away, self-styled the "Knights of the Umbrella and the Bundle," Thoreau keeping notes, which as often as not drew upon what earlier travelers had written of the St. Lawrence and its environs. To Thoreau, Canada appeared "as old as Normandy itself, and realized much that I had heard of Europe and the Middle Ages. Even the names of humble Canadian villages affected me as if they had been those of the renowned cities of antiquity. To be told by a habitant, when I asked the name of a village in sight, that it is *St. Feréol* or *St. Anne,* the *Guardian Angel* or the *Holy Joseph's;* or of a mountain, that it was *Bélange* or *St. Hyacinthe!* As soon as you leave the States, these saintly names begin. *St. Johns* is the first town you stop at . . . , and thence-forward, the names of the mountains, and streams, and villages reel, if I may so speak, with the intoxication of poetry,—*Chambly, Longueuil, Pointe aux Trembles, Bartholomy,* etc., etc.; as if it needed only a little foreign accent, a few more liquids and vowels perchance in the language, to make us locate our ideals at once. I began to dream of Provence and the Troubadours, and of places and things which have no existence on the earth. They veiled the Indian and the primitive forest, and the woods toward Hudson's Bay were only as the forests of France and Germany. I could not at once bring myself to believe that the inhabitants who pronounced daily those beautiful and, to me, significant names lead as prosaic lives as we of New England. In short, the Canada which I saw was not merely a place for railroads to terminate in and for criminals to run to."

They visited waterfalls ("It was evident that this was the country for waterfalls; that every stream that empties into the St. Lawrence, for some hundreds of miles, must have a great fall or cascade on it . . ."), fortifications ("The most modern fortifications have an air of

101

antiquity about them; they have the aspect of ruins in better or worse repair from the day they are built, because they are not really the work of this age. The very place where the soldier resides has a peculiar tendency to become old and dilapidated, as the word *barrack* implies. I couple all fortifications in my mind with the dismantled Spanish forts to be found in so many parts of the world; and if in any place they are not actually dismantled, it is because that there the intellect of the inhabitants is dismantled. The commanding officer of an old fort near Valdivia in South America, when a traveler remarked to him that, with one discharge, his gun-carriages would certainly fall to pieces, gravely replied, 'No, I am sure, sir, they would stand two.' Perhaps the guns of Quebec would stand three."), and observed that the churches in Canada were magnificent in contrast to the houses. "The churches were very picturesque, and their interior much more showy than the dwelling-houses promised. They were of stone, for it was ordered, in 1699, that that should be their material. They had tinned spires, and quaint ornaments. . . . In Beauport . . . we turned aside to look at a church which was just being completed,—a very large and handsome edifice of stone, with a green bough stuck in its gable, . . . The comparative wealth of the Church in this country was apparent; for in this village we did not see one good house besides. They were all humble cottages; and yet this appeared to me a more imposing structure than any church in Boston."

They sampled Canadian fruit ("They said they had three kinds of plums growing wild,—blue, white, and red, the two former much alike and the best. Also they asked me if I would have . . . some apples, and got me some. They were exceedingly fair and glossy, and it was evident that there was no worm in them; but they were as hard almost as a stone, as if the season was too short to mellow them."), remarked the insularity of the average Canadian's way of living ("Every New England house . . . has a front and principal door opening to the great world . . . but the Canadian's door opens into his backyard and farm alone, and the road which runs behind his house leads only from the church of one saint to that of another."), and viewed the scenery at Quebec with a critical eye ("Too much has not been said about the scenery of Quebec. The fortifications of Cape Diamond are omnipresent. They preside, they frown over the river and surrounding country. You travel ten, twenty, thirty miles up or down the river's banks, you ramble fifteen miles amid the hills on either side, and then, when you have long since forgotten them, perchance slept on them by the way, at a turn of the road or of your body, there they are still, with their geometry against the sky. . . . I associate the beauty of Quebec with the steel-like and flashing air, which may be peculiar to that season of the year . . .").

In a week the "honest walk" was done. Thoreau was back in Concord. He had traveled eleven hundred miles, at a total cost of $12.75. He would still, he recorded, like "right well to make a longer excursion on foot through the wilder parts of Canada." To tell the truth, he had not seen very much of Canada, he had barely covered a small portion of its inhabited surface, and his observations did not match those he had made in Maine or on Cape Cod, to say nothing of the continuing observations of his native place.

He was aware of the fleetness of his visit, for when his townsmen expected him to lecture on the subject "because I had *visited* it," he reflected that he had "visited

103

it as the bullet visits the wall at which it is fired, and from which it rebounds as quickly. . . ." His explorations of Concord were in depth. He continued them, resuming his habits and his way of life, and demonstrating that no matter how many times a man walked a familiar path he might learn something new with each walk.

He sampled the wild apples. "I pluck them . . . fruit of old trees that have been dying ever since I was a boy and are not yet dead. . . . Frequented only by the woodpecker, deserted now by the farmer, who has not faith enough to look under the boughs. Food for walkers. Sometimes apples red inside, perfused with a beautiful blush, faery food, too beautiful to eat,—apple of the evening sky, of the Hesperides. . . . The apples are now thawed. . . . Those which a month ago were sour, crabbed, and uneatable are now filled with a rich, sweet cider which I am better acquainted with than with wine. . . . Let the frost come to freeze them first solid as stones, and then the sun or a warm winter day—for it takes but little heat—to thaw them, and they will seem to have borrowed a flavor from heaven through the medium of the air in which they hang."

He went one evening to visit an Indian encampment and pursued his interests in their ways of living. He learned about hunting moose and caribou, how to use moose horns, how to imitate the sounds of moose and deer, how to cure the skin of these animals. He put into his journal crude drawings of their spears and traps. He added to his store of Indian lore because he hoped some day to write a book about the Indians. "Did not know use of eye in axe," he wrote in his journal. "Put a string through it and wore it round neck."

The year turned. On January 1, 1851, Thoreau lectured in Clinton on the subject of Cape Cod. While he was there, he visited the gingham-mills and set down in his journals the details of weaving. "I am struck by the fact that no work has been shirked when a piece of cloth is produced. Every thread has been counted in the finest web; it has not been matted together. The operator has succeeded only by patience, perseverance, and fidelity."

Later in the month he again lectured on his life at Walden, this time at Medford, and in May he spoke in Worcester once more on *Walking*. The day after his Worcester lecture he walked to Asnebumskit Hill in Paxton because it was said to be the highest land in Worcester County, next to Wachusett. "A very extensive view, but the western view not so much wilder as I expected. See Barre, about fifteen miles off, and Rutland, etc., etc. Not so much forest as in our neighborhood; high, swelling hills, but less shade for the walker."

In April of that year Thoreau, who had never been an Abolitionist, no matter how much he was opposed to slavery, was upset when Thomas Sims, a Negro living in Boston, was seized and sent back into slavery. He thought the Fugitive Slave Law monstrous cruelty and Massachusetts' adherence to it shameful. He took a crumb of comfort in the fact that Daniel Foster of Concord stood at the wharf as the Negro was taken away and read a prayer. "I could not help feeling a slight degree of pride because, of all the towns in the Commonwealth, Concord was the only one distinctly named as being represented in that new tea-party."

He held forth at length in his journal, expressing his convictions. "I wish my townsmen to consider that, whatever the human law may be, neither an individual nor a nation can ever deliberately commit the least act of injustice without having to pay the penalty for it. . . . I hear a good deal said about trampling this law under foot. Why, one need not go out of his way to do that. This law lies not at the level of the head or the reason. Its natural habitat is in the dirt. It was bred and has its life only in the dust and mire, on a level with the feet; and he who walks with freedom, unless, with a sort of quibbling and Hindoo mercy, he avoids treading on every venomous reptile, will inevitably tread on it, and so trample it under foot.

"It has come to this, that the friends of liberty, the friends of the slave, have shuddered when they have understood that his fate has been left to the legal tribunals, so-called, of the country to be decided. The people have no faith that justice will be awarded in such a case. . . . I would much rather trust to the sentiment of the people, which would itself be a precedent to posterity. . . .

"I think that recent events will be valuable as a criticism on the administration of justice in our midst, or rather as revealing what are the true sources of justice in any community. It is to some extent fatal to the courts when the people are compelled to go behind the courts. . . . As for measures to be adopted, among others I would advise abolitionists to make as earnest and vigorous and persevering assault on the press, as they have already made, and with effect too, on the church." Somewhat cautiously, he admitted that he did not believe "that the North will soon come to blows with the South on this question."—but he was manifestly not averse to the idea of war, for he added, "It would be too bright a page to be written in the history of the race at present."

He expressed his disgust and fury with the press, the editors of which, he maintained, supported the Fugitive Slave Law solely to "secure the approbation of their patrons, and also, one would think, because they are not aware that a sounder sentiment prevails to any extent." He fulminated for a month, pondering a talk on the subject, for which his jottings in the journal were notes.

The household abounded with Abolitionists. His late sister Helen had been an ardent Abolitionist; so were Mrs. Ward and Aunt Maria. They read Garrison's paper, *The Liberator;* so did Thoreau, who excepted it from his general condemnation of the press in the matter of slavery. But Thoreau did not belong to any of the abolitionist societies. He had a pronounced aversion to "reform" of people. But he lent a hand to aid fugitive slaves escape to Canada more than once, and the next time, after the Sims case, that the opportunity afforded itself, Thoreau did not hesitate to do what he could.

The occasion was the following October, on the first day of which at "5 P.M." he "put a fugitive slave, who has taken the name of Henry Williams, into the cars for Canada. He escaped from Stafford County, Virginia, to Boston last October; has been in Shadrach's place at the Cornhill Coffee-House; had been corresponding through an agent with his master, who is his father, about buying himself, his master asking $600, but he having been able to raise only $500. Heard that there were writs out for two Williamses, fugitives, and was informed by his fellow-servants and employer that Augerhole Burns and others of the police had called for him when he was out. Accordingly fled to Concord last night on foot, bringing a letter to our family from Mr. Lovejoy of Cambridge and another which Garrison had formerly given him on another occasion. He lodged with us, and waited in the house till funds were collected with which to forward him. Intended to dispatch him at noon through to Burlington, but when I went to buy his ticket, saw one at the

107

depot who looked and behaved so much like a Boston policeman that I did not venture that time. An intelligent and very well-behaved man, a mulatto. . . .

"The slave said he could guide himself by many other stars than the north star, whose rising and setting he knew. They steered for the north star even when it had got round and appeared to them to be in the south. They frequently followed the telegraph when there was no railroad. The slaves bring many superstitions from Africa. The fugitives sometimes superstitiously carry a turf in their hats, thinking that their success depends on it."

But essentially slavery—and indeed all the concerns of his fellowmen—were secondary issues with Thoreau. His primary interest continued to be in the place he found himself, his native place, in men only insofar as they lived in the same place, especially those close to the land, like Therien and George Minott, and in aspects of nature seen and studied from time to time; he wrote about cobwebs, muskrat houses ("They have reduced life to a lower scale than Diogenes."), acorns, witchhazel ("an extremely interesting plant. . . . Its blossoms smell like the spring, like the willow catkins; by their color as well as fragrance they belong to the saffron dawn of the year, suggesting amid all these signs of autumn, falling leaves and frost, that the life of Nature, by which she eternally flourishes, is untouched."), the hooting of owls, new-fallen leaves, a moonlight walk ("It is as if you were walking in night up to your chin."), and little Johnny Riordan, the child of Irish parents left behind by the building of the Fitchburg Railroad ("They showed me Johnny Riordan today, with one thickness of ragged cloth over his little shirt for all this cold weather, with shoes with large holes in the toes, into which the snow got, as he said, without an outer garment, to walk a mile to school every day over the bleakest of causeways,—the clothes with countless patches, which hailed from, claimed descent from, were originally identical with, pantaloons of mine, which set as if his mother had fitted them to a tea-kettle first. This little mass of humanity, this tender gobbet for the fates, cast into a cold world with a torn lichen leaf wrapped about him,—Oh, I should rather hear that America's first-born were all slain than that his little fingers and toes should feel cold while I am warm. Is man so cheap that he cannot be clothed but with a mat, a rag, that we should bestow on him our *cold* victuals? Are there any fellow-creatures to whom we abandon our rags, to whom we give our old clothes and shoes when they will not fend the weather from ourselves? Let the mature rich wear the rags and insufficient clothing; let the infant poor wear the purple and fine linen. I shudder when I think of the fate of innocency. Our charitable institutions are an insult to humanity. A charity which dispenses the crumbs that fall from its overloaded tables, which are left after its feasts!'').

And in the middle of the following April Thoreau had one of those adventures in nature which were events in his days. Rounding the corner of Hubbard's Grove, he happened upon the first woodchuck of the season, and proceeded to make its acquaintance. "I ran along the fence and cut him off, or rather overtook him, though he started at the same time. When I was only a rod and a half off, he stopped, and I did the same; then he ran again, and I ran up within three feet of him, when he stopped again, the fence being between us. I squatted down and surveyed him at my leisure. His eyes were dull black and rather inobvious, with a faint chestnut (?) iris, with but little expression and that more of resignation than of anger. The general aspect was a coarse grayish brown, a sort of grisel (?). A lighter brown next the skin, then black or very dark brown and tipped with whitish rather loosely. The head between a squirrel and a bear, flat on the top and dark brown . . ."

He cornered the woodchuck, touched it with a stick, tried to open its gritting jaws with the stick. He got up next to it. "We sat looking at one another about half an hour, till we began to feel mesmeric influences. . . . He would not stir as long as I was looking at him or could see him. . . . I sat down by his side within a foot. I talked to him *quasi* forest lingo, baby-talk, at any rate in a conciliatory tone, and thought I had some influence on him. . . . With a little stick I lifted one of his paws to examine it, and held it up at pleasure. I turned him over to see what color he was beneath . . . I laid my hand on him. If I had had some food, I could have ended with stroking him at my leisure. . . . I respect him as one of the natives." Such intimate encounters added a dimension to his existence.

In February, 1852, he lectured in Plymouth, but he was evidently not as much interested in his audience or their reaction as he was in the evergreen winterberry and the descendants of the Pilgrims still alive in that town, and on the next day he was back on the railroad near Walden Pond "reminded of spring by the quality of the air. The cock-crowing and even the telegraph harp prophesy it . . ." He also lectured in Lincoln, but lecturing did not loom large in his journal, which he filled from day to day with sensitive entries about life in and around Concord.

Horace Greeley, still hoping to bring Thoreau to the attention of a wider audience than he had, wrote him that while he was not well enough known to lecture successfully in New York, he was yet "a better speaker than many, but a far better writer still," and proposed that perhaps Thoreau might "swap" some of his "woodnotes wild" for "dollars." He urged him to write articles Greeley might sell for him.

Thoreau responded by sending him some articles—*The Iron Horse* and *A Poet Buying a Farm*—and proposing to send his account of the Canadian excursion. Within a month, Greeley had placed the two articles with *Sartain's Union Magazine* "for a low price," and had a letter from John Sartain, the editor, setting forth that "Mr. T. might send us some further contributions, and shall at least receive prompt and courteous decision respecting them." Greeley, however, was a little dubious about such a long article on Canada as Thoreau proposed and suggested that Thoreau break it up into three or four parts.

Once more Greeley proposed that Thoreau write an article on Emerson, a review of the man and his work— "Let it be calm, searching, and impartial; nothing like adulation, but a just summing up of what he is and what he has done." He was certain that he could find a place for this in the *Westminster Review,* and would pay Thoreau $50 for it—in advance, if Thoreau wished it. Thoreau did not wish it. Thoreau did not want to write about Emerson at all, still holding that it would be a presumption upon their friendship for him to do so.

Thoreau sent in his account of the Canadian trip—*A Yankee in Canada.* It was accepted by his old friend, George W. Curtis, editor of *Putnam's Magazine,* to be run in five instalments early in 1853. Curtis was also interested in seeing *Cape Cod,* and Thoreau sent him the first hundred pages later in the year. But Thoreau was unfortunate in his relations with *Putnam's*—friend or not, Curtis took it upon himself to censor Thoreau's manuscript and rid it of what Greeley called Thoreau's "defiant Pantheism."

Thoreau was outraged by the censoring of his work. He wrote Greeley, "I am sorry that my manuscript should be so mangled, insignificant as it is, but I do not know how I could have helped it fairly, since I was born to be a pantheist—if that be the name of me, and I do the deeds of one." He withdrew the final two chapters of *A Yankee in Canada* from *Putnam's*.

Though he considered his profession that of lecturing, and his employment, apart from making pencils on occasion, surveying, he was now writing more than ever. His entries in his journal for 1852 filled 750 pages. Nor was he alone concerned with nature in Concord, though he kept his townsmen out of his journal except for his recurring notes about the Irish and the trappers, muskrat-hunters, and woodsmen he encountered. Yet he was acquainted with the events of life in Concord, and viewed them with an amused detachment.

He wrote to Sophia that "Mr. Pierce the presidential candidate was in town . . . visiting Hawthorne whose college chum he was, and . . . Hawthorne is writing a life of him for electioneering purposes." He added, "Concord is just as idiotic as ever in relation to the spirits and their knockings. Most people here believe in a spiritual world which no respectable junk bottle which had not met with a slip—would condescend to contain even a portion of for a moment . . .—in spirits which the very bull frogs in our meadows would blackball. . . . The hooting of owls—the croaking of frogs—is celestial wisdom in comparison."

He continued to live very much in the bosom of his family, for all his wandering abroad. He enjoyed their company, if he sometimes vexed them. "My Aunt Maria," he wrote in his journal March 28, 1853, "asked me to read the life of Dr. Chalmers, which, however, I did not

112

promise to do. Yesterday, Sunday, she was heard through the partition shouting to my Aunt Jane, who is deaf, 'Think of it! He stood half an hour to-day to hear the frogs croak, and he wouldn't read the life of Chalmers.' "

In that same month he was asked to fill out a blank for possible membership in the Association for the Advancement of Science. He was somewhat amused and wrote, "Now, though I could state to a select few that department of human inquiry which engages me, and should be rejoiced at an opportunity to do so, I felt that it would be to make myself the laughing-stock of the scientific community to describe or attempt to describe to them that branch of science which specially interests me, inasmuch as they do not believe in a science which deals with the higher law. . . . The fact is I am a mystic, a transcendentalist, and a natural philosopher to boot. . . . How absurd that, though I probably stand as near to nature as any of them, and am by constitution as good an observer as most, yet a true account of my relation to nature should excite their ridicule only! If it had been the secretary of an association of which Plato or Aristotle was the president, I should not have hesitated to describe my studies at once and particularly." Nevertheless, later in the year he did specify on the blank as a branch of science in which he felt especial interest "The Manners & Customs of the Indians of the Algonquin Group previous to contact with the civilized man."

He was considerably less loath to answer inquiries about his attitudes sent him by Harrison Blake early that year. "As to whether what you speak of as the 'world's way' (Which for the most part is my way) or that which is shown me, is the better, the former is imposture, the latter is truth. I have the coldest confidence in the last. . . . My hours are not 'cheap in such a way that *I* doubt

113

whether the world's way would not have been better,' but cheap in such a way, that I doubt whether the world's way, which I have adopted for the time, could be worse. The whole enterprise of this nation which is not an upward, but a westward one, toward Oregon, California, Japan &c, is totally devoid of interest to me, whether performed on foot or by a Pacific railroad. . . .

"As it respects these things I have not changed an opinion one iota from the first. As the stars looked to me when I was a shepherd in Assyria, they look to me now a New Englander. The higher the *mt.* on which you stand, the less change in the prospect from year to year, from age to age. . . . I have had but one *spiritual* birth . . . , and now whether it rains or snows, whether I laugh or cry, fall farther below or approach nearer my standard, whether Pierce or Scott is elected—not a new scintillation of light flashes on me, but ever and anon, though with longer intervals, the same surprising & everlastingly new light dawns to me, with only such variations as in the coming of the natural day, with which indeed, it is often coincident. . . .

"I very rarely indeed, if ever, 'feel any itching to be what is called useful to my fellowmen.' . . . What a foul subject is this, of doing good, instead of minding ones life, which should be his business. . . . Instead of taking care to flourish & smell & taste sweet and refresh all mankind to the extent of our capacity & quality. People will sometimes try to persuade you that you have done something from that motive, as if you did not already know enough about it. If I ever *did* a man any good, in their sense, of course it was something exceptional, and insignificant compared with the good or evil which I am constantly doing by being what I am. . . .

114

"The problem of life becomes one cannot say by how many degrees more complicated as our material wealth is increased . . . since the problem is not merely nor mainly to get life for our bodies, but by this or a similar discipline to get life for our souls . . . If I accomplish as much more in spiritual work as I am richer in worldly goods, then I am just as worthy, or worth just as much as I was before, and no more. I see that, in my own case, money *might* be of great service to me, but probably it would not be, for the difficulty ever is that I do not improve my opportunities, and therefore I am not prepared to have my opportunities increased. . . .

"How prompt we are to satisfy the hunger & thirst of our bodies; how slow to satisfy the hunger & thirst of our *souls*. Indeed we who would be practical folks cannot use this word without blushing because of our infidelity, having starved this substance almost to a shadow. We feel it to be as absurd as if a man were to break forth into a eulogy on *his dog* who hasn't any. An ordinary man will work every day for a year at shovelling dirt to support his body, or a family of bodies, but he is an extraordinary man who will work a whole day in a year for the support of his soul."

Thoreau's home life at this time, as well as his life in the woods, was happily harmonious. He often took members of the family on boat rides and chronicled the little adventures of these rides faithfully, as on the occasion in May, 1853, when he and Sophia rowed past "Mr. Prichard's land, where the river is bordered by a row of elms and low willows, at 6 P.M." and "heard a singular note of distress as it were from a catbird"—which resulted in their rescue of a kitten and its addition to the household. Moreover, he took a more active part in the pencil-making business by turning his hand to an improvement in the graphite—or plumbago—used by the Thoreaus in their business.

On September 13 of that year Thoreau made a second trip to the Maine woods. This time his guide was an Indian, Joe Aitteon—"a good-looking Indian, twenty-four years old, apparently of unmixed blood, short and stout, with a broad face and reddish complexion, and eyes, methinks, narrower and more turned up at the outer corners than ours . . ." He could thus pursue his "special interest" in Indian lore at the same time that he gathered further data on the wilderness about which he planned more essays and lectures.

The goal this time was Chesuncook, just beyond the limits of Thoreau's first excursion into the Maine woods. Before reaching that lake, Thoreau lent a hand to Joe's hunting a moose, in which Thoreau's chief pleasure was the information he gained about the animal. "The distance from the tips of the hoofs of the fore-feet, stretched out, to the top of the back between the shoulders, was seven feet and five inches. . . . The extreme length was eight feet and two inches." But data about moose and hedgehogs soon gave way to rhapsodic appreciations of pine trees and night in the forest, and to Indian lore. "I asked our hosts what *Musketaquid*, the Indian name of Concord . . . meant; but they changed it to *Musketicook*, and repeated that, and Tahmunt said that it meant Dead Stream, which is probably true. *Cook* appears to mean stream, and perhaps *quid* signifies the place or ground."

The second Maine excursion lasted two weeks. By September 28, Thoreau was back in Concord, his journal filled with notes, measurements, drawings—of Indian canoes—, and the material for another lecture. In Concord

116

the elm leaves were falling, and the fringed gentian was in blossom. And in Concord he had at last to face a melancholy problem which had been pressed upon him from time to time by the publisher ("falsely so-called"), who had brought out *A Week on the Concord and Merrimack Rivers* in 1849.

The indisputable fact was that Thoreau's book had not sold at all well. It had come out like a woodland flower and remained unplucked, with but the modest appreciation of a few passersby. Since Thoreau had himself paid for the publication of the book, unsold copies belonged to him. The publisher, Munroe, had written Thoreau from time to time asking what disposition he should make of the unsold copies. At length he wrote that October that he could use the room they occupied in storage. Thoreau wrote at last and instructed him to send them—250 bound copies, and 450 sets of sheets—to Concord.

On October 28 Thoreau wrote philosophically that "they have arrived to-day by express, filling the man's wagon,—706 copies out of an edition of 1000 which I bought of Munroe four years ago and have been ever since paying for, and have not quite paid for yet. The wares are sent to me at last, and I have an opportunity to examine my purchase. They are something more substantial than fame, as my back knows, which has borne them up two flights of stairs to a place similar to that to which they trace their origin. Of the remaining two hundred and ninety and odd, seventy-five were given away, the rest sold. I have now a library of nearly nine hundred volumes, over seven hundred of which I wrote myself. Is it not well that the author should behold the fruits of his labor? My works are piled up on one side of my chamber half as high as my head, my *opera omnia*. This is authorship; these are the work of my brain. There was just one piece of good luck in the venture. The unbound were tied up by the printer four years ago in stout paper wrappers, and inscribed,—

H. D. Thoreau's
Concord River
50 cops.

So Munroe had only to cross out 'River' and write 'Mass.' and deliver them to the expressman at once. I can see now what I write for, the result of my labors.

"Nevertheless, in spite of this result, sitting beside the inert mass of my works, I take up my pen to-night to record what thought or experience I may have had, with as much satisfaction as ever. Indeed, I believe that this result is more inspiring and better for me than if a thousand had bought my wares. It affects my privacy less and leaves me freer."

He was not quite free of this initial venture in publishing. He was still in debt $100, and this had to be paid off. Before he had settled this debt, he "was obliged to manufacture a thousand dollars' worth of pencils and slowly dispose of and finally sacrifice them." Even a man with considerably more self-confidence than Thoreau might have grown discouraged.

CHAPTER 8

Walden

*If one listens to the faintest but constant sug-
gestions of his genius, which are certainly true, he
sees not to what extremes, or even insanity, it may
lead him; and yet that way, as he grows more resolute and faithful, his road lies. The faintest assured
objection which one healthy man feels will at length
prevail over the arguments and customs of mankind. No man ever followed his genius till it misled
him. Though the result were bodily weakness, yet
perhaps no one can say that the consequences were
to be regretted, for these were a life in conformity to
higher principles. If the day and the night are such
that you greet them with joy, and life emits a fragrance like flowers and sweet-scented herbs, is more
elastic, more starry, more immortal,—that is your
success. All nature is your congratulation, and you
have cause momentarily to bless yourself. The greatest gains and values are farthest from being appreciated. We easily come to doubt if they exist. We
soon forget them. They are the highest reality.
Perhaps the facts most astounding and most real
are never communicated by man to man. The true
harvest of my daily life is somewhat as intangible
and indescribable as the tints of morning or evening. It is a little star-dust caught, a segment of the
rainbow which I have clutched.* —WALDEN

FAR from being discouraged by the failure of his first book, Thoreau anticipated the publication of his second. Thoreau had been in correspondence with Ticknor & Fields of Boston about *Walden, or Life in the Woods* during late 1853; by early 1854, Thoreau had been advised that Ticknor & Fields planned to publish the book later that year, so that, when Horace Greeley wrote him early in March to ask that he collect and arrange his miscellaneous lectures and articles in the hope of finding a publisher to bring them out in book form, Thoreau was delighted to be able to tell Greeley that *Walden* was soon to appear. Thoreau pointed out that the publishers had not yet announced the book, but its acceptance was certain.

Greeley replied, "I shall announce it at once, whether Ticknor does or not." Further, Greeley made plans to publish excerpts from the book with the intention of arousing public interest in a book which Ticknor described to his firm's agent in London as "no common book. . . . It belongs to the same class of works with Mr. Emerson's writings & will be likely to attract attention."

Perhaps Thoreau felt that publication of a second book might gain him, if not prestige, some further respect—not that it could have mattered very much to him. For all that he had once taught and did some writing and lectured, Thoreau was hardly more to Concord than an assistant at pencil-making and a surveyor. These were the occupations which were visible and which earned him fees admissible as earnings to his townsmen.

Thoreau could have had no illusions about his status. A post-office loafer once taunted him, together with Emerson and Channing, as "the walkers." Thoreau asked, "Do you miss any of your wood?" and was told, "No, I hain't worried any yet." And Sam Staples ("whom I never call Sam, however") thought nothing of calling out to Thoreau casually, "Thoreau, are you going up the street pretty soon? Well, just take a couple of these handbills along and drop one in at Hoar's piazza and one at Holbrook's, and I'll do as much for you another time." Thoreau could write in his journal, "There is some advantage in being the humblest, cheapest, least dignified man in the village, so that the very stable boys shall damn you. Methinks I enjoy that advantage to an unusual extent. There is many a coarsely well-meaning fellow, who knows only the skin of me, who addresses me familiarly by my Christian name. I get the whole good of him and lose nothing myself."

Apart from such a wry note or two in the course of his journal, Thoreau left no evidence to suggest that he was unduly troubled by the impression he might make on his townsmen or the wider world, and he was very probably surprised when Charles Scribner wrote to him that May asking for biographical and bibliographical data to be published in a new Scribner book, *An Encyclopaedia of American Literature*. He went on about his business—surveying, doing some good turns for the Irish who seemed to be in constant if cheerful need, inspecting fences and streams, keeping account of thunderstorms and the arrival and departure of birds, collecting a cicada he could not certainly identify and sending it to Thaddeus Harris at Cambridge to be identified, only to be asked for further specimens.

And, as always, he walked—usually in the afternoon, but now increasingly at twilight and by moonlight. They were not always bucolic idyls. Thoreau once called them "those rough all-day walks across lots?— . . . picking our way over quaking meadows and swamps and occasionally slipping into the muddy batter midleg deep; jumping

121

or fording ditches and brooks; forcing our way through dense blueberry swamps, where there is water beneath and bushes above; then brushing through extensive birch forests all covered with green lice, which cover our clothes and face; then, relieved, under larger wood, more open beneath, steering for some more conspicuous trunk; now along a rocky hillside where the sweet-fern grows for a mile, then over a recent cutting, finding our uncertain footing on the cracking tops and trimmings of trees left by the choppers; now taking a step or two of smooth walking across a highway; now through a dense pine wood, descending into a rank, dry swamp, where the cinnamon fern rises above your head, with isles of poison-dogwood; now up a scraggy hill covered with shrub oak, stooping and winding one's way for half a mile, tearing one's clothes in many places and putting out one's eyes, and finding at last that it has no bare brow, but another slope of the same character; now through a corn-field diagonally with the rows; now coming upon the hidden melon-patch; seeing the back side of familiar hills and not knowing them. . . ."

On the ninth of August *Walden* was published. It was produced by Ticknor & Fields at a cost of 43 cents a copy, to sell for a dollar. Almost at once it brought a disciple to Thoreau—one Daniel Ricketson of New Bedford. He wrote to Thoreau three days after publication of *Walden,* writing him the kind of letter every author is gratified to receive. He hastened "to thank you for the great degree of satisfaction" *Walden* had given him. "I hail with pleasure every original production in literature which bears the stamp of a genuine and earnest love for the true philosophy of human life.—Such I assure you I esteem your book to be. To many, and to most, it will appear to be the wild musings of an eccentric and strange mind . . .

But to me the book appears to evince a mind most thoroughly self possessed, highly cultivated with a strong vein of common sense. The whole book is a prose poem . . . and at the same time as simple as a running brook." He addressed Thoreau as "Dear Mr. Walden," and echoed Thoreau in his long letter—"O how much we lose by civilization!"

Even before the book's publication, Horace Greeley had published a summary and more than three columns of extracts from *Walden*. This generous space devoted to the book in so widely-read a newspaper undoubtedly sent the book off to a modest start in sales; it gave much more of a sampling of Thoreau than any review could have done. Other reviews were less generous, but on the whole, favorable. *Graham's Magazine* called Thoreau a Transcendentalist, one of those people "who lay the greatest stress on the 'I'." *Putnam's* wondered why, if Thoreau liked the Walden experiment so much, he did not "stick to it?" and carped a little about his book, but on the whole pronounced it a good book—"there have been a good many lives spent and a good deal of noise made about them, too, from the sum total of whose results not half so much good could be extracted as may be found in this little volume. Many a man will find pleasure in it, and many a one, we hope will be profited by its counsels. A tour in Europe would have cost a good deal more, and not have produced half as much. . . . We heartily recommend . . . him to the class of readers who extract thoughts as well as words from an author . . ." And Edwin Morton of the class of 1855, reviewing both Thoreau's books in the *Harvard Magazine*, thought *Walden* "less artistic than its predecessor," but called both of them "rare books," while an anonymous reviewer in *The Knickerbocker*, sneering at town and

123

rural humbugs, nevertheless conceded that *Walden* "should be extensively read" because "it encourages the belief, which in this utilitarian age enough needs encouragement, that there is some other object to live for except 'to make money.' "

Walden was Thoreau's *apologia* for his way of life. It was meant to contain more of his philosophy, as plainly set forth as he could set it forth, than his first book. It was not intended for people who were satisfied with their lives as much as for those who lived "lives of quiet desperation." Out of his journal and the Walden experience Thoreau put into his book his thoughts on four central themes—the economic condition of men, life close to nature and its rewards, the "higher laws" man understands through a life close to nature, and the quiet desperation of the lives so many men lead. It was never meant for idle readers who did not want to be made to think, and it could be little appreciated by anyone who did not also, like Thoreau, value nonconformity and individuality.

Yet for Thoreau, by all the evidence, the book was an accomplished thing, and thus in a sense a closed chapter in his life. His lengthy journal for that summer is concerned with many things—the flight of an eagle, the nest of a snapping turtle, a nighthawk, harvest flies, river clams, the great fringed orchis, the sheen of the fields, the opening of flowers, the necessity of privacy ("My attic chamber has compelled me to sit below with the family at evening for a month. I feel the necessity of deepening the stream of my life; I must cultivate privacy. It is very dissipating to be with people too much. . . . I cannot spare my moonlight and my mountains for the best of man I am likely to get in exchange."), sailing on Fair Haven, the sting of a wasp, and scores of other subjects, most notably the affair of the slave, Anthony Burns—but of *Walden* there was set down only the briefest of notes, under date of August 9, " 'Walden' published," though perhaps his entry of September 2 was intended to be related to the book—"My faults are: / Paradoxes,—saying just the opposite,—a style which may be imitated. / Ingenius. / Playing with words,—getting the laugh,—not always simple, strong, and broad. / Using current phrases and maxims, when I should speak for myself. / Not always earnest. / 'in short,' 'in fact,' 'alas!' etc. / Want of conciseness."—however applicable these words might have been to his lectures—and neither of these entries was included in proper sequence in the body of the journal; both were written on the inside cover page of the manuscript, and may not have been intended as integral portions of the journal.

The affair of Anthony Burns was similar to that of Sims. Burns, another runaway Negro slave, had been arrested in Boston and returned to Virginia in a government cutter, in May of that year. Thoreau's reaction spilled over in the pages of the journal, and at length; it did more—out of his cold fury, Thoreau assembled from his notes on both the Sims and Burns cases, a fiery paper which he delivered under the title of *Slavery in Massachusetts* as an address before the Anti-Slavery Convention meeting in Framingham, Massachusetts, on Independence Day, and which William Lloyd Garrison then published on July 21 in the *Liberator*.

It was an address that brought Thoreau more reaction than *Walden* did, for the time being. Thoreau's attack was against the moral weakness of the North, not against slavery, for of slavery as an institution he did not profess to know enough to speak. "The whole military force of the State is at the service of a Mr. Suttle, a slaveholder

125

from Virginia, to enable him to catch a man whom he calls his property; but not a soldier is offered to save a citizen of Massachusetts from being kidnapped!" he cried. "The law will never make men free; it is men who have got to make the law free. . . . I would remind my countrymen that they are to be men first, and Americans only at a late and convenient hour. . . . I feel that, to some extent, the State has fatally interfered with my lawful business. . . . We have used up all our inherited freedom. If we would save our lives, we must fight for them." Thoreau was still hearing about his Framingham lecture two months after publication of *Walden*.

In the meantime, Thoreau had met another young writer who was to become a lifelong correspondent. This was Thomas Cholmondeley of England. He had come to Concord primarily to visit Emerson that summer but found himself much taken by Thoreau, and began to take walks with Thoreau. He was still in the vicinity—"staying at our house," Thoreau wrote to Blake—in October, asking Thoreau "to teach him *botany*—i.e., anything which I know—and also to make an excursion to some mountains with him." He proposed to Blake that Cholmondeley might come along to visit Blake when Thoreau went, bound to walk to Wachusett, a proposal Blake eagerly accepted.

On October 19th Thoreau left for Westminster by train, and with Blake walked the six miles to the top of Wachusett where, the following morning, they "Saw the sun rise from the mountain-top. . . . It was worth the while to see westward the countless hills and fields all apparently flat, now white with frost. A little white fog marked the site of many a lake and the course of the Nashua, and in the east horizon the great pond had its own fog mark in a long, low bank of cloud." It must have been a nostalgic walk, reminding Thoreau of his first walk there in May, 1842, when he had set down a poem to celebrate Wachusett, "who like me / Standest alone without society."

Daniel Ricketson constantly urged Thoreau to visit him at New Bedford, where Ricketson spent a great deal of his time in a shanty—"in study and meditation," as Ricketson told Thoreau. Ricketson bore a certain kinship to Thoreau, but he was more gregarious, more inclined to seek out people, whereas Thoreau gave the impression of only tolerating the company of others. Later that year Thoreau visited New Bedford and Ricketson, who lived near the Acushnet River north of the town, and, as usual, took notes on the setting, which, though in latitude only different "about a degree" was "far more in climate."

But, such occasional visits away from Concord notwithstanding, it was Concord and its environs which Thoreau traveled with the greatest pleasure and the continuing affection he had had for this place all his life. He surveyed between visits, he sailed to Ball's Hill with Channing, paddled up river to Clamshell, walked to Walden along the railroad or by way of Hubbard Bridge, went up the north bank of the Assabet with Channing, skated up river to Fair Haven—again with Channing whose "skates are not the best," and who was "beside . . ." a "far from an easy skater, so that, as he said, it was killing work for him. Time and again the perspiration actually dropped from his forehead on to the ice, and it froze in long icicles on his beard. Yet he kept up his spirits and his fun, said he had seen much more suffering than I . . ."

Thoreau's sympathy was limited. He was a sprightly skater himself, capable of leaping aloft and cavorting

127

on the ice, and his interests were in the face of the country. "The shadows on the snow are indigo-blue. The pines look very dark. The white oak leaves are a cinnamon-color, the black and red (?) oak leaves a reddish brown or leather-color. I see mice and rabbit and fox tracks on the meadow. Once a partridge rises from the alders and skims across the river at its widest part . . . I see the track of an otter made since yesterday morning. How glorious the perfect stillness and peace of the winter landscape!"

Meanwhile, *Walden* was selling slowly but steadily, and an awareness of Thoreau as a writer was growing. Charles Sumner, later Senator from Massachusetts, wrote from Boston that reading only the early chapters of the book satisfied him that Thoreau had "made a contribution to the permanent literature of our mother tongue," and from Fr. Adrien Rouquette the author of *Walden* received a gift of three volumes of Rouquette's work, including Rouquette's *Wild Flowers;* in return, Thoreau sent him a complimentary copy of *A Week on the Concord and Merrimack Rivers,* a book for which an increasing number of readers of *Walden* were beginning to ask.

When Cholmondeley left Concord in November, he carried with him letters of introduction from Thoreau to Bronson Alcott and Dr. Thaddeus W. Harris, the Harvard librarian, for whom Thoreau had been gathering grubs, and from whom he had been borrowing such books as Wilson's translation of the *Vishnoo Purana.* Cholmondeley was bound for home and involvement in the Crimean War, and Thoreau that late autumn and winter went on a series of lectures.

He lectured first in Philadelphia, and hoped thereafter for an invitation to make a Western tour. It was not forthcoming. The Library Association of Akron, Ohio, asked him to lecture there, but since there were no other inquiries from the middle west, Thoreau would not go. Instead, he prepared a new lecture. He went through his voluminous journal for 1854 and wrote *Getting a Living*, which was later to become more widely known as *Life without Principle*.

This lecture was for Thoreau what *Self-Reliance* was for Emerson. It was a statement of Thoreau's philosophy. It was a Transcendental attack on materialism, in the course of which Thoreau also struck at public opinion and the influence of organized religion. It was a strong plea for fundamental principles—that is, the principles Thoreau recognized as valid. It was a good, sound lecture, though Thoreau's contempt for the way of life chosen by the mass of men in their desire for wealth or fame or whatever worthless will-o-the-wisp they followed all their years, shone through.

He expressed his bitterness at being told what to lecture about, as he sometimes was. "I take it for granted, when I am invited to lecture anywhere . . . that there is a desire to hear what *I think* on some subject, though I may be the greatest fool in the country, and not that I should say pleasant things merely, or such as the audience will assent to; and I resolve accordingly, that I will give them a strong dose of myself."

He decried "the way in which we spend our lives. . . . I think that there is nothing, not even crime, more opposed to poetry, to philosophy, ay, to life itself, than this incessant business. . . . If a man walk in the woods for love of them half of each day, he is in danger of being regarded as a loafer; but if he spends his whole day as a speculator, shearing off those woods and making earth bald before her time, he is esteemed an industrious and enterprising citizen. As if a town had no interest in its forests but to cut them down!"

His contempt for money as an end in itself was made bitterly clear. "I have been surprised when one has with confidence proposed to me, a grown man, to embark in some enterprise of his, as if I had absolutely nothing to do, my life having been a complete failure hitherto." And he publicly prized his freedom. "Perhaps I am more than usually jealous with respect to my freedom. I feel that my connection with and obligation to society are still very slight and transient. Those slight labors which afford me a livelihood, and by which it is allowed that I am to some extent serviceable to my contemporaries, are as yet commonly a pleasure to me, and I am not often reminded that they are a necessity. So far I am successful. But I foresee that if my wants should be much increased, the labor required to supply them would become a drudgery. If I should sell both my forenoons and afternoons to society, as most appear to do, I am sure that for me there would be nothing left worth living for. I trust that I shall never thus sell my birthright for a mess of pottage."

He held that the gold-rush to California reflected "the greatest disgrace on mankind. That so many are ready to live by luck, and so get the means of commanding the labor of others less lucky, without contributing any value to society! And that is called enterprise!" and added that, after reading Howitt's account of Australian gold mining, "I was thinking, accidentally, of my own unsatisfactory life, doing as others do; and with that vision of the diggings still before me, I asked myself why *I* might not be washing some gold daily, though it were only the finest particles—why *I* might not sink a shaft down to the gold within me, and work that mine. *There* is a Ballarat, a Bendigo for you—what though it were a sulky-gully? At any rate, I might pursue some path, however solitary and narrow and crooked, in which I could walk with love and reverence. Wherever a man separates from the multitude, and goes his own way in this mood, there indeed is a fork in the road, though ordinary travelers may see only a gap in the paling. His solitary path across lots will turn out the *higher way* of the two. . . . A man had better starve at once than lose his innocence in the process of getting his bread."

He scorned the press, he ridiculed the concept of freedom that prevailed in the nation. "Do we call this the land of the free? What is it to be free from King George and continue the slaves of King Prejudice? What is it to be born free and not to live free? What is the value of any political freedom, but as a means to moral freedom? Is it a freedom to be slaves, or a freedom to be free, of which we boast? We are a nation of politicians, concerned about the outmost defenses only of freedom. It is our children's children who may perchance be really free. We tax ourselves unjustly. There is a part of us which is not represented. It is taxation without representation. We quarter troops, we quarter fools and cattle of all sorts upon ourselves. We quarter our gross bodies on our poor souls, till the former eat up all the latter's substance."

While this lecture was not stylistically the equal of *Walden,* yet it remained the most succinct statement of Thoreau's principles. He wrote a footnote to it to Blake in mid-December: "The world rests on principles. The wise gods will never make underpinning of a man. But as long as he crouches, and skulks, and shirks his work, every creature that has weight will be treading on his toes and crushing him; he will himself tread with one foot on the other foot."

Thoreau first delivered this lecture at New Bedford the day after Christmas, 1854. In order to make the personal acquaintance of Daniel Ricketson, he went to New Bedford the day before. Ricketson was clearing snow before his house when Thoreau came, clad in a long, dark overcoat, wearing a soft dark hat, and carrying in one hand an umbrella, in the other a portmanteau. "As he came near to me I gave him the usual salutation," wrote Ricketson in his memoirs. He supposed Thoreau to be "either a pedlar or some way-traveller." Subsequently, he sketched Thoreau in his traveling clothes, one of the few such sketches of Thoreau extant.

The two men were congenial. Thoreau at New Bedford—and on the 28th of December at Nantucket, where he delivered his new lecture for the second time—filled his journal with notes about the region. He did not neglect a partial listing of Ricketson's library, stressing the many wood-engravings by Bewick illustrating books on Ricketson's shelves. The weather in New Bedford delighted him. ("It was wonderfully warm and pleasant . . . I felt the winter breaking up in me . . .") He traveled to Nantucket in misty rain, which continued throughout the day of his lecture there, though he went about in it and examined some of Captain Gardiner's experiments in raising pine trees.

Of what his audiences thought of his lecture there is no record. One can imagine their reaction. Hold up a man's morals for scrutiny and he will laugh with you; but ridicule his love of money or fame and you cut into a sensitive nerve indeed.

On the 29th Thoreau left Nantucket early in the morning for Concord in a fog "so thick that we were lost on the water. . . . Whistled and listened for the locomotive's answer, but probably heard only the echo of our own whistle at first, but at last the locomotive's whistle and the life-boat bell."

By the end of the month he was again on the river to Fair Haven Pond, celebrating the glory of the winter landscape.

CHAPTER 9

Surveyor of Concord

Live in each season as it passes; breathe the air, drink the drink, taste the fruit, and resign yourself to the influences of each. Let them be your only diet drink and botanical medicines. In August live on berries, not dried meats and pemmican, as if you were in shipboard making your way through a waste ocean, or in a northern desert. Be blown on by all the winds. Open all your pores and bathe in all the tides of Nature, in all her streams and oceans, at all seasons. Miasma and infection are from within, not without. The invalid, brought to the brink of the grave by an unnatural life, instead of imbibing only the great influence that Nature is, drinks only the tea made of a particular herb, while he still continues his unnatural life,—saves at the spile and wastes at the bung. He does not love Nature or his life, and so sickens and dies, and no doctor can cure him. Grow green with spring, yellow and ripe with autumn. Drink of each season's influence as a vial, a true panacea of all remedies mixed for your especial use. The vials of summer never made a man sick, but those which he stored in his cellar. Drink the wines, not of your bottling, but Nature's bottling; not kept in goat-skins or pig-skins, but the skins of a myriad fair berries. Let Nature do your bottling and your pickling and preserving. For all Nature is doing her best each moment to make us well. She exists for no other end. Do not resist her. With the least inclination to be well, we should not be sick.

134

Men have discovered—or think they have discovered—the salutariness of a few wild things only, and not of all nature. Why, 'nature' is but another name for health, and the seasons are but different states of health. Some men think that they are not well in spring, or summer, or autumn, or winter; it is only because they are not well in them.

—JOURNAL, 1853

HALF way through this thirty-eighth year of his life, Thoreau was at his peak of energy and good spirits; before he had completed it, his strength had begun to ebb, and he was not thereafter to regain the fine health he had known most of his adult life. He began the year with a lecture at Worcester—presumably *Getting a Living*—and noted that the Antiquarian Library in that city "is richer in pamphlets and newspapers than Harvard."

The first report he had on the subject matter of this lecture came to hand a few days after his return from Worcester. Ricketson wrote him: "I have heard several sensible people speak well of your lecture before the New Bedford Lyceum, but conclude it was not generally understood." This was perhaps not more than Thoreau had expected.

During that first month of 1855 Thoreau saw the pleasant review of his work published in the *Harvard Magazine*. Subsequently, while in Cambridge, Thoreau stopped at Holworthy Hall to call on the editor, F. B. Sanborn. In Sanborn's absence, he left a copy of *A Week on the Concord and Merrimack Rivers* for the writer of the review. Sanborn was at that time a senior in college. Though he saw Thoreau not long after Thoreau's call at Holworthy Hall, when Thoreau came into the library where Sanborn then was, he had not known that Tho-

135

reau had called on him. He wrote to Thoreau on the thirtieth, asking to "seek" him out when next he came to Concord.

Of *Walden* he wrote to thank Thoreau "for the new light it shows me the aspects of Nature in, and for the marvelous beauty of your descriptions," though he did not think Thoreau's philosophy "worth a straw." Thoreau replied to Sanborn that he would be glad to welcome him at any time in Concord. Within two months Sanborn was not only visiting Thoreau; he was seeing him frequently, for he had taken over the teaching of school in Concord, and was soon taking his meals at the Thoreau house. Teaching, however, was not Sanborn's only occupation; with almost clinical interest he was compiling notes on the lives and activities of those people who made Concord what he had called, when writing from Cambridge, "a sort of Mecca for our pilgrimages," —Emerson, Channing, and Thoreau chief among them.

Economically, Thoreau's position had now improved to the extent that he need not any longer worry about how to make ends meet and still do very much as he liked. Though the sales of pencils had fallen off, the demand for graphite had increased to such a point that the Thoreau family had moved up a notch or two in the social scale of Concord. Contributing even more to Thoreau's satisfaction was the steady sale of *Walden*, which, within a year of publication had sold over a thousand copies and had stimulated enough of a demand for *A Week on the Concord and Merrimack Rivers* to impel Thoreau to propose to Ticknor & Fields that it might be time to republish that book, though there were still copies of the first and only edition to be had from Thoreau and from his current publishers, who had been getting ten copies at a time from Thoreau's stock in the attic room.

Thoreau could now, in view of his improved circumstances, enjoy the Concord countryside to the full. Small wonder that on a day of winter thaw he could write ecstatically in his journal, "Perhaps what most moves us in winter is some reminiscence of far-off summer. How we leap by the side of the open brooks! What beauty in the running brooks! What life! What society! The cold is merely superficial; it is summer still at the core, far, far within. It is in the cawing of the crow, the crowing of the cock, the warmth of the sun on our backs. . . . It mingles with the slight murmur of the village, the sound of children at play, as one stream empties gently into another, and the wild and tame are one. . . . Ah, bless the Lord, O my soul! bless him for wildness, for crows that will not alight within gunshot! and bless him for hens, too, that croak and cackle in the yards!"

He went out into the country around Concord almost daily, save only on those days when he went to Cambridge or perhaps to Boston, after books, or to carry specimens to Harris. He skated often for many miles, especially delighting to do so in gently falling snow, and did not mind on occasion skating "into a crack" and sliding "on my side twenty-five feet." He enjoyed walking in snowstorms, with Channing or by himself, especially in deep woods where the snow "had lodged not only on the oak leaves and the evergreens, but on every twig and branch . . . the trunks also being plastered with snow, a peculiar soft light was diffused around, very unlike the ordinary darkness of the forest, as if you were inside a drift or snow house."

He made diagrams of snow drifts to illustrate his notes

and measured the rise and fall of the river and the brooks, especially during freshets. "It is surprising how much work will be accomplished in . . . a night, . . . so many a brook will have run itself out and now be found reduced within reasonable bounds." He made drawings of birds, of pine cones and scales, of animal tracks, of ice cakes and worm borings and grains of ice. He caught a flying squirrel with the intention of taming it; he failed, and released it again. He made careful studies of the notes of birds, and one March day he tried to imitate the honking of geese in an effort to attract them: "I found myself flapping my sides with my elbows, as with wings, and uttering something like the syllables *mow-ack* with a nasal twang and twist in my head; and I produced their note so perfectly in the opinion of hearers that I thought I might possibly draw a flock down."—an opinion which the geese moving north evidently did not share.

He kept all his usual records—of the first frogs, the first redwing, the first bluebird to be seen or heard—all first things, indeed ("The skunk-cabbage open yesterday,—the earliest flower this season. . . . Some twenty minutes after sundown I hear the first *booming* of a snipe. . . . At sunset after the rain, the robins and song sparrows fill the air along the river with their song."). On one day he found a dead merganser, not long since shot; he took it home ("a perfectly fresh and very beautiful bird, and as I raise it, I get sight of its long, slender vermilion bill (color of red sealing-wax) and its clean, bright-orange legs and feet, and then of its perfectly smooth and spotlessly pure white breast and belly, tinged with a faint salmon . . ."), and stuffed it ("It is wonderful that a man, having undertaken such an enterprise, ever persevered in it to the end, and equally wonderful that he succeeded.'').

He was continuing to be, and proud to be, as he put it in *Walden,* "anxious to improve the nick of time, and notch it" on his stick, "to stand on the meeting of two eternities, the past and future, which is precisely the present moment." He was still, as always, "reporter to a journal, of no very wide circulation . . . self-appointed inspector of snow-storms and rain-storms . . . surveyor . . . of forest paths and all across-lots routes, keeping them open, and ravines bridged and passable at all seasons, where the public heel had testified to their utility. . . ." with "an eye to the unfrequented nooks and corners of the farm." He was faithfully minding his "business, till it became more and more evident that my townsmen would not after all admit me into the list of town officers, nor make my place a sinecure with a modest allowance."

Nevertheless, eccentric though they may have thought Thoreau, accustomed as they were to thinking him a loafer and a college graduate who had thrown away his "chances," Thoreau's townsmen accepted him for what he was.

But the spring of 1855 was not all balm and delight. Perhaps, as Miss Minott said Dr. Spring had told her, "when the sap began to come up into the trees then the diseases of the human body come out. The idea is that man's body sympathizes with the rest of nature, and his pent-up humors burst forth like the sap from wounded trees. This with the mass may be that languor or other weakness commonly called spring feelings." What troubled Thoreau that April and thereafter for some months was not spring fever, however, nor was it

139

only bronchitis. It was a general weakness, amounting to a decline in his health, which affected his legs and made walking—his greatest pleasure—doubly difficult. Yet he persisted in it and would not be daunted, though he betrayed a certain melancholy from time to time in his notes, and told Blake he had been "good for nothing but to lie on my back and wait for something to turn up."

He added, "I should feel a little less ashamed if I could give any name to my disorder, but I cannot, and our doctor cannot help me to it, and I will not take the name of any disease in vain. However, there is one consolation in being sick, and that is the possibility that you may recover to a better state than you were ever in before. I expected in the winter to be deep in the woods of Maine in my canoe long before this, but I am so far from that that I can only take a languid walk in Concord streets." This in June. Maine was out of the question, but within a month he did go with Channing to Cape Cod to sit in the sun and hope that this might improve his health and vaporize his melancholy.

The illness might possibly have been an assault upon his lungs. It could have been brought about by the inhalation of the graphite dust which was the core of the Thoreau business which now supported Cynthia and John, Sophia and Henry comfortably. It was not until the year was almost out that Thoreau regained the assurance he hoped for in his legs. Yet he was not the same in strength; he was never to be in the same health as he had been before the onset of the illness, though he was not to be put off from his continuing exploration of Concord and its environs.

That spring, too, Thoreau was involved in another struggle with an editor. George William Curtis had ac-

140

cepted for publication Thoreau's account of Cape Cod, which Curtis proposed to run in five chapters in *Putnam's*. Curtis thought some of Thoreau's views "heretical." Thoreau attempted at first to compromise by revising his copy. But Thoreau's revision was of style in the interests of clarity; he wanted to make his position perfectly clear, or more clear than it already was; and it was already too clear for Curtis. He could not revise his attitude or compromise with his convictions, and Curtis was too conservative to permit Thoreau their free expression for the fear—to which all editors are prone—of giving offense to many of the more conservative readers of *Putnam's*.

What Thoreau would not do, Curtis did. He made deletions in Thoreau's manuscript before sending it to the printer. This Thoreau would not tolerate. Much as he appreciated the monthly $35 stipend he received, he withdrew the balance of *Cape Cod* after three instalments had appeared in the magazine. He intended to remain a man of principle and if no further word of his appeared in print.

Meanwhile, Horace Greeley, still interested in Thoreau's place in the world of letters, wrote to urge him to send review copies of *Walden*—accompanied by copies of his first book—to the *Westminster Review* and to Dickens's *Household Words* in England, since these journals ought to print reviews of the books and perhaps find some interest among British publishers who might bring out a British edition of one or both books. George Eliot reviewed *Walden* in the *Westminster Review* within a few months, but this favorable review brought no immediate inquiry from any British publisher.

By early autumn Thoreau was beginning to regain his vigor. He was still dubious about making excursions far from Concord. He wrote Ricketson in late September, "I am so wedded to my way of spending a day—require such broad margins of leisure, and such a complete wardrobe of old clothes, that I am ill fitted for going abroad. Pleasant is it sometimes to sit, at home, on a single egg all day, in your own nest, though it may prove at last to be an egg of chalk. The old coat that I wear is Concord—it is my morning robe & study gown, my working dress and suit of ceremony, and my night-gown after all. Cleave to the simplest ever—Home—home—home. *Cars* sound like *cares* to me."

Ricketson visited him, and later, Blake, to whom he wrote after his return home: "Thank you! thank you for going a-wooding with me,—and enjoying it,—for being warmed by my wood fire. I have indeed enjoyed it much alone. I see how I might enjoy it yet more with company,—how we might help each other to live. And to be admitted to Nature's hearth costs nothing. None is excluded, but excludes himself. You have only to push aside the curtain. . . .

"Talk of burning your smoke after the wood has been consumed! There is a far more important and warming heat, commonly lost, which precedes the burning of the wood. It is the smoke of industry, which is incense. I had been so thoroughly warmed in body and spirit, that when at length my fuel was housed, I came near selling it to the ash-man, as if I had extracted all its heat."

By late November Thoreau had recovered his health sufficiently to go boating and to load a pine log from the Assabet into his boat so that he could take it home and make wheels "to roll my boat into winter quarters upon. So I sawed off two thick rollers from one end, pierced them for wheels, and then of a joist which I had found drifting on the river in the summer I made an axletree,

142

and on this I rolled my boat out." Boating afforded him much pleasure, and made up in part for the absence of the long walks he had abandoned for the duration of his illness. Very often, those visitors he could not persuade to go sauntering with him, could readily enough be induced to go boating. Writing later, George Curtis recalled boating with Thoreau as one of the "most vivid recollections of my life in Concord." They had gone boating one evening and went along the river in the darkness. "We lighted a huge fire of fat pine in an iron crate beyond the bow of the boat and drifted slowly through an illuminated circle of the ever-changing aspect of the river bed."

On Indian Summer days that November he could not keep to the house. "It is akin to sin to spend such a day in the house," he wrote in his journal. "This, too, is the *recovery* of the year,—as if the year, having nearly or quite accomplished its work, and abandoned all design, were in a more favorable and poetic mood, and thought rushed in to fill the vacuum. . . ." He was much on the river, watching for tortoises, blue herons, bitterns, and enjoying the water. "This is the aspect under which the Musketaquid might be represented at this season: a long, smooth lake, reflecting the bare willows and button-bushes, the stubble, and the wool-grass on its tussock, a muskrat-cabin or two conspicuous on its margin amid the unsightly tops of pontederia, and a bittern disappearing on undulating wing around a bend."

On the last day of that month, Thoreau received through Nichols & Company of Boston a shipment of books Thomas Cholmondeley had selected for him. They had been dispatched by Chapman of London, since Cholmondeley had gone to the Crimea, as he had expected to do. Knowing of Thoreau's interest in Indian literature and thought, Cholmondeley had gone to considerable pains to assemble a shelf of books for Thoreau. The shelf included Wilson's *Rig Veda Sanhita,* a translation of the *Mandukya Upanishads,* Wilson's *Vishnu Purana,* Haughton's *Institutes of Menu,* the *Sankhya Karika,* the *Bhagavat Geeta,* Wilson's *Sakuntala,* the *Bhagavita Purana,* the Chevalier Bunsen's *Christianity and Mankind,* and others.

Thoreau was delighted to have them. He built cases for them made in part of driftwood he had salvaged from the Concord River, and wrote Cholmondeley to thank him for his "princely gift." To Blake he wrote, "I have not made out the significance of this godsend yet," though he had "not dipped far into the new ones yet."

Welcome as the books were, they came at a time when Thoreau would have little opportunity to read. Having regained the confidence in his legs that he had almost lost during the travail of his inexplicable illness, he was up and about that winter as often as he might be. Even days of sub-zero weather did not keep him in the house, nor did deep snow. That winter of 1855–1856 was a winter of very heavy snow. At one time Thoreau carefully measured sixteen inches on the level, and by the time the snow was decreasing, he noted in his journal that for a two month period beginning early in January there had never been less than a foot of snow on the level in the environs of Concord.

He went out in all weather, even daring the biting northwest wind in sub-zero weather. He had now grown a beard, a sort of Quaker beard, covering his throat. He was photographed early in 1856 in Worcester, by D. B. Maxham, who took on that occasion the most often-reproduced photograph of Thoreau. Beards were at that

144

time coming back into fashion, but it is unlikely that Thoreau grew one for any other reason but to protect his throat on his frequent hiking excursions.

He needed such protection that winter, for he had not, in fact, so much regained his former health as improved upon his recent condition. He could not in truth say of his physical condition what he could write of his financial circumstances that January in his journal: "Within the last five years I have had the command of a little more money than in the previous five years, for I have sold some books and some lectures; yet I have not been a whit better fed or clothed or warmed or sheltered, not a whit richer, except that I have been less concerned about my living, but perhaps my life has been the less serious for it, and, to balance it, I feel now that there is a possibility of failure." Nothing was set down in his journal about the modest success of *Walden*, though he wrote Calvin Greene in Michigan that *Walden* had now sold over two thousand copies, in "an audience of excellent character . . . I should consider it a greater success to interest one wise and earnest soul, than a million unwise & frivolous."

His journal is filled with his accounts of Nature in Concord, and his thoughts rooted in Nature, with measurements of trees, snow depths, ice depths, records of his walking out and what he saw on such excursions—how the weeds looked against the snow, and the sunsets ("The colors of the west seem more than usually warm, perhaps by contrast with this simple snow-clad earth over which we look and the clear cold sky,—a sober but extensive redness, almost every night passing into a dun."), how the sap ran from the sugar maples and how he made maple sugar ("I put in saleratus and a little milk while boiling, the former to neutralize the acid, and the latter

145

to collect the impurities in a skum. After boiling it till I burned it a little, and my small quantity would not flow when cool, but was as hard as half-done candy, I put it on again, and in a minute it was softened and turned to sugar.").

He attended the felling of a giant old Concord elm— "so to speak, the funeral of this old citizen of the town,— I who commonly do not attend funerals,—as it became me to do. I was the chief if not the only mourner there. I have taken the measure of his grandeur; have spoken a few words of eulogy at his grave, . . . But there were only the choppers and the passers-by to hear me. Further the town was not represented; the fathers of the town, the selectmen, the clergy were not there. But I have not known a fitter occasion for a sermon of late." And that same month he set down in his journal again his admiration for Emerson's paternal aunt, Miss Mary, whom he had only the previous month described to Blake as "the youngest person in Concord, though about eighty,—and the most apprehensive of a genuine thought; earnest to know of your inner life; most stimulating society; and exceedingly witty withal. She says they called her old when she was young, and she has never grown any older."

Early in March Thoreau wrote to Ricketson: "This has indeed been a grand winter for me & for all of us. I am not considering how much I have enjoyed it. What matters it how happy or unhappy we have been, if we have minded our business and advanced our affairs. I have made it a part of my business to wade in the snow & take the measure of the ice. The ice on one of our ponds was just two feet thick on the first of March—and I have to-day been surveying a wood-lot where I sank about two feet at every step."

He added that he missed Channing, who was in New

Bedford: " 'But O the heavy change' now he is gone!" and went on to indite a fond description of his walking companion in a memorable portrait. "The C you have seen & described is the real Simon Pure. You have seen him. Many a good ramble may you have together. You will see in him still more *of the same kind*—to attract & to puzzle you. How to serve him most effectually has long been a problem with his friends. Perhaps it is left for you to solve it. I suspect that the most that you or any one can do for him is to appreciate his genius—to buy & read, & cause others to buy & read his poems. That is the hand which he has put forth to the world—Take hold of that. Review them if you can. Perhaps take the risk of publishing something more which he may write.

"Your knowledge of Cowper will help you to know C. He will accept sympathy & aid, but he will not bear questioning—unless the aspects of the sky are particularly auspicious. He will even be 'reserved & enigmatic,' & you must deal with him at arm's length.

"I have no secrets to tell you concerning him, and do not wish to call obvious excellences & defects by far-fetched names. I think I have already spoken to you more, and more to the purpose, on this theme, than I am likely to write now—nor need I suggest how witty & poetic he is—and what an inexhaustible fund of good-fellowship you will find in him."

Later that month Thoreau's favorite uncle, Charles Dunbar, died. He was 76. He was buried next day, and Thoreau noted in his journal, "He was born in February, 1780, the winter of the Great Snow, and he dies in the winter of another great snow,—a life bounded by great snows."

That March, too, Horace Greeley wrote to suggest that Thoreau come to live with the Greeley family, to teach his two children, at Chappaqua. Thoreau did not reject the suggestion outright, and Greeley hastened to assure him "that money shall not divide us . . . I am very sure that I shall be willing to pay such sum as you will consider satisfactory." Pending the return of Mrs. Greeley from Europe, Thoreau agreed to begin his residence at Chappaqua by July first. But he did not, after all, go.

Perhaps he did not relish the prospect of further tutoring, any more than he looked forward to much lecturing. He had written Calvin Greene in May, "lecturing has commonly proved so foreign & irksome to me, that I think I could only use it to acquire the means with which to make an independent tour another time." And he wrote to Ricketson later that year, in reply to an invitation to teach during the coming winter, "I find that I cannot entertain the idea. It would require such a revolution of all my habits, I think, as would sap the very foundation of me. I am engaged to Concord & my very private pursuits by 10,000 ties, & it would be suicide to cut them. If I were weaker, & not somewhat stronger physically, I should be more tempted. I am so busy that I cannot even think of visiting you. The days are not long enough or I am not strong enough to do the work of the day before bed-time."—which very probably accounts fully for Thoreau's ultimate decision not to go to Chappaqua to live.

There were occasions, however, on which Thoreau did not do as he wanted—however few in number. One such occurred August 8, 1856, when, coming from the house "thinking to empty my boat and go a-meditating along the river," Thoreau discovered that his father's pig had escaped. "Here was an ugly duty not to be shirked,—a wild shoat that weighed but ninety to be tracked, caught,

148

and penned,—an afternoon's work, at least (if I were lucky enough to accomplish it so soon), prepared for me, quite different from what I had anticipated." He could not ignore that duty. "Do the duty that lies nearest to thee." He began to track the pig from the corner where he escaped, "making a step of his trough." The tracks were plain enough where the pig went through the garden and along the front yard walk. Presently he caught sight of the pig up the street; unhappily, the pig also caught sight of him and led him a merry chase, through town, across lots, to the river's edge, Thoreau after him. "Each neighbor whose garden I traverse tells me some anecdote of losing pigs, or the attempt to drive them, by which I am not encouraged."

Thoreau's account of this event is filled with humor and a sense of comedy. "Twice he ran up the narrow street, for he knew I did not wish it, but though the main street was broad and open and no traveller in sight, when I tried to drive him past this opening he invariably turned his piggish head toward me, dodged from side to side, and finally ran up the narrow street or down the main one, as if there were a high barrier erected before him. But really he is no more obstinate than I. I cannot but respect his tactics and his independence. He will be he, and I may be I."

A passing Irishman was engaged to help, and the pig was finally chased into a carriage-manufactory, and after some further difficulties was roped. Driving the pig home was not easy, but Thoreau did at least get home at dark, "wet through and supperless, covered with mud and wheel-grease, without any rare flowers."

Early in September Thoreau went to Brattleboro, Vermont, to visit Charles Frost and Mary Brown. He climbed the hills there, and walked up the bank of the Connecticut River—("The Concord is worth a hundred of it for my purposes. It looks narrow as well as shallow.")—and went botanizing. He climbed Chesterfield Mountain with Frances and Mary Brown. He recorded that the most interesting thing he saw in Brattleboro "was the skin and skull of a panther . . . which was killed, according to a written notice attached, on the 15th of June by the Saranac Club of Brattleboro, six young men, on a fishing and hunting excursion. . . . I was surprised at its great size and apparent strength. It gave one a new idea of our American forests and the vigor of nature here."

He remained there five days and then went to Walpole, New Hampshire, to visit with Bronson Alcott and his family. For part of the way he walked, ascending Fall Mountain "with a heavy valise on my back." He explored the country around Alcott's house, and spent some time listing the plants he found during his week away from Concord, for by the thirteenth he was rowing up the Assabet to gather ripe grapes.

For all the vigor with which he had tramped the New England hills, he was well aware that his former strength had not fully returned, for when he wrote to Thomas Cholmondeley in October, thanking him again for the books he had sent and hinting at the coming of the Civil War ("perhaps a more serious war still is breaking out here. I seem to hear its distant mutterings, though it may be long before the bolt will fall in our midst. There has not been anything which you could call union between the North and South in this country for many years, and there cannot be so long as slavery is in the way."), he gave Cholmondeley "but a poor account" of himself.

"I got 'run down' they say," he wrote, "more than a year ago, and have not yet got fairly up again. It has not touched my spirits however, for they are as indifferently tough, as sluggishly resilient, as a dried fungus. I would it were the kind called punk; that they might catch and retain some heavenly spark. I dwell as much aloof from society as ever: find it just as impossible to agree in opinion with the most intelligent of my neighbors; they not having improved one jot, nor I either. I am still immersed in nature, have much of the time a living sense of the breadth of the field on whose verge I dwell."

That autumn, Marcus Spring, the philanthropic patron of Eagleswood near Perth Amboy, invited Thoreau, at Alcott's suggestion, to survey the two hundred acres and lecture at the same time. Eagleswood was primarily a school for young people; Spring wanted to prepare young people for maturity in a home-like environment which included brilliant conversationalists and a leavening of Abolitionists. The school at Eagleswood was run by Theodore Weld, and included, among others, Caroline Kirkland, a Western story writer. Thoreau went, surveyed, conversed, lectured.

But he was his customary prickly self, which is to say he made no concessions to his fellow lecturers or to his students. He wrote his sister Sophia in November, "This is a queer place—There is one large long stone building, . . . in which I do not know exactly who or how many work—. . . a few shops & offices, an old farm house and Mr. Spring's perfectly private residence within 20 rods of the main building. 'The City of Perth Amboy' is about as big as Concord, and Eagleswood is 1¼ miles S W of it, on the bay side. . . . Saturday evening I went to the school room, hall, or what not, to see the children & their teachers & patrons dance. Mr. Weld, a kind looking man with a long white beard, danced with them, & Mr.

Cutler his assistant, lately from Cambridge, who is acquainted with Sanborn, Mr. Spring—and others. This Sat. eve-dance is a regular thing . . . They take it for granted that you want *society!"*

Not that Thoreau had any objection to dancing. He danced himself, especially in a pixielike mood on occasion at Ricketson's shanty when he deliberately trod on Alcott's toes. For the children of Concord he improvised dances, played his flute, popped corn, played juggler tricks, made willow whistles and trumpets out of squash leaf stems, and sang his favorite songs—*Canadian Boat Song, Tom Bowling* ("Here a sheer hulk lies poor Tom Bowling, / The darling of our crew; / No more he'll hear the tempest howling, / For death has broached him to.").

"On Sunday evening," he went on in his letter to Sophia, "I read the moose-story to the children to their satisfaction. Ever since I have been constantly engaged in surveying Eagleswood—through woods, ravines, marshes & along the shore, dodging the tide—through catbriar mud & beggar ticks—having no time to look up or think where I am . . ." He wrote Blake with more appreciation of the lectures that he had given "with rare success" that he was "aware that what I was saying was silently taken in by their ears."

Of more importance, perhaps, was the fact that through Alcott's visits, Thoreau got into New York. Alcott took him to spend a day with Alice Cary, the poet, at Greeley's farm. They heard Henry Ward Beecher preach what Thoreau thought was rather a "pagan" sermon, and finally, a day or two later, they went to call on a man as independent and individual as Thoreau—Walt Whitman, whose *Leaves of Grass*—hailed by Emerson— had been published in 1855. Both Thoreau and Whitman were reserved, as if each feared to commit himself too readily, but it was not the reserve of hostility, rather of uncertainty.

Whitman in his red-flannel undershirt, overalls, and calico jacket impressed Thoreau, an impression that grew after Thoreau returned to Eagleswood, for he wrote Blake of the meeting and Whitman—"He is apparently the greatest democrat the world has seen. Kings and aristocracy go by the board at once, as they have long deserved to. A remarkably strong though coarse nature, of a sweet disposition, and much prized by his friends. Though peculiar and rough in his exterior, . . . he is essentially a gentleman. I am still somewhat in a quandary about him,—feel that he is essentially strange to me, at any rate . . ."

He added, some weeks later, "That Walt Whitman . . . is the most interesting fact to me at present. I have just read his 2nd edition (which he gave me) and it has done me more good than any reading for a long time. Perhaps I remember best the poem of Walt Whitman an American & the Sun Down Poem. . . . But . . . he has spoken more truth than any American or modern that I know. . . . Of course Walt Whitman can communicate to us no experience, and if we are shocked, whose experience is it that we are reminded of? . . .

"We ought to rejoice greatly in him. He occasionally suggests something a little more than human. . . . He is awfully good. . . .

"Since I have seen him, I find that I am not disturbed by any brag or egoism in his book. He may turn out the least of a braggart of all, having a better right to be confident.

"He is a great fellow."

He returned to Concord from Eagleswood in a little over a month, as the year was drawing to its close. A long, friendly letter from Cholmondeley came to hand, but Thoreau must have wondered just how well Cholmondeley understood him after all when his British correspondent could write, "You are not living altogether as I could wish. You ought to have society. A college, a conventual life is for you. You should be the member of some society not yet formed. You want it greatly, and without this you will be liable to moulder away as you get older. . . . Your love for, and intimate acquaintance with, Nature is ancillary to some affection which you have not yet discovered."

On the last day of 1856, Thoreau, faithful to his ideal of existence, wrote to Blake in response to another invitation to lecture in Worcester before the winter was out, "O solitude! obscurity! meanness! I never triumph so as when I have the least success in my neighbor's eyes. The lecturer gets fifty dollars a night; but what becomes of his winter? What consolation will it be hereafter to have fifty thousand dollars for living in the world? I should like not to exchange *any* of my life for money."

CHAPTER 10

The Language of the Fields

Still we live meanly, like ants; though the fable tells us that we were long ago changed into men; like pygmies we fight with cranes; it is error upon error, and clout upon clout, and our best virtue has for its occasion a superfluous and evitable wretchedness. Our life is frittered away by detail. An honest man has hardly need to count more than his ten fingers, or in extreme cases he may add his ten toes, and lump the rest. Simplicity, simplicity, simplicity! I say, let your affairs be as two or three, and not a hundred or a thousand; instead of a million count half a dozen, and keep your accounts on your thumb-nail. —WALDEN

"How I love the simple, reserved countrymen, my neighbors, who mind their own business and let me alone," wrote Thoreau in his journal late in 1856, "who never waylaid nor shot at me, to my knowledge, when I crossed their fields, though each one has a gun in his house. For nearly twoscore years I have known, at a distance, these long-suffering men, whom I never spoke to, who never spoke to me, and now feel a certain tenderness for them, as if this long probation were but the prelude to an eternal friendship. What a long trial we have withstood, and how much more admirable we are to each other, perchance, than if we had been bedfellows! I am not only grateful because Veias, and Homer, and Christ, and Shakespeare have lived, but

I am grateful for Minott, and Rice, and Melvin, and Goodwin, and Puffer even."

At his accustomed rounds, Thoreau met these countrymen with more ease than he met the audiences to which he lectured. Yet he continued to lecture. He promised Blake that he would lecture again in Worcester in February, once more on *Walking*, but a month before that occurrence he wrote in his journal: "For some years past I have partially offered myself as a lecturer; have been advertised as such several years. Yet I have had but two or three invitations to lecture in a year, and some years none at all. I congratulate myself on having been permitted to stay at home thus, I am so much richer for it. I do not see what I should have got of much value, but money, by going about, but I do see what I should have lost."

Despite a certain coolness which had come between Thoreau and the Emerson household, he was still on occasion dining there, to meet and talk about turtles with Agassiz, or to explore Eddy Emerson's snow cave—"a hole about two and a half feet wide and six feet long, into a drift, a little winding . . . I observed, as I approached in a course at right angles with the length of the cave, that the mouth of the cave was lit as if the light were close to it, so that I did not suspect its depth. Indeed, the light of this lamp was remarkably reflected and distributed. . . . I think that one lamp would light sufficiently a hall built of this material. . . . We afterward buried the lamp in a little crypt in this snowdrift and walled it in, and found that its light was visible, even in this *twilight*, through fifteen inches' thickness of snow."

Before going to Worcester, Thoreau lectured in Fitchburg. He had lectured in Amherst, New Hampshire, in

December, taken a month's freedom from lectures, and then in February delivered *Walking* at Fitchburg and Worcester. "Sometimes," he wrote after the Fitchburg lecture, "when, in conversation or a lecture, I have been grasping at, or even standing and reclining upon, the serene and everlasting truths that underlie and support our vacillating life, I have seen my auditors standing on their *terra firma*, the quaking earth, . . . and compassionately or timidly watching my motions as if they were the antics of a rope-dancer or mountebank pretending to walk on air . . ."

Thoreau was becoming more aware of the need for conservation of the nation's natural resources. It could hardly have been otherwise with so observant a walker. In his decades of tramping through the countryside he had witnessed the decline in numbers of the wild pigeons, the danger to fish in industrial growth along the rivers, the wanton felling of woodlands and even of old trees in Concord itself. His journal reflected his distress at the loss of familiar trees. "Every larger tree which I knew and admired is being gradually culled out and carried to mill. I see one or two more large oaks in Hubbard's woods lying high on stumps, waiting for snow to be removed. I miss them as surely and with the same feeling that I do the old inhabitants out of the village street." But he was also aware that there was little he could do about it. "No doubt there is *some* compensation for this loss, but I do not at this moment see clearly what it is."

In February, Sanborn brought a Concord visitor to lunch at the Thoreau house. This was John Brown, already widely known throughout the east because he was the leader of the anti-slavery forces in Kansas, which was ever since the opening of Kansas to settlement in

1855 a battleground between pro-slavery and anti-slavery groups. Brown himself had led violent raids and participated in the Pottawatomie massacre of pro-slavery colonists near Dutch Henry's Crossing at Pottawatomie Creek. He was now touring the east in an effort to raise funds for the cause against slavery. Sanborn had persuaded him to come to Concord to meet some of the leading citizens. Emerson joined them at Thoreaus' and they talked with Brown. At Thoreaus' Brown spoke passionately but quietly of liberty and the rights of all men, black as well as white, and told his listeners something of his history.

At the Town House that night, speaking to the people who had come to hear him, something of the violence in him burst forth when he spoke wildly and bitterly, with many gestures, of the way his son John had been treated in Kansas. He talked about his trials—with one son murdered, another crazed, and told his listeners in ringing words that he and his remaining sons would never stop fighting to free Kansas from slavery. And next day at Emerson's he held forth again, gentler now, entertaining young Eddy with animal stories.

Thoreau was impressed by him and made a donation. So did many others, including Emerson. But of them all, Thoreau's impression of Brown went deepest, and it was to show through later.

Meanwhile, Thoreau's excursions to Walden, Fair Haven, up the Assabet, to Conantum, Hubbard's Close and all the old places continued unabated. But he was planning excursions farther afield in 1857. Though he wrote to Ricketson April first that he wished "there were a few more signs of spring in myself—however, I take it that there *are* as many within us as we think we hear *without* us. I am decent for steady pace, but not yet for

158

a race."—he followed the letter to New Bedford. There he, Alcott, Channing and Ricketson had many lively conversations, but, as usual, he was often alone, by choice. He "caught a croaking frog in some smooth water," studied frog spawn ("in very handsome spherical masses of transparent jelly . . . suspended near the surface of some weed"), visited the New Bedford Library, gathered bayberries, picked up scallop shells, watched the smelt fishermen, spent a rainy day in Ricketson's shanty, and visited the Marlborough ponds at long last.

He set out to walk around Little Quitticus, and outwalked Ricketson ("the water being high,—higher than anciently even, on account of dams,—we had to go round the swamp at the south end . . . and R. gave it up. I went to Long Pond and waited for him . . ."). While waiting for his host, Thoreau examined the turtles in the area and made notes on the back of a lottery circular. Another day of rain followed—a day of conversation in the shanty, no doubt.

On April 16 he was back in Concord, getting birch sap, and telling Sanborn how, a month previous, he had been needled in the post-office by Abel Brooks about his "walkers" society. Sanborn told him that when first he had come to Concord and boarded at Holbrook's, he had asked Holbrook how many religious societies there were in town. Holbrook had told him there were three—"the Unitarian, the Orthodox, and the Walden Pond Society. I asked Sanborn with which Holbrook classed himself. He said he believes that he put himself with the last."

He resumed his walks about Concord, but he also spent much time in his boat, rowing up the Assabet and sailing to Ball's Hill. He made notes on lichens and mosses, and was distressed at sight of a dead snake ("I have the same objection to killing a snake that I have to

159

the killing of any other animal, yet the most humane man that I know never omits to kill one."). He heard the first toad song and built a fence as well as an arbor for Emerson. He added to his modest wardrobe—

"Within a week I have had made a pair of corduroy pants, which cost when done $1.60. They are of that peculiar clay-color, reflecting the light from portions of their surface. They have this advantage, that, beside being very strong, they will look about as well three months hence as now,—or as ill, some would say. Most of my friends are disturbed by my wearing them. I can get four or five pairs for what one ordinary pair would cost in Boston, and each of the former will last two or three times as long under the same circumstances. The tailor said that the stuff was not made in this country; that it was worn by the Irish at home, and now they would not look at it, but others would not wear it, durable and cheap as it is, because it is worn by the Irish. Moreover, I like the color on other accounts. Anything but black clothes."

Late in May Ricketson returned his visit. Thoreau took him by boat to Fair Haven, where they bathed, finding "the water unexpectedly warm and the air also delicious. Thus we are baptized into nature." Ricketson, however, never stayed long; he was apparently too restless to stay in one place, other than his shanty, very long.

On June 12, 1857, Thoreau set out for Cape Cod. He went alone this time. As usual, he made copious notes. Perhaps he intended to add to his store of writing about Cape Cod, but nothing of this excursion was subsequently used either on the lecture platform or in print. At Clark's Island, B. M. Watson told Thoreau solemnly that Daniel Webster once saw "the sea-serpent . . . with a head somewhat like a horse's raised some six feet above the water, and his body the size of a cask trailing behind. He was careering over the bay, chasing the mackerel. . . . On the sail homeward, Webster having had time to reflect on what had occurred, at length said to Peterson, 'For God's sake, never say a word about this to any one, for if it should be known that I have seen the sea-serpent, I should never hear the last of it, but wherever I went should have to tell the story to every one I met.' So it has not leaked out till now."

After a ride to Manomet with Watson and his wife, Thoreau started off by himself, shouldering his pack to walk along the shore. He went along taking note of the vegetation, listening to the booming of a bittern ("I heard distinctly two or three dry, hard sucks, as if the bird were drawing up water from the swamp, and then the sounds usually heard, as if ejecting it"), watching laying turtles, and, after walking seven miles that day, spent the night at the house of one Samuel Ellis. The Ellises were accustomed to taking in pedlars, which they thought Thoreau to be—as Ricketson had once thought him, too, which conveys the undeniable impression that —on his excursions at least—Thoreau wore the general appearance of a pedlar. There he made the acquaintance of a genuine pedlar who arrived after him with a horse and cart, "a simple and well-behaved boy of sixteen or seventeen only, peddling cutlery, who said that he started from Conway . . . In answer to my question how he liked peddling, he said that he liked it on some accounts, it enabled him to see the world. I thought him an unusually good specimen of Young America."

Next day he set out again, after listening to his host's morning prayers thanking God "that we 'of all the pale-faces were preserved alive,'" and musing—"What's the use of ushering the day with prayer, if it is . . . con-

161

secrated to turning a few more pennies merely?" He walked along a sandy road half a mile from the Atlantic, observing the snake rail fences, met and talked with an Indian, watched the "piping plover," and skipping beach-flies. At Scusset he took the train to Sandwich.

Once again out of "the cars," he went on his way with chart and compass by means of which he could "generally find a shorter way than the inhabitants can tell me." He went on to Friends Village, "a continuous street, for five miles at least, without a distinct village, the houses but a few rods apart all the way on each side. . . . As in Canada along the St. Lawrence, you never got out of the village, only came to a meeting-house now and then. . . . But all this street had a peculiarly Sabbath-day appearance, for there was scarcely an inhabitant to be seen, and they were commonly women or young children, for the greater part of the able-bodied men were gone to sea . . ."

He recorded his despondency at walking in settled regions, "but when I come out upon a bare and solitary heath am at once exhilarated. This is a common experience in my travelling. I plod along, thinking what a miserable world this is and what miserable fellows we that inhabit it, wondering what it is tempts men to live in it; but anon I leave the towns behind and am lost in some boundless heath, and life becomes gradually more tolerable, if not even glorious." He walked to the ponds between Harwich and Brewster where he "met with the first cranberry-patch . . . a handsome, perfectly level bed, a field, a redeemed meadow, adjoining the pond, the plants in perfectly straight rows eighteen inches apart, in coarse white sand which had been carted in."

He walked through mizzling rain and fog to Truro.

On the way he picked up a Mother Carey's chicken, washed up dead on the beach, and carried it along, "tied to the tip of my umbrella, dangling outside. When the inhabitants saw me come up from the beach this stormy day, with this emblem dangling from my umbrella, and saw me set it up in a corner carefully to be out of the way of cats, they may have taken me for a crazy man." This must have afforded Thoreau some amusement; he did not mind being taken for what he was or what he was not, as long as people did not take him for what they thought he ought to be.

The fog held for five days, but Thoreau was out in it, nothing daunted, though some of the Cape dwellers "denied that it was fog at all. They said with some asperity that it was rain. Yet more rain would have fallen in a smart shower in the country in twenty minutes than in these five days on the Cape." When the fog cleared, Thoreau went to Provincetown, "straight across the country to the Bay where the new road strikes it, directly through the pine plantation," and spent the night in an attic chamber at the Pilgrim House ("It would be worth the while to send a professor there, one who was also skilled in entomology.") He added, as he put it, considerable "to my knowledge of the natural history of the cat and the bedbug. . . . At still midnight, when, half awake, half asleep, you seem to be weltering in your own blood on a battlefield, you hear the stealthy tread of padded feet belonging to some animal of the cat tribe, perambulating the roof within a few inches of your head."

He reached home late in the afternoon of June 22nd, and was soon out at Farmer's Owl-Nest Swamp looking for a long-eared owl's nest near the top of a white pine, thirty feet from the ground. Thoreau climbed the tree to look at it, untroubled by the distress of the owl; the nest was empty. "It was made of twigs rather less than an eighth of an inch thick and was almost flat above, only an inch lower in the middle than at the edge, about sixteen inches in diameter and six or eight inches thick, with the twigs in the midst, and beneath was mixed sphagnum and sedge from the swamp beneath, and the lining or flooring was coarse strips of grape-vine bark; the whole pretty firmly matted together. How common and important a material is grape-vine bark for birds' nests! Nature wastes nothing."

A fortnight after he had resumed his accustomed rounds and spent a day on the Assabet with Blake, he recorded a footnote on Cape Cod. "Some of the inhabitants of the Cape," he wrote July 7, "think that the Cape is theirs and all occupied by them, but in my eyes it is no more theirs than it is the blackbirds', and in visiting the Cape there is hardly more need of my regarding or going through the villages than of going through the blackbirds' nests. I am inclined to leave them both on one side, or perchance I just glance into them to see how they are built and what they contain. I know that they have *spoken for* the whole Cape, and lines are drawn on their maps accordingly, but I know that these are imaginary, having perambulated many such, and they would have to get me or one of my craft to find them for them. For the most part, indeed with very trifling exceptions, there were no human beings there, only a few imaginary lines on a map."

Next day he wrote to Calvin Greene that he had not published anything for some time, but his pen was not idle. "I like a private life, & cannot bear to have the public in my mind." He wrote also that he was "very little of a traveller," and in the sense that Thoreau meant it this was true, for he had reference to an extended Western trip. But he was even then thinking of yet another trip into the Maine woods. He asked his cousin in Bangor, George Thatcher, to accompany him. George could not do so. Thoreau then turned to Edward Hoar—that same companion with whom Thoreau had accidentally set fire to the Concord woods thirteen years before. On July 20th, they set out for Maine to engage a guide and plunge once more into the wilderness.

Their guide was an Indian, Joe Polis ("stoutly built, perhaps a little above the middle height, with a broad face, and . . . perfect Indian features and complexion"). Polis proved to be well informed in the very subjects Thoreau wanted to study in preparation for the book on Indian life he planned to write but never wrote. Polis, a Penobscot, knew the country into which they planned to go—up to the Allegash Lakes by way of Moosehead—and persuaded them to return not by the route they had originally chosen, but by the East Branch of the Penobscot River, since it led through wilder country.

They set out from Bangor in rain which stayed with them for miles. Thoreau and Hoar each carried a large knapsack, "as full as it would hold," with provisions and utensils in two large India-rubber bags. Polis had only an axe, a gun, a blanket, tobacco and a pipe. Thoreau observed the impressive simplicity of the Indian's equipment. It was still raining when they reached Moosehead Lake on the evening of July 23d; so they stayed in a tavern that night and launched the canoe into the lake next morning, at four o'clock. The canoe was more compact than Thoreau had thought it might be, but it was new and staunch, and carried the six hundred pounds of travelers and baggage without difficulty. Off

165

they went, the Indian "on a cross-bar in the stern, but we flat on the bottom . . . and one of us commonly paddled with the Indian."

Thoreau, as usual, made copious notes, adding to his lists of trees, shrubs and flowers. But he was as much interested in what Joe Polis did and what the Indian could tell him of Indian life and lore as he was in the wilderness through which they passed. His notes are studded with Indian words and their meanings—"*Allegash,* hemlock-bark. . . . *Penobscot,* Rocky River. *Puapeskou,* stone. . . . *Sebago* or *Sebec,* large open water." Polis sang for them in "a slow, somewhat nasal, yet musical chant, in his own language. . . . His singing carried me back to the period of the discovery of America, to San Salvador and the Incas, when Europeans first encountered the simple faith of the Indian. There was, indeed, a beautiful simplicity about it; nothing of the dark and savage, only the mild and infantile."

The Indian constantly surprised his employers. On their first night in camp he announced that a sound he heard was made by a snake. "He imitated it at my request," Thoreau noted, "making a low whistling note,—*pheet—pheet,*—two or three times repeated, somewhat like the peep of the hylodes, but not so loud. In answer to my inquiries, he said that he had never seen them while making it, but going to the spot he finds the snake."

Thoreau plied Polis with questions. Even such a natural phenomenon as phosphorescent wood which Thoreau found that first night—a find which Thoreau felt "paid for" his journey—is set down in its Indian name, *Artoosoqu'*. Polis fascinated Thoreau by the variety of experiences he or "his folks" before him had had. "Nature must have made a thousand revelations to them which are still secrets to us," observed Thoreau. He was

166

somewhat surprised next day to be chided by Polis because he confessed, in answer to an inquiry from the Indian, that he did not go to church on Sunday, but sat in his chamber reading in the morning and went to walk in the afternoon. And he must have been taken aback when, in response to a question about how he did something, Polis replied, "Oh, I can't tell *you*. Great difference between me and white man."

Thoreau's account of this last trip to the Maine woods is filled with the customary observations about a great variety of things—the note of the white-throated sparrow ("a very inspiriting but almost wiry sound"), the Creeping Snowberry ("It had a slight checkerberry flavor . . ."), the larch woods ("tall and slender trees with fantastic branches"), the great purple-fringed orchis ("It is remarkable that such delicate flowers should here adorn these wilderness paths."), the No-see-ems ("the little midge . . . *Simulium nocivum* . . . a kind of sand-fly. . . . They are said to get under your clothes, and produce a feverish heat . . ."), the voice of the loon ("a very wild sound, quite in keeping with the place and the circumstances of the traveler, and very unlike the voice of a bird. I could lie awake for hours listening to it, it is so thrilling."), the portages ("a tangled and perplexing thicket, through which we stumbled and threaded our way") but the account of the excursion is primarily an account of a trip with an Indian, what he did, what he said, what he thought. Thoreau learned more from Joe Polis about the way in which human beings adapted to a wilderness environment than he did of nature on this journey.

Thoreau reached home early in the morning of August 8th, and found half a dozen glow-worms, sent by B. M. Watson from Plymouth, waiting for his examina-

167

tion. He wrote Watson that two of them remained just about as bright as at first. "It was a singular coincidence that I should find these worms awaiting me, for my mind was full of a phosphoresence which I had seen in the woods." He fell readily into his customary pattern, but delayed answering most of his mail for ten or twelve days.

To Blake he wrote on August 18th about his Maine excursion, "I have had a quite profitable journey, chiefly from associating with an intelligent Indian. . . . Having returned, I flatter myself that the world appears in some respects a little larger, and not, as usual, smaller and shallower, for having extended my range. I have made a short excursion into the new world which the Indian dwells in, or *is*. He begins where we leave off. It is worth the while to detect new faculties in man,—he is so much the more divine; and anything that fairly excites our admiration expands us. The Indian, who can find his way so wonderfully in the woods, possesses so much intelligence which the white man does not,—and it increases my own capacity, as well as faith, to observe it. I rejoice to find that intelligence flows in other channels than I knew. It redeems for me portions of what seemed brutish before.

"It is a great satisfaction to find that your oldest convictions are permanent. With regard to essentials, I have never had occasion to change my mind. The aspect of the world varies from year to year, as the landscape is differently clothed, but I find that the *truth* is still *true* . . ." Truth as much as freedom was still Thoreau's grail.

To Ricketson he wrote on the same day the sparest of accounts of his two trips—to Cape Cod and the Maine woods—and at length about Wilson Flagg's *Studies in the Field & Forest* ("he is not alert enough. He wants stirring up with a pole."), and struck off some pointed lines on literary style.

"As for style of writing—if one has any thing to say, it drops from him simply & directly, as a stone falls to the ground, for there are no two ways about it, but down it comes, and he may stick in the points and stops whenever he can get a chance. New ideas come into this world somewhat like falling meteors, with a flash and an explosion, and perhaps somebody's castle roof perforated. To try to polish the stone in its descent, to give it a peculiar turn and make it whistle a tune perchance, would be of no use, if it were possible. Your polished stuff turns out not to be meteoric, but of this earth.— However there is plenty of time, and Nature is an admirable schoolmistress."

His excursions behind him, Thoreau spent the remainder of that year at home, declining invitations to visit anywhere. His father was ill—"quite sick with the jaundice . . . this, added to his long standing cold, has reduced him very much," and it was upon Thoreau that the work of the graphite business now devolved. The business may have diminished somewhat temporarily because of the panic of 1857, but it was probably not much affected by it.

Yet Thoreau took notice of the panic. It was unusual for him to pay much attention to what went on very far from Concord, except in the domain of ideas. He wrote Blake in mid-November what amounted to a lecture on hard times. "They make a great ado nowadays about hard times. . . . It is not enough to be industrious; so are the ants. What are you industrious about? . . . The merchants and company have long laughed at transcendentalism, higher laws, etc., crying, 'None of your moonshine,' as if they were anchored to something not only definite, but sure and permanent. . . . But there is the moonshine still, serene, beneficent, and unchanged."

He went on excursions about Concord with redoubled energy. This was only to be expected. When the graphite business made greater demands upon his time, he was all the more eager to be up and about his real business, as chronicler of the wild in man and nature and inspector of that corner of the world which he had made so intimately his own. He resented visitors who kept him from his walks. He chafed at them in his journal, October 7th, when he wrote, "I do not know how to entertain one who can't take long walks. The first thing that suggests itself is to get a horse to draw them, and that brings us at once into contact with stablers and dirty harness, and I do not get over my ride for a long time. I give up my forenoon to them and get along pretty well, the very elasticity of the air and promise of the day abetting me, but they are as heavy as dumplings by mid-afternoon. If they can't walk, why won't they take an honest nap and let me go in the afternoon? But, come two o'clock, they alarm me by an evident disposition to sit. In the midst of the most glorious Indian-summer afternoon, there they sit, breaking your chairs and wearing out the house, with their backs to the light, taking no note of the lapse of time."

But a month later, when he wrote to Blake, he was indignant at the idea that he should listen to lectures. Dr. Reinhold Solger was lecturing in Concord, to Sanborn's students. Emerson and Alcott had listened to Dr. Solger on the subject of geography, and Emerson asked Thoreau if he, too, would not go to listen to the speaker. "What," he wrote Blake, "to be sitting in a meeting-house cellar at that time of day, when you might possibly be out-doors! I never thought of such a thing. What was the sun made for? If he does not prize daylight, I do. Let him lecture to owls and dormice. He must be a wonderful lecturer indeed who can keep me indoors at such an hour, when the night is coming in which no man can walk."

He was happy to be home, and all his life consistent in this. His journal was the repository for his convictions about his relation to his home place. Late in November he set down lines which were profoundly true for him, as they are true for thousands of other men and women less articulate than Thoreau. "A man is worth most to himself and to others, whether as an observer, or poet, or neighbor, or friend, where he is most himself, most contented and at home. There his life is the most intense and he loses the fewest moments. Familiar and surrounding objects are the best symbols and illustrations of his life. . . . The poet has made the best roots in his native soil of any man, and is the hardest to transplant. The man who is often thinking that it is better to be somewhere else than where he is excommunicates himself. If a man is rich and strong anywhere, it must be on his native soil. Here I have been these forty years learning the language of these fields that I may the better express myself."

CHAPTER 11

"Conformity Is Death"

> *We talk about a* representative *government; but what a monster of a government is that where the noblest faculties of the mind, and the* whole *heart, are not* represented. *A semi-human tiger or ox, stalking over the earth, with its heart taken out and the top of its brain shot away. . . .*
>
> *The only government that I recognize—and it matters not how few are at the head of it, or how small its army—is that power that establishes justice in the land, never that which establishes injustice.*
>
> —A PLEA FOR CAPTAIN JOHN BROWN

IT was true, as Thoreau had written his correspondents, that he had not recently published very much. In this respect, however, 1858 opened auspiciously for him. A new magazine had begun publication in Boston in 1857, and its editor, James Russell Lowell, asked for something from Thoreau—either directly, or through Emerson. Thoreau wrote Lowell late in January that he had been busy surveying, and had scarcely "had time to 'think' of your proposition." But he was not inclined to send in the account he had written of the most recent expedition to Maine because Joe Polis could read, and Thoreau reported his words and deeds too faithfully; "I could not face him again." He sent him instead his account of the second expedition, *Chesuncook*. Lowell accepted it and scheduled it for the June and July issues of *The Atlantic Monthly*.

172

It seems to have been Thoreau's pattern as a writer to be solicited for material; he put his work on offer very seldom, and Horace Greeley's activity on behalf of Thoreau's work exceeded his own. Clearly, he considered that his primary business was still keeping the accounts of Concord—the records of its wood life, the annals of its meadows, ponds, rivers; publication was secondary. His income from the graphite business and his occasional lectures was evidently enough to satisfy his small needs, and such income as he might gain from publication must not have seemed to Thoreau worth the effort of putting himself out to get it.

The records he kept, such as survive, were meticulous. When Thomas Wentworth Higginson wrote him in January, 1858, to ask about the possibility of going to Quebec by way of the Allegash, Thoreau could give an account of his journey ("We went about 325 miles with the canoe [including 60 miles of Stage between Bangor & Oldtown] were out 12 nights, & spent about 40 dollars apiece, which was more than was necessary. We paid the Indian, who was a very good one, $1.50 per day & 50 cts. per week for his canoe.") and of his needs on the excursion that was as detailed as anyone could wish ("We *used* [3 of us] exactly 26 lbs. of hard bread, 14 lbs. of pork, 3 lbs. of coffee, 12 lbs. of sugar [& could have used more] besides a little tea, Ind. meal, & rice & plenty of berries & moosemeat. This was faring very luxuriously. I had not formerly carried coffee—sugar, or rice. But for solid food, I decide that *it is not worth the while to carry anything but hard bread & pork*, whatever your tastes & habits may be. These wear best—& you have no time nor dishes in which to cook any thing else. Of course you will take a little Ind. meal to fry fish in—& half a dozen lemons also, if you have sugar—will be very refreshing—for the

173

water is warm. . . . Don't forget an India rubber knapsack—with a large flap—plenty of *dish cloths*—old newspapers, strings, & 25 feet of strong cord."). To this and
more, Thoreau added that he "could be more particular,
but perhaps have been too much so already."

Perhaps because the panic of the preceding year made
the demand for graphite lessen a little, Thoreau was
abroad very often, both at surveying and at his walks
through the neighborhood. His entries in his journal for
that year were at length and much varied. He had his
lichen days, his frog days, his turtle days—days on which
he was particularly aware of or interested in certain
phenomena of nature. He was as likely to start off from
lichens into philosophical asides about his fellowmen
("How protean is life! One may eat and drink and sleep
and digest, and do the ordinary duties of a man, and
have no excuse for sending for a doctor, and yet he may
have reason to doubt if he is as truly alive or his life is
as valuable and divine as that of an oyster. He may be
the very best citizen in the town, and yet it shall occur
to him to prick himself with a pin to see if he is alive.
It is wonderful how quiet, harmless, and ineffective a
living creature may be. No more energy may it have than
a fungus that lifts the bark of a decaying tree. I raised
last summer a squash which weighed 123½ pounds. If
it had fallen on me it would have made as deep and
lasting an impression as most men do.") as he was to
learn, by dint of cutting holes in the ice at Gowing's
Swamp that "sphagnum will grow on the surface of water
five feet deep!"

That winter being open, deep snow did not limit
Thoreau's hikes nor impede his surveying. He observed
"that herbaceous plants show less greenness than usual
. . . , having been more exposed for want of a snowy

174

covering" and that tea made of spruce was "in spite of a slight piny or turpentine flavor . . . unexpectedly good." He was ever the inquirer, not in a narrowly scientific sense, but rather in that of the naturalist. He observed, he appreciated, he chronicled, he probed and learned, but his goal was not fundamentally scientific.

He was interested in tree rings ("in that oak stump on the ditch-bank by Trillium Wood . . . between the twentieth and twenty-seventh rings there was only about three-sevenths of an inch, though before and after this it grew very fast and seven spaces would make nearly two inches. The tree was growing lustily till twenty years old, and then for seven years it grew only one fourth or one fifth part as fast as before and after. I am curious to know what happened."), in the entrances to burrows ("Those small holes in the ground,—musquash, mice, etc.,—thickly beset with crystals of frost, remind me of the invisible vapor issuing thence which may be called Earth's breath, though you might think it were the breath of a mouse."), in snow buntings ("They are trotting about briskly over the snow amid the weeds,—apparently pigweed and Roman wormwood,—as it were to keep their tocs warm, hopping up to the weeds. Then they restlessly take to wing again, and as they wheel about one, it is a very rich sight to see them dressed in black and white uniforms, alternate black and white, very distinct and regular."), in a Chippewa Indian who came to speak in Concord early in March and whom he plied with questions, in the language of the Indians ("It reveals to me a life within a life, or rather a life without a life, as it were threading the woods between our towns still, and yet we can never tread in its trail. The Indian's earthly life was as far off from us as heaven is."), in the cry of a flicker ("how that single sound peoples and enriches all the woods and fields!"), in the view from Fair Haven Hill ("I think that Concord affords no better view. It is always incredibly fair, but ordinarily we are mere objects in it, and not witnesses of it. I see . . . a valley extending southwest and northeast and some two miles across, . . . with a broad, yellow meadow tinged with brown at the bottom, and a blue river winding slowly through it northward, with a regular edging of low bushes on the brink, of the same color with the meadow. . . . Such is the dwelling-place of man; but go to the caucus in the village to-night or to a church to-morrow, and see if there is anything said to suggest that the inhabitants of those houses know what kind of world they live in.").

That spring Thoreau corrected proofs of *Chesuncook,* and the first part of that account appeared in the June issue of *The Atlantic Monthly.* In June Thoreau climbed Monadnock, which reared almost four thousand feet northwest of Concord; Blake accompanied him. They carried packs on their backs and mounted to the summit to watch the sun set, though they lost their way coming back down ("nothing is easier than to lose your way here, where so little trail is left upon the rocks"). Thoreau was struck by the insistence of hikers in carving names into the rocks. "These sculptors seemed to me to court such alliance with the grave as they who put their names over tombstones along the highway. . . . Apparently a part of the regular outfit of mountain-climbers is a hammer and cold-chisel, . . . Certainly you could not hire a stone-cutter to do so much engraving for less than several thousand dollars. But no Old Mortality will ever be caught renewing these epitaphs. It reminds what kind of steeps do climb the false pretenders to fame, whose chief exploit is the carriage of the tools with which to inscribe their names. For speaking epitaphs they are,

176

and the mere name is a sufficient revelation of the character. They are all of one trade,—stone-cutters, defacers of mountain-tops. 'Charles & Lizzie!' Charles carried the sledge-hammer, and Lizzie the cold-chisel. Some have carried up a paint-pot, and painted their names on the rocks."

They spent all the next day there, Thoreau industriously setting down the names of all the plants growing on the heights, and the two of them exploring the mountain. "But the most interesting part of this walk," he wrote, on the way back to Concord next day, "was the three miles along the railroad between State Line and Winchendon Station. . . . The railroad runs very straight for long distances here through a primitive forest." By June fifth, Thoreau was once again surveying in the northeast part of Lincoln.

Later that month the July issue of *The Atlantic Monthly* carrying the second part of *Chesuncook* came out. Much to his anger, Thoreau discovered that his proofs had once again been tampered with by an editor. James Russell Lowell, who lived in a more social and academic milieu than Thoreau did, and who was far more sensitive to the opinions of the public than Thoreau could be, deleted one pantheistic sentence which would certainly have disturbed some men of the cloth who might have read Thoreau's account of his excursion. On June 22, Thoreau wrote him a cold, stiff letter of protest—

"When I received the proof of that portion of my story printed in the May number of your magazine, I was surprised to find that the sentence—'It is as immortal as I am, and perchance will go to as high a heaven, there to tower above me still.'—(which comes directly after the words 'heal my cuts,' page 230, tenth line from the top,) had been crossed out, and it occurred to me that, after all, it was of some consequence that I should see the proofs; supposing, of course, that my 'Stet' &c in the margin would be respected, as I perceive that it was in other cases of comparatively little importance to me. However, I have just noticed that that sentence was, in a very mean and cowardly manner, omitted. I hardly need to say that this is a liberty which I will not permit to be taken with my MS. The editor has, in this case, no more right to omit a sentiment than to insert one, or put words into my mouth. I do not ask anybody to adopt my opinions, but I do expect that when they ask for them to print, they will print them, or obtain my consent to their alteration, or omission. I should not read many books if I thought that they had been thus expurgated. I feel this treatment to be an insult, though not intended as such, for it is to presume that I can be hired to suppress my opinions.

"I do not mean to charge you with this omission, for I cannot believe that you knew anything about it, but there must be a responsible editor somewhere, and you, to whom I entrusted my MS. are the only party that I know in this matter. I therefore write to ask if you sanction this omission, and if there are any other sentiments to be omitted in the remainder of my article. If you do not sanction it—or whether you do or not—will you do me the justice to print that sentence, as an omitted one, indicating its place, in the August number?

"I am not willing to be associated in any way, un- necessarily, with parties who will confess themselves so bigoted & timid as this implies. I could excuse a man who was afraid of an uplifted fist, but if one habitually manifests fear at the utterance of a sincere thought, I must think that his life is a kind of nightmare continued

178

into broad daylight. It is hard to conceive of one so completely derivative. Is this the avowed character of *The Atlantic Monthly?* I should like an early reply."

No record of Lowell's reply has been found. Presumably, therefore, no reply was made, for Thoreau's subsequent refusal to submit anything further to *The Atlantic Monthly* as long as Lowell remained its editor suggests that he heard nothing from Lowell, and that therefore Lowell condoned the deletion of the disputed sentence.

Having put himself on record unmistakably, Thoreau patently considered the episode finished. He busied himself with plans for an excursion to the White Mountains and asked Blake to accompany Edward Hoar and himself; a day later he proposed that Blake's friend, Theophilus Brown, also go along. Neither, however, found it possible to go immediately, but promised to join Thoreau later. Thoreau and Hoar went alone, starting the second day of July "in a private carriage,"—a horse and covered wagon Hoar had arranged for. They drove to Merrimack and stopped overnight at a tavern there. Thoreau, as was his custom, went out for an evening walk finding that "The wood thrush sings almost wherever I go, eternally reconsecrating the world, morning and evening, for us." He walked whenever he could do so en route ("You have to sacrifice so much to the horse. You cannot choose the most agreeable places in which to spend the noon, commanding the finest views, because commonly there is no water there, or you cannot get there with your horse.").

Their goal was Mount Washington, the highest point in New England. They reached the base of the mountain late on the fifth day of their excursion, hired a local man to help with their baggage, and began the ascent next day. On the second day of the ascent they reached the summit and camped there. They managed with the help of their guide, Wentworth—to set a spreading fire, which did not, however, approximate the damage done at Concord by Thoreau and Hoar. Here Blake and Brown finally joined them, and they slept five in the tent that night, while rain put out their fire.

On July 9th, Thoreau, continuing his exploration of the ravines, miscalculated a jump, and sprained his ankle. He spent a sleepless night, in consequence, and could not walk next day. That day of inactivity was one in which he was much troubled—as Blake and Brown had been on their ascent—by black flies ("They compelled me most of the time to sit in the smoke, which I preferred to wearing a veil. They lie along your forehead in a line, where your hat touches it, or behind your ears, or about your throat [if not protected by a beard], . . . and there suck till they are crushed. . . . Anything but mosquitoes by night.").

By the twelfth of July they had begun the descent of Mt. Washington; a week later Thoreau was back in Concord setting down a list of necessities for such an excursion—"Three strong check shirts. Two pairs socks. Neck ribbon and handkerchief. Three pocket-handkerchiefs. . . . A large, broad india-rubber knapsack, with a *broad* flap. . . . Pins, needles, thread. . . . A cap to lie in at night. . . . Veil and *gloves* (or enough millinet to cover all at night). . . . Botany, spyglass, microscope. Tape, insect-boxes. . . . Hard-bread (sweet crackers good); a moist, sweet plum cake very good and lasting; pork, corned beef or tongue, sugar, tea or coffee, and a little salt."

He was scarcely settled into his Concord routine once more before, at the time of the autumnal equinox, he was off to Cape Ann with Channing. He visited with his

180

friends, the Russells, and on this excursion he and Channing spent some time in Marblehead, Salem and Rockport, where they walked for the most part and prepared their own meals, using, "as usual, dead bayberry bushes for fuel. . . . They make a very quick fire, and I noticed that their smoke covered our dippers with a kind of japan which did not crack or come off nearly so much as ordinary soot."

They stayed only four days. On September 25th he went "a-graping up Assabet with some young ladies." Perhaps he had mellowed a little since he wrote in his journal seven years before, on the occasion of a party at Emerson's, "I confess that I am lacking a sense, perchance, in this respect, and I derive no pleasure from talking with a young woman half an hour simply because she has regular features. The society of young women is the most unprofitable I have ever tried. They are so light and flighty that you can never be sure whether they are there or not there. I prefer to talk with the more staid and settled, *settled for life,* in every sense."

He went to work at a possible lecture on the subject of autumnal tints and wrote Ricketson to learn "how much our trees differ from English & European ones in this respect." Ricketson sent him the information he required, and asked him to visit again at New Bedford. But Thoreau would not leave Concord again at this time because his father was ill and did not appear to be mending. Cholmondeley, on his way from Canada to Jamaica, visited Thoreau early that December, but for the most part that autumn and winter Thoreau was writing, keeping his journal, and devoting ever more time to the business of manufacturing graphite since his father was too ill to work.

His friends made repeated efforts to draw Thoreau

181

into their company. He was invited to Emerson's, to "an Alcottian conversation," to meet Henry James ("a hearty man enough, with whom you can differ very satisfactorily, on account of both his doctrines and his good temper"). He went to a meeting of the Saturday Club at the Parker House; its members included Emerson, Longfellow, Holmes, Agassiz, Lowell, and other distinguished literary men. Thoreau "found it hard to see through the cigar smoke, and men were deposited about in chairs over the marble floor, as thick as legs of bacon in a smokehouse. It was all smoke, and no salt, Attic or other."

He wrote to Blake, "The doctors are all agreed that I am suffering from want of society. Was never a case like it. First, I did not know that I was suffering at all. Secondly, as an Irishman might say, I had thought it was indigestion of the society I got." His journal reflected his reaction. "All the community may scream," he wrote December 27, "because one man is born who will not do as it does, who will not conform because conformity to him is death,—he is so constituted. They know nothing about his case; they are fools when they presume to advise him. The man of genius knows what he is aiming at; nobody else knows. And he alone knows when something comes between him and his object. In the course of generations, however, men will excuse you for not doing as they do, if you will bring enough to pass in your own way."

Thoreau's father declined steadily in health. On January 13, 1859, he retired to his bedroom and did not come out of it again. His illness was now quite clearly terminal, and he died in mid-afternoon February third. Though Thoreau had made little mention of his father's illness in his journal, his entry for that date briefly sketched his father's history and added, "As far as I know, Father, when he died, was not only one of the oldest men

182

in the middle of Concord, but the one perhaps best acquainted with the inhabitants, and the local, social, and street history of the middle of the town, for the last fifty years. He belonged in a peculiar sense to the village street; loved to sit in the shops or at the post-office and read the daily papers." And, after a few paragraphs about the Indians, he added, "I perceive that we partially die ourselves through sympathy at the death of each of our friends or near relatives. Each such experience is an assault on our vital force. It becomes a source of wonder that they who have lost many friends still live. After long watching around the sick-bed of a friend, we, too, partially give up the ghost with him, and are the less to be identified with this state of things."

A few days later he answered a letter of sympathy from Ricketson ("I was much impressed with his good sense, his fine social nature, and genuine hospitality."), "I am glad to read what you say about his social nature. I think I may say that he was wholly unpretending; and there was this peculiarity in his aim, that, though he had pecuniary difficulties to contend with the greater part of his life, he always studied merely how to make a *good* article, pencil or other . . ."

Thoreau speedily resumed his way of life, watching the muskrat-hunters ("I meet these gods of the river and woods with sparkling faces . . . while the dull regular priests are steering their parish rafts in a prose mood"), and keeping the annals of Concord. The birds may not have sounded as sweet to him as before the death of his father, as he noted, but he was none the less given to attending their affairs. He gave another lecture, this time on *Autumnal Tints*, on February 22 at Worcester. And, the necessity of running the graphite business notwithstanding, he took a major job of surveying—this time

183

measuring the water depths of the constantly flooding Concord, Sudbury, and Assabet Rivers, and set down the history of the bridges crossing them, and their abutments. He thought himself as much civil engineer as surveyor.

The spring and summer wore away. Though Thoreau was out on his rounds as much as circumstances permitted, he was plainly kept busier than he liked with the graphite business. Late in September he wrote to Blake, "I feel and think rather too much like a business man, having some very irksome affairs to attend to these months and years on account of my family. This is the way I am serving King Admetus, confound him! If it were not for my relations, I would let the wolves prey on his flocks to their bellies' content." He lacked the time for writing, if not for hiking. "It is easy enough to maintain a family, or a state, but it is hard to maintain these children of your brain . . ."

In October John Brown was again in Concord. Thoreau heard him talk at the Town Hall. Brown was on his way to Virginia to lead the raid on Harper's Ferry, but, of course, he let drop no hint of his plans. Soon after, Blake visited Thoreau; they walked to and around Flint's Pond, and Thoreau made a list of all autumn berries to be seen up to the middle of October and after. Next day, the fifteenth, Thoreau set down a plea for town parks— "Each town should have a park, or rather a primitive forest, of five hundred or a thousand acres, where a stick should never be cut for fuel, a common possession forever, for instruction and recreation. . . . All Walden Wood might have been preserved for our park forever, with Walden in its midst, and the Easterbrooks Country, an unoccupied area of some four square miles, might have been our huckleberry-field. . . . A town is an institution which deserves to be remembered."

184

In Virginia, Brown led eighteen of his men in an attack on Harper's Ferry, hoping to foment a slave insurrection and establish a free state in the Appalachians from which to spread rebellion to the south. The insurrection did not take place, and Brown and those of his followers who survived were taken prisoner by forces under Colonel Robert E. Lee. By the nineteenth of October, word of that abortive stroke against the institution of slavery had reached Concord and so excited Thoreau that he wrote two thousand words about the event in his journal. He looked past all legal questions and saw only that here was a man who had dared at last to strike out against an abhorrent situation. However much Thoreau disliked violence, he was prepared to support violence against an institution about which he felt so strongly.

In subsequent days, he poured more of his thoughts about Brown and slavery into his journal, and by the end of that month he had reassembled these paragraphs into a lecture and announced that he would speak in Concord on behalf of John Brown. He was advised not to, that feeling was against Brown and his rash act. When the selectmen refused to ring the bell of the Town Hall to announce the hour of the lecture, Thoreau did it himself. He delivered his lecture to a partially hostile audience October 30.

Though he outlined Brown's life, his lecture was not so much a plea for Brown, as it was a defense of principle, an urgent plea that civil disobedience be continued, and that, if all else failed, violence in a good cause could be condoned. He spoke forcefully, with deep conviction, and if he did not dispel entirely the hostility of his audience, he abated it. He was particularly vehement about the attitude of the press in its condemnation of John Brown. "The newspapers seem to ignore, or perhaps are

185

really ignorant, of the fact that there are at least as many as two or three individuals to a town throughout the North who think much as the present speaker does about him and his enterprise. I do not hesitate to say that they are an important and growing party. We aspire to be something more than stupid and timid chattels, pretending to read history and our Bibles, but desecrating every house and every day we breathe in. . . . Why do they still dodge the truth? They are so anxious because of a dim consciousness of the fact, which they do not distinctly face, that at least a million of the free inhabitants of the United States would have rejoiced if it had succeeded. They at most only criticise the tactics."

He asserted that his respect for those fellowmen who were content to follow the path of least resistance in a matter involving so basic a principle was not very high. "Such do not know that like the seed is the fruit, and that, in the moral world, when good seed is planted, good fruit is inevitable, and does not depend on our watering and cultivating; that when you plant, or bury, a hero in his field, a crop of heroes is sure to spring up. This is a seed of such force and vitality, that it does not ask our leave to germinate."

He made no attempt to explain away Brown's defiance of law but put himself squarely on the side of John Brown. "I speak for the slave when I say that I prefer the philanthropy of Captain Brown to that philanthropy which neither shoots me nor liberates me. At any rate, I do not think it is quite sane for one to spend his whole life in talking or writing about this matter, unless he is continuously inspired, and I have not done so. A man may have other affairs to tend to. I do not wish to kill nor to be killed, but I can foresee circumstances in which both these things would be by me unavoidable. . . .

"These men, in teaching us how to die, have at the same time taught us how to live. If this man's acts and words do not create a revival, it will be the severest possible satire on the acts and words that do. It is the best news that America has ever heard. It has already quickened the feeble pulse of the North, and infused more and more generous blood into her veins and heart than any number of years of what is called commercial and political prosperity could."

Thoreau's plea for Brown was certainly his most successful and powerful address. It was received by his audience with much sympathy and so much applause that the echoes of it reached into Boston. He was asked to repeat it at Theodore Parker's Boston Temple, where it met with the enthusiastic response of the largest audience Thoreau had ever had. Two days later he gave it in Worcester, again to a responsive audience. The newspapers reported it, somewhat garbled, to be sure, but word of Thoreau's defense of Brown was carried in the nation's press. Even Calvin Greene, in faraway Detroit, heard about his plea and wrote about it.

Yet Thoreau was not an Abolitionist. He belonged to no society, no group, however much they might rally behind him. His was the reaction of a man of principle, not of the spokesman for a group committed to a cause. He was not yet done with John Brown. On the second of December he spoke again at the Town Hall at a memorial service for Brown. On the third he drove one of Brown's men, Francis Merriam, to Acton; Merriam was on his way to Canada, for the government was pressing the search for all Brown's fellow conspirators, and even Sanborn absented himself from Concord for a while.

Merriam was unbalanced. Thoreau noted that he "was betrayed by his eyes, which had a glaring film over them and no serene depth into which you could look." Merriam wanted to go to Emerson's house, and told Thoreau certain things he did not want Sanborn to know. "Said 'I know I am insane,'—and I knew it too." Merriam thought Thoreau might be Emerson, but when he was assured that this was not so, he wanted to leave the conveyance. Thoreau discharged the mission successfully.

Then he went back to his beloved ponds, meadows, rivers and hills. On the last day of that active year he was hiking up the Assabet to the sweet-gale meadow, making notes on seed-heads, catkins, tree sparrows, trees, ice-cutters, and reflecting, "How vain to try to teach youth, or anybody, truths! They can only learn them after their own fashion, and when they are ready. I do not mean by this to condemn our system of education, but to show what it amounts to," and concluding that "A man thinks as well through his legs and arms as his brain."—quite as if the attack on Harper's Ferry and the execution of John Brown had never taken place.

CHAPTER 12

"...I Would Know Better How It Would End"

> *I learned this, at least, by my experiment: that if one advances confidently in the direction of his dreams, and endeavors to live the life which he has imagined, he will meet with a success unexpected in common hours. He will put some things behind, will pass an invisible boundary; new, universal, and more liberal laws will begin to establish themselves around and within him; or the old laws be expanded, and interpreted in his favor in a more liberal sense, and he will live with the license of a higher order of beings. In proportion as he simplifies his life, the laws of the universe will appear less complex, and solitude will not be solitude, nor poverty poverty, nor weakness weakness. If you have built castles in the air, your work need not be lost; that is where they should be. Now put the foundations under them.* —WALDEN

WITH the beginning of 1860, Thoreau was at work on two major projects. One, to which he referred as his *Kalendar of Concord*, was to be something similar to but more intimate than Gilbert White's *Natural History of Selborne*. The other was a study of *The Dispersion of Seeds*, undoubtedly intended to be ultimately part of the larger project, the *Kalendar*.

But his writing time was sadly cut into by the hours he

was forced to give to the graphite business. Nor would he decrease his sauntering time and the compilation of his journal. He was much at Walden that winter, and at Fair Haven, where one January day he watched the snow-fleas. "There are a dozen or twenty to a square rod on the very middle of the pond. When I approach one, it commonly hops away, and if it gets a good spring it hops a foot or more, so that it is lost to me. Though they are scarcely the twentieth of an inch long they make these surprising bounds, or else conceal themselves by entering the snow."

Early in February he delivered a new lecture to the Concord Lyceum. This was *Wild Apples*. When the weather did not permit his hiking, he went into Cambridge and took books from the library. That February he was reading Conrad Gesner's *History of Four-footed Beasts* and reflecting, "We cannot spare the very lively and lifelike descriptions of some of the old naturalists. They sympathize with the creatures which they describe."

In February also, James Redpath wrote to Thoreau for an account of John Brown's Battle of Black Jack, Kansas, about which Brown had told Thoreau on the occasion of his visit to the Thoreaus. Redpath had been an assistant of Brown—but not a participant—in the Harper's Ferry attack. The correspondence thus opened led to publication of *A Plea for Captain John Brown* and Thoreau's memorial comments in an anthology of articles edited by Redpath under the title of *Echoes of Harper's Ferry* later in 1860.

In May he wrote a curious letter to Blake, philosophizing about the state of mankind in the world. "Men & boys are learning all kinds of trades but how to make *men* of themselves. They learn to make houses, but they are not so well housed, they are not so contented in their houses, as the woodchucks in their holes. What is the use of a house if you haven't got a tolerable planet to put it on? If you can not tolerate the planet it is on? Grade the ground first. If a man believes and expects great things of himself it makes no odds where you put him, or what you show him . . . he will be surrounded by grandeur. He's in the condition of a healthy & hungry man, who says to himself—How sweet this crust is!"

Thoreau, at least, was not discontented with his attic room, and the stacks of his first book, which were slowly diminishing in response to the orders which came in to him still from isolated readers of *Walden* in various parts of the country. After the details of the graphite business and his hours of sauntering about Concord, he retired almost every evening to his attic room and wrote until it was time to go to bed.

In July Thoreau saw Hawthorne once more. Hawthorne had been abroad, acting as American consul at Liverpool; now he had returned to Concord. Thoreau wrote his sister Sophia, then visiting in Campton, New Hampshire, that Hawthorne had not altered "except that he was looking pretty brown after his voyage. He is as simple & child-like as ever." Thoreau was much concerned this month with the temperature of the brooks and the ponds around Concord, and filled his journal with details about the "cold brooks" and those filled with warmer water.

That summer he was ready for another excursion. He asked Channing to go with him to Monadnock, and, after some delay, Channing agreed to go. They left Concord on the morning of August fourth and were gone six days. They did not always enjoy fair weather. Thoreau filled his journal with all manner of data about the plants, rocks, streams, only occasionally pausing to admire the view. "Each day, about an hour before sunset, I got sight, as it were accidentally, of an elysium beneath me. The smoky haze of the day, suggesting a furnace-like heat, a trivial dustiness, gave place to a clear transparent enamel, through which houses, woods, farms, and lakes were seen as in a picture indescribably fair and expressly made to be looked at."

In an account of the excursion written to Blake that September, "We went up in the rain—wet through, and found ourselves in a cloud there at mid *pm*. in no situation to look about for the best place for a camp. So I proceeded at once, through the cloud, to that memorable stone 'chunk yard,' in which we made our humble camp once, and there, after putting our packs under a rock, having a good hatchet, I proceeded to build a substantial house, which Channing declared the handsomest he ever saw. (He never camped out before, and was, no doubt, prejudiced in its favor.) This was done about dark, and by that time we were nearly as wet as if we had stood in a hogshead of water. We then built a fire before the door, directly on the site of our little camp of two years ago. Standing before this, and turning round slowly, like meat that is roasting, we were as dry if not drier than ever after a few hours, & so, at last, we 'turned in.' . . .

"We & the *mt.* had a sound season, as the saying is. How glad we were to be wet in order that we might be dried!—how glad we were of the storm which made our house seem like a new home to us! . . . Our next house was more substantial still. One side was rock, good for durability, the floor the same, & the roof which I made would have upheld a horse. I stood on it to do the shingling."

Channing, however, was not as good a camper as Thoreau. He worried a little about "what was the largest beast that might nibble his legs there," and was presently ready

192

to "*de-camp*," a day sooner than Thoreau had counted on. Their camp was well concealed, for "Five hundred persons at least came onto the *mt.* while we were there, but not one found our camp."

Once back in Concord, Thoreau was not inclined to go abroad again that year. He declined an invitation from Ricketson to come to New Bedford. "I have enjoyed very much my visits to you and my rides in your neighborhood, and am sorry that I cannot enjoy such things oftener; but life is short, and there are other things also to be done. I admit that you are more social than I am, and far more attentive to 'the common courtesies of life' but this is partly for the reason that you have fewer or less exacting private pursuits." Ricketson had chided him for not writing. "Not to have written a note for a year," Thoreau replied, "is with me a very menial offence. I think that I do not correspond with any one so often as once in six-months."

Early in September, however, Thoreau spoke in Lowell, Massachusetts, where he walked along the Merrimack River on a suddenly crisp morning, seeing "very large plants of the lanceolate thistle, four feet high and very branching." No word of his lecture is set down in his journal. He wrote instead of "the dew on a fine grass in the meadows, which was almost as white and silvery as frost when the rays of the newly risen sun fell on it," seen from the windows of the train as he rode the next morning from Lowell to Boston on his way home. Next day, back in his pattern, he was summoned by George Melvin to look at a lynx killed on the Carlisle road.

He now had ready—despite his excursions in and away from Concord, and despite the press of the graphite business—part of his *Dispersion of Seeds*. This was *The Succession of Forest Trees*, one of the products of his study of tree rings. He delivered it as a lecture before the Middlesex Agricultural Society, which planned to include it in its "Report" later in the year. Before this, however, it occurred to Thoreau that Horace Greeley, who had frequently asked for something from Thoreau's pen, might be interested in seeing it; so he dispatched it to Greeley for the *Tribune,* where Greeley printed it October sixth.

Early in November, writing to Ricketson, Thoreau mentioned his "out-door harvest this fall," and said it had been "one Canada Lynx, a fierce looking fellow, which, it seems, we have hereabouts; eleven barrels of apples from trees of my own planting; and a large crop of white oak acorns which I did not raise." That autumn's harvest, fatefully, had yet another aspect; on the third of December he went out to Smith's Hill to count the rings in some hickory trees. The day was damp and cold. He lay on the ground, the better to count the rings in a trunk broken from the stump too high for him to see. He caught cold.

On his way home he had an argument with Sam Staples and another Concord man, named Walcott, who declared that John Brown had done wrong. "When I said that I thought he was right, they agreed in asserting that he did wrong because he threw his life away, and that no man had a right to undertake anything which he knew would cost him his life. I inquired if Christ did not foresee that he would be crucified if he preached such doctrines as he did, but they both, though as if it was their only escape, asserted that they did not believe that he did. Upon which a third party threw in, 'You do not think that he had so much foresight as Brown.' Of course, they as good as said that, if Christ *had* foreseen that he would be crucified, he would have 'backed out.' Such are the principles and the logic of the mass of men."

Snow fell next day, and Thoreau was confined to the

194

house. He was still stirred by his argument with Walcott and Staples of the previous day, added to by an article in the *New York Tribune* about a demand levied upon an escaped slave in Toronto. "Talk about slavery!" he wrote. "It is not the peculiar institution of the South. It exists wherever men are bought and sold, wherever a man allows himself to be made a mere thing or a tool, and surrenders his inalienable rights of reason and conscience. Indeed, this slavery is more complete than that which enslaves the body alone."

Though his cold did not improve, he went to lecture at Waterbury a week later, but on his return he was kept to the house, not alone by his own illness, but also by that of his mother, now confined to her bed. He had to decline an invitation from the curator of the Concord Lyceum to entertain Wendell Phillips when he came to Concord to lecture that month. His mother slowly improved; Thoreau's improvement was slower and not lasting.

For much of that winter he stayed at home. His journal for 1861 opened with paragraphs clearly intended for a lecture—on wild berries ("I think that our various species of berries are our *wild fruits* to be compared with the more celebrated ones of the tropics")—and went on with the contents of a crow's stomach brought to him by the younger Horace Mann, quotations from books under study, notes on the depth of the snow ("two feet deep on a level now"), a screech owl caught in Hastings's barn on the meeting-house avenue, also brought by Mann, reports of Walden brought by Channing—but his entries were no longer daily, and longer hiatuses occurred.

On March 22nd he wrote Ricketson, "To tell the truth, I am not on the alert for the signs of spring, not having had any winter yet. I took a severe cold about the 3 of Dec., which at length resulted in a kind of bronchitis, so that I have been confined to the house ever since, excepting a very few experimental trips as far as the P.O. in some particularly mild noons. My health otherwise has not been affected in the least, nor my spirits. I have simply been imprisoned for so long; & it has not prevented my doing a good deal of reading & the like."

On May 3d he wrote Blake, "I am still as much an invalid as when you & Brown were here, if not more of one, and at this rate there is danger that the cold weather may come again, before I get over my bronchitis. The Doctor accordingly tells me that I must 'clear out,' to the West Indies, or elsewhere, he does not seem to care much where." The Indies were out of the question "on account of their muggy heat in the summer," and the cost of a trip to Europe was beyond him. He thought of going to Minnesota. "The inland air may help me at once, or it may not." He tried to persuade Blake to go along; Blake could not go. He next tried Channing, who was loath to be gone from Concord for so long.

At last he turned to young Horace Mann, who had been supplying him with specimens throughout the winter. Mann was the son of the famous educator of the same name, who had died in August, 1859, after which his family had moved to Concord. Mann accepted his invitation, and on Sunday, May 12, they set out, going by way of Worcester where they paused to visit Blake and Brown and another man—"a dry humorist, a gentlemen who has been a sportsman and was well acquainted with dogs." Thence to Albany and Schenectady, and so westward.

At this point, Thoreau virtually abandoned his journal. He was a sick man, and he was well aware of it. He had now grown a bushy beard, and looked much older than his 44 years. His illness prevented him from appreciating the journey. He could have written an outstanding account of this longest excursion, had he been in good health. One aspect of the passing landscape caught his eye. "I began to notice from the cars a tree with handsome rose-colored flowers. At first I thought it some variety of thorn; but it was not long before the truth flashed on me, that this was my long-sought Crab-Apple." To find this tree had long been an ambition of Thoreau's, yet wherever the train stopped, there seemed to be none.

In Minnesota at last he saw the wild pigeon, he studied the wild gophers, and observed the greater wildness of the country—but he did so as a sick man does, not with the fever of discovery and the compulsion to communicate his discoveries. And at last he found the wild crab-apple —"about eight miles west of St. Anthony's Falls; touched it and smelled it, and secured a lingering corymb of flowers for my herbarium." This discovery alone stood out in his memory and was embodied in his revision of *Wild Apples*.

On June 25 he wrote Sanborn from Redwing, Minnesota, that he had "performed this journey in a very dead and alive manner." The Civil War had begun, but "I am not even so well informed as to the progress of the war as you suppose. . . . The people of Minnesota have seemed to me more cold—to feel less implicated in this war, than the people of Massachusetts." He wrote at length of the landscape. "The grand feature hereabouts is, of course, the Mississippi River. Too much can hardly be said of its grandeur, & the beauty of this portion of it. . . . it flows from the pine to the palm."

At last he was close to more Indians than he had ever known before. The Sioux were still very much in Minnesota, and still menacing the white man's way of life, as the New Ulm uprising next year was to prove. But his

197

interest in the Indians had flagged with his health. "After spending some three weeks in and about St. Paul, St. Anthony, and Minneapolis, we made an excursion in a steamer some 300 or more miles up the Minnesota (St. Peter's) River, to Redwood, and the Lower Sioux Agency, in order to see the plains & the Sioux, who were to receive their annual payment there. . . .

"A regular council was held with the Indians, who had come in on their ponies, and speeches were made on both sides thro' an interpreter, quite in the described mode; the Indians, as usual, having the advantage in point of truth and earnestness, and therefore of eloquence. The most prominent chief was named Little Crow. They were quite dissatisfied with the white man's treatment of them & probably have reason to be so. . . .

"In the afternoon the half naked Indians performed a dance, at the request of the Governor, for our amusement & their own benefit & then we took leave of them & of the officials who had come to treat with them."

But Thoreau was now ready for home. "Our faces are set toward home. Will you please let my sister know that we shall *probably* start for Milwaukee & Mackinaw in a day or 2 . . . *via Prairie du Chien* & not La Crosse."

Home again, Thoreau thought himself in somewhat better health. He wrote Ricketson in August that he was "considerably, yet not essentially better, my cough still continuing." He added that he might be obliged "to go to another climate again very soon," and complained that his "ordinary pursuits, both indoor and out, have been for the most part omitted, or seriously interrupted—walking, boating, scribbling, &c. Indeed, I have been sick so long that I have almost forgotten what it is to be well, yet I feel that it all respects only my envelope." Two months later, in mid-October, he wrote Ricketson that he

198

had been riding about in a wagon owned by Edward Hoar, "every other day." But his letter was short. "It is easy to talk, but hard to write."

By the beginning of 1862, it was evident to Thoreau that he was not improving, and that in all probability he would not get better. As so often happens to literary men, at this point in his life, when it was all but over, there was a rising tide of appreciation of his work. Myron Benton wrote him from Dutchess County, New York, "I read and re-read your books with ever fresh delight. Nor is it pleasure alone; there is a singular spiritual healthiness with which they seem imbued,—the expression of a soul essentially sound, so free from any morbid tendency." Thoreau replied two months later to say, "if I were to live, I should have much to report on Natural History generally. You ask particularly after my health. I *suppose* that I have not many months to live; but, of course, I know nothing about it. I may add that I am enjoying existence as much as ever, and regret nothing."

Theophilus Brown wrote that "The demand for your books here seems to be rather on the increase," and ordered two copies of *A Week on the Concord and Merrimack Rivers*, of which Thoreau had by this time disposed of slightly over a hundred copies. At the same time, Ticknor & Fields, Thoreau's publishers, proposed bringing out his first book again—which meant binding the unbound sheets Thoreau took over from Munroe—and bringing out a second edition of *Walden*, from which Thoreau indicated that he wanted the subtitle, *Life in the Woods,* deleted.

Ticknor & Fields had also, in late 1859, taken over *The Atlantic Monthly*. The new editor was James T. Fields, who wrote Thoreau for contributions to the magazine. Thoreau replied in February, making clear that he

199

"should expect no sentiment or sentence be altered or omitted without my consent." He sent in *Autumnal Tints* and, a few days later, *The Higher Law,* which, at Fields's suggestion, he retitled *Life without Principle.* Then he got to work at revision of *Walking, Wild Apples, Night and Moonlight.*

He was dying, and knew it, of tuberculosis. But next to sauntering through the countryside he loved, he must have enjoyed, as far as was possible, lingering over the sentences and paragraphs he had written in healthier days. "I wish to speak a word for Nature, for absolute freedom and wildness, as contrasted with a freedom and culture merely civil,—to regard man as an inhabitant, or a part and parcel of Nature, rather than a member of society. . . . the walking of which I speak . . . is itself the enterprise and adventure of the day. . . . I believe in the forest, and in the meadow, and in the night in which the corn grows."

One cannot doubt that he walked his beloved lanes and byways in spirit in these months, and lived again those afternoons and nights in Nature. "Night is . . . less profane than day. . . . It must be allowed that the light of the moon, sufficient though it is for the pensive walker, and not disproportionate to the inner light we have, is very inferior in quality and intensity to that of the sun. But the moon is not to be judged alone by the quantity of light she sends to us, but also by her influence on the earth and its inhabitants. . . . I speak out of the night. . . . the beauty of moonlight is seen over lonely pastures where cattle are silently feeding. . . . Every plant and field and forest emits its odor now, swamp-pink in the meadow and tansy in the road . . . We hear the tinkling of rills which we never detected before. . . . The stars are the jewels of the night, . . . a man could get along with *them,*—though he was considerably reduced in his circumstances,— . . . a kind of bread and cheese that never failed. . . . Great restorer of antiquity, great enchanter. . . . New and old things are confounded. . . . Consider the moonlight, so civil, yet so savage!"

As he weakened, his sister Sophia took letters at his dictation, and helped with the revision of his essays, all destined for *The Atlantic Monthly*. His friends came to call, even to Sam Staples, his onetime jailer, who had since on occasion served as Thoreau's rodman when he surveyed the town. He told Emerson later that he had never spent an hour with more satisfaction; "Never saw a man dying with so much pleasure and peace." His Aunt Louisa asked Thoreau whether he had made his peace with God; Thoreau replied, "I never knew that we had quarrelled." Channing mourned his approaching solitude; Thoreau told him, "It is better some things should end."

Another visitor strove to comfort Thoreau by pointing out that death was the common lot of all people. Thoreau replied, "When I was a boy, I learned that I must die, so I am not disappointed now; death is as near to you as it is to me." He fretted a little because the children did not come oftener to see him. "I love them as if they were my own," he said. And to another well-meaning visitor who sought to talk to him about the next world, he said only, "One world at a time."

On the morning of May sixth, a fine, sunny morning, just after a neighbor had brought him some hyacinths, he sank back on his couch, closed his eyes, murmured "moose" and "Indian," and slept quietly away in his forty-fifth year.

He was buried from the parish church at a public funeral at which Emerson spoke. He said of Thoreau that "No truer American existed" and praised his "wonderful fitness of body and mind. He could pace sixteen rods more accurately than another man could measure them with rod and chain. He could find his path in the woods at night, he said, better by his feet than his eyes. He could estimate the measure of a tree very well by his eyes; he could estimate the weight of a calf or a pig, like a dealer. From a box containing a bushel or more of loose pencils, he could take up with his hands fast enough just a dozen pencils at every grasp. He was a good swimmer, runner, skater, boatman, and would probably outwalk most countrymen in a day's journey. And the relation of body to mind was still finer than we have indicated."

He praised his "robust common sense, armed with stout hands, keen perceptions, and strong will" as well as his "excellent wisdom." And, prophetically, he concluded with, "The country knows not yet, or in the least part, how great a son it has lost. It seems an injury that he should leave in the midst his broken task, which none else can finish,—a kind of indignity to so noble a soul, that he should depart out of Nature before yet he has been really shown to his peers for what he is. But he, at least, is content. His soul was made for the noblest society; he had in a short life exhausted the capabilities of this world; wherever there is knowledge, wherever there is virtue, wherever there is beauty, he will find a home."

After this long eulogy, Thoreau was carried to his grave in the New Burying Ground, at the foot of Bedford Street, though some years later his remains were removed to the Sleepy Hollow Cemetery. Concord had lost its most distinguished son, and the nation a man and writer unique in any age.

Afterword

One of the great names in American literature is the name of Henry Thoreau. Yet only after sixty years is he slowly coming into his own.

—VERNON L. PARRINGTON
Main Currents in American Thought

THOREAU'S fame was slow to grow, his influence slow to spread. Yet neither spread as fast as that very materialism he so scorned. Emerson's eulogy was published in the August 1862 issue of *The Atlantic Monthly,* and various other tributes found their way into print. The essays Thoreau had revised in the months of his long dying came rapidly into print in *The Atlantic Monthly,* and Ticknor & Fields reprinted *Walden* in 1863, 1864, and 1866; even *A Week on the Concord and Merrimack Rivers* was reprinted in 1862 and again in 1868. In 1863 the same publishers brought out the essays collected under the title of *Excursions,* in 1864 *The Maine Woods,* and in 1865 both *Cape Cod* and Emerson's selection of Thoreau's letters. These books found a waiting and slowly growing audience, despite a somewhat deprecatory view of Thoreau as an eccentric written by James Russell Lowell and published in *The North American Review.*

In 1873 Ellery Channing's biography of Thoreau—*Thoreau, the Poet-Naturalist,*—appeared; but this, which was more Channing than Thoreau, added nothing to his then small fame. Sanborn's biography came in 1882; it was scarcely more satisfying. It took an Englishman, H. S. Salt, to write a balanced life of Thoreau in 1890, and a Frenchman, Léon Bazalgette, in *Henry Thoreau. Sauvage* (1924), to point out that Thoreau's significance was greater than his age had suspected.

Thoreau's influence, by the turn of the century, was instanced by more than one world leader, and in various parts of the world. Count Leo Tolstoi wrote in 1901 of it in *A Message to the American People*—published, ironically, in that very same magazine which had given space to Lowell's deprecation of Thoreau. The British Labor Party, which grew out of the theories of Karl Marx and William Morris, urged members to buy and carry with them a pocket edition of *Walden,* as best embodying their essential philosophy. And the Mahatma Gandhi took from Thoreau's *Civil Disobedience* the philosophy of passive resistance which led to India's freedom, while countless numbers of writers—William Butler Yeats, W. H. Hudson, H. M. Tomlinson, many another—testified to the importance of Thoreau in their lives. His native country has only recently recognized Thoreau's significance to the extent of including *Walden* among less than a score of essential classics of democracy and distributed throughout the world in many languages by the United States Information Agency.

Today, a century after his death, the name of Henry D. Thoreau appears on every list of that small handful of American writers considered to be the greatest.

Bibliographical Notes

THE reader who wishes to read Thoreau or to learn more about him and his work will find, as I did, certain books indispensable. Foremost among them is *The Writings of Henry David Thoreau* (Walden Edition, in 20 volumes: Houghton Mifflin Company, 1906). The student ought to avoid the four volumes of the *Journal* edited by Harrison Blake, because of the unhappily arbitrary arrangement of the entries, which destroys the continuity of the *Journal*. Next to the Walden Edition of Thoreau stands *The Correspondence of Henry David Thoreau*, edited by Walter Harding and Carl Bode (New York University Press, 1958). These are the basic sources necessary to any knowledge of the writings of Thoreau. In addition, the reader will want *A Thoreau Handbook*, by Walter Harding (New York University Press, 1959), the best available guide through Thoreau scholarship.

The early biographies of Thoreau are all interesting —*Thoreau, the Poet-Naturalist*, by William Ellery Channing (Roberts, 1873); *Henry D. Thoreau*, by F. B. Sanborn (Houghton Mifflin Company, 1882); *The Life of Henry David Thoreau*, by Henry S. Salt (Richard Bentley & Son, London, 1890—the best of the biographies before 1900)—but perhaps the most complete, despite several moot points in the text, is *Thoreau*, by Henry Seidel

205

Canby (Houghton Mifflin Company, 1939). Also of value to the student interested in Thoreau's background is *Concord: American Town,* by Townsend Scudder (Little, Brown and Company, 1947).

The student who wishes merely to sample Thoreau will find four very fine samplers available. First among them is *The Portable Thoreau,* edited by Carl Bode (The Viking Press, 1947); this has no peer. Three books which are cross-sections of the *Journal* seemed to me especially effective in conveying the flavor of that remarkable work; these are *The Heart of Thoreau's Journals,* edited by Odell Shepard (Houghton Mifflin Company, 1927), *Men of Concord,* edited by F. H. Allen (Houghton Mifflin Company, 1936), and *H. D. Thoreau: A Writer's Journal,* edited by Laurence Stapleton (Dover Publications, 1962).

Finally, that scholar who wishes to delve more deeply into Thoreau's relation to his world will find two books of especial importance—*Henry David Thoreau,* by Joseph Wood Krutch (William Sloane Associates, 1948), and *The Shores of America: Thoreau's Inward Exploration,* by Sherman Paul (The University of Illinois Press, 1958).

AUGUST DERLETH

Sauk City, Wisconsin

Index

211

AUGUST DERLETH

began writing in 1922 at the age of thirteen. Since then many short stories, essays, reviews, poems, novels and other books have appeared under the August Derleth byline or one of his pen names. His most widely popular novels have been *Wind Over Wisconsin, The Shield of the Valiant* and *Bright Journey*. His Sac Prairie Saga was projected as a group of approximately fifty books designed to portray the social and economic life and history of a typical Wisconsin village from about 1830 to 1950. Many of these books have already been published. Mr. Derleth has spent practically all his life in Sauk City, Wisconsin, where he was born and where he still makes his home.